LUCY IN THE SKY

Written by
Kiara Brinkman

Art by
Sean Chiki

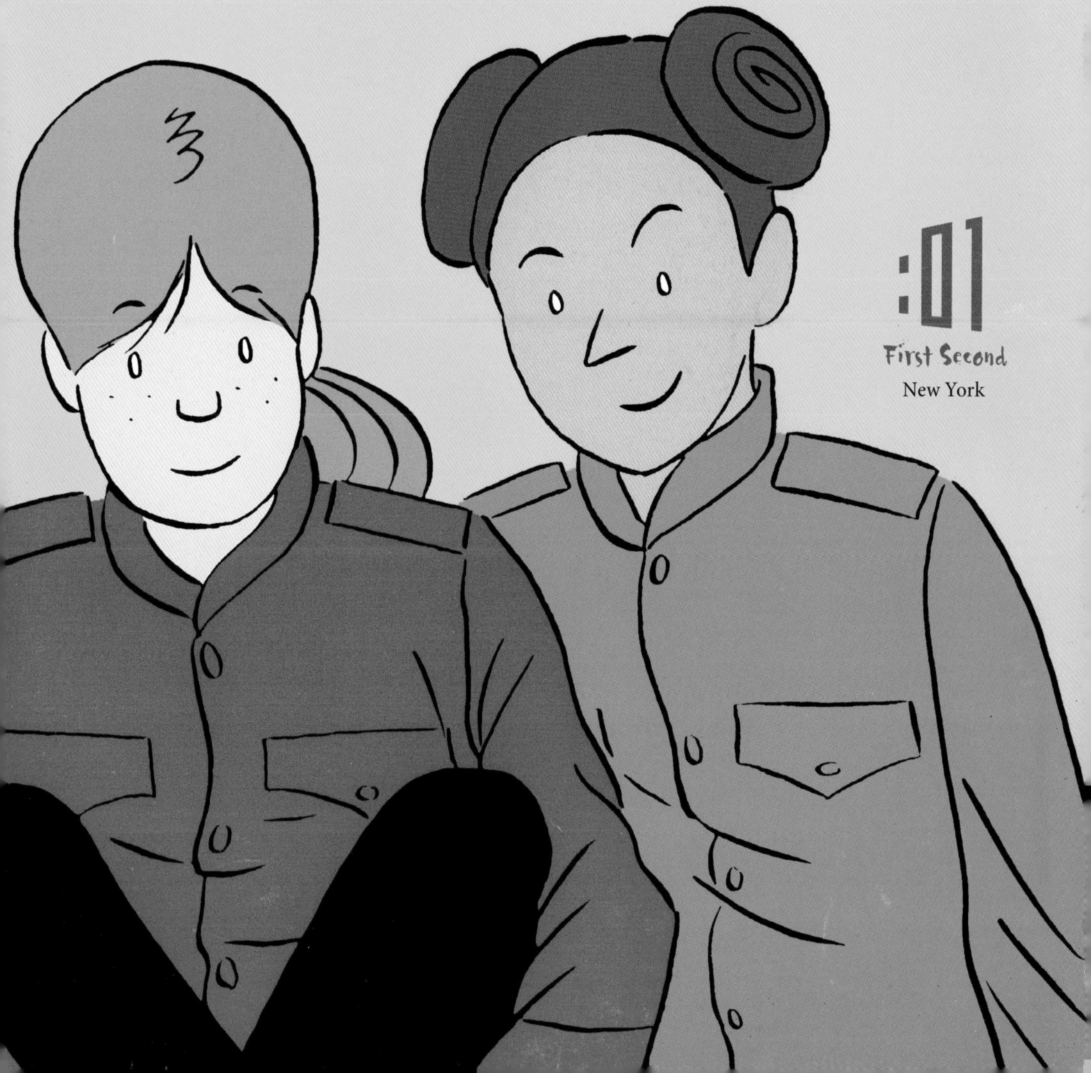

First Second
New York

1. LUCY SUTCLIFFE
2. VANESSA TAKAHASHI
3. GEORGIANNA BIRK
4. RUPA KHANNA
5. KATE
6. RYAN
7. CONNOR
8. PETE
9. ISABEL TRANTON
10. DANIEL SUTCLIFFE
11. ELEANOR "COOKIE" TRANTON
12. EMILY
13. MR. DOYLE
14. MAYA
15. MRS. TAKAHASHI
16. CAMILLE
17. MR. KHANNA
18. MRS. KHANNA
19. MRS. SCOTT
20. MR. TAKAHASHI

Text © 2021 by Kiara Brinkman
Illustration © 2021 by Sean Chiki
Published by First Second, an imprint of Roaring Brook
Press, a division of Holtzbrinck Publishing Holdings Limited
Partnership. 120 Broadway, New York, NY 10271.
All rights reserved.
Library of Congress Control Number: 2019947778
First edition, 2021. Edited by Calista Brill and Robyn
Chapman. Cover design by Kirk Benshoff. Interior book
design by Molly Johanson. Special thanks to Sarah Myer.
Printed in China by 1010 Printing International Ltd.,
North Point, Hong Kong.
Penciled with a Pentel Graph Gear 500 mechanical pencil with 0.5
HB lead on Strathmore drawing paper. Traced onto Strathmore
bristol board with an Artograph LightPad. Inked with a Hunt 56
dip pen and Winsor & Newton calligraphy ink. Lettered with a
Pigma Micron 08 pen. Colored digitally in Photoshop.
Our books may be purchased in bulk for promotional,
educational, or business use. Please contact your local
bookseller or the Macmillan Corporate and Premium Sales
Department at MacmillanSpecialMarkets@macmillan.com.
Paperback ISBN: 978-1-62672-720-5
Hardcover ISBN: 978-1-62672-721-2
Paperback: 10 9 8 7 6 5 4 3 2 1
Hardcover: 10 9 8 7 6 5 4 3 2 1
Don't miss your next favorite book from First Second!
For the latest updates go to firstsecondnewsletter.com and
sign up for our enewsletter.

LUCY IN THE SKY

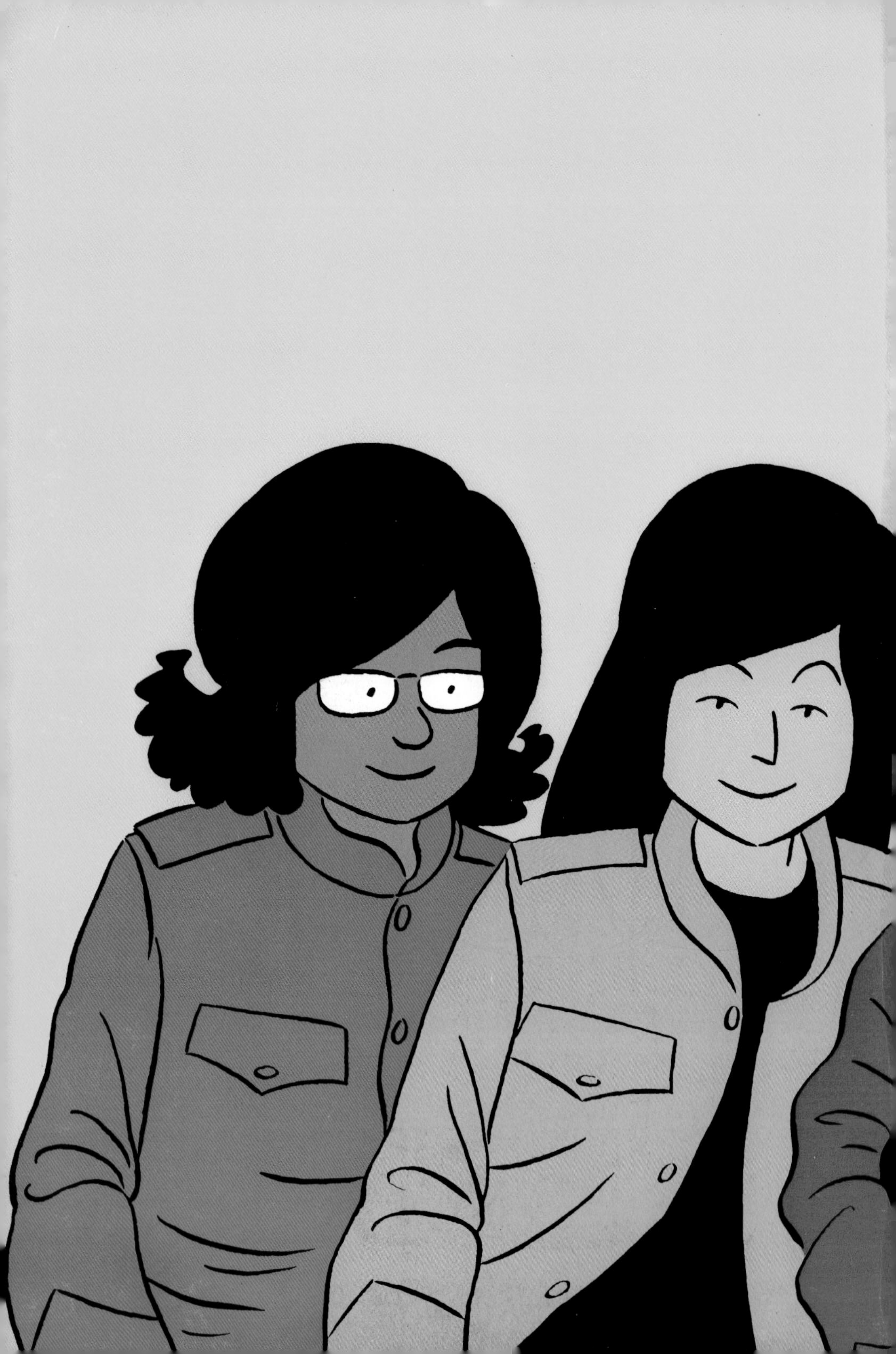

FOR ESMÉ

WITH LOVE AND
SQUALOR

fall
2012

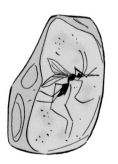

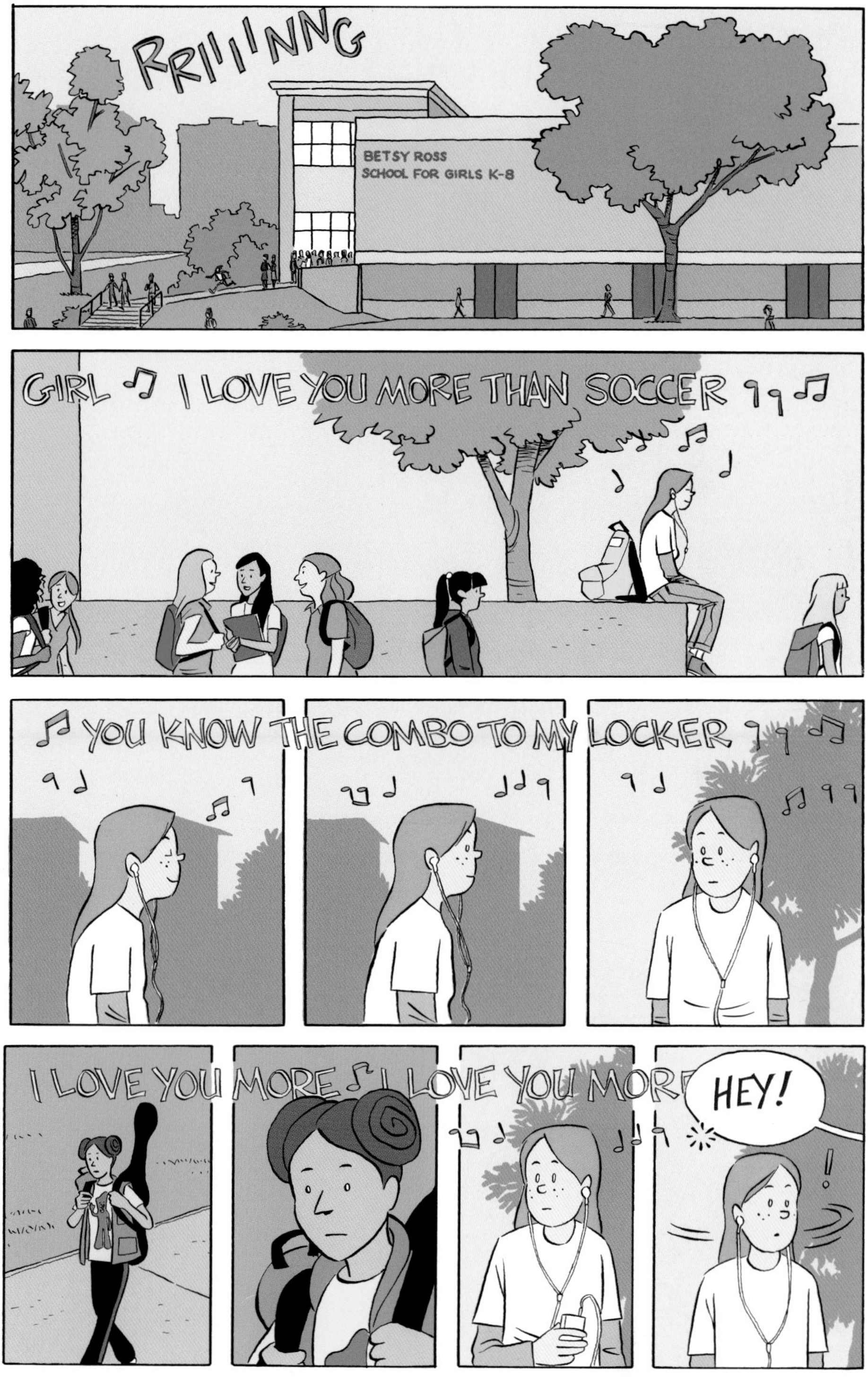
RRIIINNG
BETSY ROSS
SCHOOL FOR GIRLS K-8
GIRL ♫ I LOVE YOU MORE THAN SOCCER ♫
♫ YOU KNOW THE COMBO TO MY LOCKER ♫
I LOVE YOU MORE ♫ I LOVE YOU MORE
HEY!

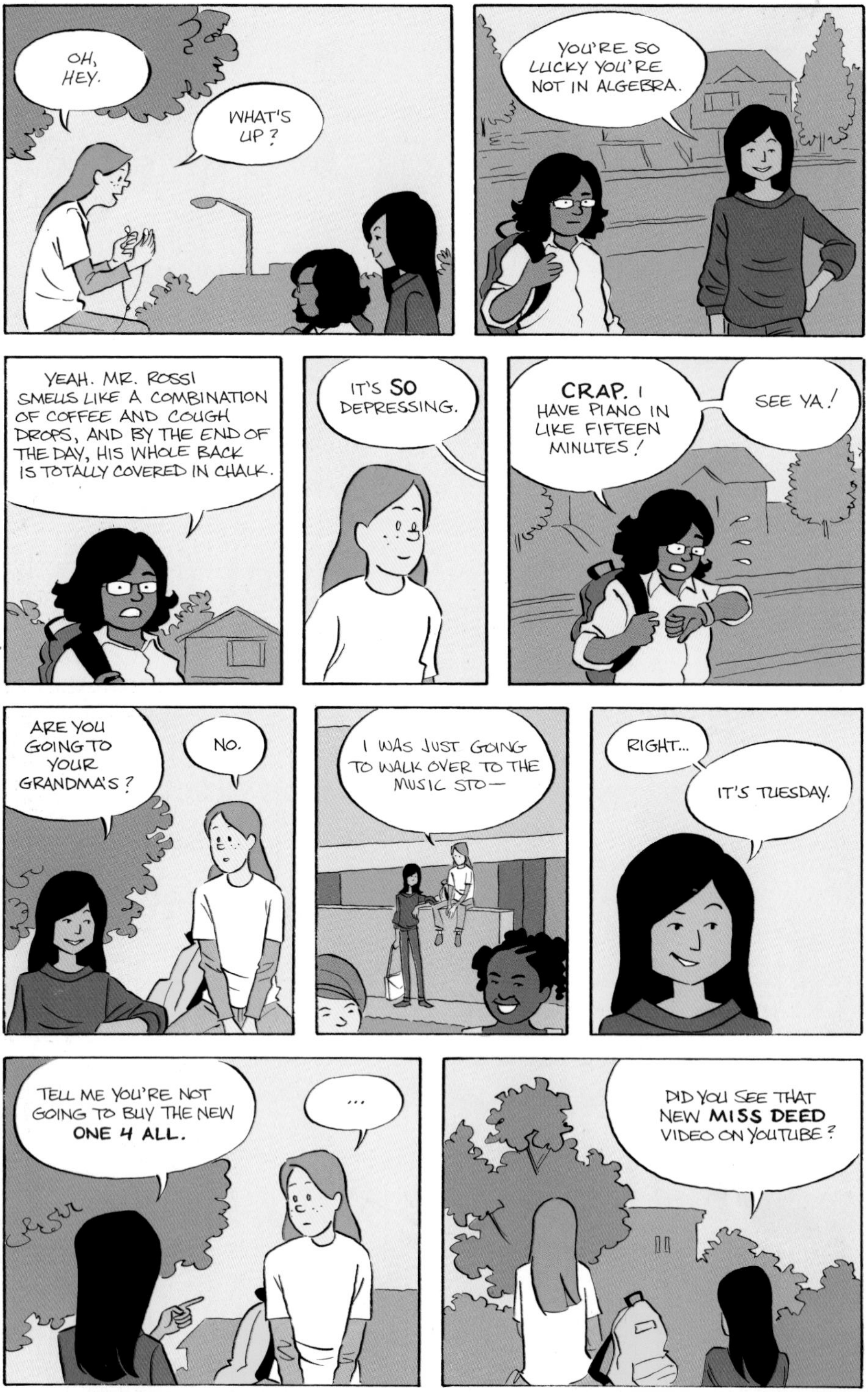
OH, HEY.
WHAT'S UP?
YOU'RE SO LUCKY YOU'RE NOT IN ALGEBRA.
YEAH. MR. ROSSI SMELLS LIKE A COMBINATION OF COFFEE AND COUGH DROPS, AND BY THE END OF THE DAY, HIS WHOLE BACK IS TOTALLY COVERED IN CHALK.
IT'S **SO** DEPRESSING.
CRAP. I HAVE PIANO IN LIKE FIFTEEN MINUTES!
SEE YA!
ARE YOU GOING TO YOUR GRANDMA'S?
NO.
I WAS JUST GOING TO WALK OVER TO THE MUSIC STO—
RIGHT...
IT'S TUESDAY.
TELL ME YOU'RE NOT GOING TO BUY THE NEW **ONE 4 ALL.**
...
DID YOU SEE THAT NEW **MISS DEED** VIDEO ON YOUTUBE?

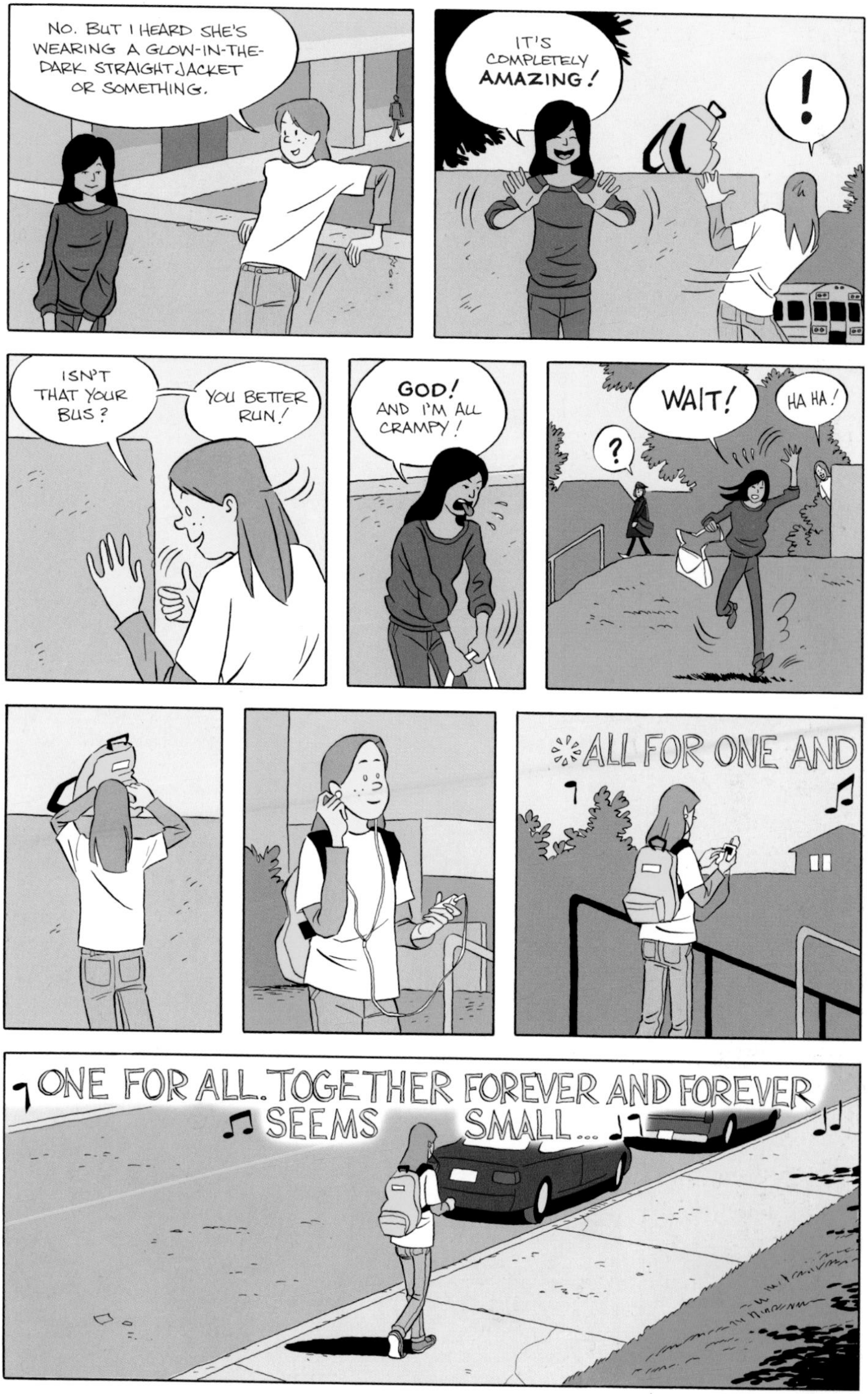
NO. BUT I HEARD SHE'S WEARING A GLOW-IN-THE-DARK STRAIGHTJACKET OR SOMETHING.
IT'S COMPLETELY AMAZING!
!
ISN'T THAT YOUR BUS?
YOU BETTER RUN!
GOD! AND I'M ALL CRAMPY!
?
WAIT!
HA HA!
ALL FOR ONE AND
ONE FOR ALL. TOGETHER FOREVER AND FOREVER
SEEMS SMALL...

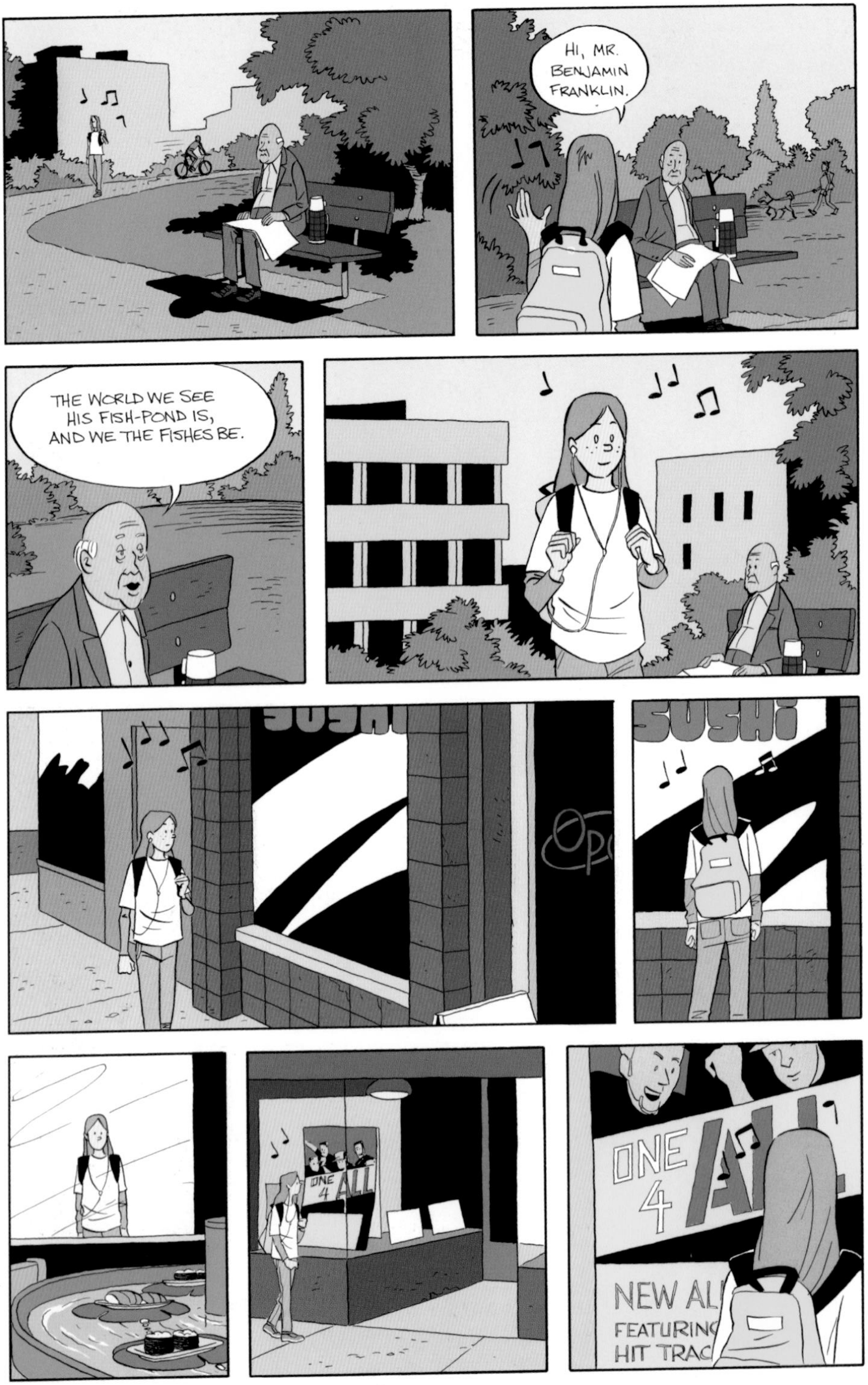
HI, MR. BENJAMIN FRANKLIN.
THE WORLD WE SEE HIS FISH-POND IS, AND WE THE FISHES BE.
SUSHI
SUSHI
ONE 4 ALL
ONE 4 ALL
NEW ALL
FEATURING
HIT TRAC

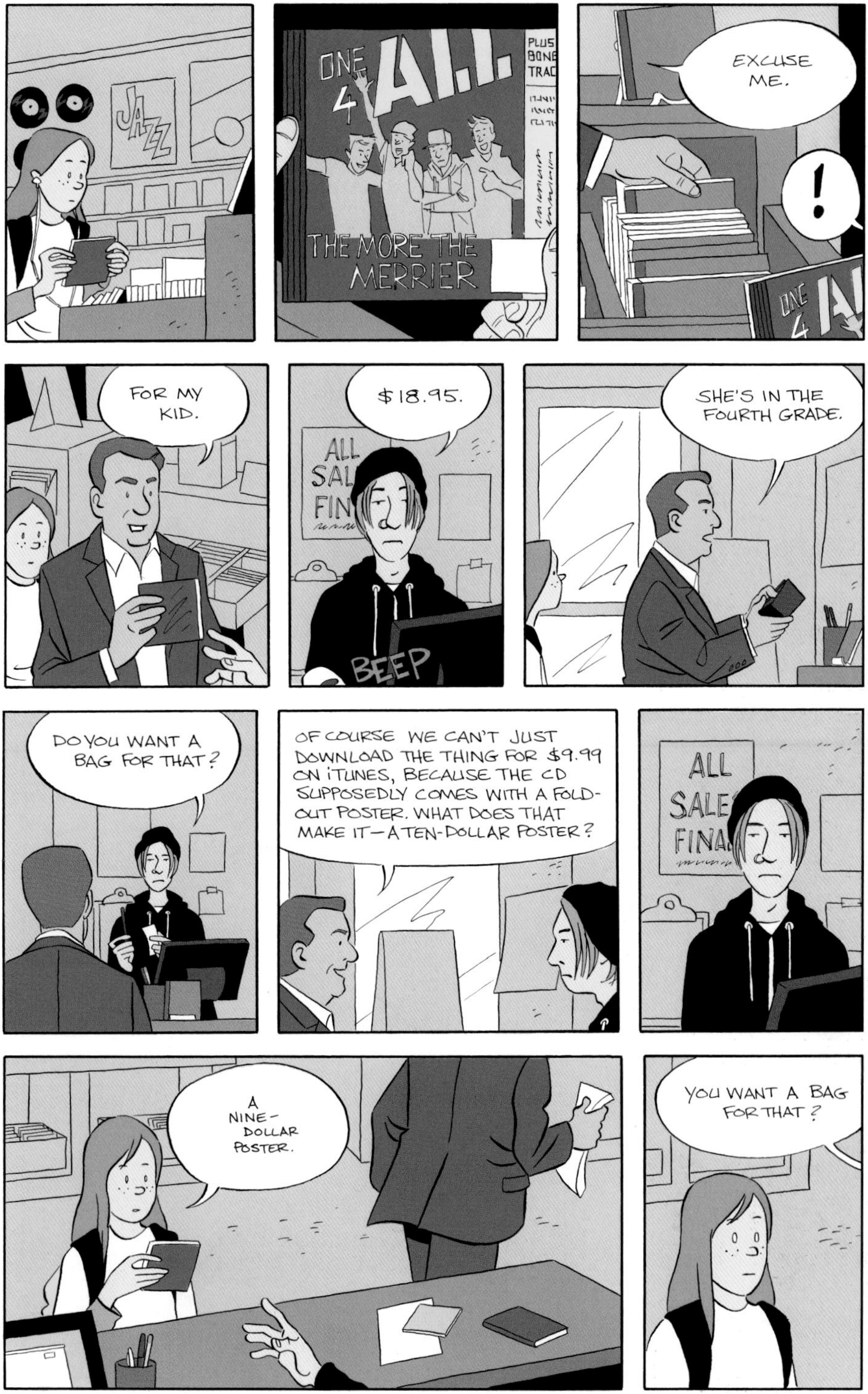
JAZZ
ONE 4 ALL
PLUS BONE TRAC
THE MORE THE MERRIER
EXCUSE ME.
!
FOR MY KID.
$18.95.
ALL SAL FIN
BEEP
SHE'S IN THE FOURTH GRADE.
DO YOU WANT A BAG FOR THAT?
OF COURSE WE CAN'T JUST DOWNLOAD THE THING FOR $9.99 ON iTUNES, BECAUSE THE CD SUPPOSEDLY COMES WITH A FOLD-OUT POSTER. WHAT DOES THAT MAKE IT—A TEN-DOLLAR POSTER?
ALL SALE FINA
A NINE-DOLLAR POSTER.
YOU WANT A BAG FOR THAT?

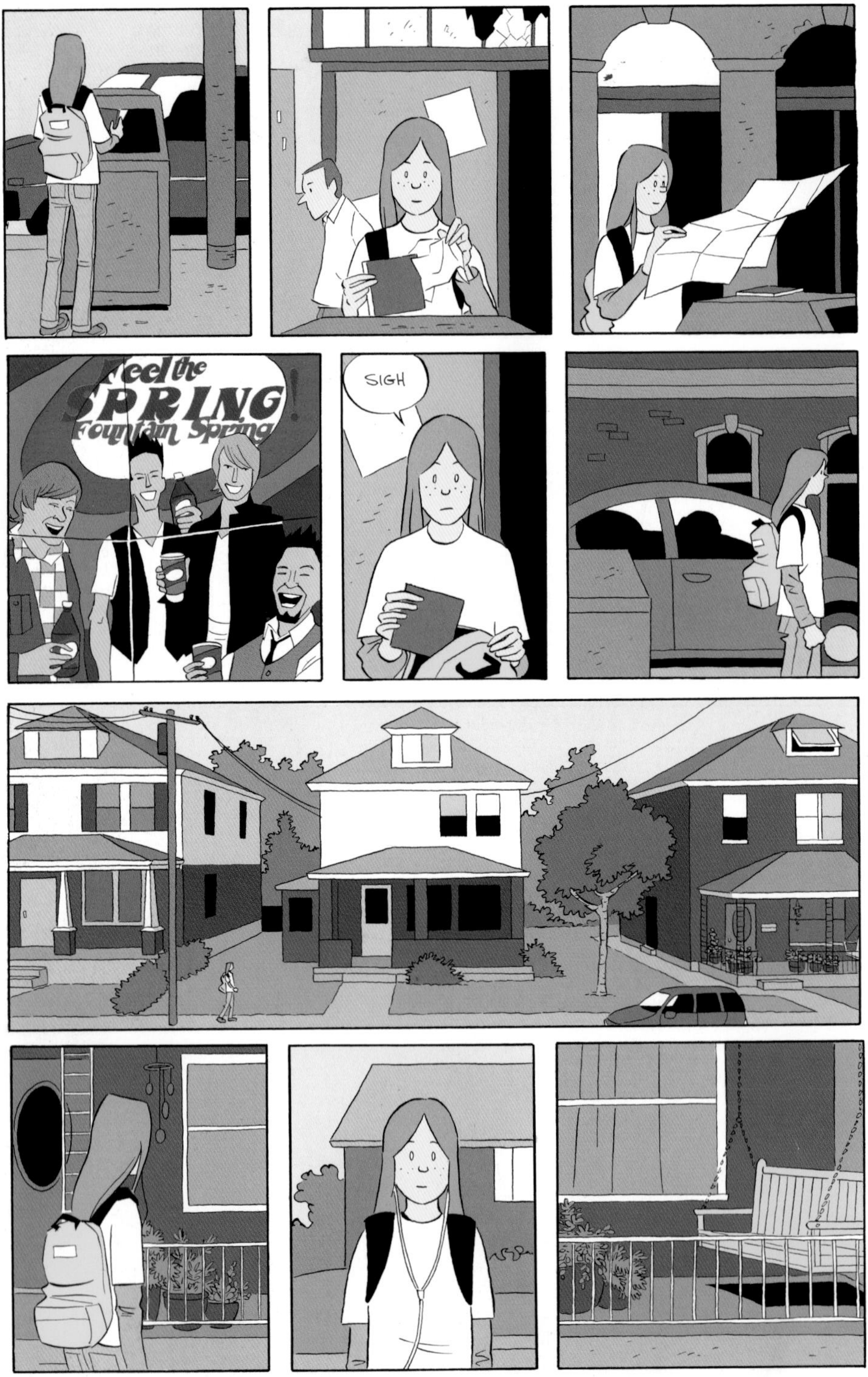
Feel the SPRING!
Fountain Spring
SIGH

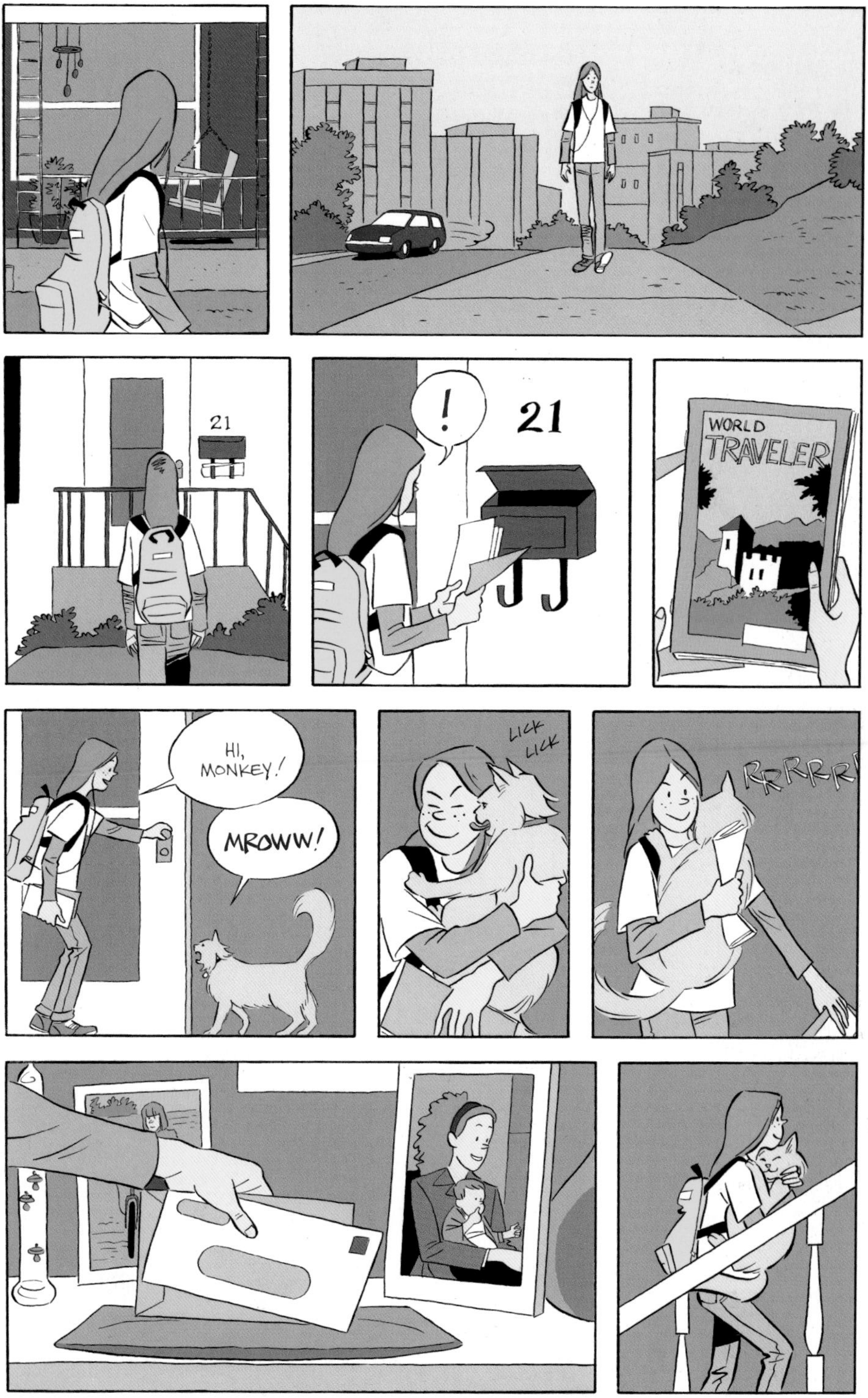
21
!
21
WORLD TRAVELER
HI, MONKEY!
MROWW!
LICK LICK
RRRRR

SJ...
WHERE ARE YOU?

SNIFF SNIFF

DID YOU HAVE A GOOD DAY?

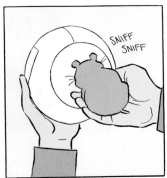

SNIFF SNIFF

HELLO
MY NAME IS
Strawberry
Jam

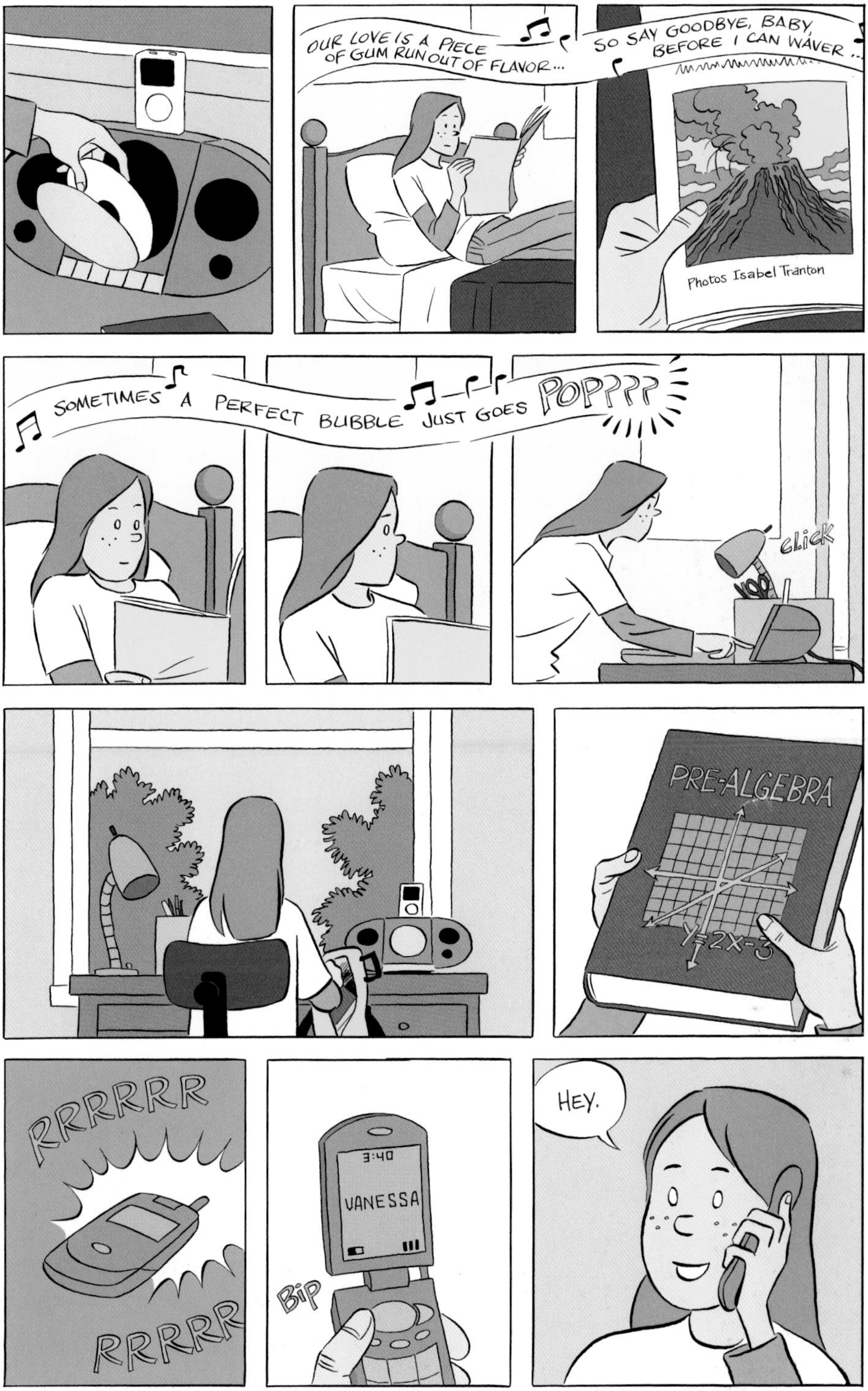

OUR LOVE IS A PIECE OF GUM RUN OUT OF FLAVOR...
SO SAY GOODBYE, BABY, BEFORE I CAN WAVER...
Photos Isabel Tranton
SOMETIMES A PERFECT BUBBLE JUST GOES POP???
CLICK
PRE-ALGEBRA
Y=2X-3
RRRRRR
RRRRR
3:40
VANESSA
Bip
HEY.

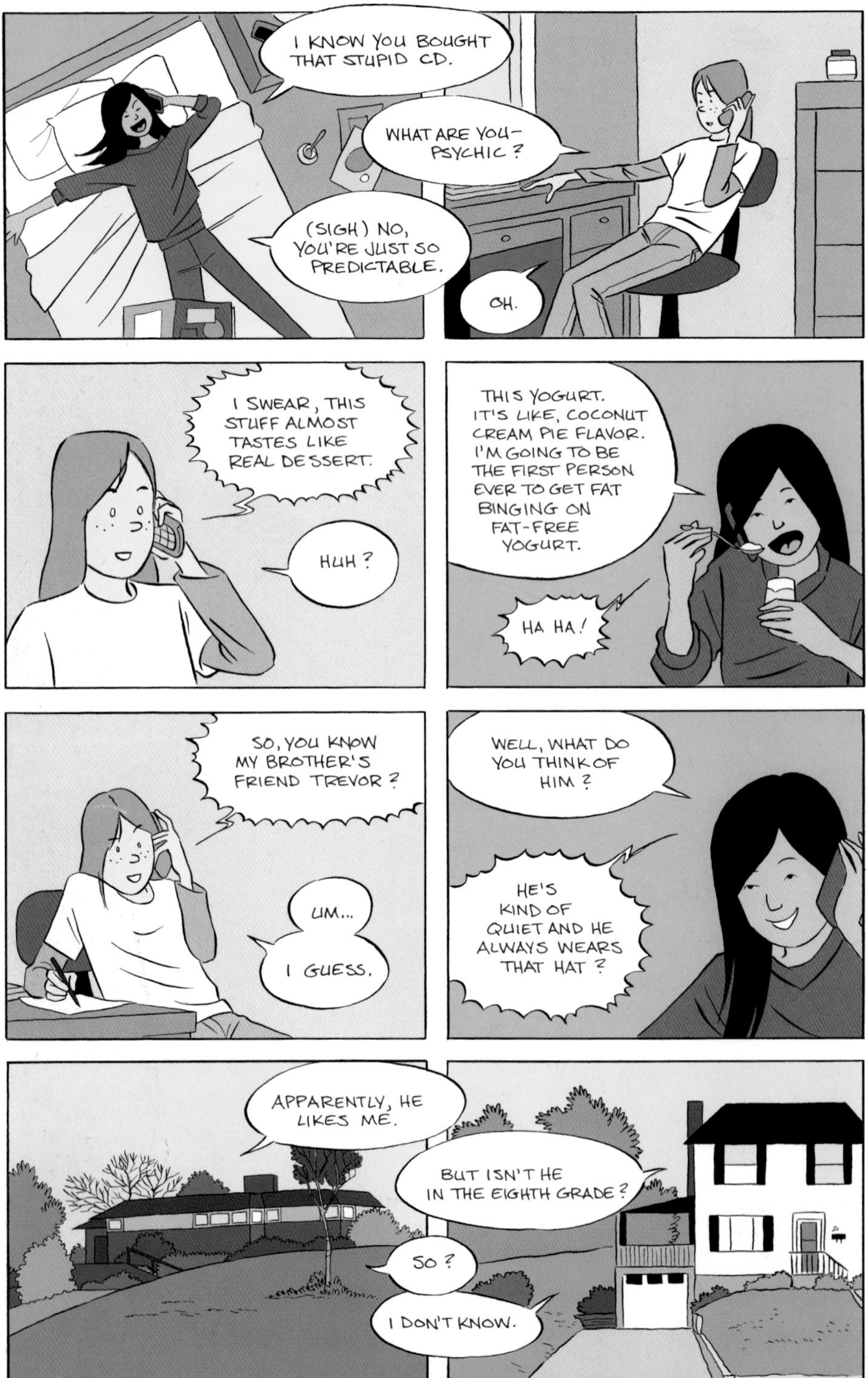
I KNOW YOU BOUGHT THAT STUPID CD.
WHAT ARE YOU- PSYCHIC?
(SIGH) NO, YOU'RE JUST SO PREDICTABLE.
OH.
I SWEAR, THIS STUFF ALMOST TASTES LIKE REAL DESSERT.
HUH?
THIS YOGURT. IT'S LIKE, COCONUT CREAM PIE FLAVOR. I'M GOING TO BE THE FIRST PERSON EVER TO GET FAT BINGING ON FAT-FREE YOGURT.
HA HA!
SO, YOU KNOW MY BROTHER'S FRIEND TREVOR?
UM...
I GUESS.
WELL, WHAT DO YOU THINK OF HIM?
HE'S KIND OF QUIET AND HE ALWAYS WEARS THAT HAT?
APPARENTLY, HE LIKES ME.
BUT ISN'T HE IN THE EIGHTH GRADE?
SO?
I DON'T KNOW.

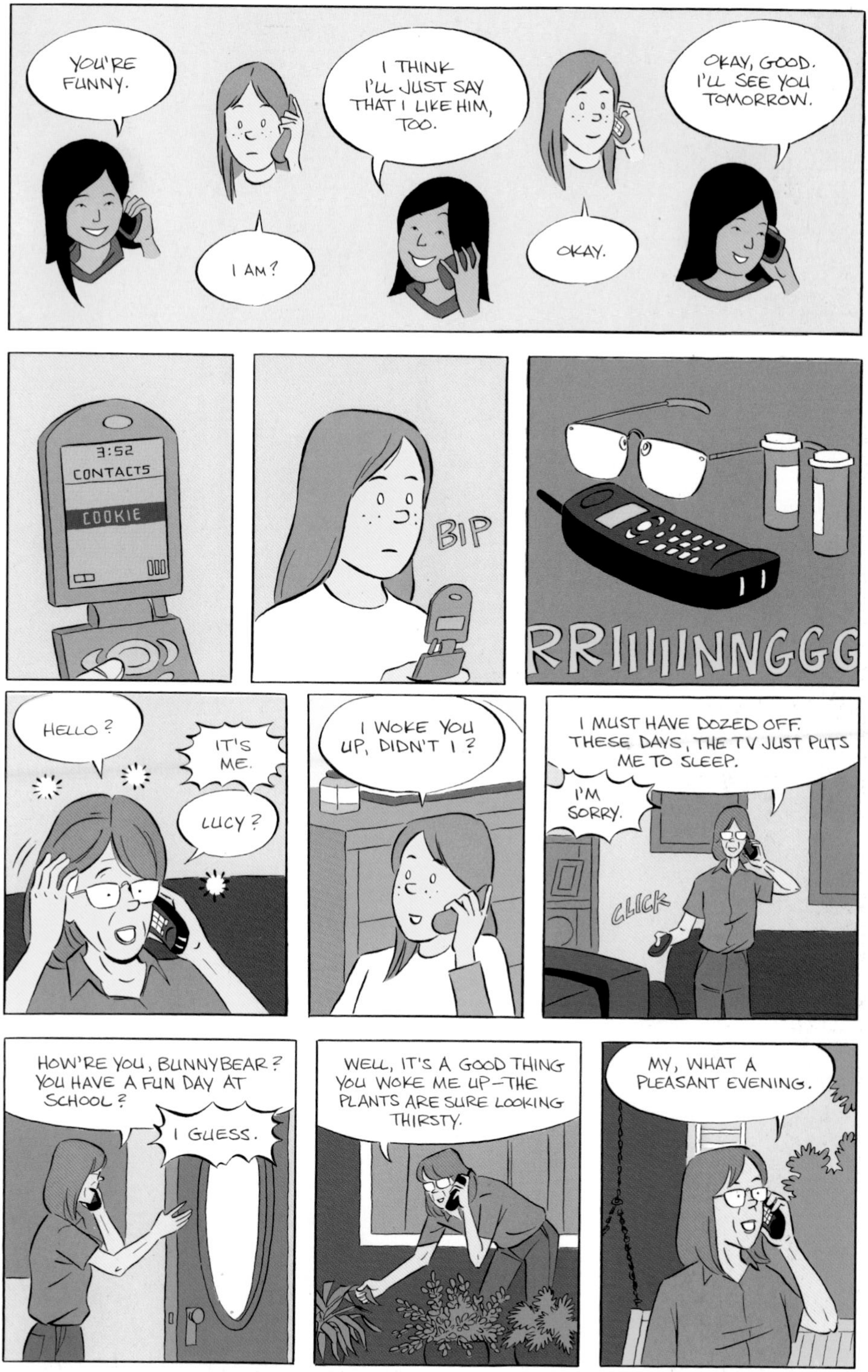
YOU'RE FUNNY.
I AM?
I THINK I'LL JUST SAY THAT I LIKE HIM, TOO.
OKAY.
OKAY, GOOD. I'LL SEE YOU TOMORROW.
3:52
CONTACTS
COOKIE
BIP
RRIIIIINNGGG
HELLO?
IT'S ME.
LUCY?
I WOKE YOU UP, DIDN'T I?
I MUST HAVE DOZED OFF. THESE DAYS, THE TV JUST PUTS ME TO SLEEP.
I'M SORRY.
CLICK
HOW'RE YOU, BUNNYBEAR? YOU HAVE A FUN DAY AT SCHOOL?
I GUESS.
WELL, IT'S A GOOD THING YOU WOKE ME UP—THE PLANTS ARE SURE LOOKING THIRSTY.
MY, WHAT A PLEASANT EVENING.

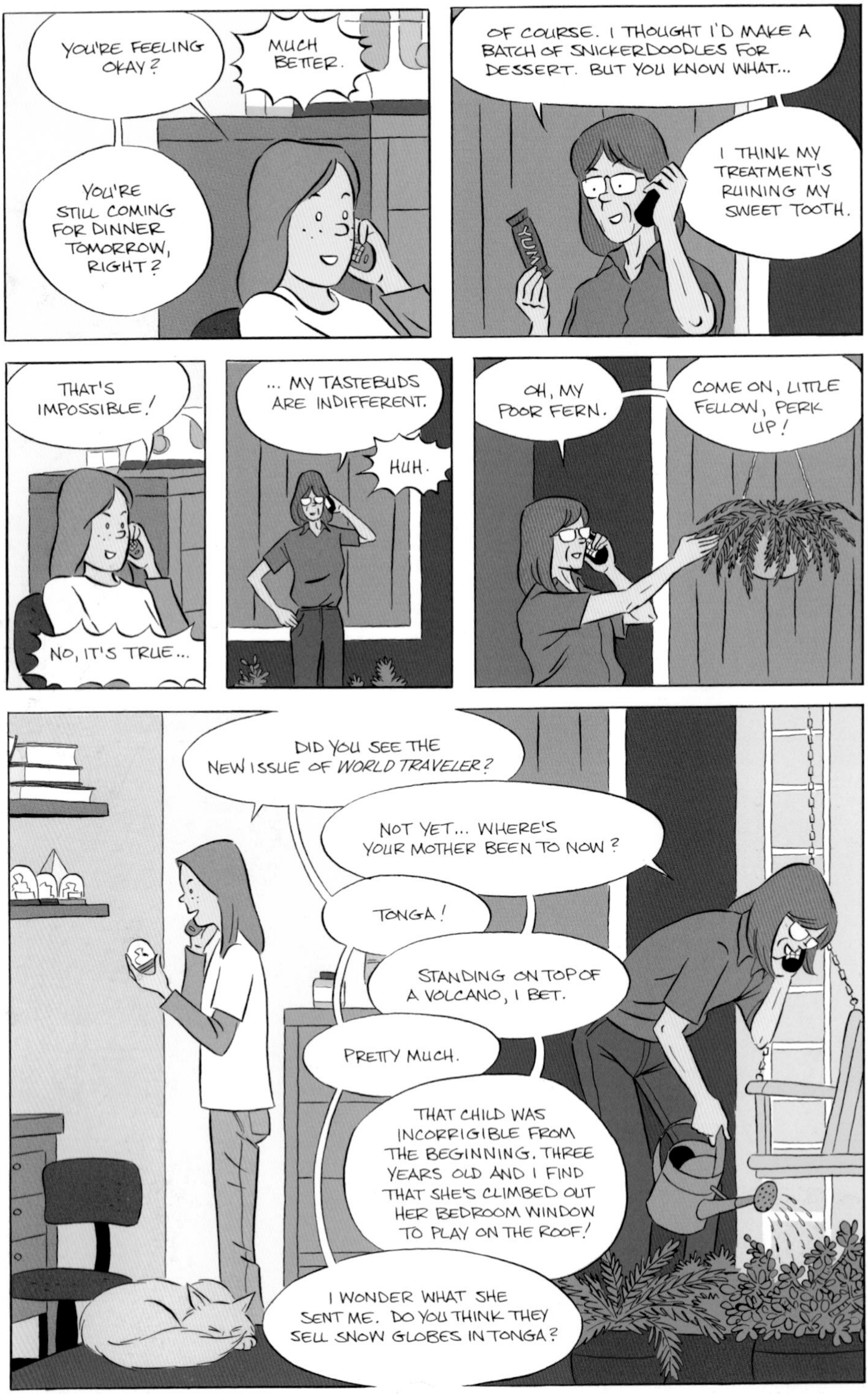
YOU'RE FEELING OKAY?
MUCH BETTER.
YOU'RE STILL COMING FOR DINNER TOMORROW, RIGHT?
OF COURSE. I THOUGHT I'D MAKE A BATCH OF SNICKERDOODLES FOR DESSERT. BUT YOU KNOW WHAT...
I THINK MY TREATMENT'S RUINING MY SWEET TOOTH.
YUM
THAT'S IMPOSSIBLE!
NO, IT'S TRUE...
... MY TASTEBUDS ARE INDIFFERENT.
HUH.
OH, MY POOR FERN.
COME ON, LITTLE FELLOW, PERK UP!
DID YOU SEE THE NEW ISSUE OF *WORLD TRAVELER*?
NOT YET... WHERE'S YOUR MOTHER BEEN TO NOW?
TONGA!
STANDING ON TOP OF A VOLCANO, I BET.
PRETTY MUCH.
THAT CHILD WAS INCORRIGIBLE FROM THE BEGINNING. THREE YEARS OLD AND I FIND THAT SHE'S CLIMBED OUT HER BEDROOM WINDOW TO PLAY ON THE ROOF!
I WONDER WHAT SHE SENT ME. DO YOU THINK THEY SELL SNOW GLOBES IN TONGA?

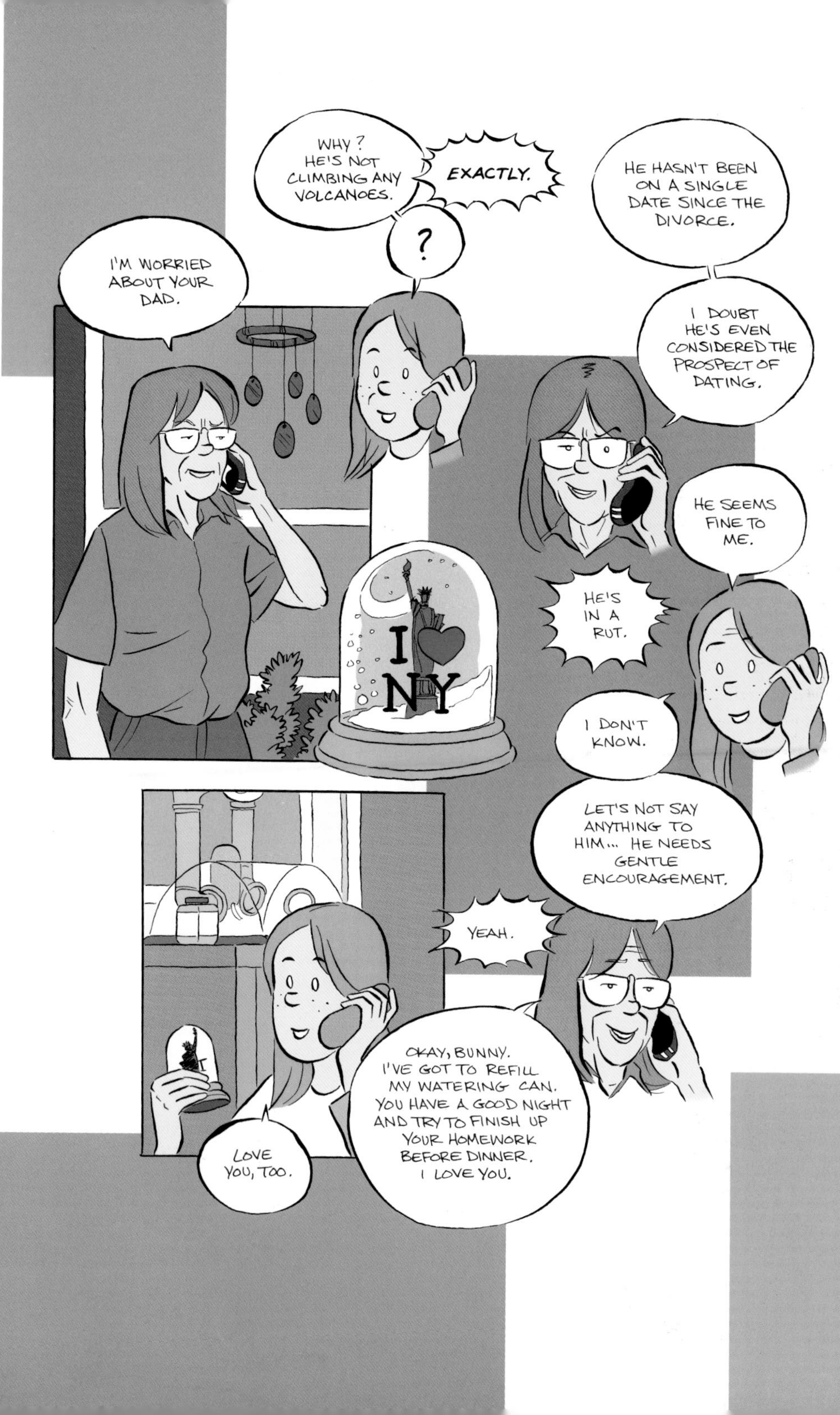
I'M WORRIED ABOUT YOUR DAD.
?
WHY? HE'S NOT CLIMBING ANY VOLCANOES.
EXACTLY.
HE HASN'T BEEN ON A SINGLE DATE SINCE THE DIVORCE.
I DOUBT HE'S EVEN CONSIDERED THE PROSPECT OF DATING.
HE SEEMS FINE TO ME.
HE'S IN A RUT.
I DON'T KNOW.
I ♥ NY
LET'S NOT SAY ANYTHING TO HIM... HE NEEDS GENTLE ENCOURAGEMENT.
YEAH.
OKAY, BUNNY. I'VE GOT TO REFILL MY WATERING CAN. YOU HAVE A GOOD NIGHT AND TRY TO FINISH UP YOUR HOMEWORK BEFORE DINNER. I LOVE YOU.
LOVE YOU, TOO.

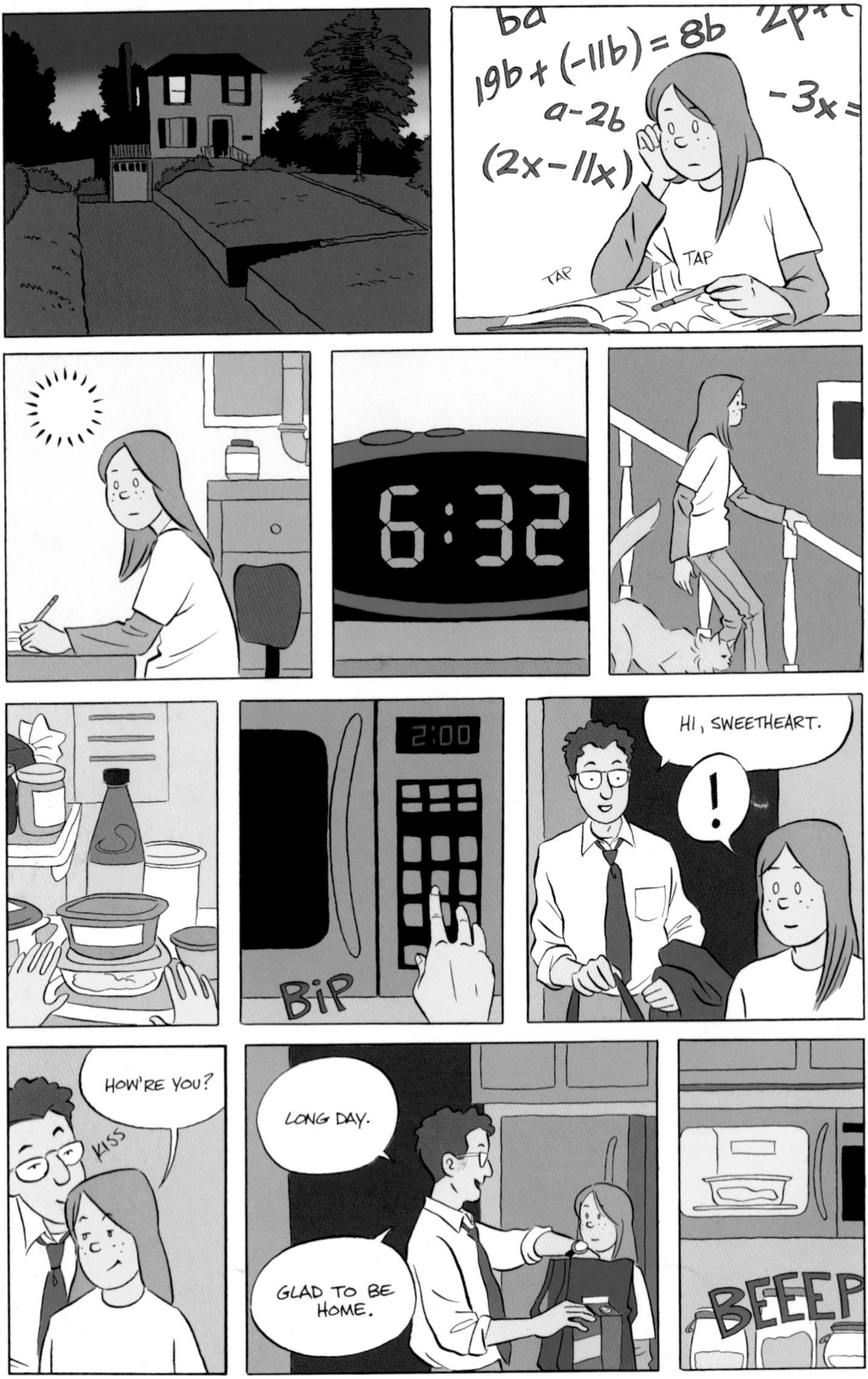
ba
19b + (-11b) = 8b
2p+
a-2b
-3x =
(2x-11x)
TAP
TAP
6:32
2:00
BIP
HI, SWEETHEART.
!
HOW'RE YOU?
KISS
LONG DAY.
GLAD TO BE HOME.
BEEEP

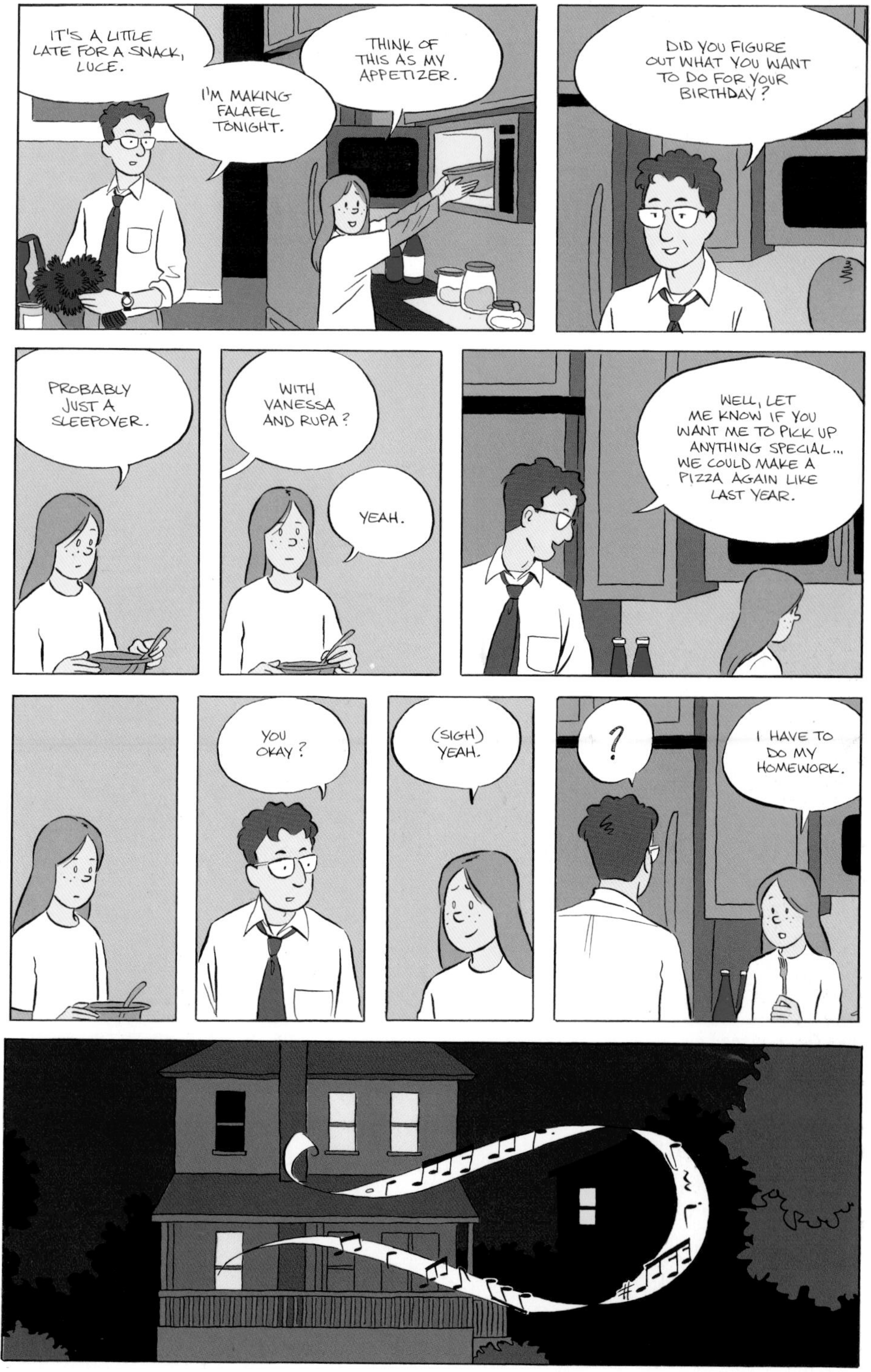
IT'S A LITTLE LATE FOR A SNACK, LUCE.
I'M MAKING FALAFEL TONIGHT.
THINK OF THIS AS MY APPETIZER.
DID YOU FIGURE OUT WHAT YOU WANT TO DO FOR YOUR BIRTHDAY?
PROBABLY JUST A SLEEPOVER.
WITH VANESSA AND RUPA?
YEAH.
WELL, LET ME KNOW IF YOU WANT ME TO PICK UP ANYTHING SPECIAL... WE COULD MAKE A PIZZA AGAIN LIKE LAST YEAR.
YOU OKAY?
(SIGH) YEAH.
?
I HAVE TO DO MY HOMEWORK.

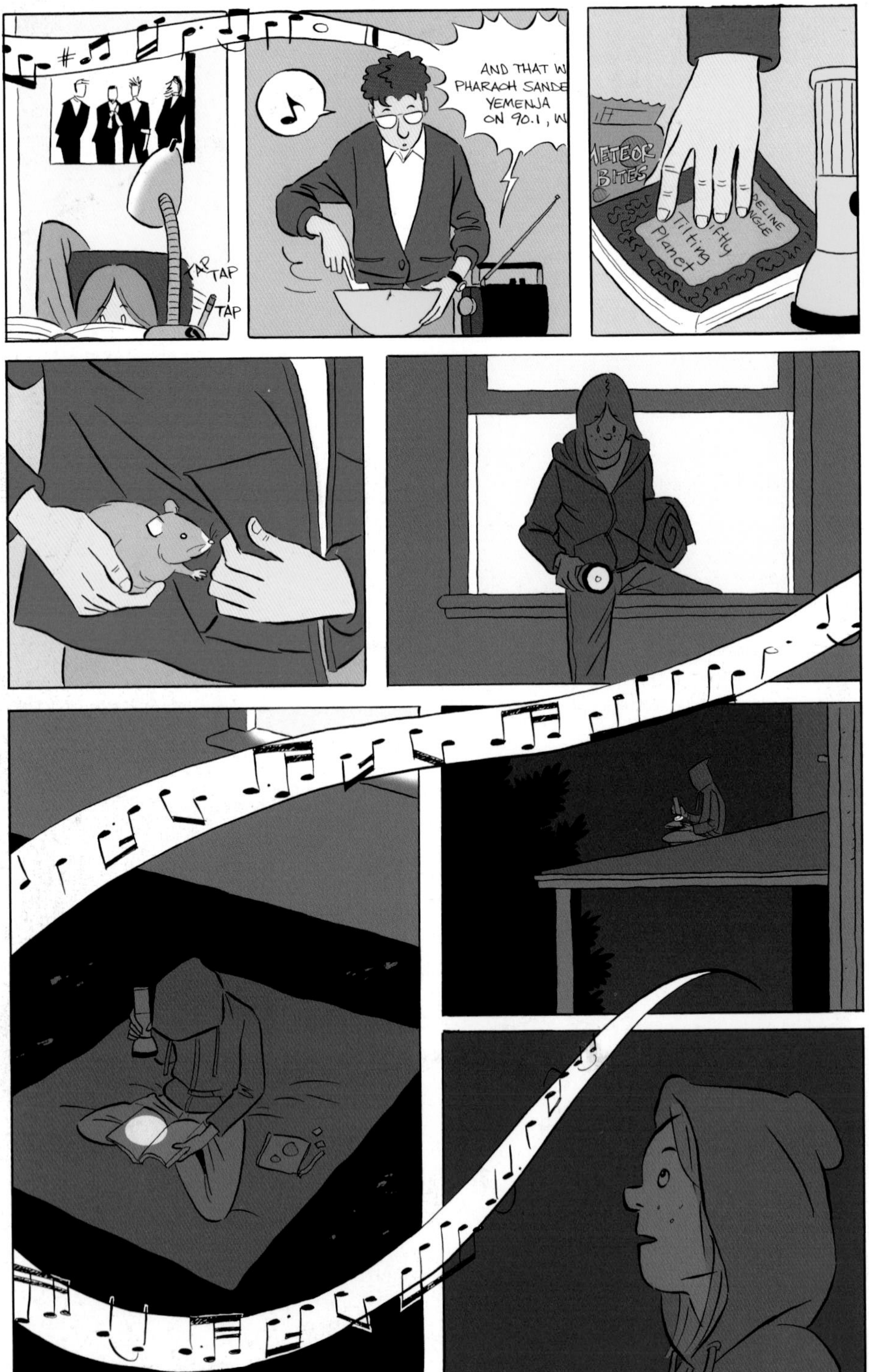
TAP TAP
TAP
AND THAT W
PHARAOH SANDE
YEMENJA
ON 90.1, W
METEOR BITES
Tilting Planet

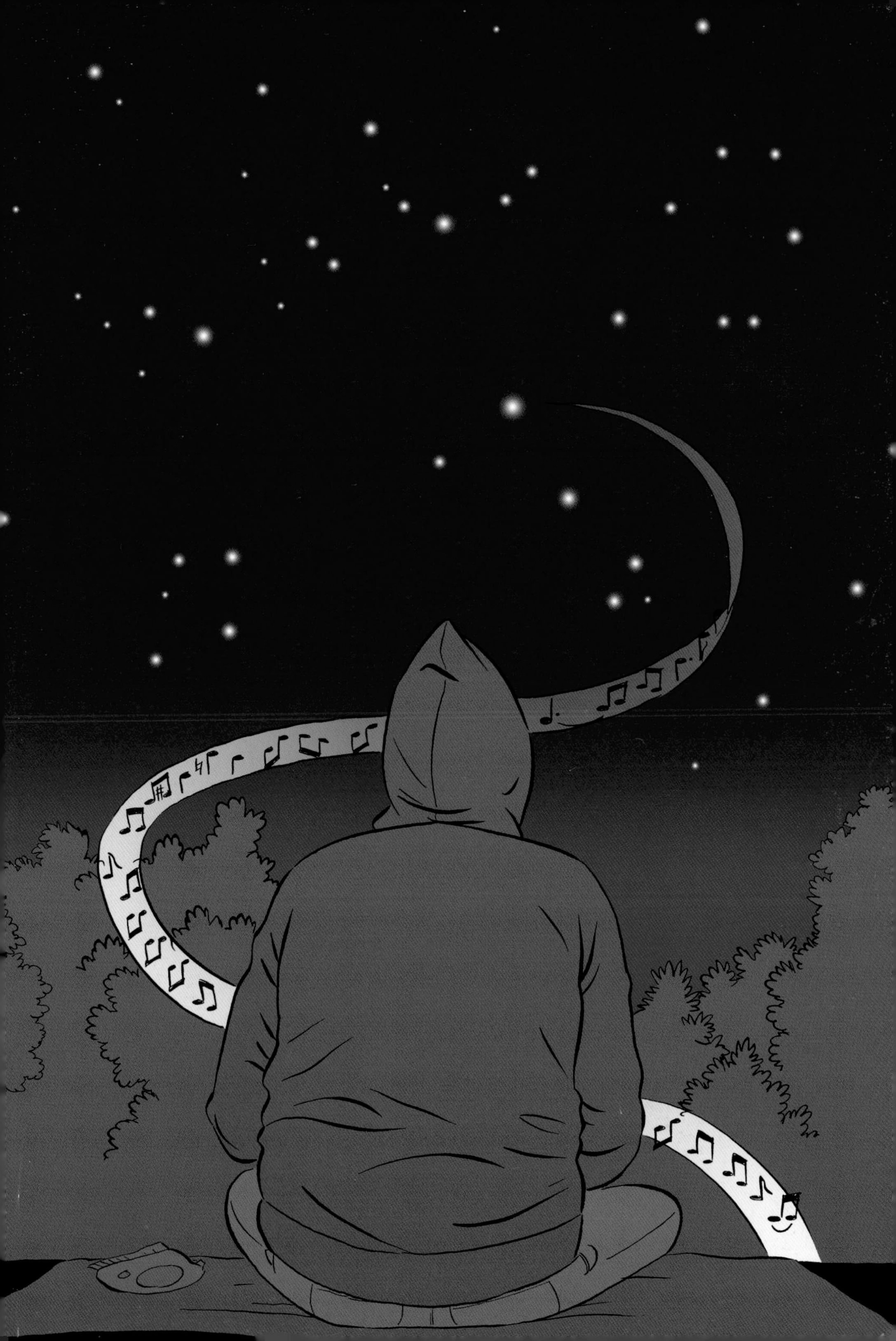

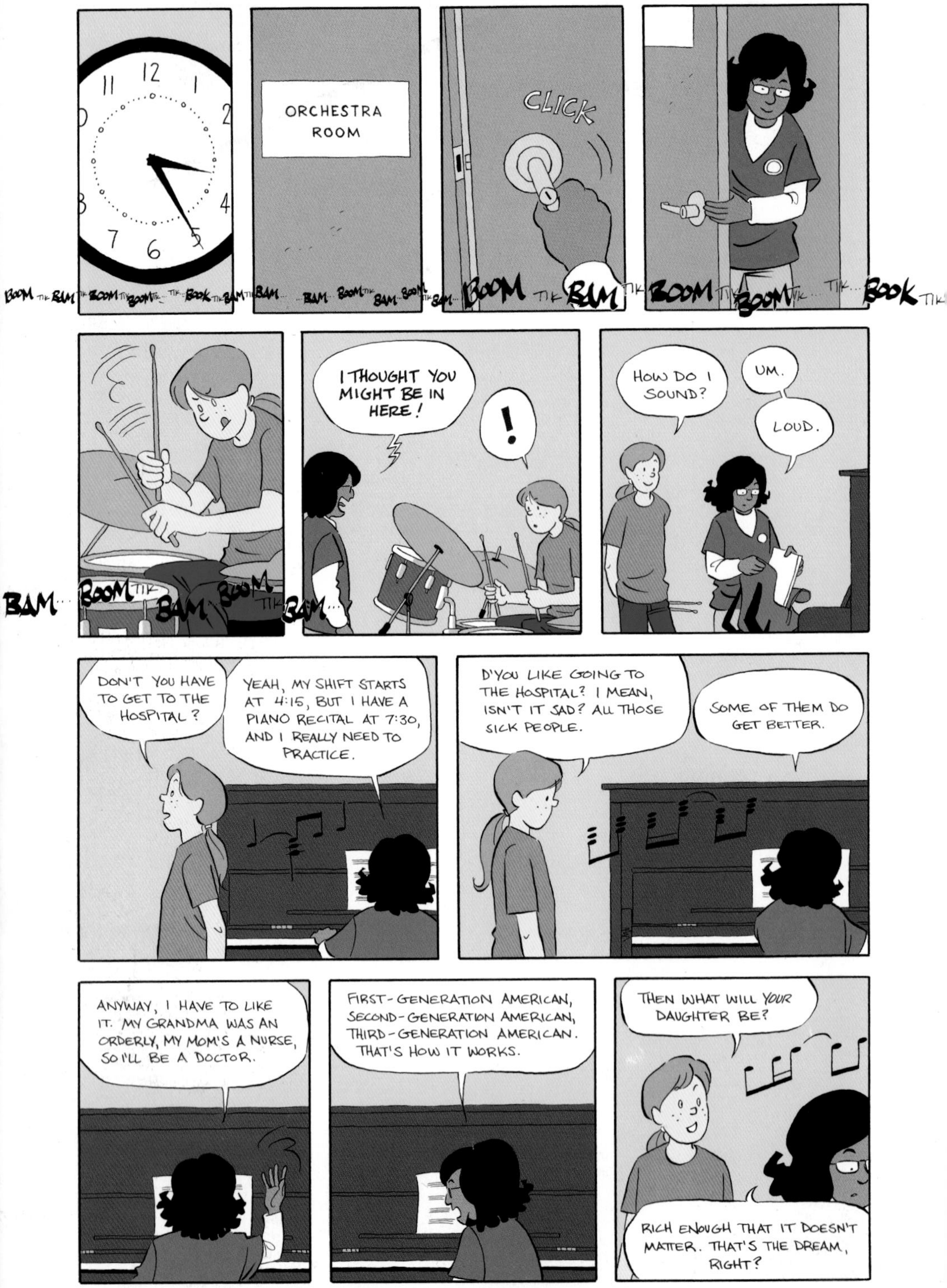
ORCHESTRA ROOM
CLICK
BOOM TIK BAM TIK BOOM TIK BOOM TIK TIK BOOK TIK BAM TIK BAM BAM BOOM TIK BAM BOOM TIK BAM BOOM TIK BAM TIK BOOM TIK BOOM TIK TIK BOOK TIK
BAM BOOM TIK BAM BOOM TIK BAM
I THOUGHT YOU MIGHT BE IN HERE!
!
HOW DO I SOUND?
UM.
LOUD.
DON'T YOU HAVE TO GET TO THE HOSPITAL?
YEAH, MY SHIFT STARTS AT 4:15, BUT I HAVE A PIANO RECITAL AT 7:30, AND I REALLY NEED TO PRACTICE.
D'YOU LIKE GOING TO THE HOSPITAL? I MEAN, ISN'T IT SAD? ALL THOSE SICK PEOPLE.
SOME OF THEM DO GET BETTER.
ANYWAY, I HAVE TO LIKE IT. MY GRANDMA WAS AN ORDERLY, MY MOM'S A NURSE, SO I'LL BE A DOCTOR.
FIRST-GENERATION AMERICAN, SECOND-GENERATION AMERICAN, THIRD-GENERATION AMERICAN. THAT'S HOW IT WORKS.
THEN WHAT WILL YOUR DAUGHTER BE?
RICH ENOUGH THAT IT DOESN'T MATTER. THAT'S THE DREAM, RIGHT?

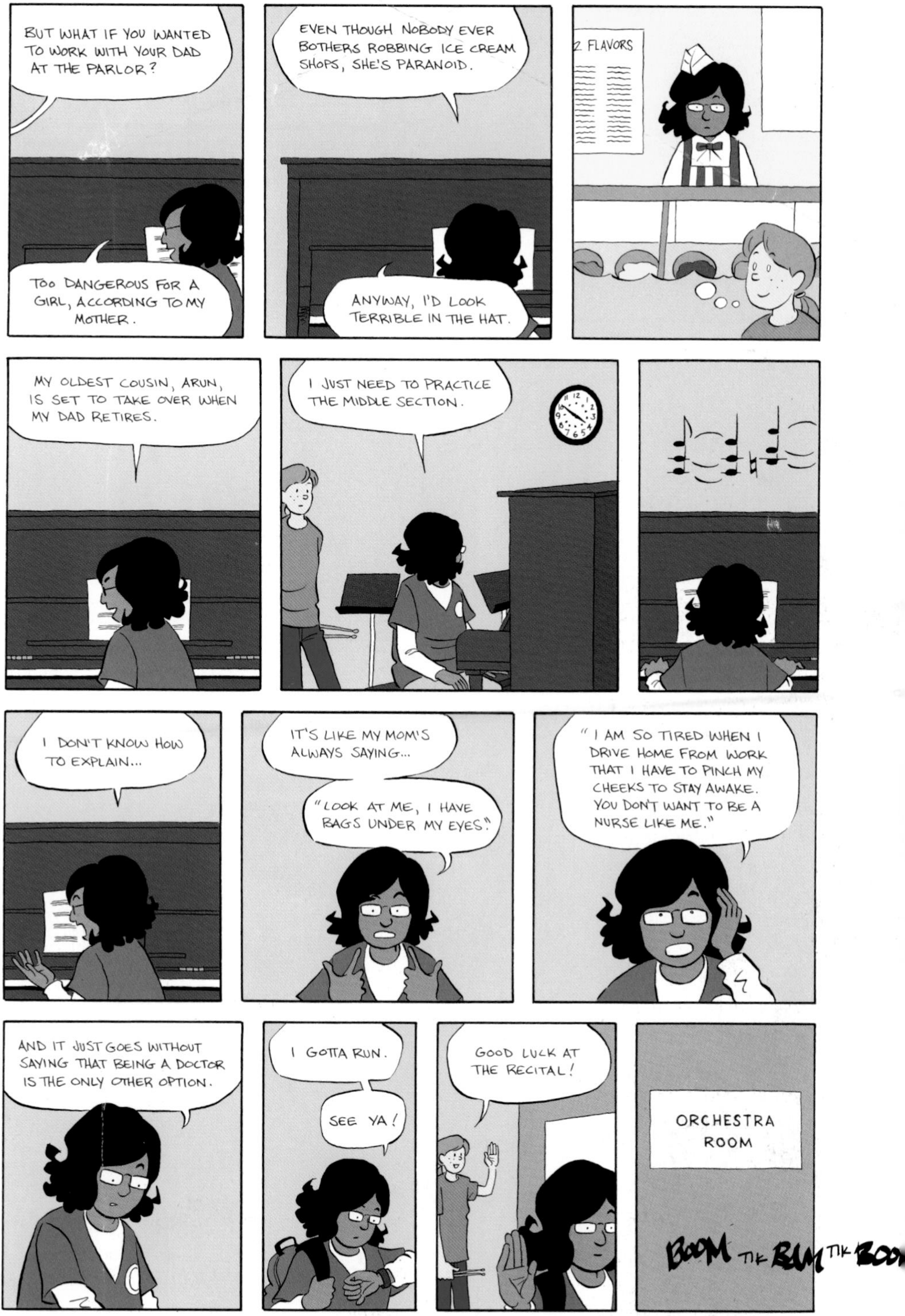

BUT WHAT IF YOU WANTED TO WORK WITH YOUR DAD AT THE PARLOR?
TOO DANGEROUS FOR A GIRL, ACCORDING TO MY MOTHER.
EVEN THOUGH NOBODY EVER BOTHERS ROBBING ICE CREAM SHOPS, SHE'S PARANOID.
ANYWAY, I'D LOOK TERRIBLE IN THE HAT.
2 FLAVORS
MY OLDEST COUSIN, ARUN, IS SET TO TAKE OVER WHEN MY DAD RETIRES.
I JUST NEED TO PRACTICE THE MIDDLE SECTION.
I DON'T KNOW HOW TO EXPLAIN...
IT'S LIKE MY MOM'S ALWAYS SAYING...
"LOOK AT ME, I HAVE BAGS UNDER MY EYES."
"I AM SO TIRED WHEN I DRIVE HOME FROM WORK THAT I HAVE TO PINCH MY CHEEKS TO STAY AWAKE. YOU DON'T WANT TO BE A NURSE LIKE ME."
AND IT JUST GOES WITHOUT SAYING THAT BEING A DOCTOR IS THE ONLY OTHER OPTION.
I GOTTA RUN.
SEE YA!
GOOD LUCK AT THE RECITAL!
ORCHESTRA ROOM
BOOM TIK BUM TIK

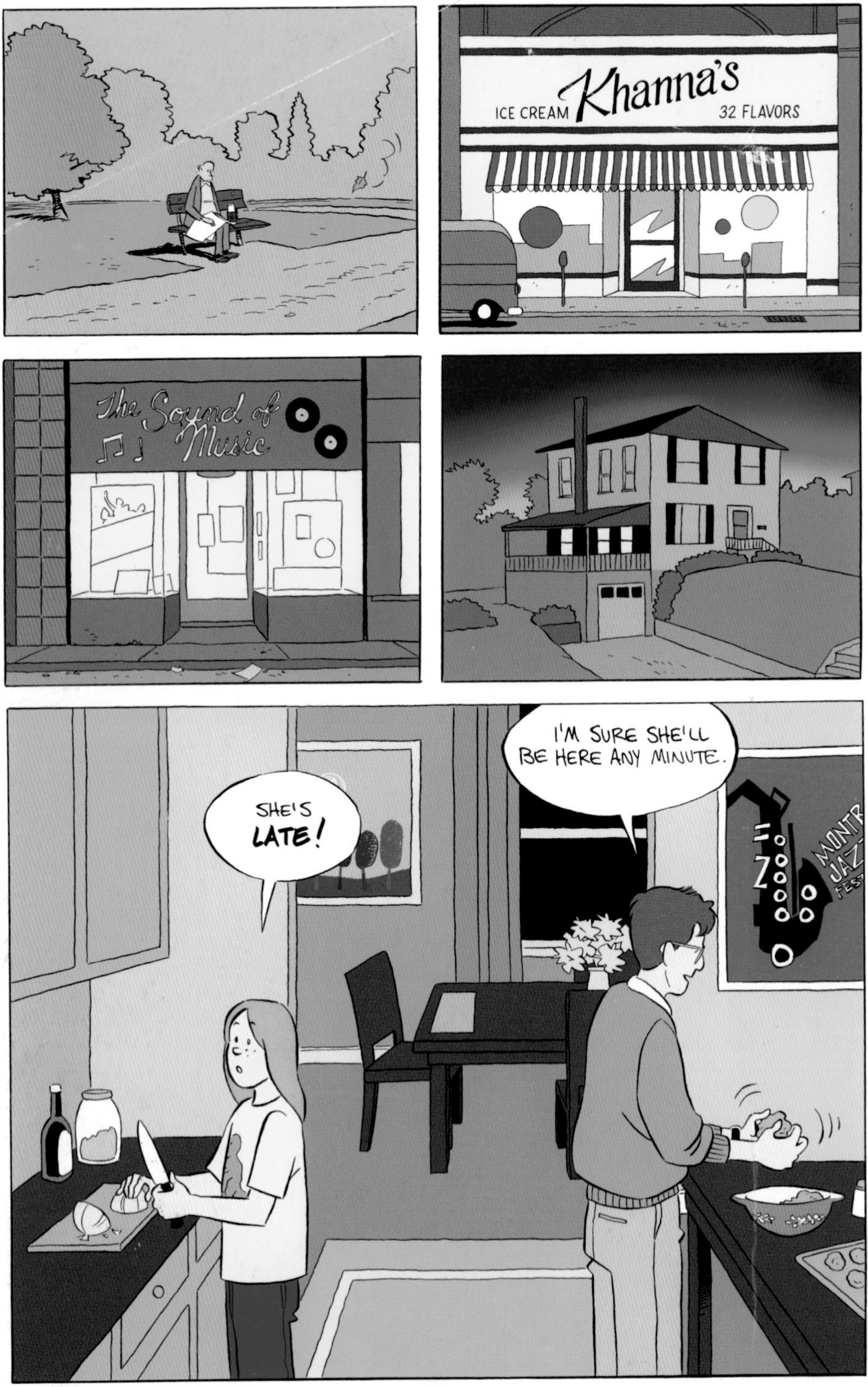
ICE CREAM
Khanna's
32 FLAVORS
The Sound of Music
SHE'S LATE!
I'M SURE SHE'LL BE HERE ANY MINUTE.

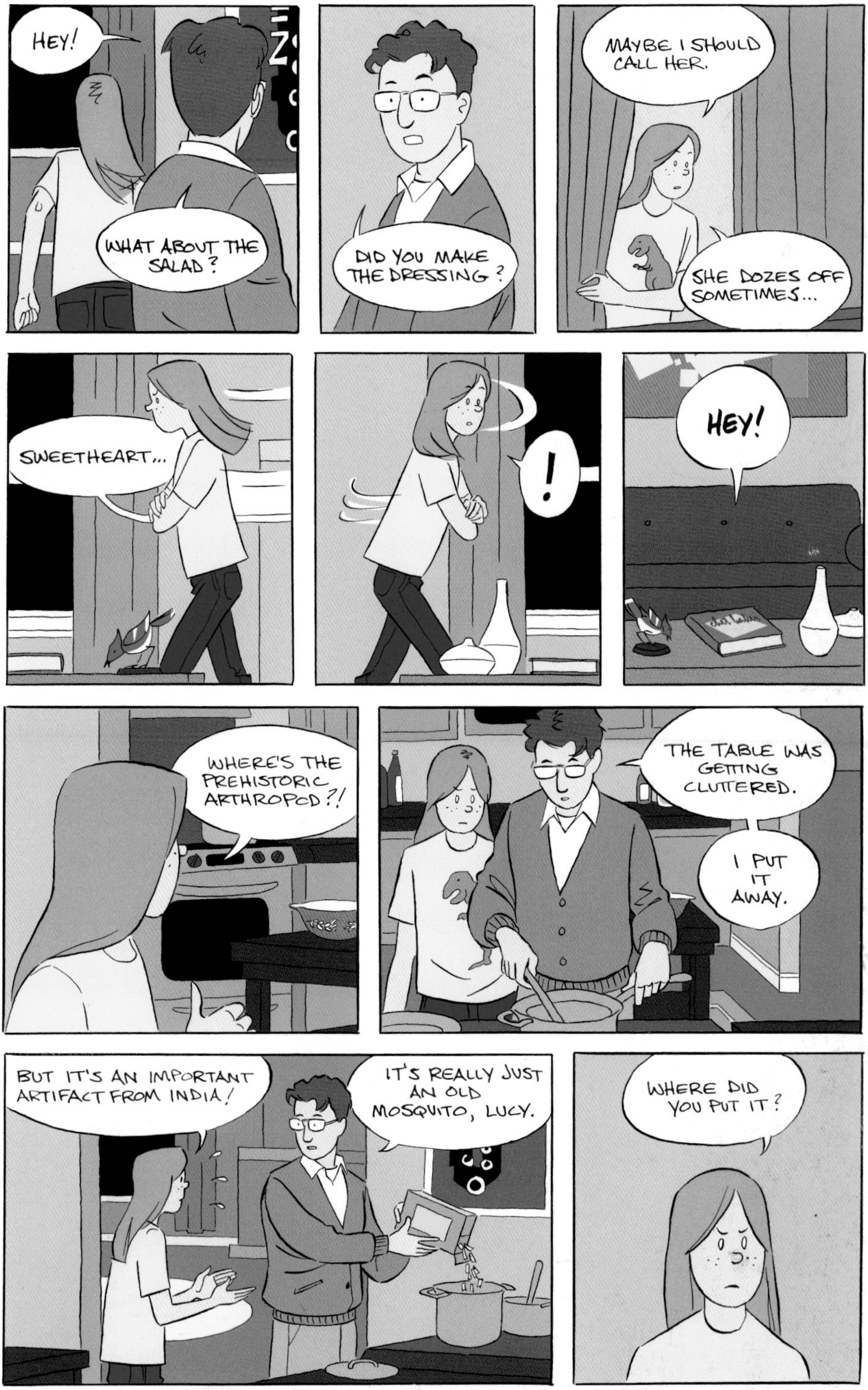
HEY!
WHAT ABOUT THE SALAD?
DID YOU MAKE THE DRESSING?
MAYBE I SHOULD CALL HER.
SHE DOZES OFF SOMETIMES...
SWEETHEART...
!
HEY!
WHERE'S THE PREHISTORIC ARTHROPOD?!
THE TABLE WAS GETTING CLUTTERED.
I PUT IT AWAY.
BUT IT'S AN IMPORTANT ARTIFACT FROM INDIA!
IT'S REALLY JUST AN OLD MOSQUITO, LUCY.
WHERE DID YOU PUT IT?

IN ONE OF THE BOXES IN THE HALLWAY CLOSET UPSTAIRS. CAN I GET IT FOR YOU LATER?

NO!

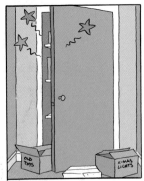

OLD TOYS

X-MAS LIGHTS

LUTZOMYIA AN

HERE YOU GO.

WHAT'S IN THIS BOX ANYWAY? IT'S SO HEAVY!

THEY'RE RECORDS. MY OLD COLLECTION.

AND SOME OF YOUR MOM'S, TOO.

HANG ON.

THANKS.

THAT'S THE PASTA.

BE BEEP

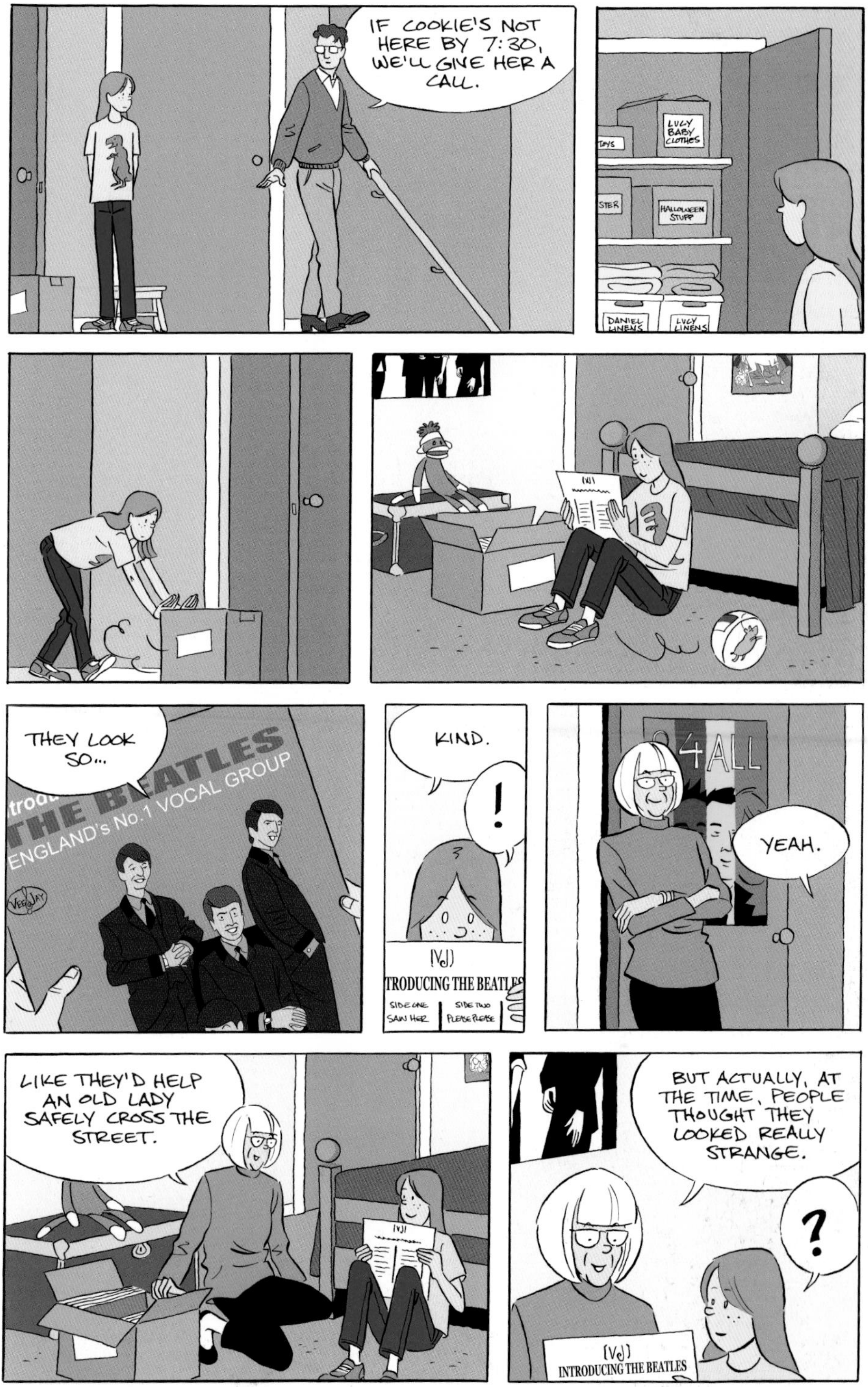
IF COOKIE'S NOT HERE BY 7:30, WE'LL GIVE HER A CALL.
LUCY BABY CLOTHES
TOYS
STER
HALLOWEEN STUFF
DANIEL LINENS
LUCY LINENS
THEY LOOK SO...
THE BEATLES
ENGLAND's No.1 VOCAL GROUP
VEE JAY
KIND.
!
INTRODUCING THE BEATLES
SIDE ONE
SIDE TWO
SAW HER
PLEASE PLEASE
4ALL
YEAH.
LIKE THEY'D HELP AN OLD LADY SAFELY CROSS THE STREET.
BUT ACTUALLY, AT THE TIME, PEOPLE THOUGHT THEY LOOKED REALLY STRANGE.
?
INTRODUCING THE BEATLES

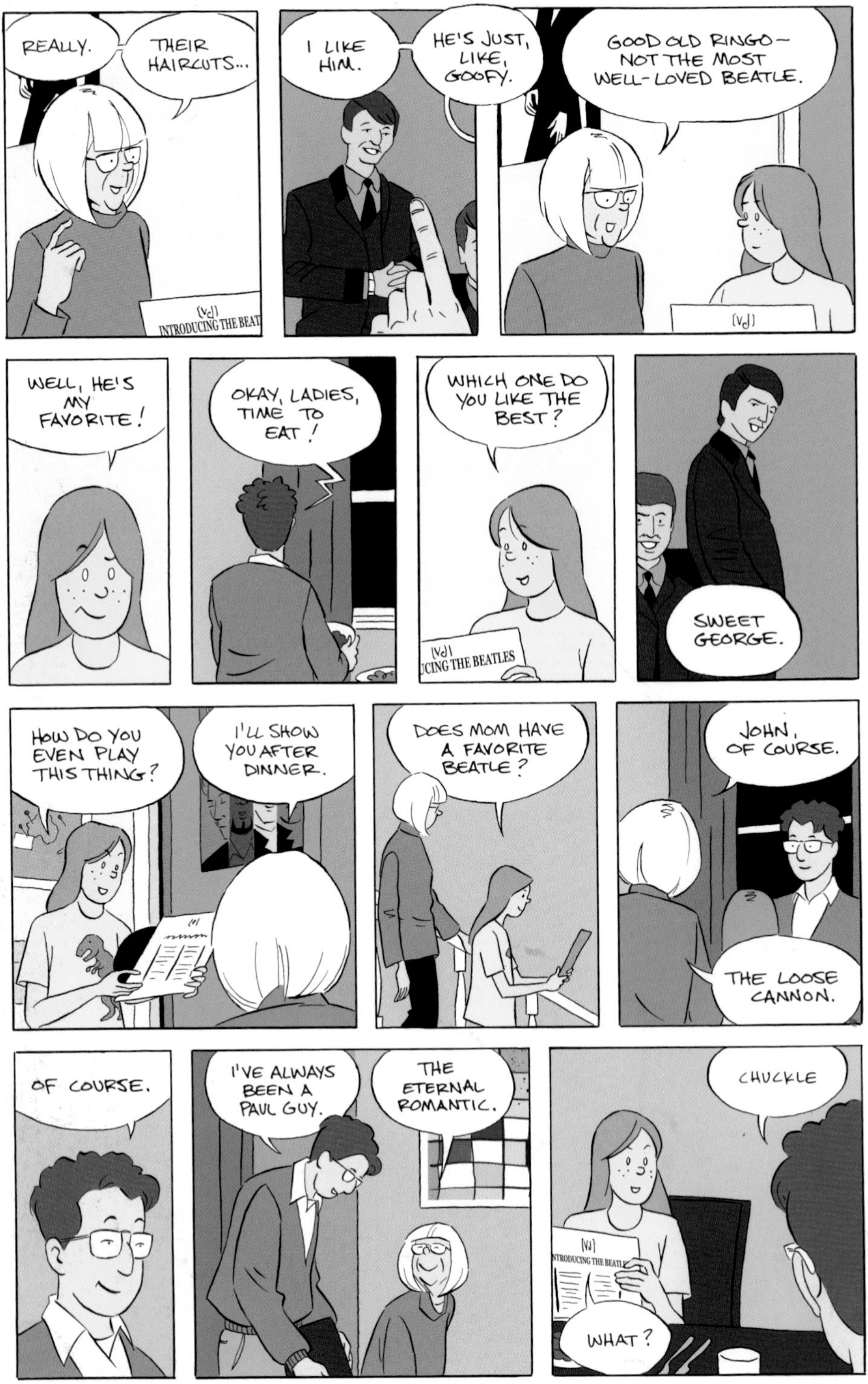
REALLY.
THEIR HAIRCUTS...
[VJ]
INTRODUCING THE BEAT
I LIKE HIM.
HE'S JUST, LIKE, GOOFY.
GOOD OLD RINGO— NOT THE MOST WELL-LOVED BEATLE.
[VJ]
WELL, HE'S MY FAVORITE!
OKAY, LADIES, TIME TO EAT!
WHICH ONE DO YOU LIKE THE BEST?
[VJ]
UCING THE BEATLES
SWEET GEORGE.
HOW DO YOU EVEN PLAY THIS THING?
I'LL SHOW YOU AFTER DINNER.
DOES MOM HAVE A FAVORITE BEATLE?
JOHN, OF COURSE.
THE LOOSE CANNON.
OF COURSE.
I'VE ALWAYS BEEN A PAUL GUY.
THE ETERNAL ROMANTIC.
CHUCKLE
[VJ]
INTRODUCING THE BEATLE
WHAT?

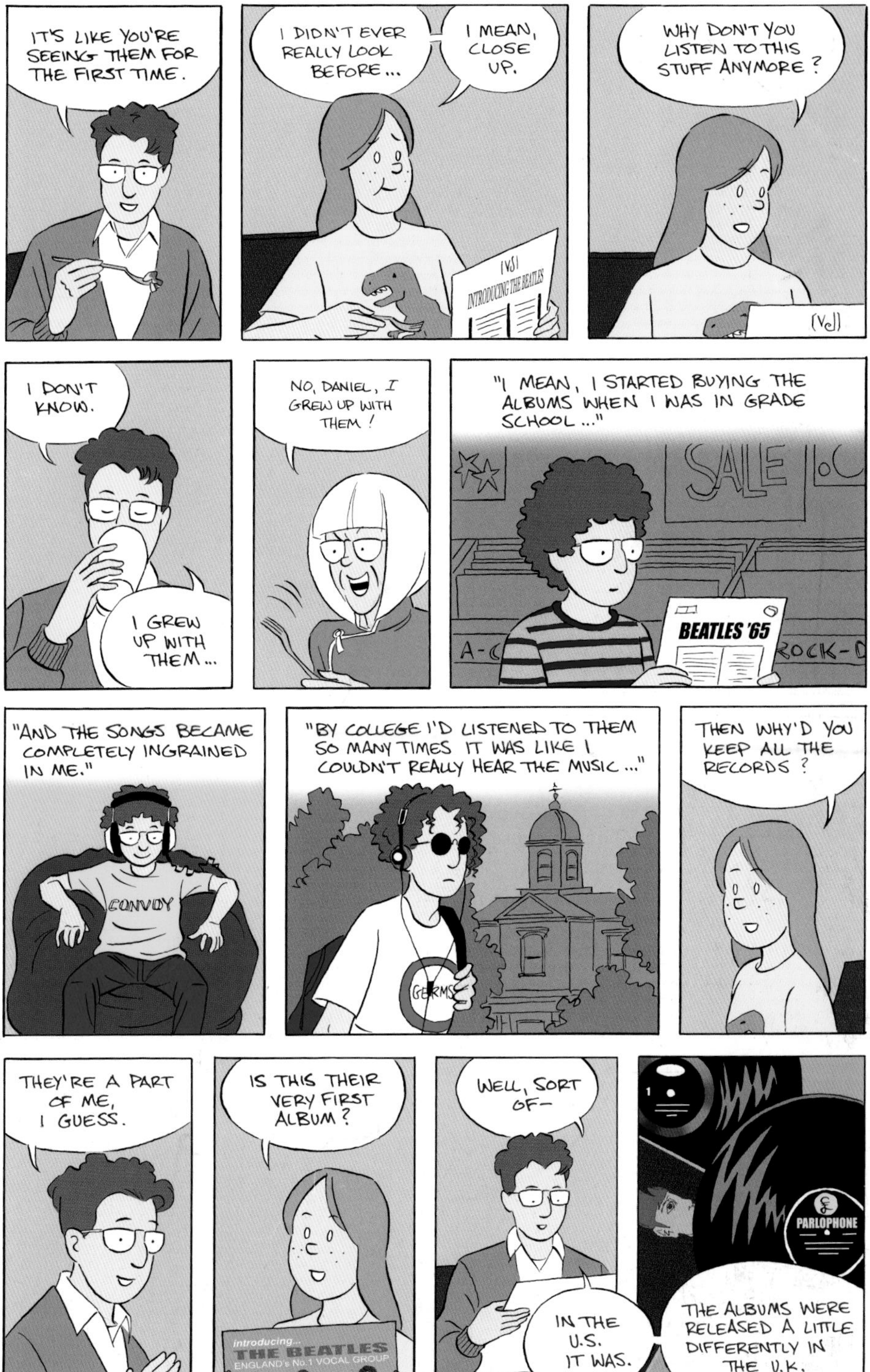
IT'S LIKE YOU'RE SEEING THEM FOR THE FIRST TIME.
I DIDN'T EVER REALLY LOOK BEFORE...
I MEAN, CLOSE UP.
INTRODUCING THE BEATLES
WHY DON'T YOU LISTEN TO THIS STUFF ANYMORE?
I DON'T KNOW.
I GREW UP WITH THEM...
NO, DANIEL, I GREW UP WITH THEM!
"I MEAN, I STARTED BUYING THE ALBUMS WHEN I WAS IN GRADE SCHOOL..."
SALE
BEATLES '65
A-C
ROCK-D
"AND THE SONGS BECAME COMPLETELY INGRAINED IN ME."
CONVOY
"BY COLLEGE I'D LISTENED TO THEM SO MANY TIMES IT WAS LIKE I COULDN'T REALLY HEAR THE MUSIC..."
GERMS
THEN WHY'D YOU KEEP ALL THE RECORDS?
THEY'RE A PART OF ME, I GUESS.
IS THIS THEIR VERY FIRST ALBUM?
introducing... THE BEATLES
ENGLAND's No.1 VOCAL GROUP
WELL, SORT OF–
IN THE U.S. IT WAS.
PARLOPHONE
THE ALBUMS WERE RELEASED A LITTLE DIFFERENTLY IN THE U.K.

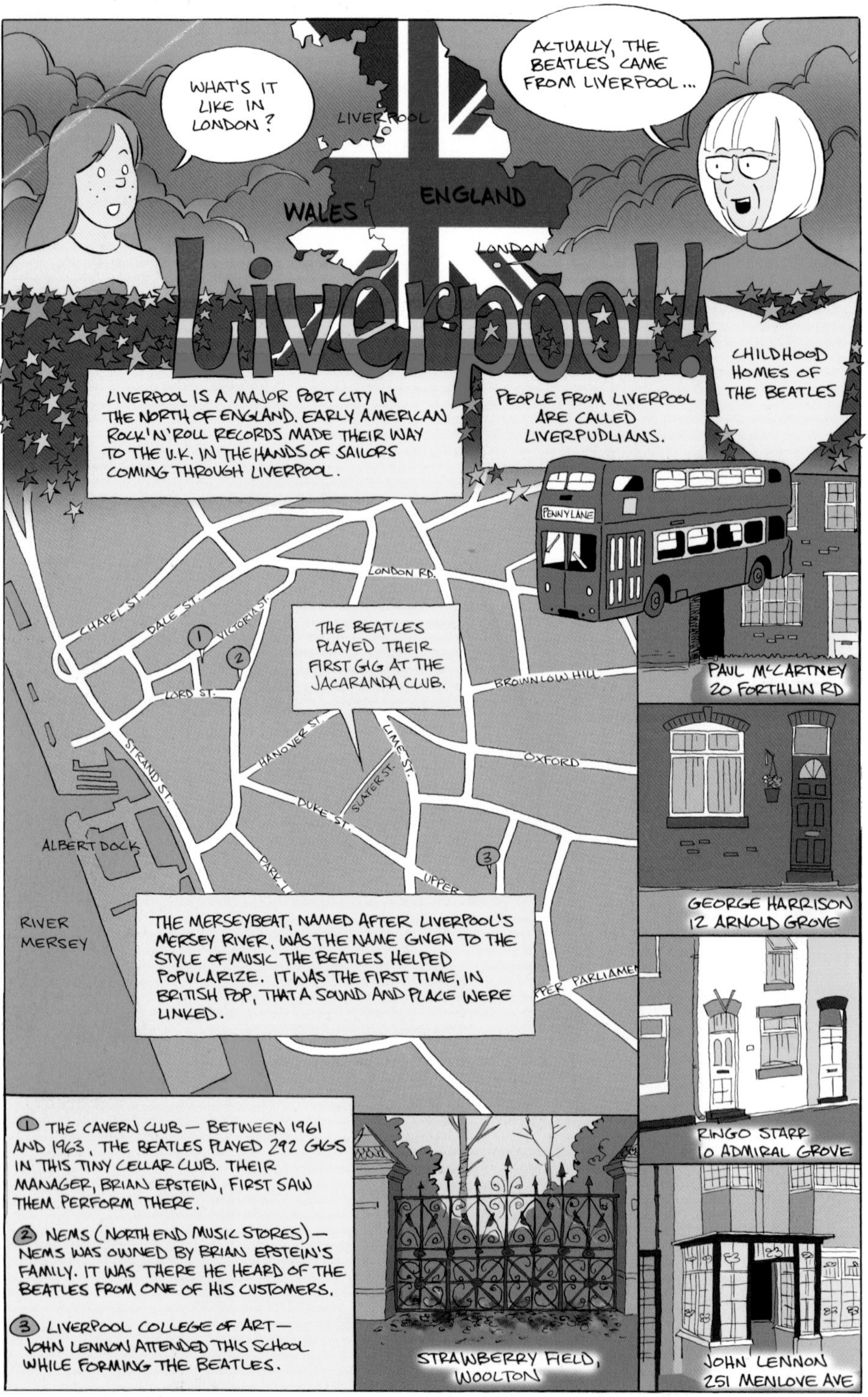

WHAT'S IT LIKE IN LONDON?
ACTUALLY, THE BEATLES CAME FROM LIVERPOOL...
LIVERPOOL
WALES
ENGLAND
LONDON
Liverpool!
LIVERPOOL IS A MAJOR PORT CITY IN THE NORTH OF ENGLAND. EARLY AMERICAN ROCK'N'ROLL RECORDS MADE THEIR WAY TO THE U.K. IN THE HANDS OF SAILORS COMING THROUGH LIVERPOOL.
PEOPLE FROM LIVERPOOL ARE CALLED LIVERPUDLIANS.
CHILDHOOD HOMES OF THE BEATLES
PENNY LANE
LONDON RD.
CHAPEL ST.
DALE ST.
VICTORIA ST.
LORD ST.
BROWNLOW HILL
STRAND ST.
HANOVER ST.
LIME ST.
SLATER ST.
DUKE ST.
OXFORD
ALBERT DOCK
PARK L
UPPER
PPER PARLIAMEN
RIVER MERSEY
THE BEATLES PLAYED THEIR FIRST GIG AT THE JACARANDA CLUB.
THE MERSEYBEAT, NAMED AFTER LIVERPOOL'S MERSEY RIVER, WAS THE NAME GIVEN TO THE STYLE OF MUSIC THE BEATLES HELPED POPULARIZE. IT WAS THE FIRST TIME, IN BRITISH POP, THAT A SOUND AND PLACE WERE LINKED.
PAUL McCARTNEY 20 FORTHLIN RD
GEORGE HARRISON 12 ARNOLD GROVE
RINGO STARR 10 ADMIRAL GROVE
JOHN LENNON 251 MENLOVE AVE
STRAWBERRY FIELD, WOOLTON
① THE CAVERN CLUB — BETWEEN 1961 AND 1963, THE BEATLES PLAYED 292 GIGS IN THIS TINY CELLAR CLUB. THEIR MANAGER, BRIAN EPSTEIN, FIRST SAW THEM PERFORM THERE.
② NEMS (NORTH END MUSIC STORES) — NEMS WAS OWNED BY BRIAN EPSTEIN'S FAMILY. IT WAS THERE HE HEARD OF THE BEATLES FROM ONE OF HIS CUSTOMERS.
③ LIVERPOOL COLLEGE OF ART — JOHN LENNON ATTENDED THIS SCHOOL WHILE FORMING THE BEATLES.

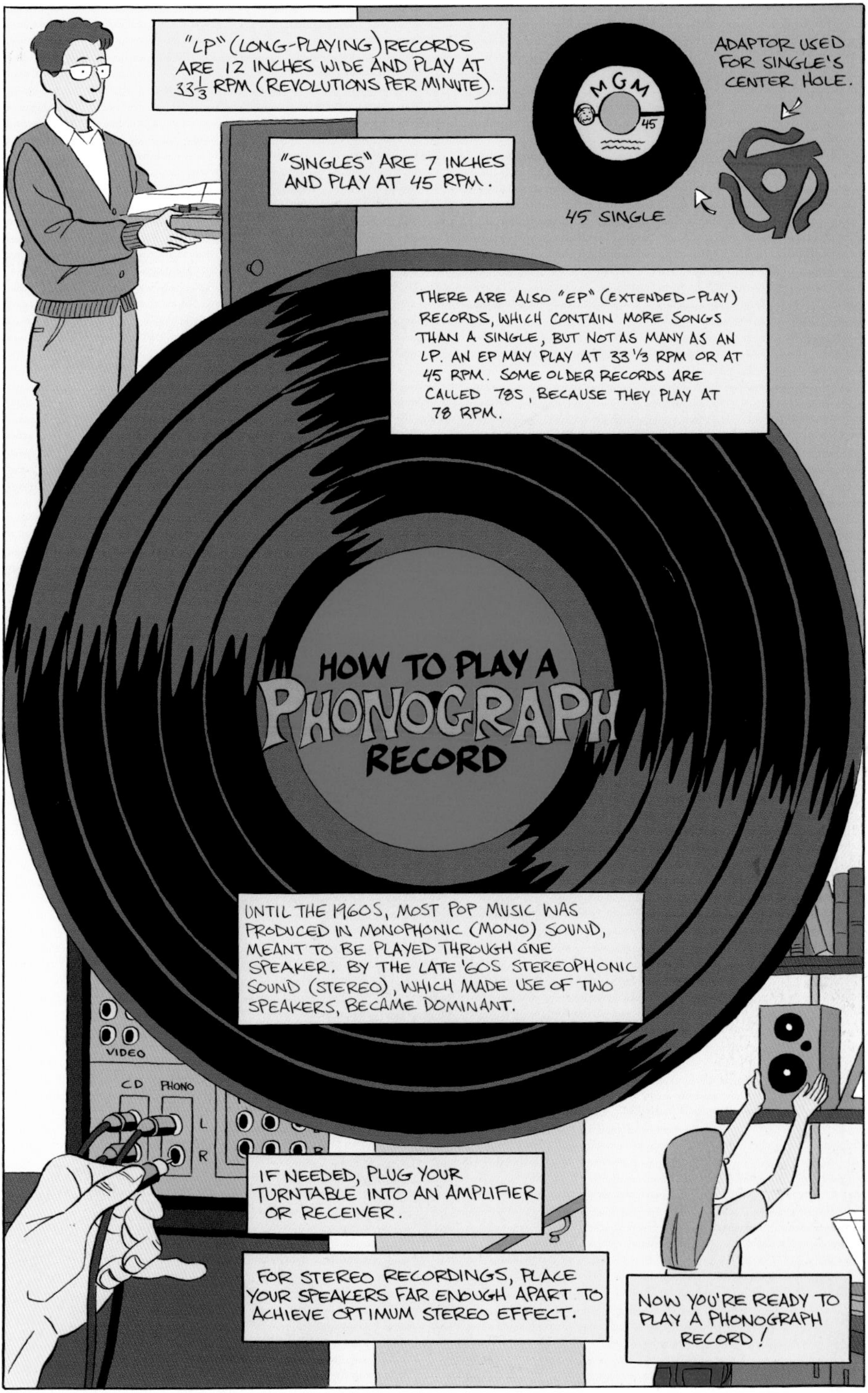
"LP" (LONG-PLAYING) RECORDS ARE 12 INCHES WIDE AND PLAY AT 33 1/3 RPM (REVOLUTIONS PER MINUTE).
MGM
45
ADAPTOR USED FOR SINGLE'S CENTER HOLE.
"SINGLES" ARE 7 INCHES AND PLAY AT 45 RPM.
45 SINGLE
THERE ARE ALSO "EP" (EXTENDED-PLAY) RECORDS, WHICH CONTAIN MORE SONGS THAN A SINGLE, BUT NOT AS MANY AS AN LP. AN EP MAY PLAY AT 33 1/3 RPM OR AT 45 RPM. SOME OLDER RECORDS ARE CALLED 78S, BECAUSE THEY PLAY AT 78 RPM.
HOW TO PLAY A PHONOGRAPH RECORD
UNTIL THE 1960S, MOST POP MUSIC WAS PRODUCED IN MONOPHONIC (MONO) SOUND, MEANT TO BE PLAYED THROUGH ONE SPEAKER. BY THE LATE '60S STEREOPHONIC SOUND (STEREO), WHICH MADE USE OF TWO SPEAKERS, BECAME DOMINANT.
VIDEO
CD
PHONO
L
R
IF NEEDED, PLUG YOUR TURNTABLE INTO AN AMPLIFIER OR RECEIVER.
FOR STEREO RECORDINGS, PLACE YOUR SPEAKERS FAR ENOUGH APART TO ACHIEVE OPTIMUM STEREO EFFECT.
NOW YOU'RE READY TO PLAY A PHONOGRAPH RECORD!

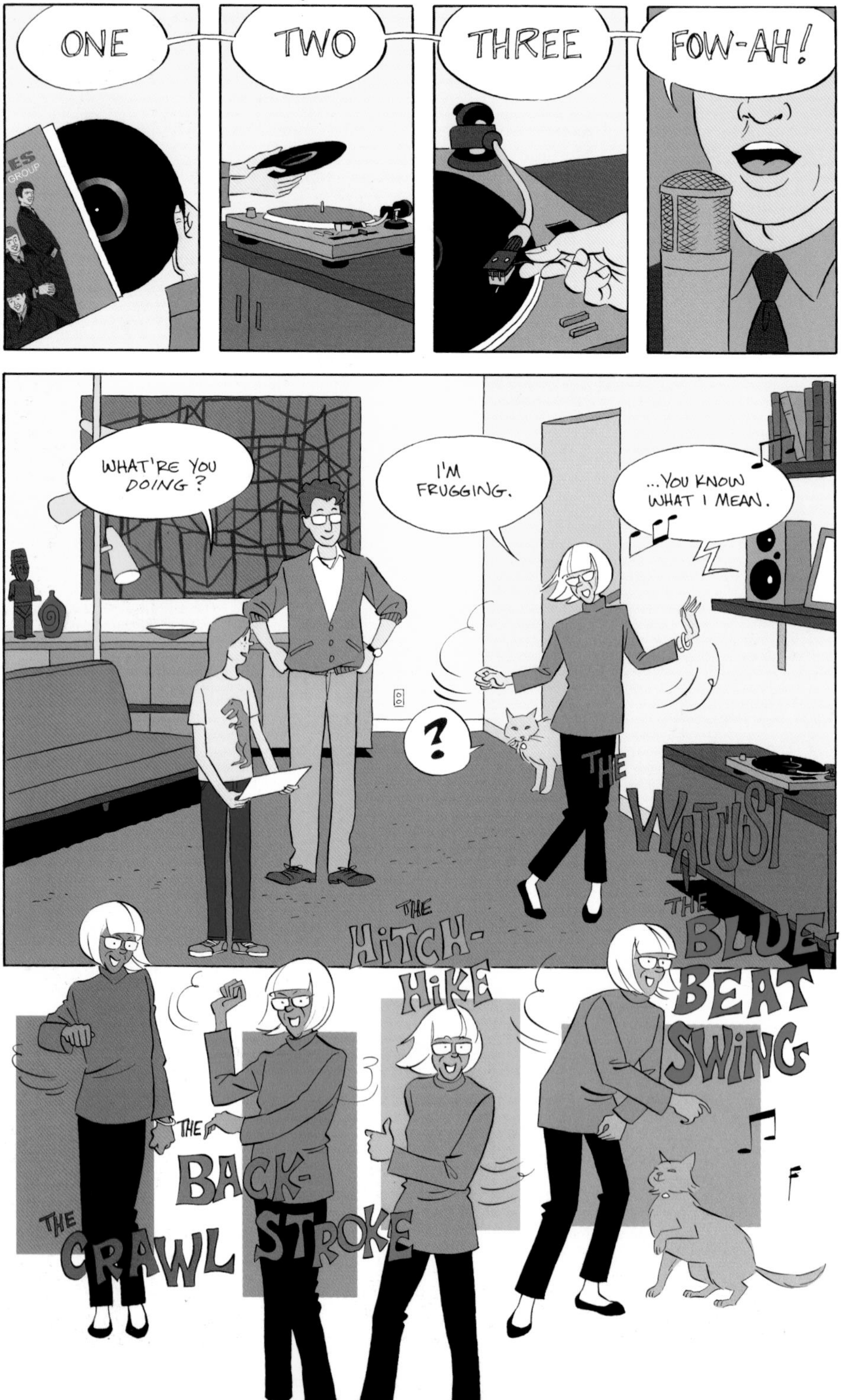
ONE
TWO
THREE
FOW-AH!
WHAT'RE YOU DOING?
I'M FRUGGING.
...YOU KNOW WHAT I MEAN.
?
THE WATUSI
THE HITCH-HIKE
THE BLUE BEAT SWING
THE BACK-STROKE
THE CRAWL

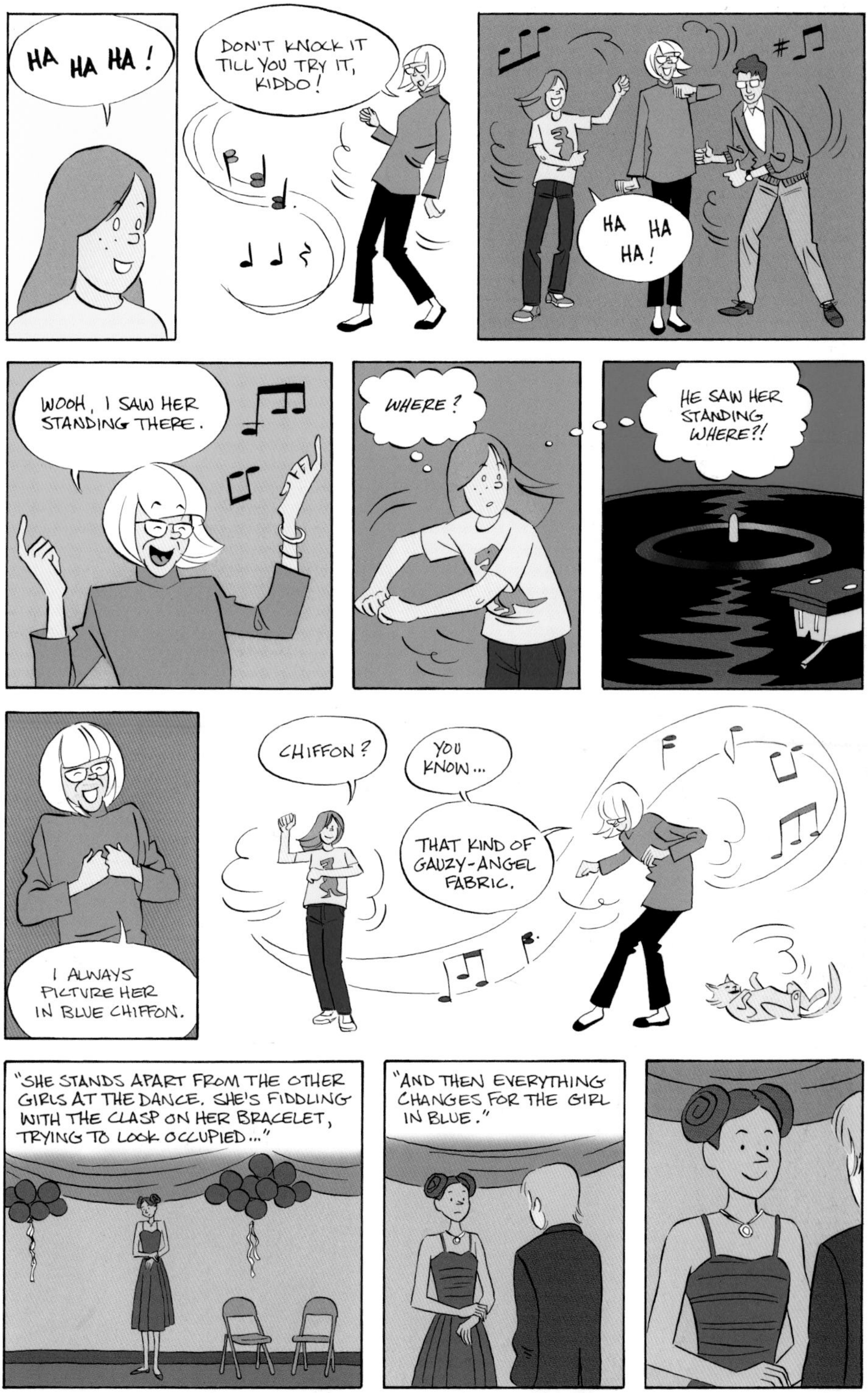
HA HA HA!
DON'T KNOCK IT TILL YOU TRY IT, KIDDO!
HA HA HA!
WOOH, I SAW HER STANDING THERE.
WHERE?
HE SAW HER STANDING WHERE?!
I ALWAYS PICTURE HER IN BLUE CHIFFON.
CHIFFON?
YOU KNOW...
THAT KIND OF GAUZY-ANGEL FABRIC.
"SHE STANDS APART FROM THE OTHER GIRLS AT THE DANCE. SHE'S FIDDLING WITH THE CLASP ON HER BRACELET, TRYING TO LOOK OCCUPIED..."
"AND THEN EVERYTHING CHANGES FOR THE GIRL IN BLUE."

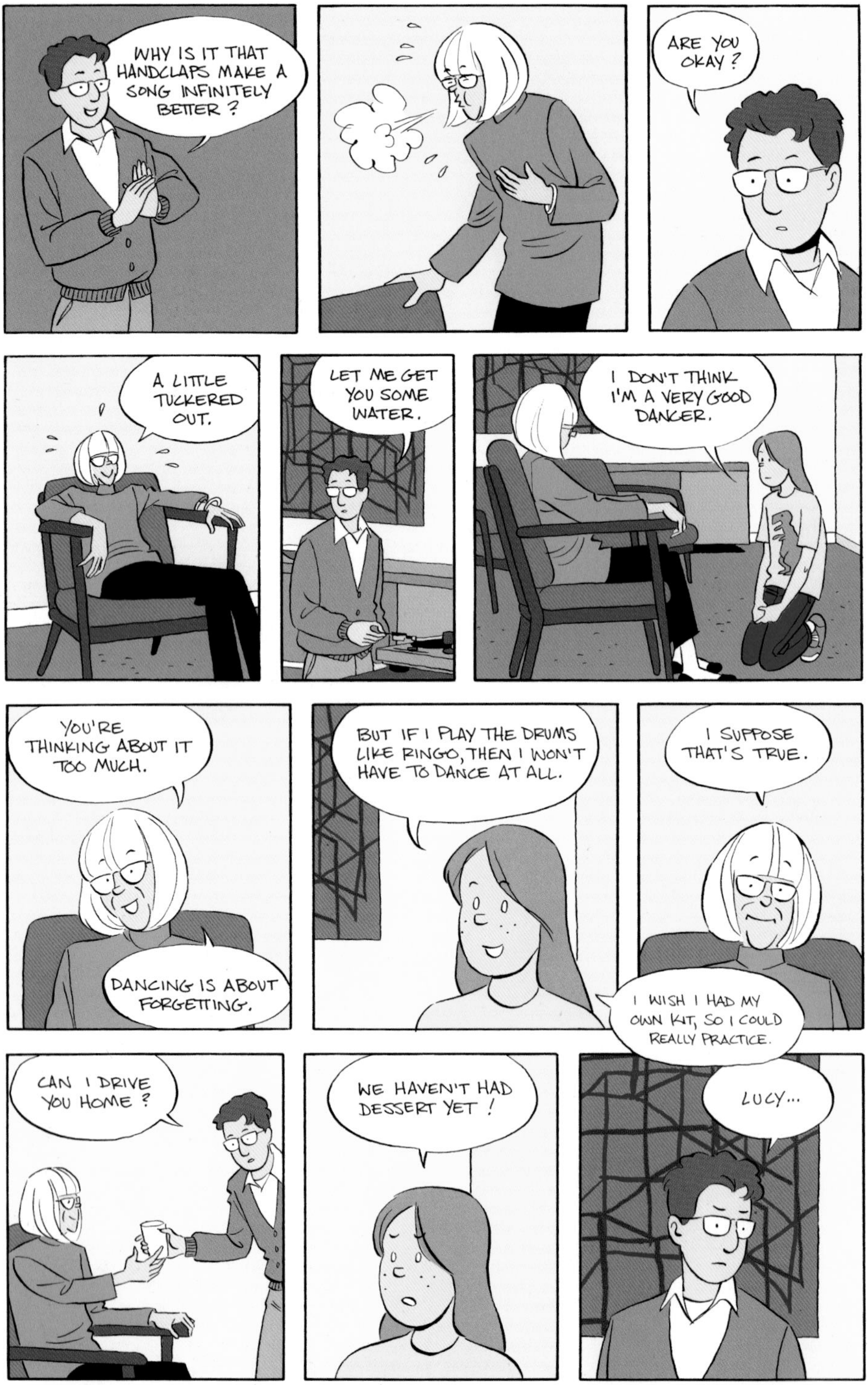
WHY IS IT THAT HANDCLAPS MAKE A SONG INFINITELY BETTER?
ARE YOU OKAY?
A LITTLE TUCKERED OUT.
LET ME GET YOU SOME WATER.
I DON'T THINK I'M A VERY GOOD DANCER.
YOU'RE THINKING ABOUT IT TOO MUCH.
DANCING IS ABOUT FORGETTING.
BUT IF I PLAY THE DRUMS LIKE RINGO, THEN I WON'T HAVE TO DANCE AT ALL.
I SUPPOSE THAT'S TRUE.
I WISH I HAD MY OWN KIT, SO I COULD REALLY PRACTICE.
CAN I DRIVE YOU HOME?
WE HAVEN'T HAD DESSERT YET!
LUCY...

THE SNICKERDOODLES ARE IN THE TUPPERWARE.

KISS

I THINK I SET THEM ON THE COUNTER NEXT TO THE FRIDGE.

YOU HAVE AN EXTRA ONE FOR ME.

OKAY?

SKRTCHH ...

MISERY!...

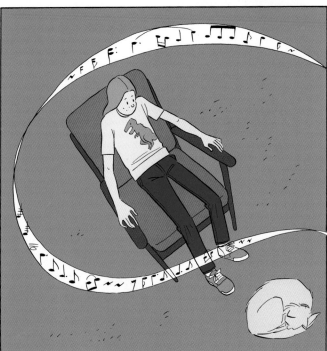

TAP TAP

TAP TAP

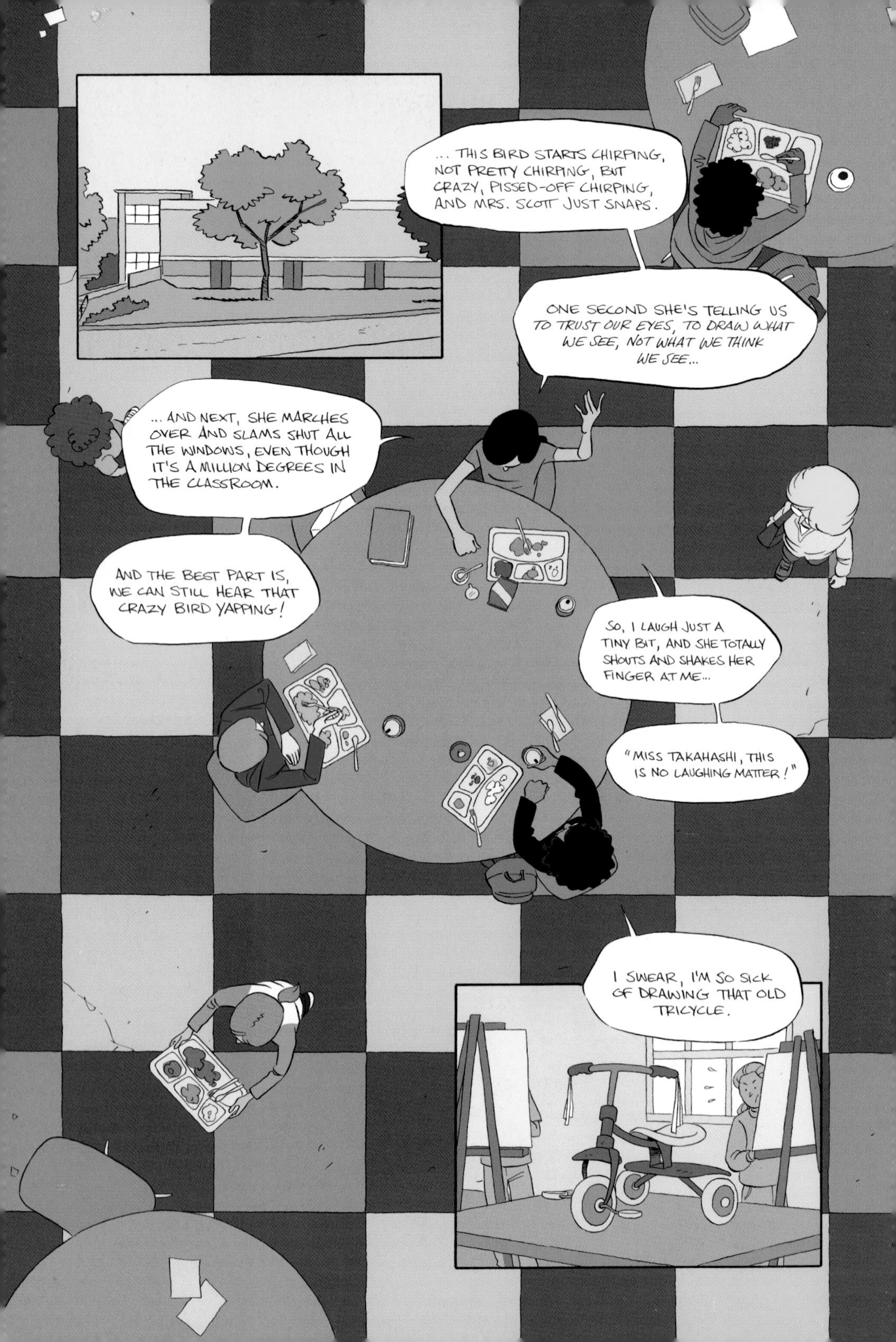
... THIS BIRD STARTS CHIRPING, NOT PRETTY CHIRPING, BUT CRAZY, PISSED-OFF CHIRPING, AND MRS. SCOTT JUST SNAPS.
ONE SECOND SHE'S TELLING US TO TRUST OUR EYES, TO DRAW WHAT WE SEE, NOT WHAT WE THINK WE SEE...
... AND NEXT, SHE MARCHES OVER AND SLAMS SHUT ALL THE WINDOWS, EVEN THOUGH IT'S A MILLION DEGREES IN THE CLASSROOM.
AND THE BEST PART IS, WE CAN STILL HEAR THAT CRAZY BIRD YAPPING!
SO, I LAUGH JUST A TINY BIT, AND SHE TOTALLY SHOUTS AND SHAKES HER FINGER AT ME...
"MISS TAKAHASHI, THIS IS NO LAUGHING MATTER!"
I SWEAR, I'M SO SICK OF DRAWING THAT OLD TRICYCLE.

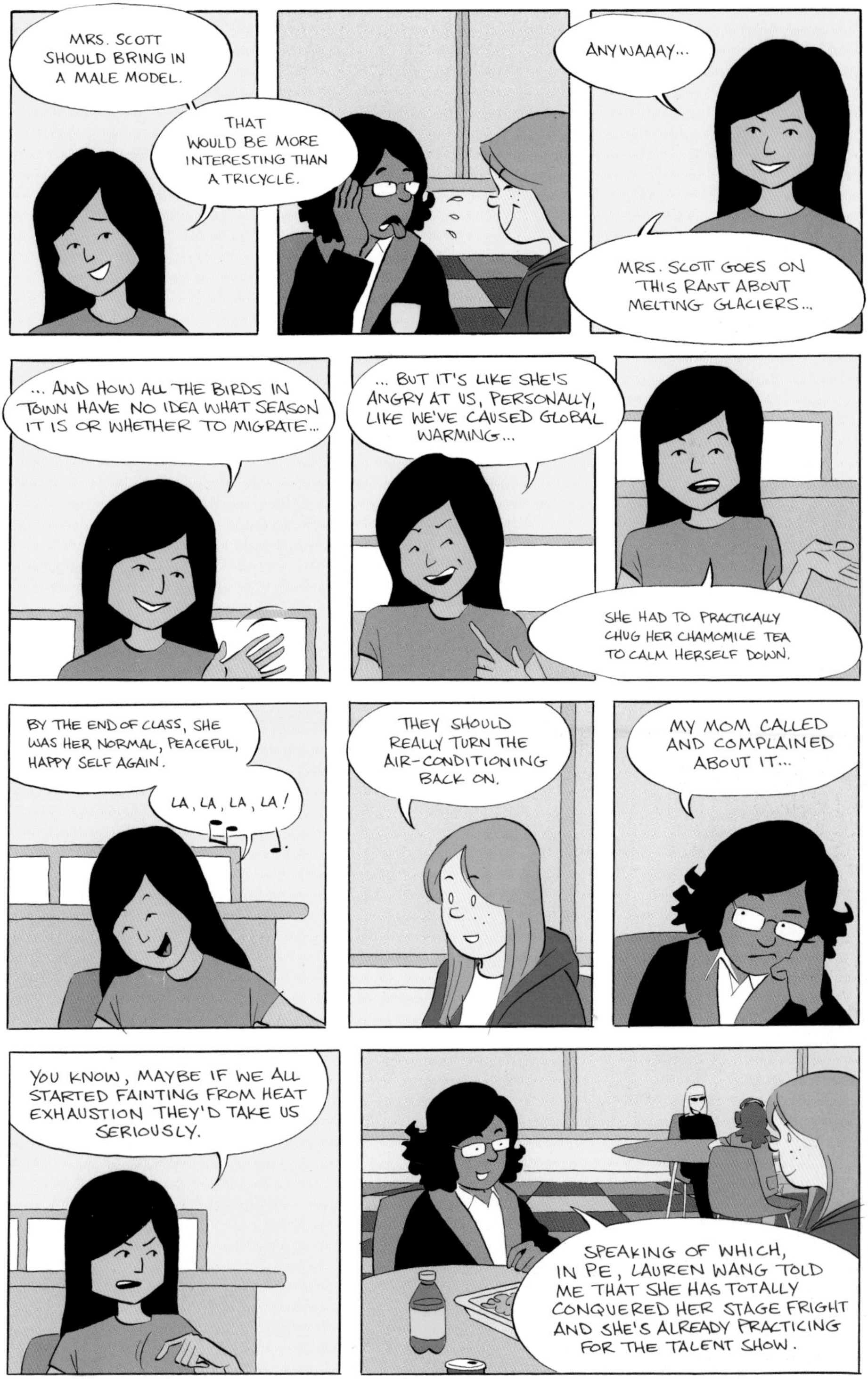
MRS. SCOTT SHOULD BRING IN A MALE MODEL.
THAT WOULD BE MORE INTERESTING THAN A TRICYCLE.
ANYWAAAY...
MRS. SCOTT GOES ON THIS RANT ABOUT MELTING GLACIERS...
... AND HOW ALL THE BIRDS IN TOWN HAVE NO IDEA WHAT SEASON IT IS OR WHETHER TO MIGRATE...
... BUT IT'S LIKE SHE'S ANGRY AT US, PERSONALLY, LIKE WE'VE CAUSED GLOBAL WARMING...
SHE HAD TO PRACTICALLY CHUG HER CHAMOMILE TEA TO CALM HERSELF DOWN.
BY THE END OF CLASS, SHE WAS HER NORMAL, PEACEFUL, HAPPY SELF AGAIN.
LA, LA, LA, LA!
THEY SHOULD REALLY TURN THE AIR-CONDITIONING BACK ON.
MY MOM CALLED AND COMPLAINED ABOUT IT...
YOU KNOW, MAYBE IF WE ALL STARTED FAINTING FROM HEAT EXHAUSTION THEY'D TAKE US SERIOUSLY.
SPEAKING OF WHICH, IN PE, LAUREN WANG TOLD ME THAT SHE HAS TOTALLY CONQUERED HER STAGE FRIGHT AND SHE'S ALREADY PRACTICING FOR THE TALENT SHOW.

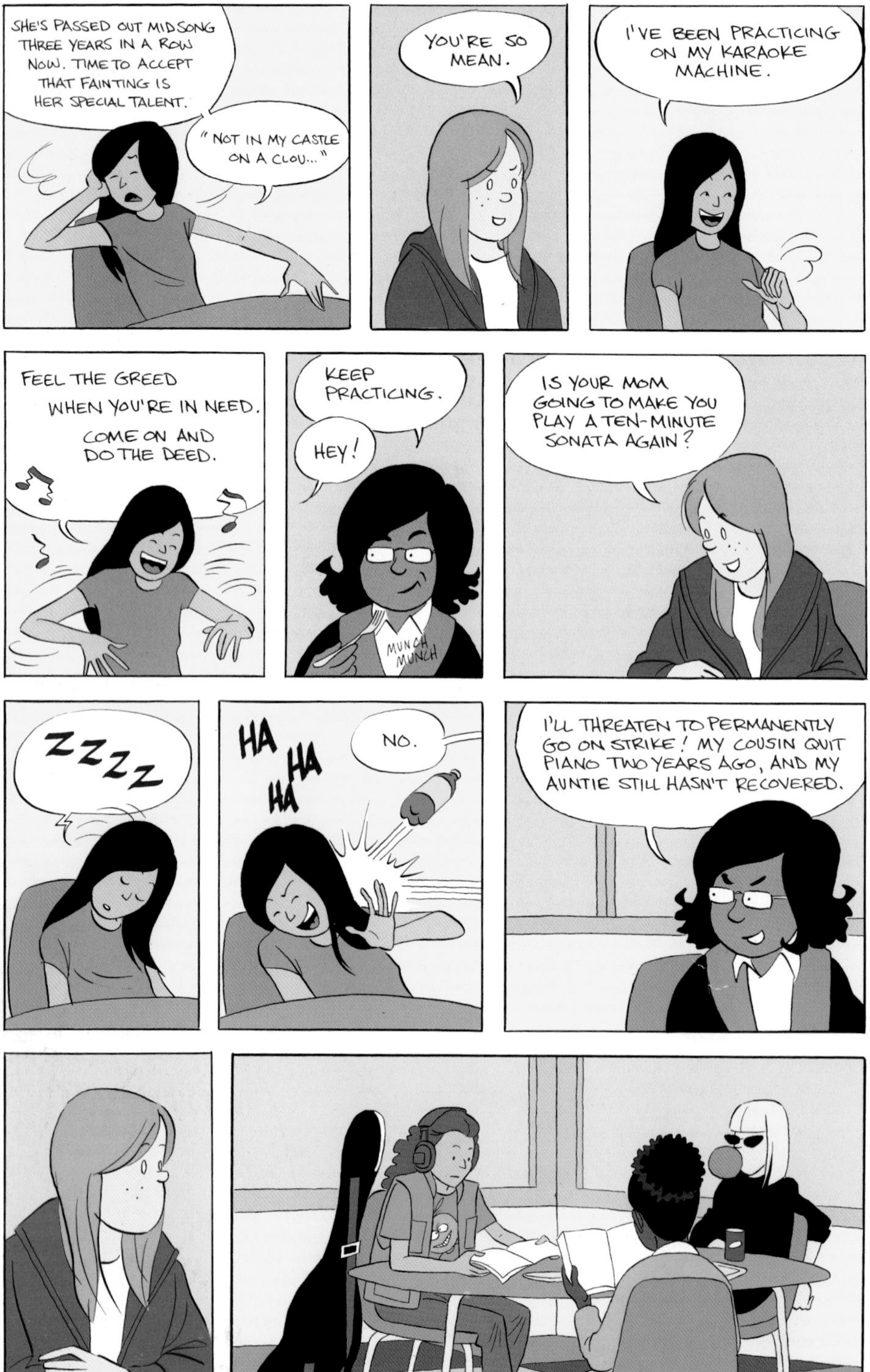
SHE'S PASSED OUT MIDSONG THREE YEARS IN A ROW NOW. TIME TO ACCEPT THAT FAINTING IS HER SPECIAL TALENT.
"NOT IN MY CASTLE ON A CLOU..."
YOU'RE SO MEAN.
I'VE BEEN PRACTICING ON MY KARAOKE MACHINE.
FEEL THE GREED WHEN YOU'RE IN NEED. COME ON AND DO THE DEED.
KEEP PRACTICING.
HEY!
MUNCH MUNCH
IS YOUR MOM GOING TO MAKE YOU PLAY A TEN-MINUTE SONATA AGAIN?
ZZZZ
HA HA HA
NO.
I'LL THREATEN TO PERMANENTLY GO ON STRIKE! MY COUSIN QUIT PIANO TWO YEARS AGO, AND MY AUNTIE STILL HASN'T RECOVERED.

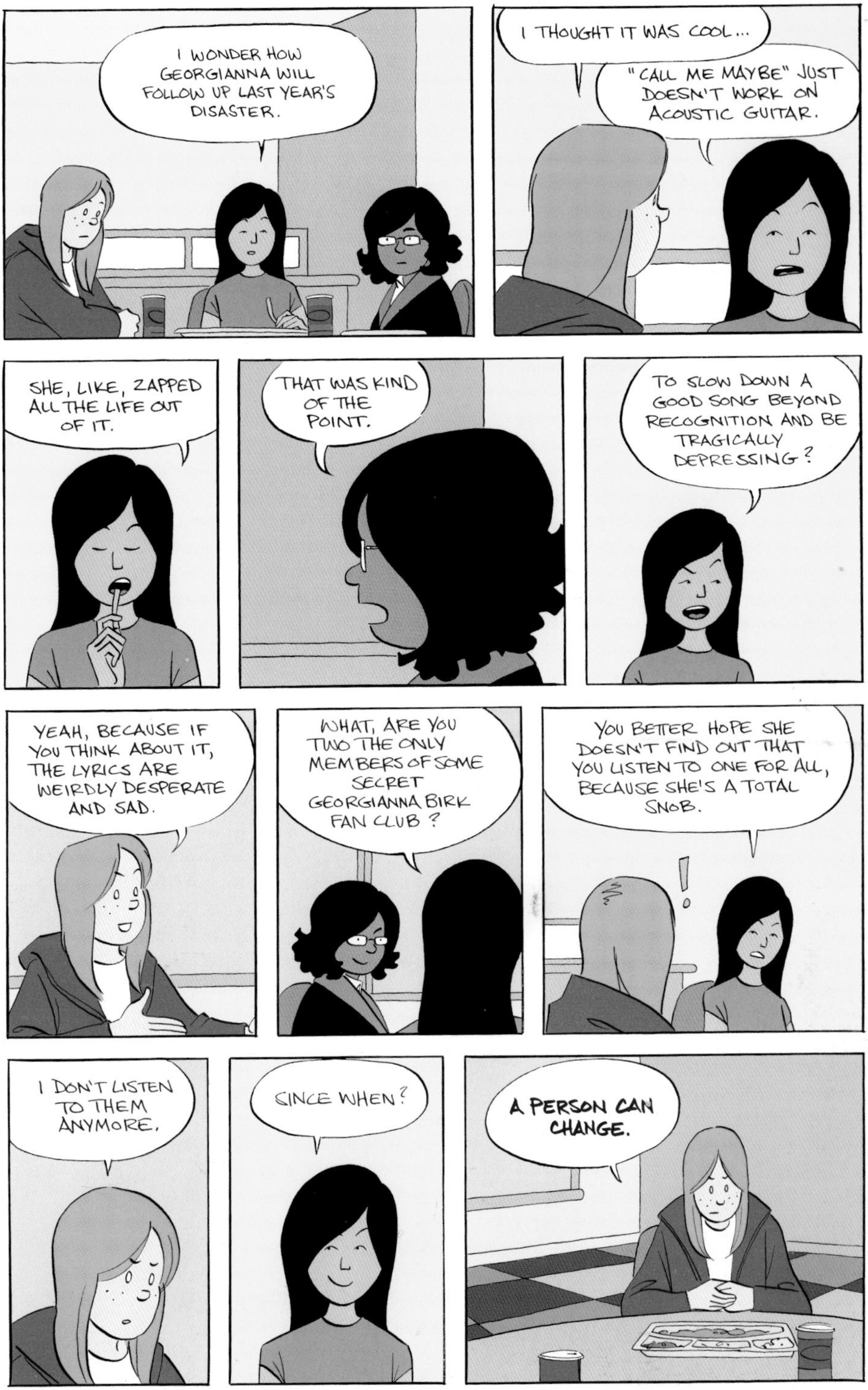
I WONDER HOW GEORGIANNA WILL FOLLOW UP LAST YEAR'S DISASTER.
I THOUGHT IT WAS COOL...
"CALL ME MAYBE" JUST DOESN'T WORK ON ACOUSTIC GUITAR.
SHE, LIKE, ZAPPED ALL THE LIFE OUT OF IT.
THAT WAS KIND OF THE POINT.
TO SLOW DOWN A GOOD SONG BEYOND RECOGNITION AND BE TRAGICALLY DEPRESSING?
YEAH, BECAUSE IF YOU THINK ABOUT IT, THE LYRICS ARE WEIRDLY DESPERATE AND SAD.
WHAT, ARE YOU TWO THE ONLY MEMBERS OF SOME SECRET GEORGIANNA BIRK FAN CLUB?
YOU BETTER HOPE SHE DOESN'T FIND OUT THAT YOU LISTEN TO ONE FOR ALL, BECAUSE SHE'S A TOTAL SNOB.
!
I DON'T LISTEN TO THEM ANYMORE.
SINCE WHEN?
A PERSON CAN CHANGE.

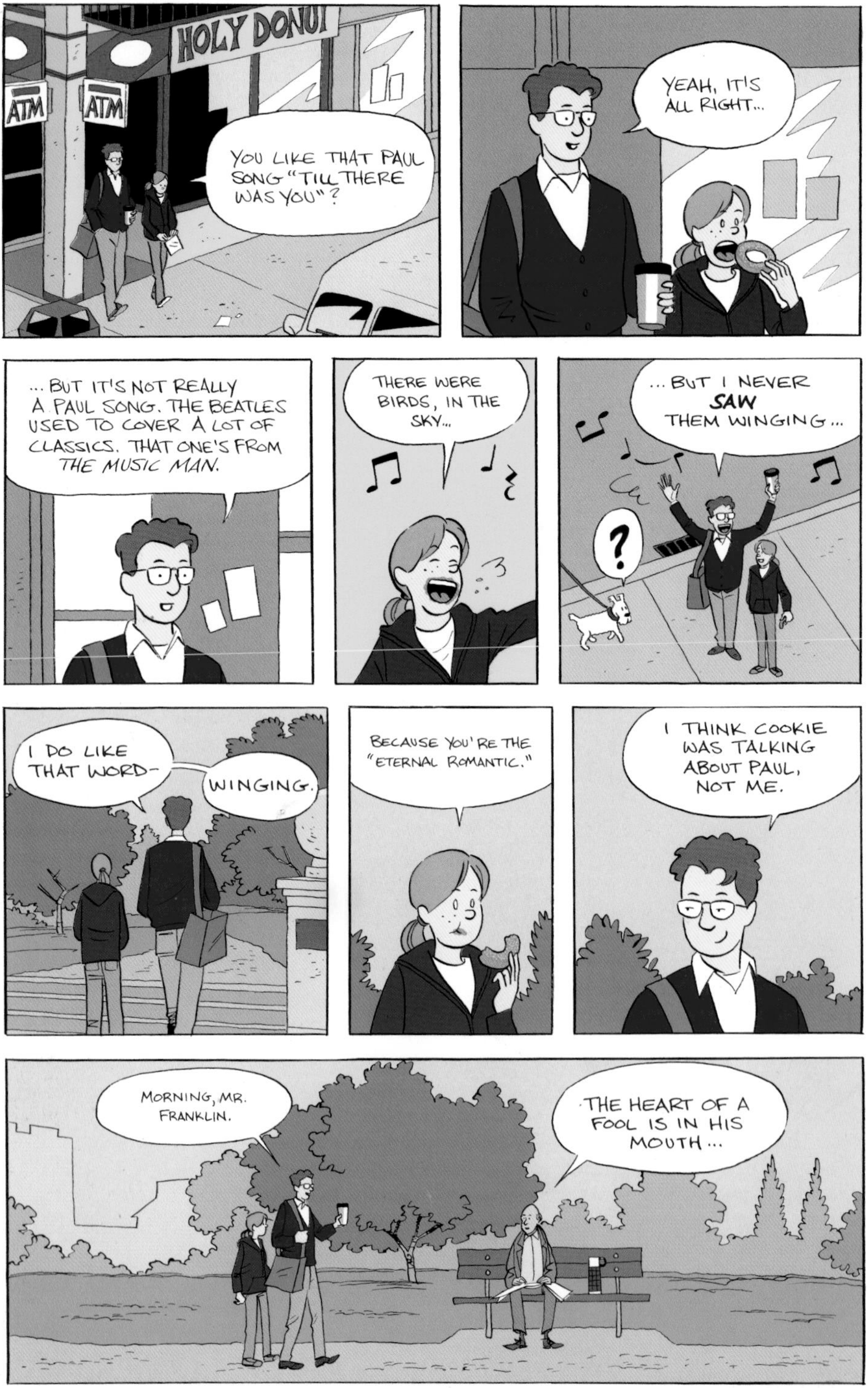
HOLY DONUT
ATM
ATM
YOU LIKE THAT PAUL SONG "TILL THERE WAS YOU"?
YEAH, IT'S ALL RIGHT...
... BUT IT'S NOT REALLY A PAUL SONG. THE BEATLES USED TO COVER A LOT OF CLASSICS. THAT ONE'S FROM *THE MUSIC MAN.*
THERE WERE BIRDS, IN THE SKY...
... BUT I NEVER **SAW** THEM WINGING...
?
I DO LIKE THAT WORD-
WINGING.
BECAUSE YOU'RE THE "ETERNAL ROMANTIC."
I THINK COOKIE WAS TALKING ABOUT PAUL, NOT ME.
MORNING, MR. FRANKLIN.
THE HEART OF A FOOL IS IN HIS MOUTH...

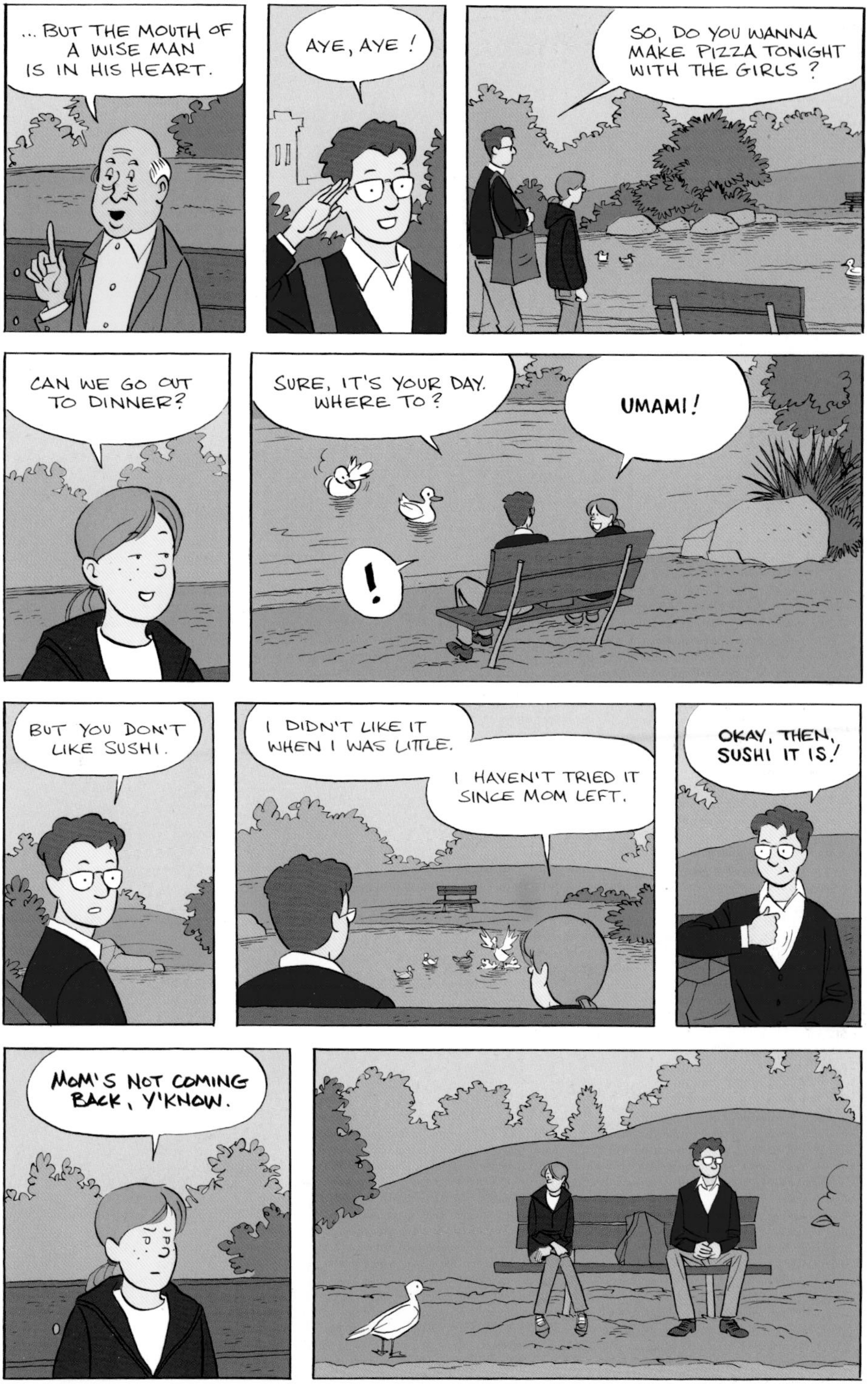
... BUT THE MOUTH OF A WISE MAN IS IN HIS HEART.
AYE, AYE!
SO, DO YOU WANNA MAKE PIZZA TONIGHT WITH THE GIRLS?
CAN WE GO OUT TO DINNER?
SURE, IT'S YOUR DAY. WHERE TO?
UMAMI!
!
BUT YOU DON'T LIKE SUSHI.
I DIDN'T LIKE IT WHEN I WAS LITTLE.
I HAVEN'T TRIED IT SINCE MOM LEFT.
OKAY, THEN, SUSHI IT IS!
MOM'S NOT COMING BACK, Y'KNOW.

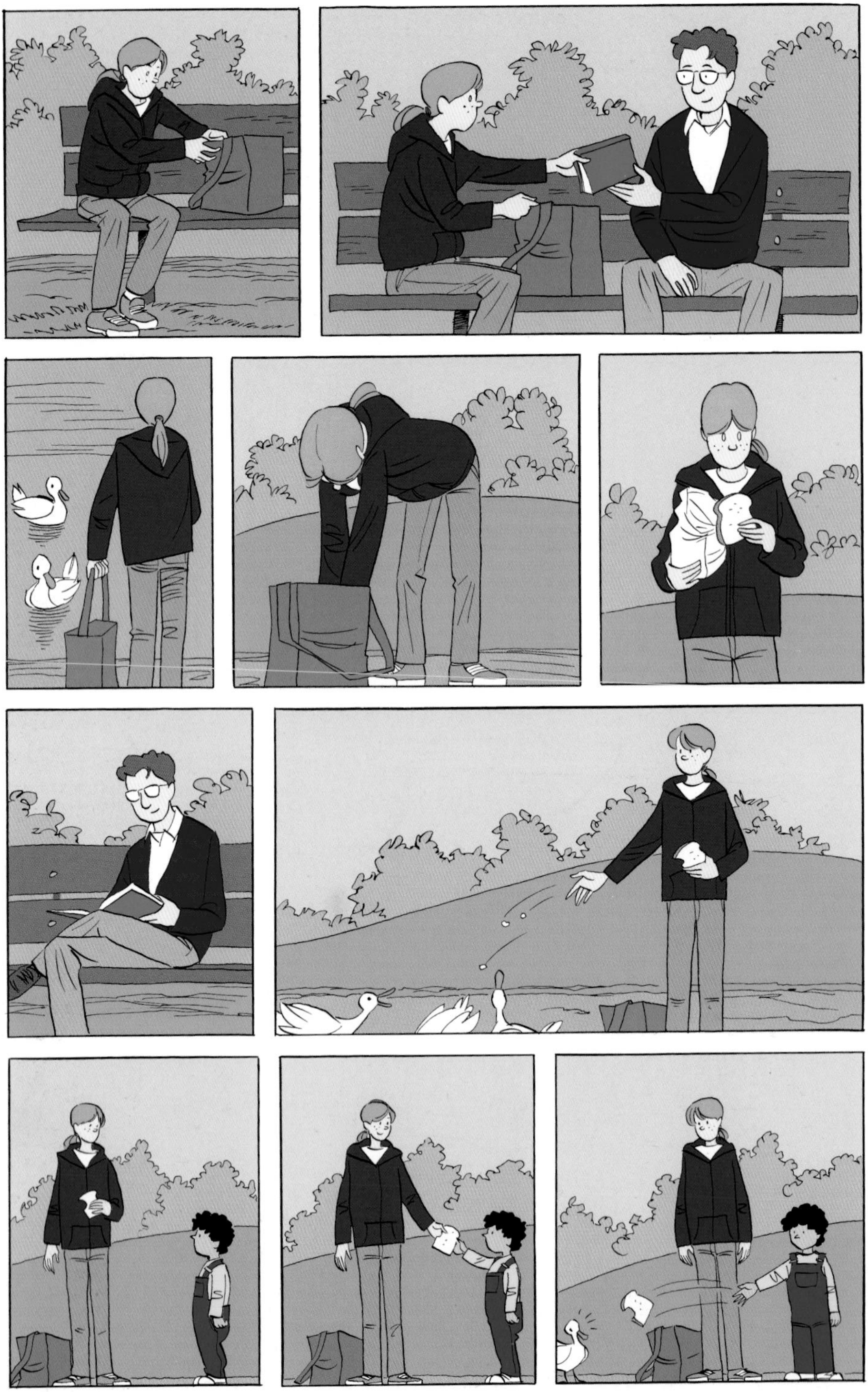

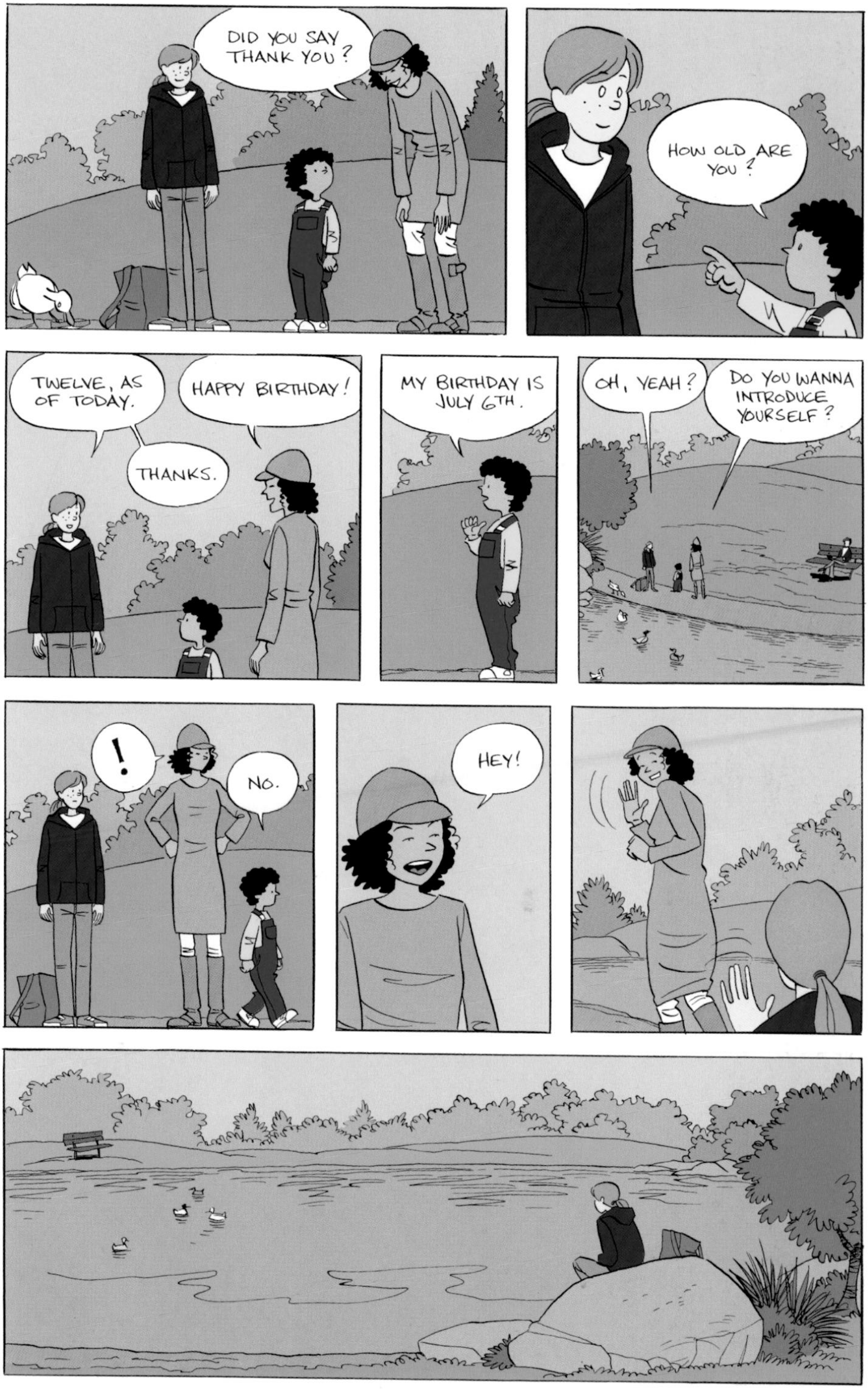
DID YOU SAY THANK YOU?
HOW OLD ARE YOU?
TWELVE, AS OF TODAY.
THANKS.
HAPPY BIRTHDAY!
MY BIRTHDAY IS JULY 6TH.
OH, YEAH?
DO YOU WANNA INTRODUCE YOURSELF?
!
NO.
HEY!

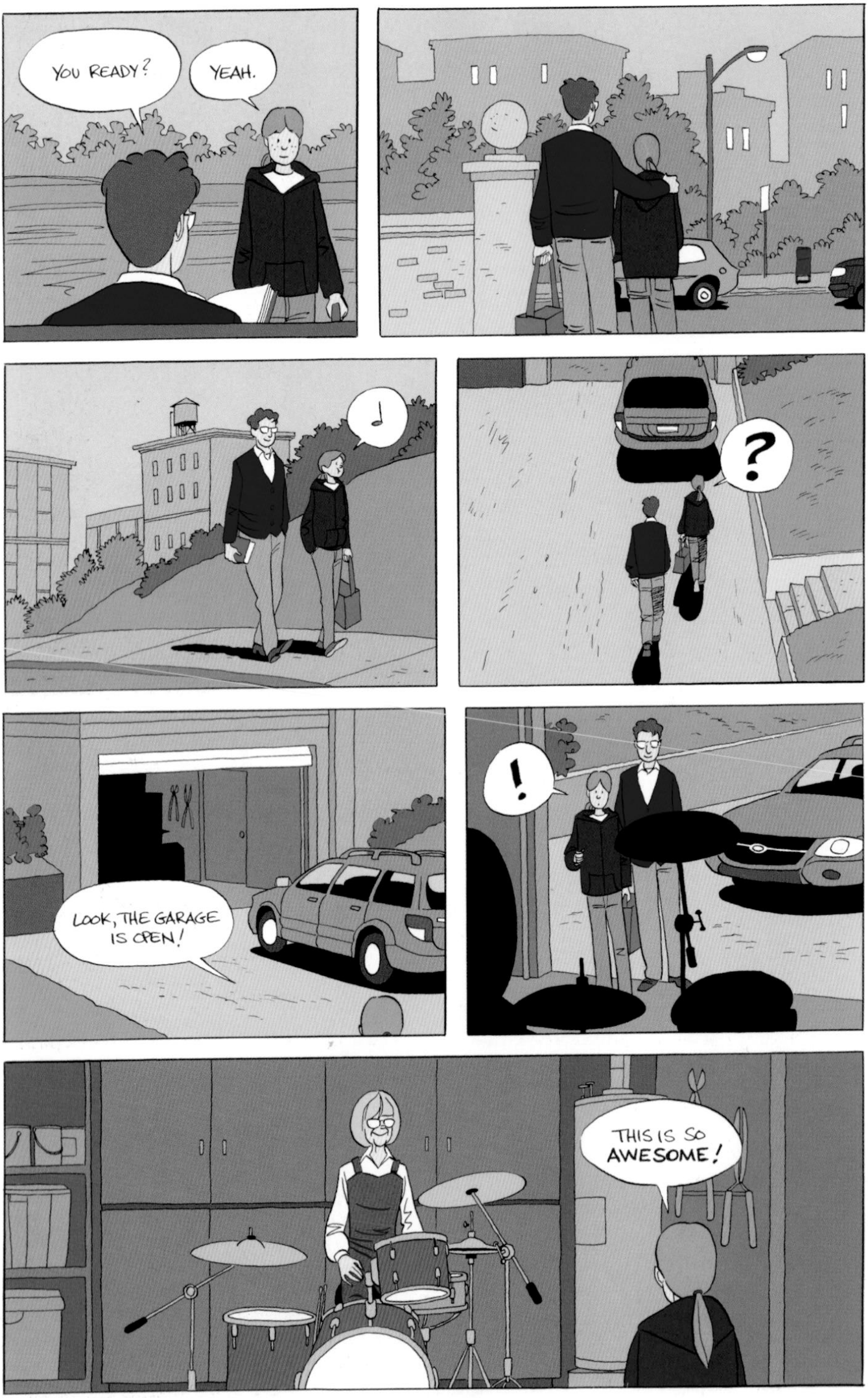
YOU READY?
YEAH.
?
!
LOOK, THE GARAGE IS OPEN!
!
THIS IS SO AWESOME!

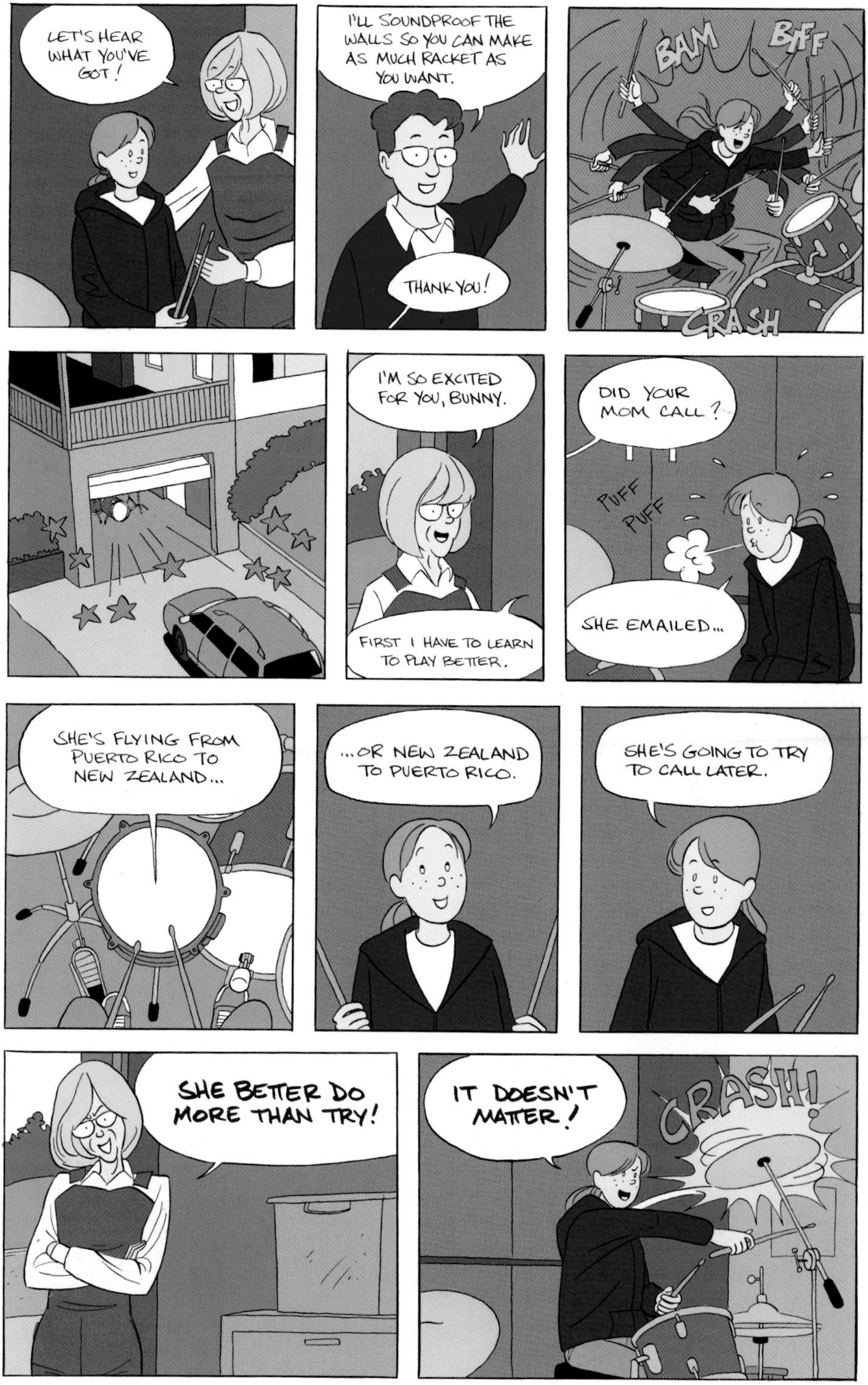
LET'S HEAR WHAT YOU'VE GOT!
I'LL SOUNDPROOF THE WALLS SO YOU CAN MAKE AS MUCH RACKET AS YOU WANT.
THANK YOU!
BAM
BIFF
CRASH
I'M SO EXCITED FOR YOU, BUNNY.
FIRST I HAVE TO LEARN TO PLAY BETTER.
DID YOUR MOM CALL?
PUFF PUFF
SHE EMAILED...
SHE'S FLYING FROM PUERTO RICO TO NEW ZEALAND...
...OR NEW ZEALAND TO PUERTO RICO.
SHE'S GOING TO TRY TO CALL LATER.
SHE BETTER DO MORE THAN TRY!
IT DOESN'T MATTER!
CRASH!

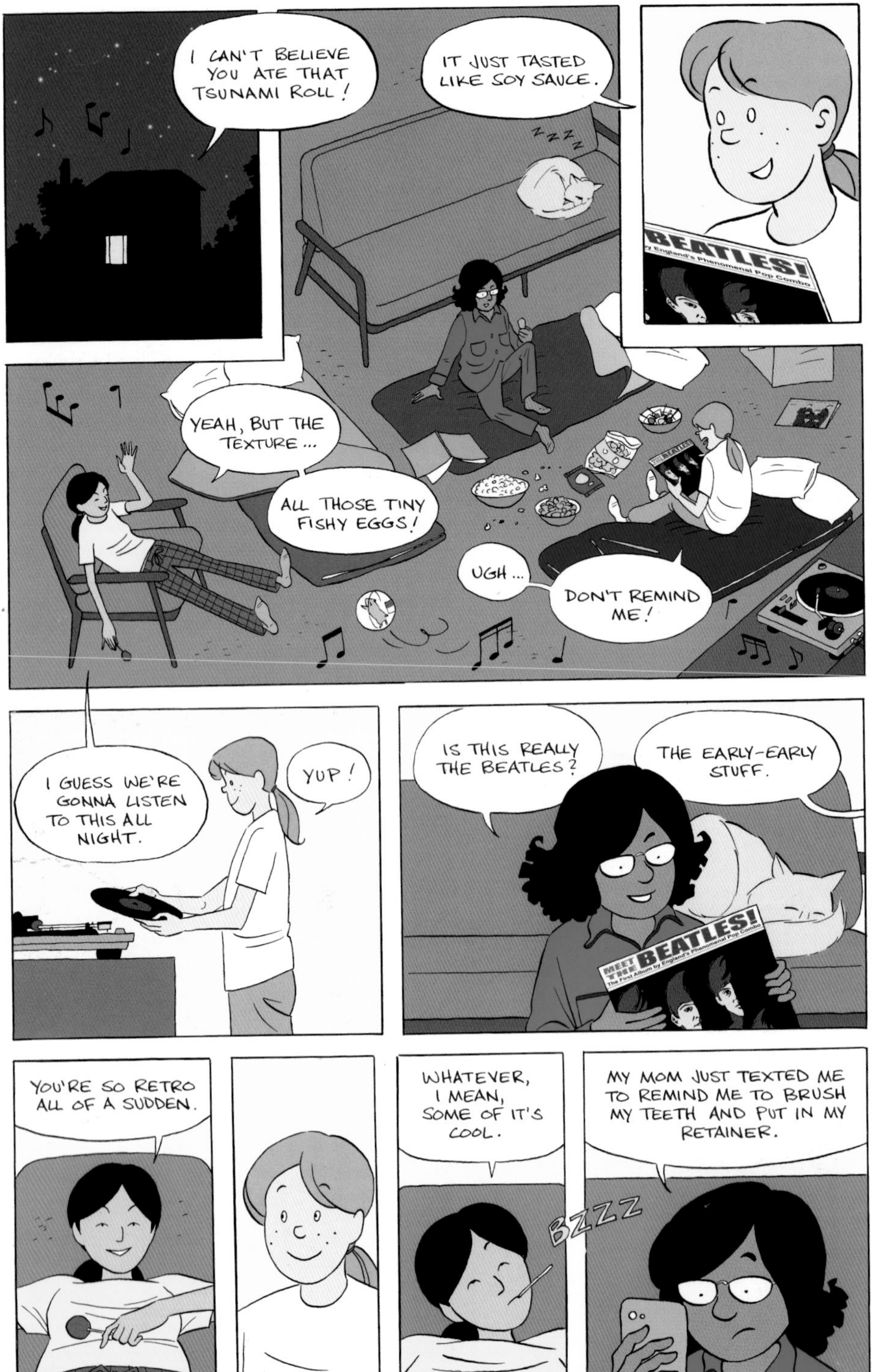
I CAN'T BELIEVE YOU ATE THAT TSUNAMI ROLL!
IT JUST TASTED LIKE SOY SAUCE.
ZZZ
YEAH, BUT THE TEXTURE...
ALL THOSE TINY FISHY EGGS!
UGH...
DON'T REMIND ME!
I GUESS WE'RE GONNA LISTEN TO THIS ALL NIGHT.
YUP!
IS THIS REALLY THE BEATLES?
THE EARLY-EARLY STUFF.
MEET THE BEATLES!
The First Album by England's Phenomenal Pop Combo
YOU'RE SO RETRO ALL OF A SUDDEN.
WHATEVER, I MEAN, SOME OF IT'S COOL.
BZZZ
MY MOM JUST TEXTED ME TO REMIND ME TO BRUSH MY TEETH AND PUT IN MY RETAINER.

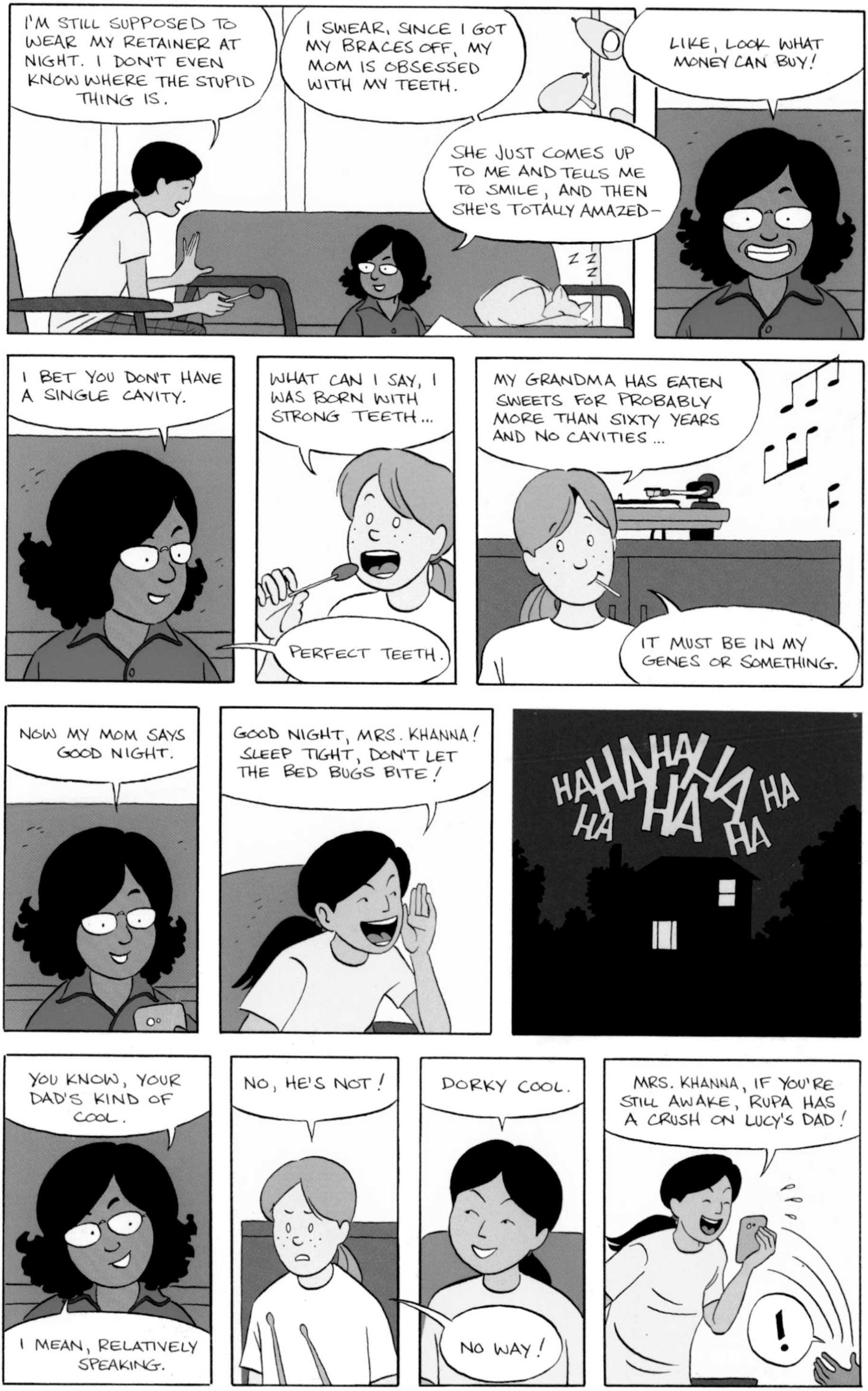
I'M STILL SUPPOSED TO WEAR MY RETAINER AT NIGHT. I DON'T EVEN KNOW WHERE THE STUPID THING IS.
I SWEAR, SINCE I GOT MY BRACES OFF, MY MOM IS OBSESSED WITH MY TEETH.
SHE JUST COMES UP TO ME AND TELLS ME TO SMILE, AND THEN SHE'S TOTALLY AMAZED—
Z Z Z
LIKE, LOOK WHAT MONEY CAN BUY!
I BET YOU DON'T HAVE A SINGLE CAVITY.
WHAT CAN I SAY, I WAS BORN WITH STRONG TEETH...
PERFECT TEETH.
MY GRANDMA HAS EATEN SWEETS FOR PROBABLY MORE THAN SIXTY YEARS AND NO CAVITIES...
IT MUST BE IN MY GENES OR SOMETHING.
NOW MY MOM SAYS GOOD NIGHT.
GOOD NIGHT, MRS. KHANNA! SLEEP TIGHT, DON'T LET THE BED BUGS BITE!
HA HA HA HA HA HA HA HA HA
YOU KNOW, YOUR DAD'S KIND OF COOL.
I MEAN, RELATIVELY SPEAKING.
NO, HE'S NOT!
DORKY COOL.
NO WAY!
MRS. KHANNA, IF YOU'RE STILL AWAKE, RUPA HAS A CRUSH ON LUCY'S DAD!
!

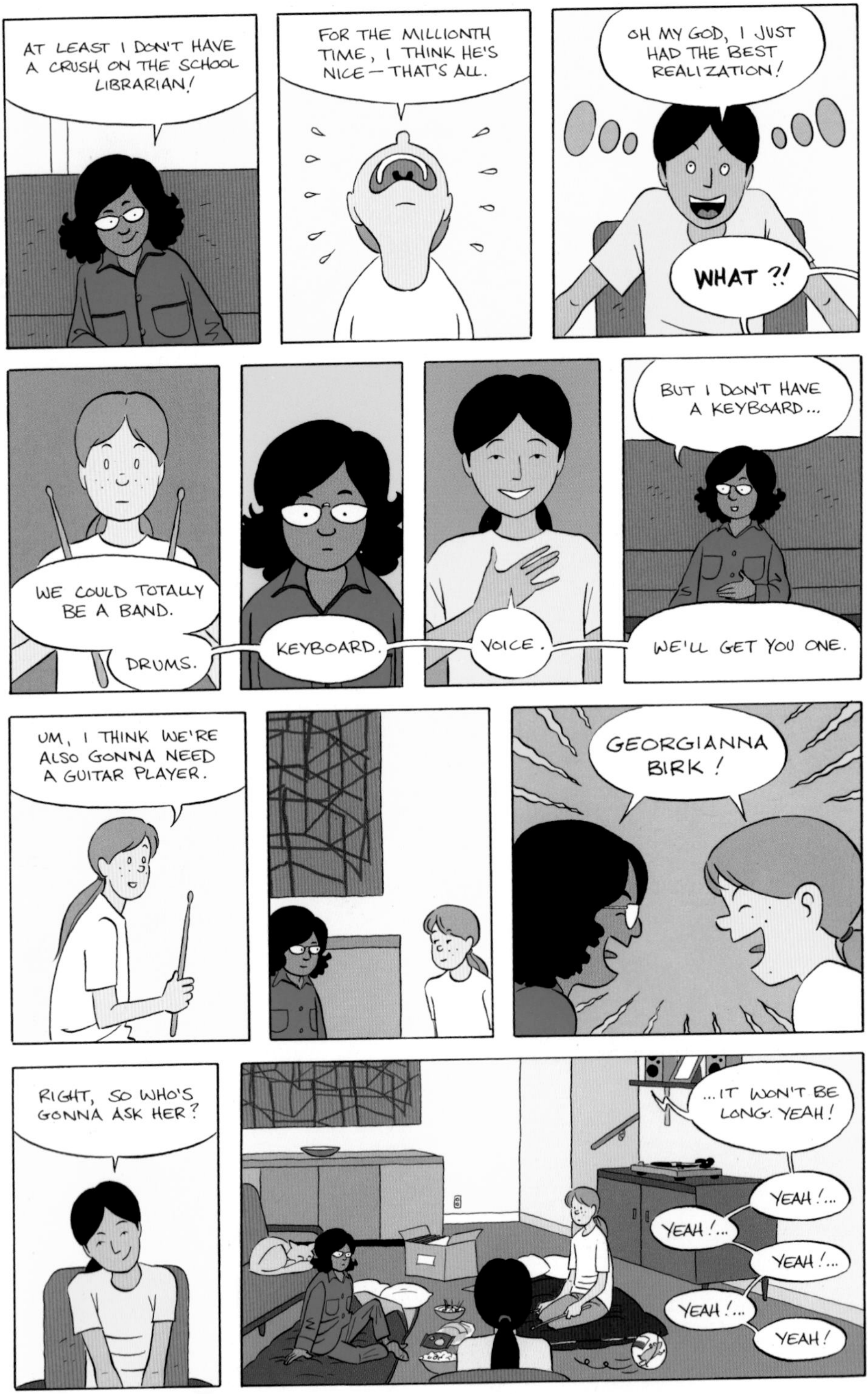
AT LEAST I DON'T HAVE A CRUSH ON THE SCHOOL LIBRARIAN!
FOR THE MILLIONTH TIME, I THINK HE'S NICE—THAT'S ALL.
OH MY GOD, I JUST HAD THE BEST REALIZATION!
WHAT ?!
WE COULD TOTALLY BE A BAND.
DRUMS.
KEYBOARD.
VOICE.
BUT I DON'T HAVE A KEYBOARD...
WE'LL GET YOU ONE.
UM, I THINK WE'RE ALSO GONNA NEED A GUITAR PLAYER.
GEORGIANNA BIRK!
RIGHT, SO WHO'S GONNA ASK HER?
...IT WON'T BE LONG. YEAH!
YEAH!...
YEAH!...
YEAH!...
YEAH!...
YEAH!

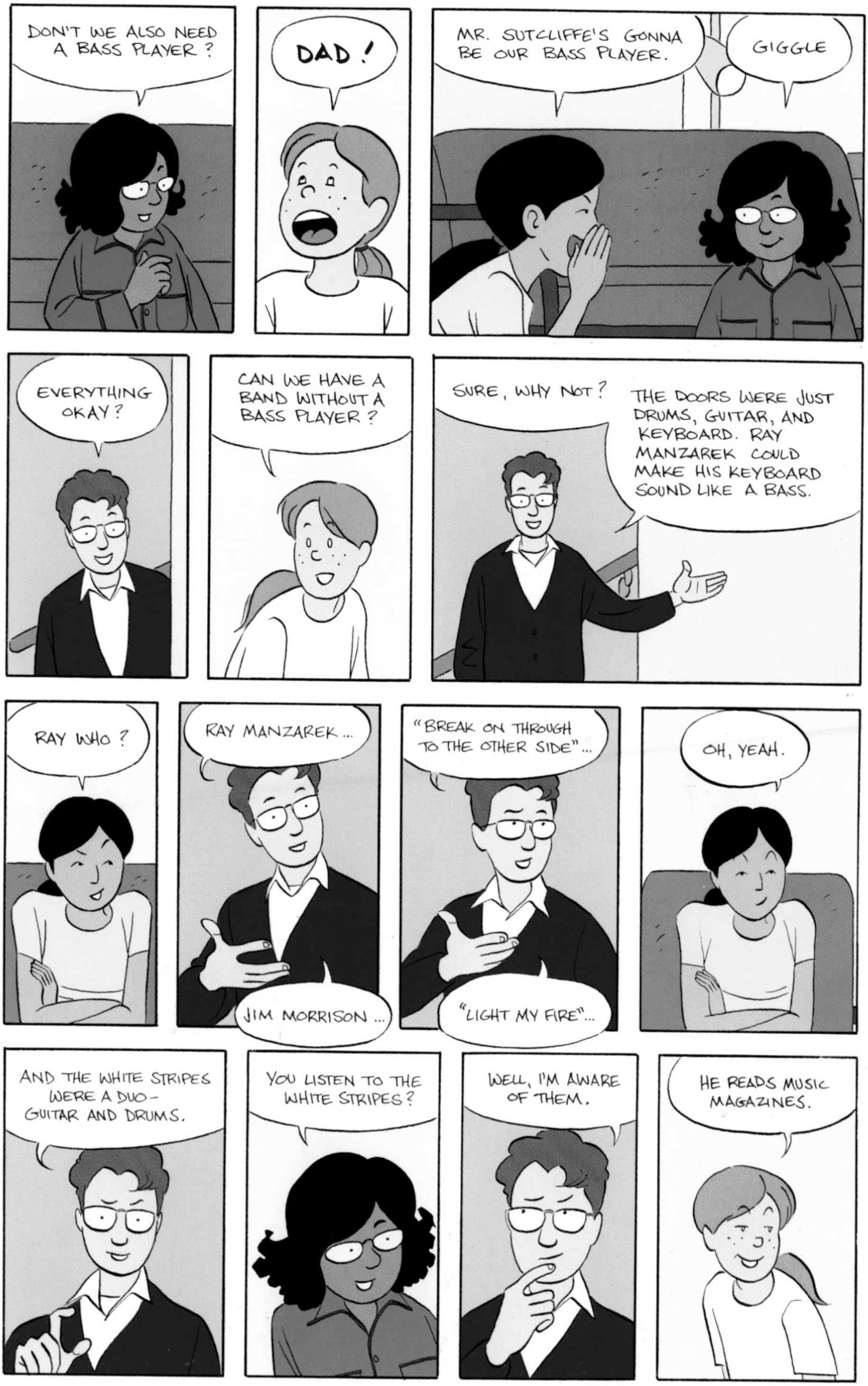
DON'T WE ALSO NEED A BASS PLAYER?
DAD!
MR. SUTCLIFFE'S GONNA BE OUR BASS PLAYER.
GIGGLE
EVERYTHING OKAY?
CAN WE HAVE A BAND WITHOUT A BASS PLAYER?
SURE, WHY NOT?
THE DOORS WERE JUST DRUMS, GUITAR, AND KEYBOARD. RAY MANZAREK COULD MAKE HIS KEYBOARD SOUND LIKE A BASS.
RAY WHO?
RAY MANZAREK...
JIM MORRISON...
"BREAK ON THROUGH TO THE OTHER SIDE"...
"LIGHT MY FIRE"...
OH, YEAH.
AND THE WHITE STRIPES WERE A DUO- GUITAR AND DRUMS.
YOU LISTEN TO THE WHITE STRIPES?
WELL, I'M AWARE OF THEM.
HE READS MUSIC MAGAZINES.

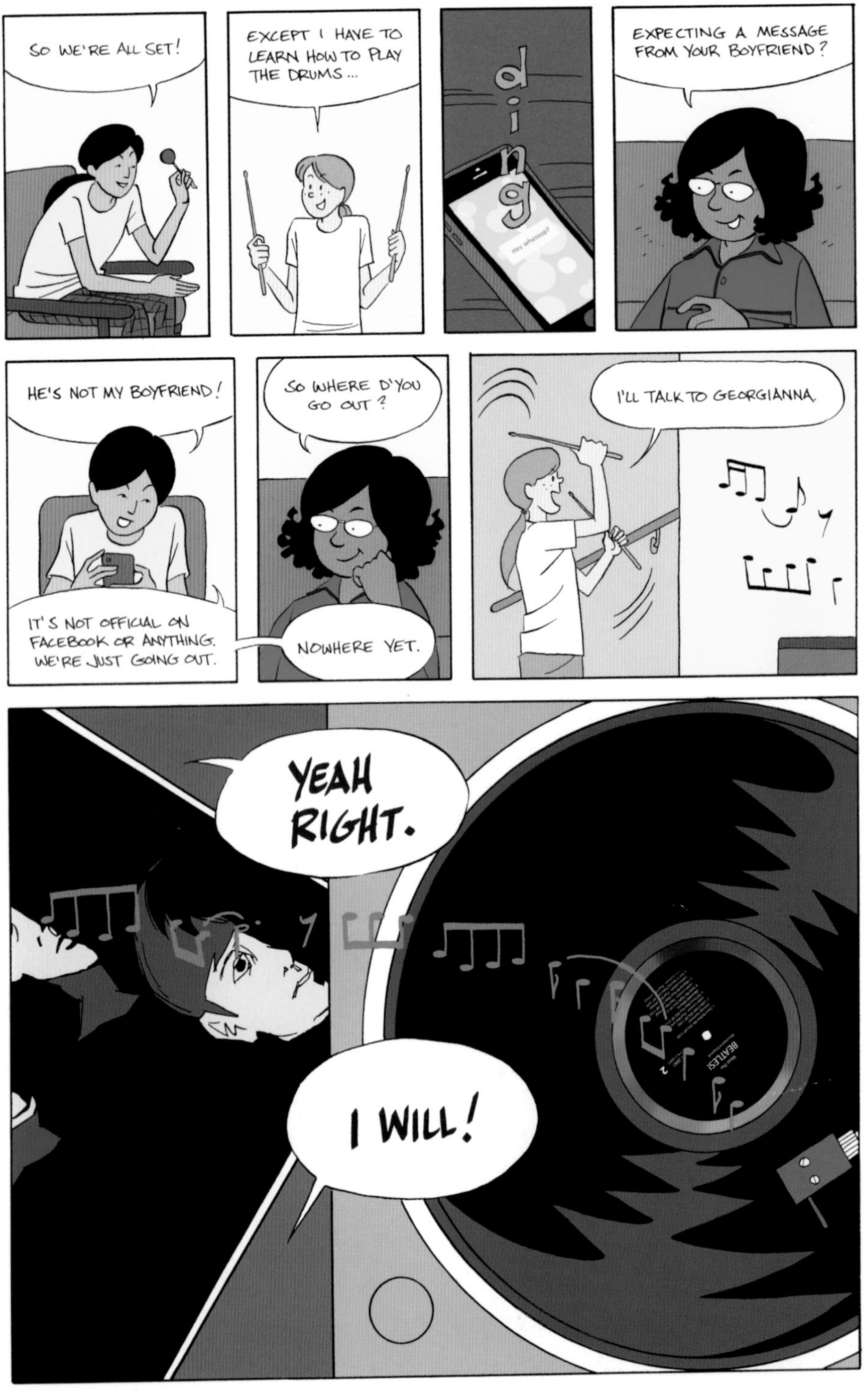
SO WE'RE ALL SET!
EXCEPT I HAVE TO LEARN HOW TO PLAY THE DRUMS...
ding
Hey whassup?
EXPECTING A MESSAGE FROM YOUR BOYFRIEND?
HE'S NOT MY BOYFRIEND!
IT'S NOT OFFICIAL ON FACEBOOK OR ANYTHING. WE'RE JUST GOING OUT.
SO WHERE D'YOU GO OUT?
NOWHERE YET.
I'LL TALK TO GEORGIANNA.
YEAH RIGHT.
I WILL!

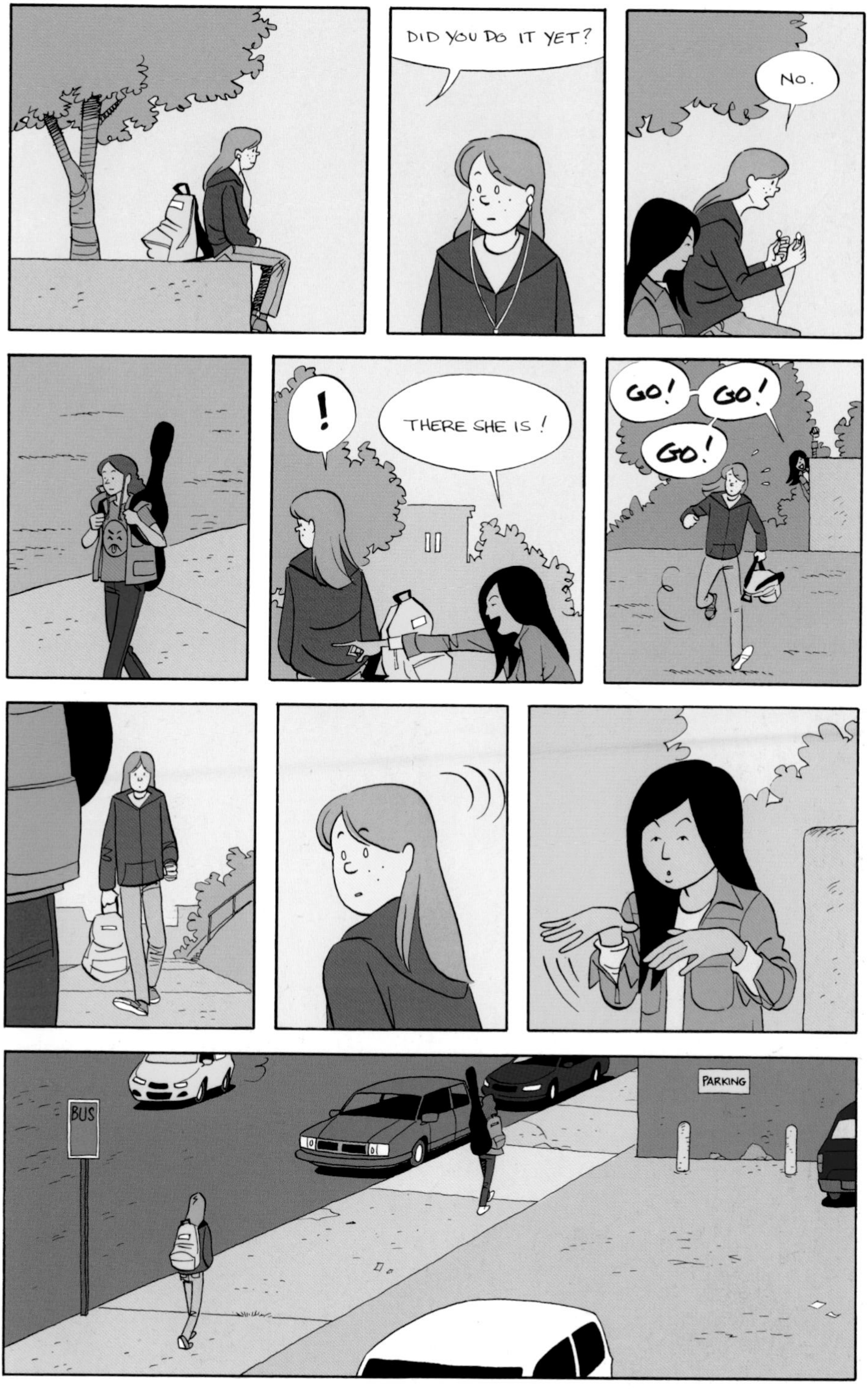
DID YOU DO IT YET?
NO.
!
THERE SHE IS!
GO!
GO!
GO!
BUS
PARKING

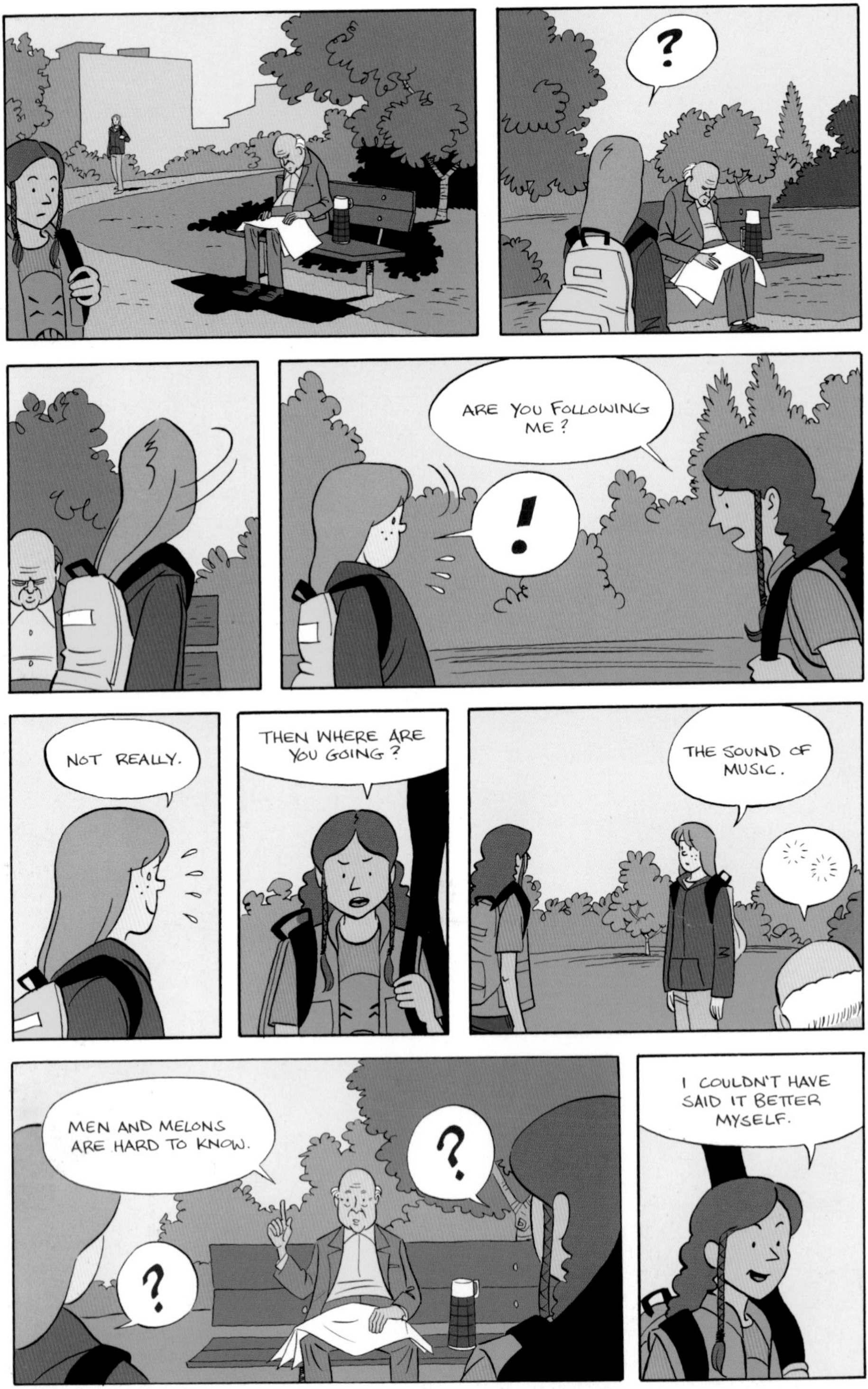
?
ARE YOU FOLLOWING ME?
!
NOT REALLY.
THEN WHERE ARE YOU GOING?
THE SOUND OF MUSIC.
MEN AND MELONS ARE HARD TO KNOW.
?
?
I COULDN'T HAVE SAID IT BETTER MYSELF.

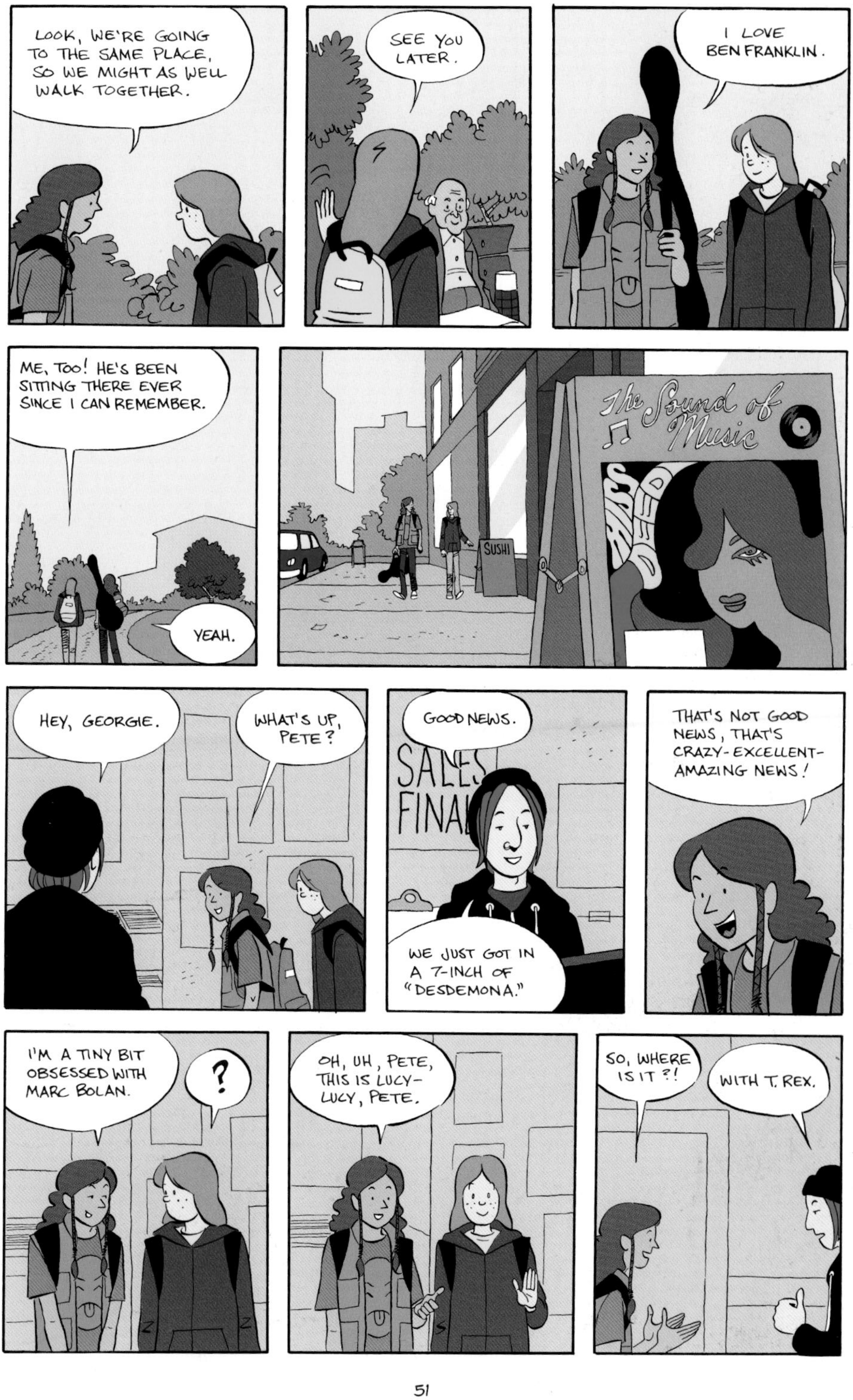
LOOK, WE'RE GOING TO THE SAME PLACE, SO WE MIGHT AS WELL WALK TOGETHER.
SEE YOU LATER.
I LOVE BEN FRANKLIN.
ME, TOO! HE'S BEEN SITTING THERE EVER SINCE I CAN REMEMBER.
YEAH.
SUSHI
The Sound of Music
HEY, GEORGIE.
WHAT'S UP, PETE?
GOOD NEWS.
SALES FINAL
WE JUST GOT IN A 7-INCH OF "DESDEMONA."
THAT'S NOT GOOD NEWS, THAT'S CRAZY-EXCELLENT-AMAZING NEWS!
I'M A TINY BIT OBSESSED WITH MARC BOLAN.
?
OH, UH, PETE, THIS IS LUCY-LUCY, PETE.
SO, WHERE IS IT?!
WITH T. REX.

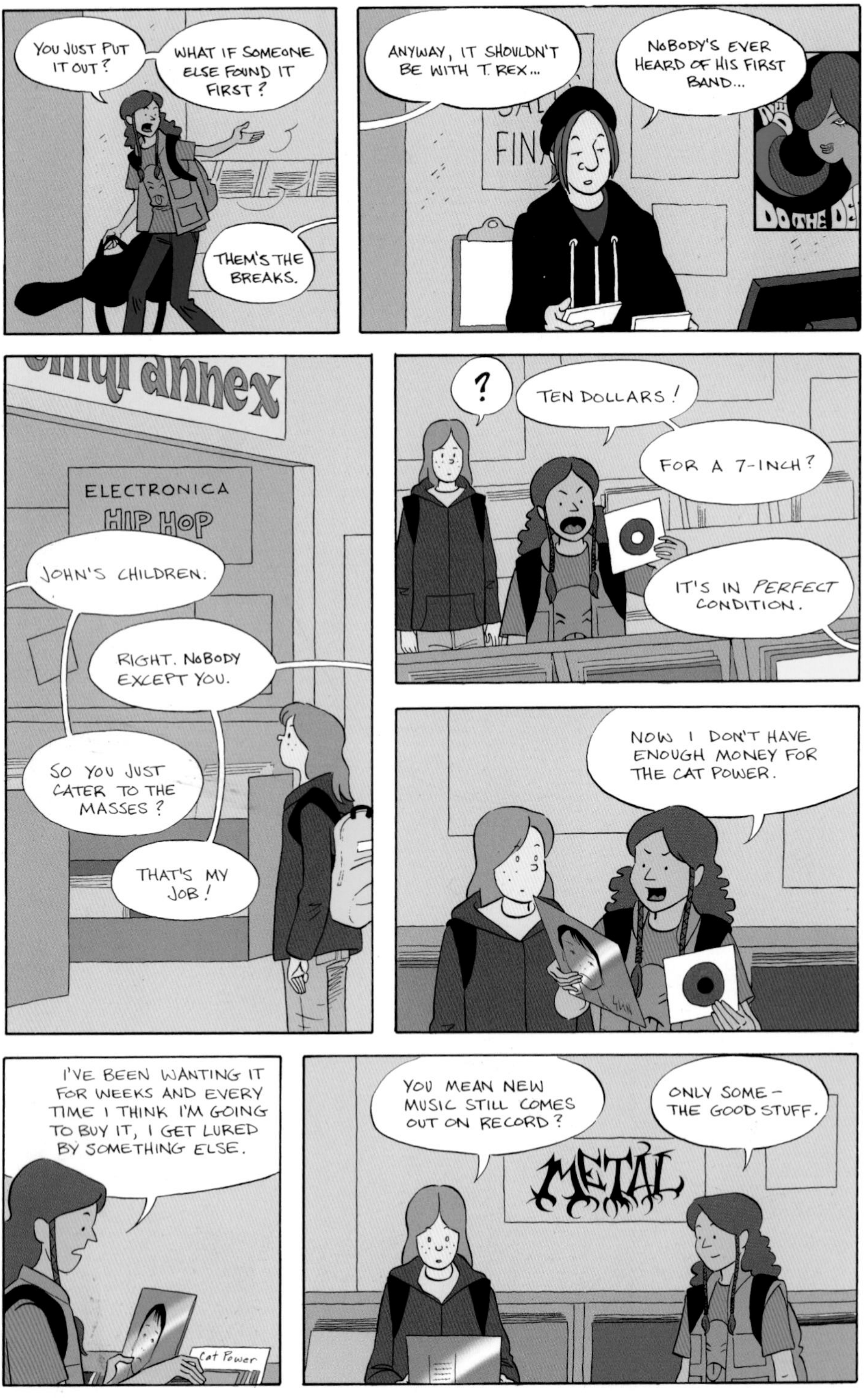

YOU JUST PUT IT OUT?
WHAT IF SOMEONE ELSE FOUND IT FIRST?
THEM'S THE BREAKS.
ANYWAY, IT SHOULDN'T BE WITH T. REX...
NOBODY'S EVER HEARD OF HIS FIRST BAND...
DO THE
ELECTRONICA
HIP HOP
JOHN'S CHILDREN.
RIGHT. NOBODY EXCEPT YOU.
SO YOU JUST CATER TO THE MASSES?
THAT'S MY JOB!
?
TEN DOLLARS!
FOR A 7-INCH?
IT'S IN *PERFECT* CONDITION.
NOW I DON'T HAVE ENOUGH MONEY FOR THE CAT POWER.
I'VE BEEN WANTING IT FOR WEEKS AND EVERY TIME I THINK I'M GOING TO BUY IT, I GET LURED BY SOMETHING ELSE.
Cat Power
YOU MEAN NEW MUSIC STILL COMES OUT ON RECORD?
ONLY SOME— THE GOOD STUFF.
METAL

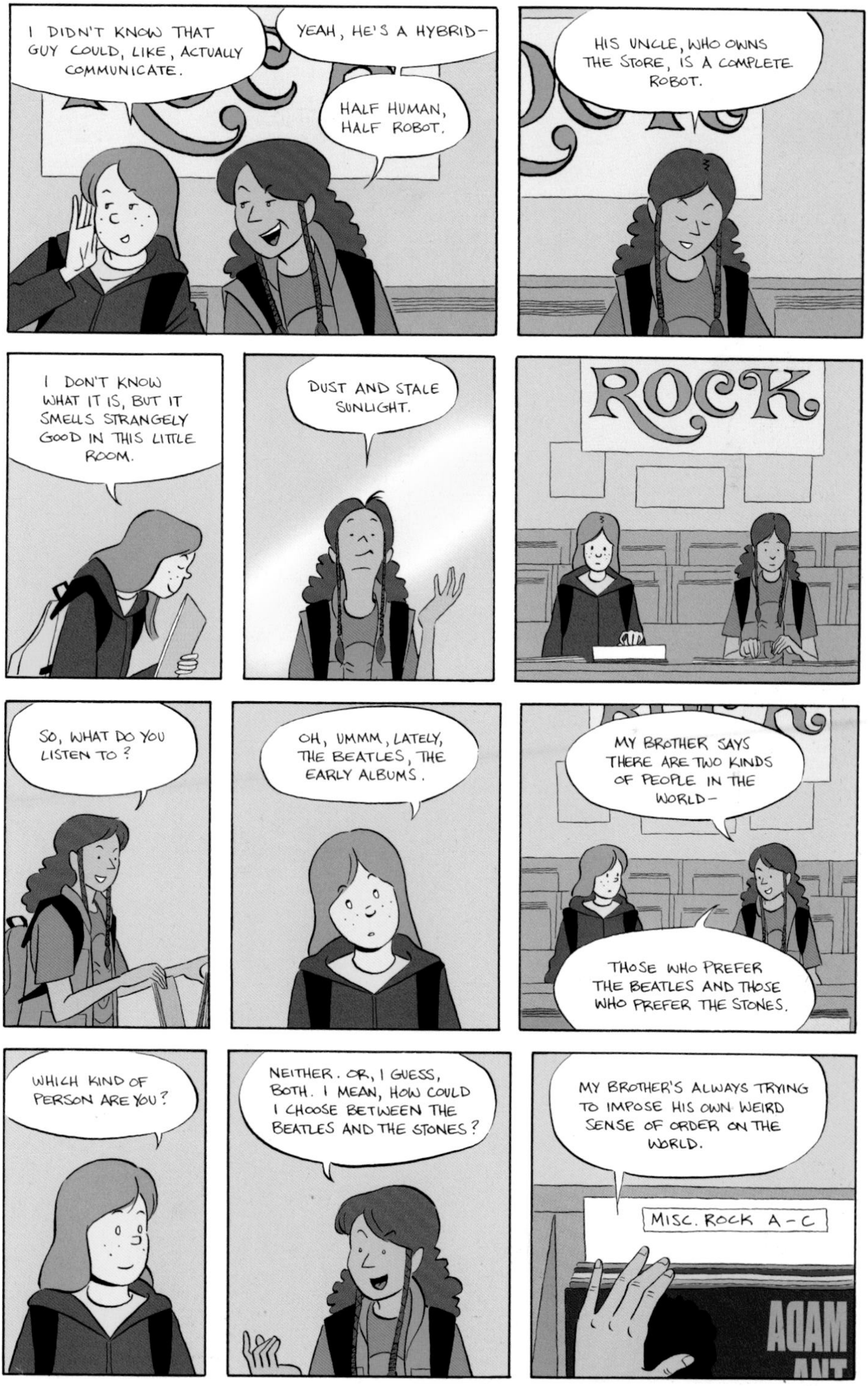
I DIDN'T KNOW THAT GUY COULD, LIKE, ACTUALLY COMMUNICATE.
YEAH, HE'S A HYBRID–
HALF HUMAN, HALF ROBOT.
HIS UNCLE, WHO OWNS THE STORE, IS A COMPLETE ROBOT.
I DON'T KNOW WHAT IT IS, BUT IT SMELLS STRANGELY GOOD IN THIS LITTLE ROOM.
DUST AND STALE SUNLIGHT.
ROCK
SO, WHAT DO YOU LISTEN TO?
OH, UMMM, LATELY, THE BEATLES, THE EARLY ALBUMS.
MY BROTHER SAYS THERE ARE TWO KINDS OF PEOPLE IN THE WORLD–
THOSE WHO PREFER THE BEATLES AND THOSE WHO PREFER THE STONES.
WHICH KIND OF PERSON ARE YOU?
NEITHER. OR, I GUESS, BOTH. I MEAN, HOW COULD I CHOOSE BETWEEN THE BEATLES AND THE STONES?
MY BROTHER'S ALWAYS TRYING TO IMPOSE HIS OWN WEIRD SENSE OF ORDER ON THE WORLD.
MISC. ROCK A–C
ADAM
ANT

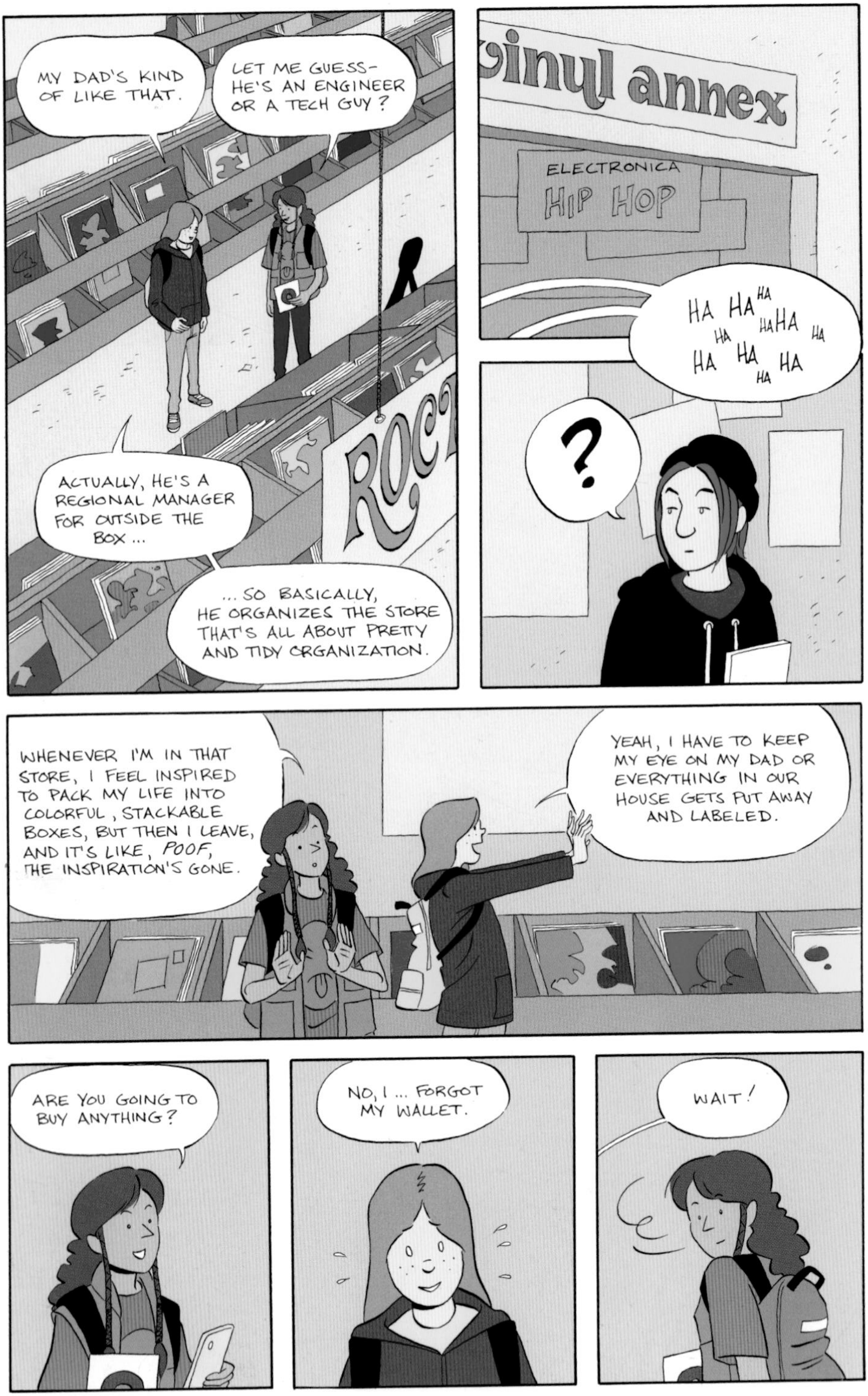
MY DAD'S KIND OF LIKE THAT.
LET ME GUESS- HE'S AN ENGINEER OR A TECH GUY?
ACTUALLY, HE'S A REGIONAL MANAGER FOR OUTSIDE THE BOX...
...SO BASICALLY, HE ORGANIZES THE STORE THAT'S ALL ABOUT PRETTY AND TIDY ORGANIZATION.
ROC
vinyl annex
ELECTRONICA
HIP HOP
HA HA HA HA HA HA HA HA HA HA HA HA
?
WHENEVER I'M IN THAT STORE, I FEEL INSPIRED TO PACK MY LIFE INTO COLORFUL, STACKABLE BOXES, BUT THEN I LEAVE, AND IT'S LIKE, *POOF*, THE INSPIRATION'S GONE.
YEAH, I HAVE TO KEEP MY EYE ON MY DAD OR EVERYTHING IN OUR HOUSE GETS PUT AWAY AND LABELED.
ARE YOU GOING TO BUY ANYTHING?
NO, I... FORGOT MY WALLET.
WAIT!

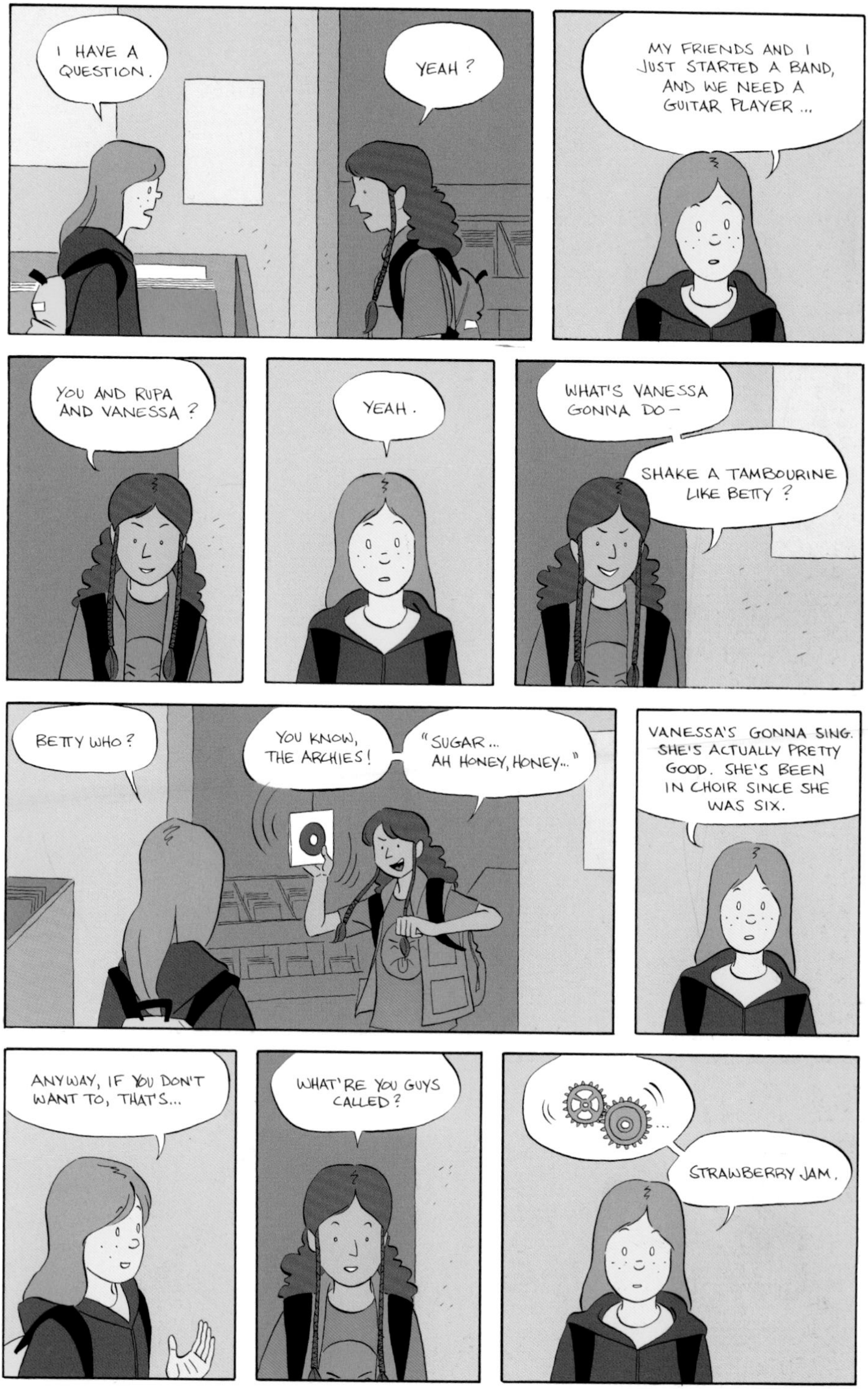
I HAVE A QUESTION.
YEAH?
MY FRIENDS AND I JUST STARTED A BAND, AND WE NEED A GUITAR PLAYER...
YOU AND RUPA AND VANESSA?
YEAH.
WHAT'S VANESSA GONNA DO-
SHAKE A TAMBOURINE LIKE BETTY?
BETTY WHO?
YOU KNOW, THE ARCHIES!
"SUGAR... AH HONEY, HONEY..."
VANESSA'S GONNA SING. SHE'S ACTUALLY PRETTY GOOD. SHE'S BEEN IN CHOIR SINCE SHE WAS SIX.
ANYWAY, IF YOU DON'T WANT TO, THAT'S...
WHAT'RE YOU GUYS CALLED?
...
STRAWBERRY JAM.

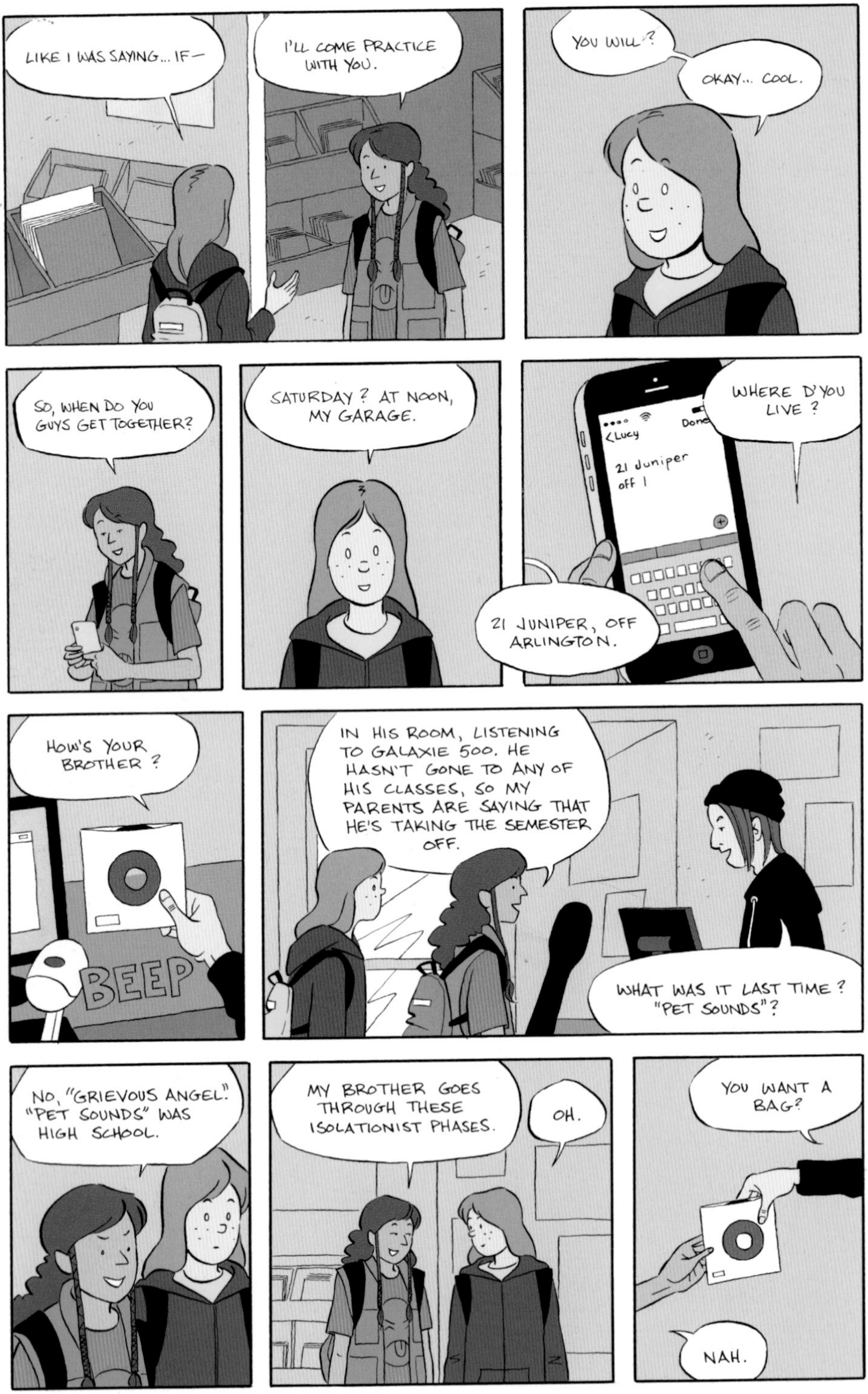
LIKE I WAS SAYING... IF—
I'LL COME PRACTICE WITH YOU.
YOU WILL?
OKAY... COOL.
SO, WHEN DO YOU GUYS GET TOGETHER?
SATURDAY? AT NOON, MY GARAGE.
WHERE D'YOU LIVE?
<Lucy
Done
21 Juniper
off 1
21 JUNIPER, OFF ARLINGTON.
HOW'S YOUR BROTHER?
BEEP
IN HIS ROOM, LISTENING TO GALAXIE 500. HE HASN'T GONE TO ANY OF HIS CLASSES, SO MY PARENTS ARE SAYING THAT HE'S TAKING THE SEMESTER OFF.
WHAT WAS IT LAST TIME? "PET SOUNDS"?
NO, "GRIEVOUS ANGEL." "PET SOUNDS" WAS HIGH SCHOOL.
MY BROTHER GOES THROUGH THESE ISOLATIONIST PHASES.
OH.
YOU WANT A BAG?
NAH.

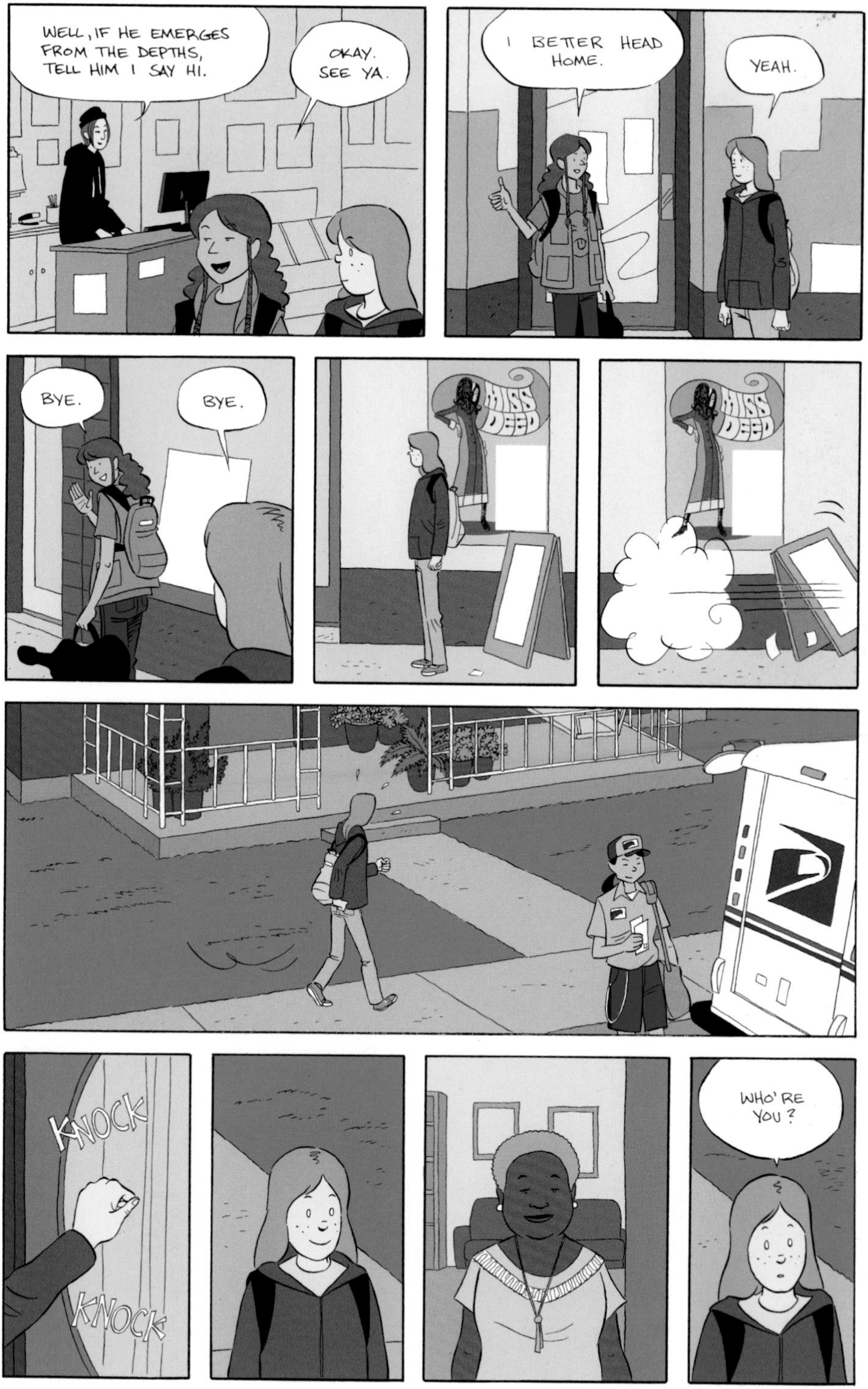
WELL, IF HE EMERGES FROM THE DEPTHS, TELL HIM I SAY HI.
OKAY. SEE YA.
I BETTER HEAD HOME.
YEAH.
BYE.
BYE.
MISS DEED
MISS DEED
KNOCK
KNOCK
WHO'RE YOU?

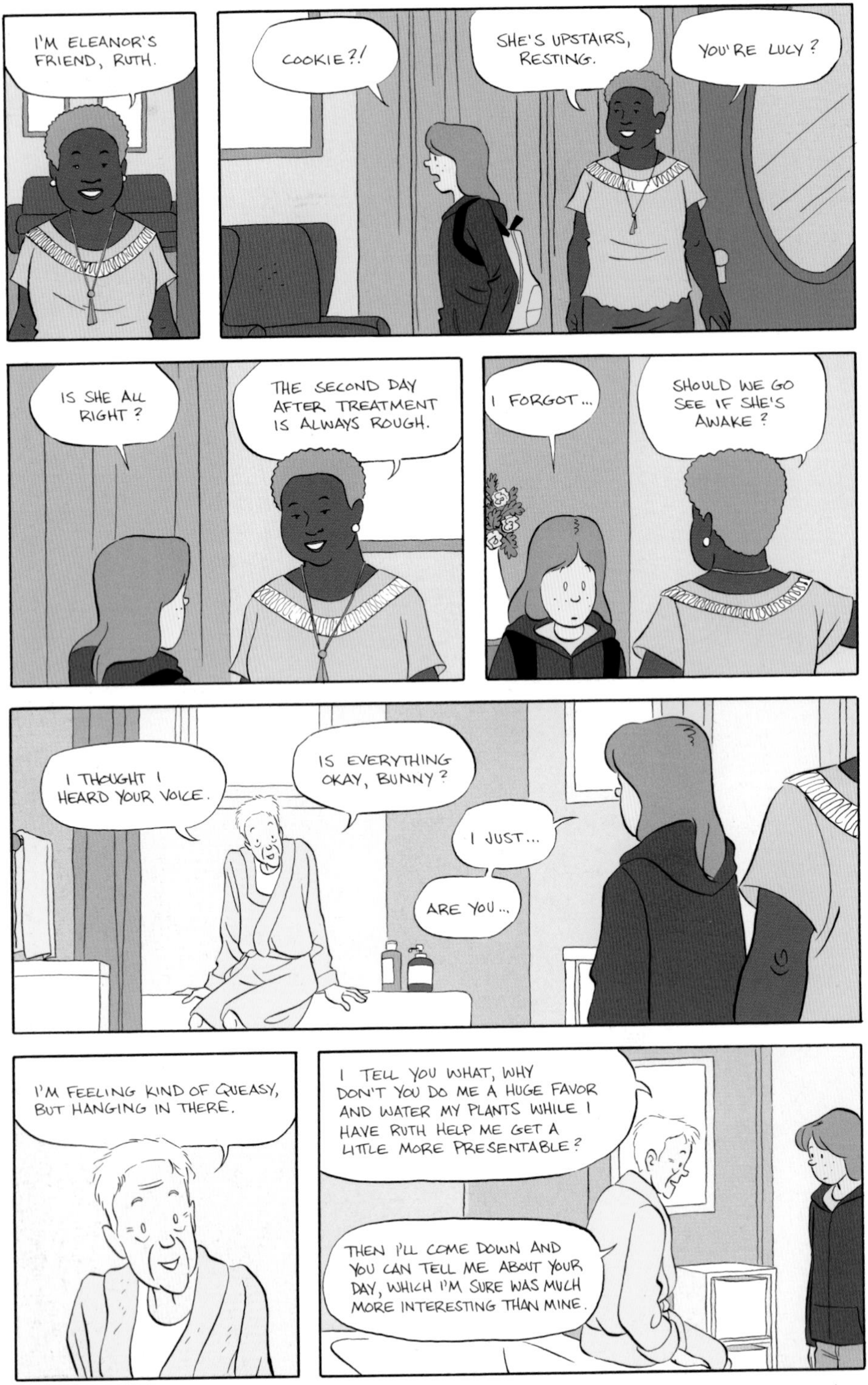

I'M ELEANOR'S FRIEND, RUTH.
COOKIE?!
SHE'S UPSTAIRS, RESTING.
YOU'RE LUCY?
IS SHE ALL RIGHT?
THE SECOND DAY AFTER TREATMENT IS ALWAYS ROUGH.
I FORGOT...
SHOULD WE GO SEE IF SHE'S AWAKE?
I THOUGHT I HEARD YOUR VOICE.
IS EVERYTHING OKAY, BUNNY?
I JUST...
ARE YOU...
I'M FEELING KIND OF QUEASY, BUT HANGING IN THERE.
I TELL YOU WHAT, WHY DON'T YOU DO ME A HUGE FAVOR AND WATER MY PLANTS WHILE I HAVE RUTH HELP ME GET A LITTLE MORE PRESENTABLE?
THEN I'LL COME DOWN AND YOU CAN TELL ME ABOUT YOUR DAY, WHICH I'M SURE WAS MUCH MORE INTERESTING THAN MINE.

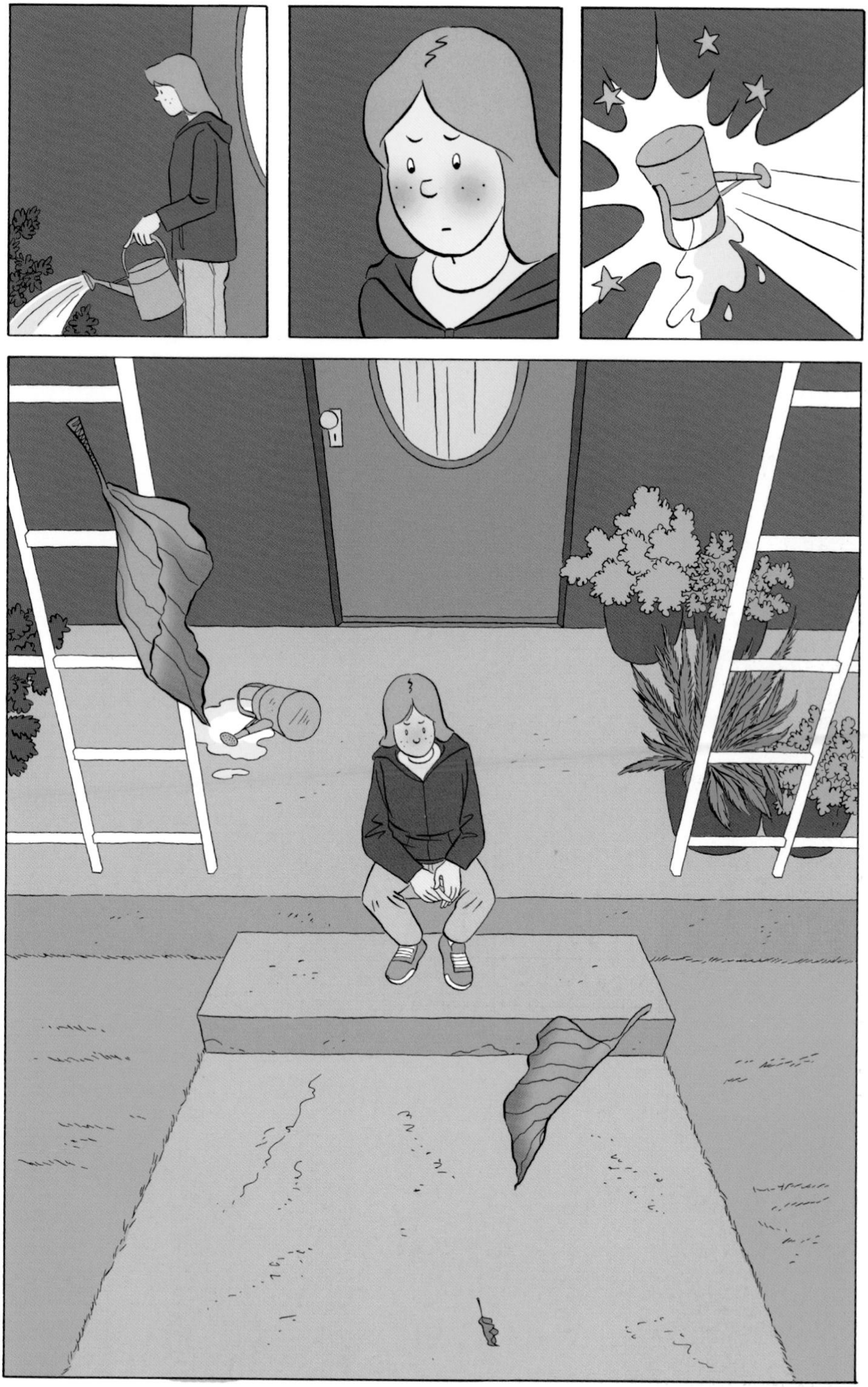

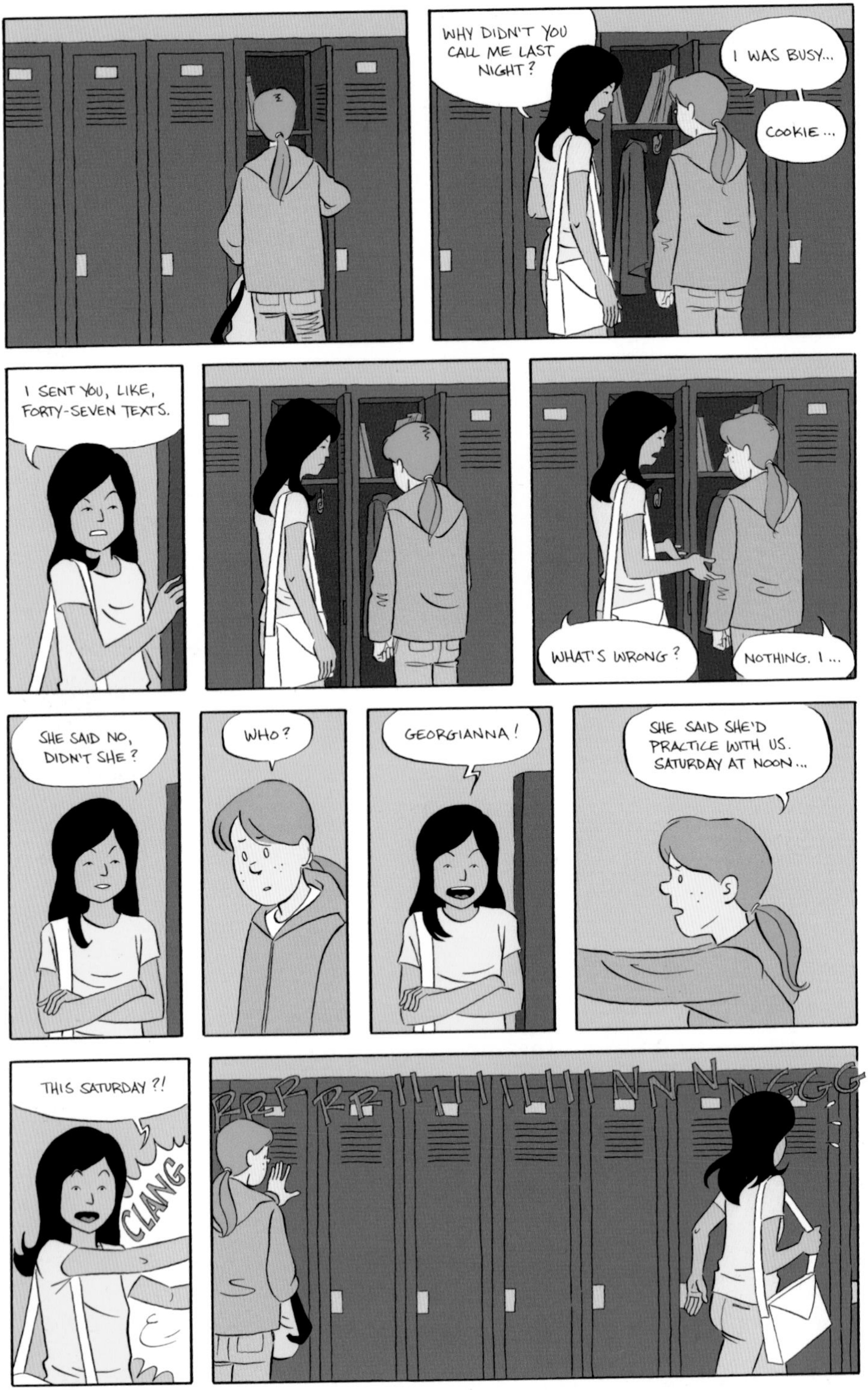
WHY DIDN'T YOU CALL ME LAST NIGHT?
I WAS BUSY...
COOKIE...
I SENT YOU, LIKE, FORTY-SEVEN TEXTS.
WHAT'S WRONG?
NOTHING. I...
SHE SAID NO, DIDN'T SHE?
WHO?
GEORGIANNA!
SHE SAID SHE'D PRACTICE WITH US. SATURDAY AT NOON...
THIS SATURDAY?!
CLANG
RRRRRRIIIIIIIIIINNNNNGGG

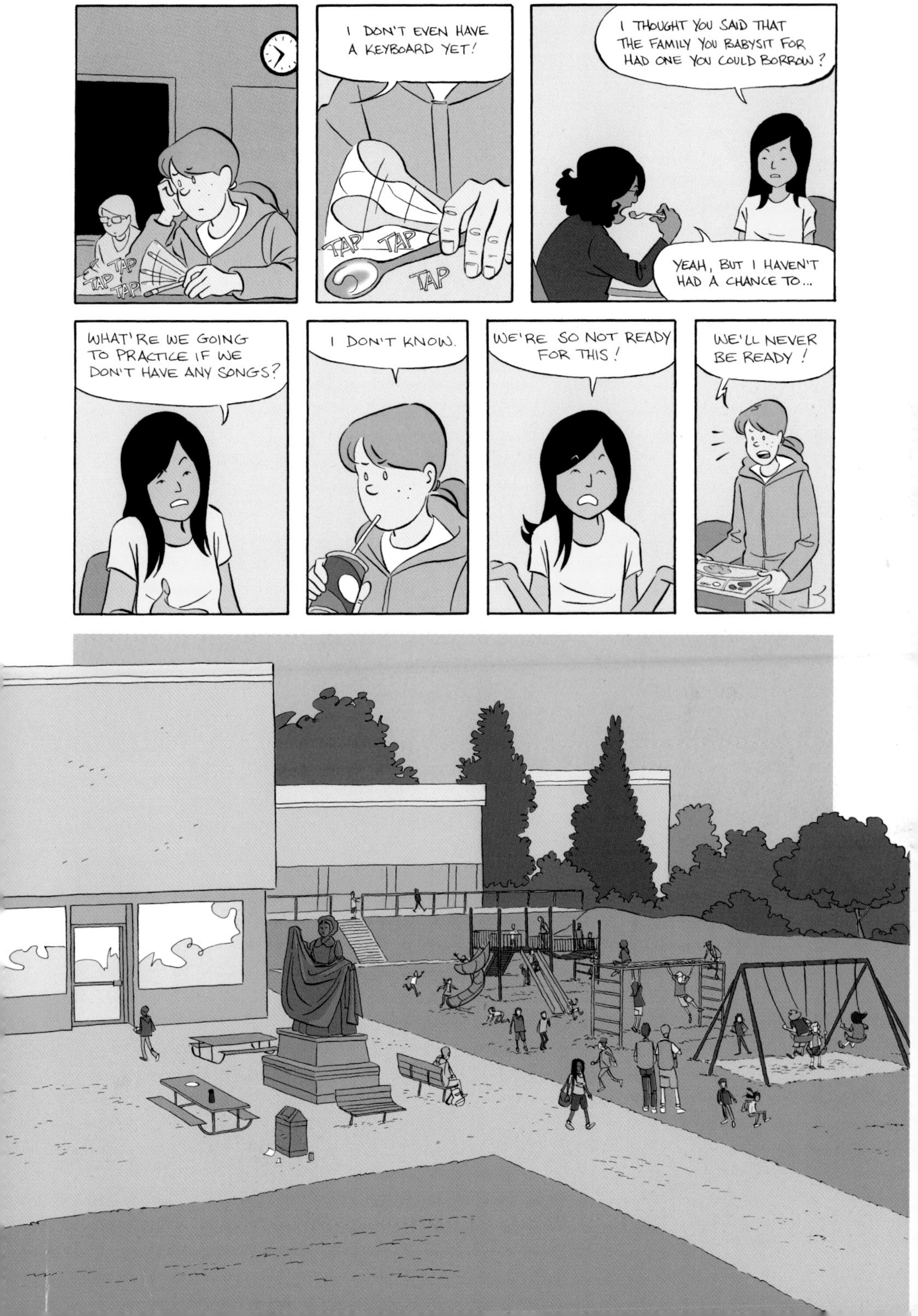
TAP TAP TAP TAP
I DON'T EVEN HAVE A KEYBOARD YET!
TAP TAP TAP
I THOUGHT YOU SAID THAT THE FAMILY YOU BABYSIT FOR HAD ONE YOU COULD BORROW?
YEAH, BUT I HAVEN'T HAD A CHANCE TO...
WHAT'RE WE GOING TO PRACTICE IF WE DON'T HAVE ANY SONGS?
I DON'T KNOW.
WE'RE SO NOT READY FOR THIS!
WE'LL NEVER BE READY!

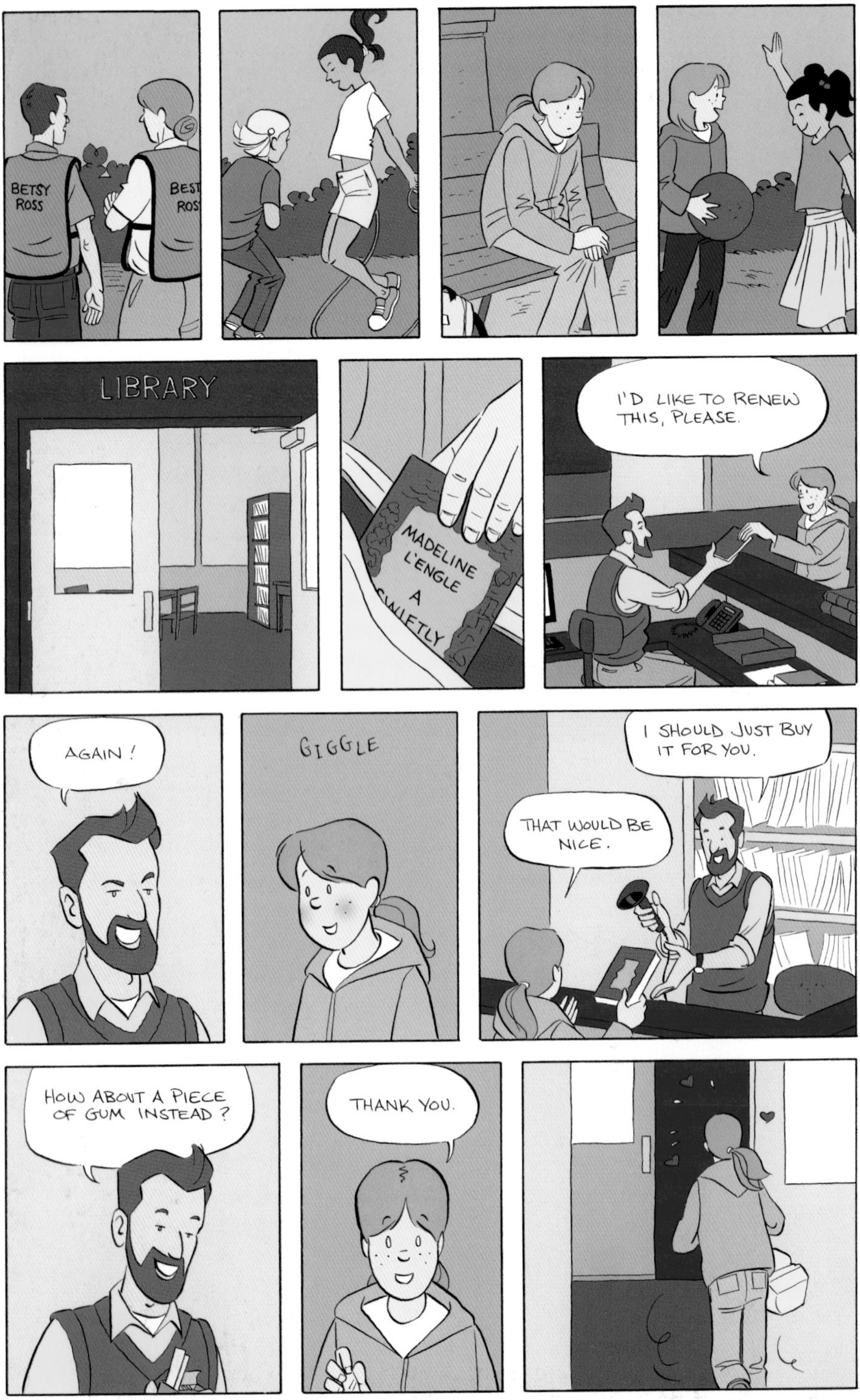
BETSY ROSS
BEST ROS
LIBRARY
MADELINE L'ENGLE A SWIFTLY
I'D LIKE TO RENEW THIS, PLEASE.
AGAIN!
GIGGLE
I SHOULD JUST BUY IT FOR YOU.
THAT WOULD BE NICE.
HOW ABOUT A PIECE OF GUM INSTEAD?
THANK YOU.

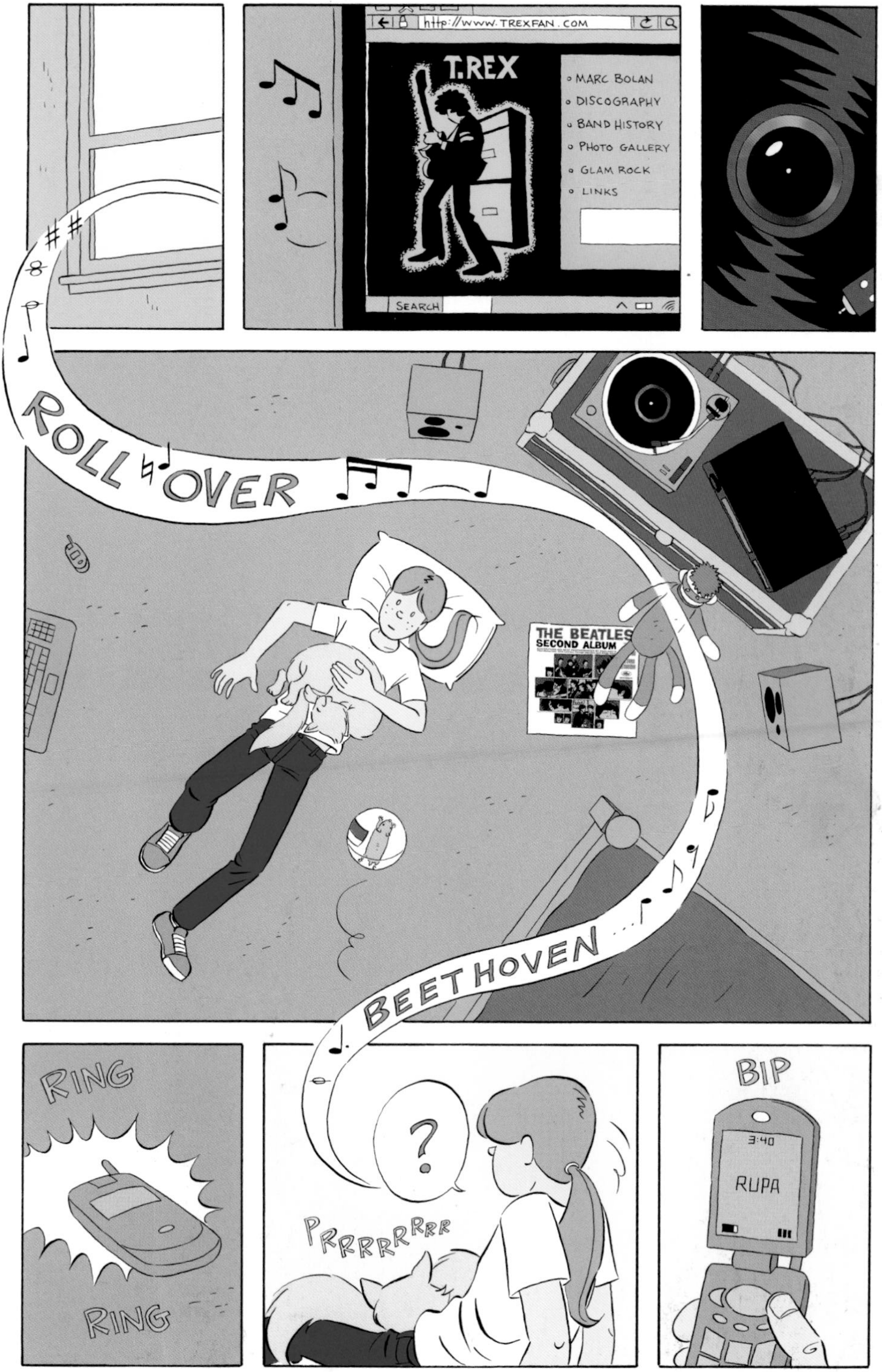
http://www.TREXFAN.COM
T.REX
MARC BOLAN
DISCOGRAPHY
BAND HISTORY
PHOTO GALLERY
GLAM ROCK
LINKS
SEARCH
ROLL OVER BEETHOVEN
THE BEATLES
SECOND ALBUM
RING
RING
?
PRRRRRRRRR
BIP
3:40
RUPA

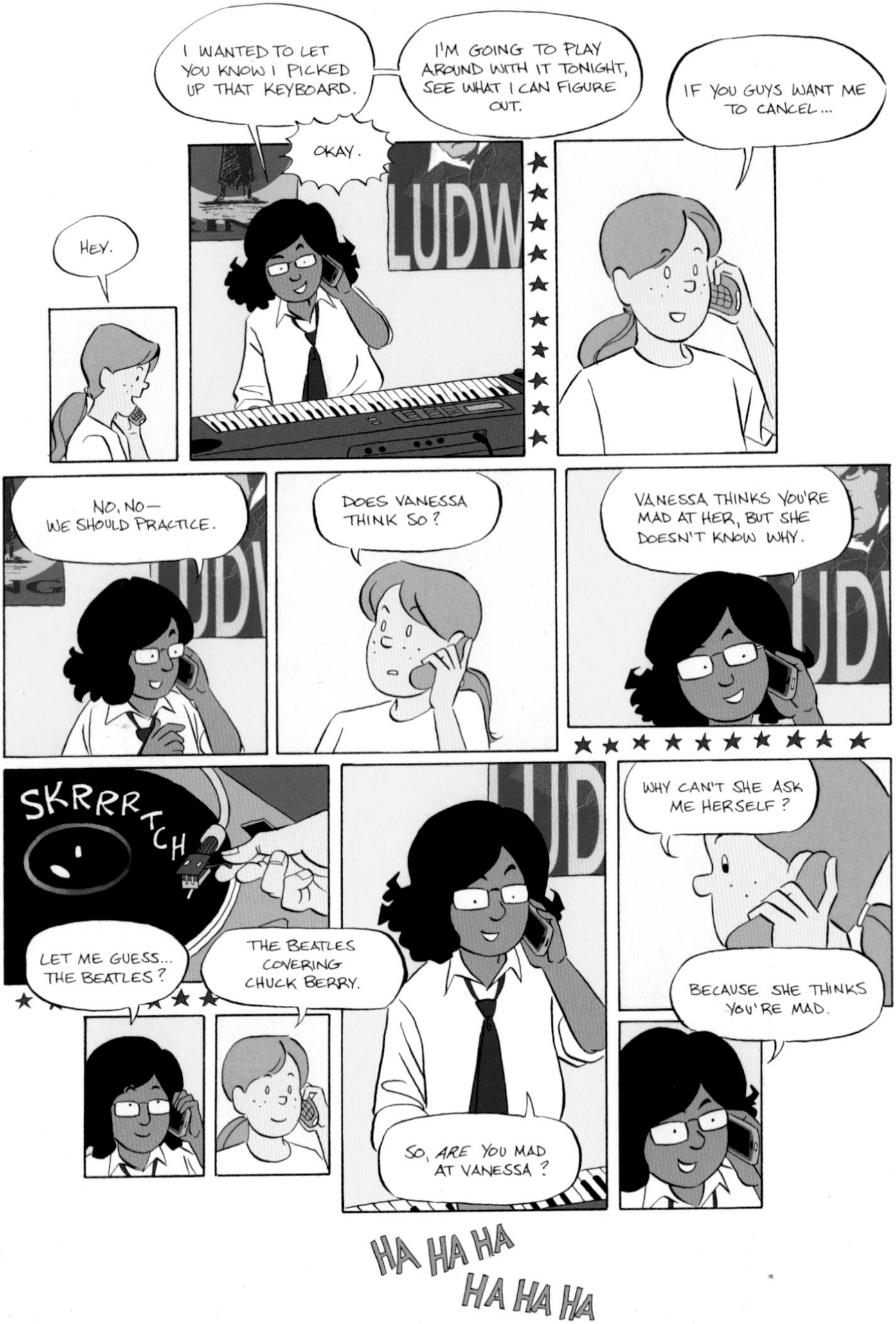
HEY.
I WANTED TO LET YOU KNOW I PICKED UP THAT KEYBOARD.
OKAY.
I'M GOING TO PLAY AROUND WITH IT TONIGHT, SEE WHAT I CAN FIGURE OUT.
IF YOU GUYS WANT ME TO CANCEL...
LUDW
NO, NO— WE SHOULD PRACTICE.
DOES VANESSA THINK SO?
VANESSA THINKS YOU'RE MAD AT HER, BUT SHE DOESN'T KNOW WHY.
SKRRRTCH
LET ME GUESS... THE BEATLES?
THE BEATLES COVERING CHUCK BERRY.
WHY CAN'T SHE ASK ME HERSELF?
BECAUSE SHE THINKS YOU'RE MAD.
SO, *ARE* YOU MAD AT VANESSA?
HA HA HA
HA HA HA

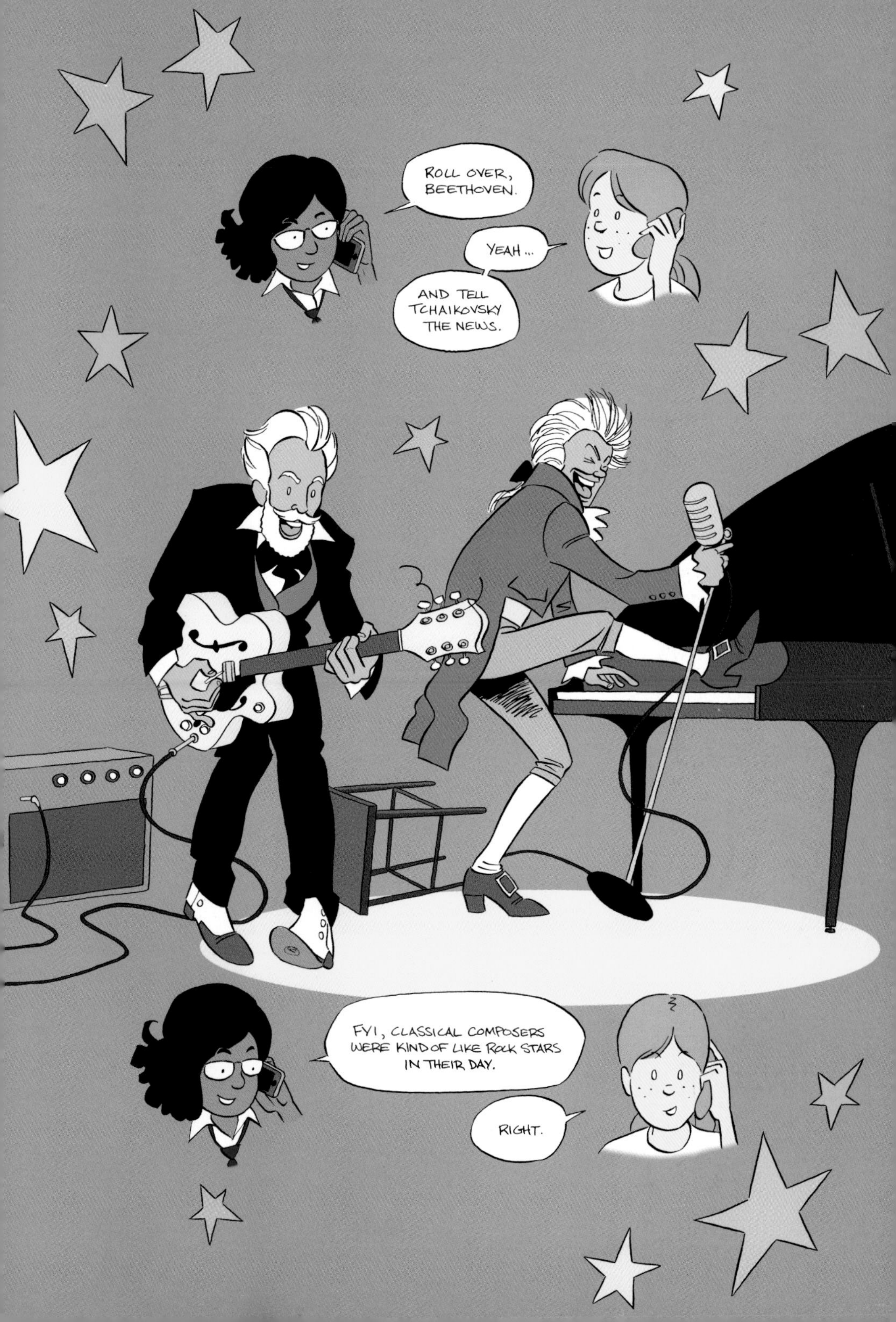
ROLL OVER, BEETHOVEN.
YEAH...
AND TELL TCHAIKOVSKY THE NEWS.
FYI, CLASSICAL COMPOSERS WERE KIND OF LIKE ROCK STARS IN THEIR DAY.
RIGHT.

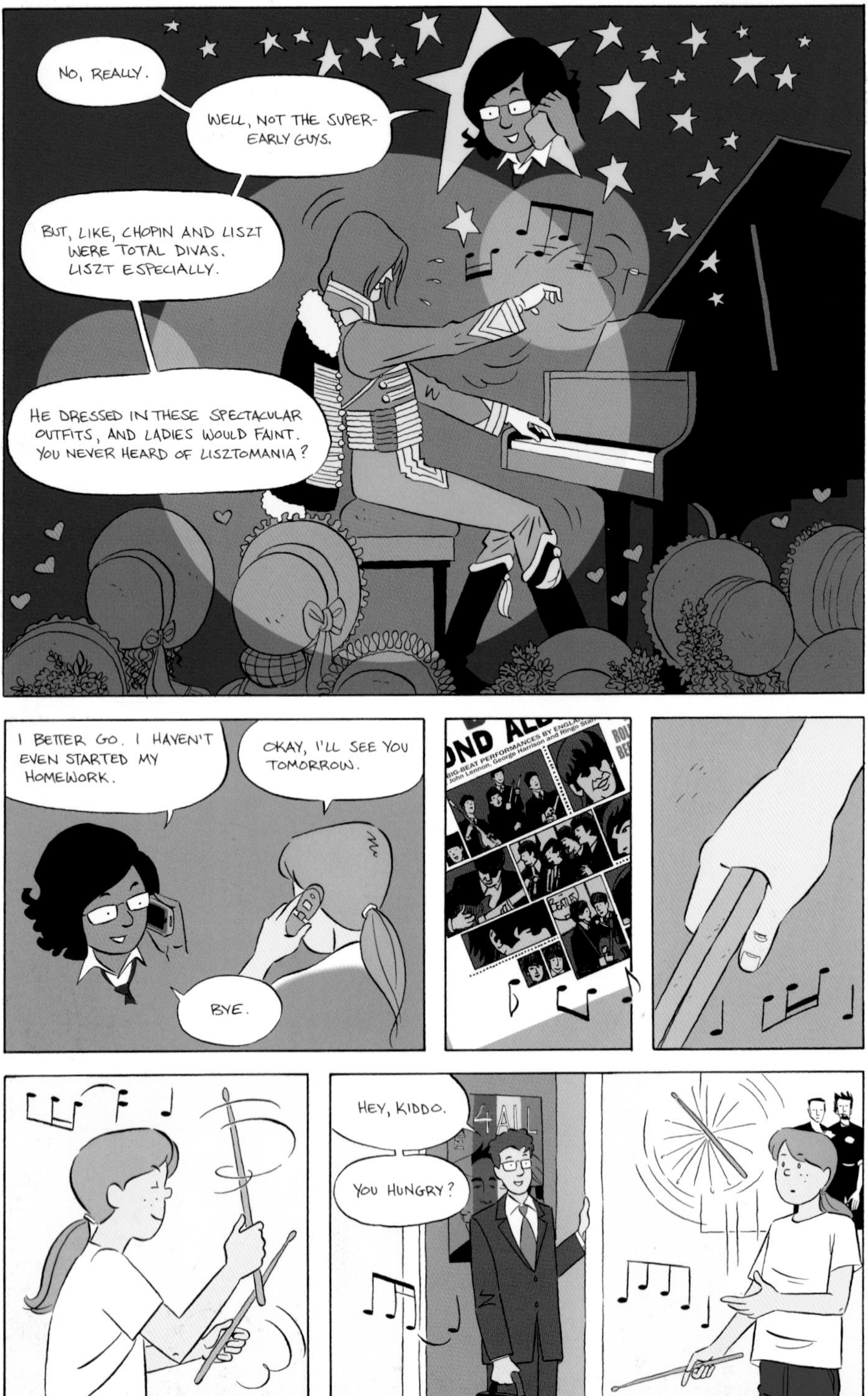
NO, REALLY.
WELL, NOT THE SUPER-EARLY GUYS.
BUT, LIKE, CHOPIN AND LISZT WERE TOTAL DIVAS. LISZT ESPECIALLY.
HE DRESSED IN THESE SPECTACULAR OUTFITS, AND LADIES WOULD FAINT. YOU NEVER HEARD OF LISZTOMANIA?
I BETTER GO. I HAVEN'T EVEN STARTED MY HOMEWORK.
OKAY, I'LL SEE YOU TOMORROW.
BYE.
BIG-BEAT PERFORMANCES BY
John Lennon, George Harrison and Ringo
BEATLES
HEY, KIDDO.
YOU HUNGRY?
4ALL

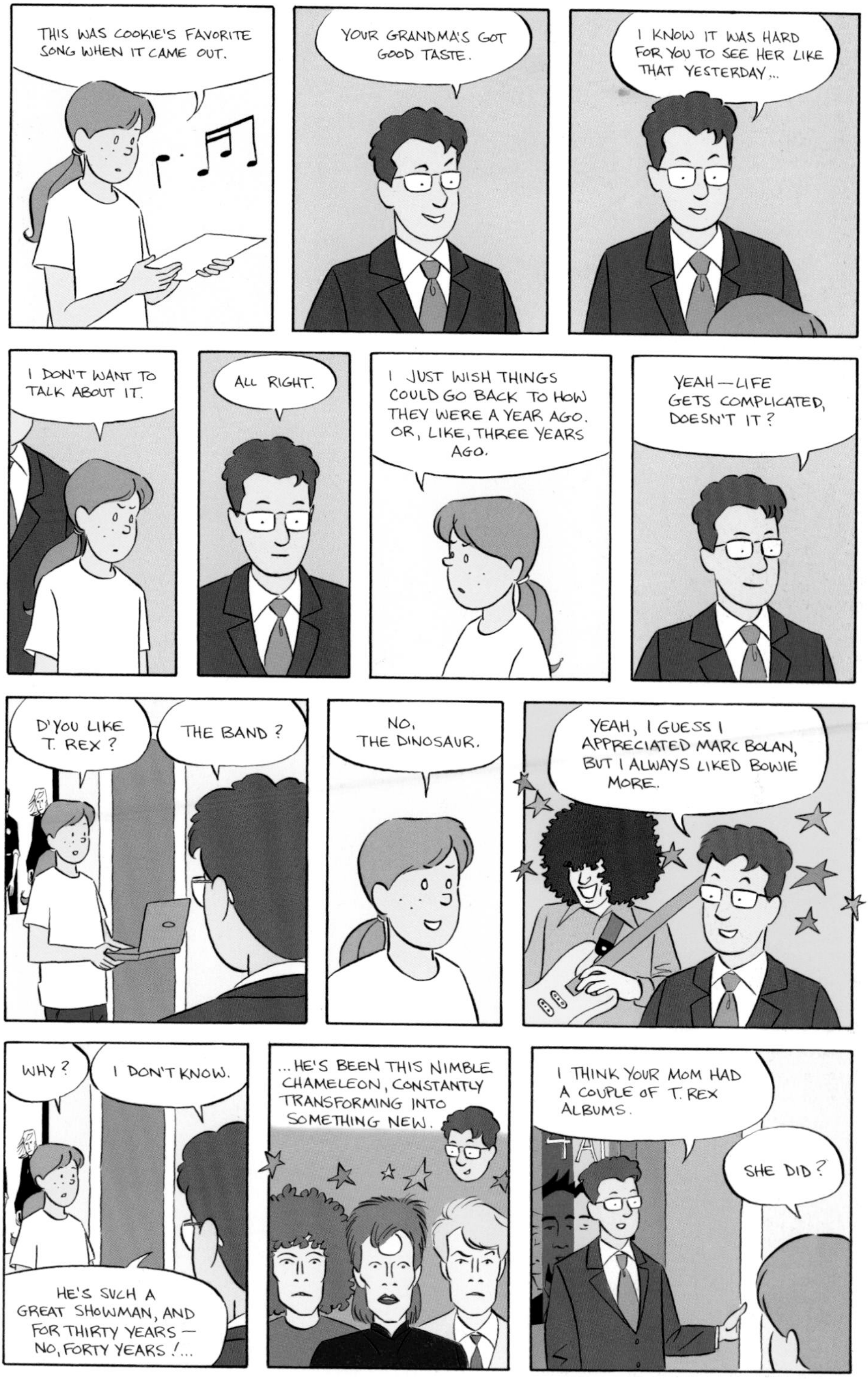
THIS WAS COOKIE'S FAVORITE SONG WHEN IT CAME OUT.
YOUR GRANDMA'S GOT GOOD TASTE.
I KNOW IT WAS HARD FOR YOU TO SEE HER LIKE THAT YESTERDAY...
I DON'T WANT TO TALK ABOUT IT.
ALL RIGHT.
I JUST WISH THINGS COULD GO BACK TO HOW THEY WERE A YEAR AGO. OR, LIKE, THREE YEARS AGO.
YEAH — LIFE GETS COMPLICATED, DOESN'T IT?
D'YOU LIKE T. REX?
THE BAND?
NO, THE DINOSAUR.
YEAH, I GUESS I APPRECIATED MARC BOLAN, BUT I ALWAYS LIKED BOWIE MORE.
WHY?
I DON'T KNOW.
HE'S SUCH A GREAT SHOWMAN, AND FOR THIRTY YEARS — NO, FORTY YEARS!...
...HE'S BEEN THIS NIMBLE CHAMELEON, CONSTANTLY TRANSFORMING INTO SOMETHING NEW.
I THINK YOUR MOM HAD A COUPLE OF T. REX ALBUMS.
SHE DID?

YOU'LL HAVE TO ASK HER.

SK RRR KUUH

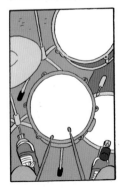

ASK ME ABOUT BIO DIESEL

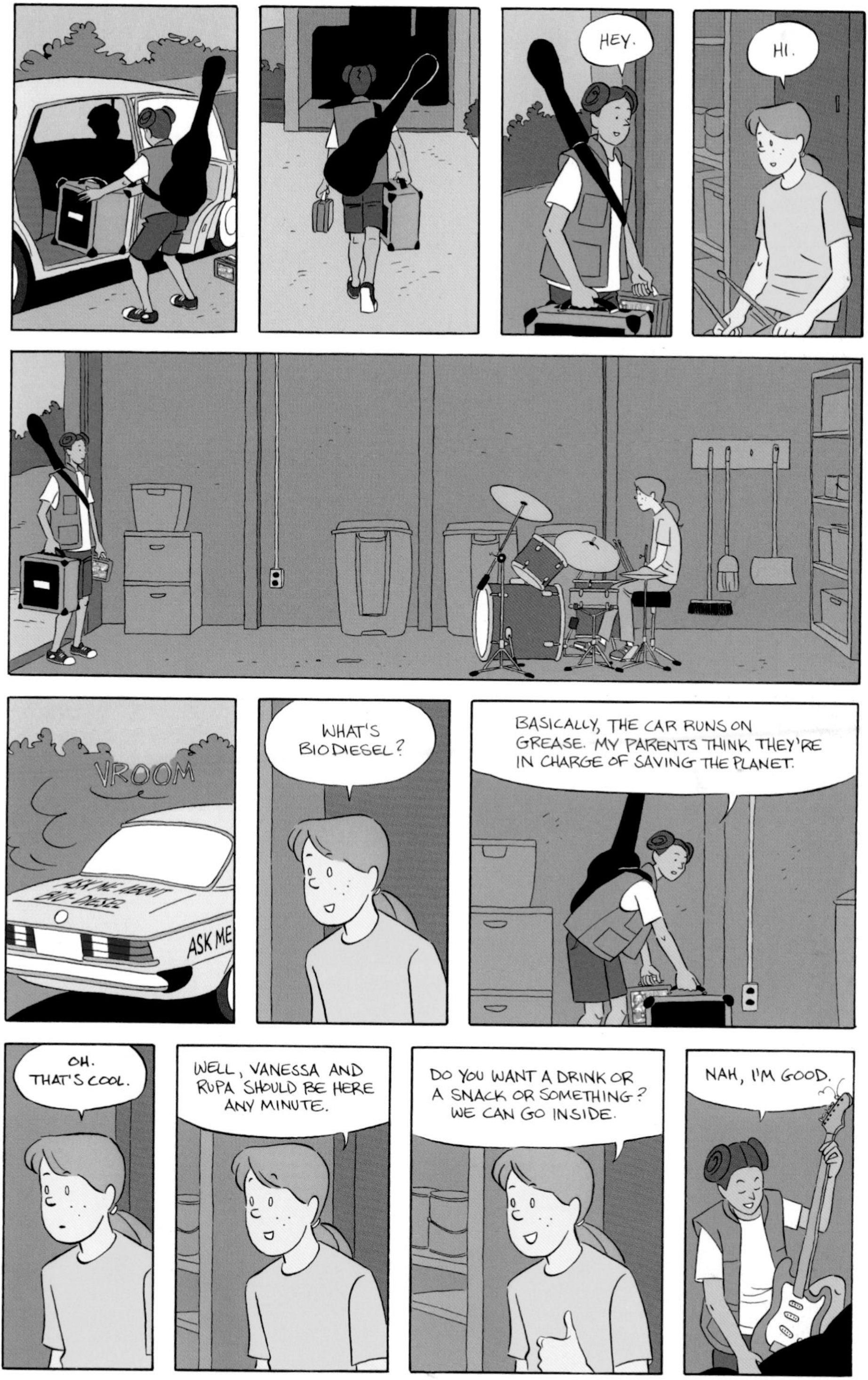
HEY.
HI.
VROOM
ASK ME ABOUT BIO-DIESEL
ASK ME
WHAT'S BIODIESEL?
BASICALLY, THE CAR RUNS ON GREASE. MY PARENTS THINK THEY'RE IN CHARGE OF SAVING THE PLANET.
OH. THAT'S COOL.
WELL, VANESSA AND RUPA SHOULD BE HERE ANY MINUTE.
DO YOU WANT A DRINK OR A SNACK OR SOMETHING? WE CAN GO INSIDE.
NAH, I'M GOOD.

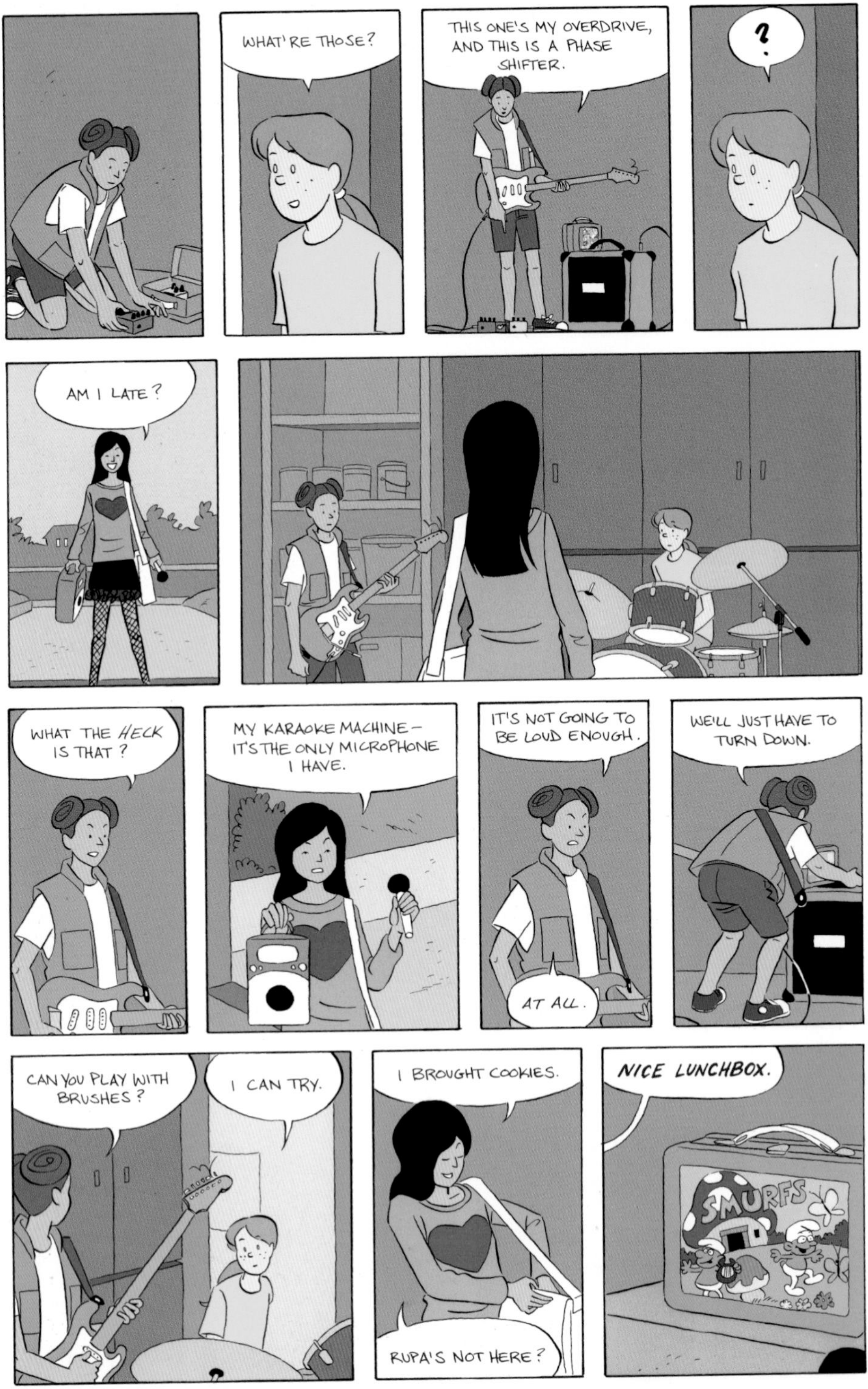
WHAT'RE THOSE?
THIS ONE'S MY OVERDRIVE, AND THIS IS A PHASE SHIFTER.
?
AM I LATE?
WHAT THE HECK IS THAT?
MY KARAOKE MACHINE— IT'S THE ONLY MICROPHONE I HAVE.
IT'S NOT GOING TO BE LOUD ENOUGH.
AT ALL.
WE'LL JUST HAVE TO TURN DOWN.
CAN YOU PLAY WITH BRUSHES?
I CAN TRY.
I BROUGHT COOKIES.
RUPA'S NOT HERE?
NICE LUNCHBOX.
SMURFS

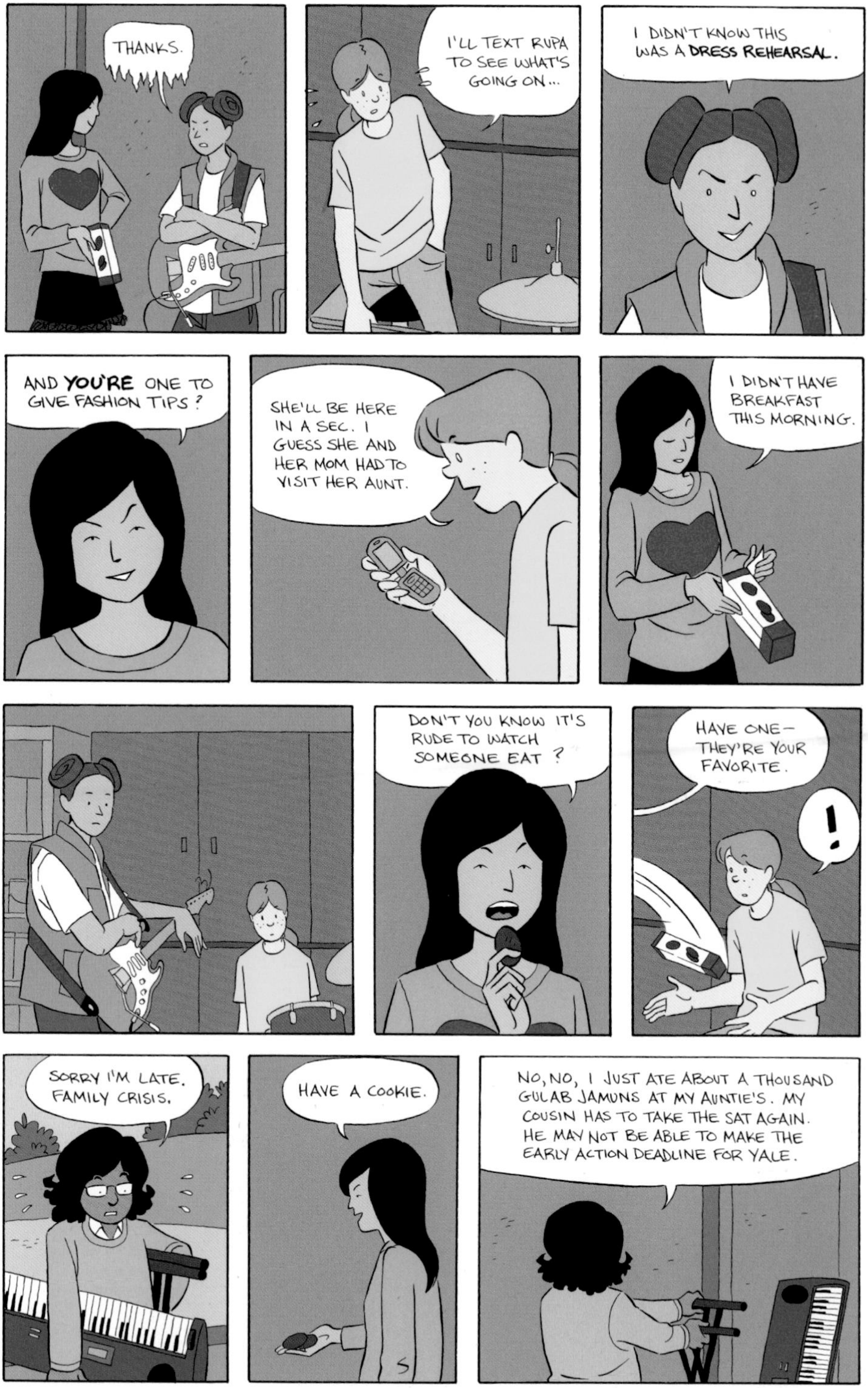
THANKS.
I'LL TEXT RUPA TO SEE WHAT'S GOING ON...
I DIDN'T KNOW THIS WAS A **DRESS REHEARSAL.**
AND **YOU'RE** ONE TO GIVE FASHION TIPS?
SHE'LL BE HERE IN A SEC. I GUESS SHE AND HER MOM HAD TO VISIT HER AUNT.
I DIDN'T HAVE BREAKFAST THIS MORNING.
DON'T YOU KNOW IT'S RUDE TO WATCH SOMEONE EAT?
HAVE ONE— THEY'RE YOUR FAVORITE.
!
SORRY I'M LATE. FAMILY CRISIS.
HAVE A COOKIE.
NO, NO, I JUST ATE ABOUT A THOUSAND GULAB JAMUNS AT MY AUNTIE'S. MY COUSIN HAS TO TAKE THE SAT AGAIN. HE MAY NOT BE ABLE TO MAKE THE EARLY ACTION DEADLINE FOR YALE.

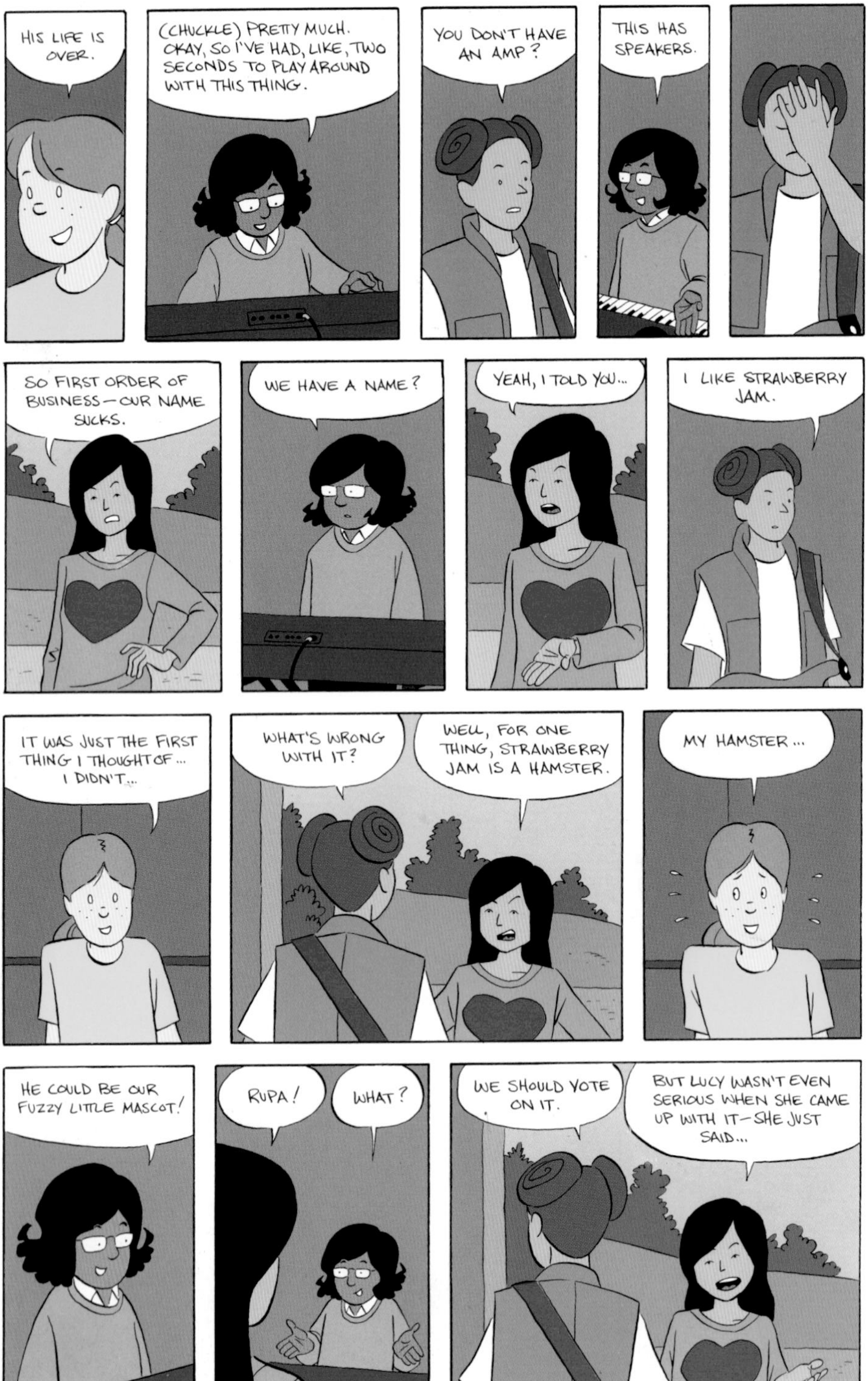
HIS LIFE IS OVER.
(CHUCKLE) PRETTY MUCH. OKAY, SO I'VE HAD, LIKE, TWO SECONDS TO PLAY AROUND WITH THIS THING.
YOU DON'T HAVE AN AMP?
THIS HAS SPEAKERS.
SO FIRST ORDER OF BUSINESS—OUR NAME SUCKS.
WE HAVE A NAME?
YEAH, I TOLD YOU...
I LIKE STRAWBERRY JAM.
IT WAS JUST THE FIRST THING I THOUGHT OF... I DIDN'T...
WHAT'S WRONG WITH IT?
WELL, FOR ONE THING, STRAWBERRY JAM IS A HAMSTER.
MY HAMSTER...
HE COULD BE OUR FUZZY LITTLE MASCOT!
RUPA!
WHAT?
WE SHOULD VOTE ON IT.
BUT LUCY WASN'T EVEN SERIOUS WHEN SHE CAME UP WITH IT—SHE JUST SAID...

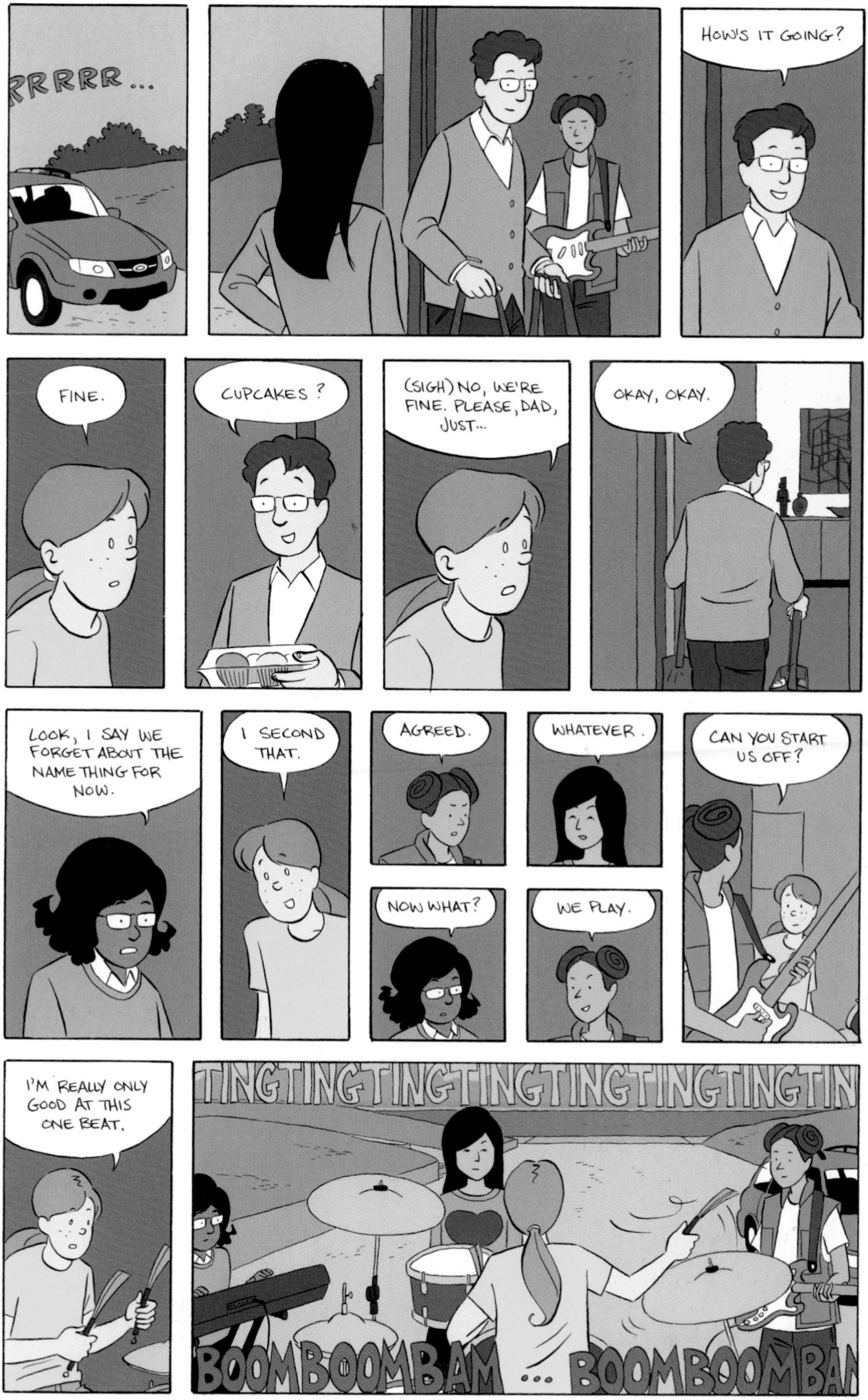
RRRRR...
HOW'S IT GOING?
FINE.
CUPCAKES?
(SIGH) NO, WE'RE FINE. PLEASE, DAD, JUST...
OKAY, OKAY.
LOOK, I SAY WE FORGET ABOUT THE NAME THING FOR NOW.
I SECOND THAT.
AGREED.
WHATEVER.
NOW WHAT?
WE PLAY.
CAN YOU START US OFF?
I'M REALLY ONLY GOOD AT THIS ONE BEAT.
TINGTINGTINGTINGTINGTINGTINGTIN
BOOMBOOMBAM ... BOOMBOOMBA

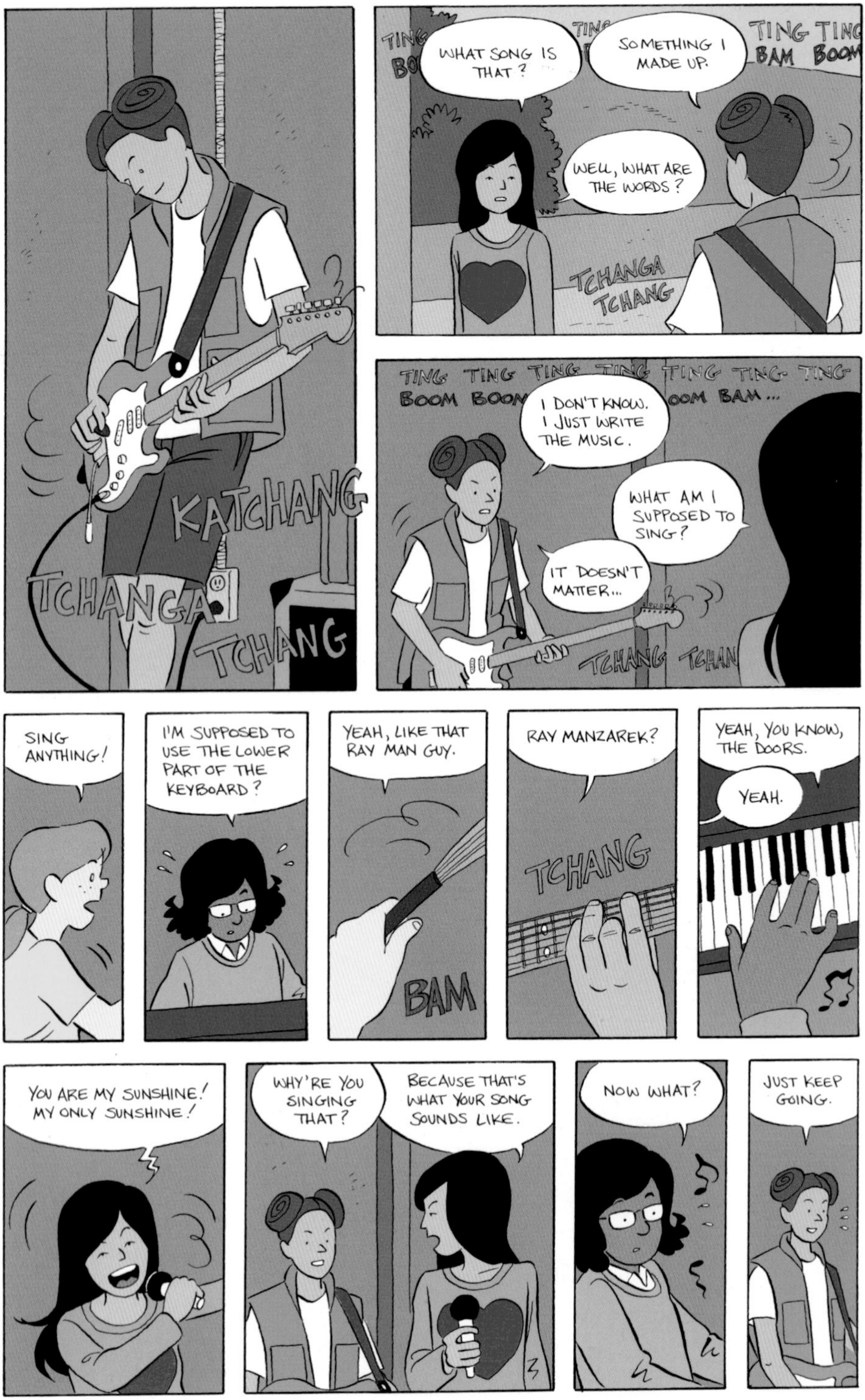
KATCHANG
TCHANGA
TCHANG
TING BOOM
WHAT SONG IS THAT?
SOMETHING I MADE UP.
TING TING BAM BOOM
WELL, WHAT ARE THE WORDS?
TCHANGA TCHANG
TING TING TING TING TING TING TING
BOOM BOOM BOOM BAM...
I DON'T KNOW. I JUST WRITE THE MUSIC.
WHAT AM I SUPPOSED TO SING?
IT DOESN'T MATTER...
TCHANG TCHAN
SING ANYTHING!
I'M SUPPOSED TO USE THE LOWER PART OF THE KEYBOARD?
YEAH, LIKE THAT RAY MAN GUY.
BAM
RAY MANZAREK?
TCHANG
YEAH, YOU KNOW, THE DOORS.
YEAH.
YOU ARE MY SUNSHINE! MY ONLY SUNSHINE!
WHY'RE YOU SINGING THAT?
BECAUSE THAT'S WHAT YOUR SONG SOUNDS LIKE.
NOW WHAT?
JUST KEEP GOING.

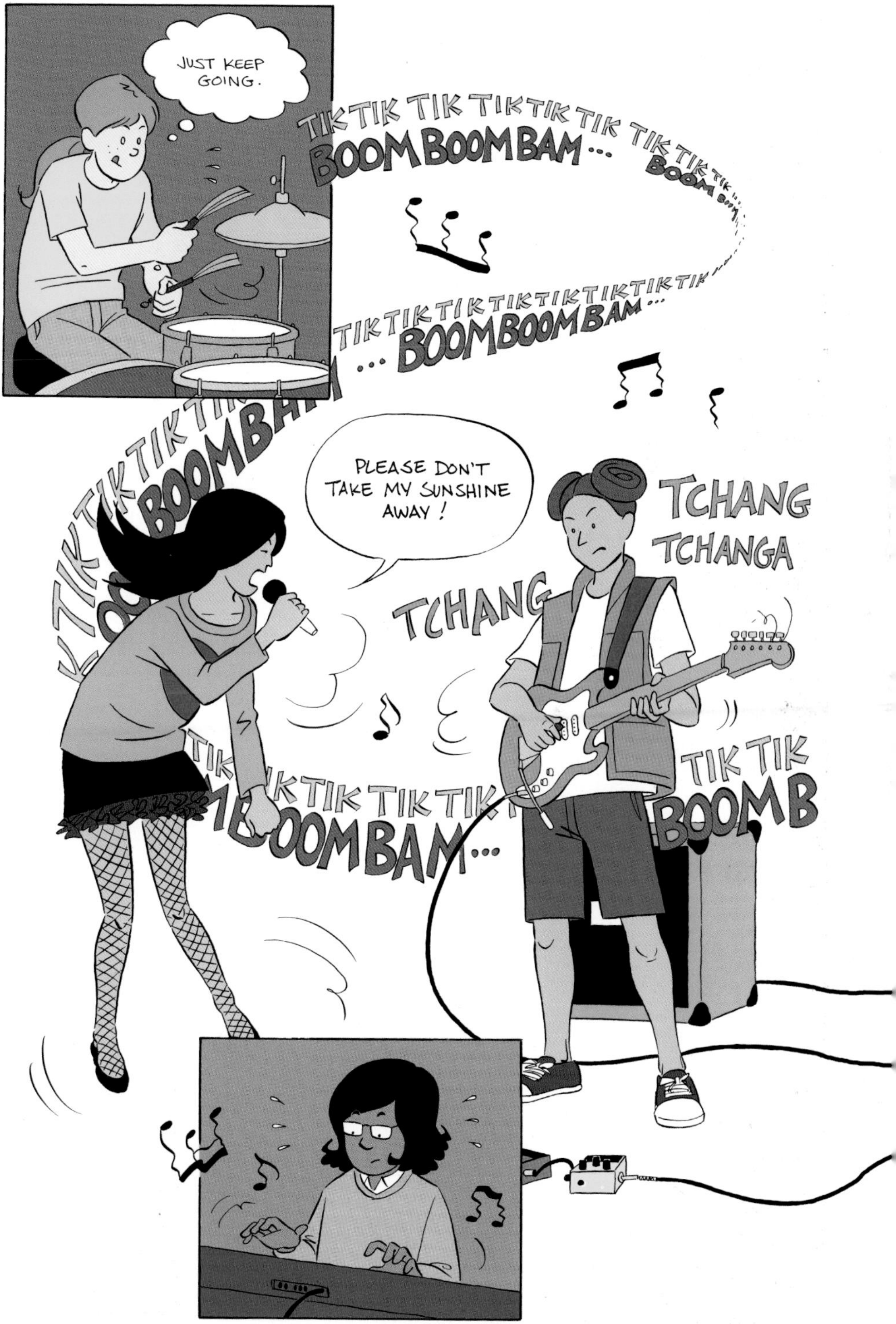
JUST KEEP GOING.
TIKTIK TIK TIKTIK TIK TIKTIK
BOOMBOOMBAM...
TIKTIKTIKTIKTIKTIKTIKTIK
BOOMBOOMBAM...
BOOMBAM
PLEASE DON'T TAKE MY SUNSHINE AWAY!
TCHANG
TCHANGA
TCHANG
TIKTIKTIKTIK
BOOMBAM...
TIKTIK
BOOMB

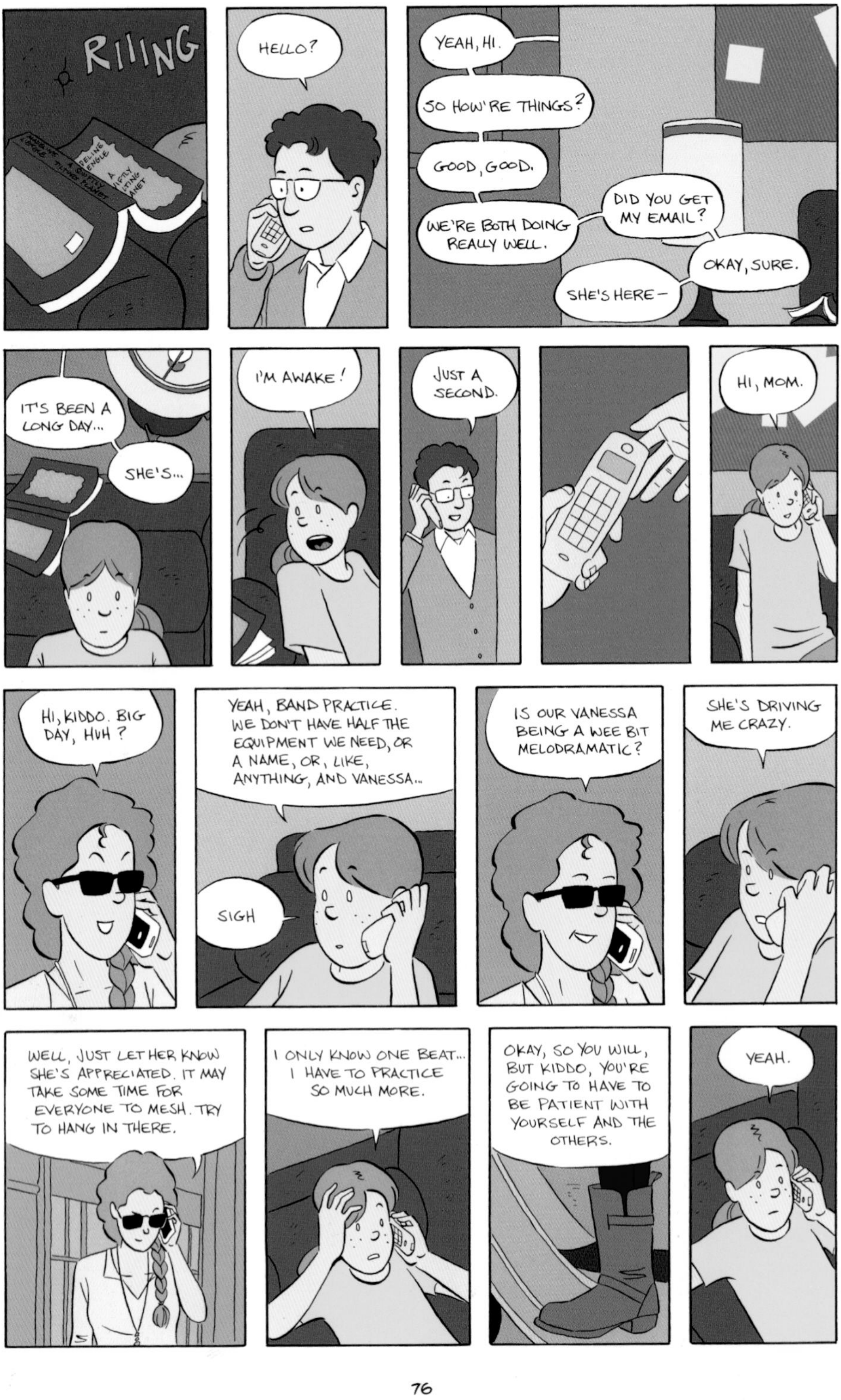
RIIING
HELLO?
YEAH, HI.
SO HOW'RE THINGS?
GOOD, GOOD.
WE'RE BOTH DOING REALLY WELL.
DID YOU GET MY EMAIL?
OKAY, SURE.
SHE'S HERE—
IT'S BEEN A LONG DAY...
SHE'S...
I'M AWAKE!
JUST A SECOND.
HI, MOM.
HI, KIDDO. BIG DAY, HUH?
YEAH, BAND PRACTICE. WE DON'T HAVE HALF THE EQUIPMENT WE NEED, OR A NAME, OR, LIKE, ANYTHING, AND VANESSA...
SIGH
IS OUR VANESSA BEING A WEE BIT MELODRAMATIC?
SHE'S DRIVING ME CRAZY.
WELL, JUST LET HER KNOW SHE'S APPRECIATED. IT MAY TAKE SOME TIME FOR EVERYONE TO MESH. TRY TO HANG IN THERE.
I ONLY KNOW ONE BEAT... I HAVE TO PRACTICE SO MUCH MORE.
OKAY, SO YOU WILL, BUT KIDDO, YOU'RE GOING TO HAVE TO BE PATIENT WITH YOURSELF AND THE OTHERS.
YEAH.

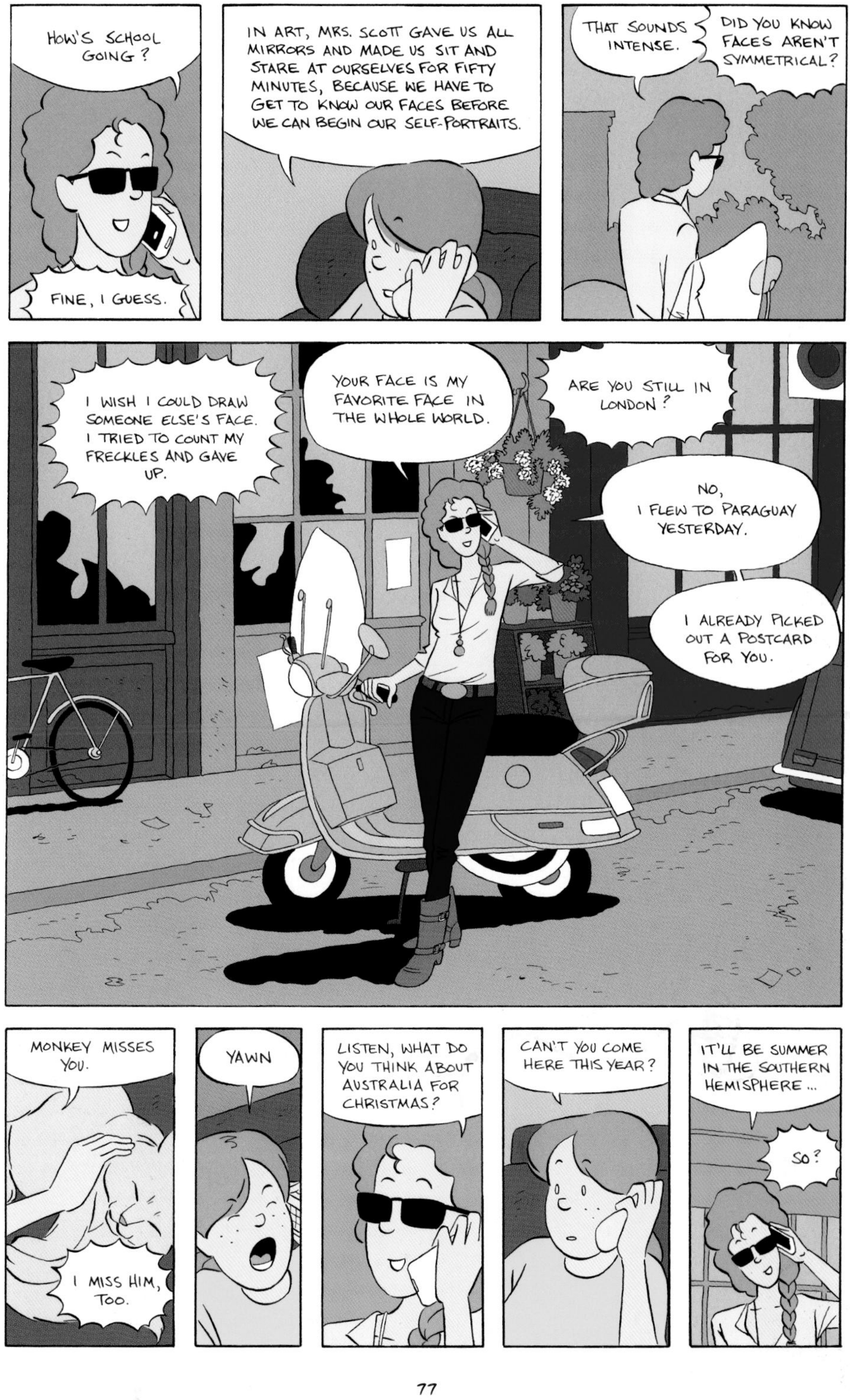
HOW'S SCHOOL GOING?
FINE, I GUESS.
IN ART, MRS. SCOTT GAVE US ALL MIRRORS AND MADE US SIT AND STARE AT OURSELVES FOR FIFTY MINUTES, BECAUSE WE HAVE TO GET TO KNOW OUR FACES BEFORE WE CAN BEGIN OUR SELF-PORTRAITS.
THAT SOUNDS INTENSE.
DID YOU KNOW FACES AREN'T SYMMETRICAL?
I WISH I COULD DRAW SOMEONE ELSE'S FACE. I TRIED TO COUNT MY FRECKLES AND GAVE UP.
YOUR FACE IS MY FAVORITE FACE IN THE WHOLE WORLD.
ARE YOU STILL IN LONDON?
NO, I FLEW TO PARAGUAY YESTERDAY.
I ALREADY PICKED OUT A POSTCARD FOR YOU.
MONKEY MISSES YOU.
I MISS HIM, TOO.
YAWN
LISTEN, WHAT DO YOU THINK ABOUT AUSTRALIA FOR CHRISTMAS?
CAN'T YOU COME HERE THIS YEAR?
IT'LL BE SUMMER IN THE SOUTHERN HEMISPHERE...
SO?

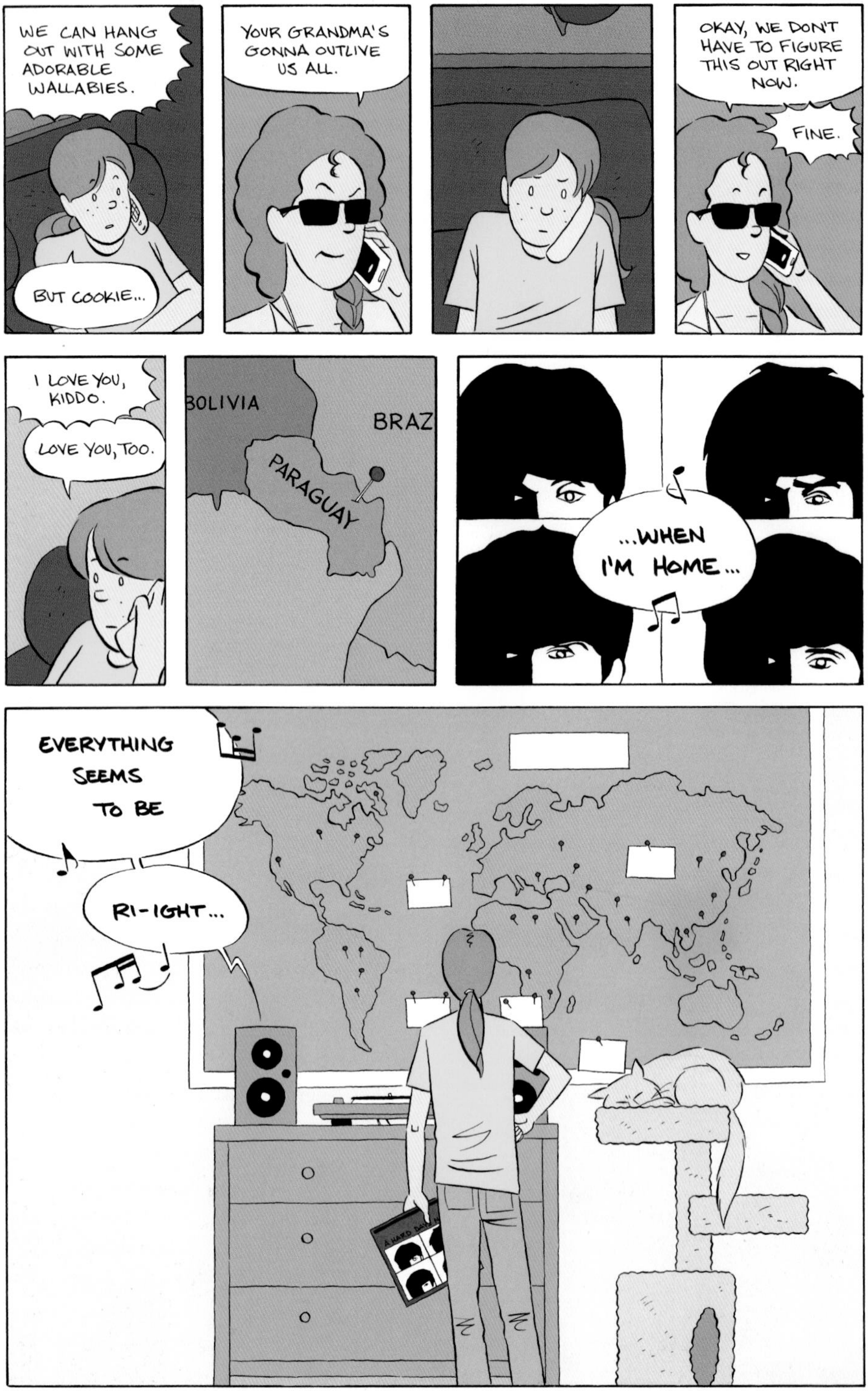
WE CAN HANG OUT WITH SOME ADORABLE WALLABIES.
BUT COOKIE...
YOUR GRANDMA'S GONNA OUTLIVE US ALL.
OKAY, WE DON'T HAVE TO FIGURE THIS OUT RIGHT NOW.
FINE.
I LOVE YOU, KIDDO.
LOVE YOU, TOO.
BOLIVIA
BRAZ
PARAGUAY
...WHEN I'M HOME...
EVERYTHING SEEMS TO BE
RI-IGHT...

41
Allerton D.

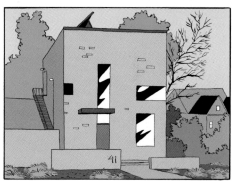

WELCOME TO THE HOME OF THE FUTURE.

HA! THE SOLAR PANELS ARE COOL.

IN THE UNLIKELY EVENT THAT OUR PLANET SHOULD BECOME TOO TOXIC, WE WILL BLAST OFF INTO SPACE AND DOCK ON THE DARK SIDE OF THE MOON.

I'LL GIVE YOU THE GRAND TOUR.

FAMILY ROOM.

KITCHEN.

THE HALLWAY. BATHROOM'S THE SECOND DOOR ON THE RIGHT. THAT'S MY ROOM...

...MY BROTHER'S ROOM.

ABANDON ALL HOPE, YE WHO ENTER HERE.

MY PARENTS' ROOM...

AND DOWN THERE'S THE DEN, BUT WE CALL IT THE GUITAR ROOM.

YOUR GUITAR HAS ITS OWN ROOM?

(CHUCKLE) I HAVE MANY GUITARS.

WANNA SEE?

SURE.

MOST OF THEM, WE FIND FOR REALLY CHEAP AND THEN FIX UP.

MY BROTHER'S AN EBAY WIZARD.

!

HOW LONG'VE YOU BEEN COLLECTING THEM?

SINCE I WAS NINE.

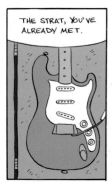

THE STRAT, YOU'VE ALREADY MET.

THIS ONE'S MOSTLY FOR SHOW. YOU CAN'T PLAY IT SITTING DOWN.

THE CASINO'S FUN, BUT IT FEEDS BACK WHEN YOU PLAY LOUD.

THIS ONE'S MY GEM: A HAGSTROM VIKING ...

...THE KIND ELVIS PLAYED IN HIS '68 COMEBACK SPECIAL.

IT STILL NEEDS A LITTLE WORK, THOUGH. THE TUNING KNOBS'LL PROBABLY HAVE TO BE REPLACED.

YOU LIKE ELVIS?

IS THAT BAD?

NO... UM...

I LIKE THE STORY OF ELVIS.

SO TRAGIC.

WHAT ABOUT DAVID BOWIE?

JUST IN GENERAL?

ISN'T HE BETTER THAN MARC BOLAN?

BOWIE IS LIKE A SUPERBEING. I'M CONVINCED HE'S FROM ANOTHER PLANET...

...AND THAT'S COOL AND EVERYTHING, BUT FOR ME...

I JUST FEEL MORE REAL LISTENING TO SOMEONE WHO'S HUMAN, WHO'S ALMOST GREAT...

...BUT NOT PERFECT, YOU KNOW?

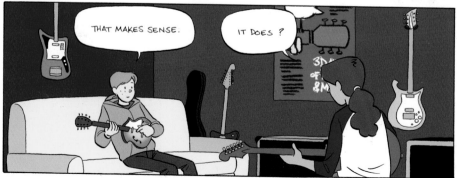

THAT MAKES SENSE.

IT DOES?

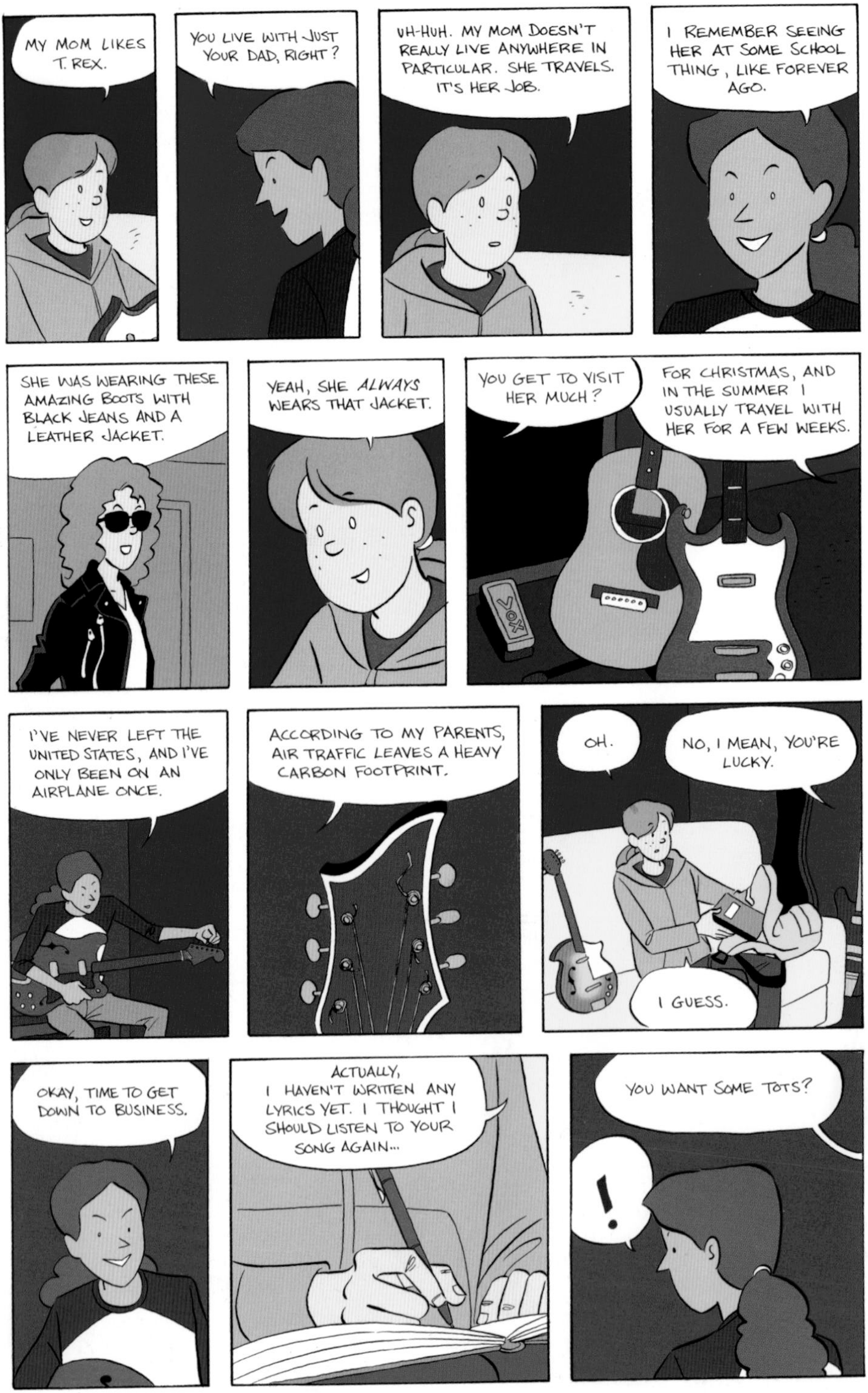
MY MOM LIKES T. REX.
YOU LIVE WITH JUST YOUR DAD, RIGHT?
UH-HUH. MY MOM DOESN'T REALLY LIVE ANYWHERE IN PARTICULAR. SHE TRAVELS. IT'S HER JOB.
I REMEMBER SEEING HER AT SOME SCHOOL THING, LIKE FOREVER AGO.
SHE WAS WEARING THESE AMAZING BOOTS WITH BLACK JEANS AND A LEATHER JACKET.
YEAH, SHE *ALWAYS* WEARS THAT JACKET.
YOU GET TO VISIT HER MUCH?
FOR CHRISTMAS, AND IN THE SUMMER I USUALLY TRAVEL WITH HER FOR A FEW WEEKS.
VOX
I'VE NEVER LEFT THE UNITED STATES, AND I'VE ONLY BEEN ON AN AIRPLANE ONCE.
ACCORDING TO MY PARENTS, AIR TRAFFIC LEAVES A HEAVY CARBON FOOTPRINT.
OH.
NO, I MEAN, YOU'RE LUCKY.
I GUESS.
OKAY, TIME TO GET DOWN TO BUSINESS.
ACTUALLY, I HAVEN'T WRITTEN ANY LYRICS YET. I THOUGHT I SHOULD LISTEN TO YOUR SONG AGAIN...
!
YOU WANT SOME TOTS?

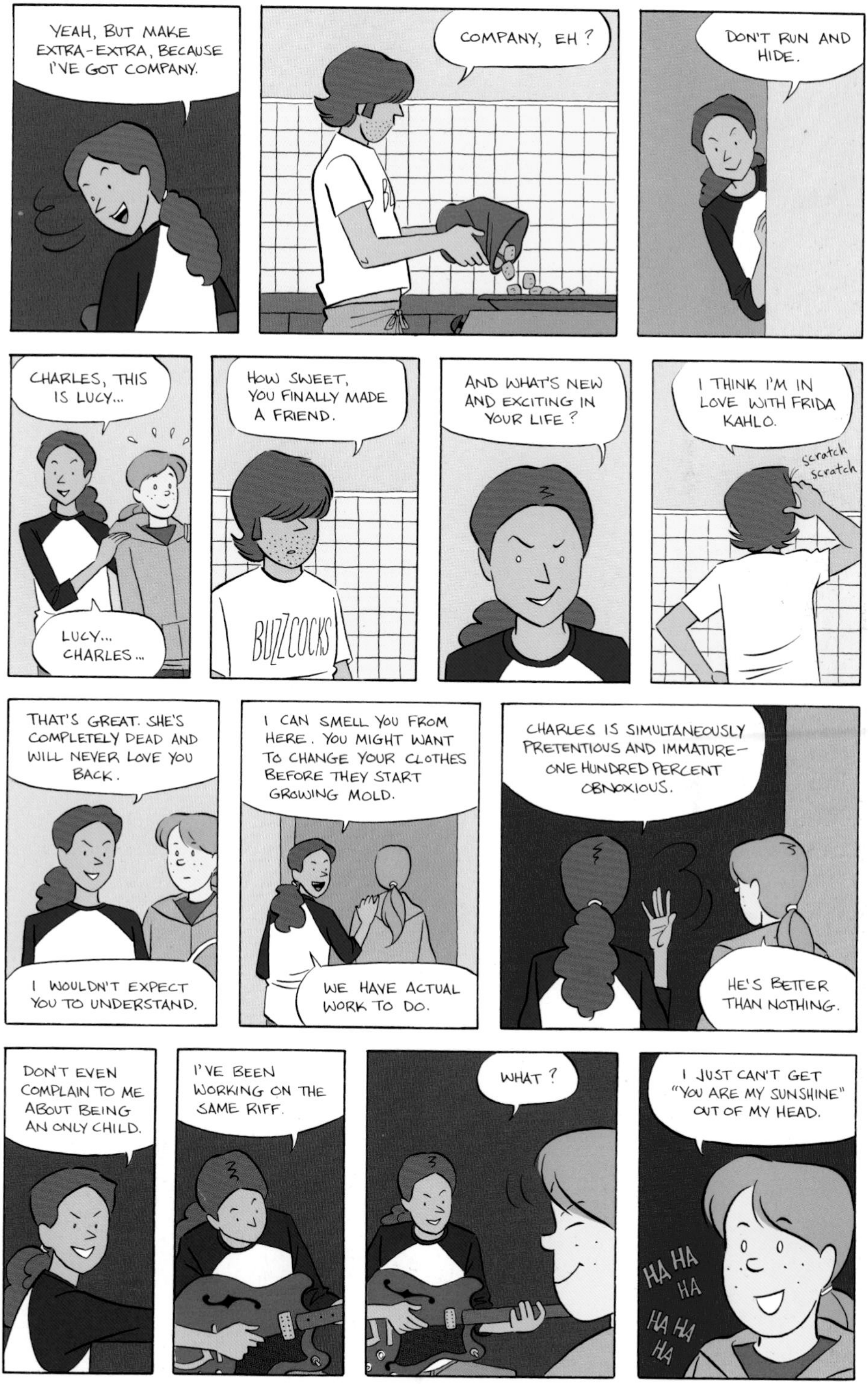
YEAH, BUT MAKE EXTRA-EXTRA, BECAUSE I'VE GOT COMPANY.
COMPANY, EH?
DON'T RUN AND HIDE.
CHARLES, THIS IS LUCY...
LUCY... CHARLES...
HOW SWEET, YOU FINALLY MADE A FRIEND.
BUZZCOCKS
AND WHAT'S NEW AND EXCITING IN YOUR LIFE?
I THINK I'M IN LOVE WITH FRIDA KAHLO.
scratch scratch
THAT'S GREAT. SHE'S COMPLETELY DEAD AND WILL NEVER LOVE YOU BACK.
I WOULDN'T EXPECT YOU TO UNDERSTAND.
I CAN SMELL YOU FROM HERE. YOU MIGHT WANT TO CHANGE YOUR CLOTHES BEFORE THEY START GROWING MOLD.
WE HAVE ACTUAL WORK TO DO.
CHARLES IS SIMULTANEOUSLY PRETENTIOUS AND IMMATURE— ONE HUNDRED PERCENT OBNOXIOUS.
HE'S BETTER THAN NOTHING.
DON'T EVEN COMPLAIN TO ME ABOUT BEING AN ONLY CHILD.
I'VE BEEN WORKING ON THE SAME RIFF.
WHAT?
I JUST CAN'T GET "YOU ARE MY SUNSHINE" OUT OF MY HEAD.
HA HA HA
HA HA HA

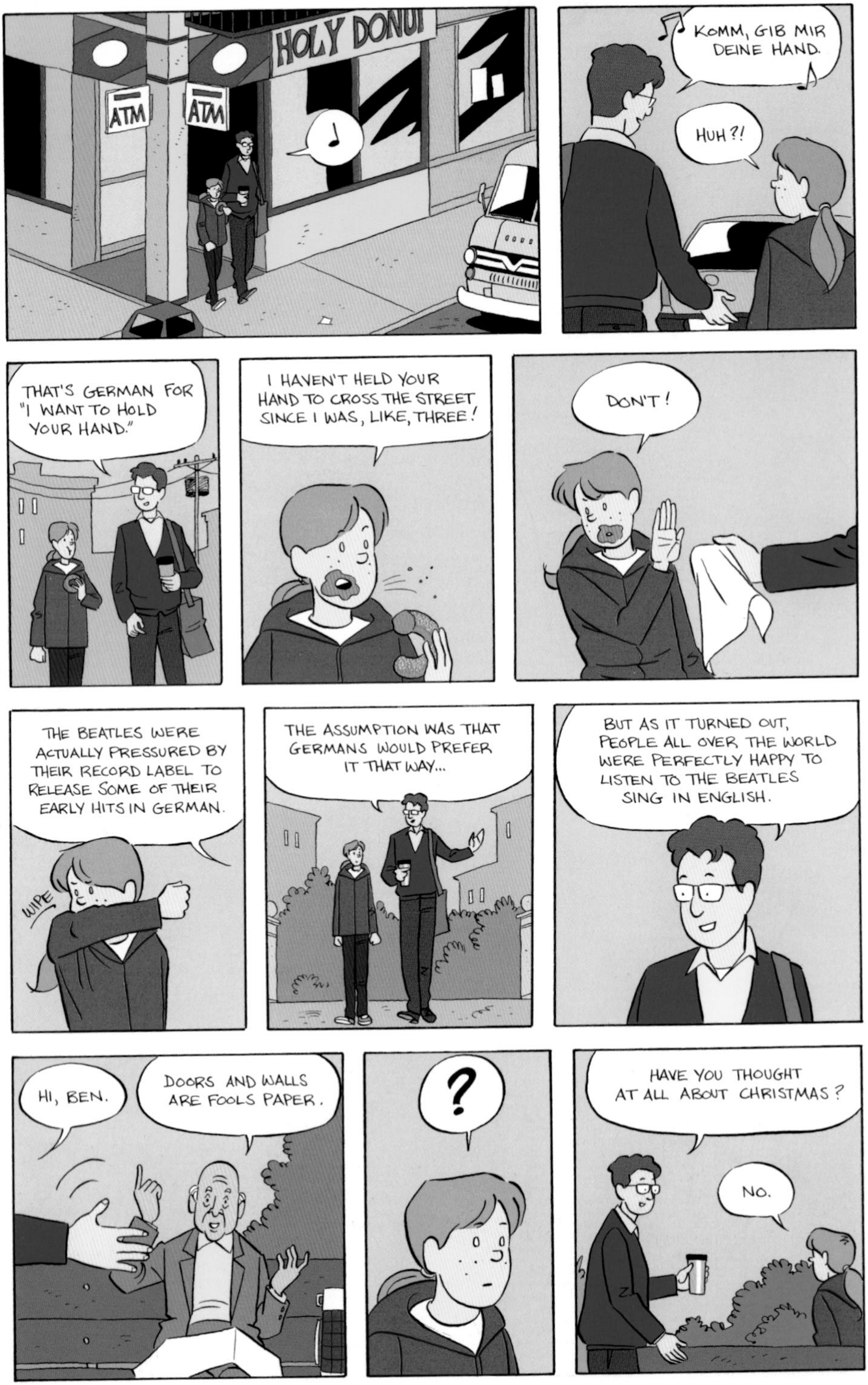
HOLY DONUT
ATM
ATM
KOMM, GIB MIR DEINE HAND.
HUH?!
THAT'S GERMAN FOR "I WANT TO HOLD YOUR HAND."
I HAVEN'T HELD YOUR HAND TO CROSS THE STREET SINCE I WAS, LIKE, THREE!
DON'T!
THE BEATLES WERE ACTUALLY PRESSURED BY THEIR RECORD LABEL TO RELEASE SOME OF THEIR EARLY HITS IN GERMAN.
WIPE
THE ASSUMPTION WAS THAT GERMANS WOULD PREFER IT THAT WAY...
BUT AS IT TURNED OUT, PEOPLE ALL OVER THE WORLD WERE PERFECTLY HAPPY TO LISTEN TO THE BEATLES SING IN ENGLISH.
HI, BEN.
DOORS AND WALLS ARE FOOLS PAPER.
?
HAVE YOU THOUGHT AT ALL ABOUT CHRISTMAS?
NO.

YOUR MOM'S GOING TO CALL TOMORROW, SO YOU MIGHT WANNA THINK ABOUT IT BEFORE THEN.

DON'T YOU WANT THE BREAD?

I HAVE WORK TO DO.

☆ LYRICS
Bees ~~in the garden~~
please ~~take my hand~~
~~~~ in cars
on the roof with stars
~~~~~~~~
Mars?

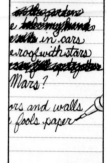

~~in the garden~~
e ~~take my hand~~
~~~~ in cars
~~~~ roof with stars
~~~~~~~~
Mars?

rs and walls
fools paper

!

HI.

HI.

IT'S A MECHANICAL PENCIL.

Bees ~~in the garden~~ please ~~leave my Ma~~ ~~A vessels~~ in ca on the roof with st ~~a bunny of inst~~ Mars?

Doors and wall are fools paper

RYAN

I'M LUCY.

YOU'RE TWELVE.

YUP. HOW OLD'RE YOU?

FIVE AND A QUARTER.

YOU'RE IN KINDERGARTEN?

UH-HUH.

WHAT'RE YOU DOING?

I'M TRYING TO WRITE A SONG.

IT'S NOT GOING SO WELL.

DO YOU WANNA FEED THE DUCKS?

OKAY.

THAT'S MY DAD OVER THERE.

HE HAS THE BREAD IN HIS BAG — YOU JUST HAVE TO ASK HIM FOR IT.

YOU SHOULD ASK HIM.

IF YOU DO IT, I'LL GIVE YOU MY PENCIL.

OKAY.

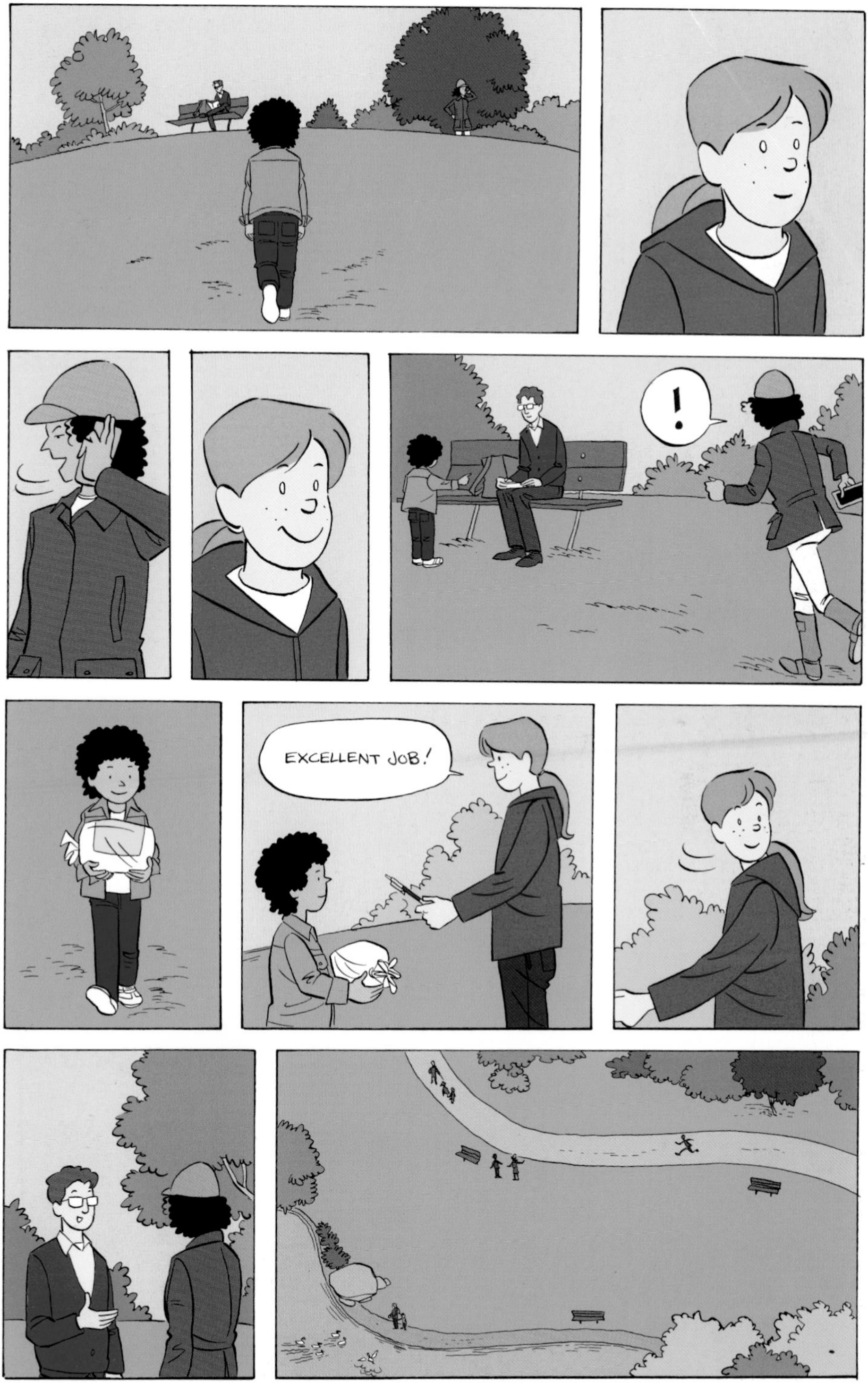
!
EXCELLENT JOB!

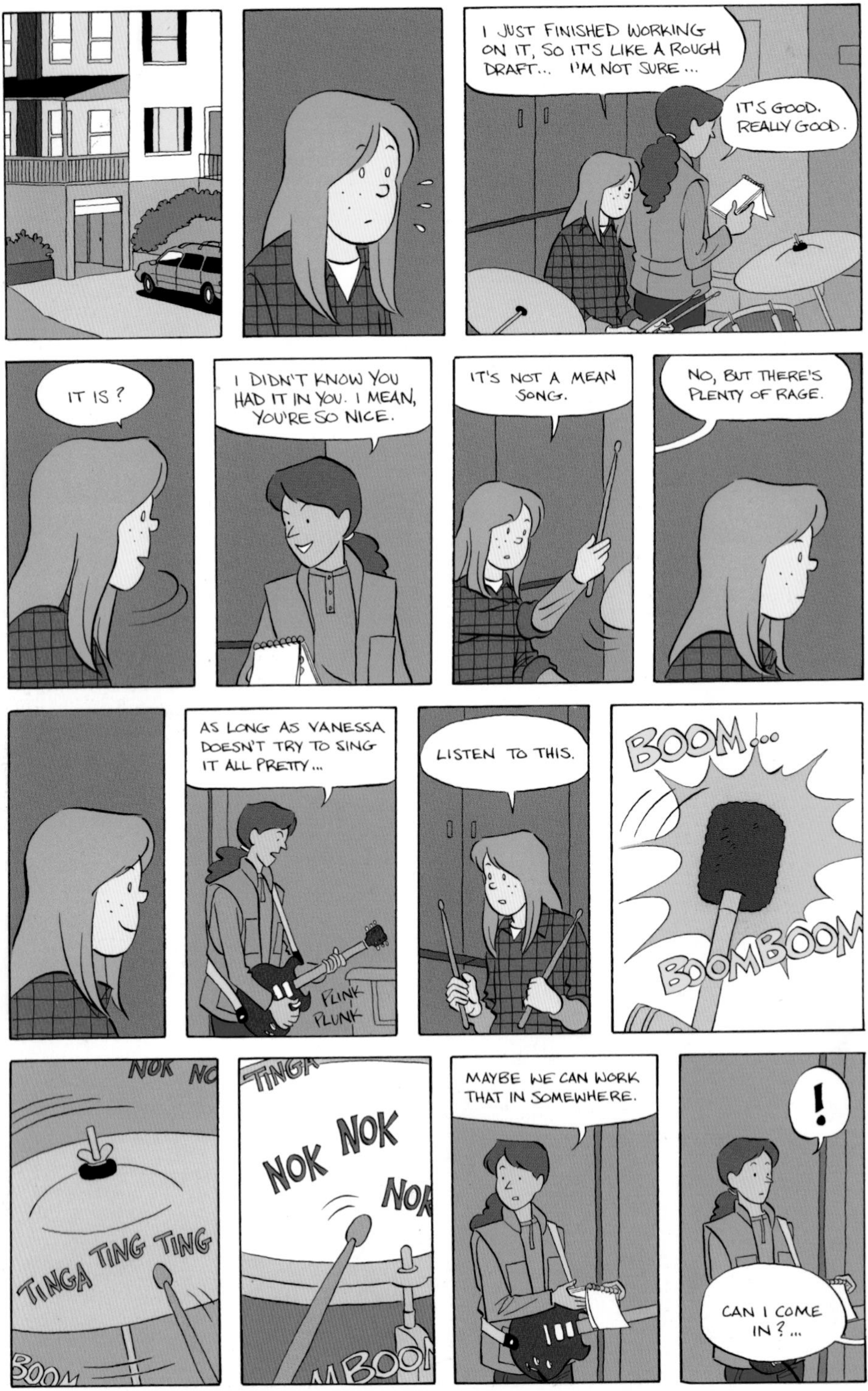
I JUST FINISHED WORKING ON IT, SO IT'S LIKE A ROUGH DRAFT... I'M NOT SURE...
IT'S GOOD. REALLY GOOD.
IT IS?
I DIDN'T KNOW YOU HAD IT IN YOU. I MEAN, YOU'RE SO NICE.
IT'S NOT A MEAN SONG.
NO, BUT THERE'S PLENTY OF RAGE.
AS LONG AS VANESSA DOESN'T TRY TO SING IT ALL PRETTY...
PLINK PLUNK
LISTEN TO THIS.
BOOM...
BOOMBOOM
NOK NO
TINGA TING TING
BOOM
TINGA
NOK NOK
NOK
MBOOM
MAYBE WE CAN WORK THAT IN SOMEWHERE.
!
CAN I COME IN?...

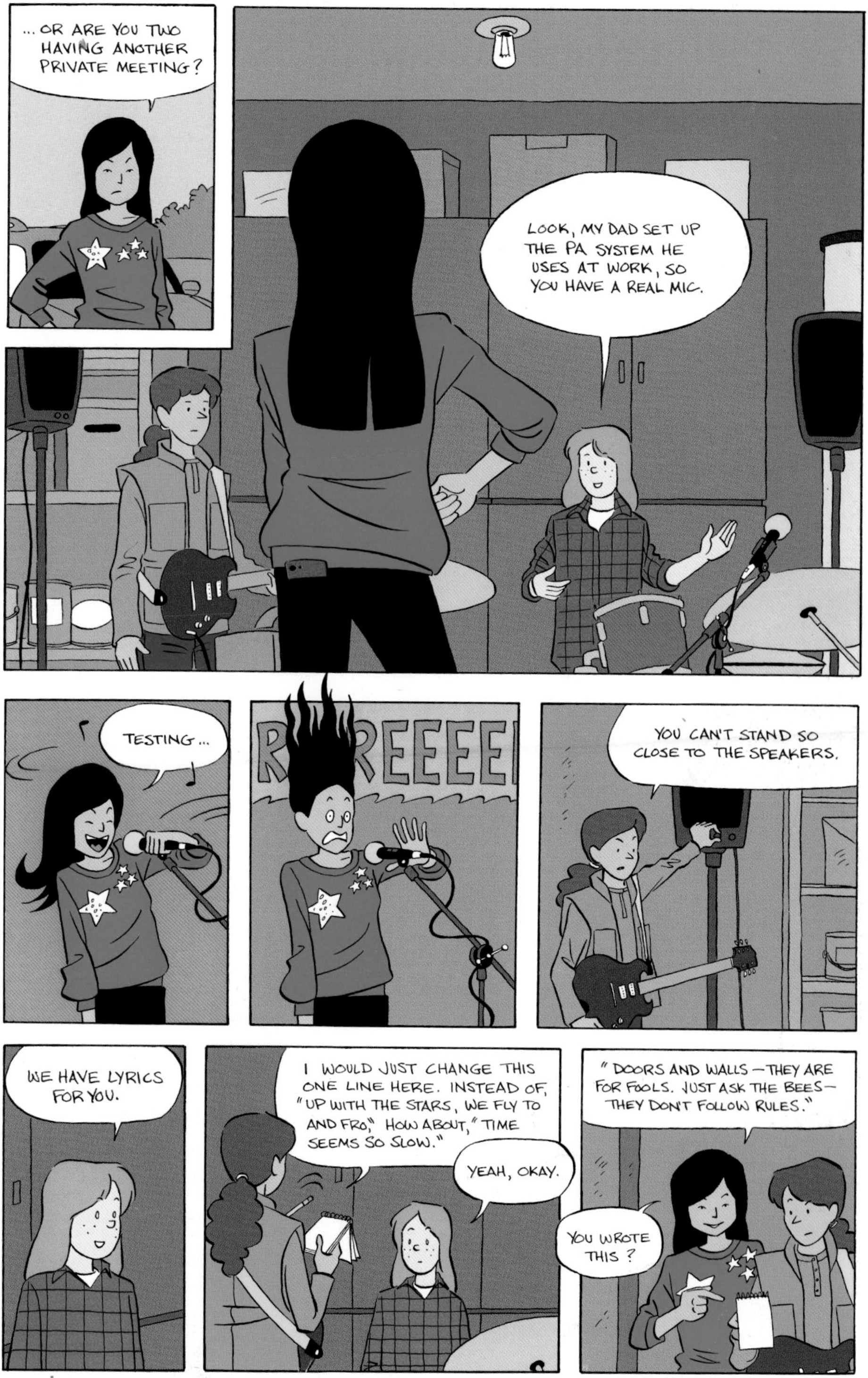
... OR ARE YOU TWO HAVING ANOTHER PRIVATE MEETING?
LOOK, MY DAD SET UP THE PA SYSTEM HE USES AT WORK, SO YOU HAVE A REAL MIC.
TESTING...
REEEEEE
YOU CAN'T STAND SO CLOSE TO THE SPEAKERS.
WE HAVE LYRICS FOR YOU.
I WOULD JUST CHANGE THIS ONE LINE HERE. INSTEAD OF, "UP WITH THE STARS, WE FLY TO AND FRO," HOW ABOUT, "TIME SEEMS SO SLOW."
YEAH, OKAY.
"DOORS AND WALLS—THEY ARE FOR FOOLS. JUST ASK THE BEES—THEY DON'T FOLLOW RULES."
YOU WROTE THIS?

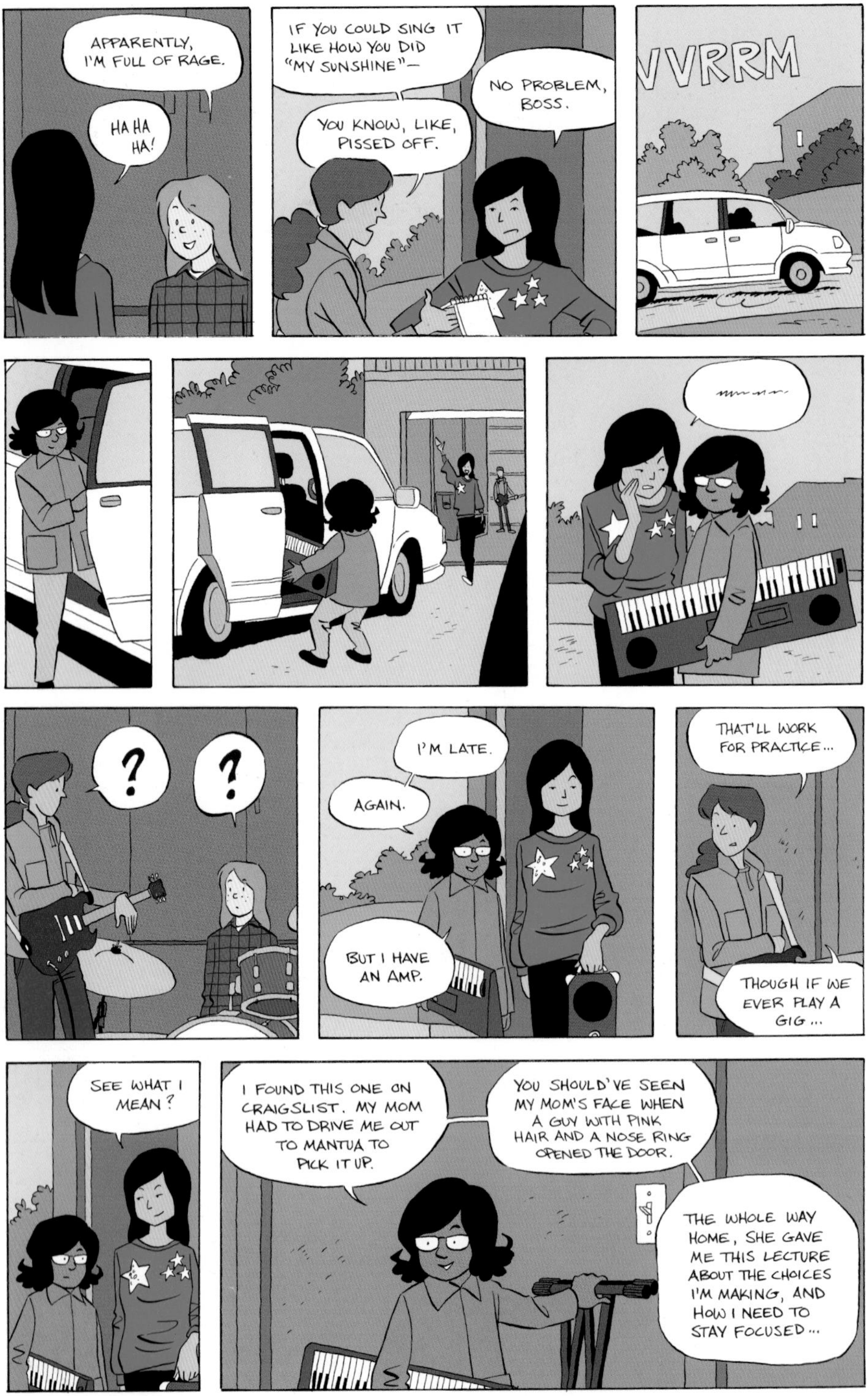
APPARENTLY, I'M FULL OF RAGE.
HA HA HA!
IF YOU COULD SING IT LIKE HOW YOU DID "MY SUNSHINE"—
YOU KNOW, LIKE, PISSED OFF.
NO PROBLEM, BOSS.
VVRRM
?
?
I'M LATE.
AGAIN.
BUT I HAVE AN AMP.
THAT'LL WORK FOR PRACTICE...
THOUGH IF WE EVER PLAY A GIG...
SEE WHAT I MEAN?
I FOUND THIS ONE ON CRAIGSLIST. MY MOM HAD TO DRIVE ME OUT TO MANTUA TO PICK IT UP.
YOU SHOULD'VE SEEN MY MOM'S FACE WHEN A GUY WITH PINK HAIR AND A NOSE RING OPENED THE DOOR.
THE WHOLE WAY HOME, SHE GAVE ME THIS LECTURE ABOUT THE CHOICES I'M MAKING, AND HOW I NEED TO STAY FOCUSED...

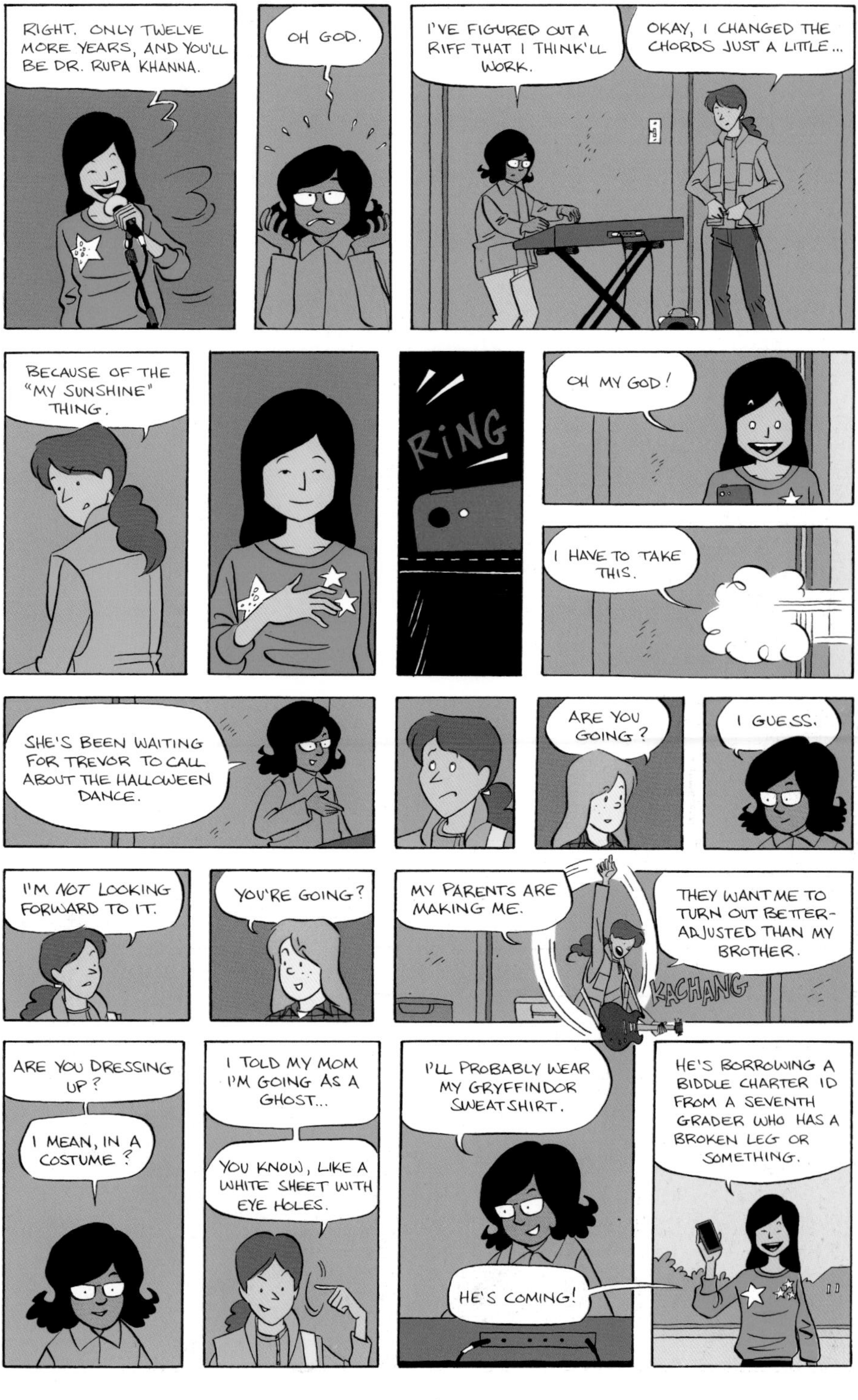
RIGHT. ONLY TWELVE MORE YEARS, AND YOU'LL BE DR. RUPA KHANNA.
OH GOD.
I'VE FIGURED OUT A RIFF THAT I THINK'LL WORK.
OKAY, I CHANGED THE CHORDS JUST A LITTLE...
BECAUSE OF THE "MY SUNSHINE" THING.
RING
OH MY GOD!
I HAVE TO TAKE THIS.
SHE'S BEEN WAITING FOR TREVOR TO CALL ABOUT THE HALLOWEEN DANCE.
ARE YOU GOING?
I GUESS.
I'M NOT LOOKING FORWARD TO IT.
YOU'RE GOING?
MY PARENTS ARE MAKING ME.
THEY WANT ME TO TURN OUT BETTER-ADJUSTED THAN MY BROTHER.
KACHANG
ARE YOU DRESSING UP?
I MEAN, IN A COSTUME?
I TOLD MY MOM I'M GOING AS A GHOST...
YOU KNOW, LIKE A WHITE SHEET WITH EYE HOLES.
I'LL PROBABLY WEAR MY GRYFFINDOR SWEATSHIRT.
HE'S BORROWING A BIDDLE CHARTER ID FROM A SEVENTH GRADER WHO HAS A BROKEN LEG OR SOMETHING.
HE'S COMING!

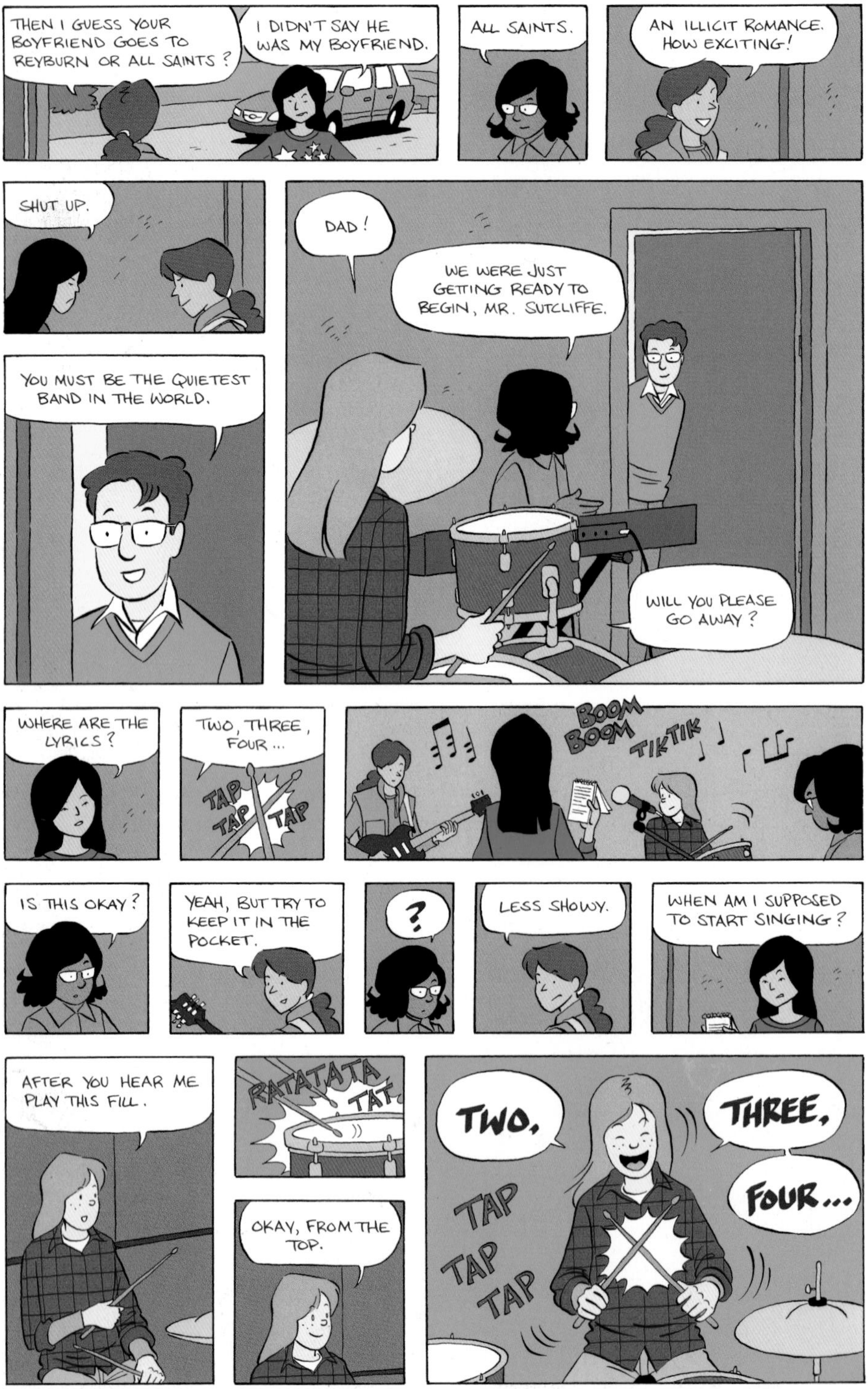
THEN I GUESS YOUR BOYFRIEND GOES TO REYBURN OR ALL SAINTS?
I DIDN'T SAY HE WAS MY BOYFRIEND.
ALL SAINTS.
AN ILLICIT ROMANCE. HOW EXCITING!
SHUT UP.
DAD!
WE WERE JUST GETTING READY TO BEGIN, MR. SUTCLIFFE.
YOU MUST BE THE QUIETEST BAND IN THE WORLD.
WILL YOU PLEASE GO AWAY?
WHERE ARE THE LYRICS?
TWO, THREE, FOUR...
TAP TAP TAP
BOOM BOOM TIKTIK
IS THIS OKAY?
YEAH, BUT TRY TO KEEP IT IN THE POCKET.
?
LESS SHOWY.
WHEN AM I SUPPOSED TO START SINGING?
AFTER YOU HEAR ME PLAY THIS FILL.
RATATATA TAT
OKAY, FROM THE TOP.
TWO,
THREE,
FOUR...
TAP TAP TAP

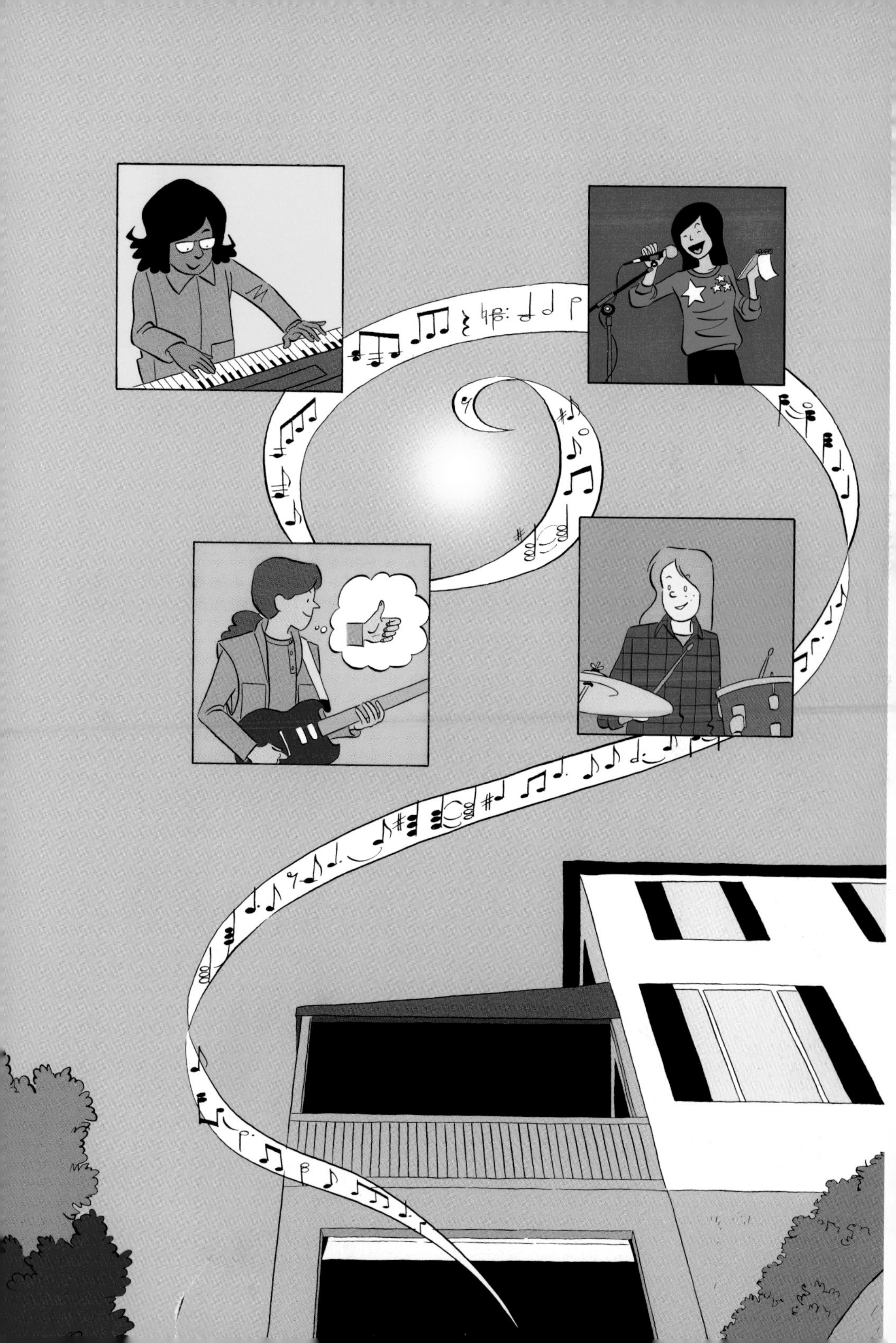

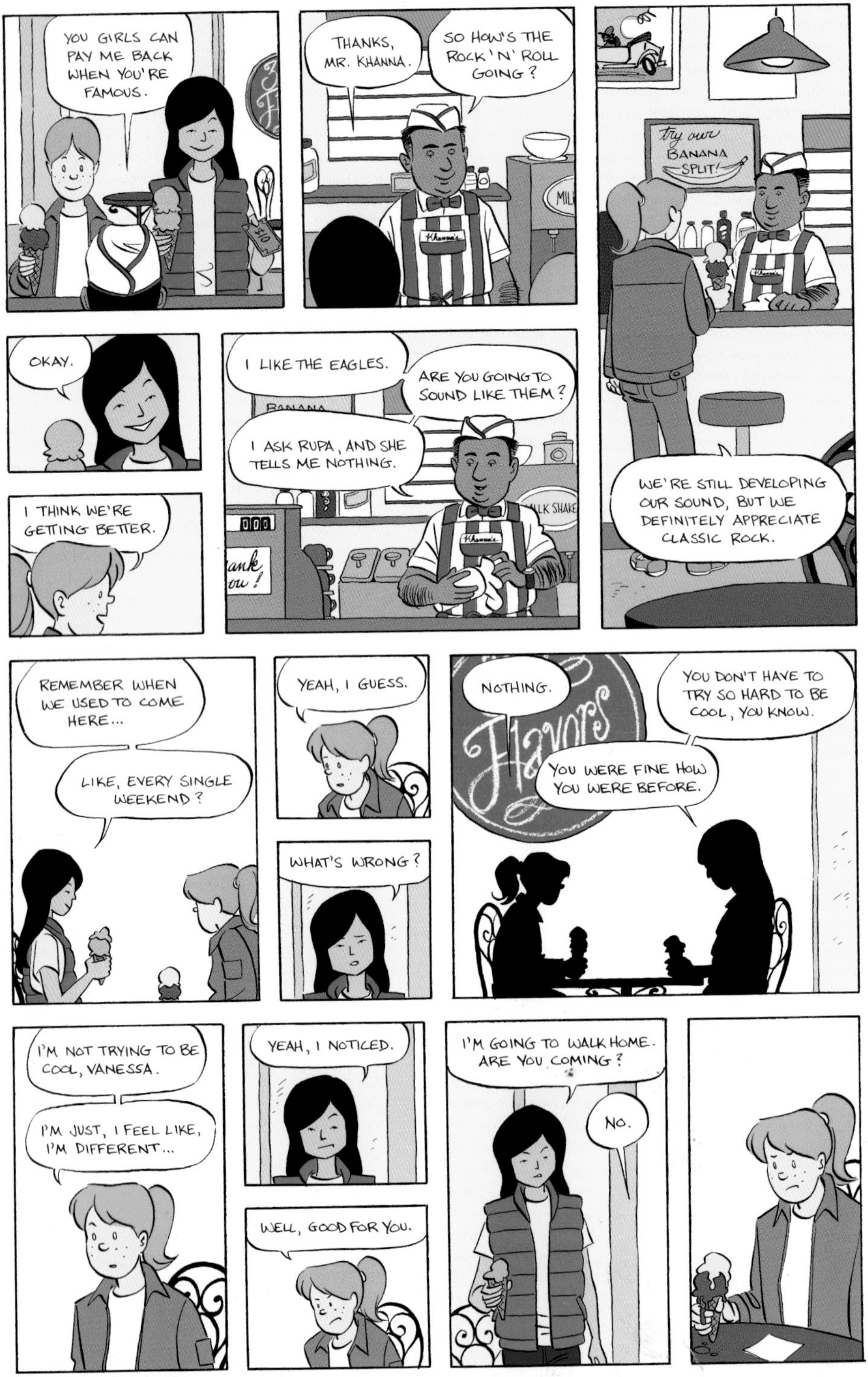

YOU GIRLS CAN PAY ME BACK WHEN YOU'RE FAMOUS.
THANKS, MR. KHANNA.
SO HOW'S THE ROCK 'N' ROLL GOING?
try our BANANA SPLIT!
OKAY.
I LIKE THE EAGLES.
ARE YOU GOING TO SOUND LIKE THEM?
I ASK RUPA, AND SHE TELLS ME NOTHING.
I THINK WE'RE GETTING BETTER.
WE'RE STILL DEVELOPING OUR SOUND, BUT WE DEFINITELY APPRECIATE CLASSIC ROCK.
REMEMBER WHEN WE USED TO COME HERE...
LIKE, EVERY SINGLE WEEKEND?
YEAH, I GUESS.
WHAT'S WRONG?
NOTHING.
YOU DON'T HAVE TO TRY SO HARD TO BE COOL, YOU KNOW.
YOU WERE FINE HOW YOU WERE BEFORE.
Flavors
I'M NOT TRYING TO BE COOL, VANESSA.
I'M JUST, I FEEL LIKE, I'M DIFFERENT...
YEAH, I NOTICED.
WELL, GOOD FOR YOU.
I'M GOING TO WALK HOME. ARE YOU COMING?
NO.

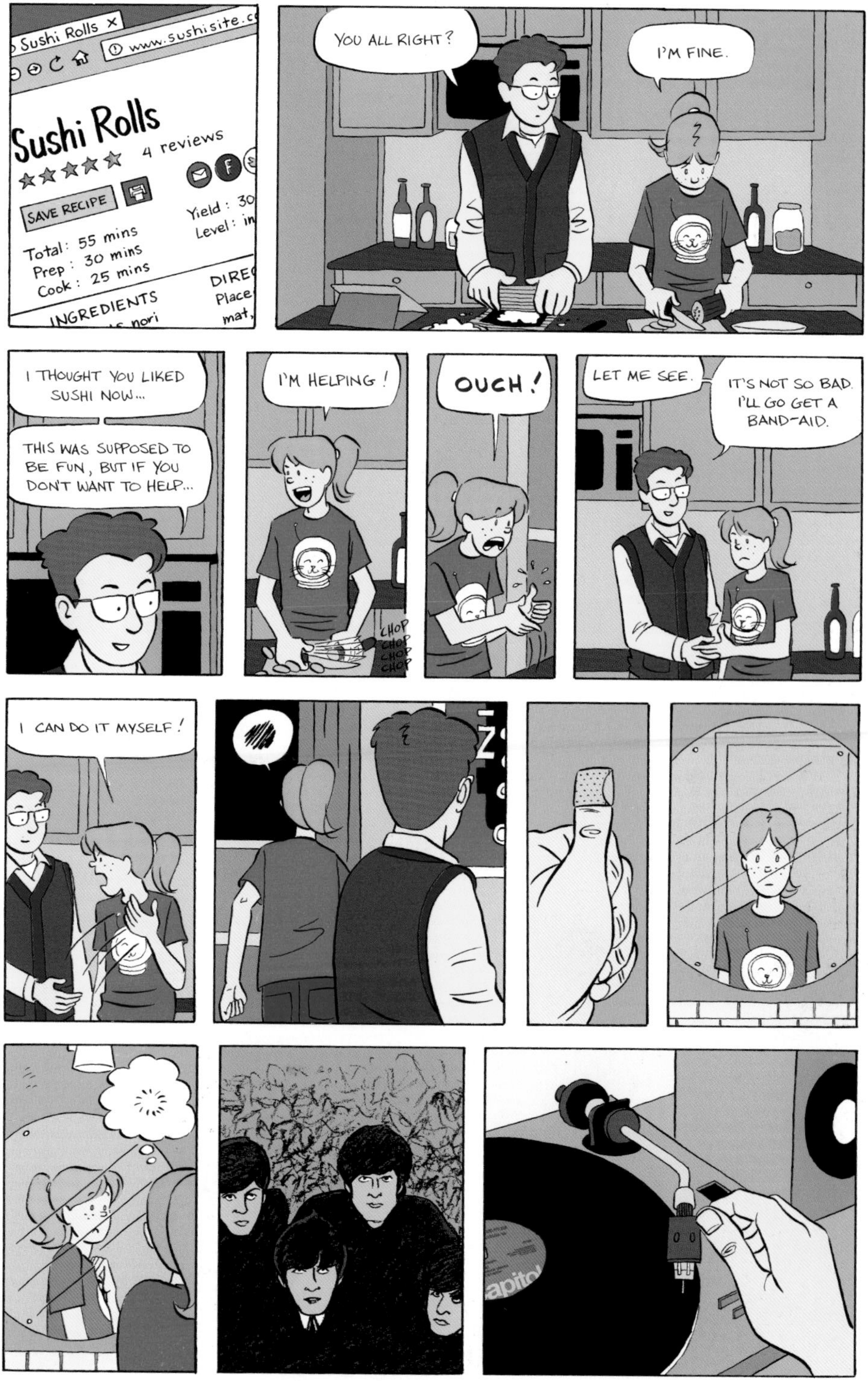

Sushi Rolls ×
www.sushisite.c
Sushi Rolls
4 reviews
SAVE RECIPE
Total : 55 mins
Prep : 30 mins
Cook : 25 mins
Yield : 30
Level : in
INGREDIENTS
DIREC
Place
mat,
YOU ALL RIGHT?
I'M FINE.
I THOUGHT YOU LIKED SUSHI NOW...
THIS WAS SUPPOSED TO BE FUN, BUT IF YOU DON'T WANT TO HELP...
I'M HELPING!
CHOP CHOP CHOP CHOP
OUCH!
LET ME SEE.
IT'S NOT SO BAD. I'LL GO GET A BAND-AID.
I CAN DO IT MYSELF!

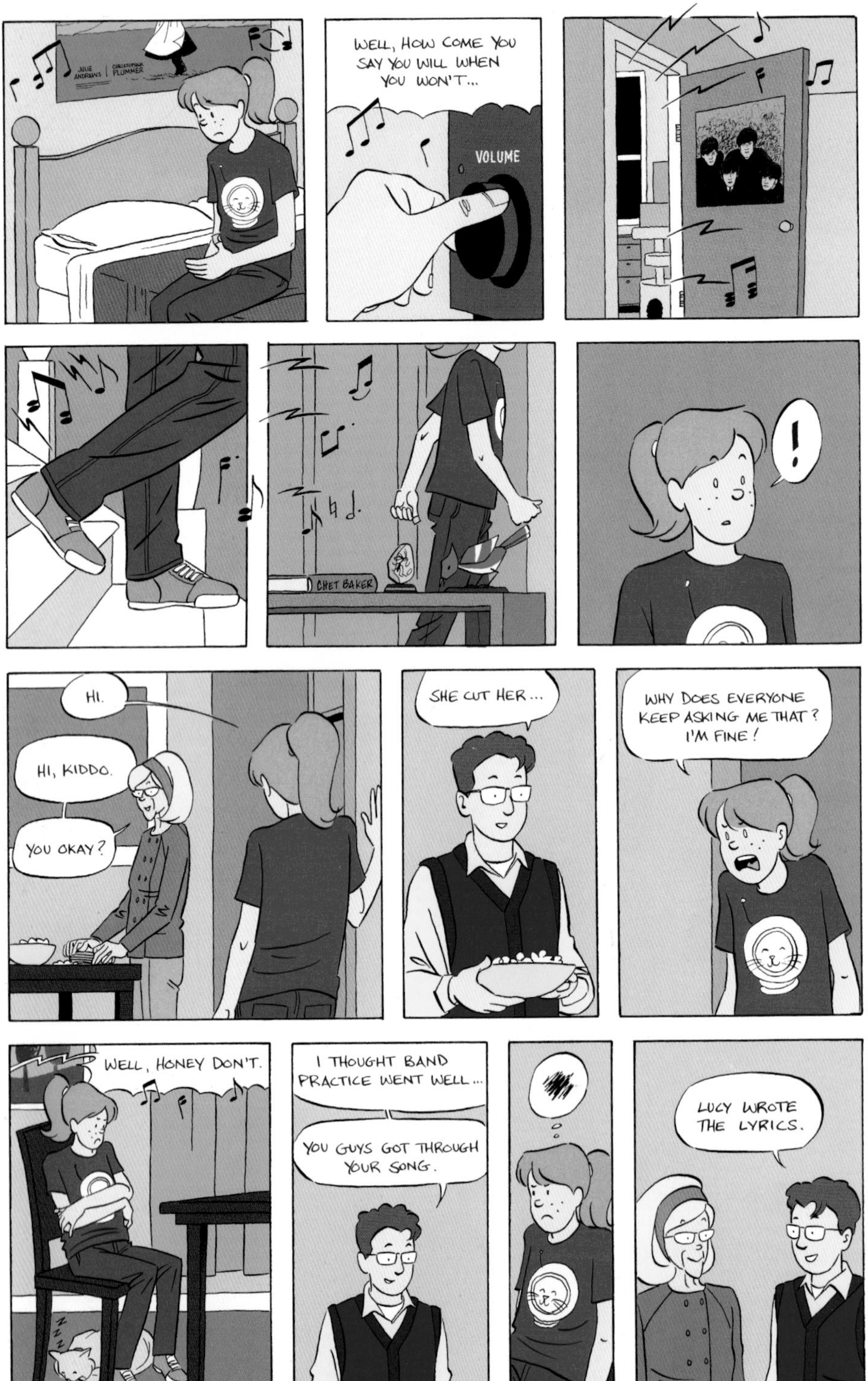
JULIE ANDREWS | CHRISTOPHER PLUMMER
WELL, HOW COME YOU SAY YOU WILL WHEN YOU WON'T...
VOLUME
CHET BAKER
!
HI.
HI, KIDDO.
YOU OKAY?
SHE CUT HER...
WHY DOES EVERYONE KEEP ASKING ME THAT? I'M FINE!
WELL, HONEY DON'T.
I THOUGHT BAND PRACTICE WENT WELL...
YOU GUYS GOT THROUGH YOUR SONG.
LUCY WROTE THE LYRICS.

DID YOU TELL MOM I WOULD GO TO AUSTRALIA?!

WHAP

NO, I HAVEN'T EVEN...

I TALKED TO HER, BUNNY. I WANT YOU TO GO. THERE'S NO REASON FOR YOU TO STAY HERE.

WHAT ABOUT WHAT *I* WANT?!

LET'S JUST CALM DOWN FOR A SECOND.

NO!

AND I'M NOT HUNGRY!

SLAM

SHE'S A WOMAN. SHE'S A WOMAN.

Capitol

BABY'S GOOD TO ME...

WHOMMP

I'M IN LOVE WITH HER AND I FEEL FINE...

FLUMP

...I FEEL FINE

SCRRKHHHKH...

Capitol

KNOCK KNOCK

HI.

HI.

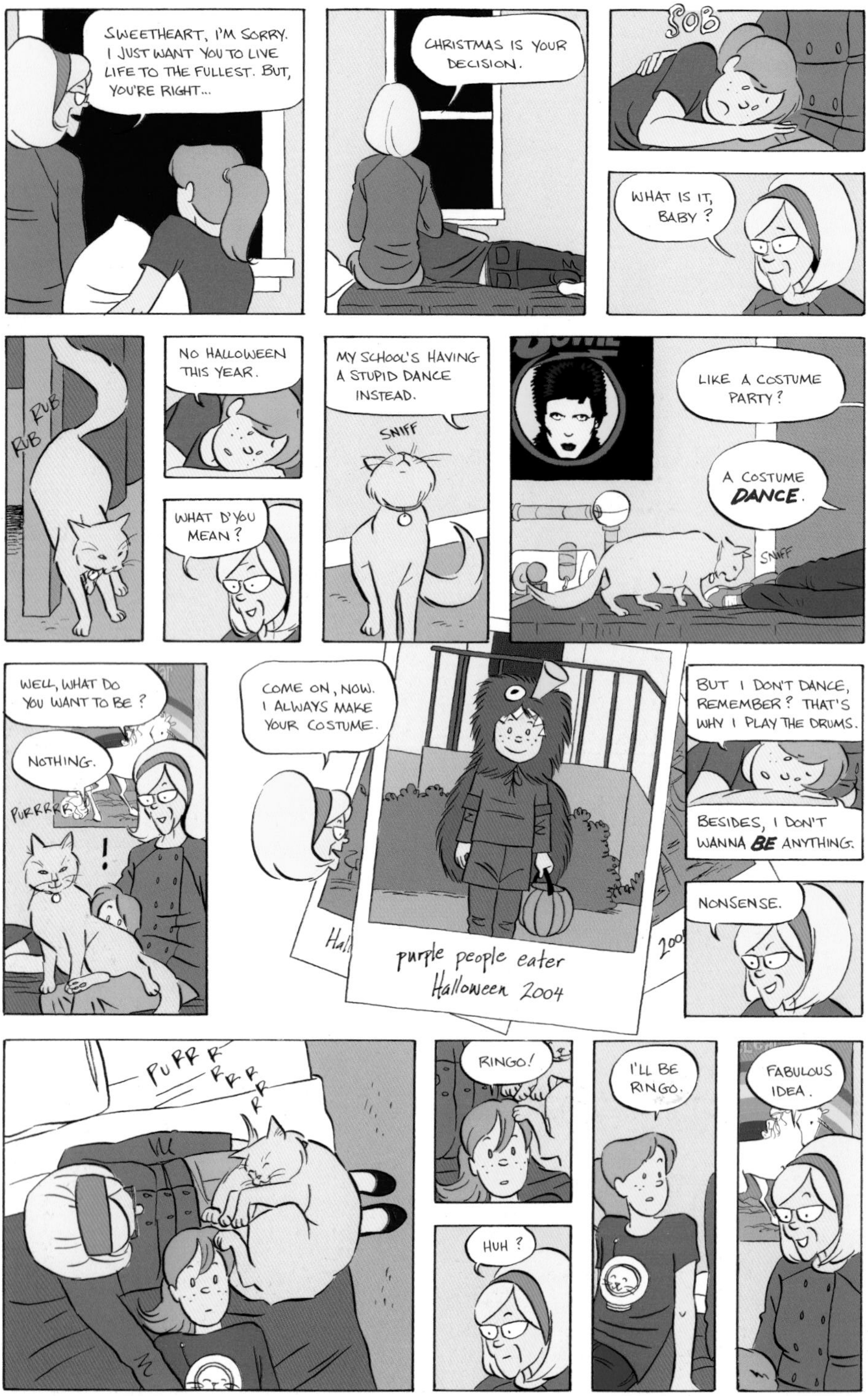
SWEETHEART, I'M SORRY. I JUST WANT YOU TO LIVE LIFE TO THE FULLEST. BUT, YOU'RE RIGHT...
CHRISTMAS IS YOUR DECISION.
SOB
WHAT IS IT, BABY ?
RUB RUB
NO HALLOWEEN THIS YEAR.
WHAT D'YOU MEAN ?
MY SCHOOL'S HAVING A STUPID DANCE INSTEAD.
SNIFF
LIKE A COSTUME PARTY ?
A COSTUME DANCE.
SNIFF
WELL, WHAT DO YOU WANT TO BE ?
NOTHING.
PURRRRR
!
COME ON, NOW. I ALWAYS MAKE YOUR COSTUME.
purple people eater
Halloween 2004
BUT I DON'T DANCE, REMEMBER? THAT'S WHY I PLAY THE DRUMS.
BESIDES, I DON'T WANNA BE ANYTHING.
NONSENSE.
PURRRRRR
RINGO!
HUH ?
I'LL BE RINGO.
FABULOUS IDEA.

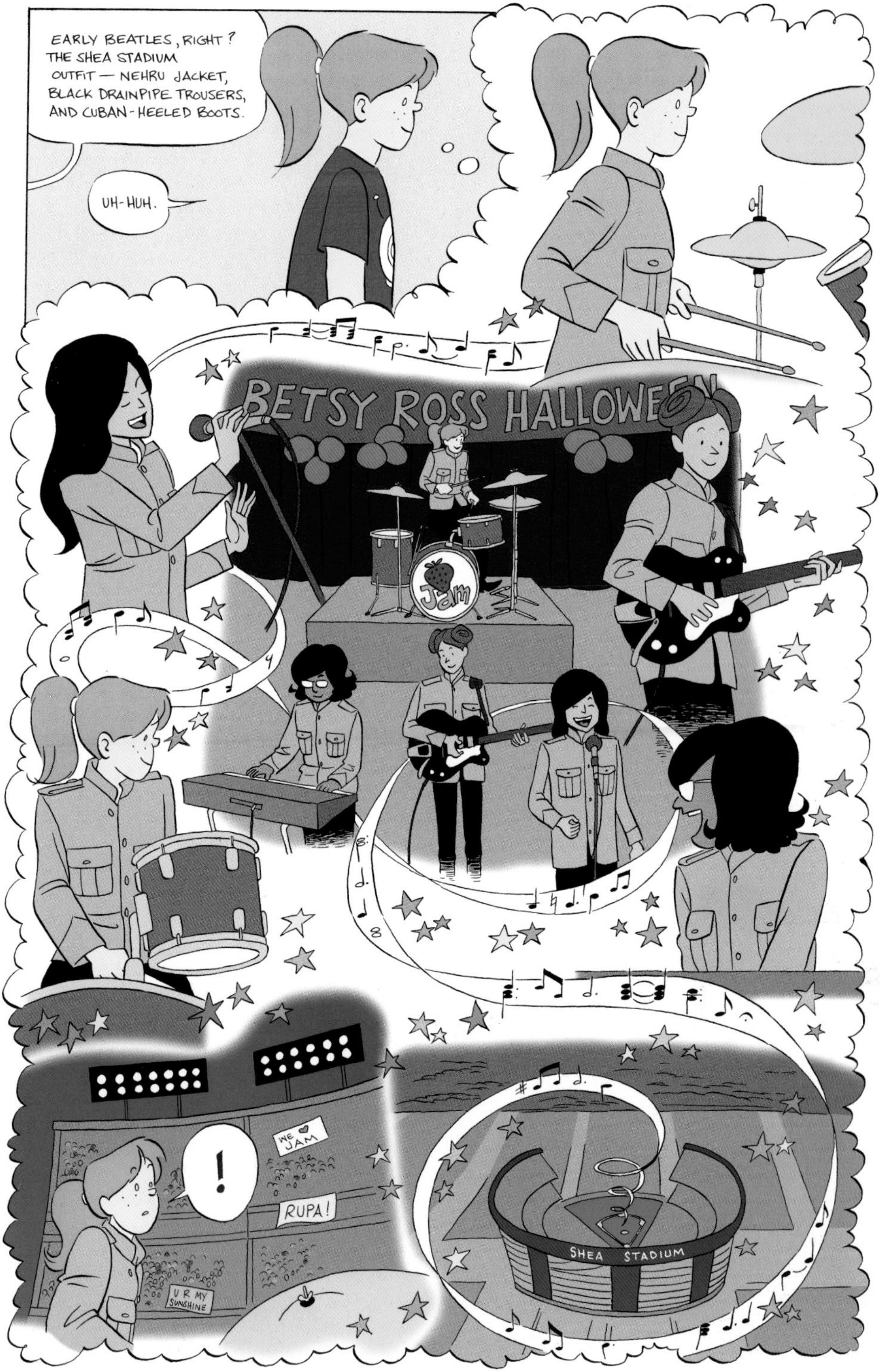
EARLY BEATLES, RIGHT? THE SHEA STADIUM OUTFIT — NEHRU JACKET, BLACK DRAINPIPE TROUSERS, AND CUBAN-HEELED BOOTS.
UH-HUH.
BETSY ROSS HALLOWEEN
Jam
WE ♥ JAM
!
RUPA!
U R MY SUNSHINE
SHEA STADIUM

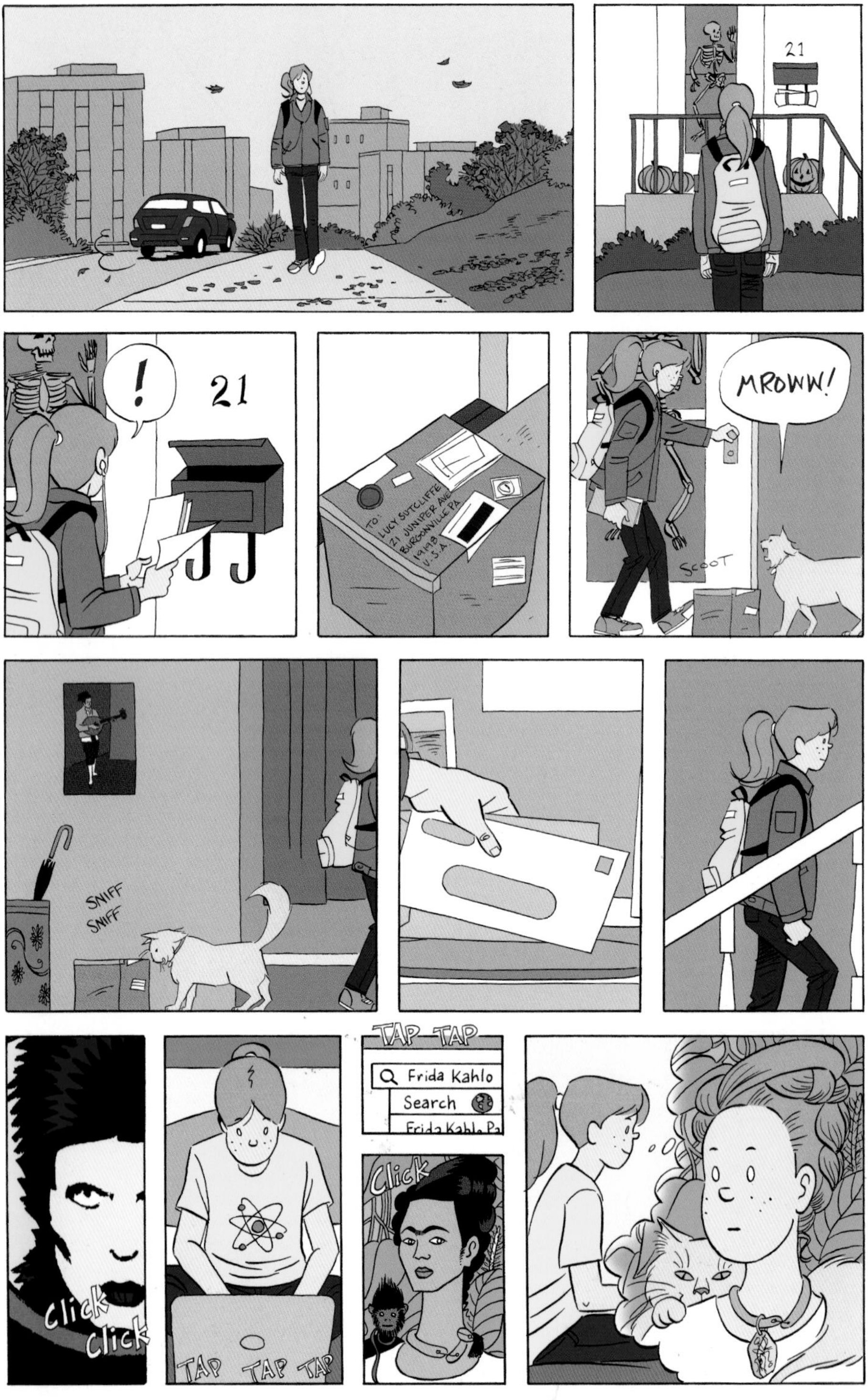

21
!
21
TO:
LUCY SUTCLIFFE
21 JUNIPER AVE
BURGONVILLE PA
19148
U.S.A.
MROWW!
SCOOT
SNIFF
SNIFF
CLICK
CLICK
TAP
TAP
TAP
TAP TAP
Frida Kahlo
Search
CLICK

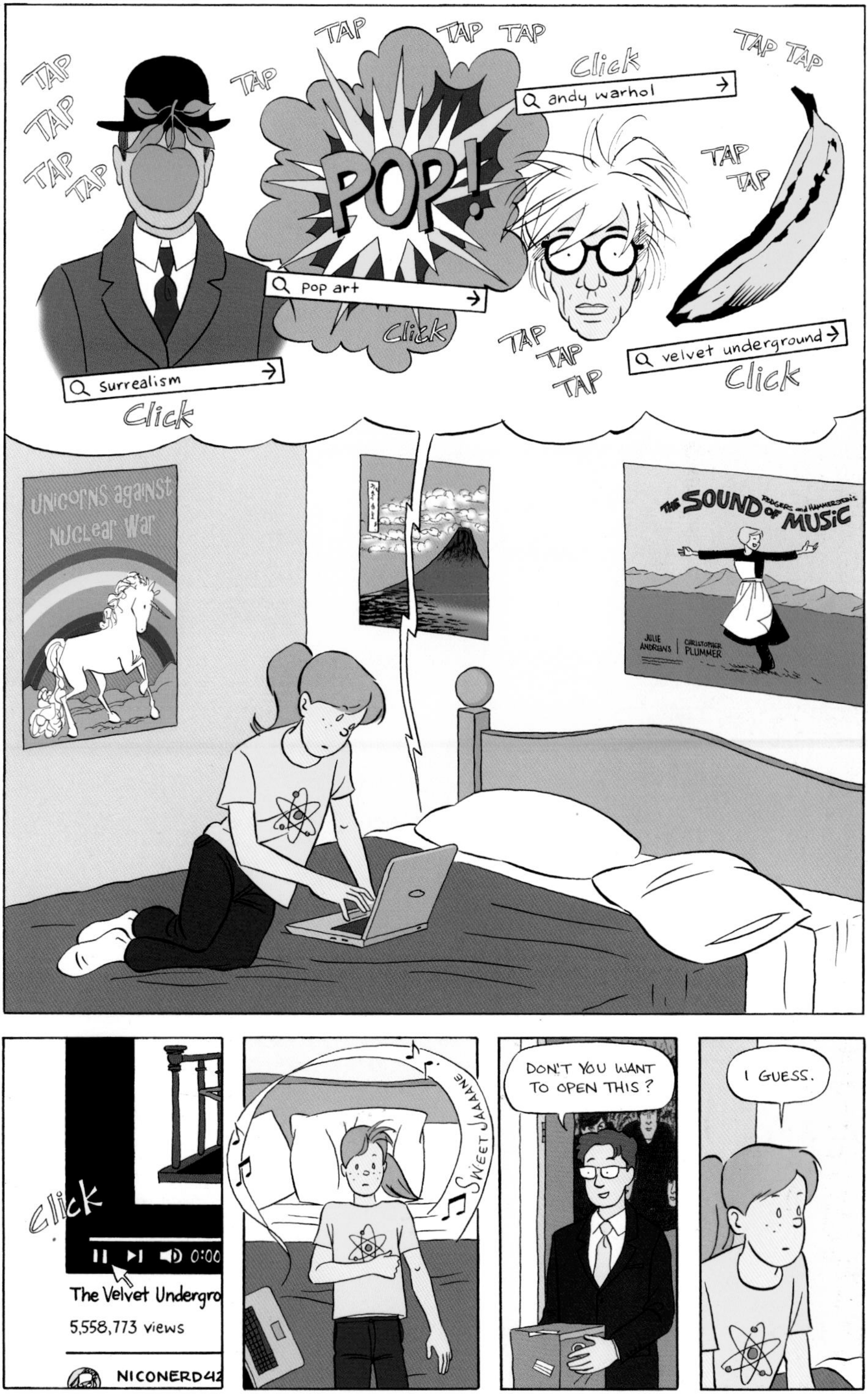

TAP
TAP
TAP
TAP
TAP
TAP
TAP TAP
POP!
Click
andy warhol
TAP TAP
TAP
TAP
pop art
Click
surrealism
Click
TAP
TAP
TAP
velvet underground
Click
UNICORNS against NUCLEAR WAR
RODGERS and HAMMERSTEIN'S
THE SOUND OF MUSIC
JULIE ANDREWS
CHRISTOPHER PLUMMER
Click
0:00
The Velvet Undergro
5,558,773 views
NICONERD42
SWEET JAAAANE
DON'T YOU WANT TO OPEN THIS?
I GUESS.

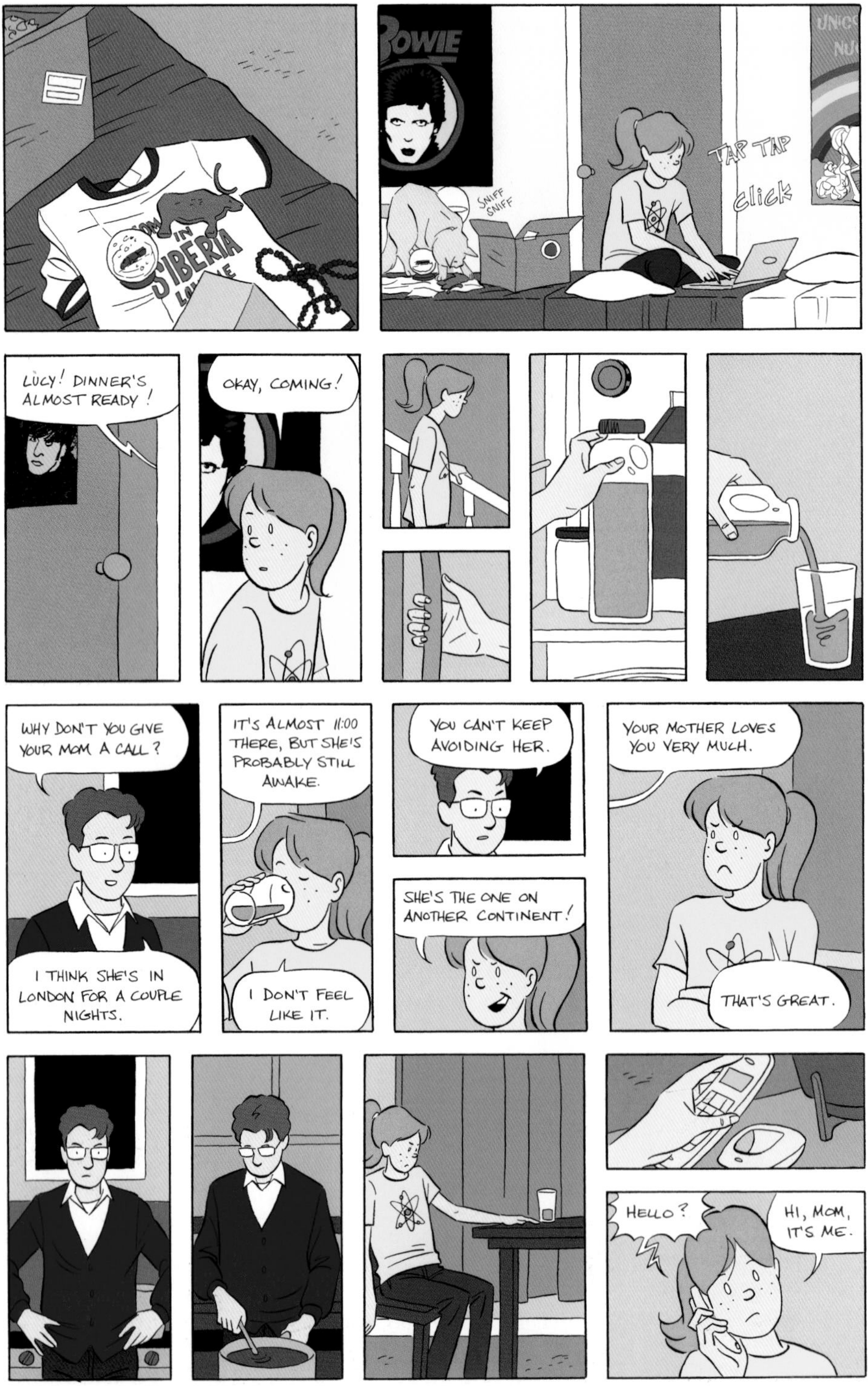

FROM IN SIBERIA
BOWIE
SNIFF SNIFF
TAP TAP
click
LUCY! DINNER'S ALMOST READY!
OKAY, COMING!
WHY DON'T YOU GIVE YOUR MOM A CALL?
I THINK SHE'S IN LONDON FOR A COUPLE NIGHTS.
IT'S ALMOST 11:00 THERE, BUT SHE'S PROBABLY STILL AWAKE.
I DON'T FEEL LIKE IT.
YOU CAN'T KEEP AVOIDING HER.
SHE'S THE ONE ON ANOTHER CONTINENT!
YOUR MOTHER LOVES YOU VERY MUCH.
THAT'S GREAT.
HELLO?
HI, MOM, IT'S ME.

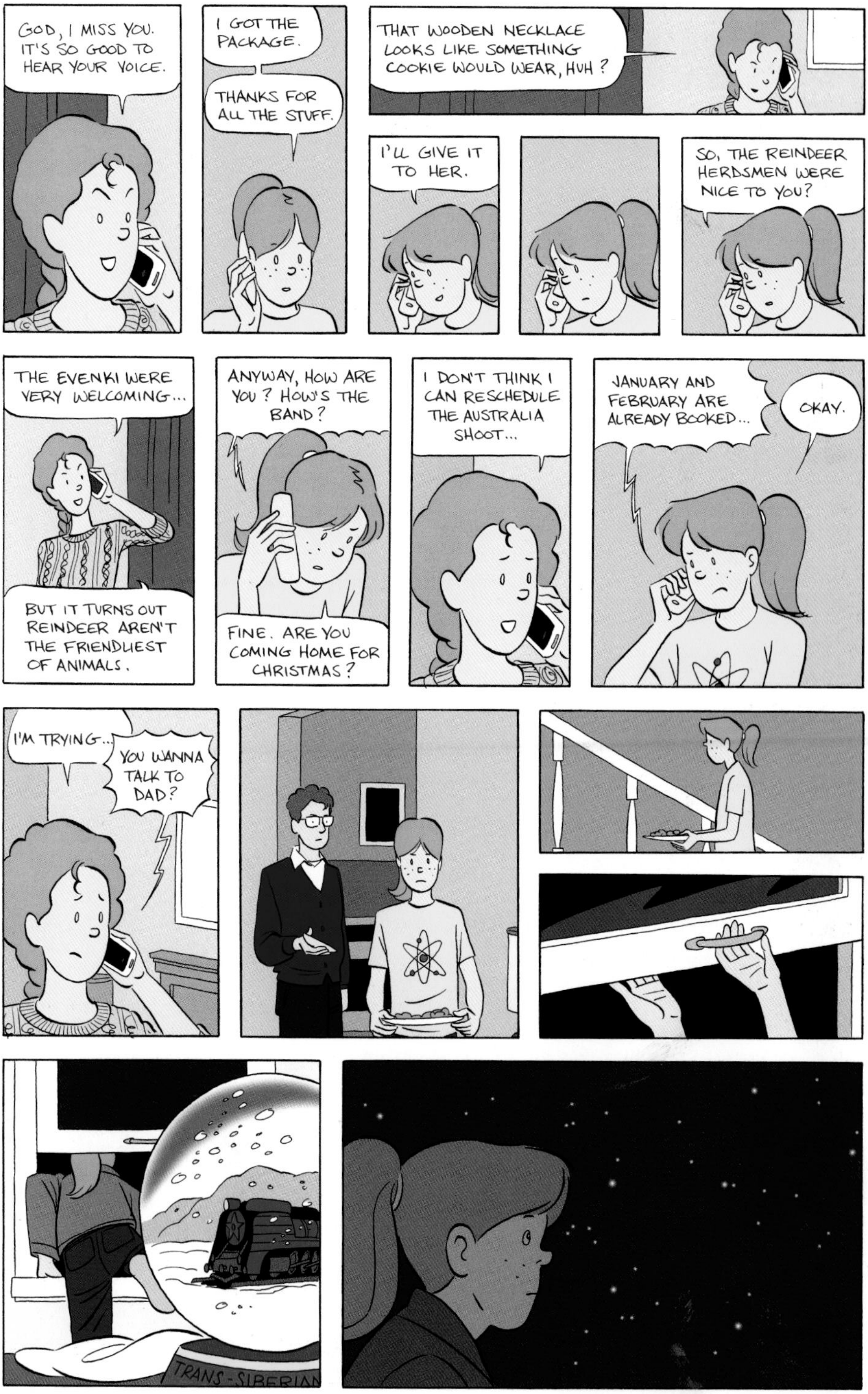
GOD, I MISS YOU. IT'S SO GOOD TO HEAR YOUR VOICE.
I GOT THE PACKAGE.
THANKS FOR ALL THE STUFF.
THAT WOODEN NECKLACE LOOKS LIKE SOMETHING COOKIE WOULD WEAR, HUH ?
I'LL GIVE IT TO HER.
SO, THE REINDEER HERDSMEN WERE NICE TO YOU?
THE EVENKI WERE VERY WELCOMING...
BUT IT TURNS OUT REINDEER AREN'T THE FRIENDLIEST OF ANIMALS.
ANYWAY, HOW ARE YOU ? HOW'S THE BAND ?
FINE. ARE YOU COMING HOME FOR CHRISTMAS ?
I DON'T THINK I CAN RESCHEDULE THE AUSTRALIA SHOOT...
JANUARY AND FEBRUARY ARE ALREADY BOOKED...
OKAY.
I'M TRYING...
YOU WANNA TALK TO DAD?
TRANS-SIBERIAN

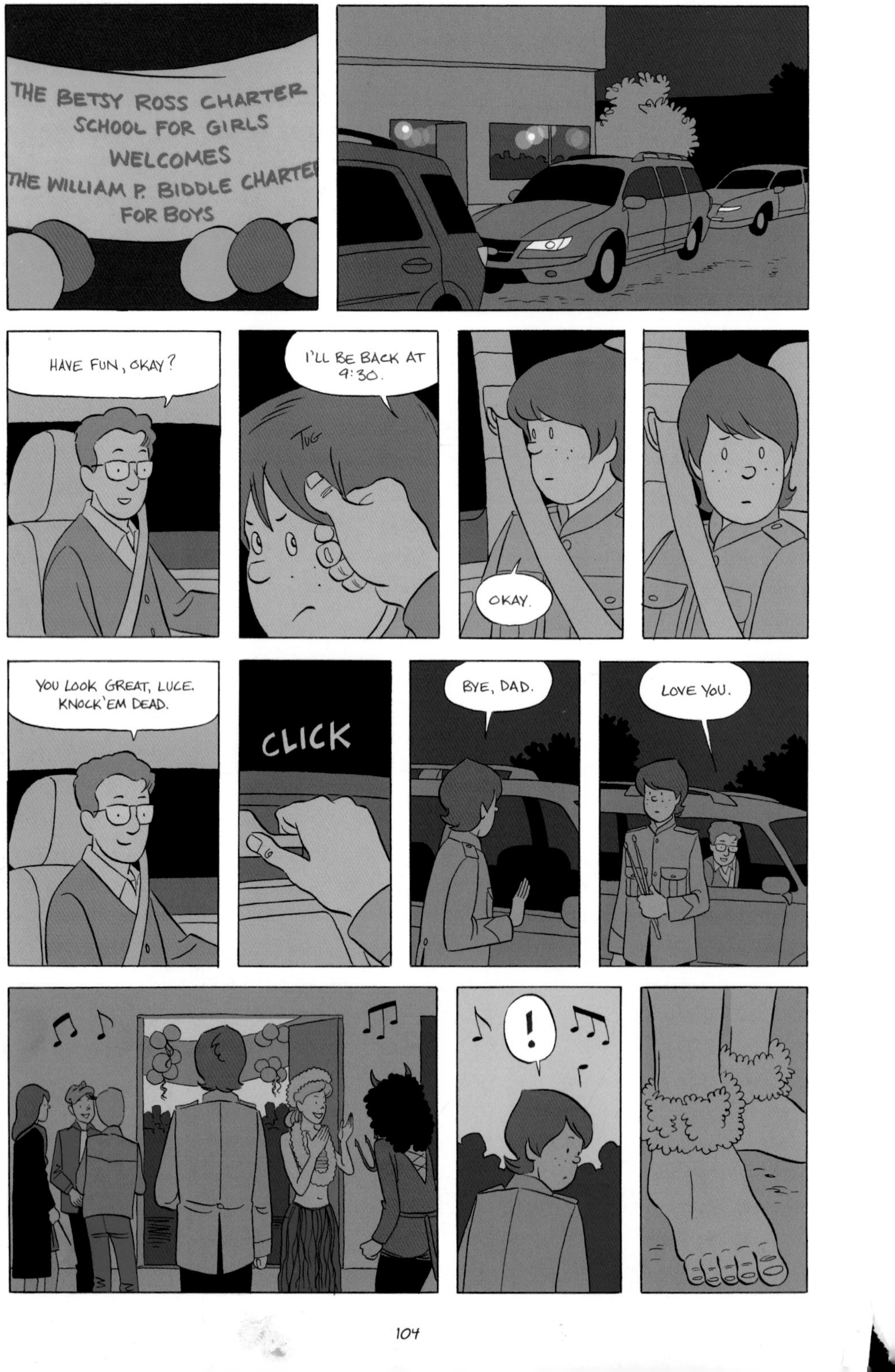
THE BETSY ROSS CHARTER SCHOOL FOR GIRLS WELCOMES THE WILLIAM P. BIDDLE CHARTE FOR BOYS
HAVE FUN, OKAY?
I'LL BE BACK AT 9:30.
TUG
OKAY.
YOU LOOK GREAT, LUCE. KNOCK'EM DEAD.
CLICK
BYE, DAD.
LOVE YOU.
!

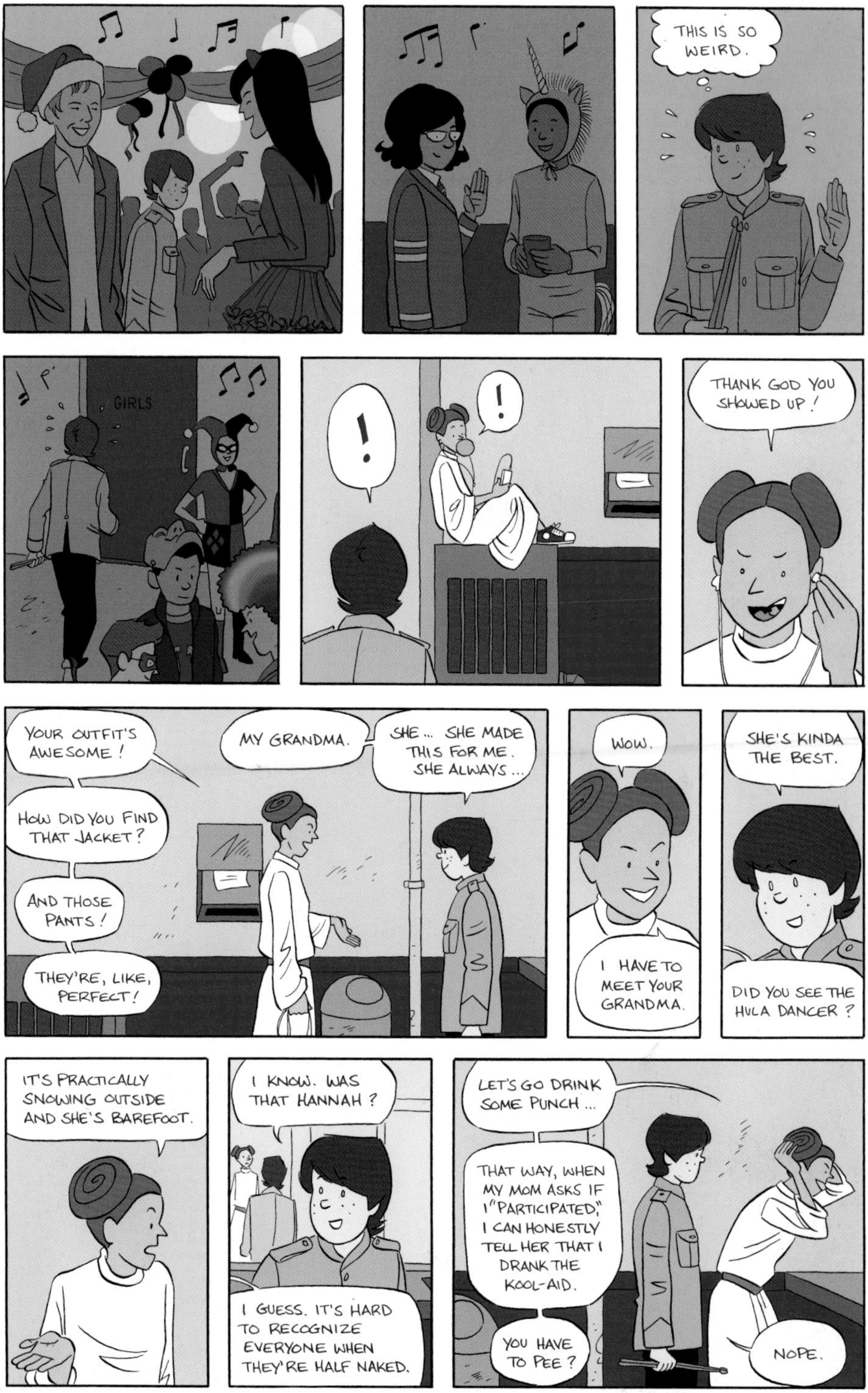
THIS IS SO WEIRD.
!
!
THANK GOD YOU SHOWED UP!
YOUR OUTFIT'S AWESOME!
HOW DID YOU FIND THAT JACKET?
AND THOSE PANTS!
THEY'RE, LIKE, PERFECT!
MY GRANDMA.
SHE... SHE MADE THIS FOR ME. SHE ALWAYS...
WOW.
I HAVE TO MEET YOUR GRANDMA.
SHE'S KINDA THE BEST.
DID YOU SEE THE HULA DANCER?
IT'S PRACTICALLY SNOWING OUTSIDE AND SHE'S BAREFOOT.
I KNOW. WAS THAT HANNAH?
I GUESS. IT'S HARD TO RECOGNIZE EVERYONE WHEN THEY'RE HALF NAKED.
LET'S GO DRINK SOME PUNCH...
THAT WAY, WHEN MY MOM ASKS IF I "PARTICIPATED," I CAN HONESTLY TELL HER THAT I DRANK THE KOOL-AID.
YOU HAVE TO PEE?
NOPE.

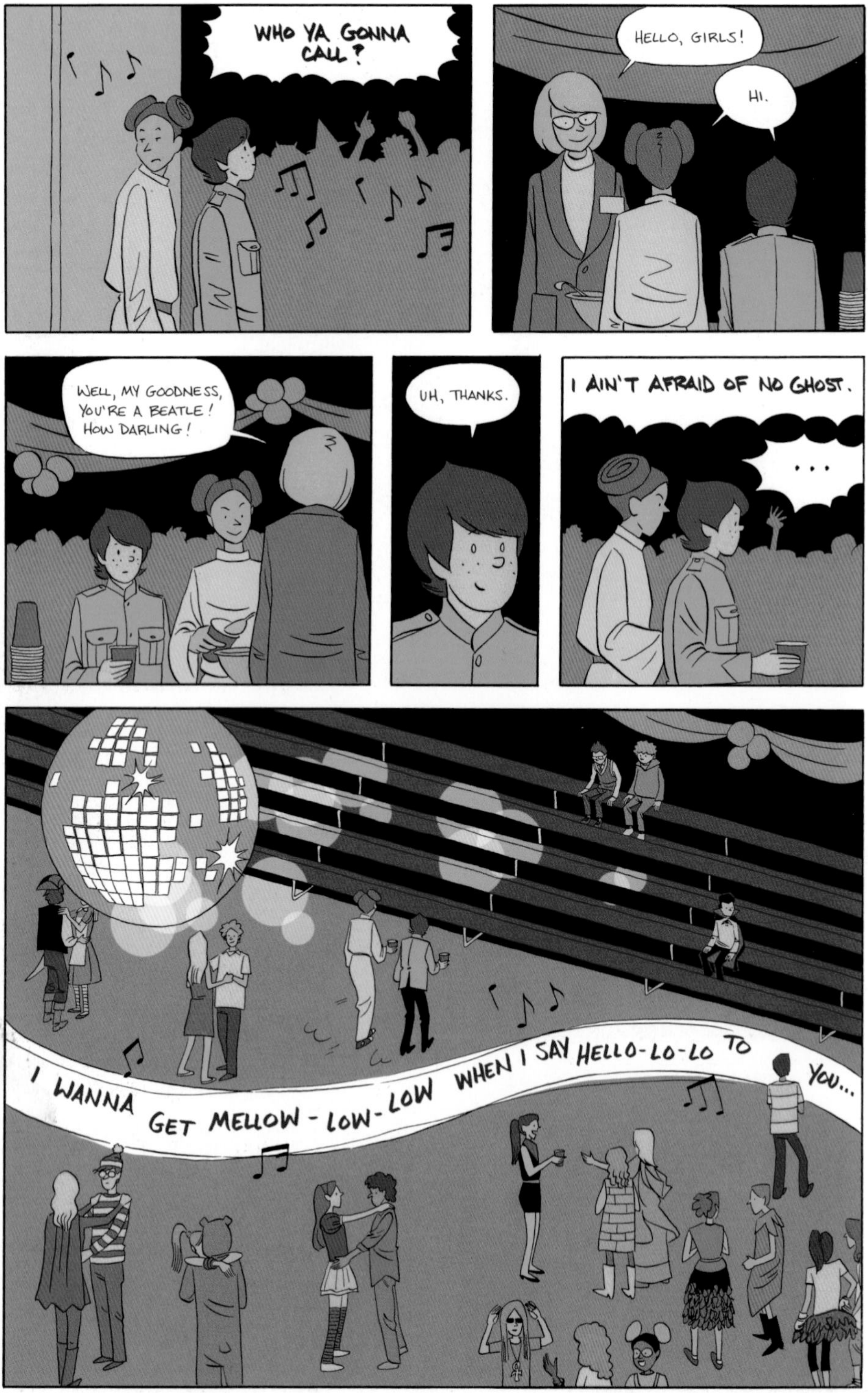
WHO YA GONNA CALL?
HELLO, GIRLS!
HI.
WELL, MY GOODNESS, YOU'RE A BEATLE! HOW DARLING!
UH, THANKS.
I AIN'T AFRAID OF NO GHOST.
. . .
I WANNA GET MELLOW-LOW-LOW WHEN I SAY HELLO-LO-LO TO YOU...

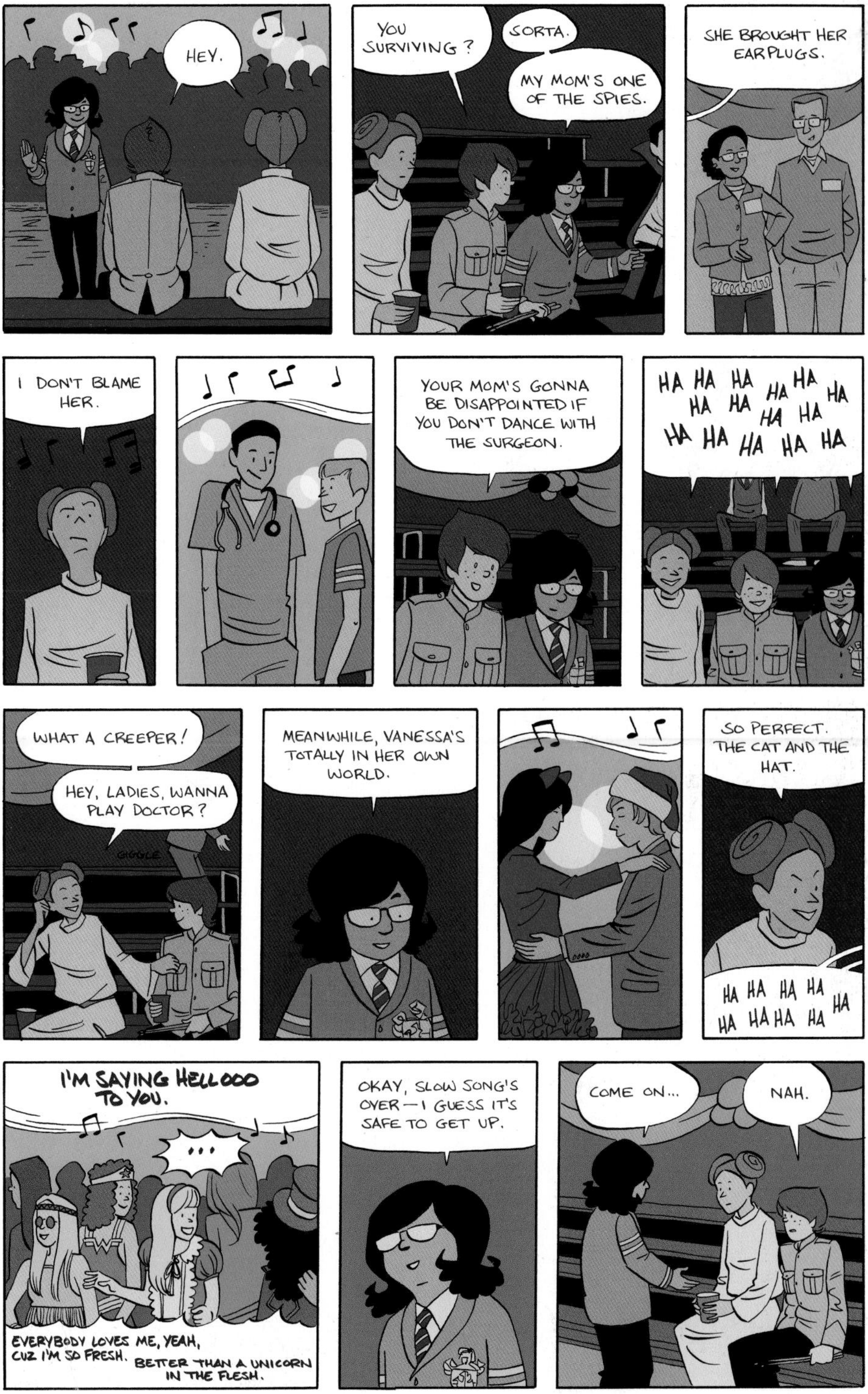

HEY.
YOU SURVIVING?
SORTA.
MY MOM'S ONE OF THE SPIES.
SHE BROUGHT HER EARPLUGS.
I DON'T BLAME HER.
YOUR MOM'S GONNA BE DISAPPOINTED IF YOU DON'T DANCE WITH THE SURGEON.
HA HA HA HA HA HA HA HA HA HA HA HA HA HA HA
WHAT A CREEPER!
HEY, LADIES, WANNA PLAY DOCTOR?
GIGGLE
MEANWHILE, VANESSA'S TOTALLY IN HER OWN WORLD.
SO PERFECT. THE CAT AND THE HAT.
HA HA HA HA HA HAHA HA HA
I'M SAYING HELLOOO TO YOU.
...
EVERYBODY LOVES ME, YEAH, CUZ I'M SO FRESH.
BETTER THAN A UNICORN IN THE FLESH.
OKAY, SLOW SONG'S OVER—I GUESS IT'S SAFE TO GET UP.
COME ON...
NAH.

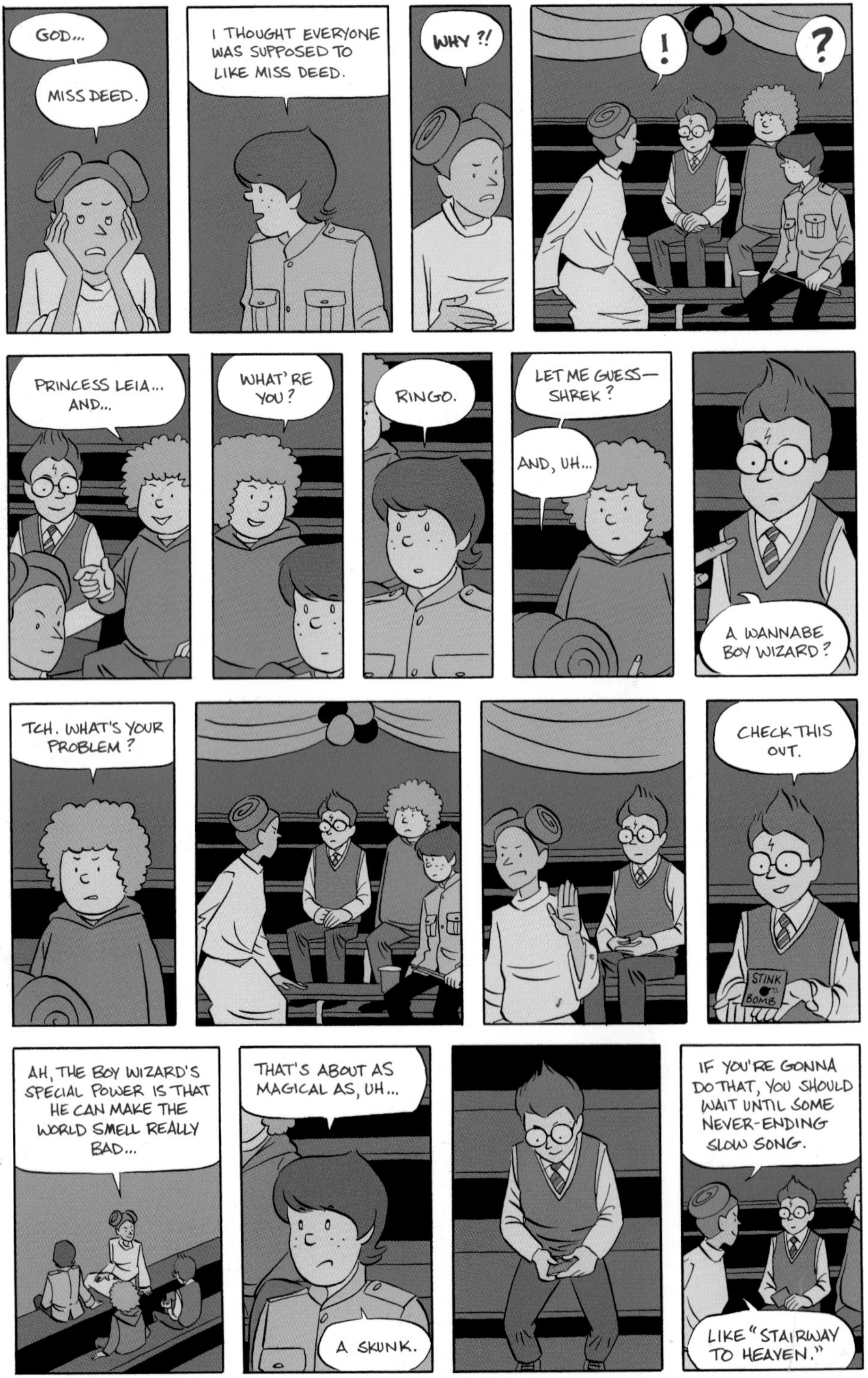
GOD...
MISS DEED.
I THOUGHT EVERYONE WAS SUPPOSED TO LIKE MISS DEED.
WHY ?!
!
?
PRINCESS LEIA... AND...
WHAT'RE YOU?
RINGO.
LET ME GUESS— SHREK?
AND, UH...
A WANNABE BOY WIZARD?
TCH. WHAT'S YOUR PROBLEM?
CHECK THIS OUT.
STINK BOMB
AH, THE BOY WIZARD'S SPECIAL POWER IS THAT HE CAN MAKE THE WORLD SMELL REALLY BAD...
THAT'S ABOUT AS MAGICAL AS, UH...
A SKUNK.
IF YOU'RE GONNA DO THAT, YOU SHOULD WAIT UNTIL SOME NEVER-ENDING SLOW SONG.
LIKE "STAIRWAY TO HEAVEN."

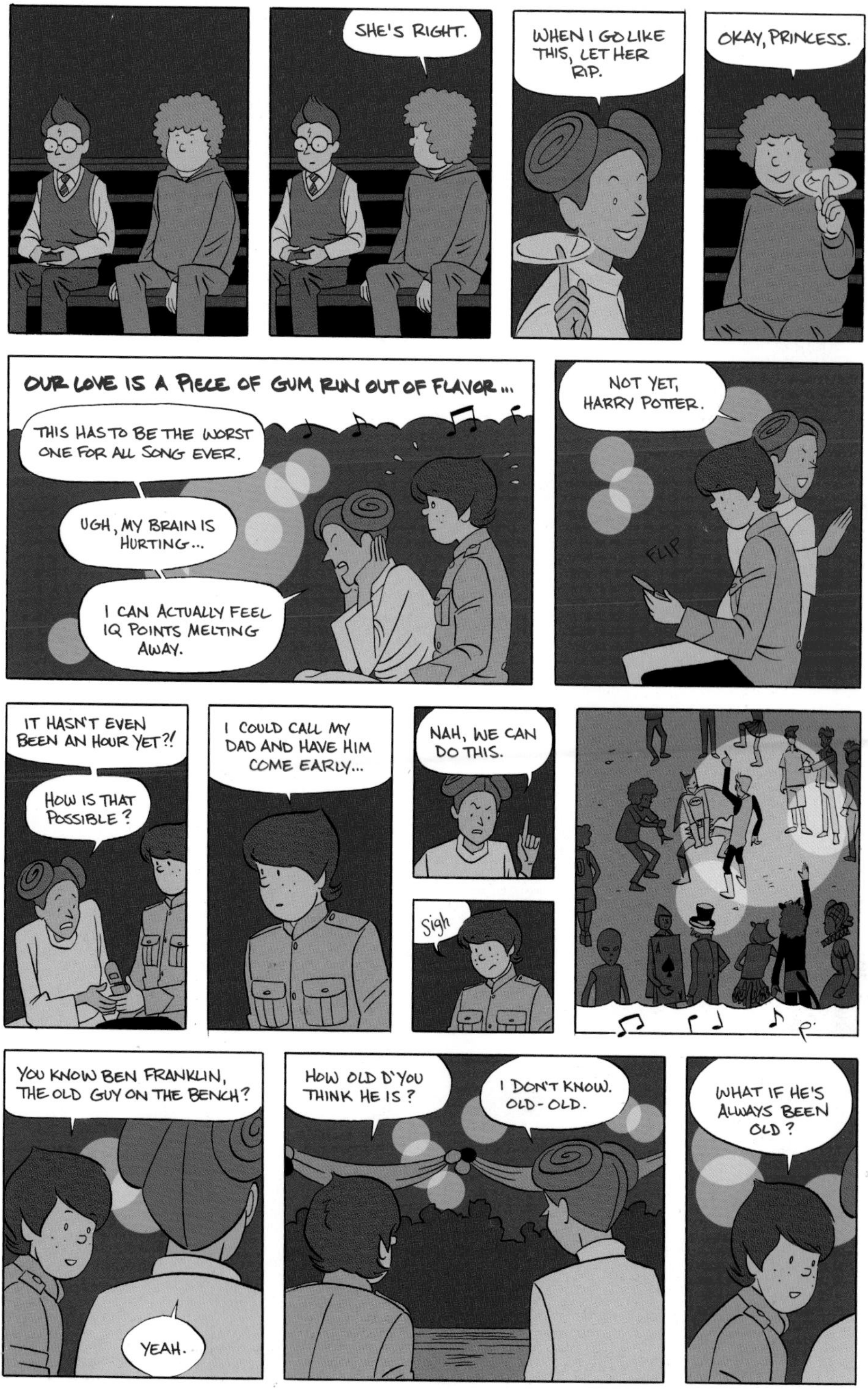

SHE'S RIGHT.
WHEN I GO LIKE THIS, LET HER RIP.
OKAY, PRINCESS.
OUR LOVE IS A PIECE OF GUM RUN OUT OF FLAVOR...
THIS HAS TO BE THE WORST ONE FOR ALL SONG EVER.
UGH, MY BRAIN IS HURTING...
I CAN ACTUALLY FEEL IQ POINTS MELTING AWAY.
NOT YET, HARRY POTTER.
FLIP
IT HASN'T EVEN BEEN AN HOUR YET?!
HOW IS THAT POSSIBLE?
I COULD CALL MY DAD AND HAVE HIM COME EARLY...
NAH, WE CAN DO THIS.
Sigh
YOU KNOW BEN FRANKLIN, THE OLD GUY ON THE BENCH?
YEAH.
HOW OLD D'YOU THINK HE IS?
I DON'T KNOW. OLD-OLD.
WHAT IF HE'S ALWAYS BEEN OLD?

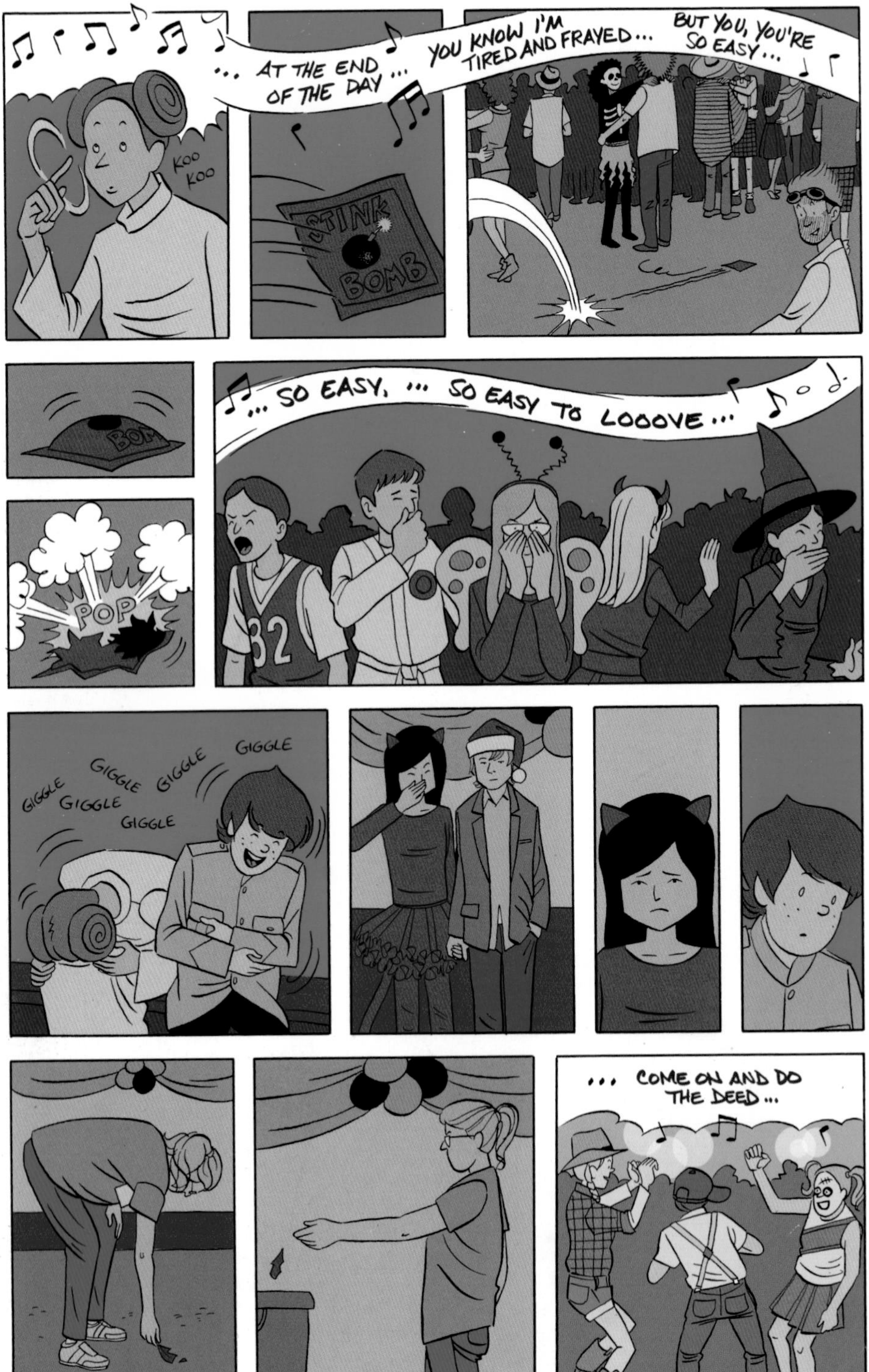
KOO KOO
... AT THE END OF THE DAY ... YOU KNOW I'M TIRED AND FRAYED ... BUT YOU, YOU'RE SO EASY ...
STINK BOMB
BOM
POP
... SO EASY, ... SO EASY TO LOOOVE ...
32
GIGGLE GIGGLE GIGGLE GIGGLE GIGGLE GIGGLE
... COME ON AND DO THE DEED ...

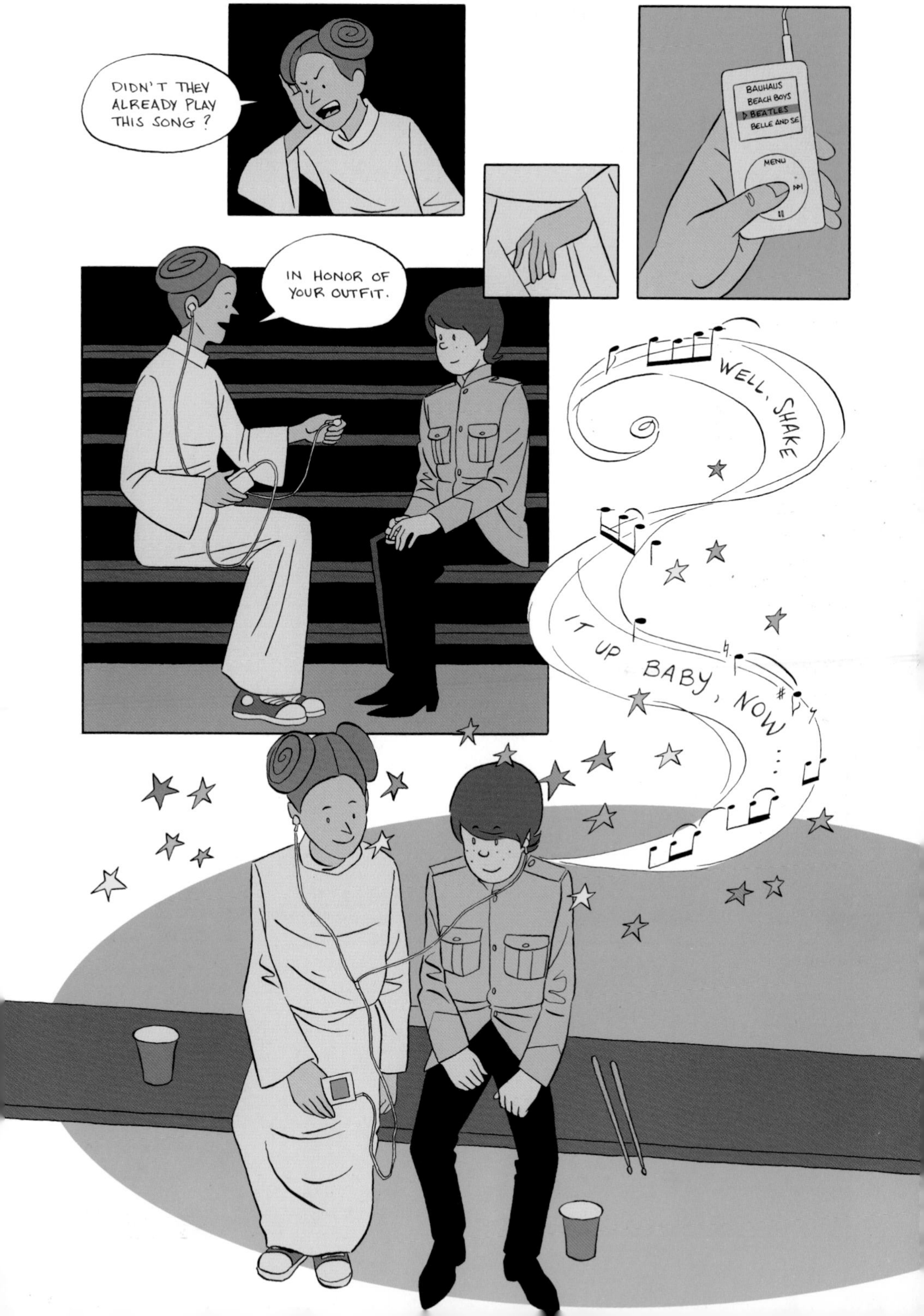

DIDN'T THEY ALREADY PLAY THIS SONG?
BAUHAUS
BEACH BOYS
BEATLES
BELLE AND SE
MENU
IN HONOR OF YOUR OUTFIT.
WELL, SHAKE IT UP BABY, NOW...

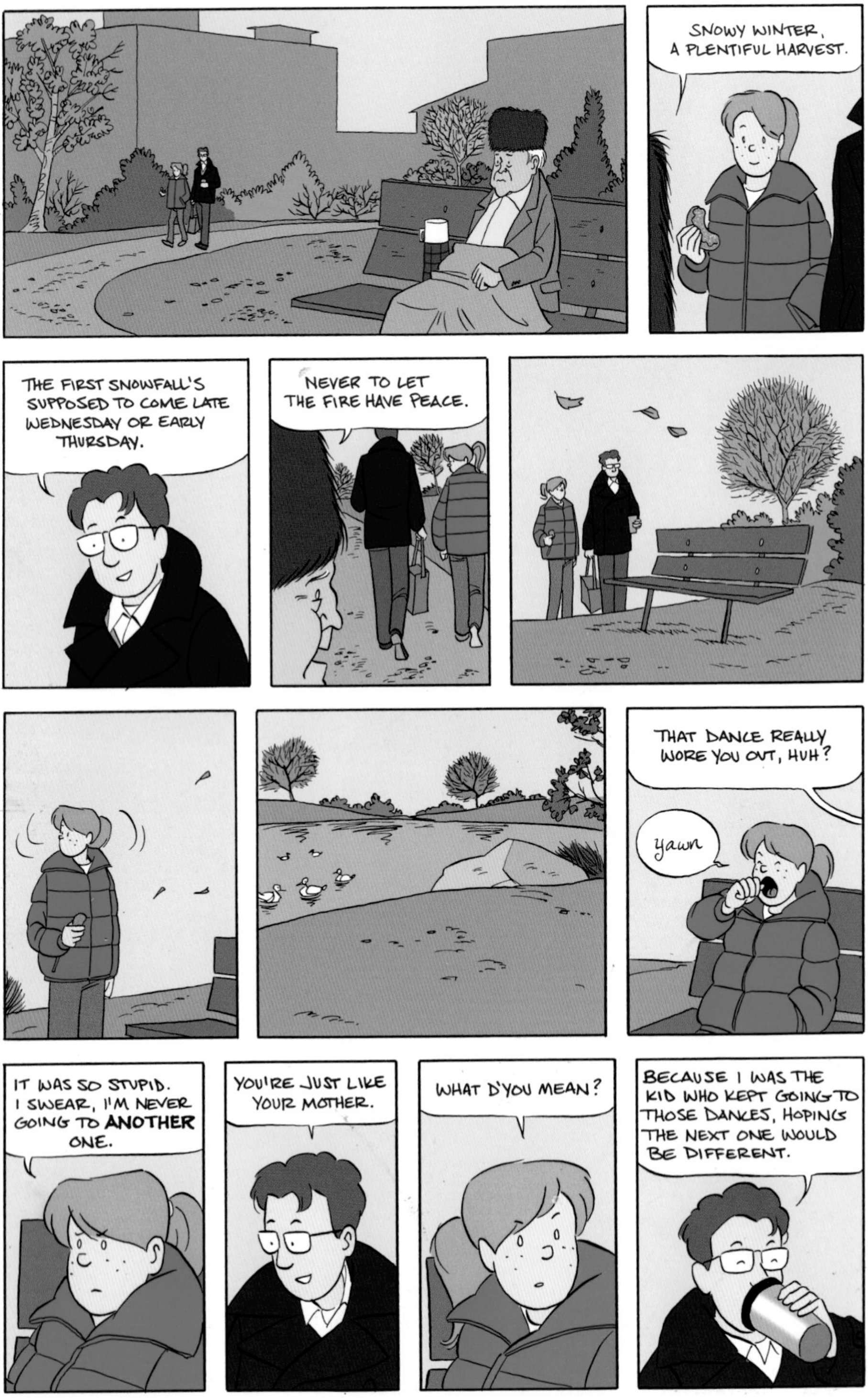
SNOWY WINTER, A PLENTIFUL HARVEST.
THE FIRST SNOWFALL'S SUPPOSED TO COME LATE WEDNESDAY OR EARLY THURSDAY.
NEVER TO LET THE FIRE HAVE PEACE.
THAT DANCE REALLY WORE YOU OUT, HUH?
yawn
IT WAS SO STUPID. I SWEAR, I'M NEVER GOING TO **ANOTHER** ONE.
YOU'RE JUST LIKE YOUR MOTHER.
WHAT D'YOU MEAN?
BECAUSE I WAS THE KID WHO KEPT GOING TO THOSE DANCES, HOPING THE NEXT ONE WOULD BE DIFFERENT.

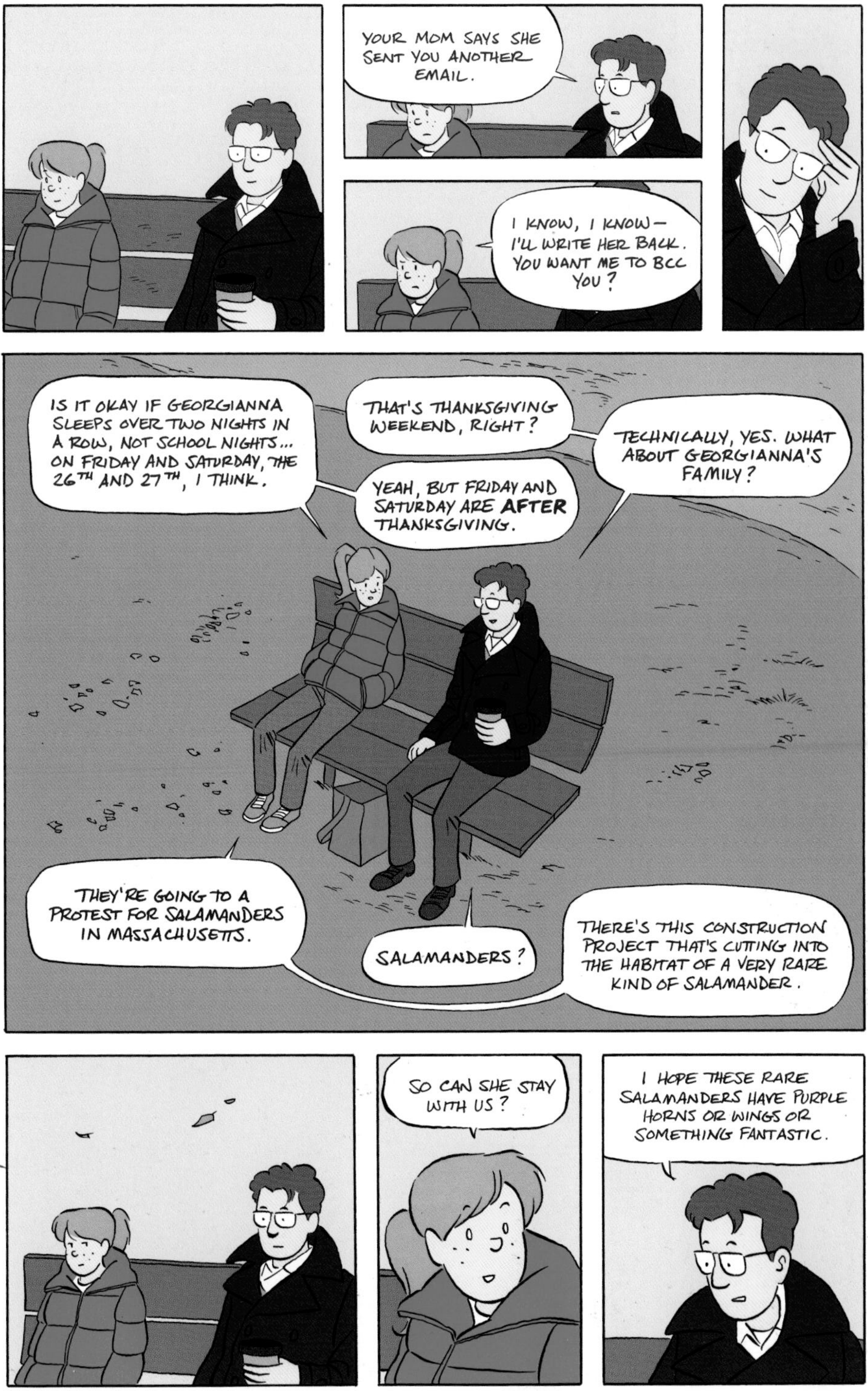

YOUR MOM SAYS SHE SENT YOU ANOTHER EMAIL.
I KNOW, I KNOW— I'LL WRITE HER BACK. YOU WANT ME TO BCC YOU?
IS IT OKAY IF GEORGIANNA SLEEPS OVER TWO NIGHTS IN A ROW, NOT SCHOOL NIGHTS... ON FRIDAY AND SATURDAY, THE 26TH AND 27TH, I THINK.
THAT'S THANKSGIVING WEEKEND, RIGHT?
YEAH, BUT FRIDAY AND SATURDAY ARE **AFTER** THANKSGIVING.
TECHNICALLY, YES. WHAT ABOUT GEORGIANNA'S FAMILY?
THEY'RE GOING TO A PROTEST FOR SALAMANDERS IN MASSACHUSETTS.
SALAMANDERS?
THERE'S THIS CONSTRUCTION PROJECT THAT'S CUTTING INTO THE HABITAT OF A VERY RARE KIND OF SALAMANDER.
SO CAN SHE STAY WITH US?
I HOPE THESE RARE SALAMANDERS HAVE PURPLE HORNS OR WINGS OR SOMETHING FANTASTIC.

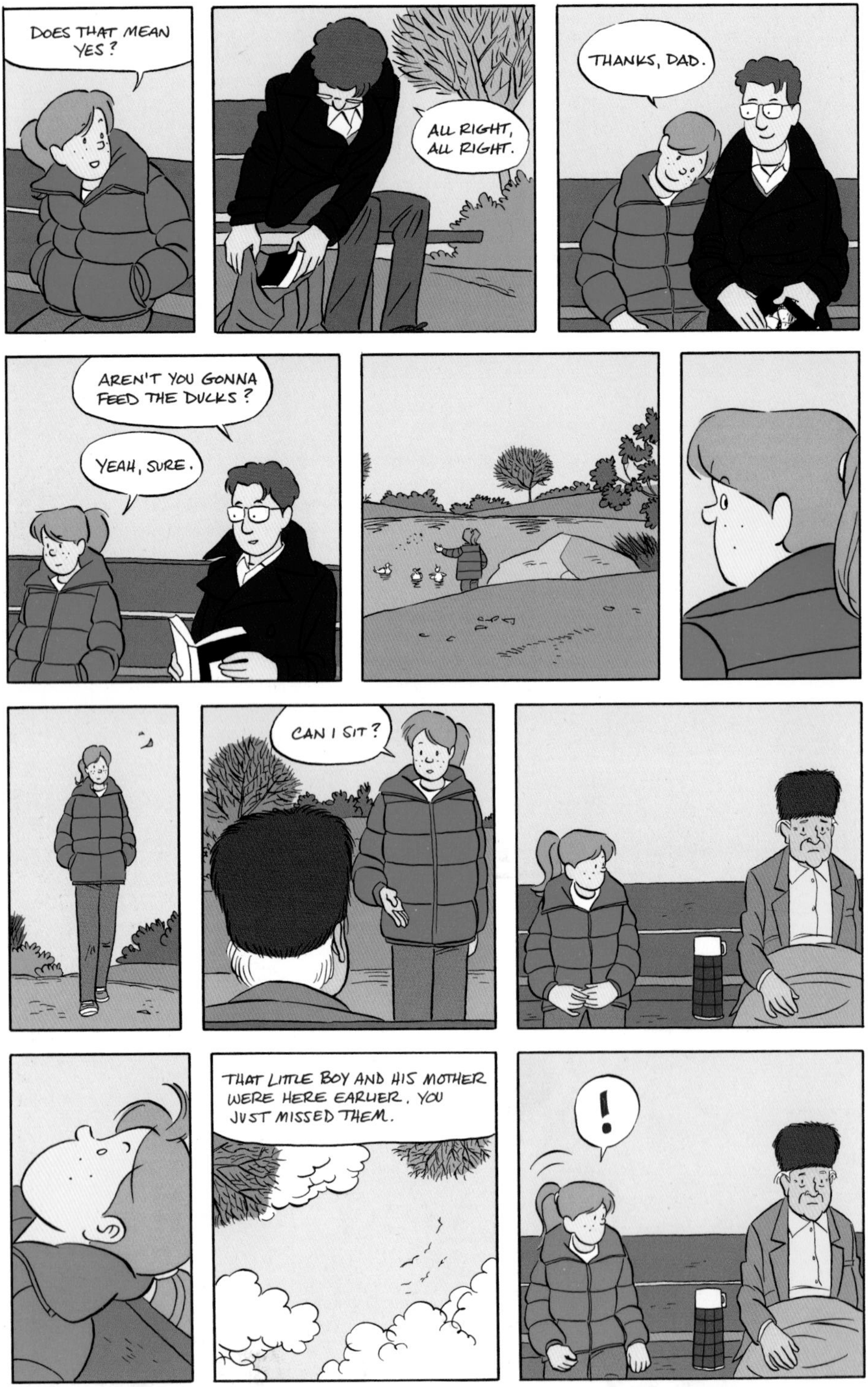
DOES THAT MEAN YES?
ALL RIGHT, ALL RIGHT.
THANKS, DAD.
AREN'T YOU GONNA FEED THE DUCKS?
YEAH, SURE.
CAN I SIT?
THAT LITTLE BOY AND HIS MOTHER WERE HERE EARLIER. YOU JUST MISSED THEM.
!

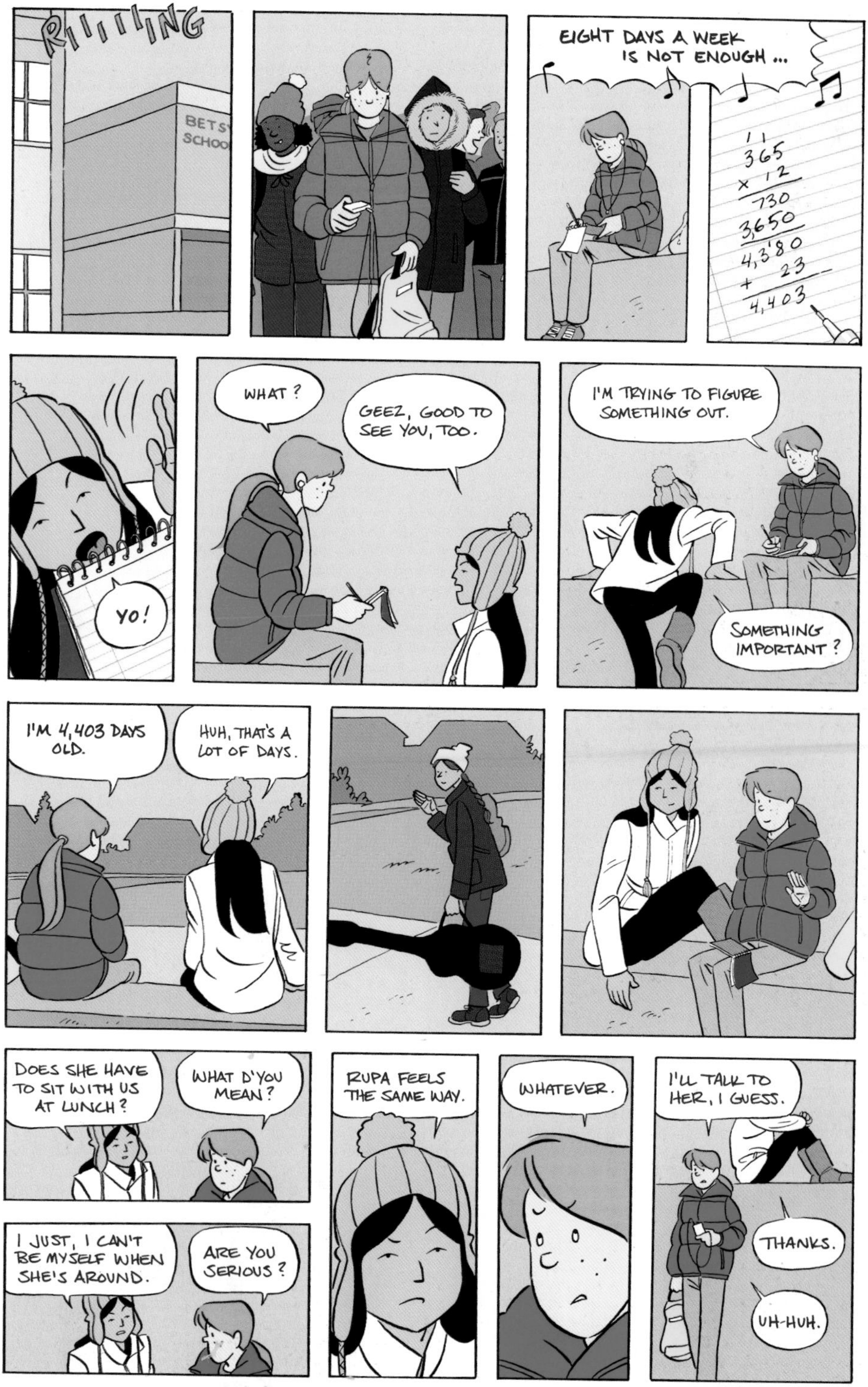
RIIIIING
BETS
SCHOO
EIGHT DAYS A WEEK IS NOT ENOUGH ...
365
× 12
730
3650
4,380
+ 23
4,403
YO!
WHAT?
GEEZ, GOOD TO SEE YOU, TOO.
I'M TRYING TO FIGURE SOMETHING OUT.
SOMETHING IMPORTANT?
I'M 4,403 DAYS OLD.
HUH, THAT'S A LOT OF DAYS.
DOES SHE HAVE TO SIT WITH US AT LUNCH?
WHAT D'YOU MEAN?
I JUST, I CAN'T BE MYSELF WHEN SHE'S AROUND.
ARE YOU SERIOUS?
RUPA FEELS THE SAME WAY.
WHATEVER.
I'LL TALK TO HER, I GUESS.
THANKS.
UH-HUH.

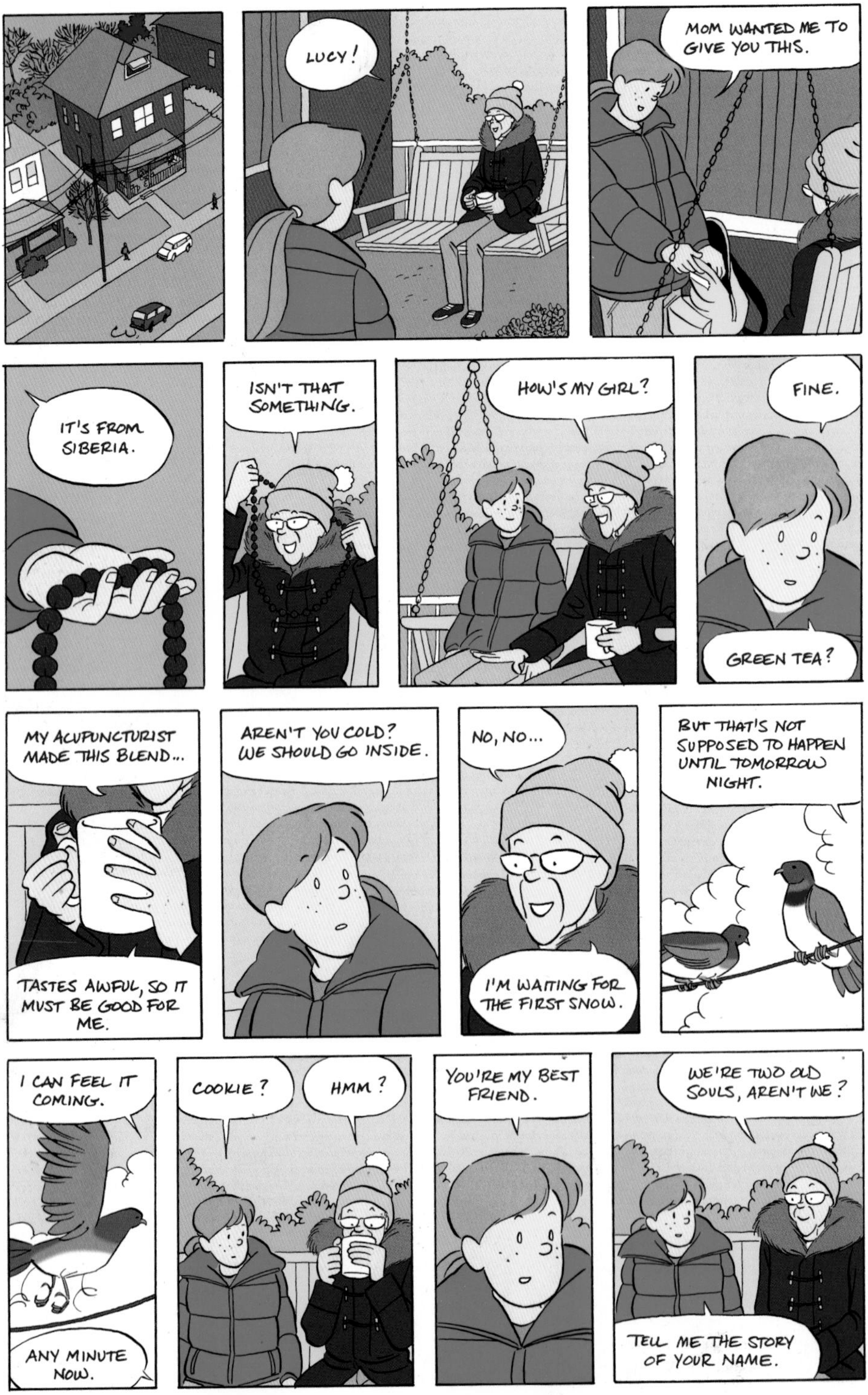
LUCY!
MOM WANTED ME TO GIVE YOU THIS.
IT'S FROM SIBERIA.
ISN'T THAT SOMETHING.
HOW'S MY GIRL?
FINE.
GREEN TEA?
MY ACUPUNCTURIST MADE THIS BLEND...
TASTES AWFUL, SO IT MUST BE GOOD FOR ME.
AREN'T YOU COLD? WE SHOULD GO INSIDE.
NO, NO...
I'M WAITING FOR THE FIRST SNOW.
BUT THAT'S NOT SUPPOSED TO HAPPEN UNTIL TOMORROW NIGHT.
I CAN FEEL IT COMING.
ANY MINUTE NOW.
COOKIE?
HMM?
YOU'RE MY BEST FRIEND.
WE'RE TWO OLD SOULS, AREN'T WE?
TELL ME THE STORY OF YOUR NAME.

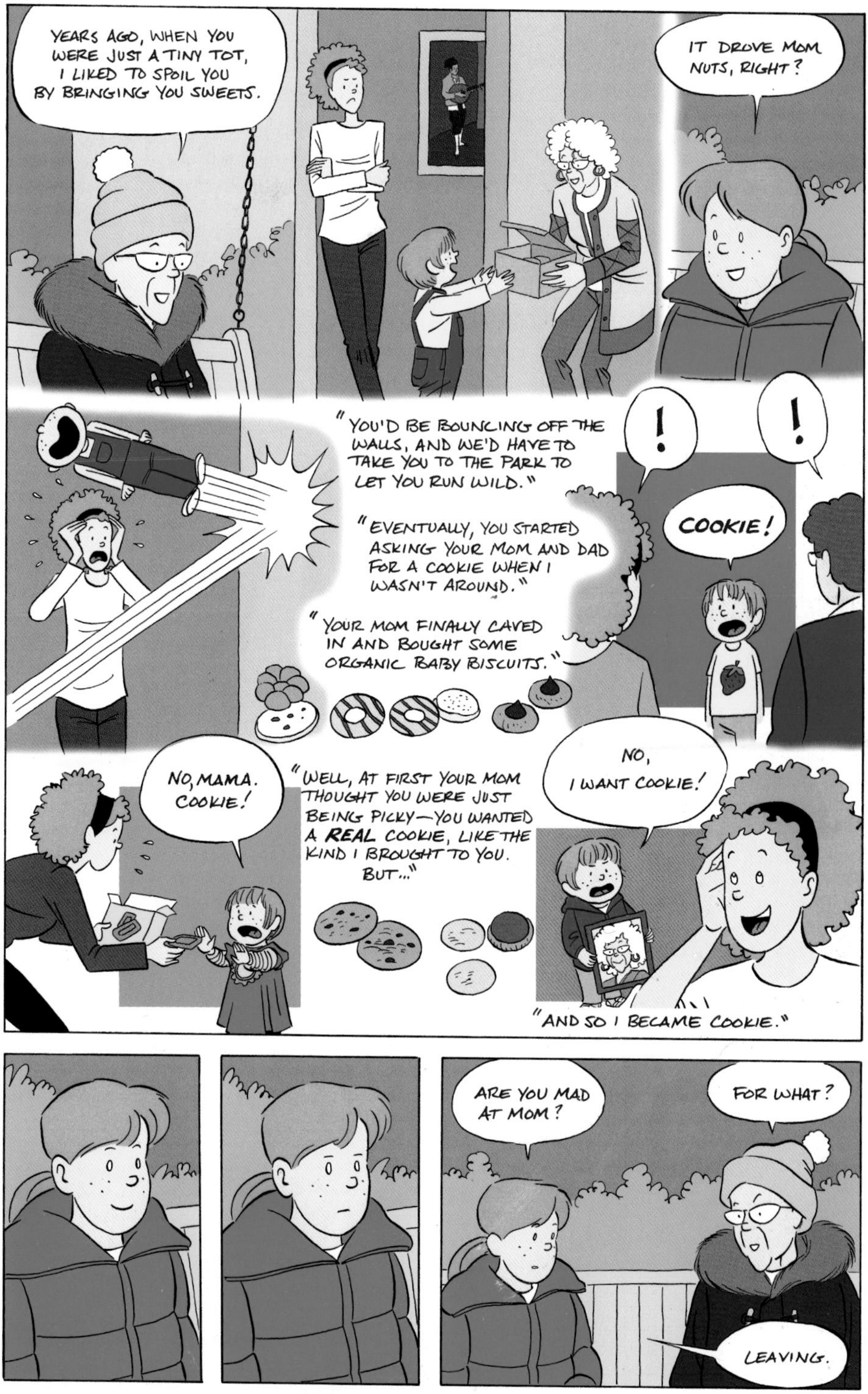
YEARS AGO, WHEN YOU WERE JUST A TINY TOT, I LIKED TO SPOIL YOU BY BRINGING YOU SWEETS.
IT DROVE MOM NUTS, RIGHT?
"YOU'D BE BOUNCING OFF THE WALLS, AND WE'D HAVE TO TAKE YOU TO THE PARK TO LET YOU RUN WILD."
!
!
"EVENTUALLY, YOU STARTED ASKING YOUR MOM AND DAD FOR A COOKIE WHEN I WASN'T AROUND."
COOKIE!
"YOUR MOM FINALLY CAVED IN AND BOUGHT SOME ORGANIC BABY BISCUITS."
NO, MAMA. COOKIE!
"WELL, AT FIRST YOUR MOM THOUGHT YOU WERE JUST BEING PICKY—YOU WANTED A REAL COOKIE, LIKE THE KIND I BROUGHT TO YOU. BUT..."
NO, I WANT COOKIE!
"AND SO I BECAME COOKIE."
ARE YOU MAD AT MOM?
FOR WHAT?
LEAVING.

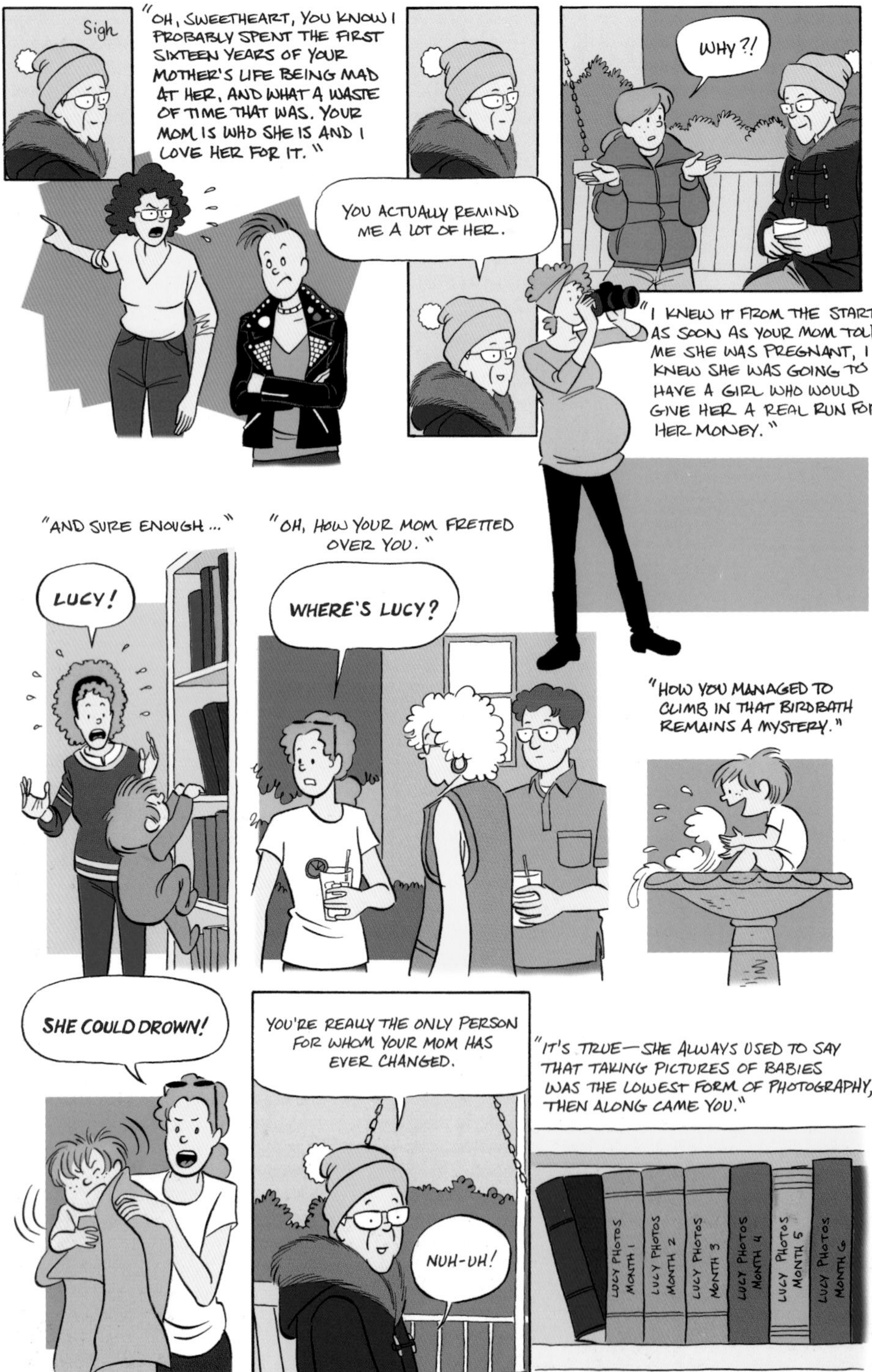
Sigh
"OH, SWEETHEART, YOU KNOW I PROBABLY SPENT THE FIRST SIXTEEN YEARS OF YOUR MOTHER'S LIFE BEING MAD AT HER, AND WHAT A WASTE OF TIME THAT WAS. YOUR MOM IS WHO SHE IS AND I LOVE HER FOR IT."
WHY?!
YOU ACTUALLY REMIND ME A LOT OF HER.
"I KNEW IT FROM THE START. AS SOON AS YOUR MOM TOLD ME SHE WAS PREGNANT, I KNEW SHE WAS GOING TO HAVE A GIRL WHO WOULD GIVE HER A REAL RUN FOR HER MONEY."
"AND SURE ENOUGH..."
LUCY!
"OH, HOW YOUR MOM FRETTED OVER YOU."
WHERE'S LUCY?
"HOW YOU MANAGED TO CLIMB IN THAT BIRDBATH REMAINS A MYSTERY."
SHE COULD DROWN!
YOU'RE REALLY THE ONLY PERSON FOR WHOM YOUR MOM HAS EVER CHANGED.
NUH-UH!
"IT'S TRUE—SHE ALWAYS USED TO SAY THAT TAKING PICTURES OF BABIES WAS THE LOWEST FORM OF PHOTOGRAPHY, THEN ALONG CAME YOU."
LUCY PHOTOS MONTH 1
LUCY PHOTOS MONTH 2
LUCY PHOTOS MONTH 3
LUCY PHOTOS MONTH 4
LUCY PHOTOS MONTH 5
LUCY PHOTOS MONTH 6

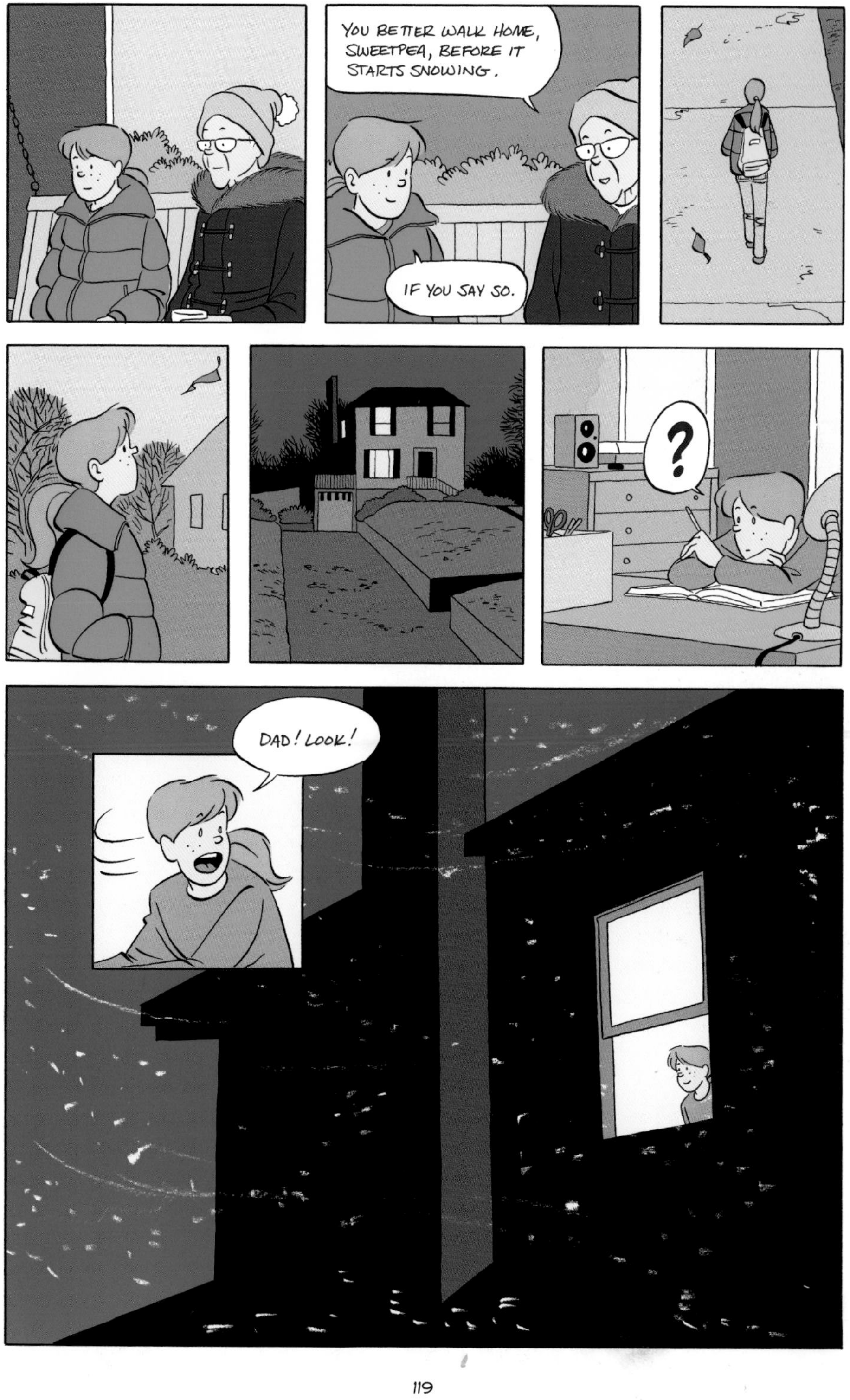
YOU BETTER WALK HOME, SWEETPEA, BEFORE IT STARTS SNOWING.
IF YOU SAY SO.
?
DAD! LOOK!

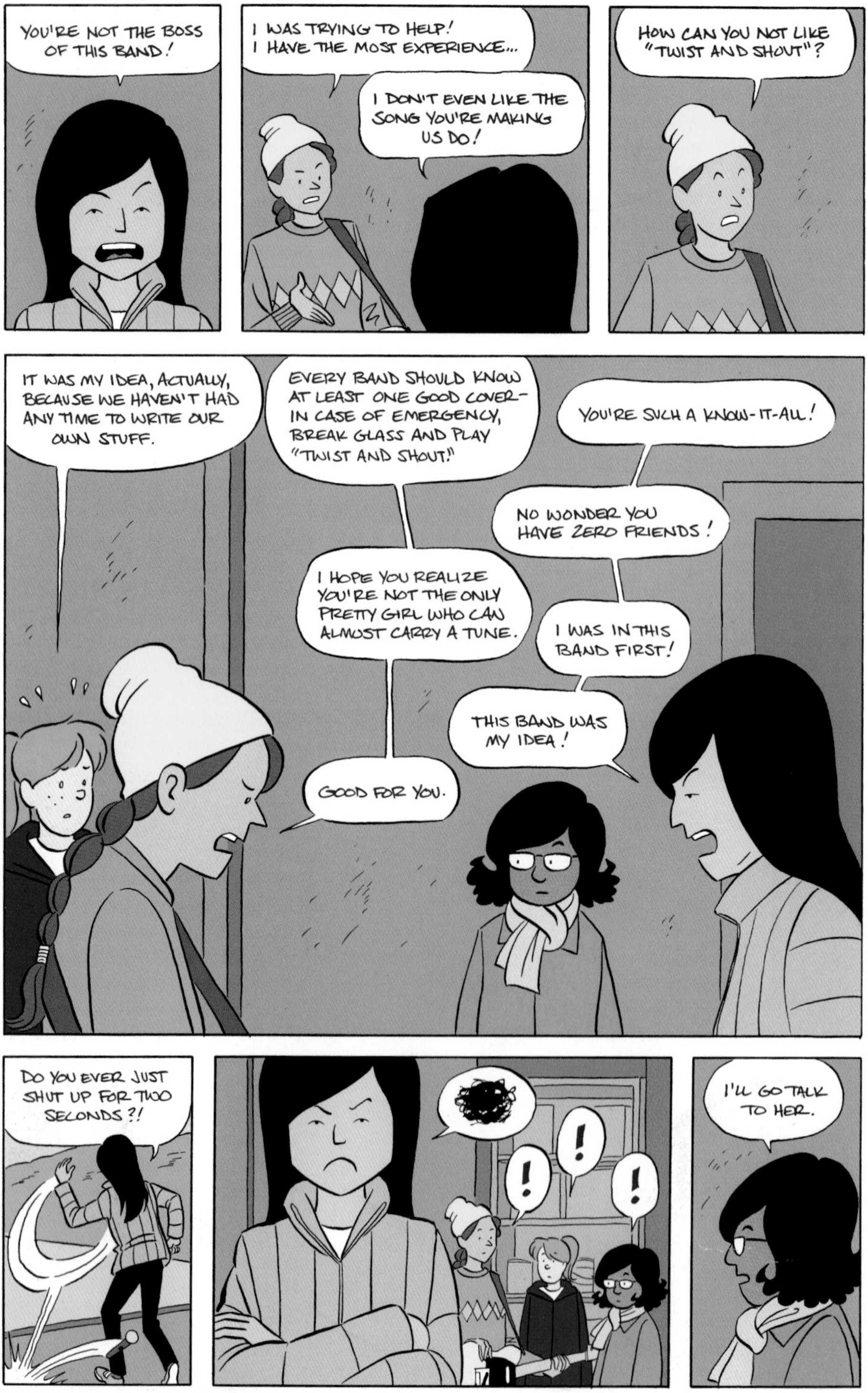
YOU'RE NOT THE BOSS OF THIS BAND!
I WAS TRYING TO HELP! I HAVE THE MOST EXPERIENCE...
I DON'T EVEN LIKE THE SONG YOU'RE MAKING US DO!
HOW CAN YOU NOT LIKE "TWIST AND SHOUT"?
IT WAS MY IDEA, ACTUALLY, BECAUSE WE HAVEN'T HAD ANY TIME TO WRITE OUR OWN STUFF.
EVERY BAND SHOULD KNOW AT LEAST ONE GOOD COVER- IN CASE OF EMERGENCY, BREAK GLASS AND PLAY "TWIST AND SHOUT."
YOU'RE SUCH A KNOW-IT-ALL!
NO WONDER YOU HAVE ZERO FRIENDS!
I HOPE YOU REALIZE YOU'RE NOT THE ONLY PRETTY GIRL WHO CAN ALMOST CARRY A TUNE.
I WAS IN THIS BAND FIRST!
THIS BAND WAS MY IDEA!
GOOD FOR YOU.
DO YOU EVER JUST SHUT UP FOR TWO SECONDS?!
!
!
!
I'LL GO TALK TO HER.

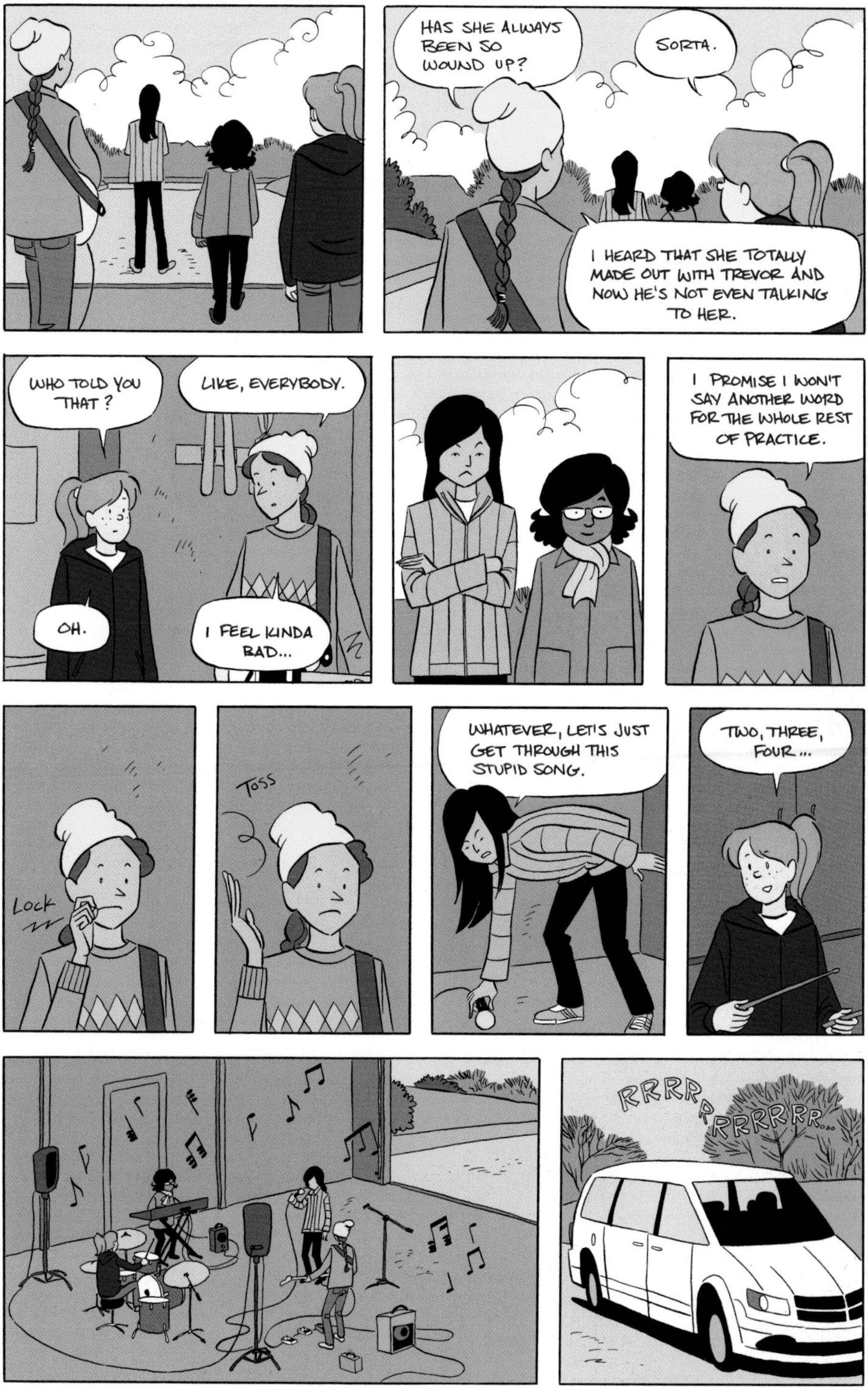

HAS SHE ALWAYS BEEN SO WOUND UP?
SORTA.
I HEARD THAT SHE TOTALLY MADE OUT WITH TREVOR AND NOW HE'S NOT EVEN TALKING TO HER.
WHO TOLD YOU THAT?
LIKE, EVERYBODY.
OH.
I FEEL KINDA BAD...
I PROMISE I WON'T SAY ANOTHER WORD FOR THE WHOLE REST OF PRACTICE.
LOCK
TOSS
WHATEVER, LET'S JUST GET THROUGH THIS STUPID SONG.
TWO, THREE, FOUR...
RRRRRRRRRRRR...

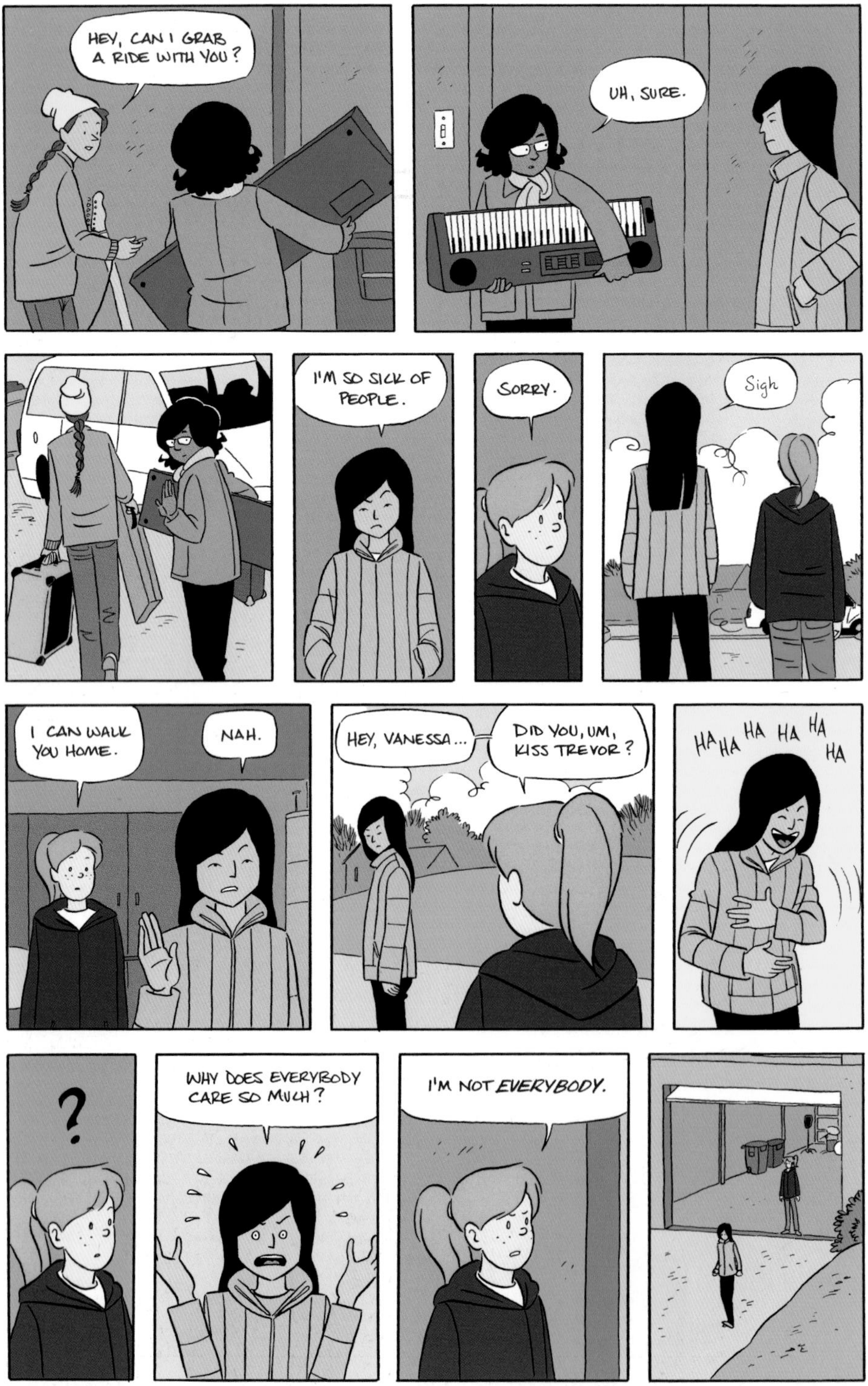
HEY, CAN I GRAB A RIDE WITH YOU?
UH, SURE.
I'M SO SICK OF PEOPLE.
SORRY.
Sigh
I CAN WALK YOU HOME.
NAH.
HEY, VANESSA...
DID YOU, UM, KISS TREVOR?
HA HA HA HA HA HA
?
WHY DOES EVERYBODY CARE SO MUCH?
I'M NOT *EVERYBODY*.

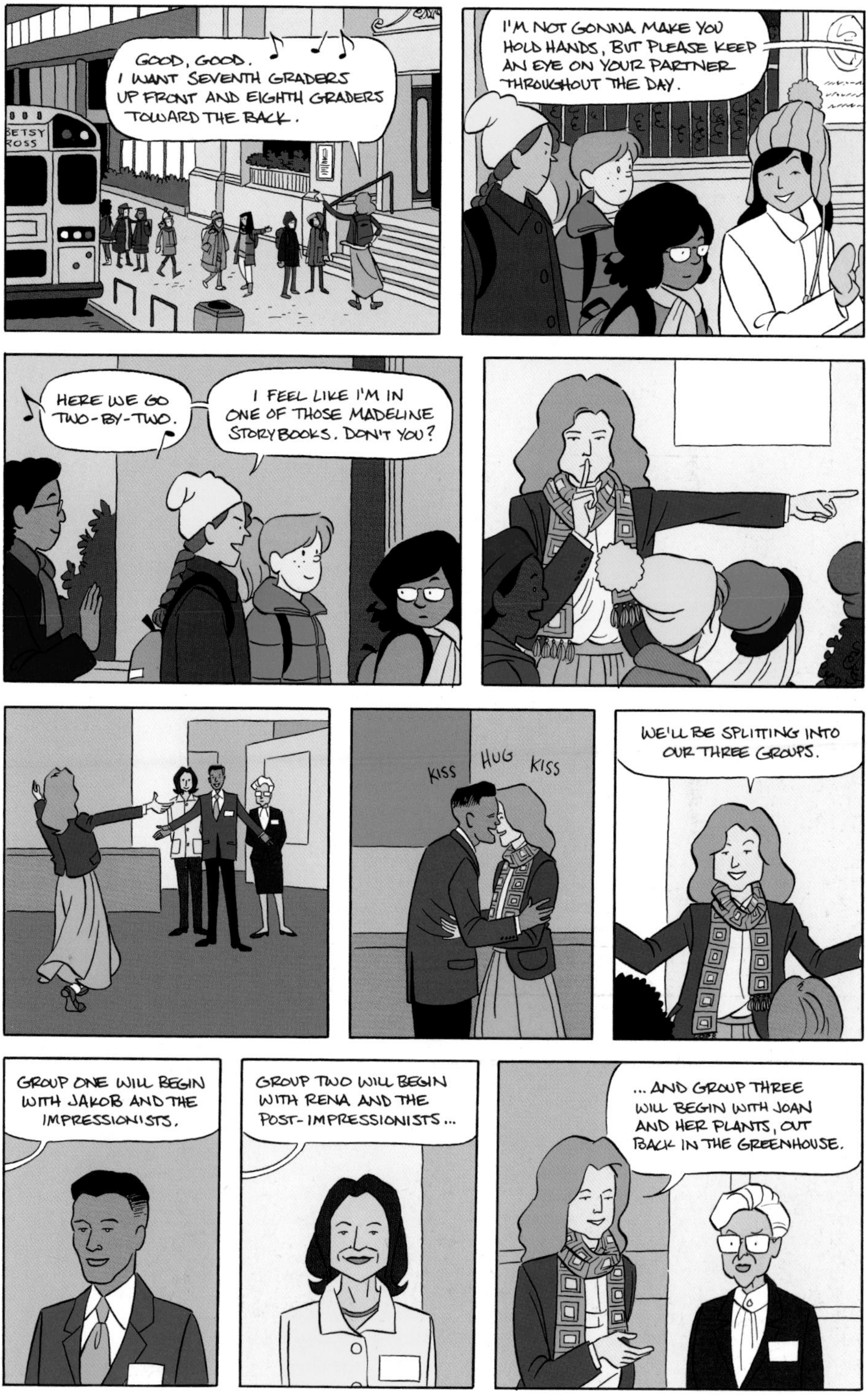
BETSY ROSS
GOOD, GOOD. I WANT SEVENTH GRADERS UP FRONT AND EIGHTH GRADERS TOWARD THE BACK.
I'M NOT GONNA MAKE YOU HOLD HANDS, BUT PLEASE KEEP AN EYE ON YOUR PARTNER THROUGHOUT THE DAY.
HERE WE GO TWO-BY-TWO.
I FEEL LIKE I'M IN ONE OF THOSE MADELINE STORYBOOKS. DON'T YOU?
KISS
HUG
KISS
WE'LL BE SPLITTING INTO OUR THREE GROUPS.
GROUP ONE WILL BEGIN WITH JAKOB AND THE IMPRESSIONISTS.
GROUP TWO WILL BEGIN WITH RENA AND THE POST-IMPRESSIONISTS...
...AND GROUP THREE WILL BEGIN WITH JOAN AND HER PLANTS, OUT BACK IN THE GREENHOUSE.

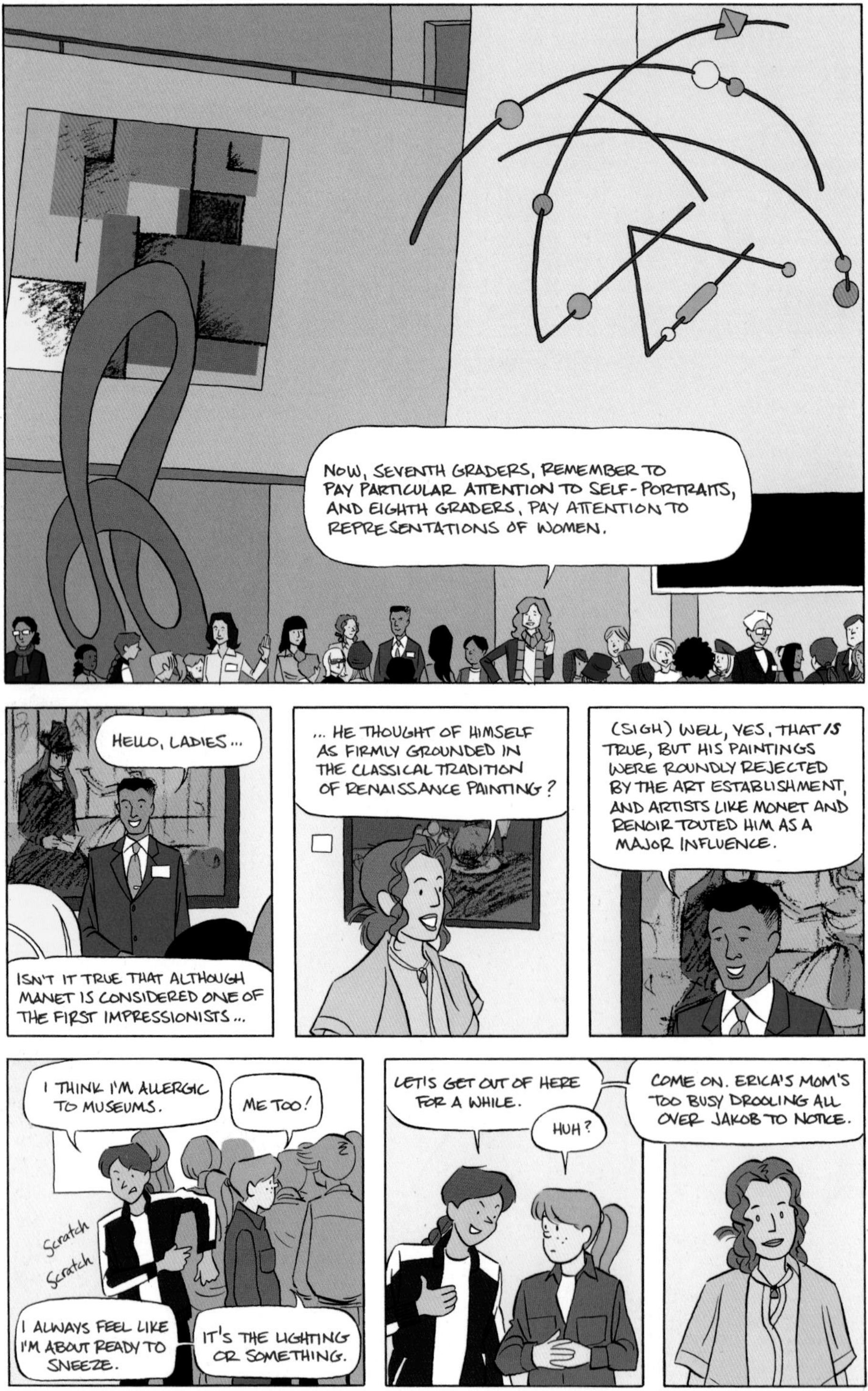
NOW, SEVENTH GRADERS, REMEMBER TO PAY PARTICULAR ATTENTION TO SELF-PORTRAITS, AND EIGHTH GRADERS, PAY ATTENTION TO REPRESENTATIONS OF WOMEN.
HELLO, LADIES...
ISN'T IT TRUE THAT ALTHOUGH MANET IS CONSIDERED ONE OF THE FIRST IMPRESSIONISTS...
...HE THOUGHT OF HIMSELF AS FIRMLY GROUNDED IN THE CLASSICAL TRADITION OF RENAISSANCE PAINTING?
(SIGH) WELL, YES, THAT IS TRUE, BUT HIS PAINTINGS WERE ROUNDLY REJECTED BY THE ART ESTABLISHMENT, AND ARTISTS LIKE MONET AND RENOIR TOUTED HIM AS A MAJOR INFLUENCE.
I THINK I'M ALLERGIC TO MUSEUMS.
ME TOO!
Scratch
Scratch
I ALWAYS FEEL LIKE I'M ABOUT READY TO SNEEZE.
IT'S THE LIGHTING OR SOMETHING.
LET'S GET OUT OF HERE FOR A WHILE.
HUH?
COME ON. ERICA'S MOM'S TOO BUSY DROOLING ALL OVER JAKOB TO NOTICE.

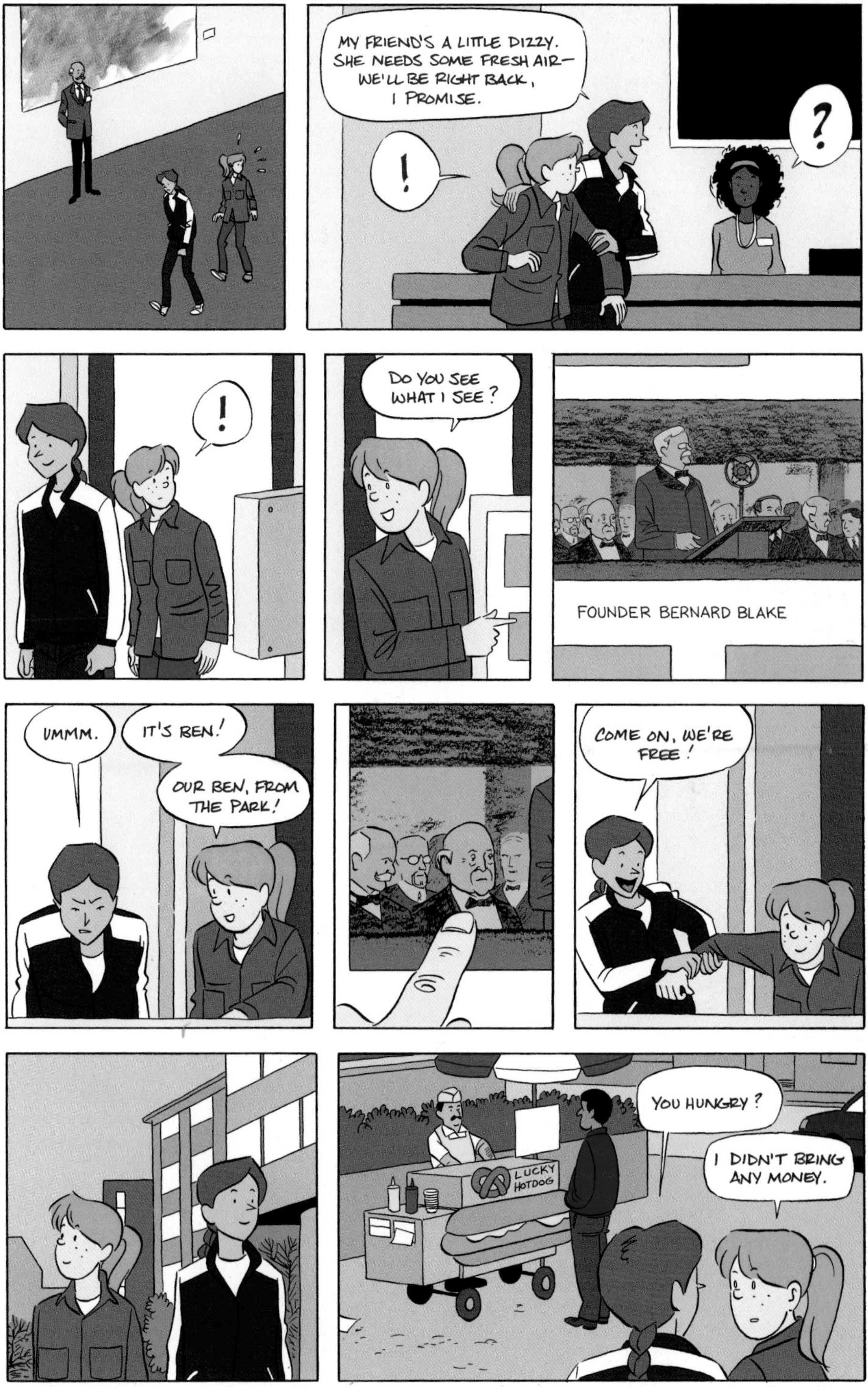
!
MY FRIEND'S A LITTLE DIZZY. SHE NEEDS SOME FRESH AIR— WE'LL BE RIGHT BACK, I PROMISE.
!
?
!
DO YOU SEE WHAT I SEE?
FOUNDER BERNARD BLAKE
UMMM.
IT'S BEN!
OUR BEN, FROM THE PARK!
COME ON, WE'RE FREE!
LUCKY HOTDOG
YOU HUNGRY?
I DIDN'T BRING ANY MONEY.

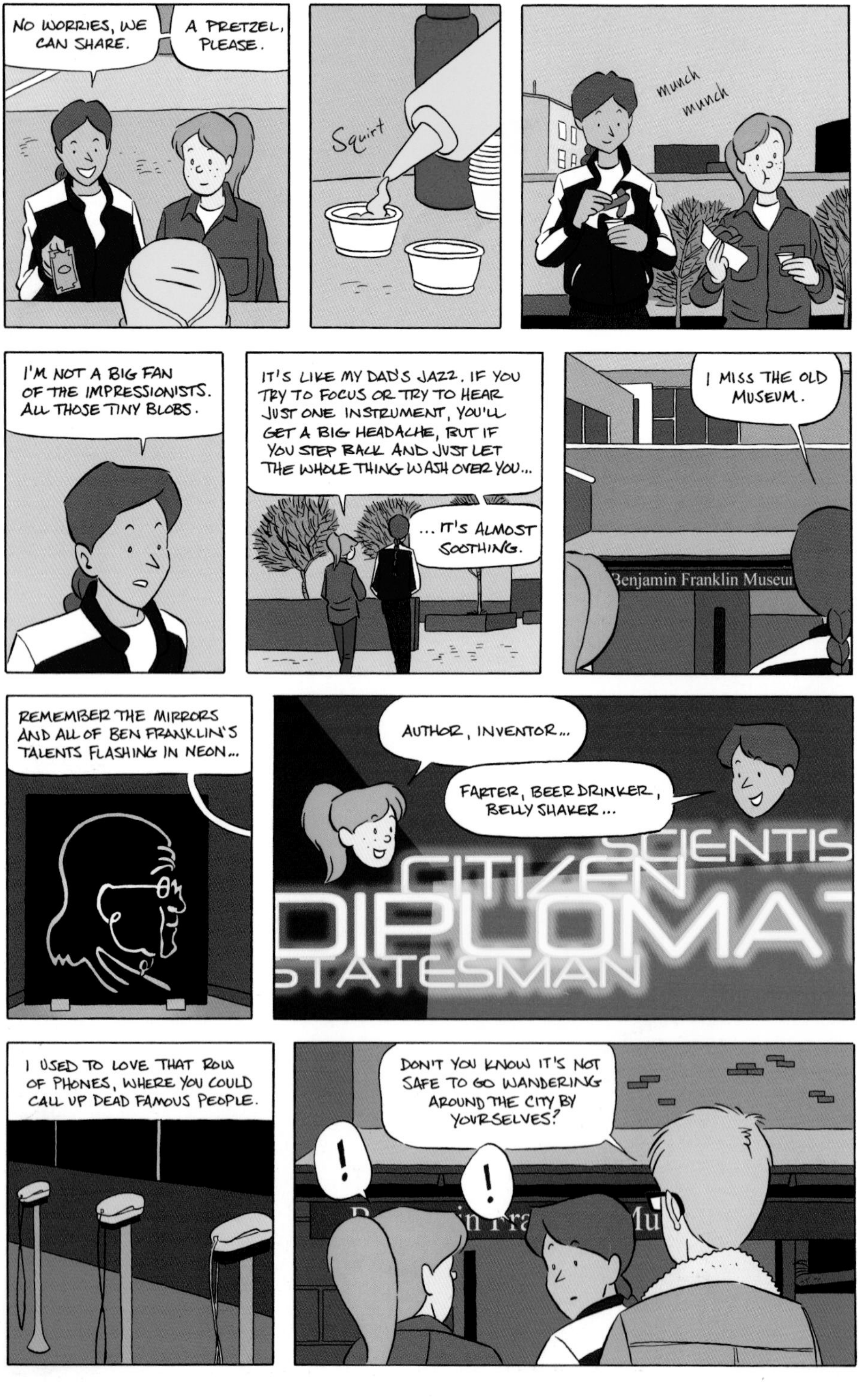

NO WORRIES, WE CAN SHARE.
A PRETZEL, PLEASE.
Squirt
munch munch
I'M NOT A BIG FAN OF THE IMPRESSIONISTS. ALL THOSE TINY BLOBS.
IT'S LIKE MY DAD'S JAZZ. IF YOU TRY TO FOCUS OR TRY TO HEAR JUST ONE INSTRUMENT, YOU'LL GET A BIG HEADACHE, BUT IF YOU STEP BACK AND JUST LET THE WHOLE THING WASH OVER YOU...
... IT'S ALMOST SOOTHING.
I MISS THE OLD MUSEUM.
Benjamin Franklin Museum
REMEMBER THE MIRRORS AND ALL OF BEN FRANKLIN'S TALENTS FLASHING IN NEON...
AUTHOR, INVENTOR...
FARTER, BEER DRINKER, BELLY SHAKER...
SCIENTIS
CITIZEN
DIPLOMAT
STATESMAN
I USED TO LOVE THAT ROW OF PHONES, WHERE YOU COULD CALL UP DEAD FAMOUS PEOPLE.
DON'T YOU KNOW IT'S NOT SAFE TO GO WANDERING AROUND THE CITY BY YOURSELVES?
!
!

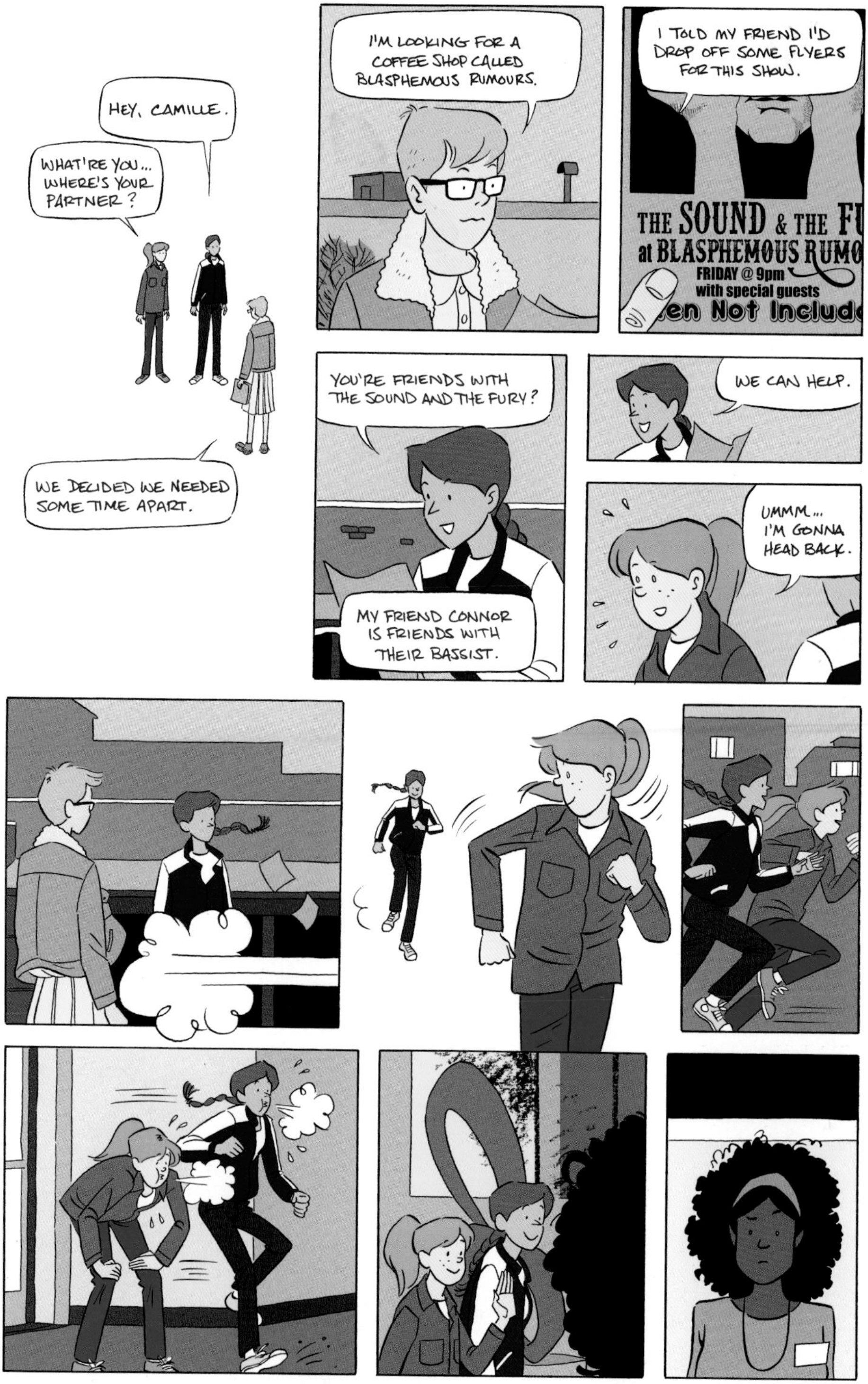
HEY, CAMILLE.
WHAT'RE YOU... WHERE'S YOUR PARTNER?
WE DECIDED WE NEEDED SOME TIME APART.
I'M LOOKING FOR A COFFEE SHOP CALLED BLASPHEMOUS RUMOURS.
I TOLD MY FRIEND I'D DROP OFF SOME FLYERS FOR THIS SHOW.
THE SOUND & THE FU
at BLASPHEMOUS RUMO
FRIDAY @ 9pm
with special guests
YOU'RE FRIENDS WITH THE SOUND AND THE FURY?
MY FRIEND CONNOR IS FRIENDS WITH THEIR BASSIST.
WE CAN HELP.
UMMM... I'M GONNA HEAD BACK.

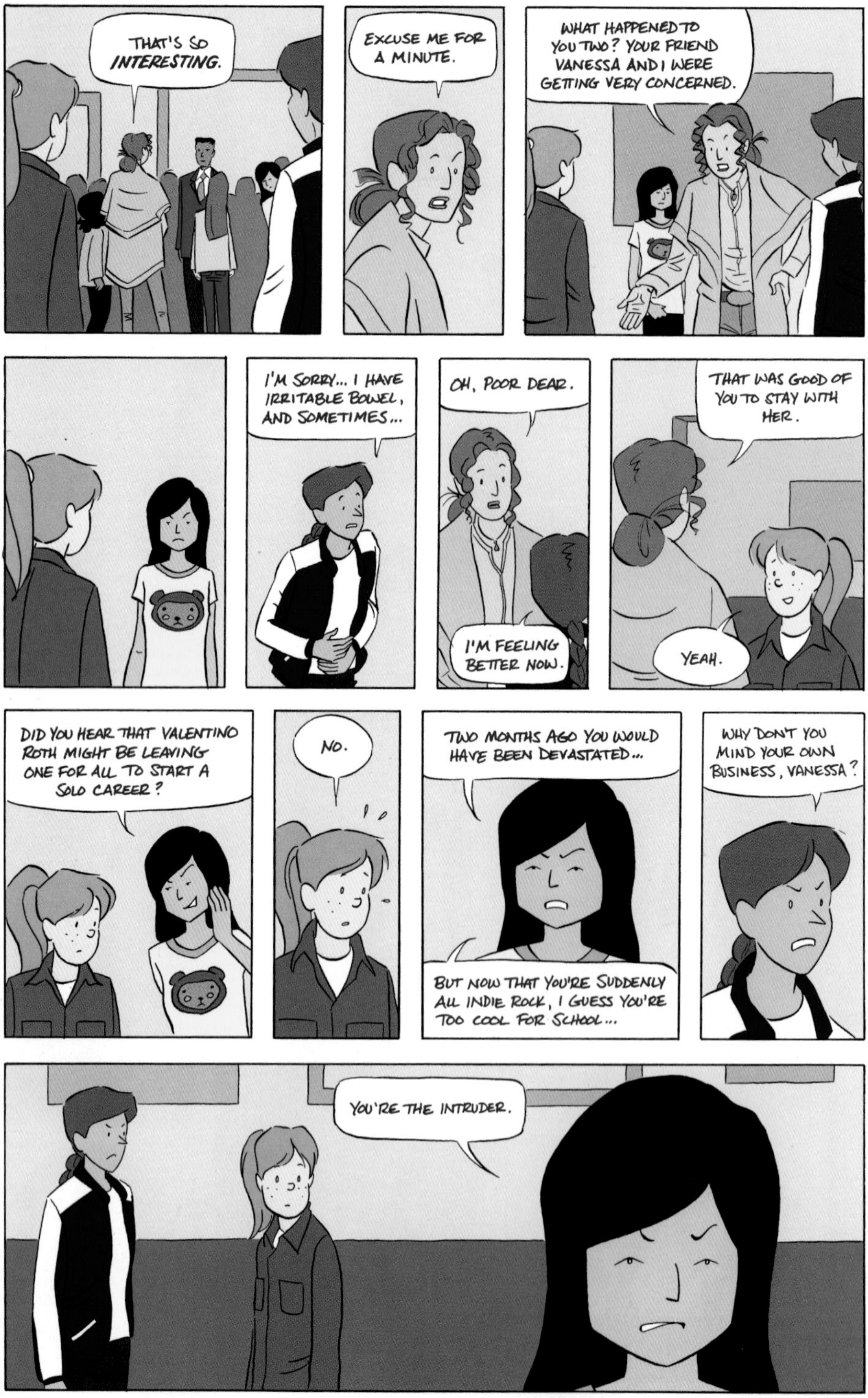
THAT'S SO INTERESTING.
EXCUSE ME FOR A MINUTE.
WHAT HAPPENED TO YOU TWO? YOUR FRIEND VANESSA AND I WERE GETTING VERY CONCERNED.
I'M SORRY... I HAVE IRRITABLE BOWEL, AND SOMETIMES...
OH, POOR DEAR.
I'M FEELING BETTER NOW.
THAT WAS GOOD OF YOU TO STAY WITH HER.
YEAH.
DID YOU HEAR THAT VALENTINO ROTH MIGHT BE LEAVING ONE FOR ALL TO START A SOLO CAREER?
NO.
TWO MONTHS AGO YOU WOULD HAVE BEEN DEVASTATED...
BUT NOW THAT YOU'RE SUDDENLY ALL INDIE ROCK, I GUESS YOU'RE TOO COOL FOR SCHOOL...
WHY DON'T YOU MIND YOUR OWN BUSINESS, VANESSA?
YOU'RE THE INTRUDER.

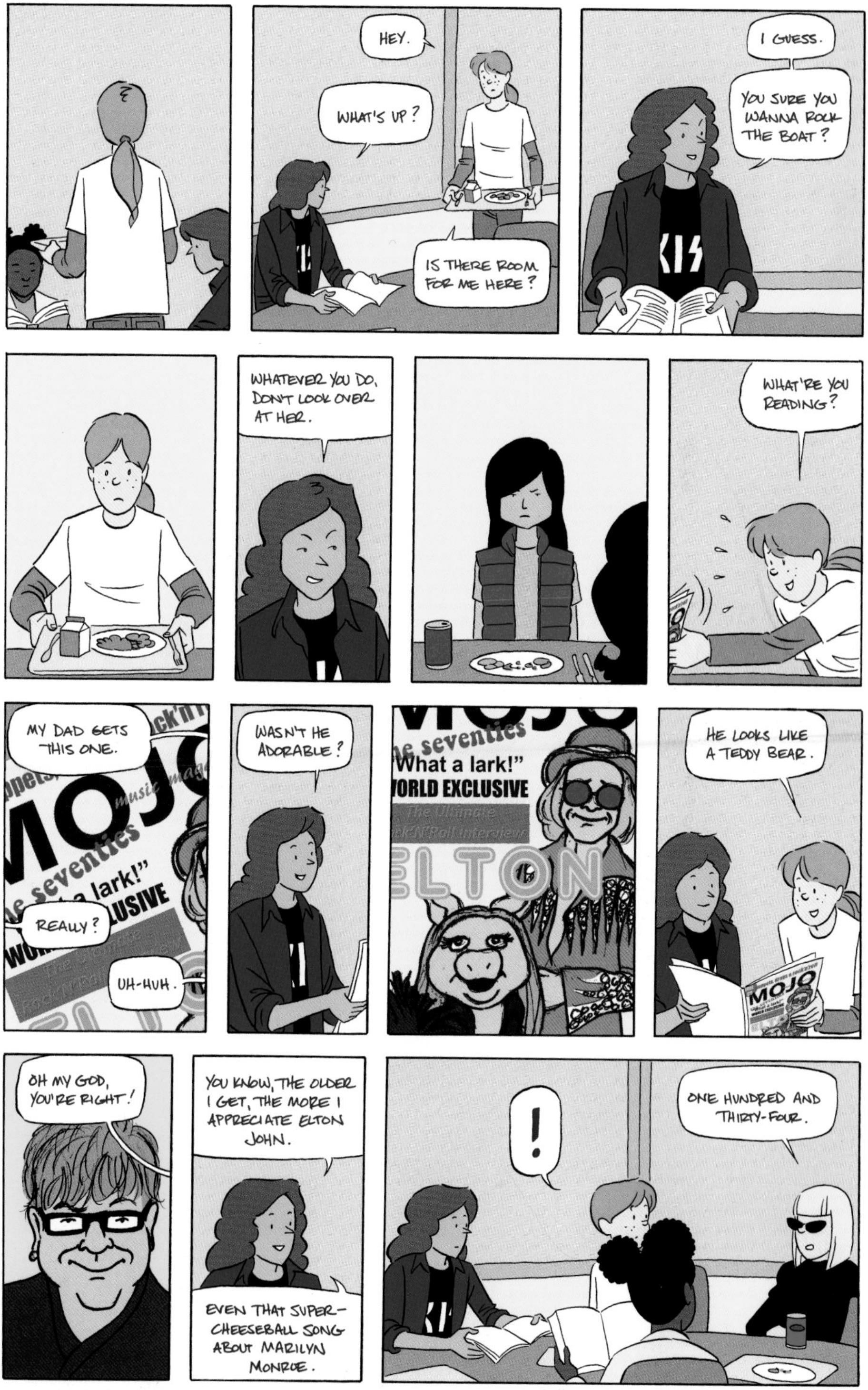
HEY.
WHAT'S UP?
IS THERE ROOM FOR ME HERE?
I GUESS.
YOU SURE YOU WANNA ROCK THE BOAT?
WHATEVER YOU DO, DON'T LOOK OVER AT HER.
WHAT'RE YOU READING?
MY DAD GETS THIS ONE.
REALLY?
UH-HUH.
WASN'T HE ADORABLE?
MOJO
the seventies
"What a lark!"
WORLD EXCLUSIVE
HE LOOKS LIKE A TEDDY BEAR.
OH MY GOD, YOU'RE RIGHT!
YOU KNOW, THE OLDER I GET, THE MORE I APPRECIATE ELTON JOHN.
EVEN THAT SUPER-CHEESEBALL SONG ABOUT MARILYN MONROE.
!
ONE HUNDRED AND THIRTY-FOUR.

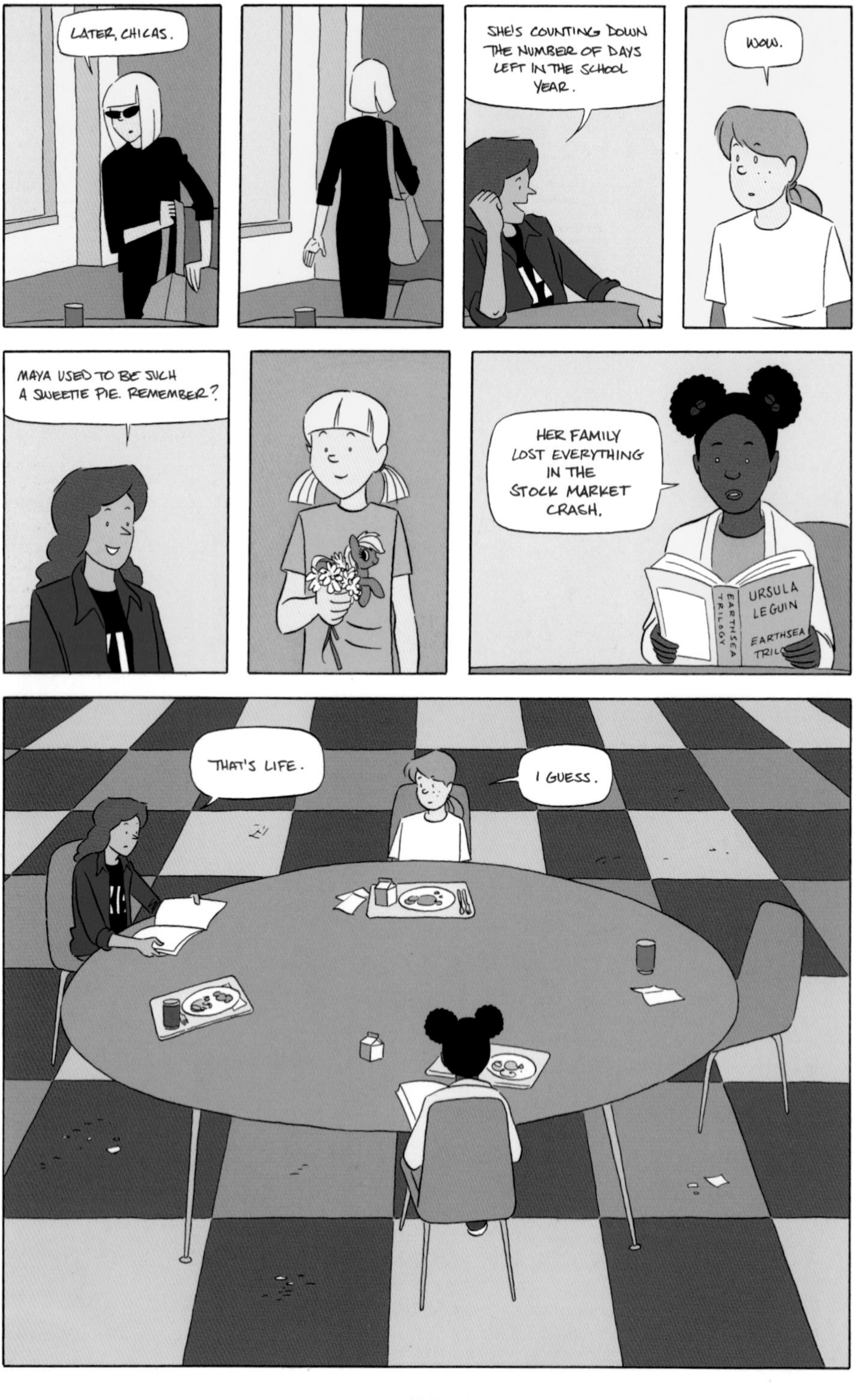
LATER, CHICAS.
SHE'S COUNTING DOWN THE NUMBER OF DAYS LEFT IN THE SCHOOL YEAR.
WOW.
MAYA USED TO BE SUCH A SWEETIE PIE. REMEMBER?
HER FAMILY LOST EVERYTHING IN THE STOCK MARKET CRASH.
URSULA LEGUIN
EARTHSEA TRILOGY
THAT'S LIFE.
I GUESS.

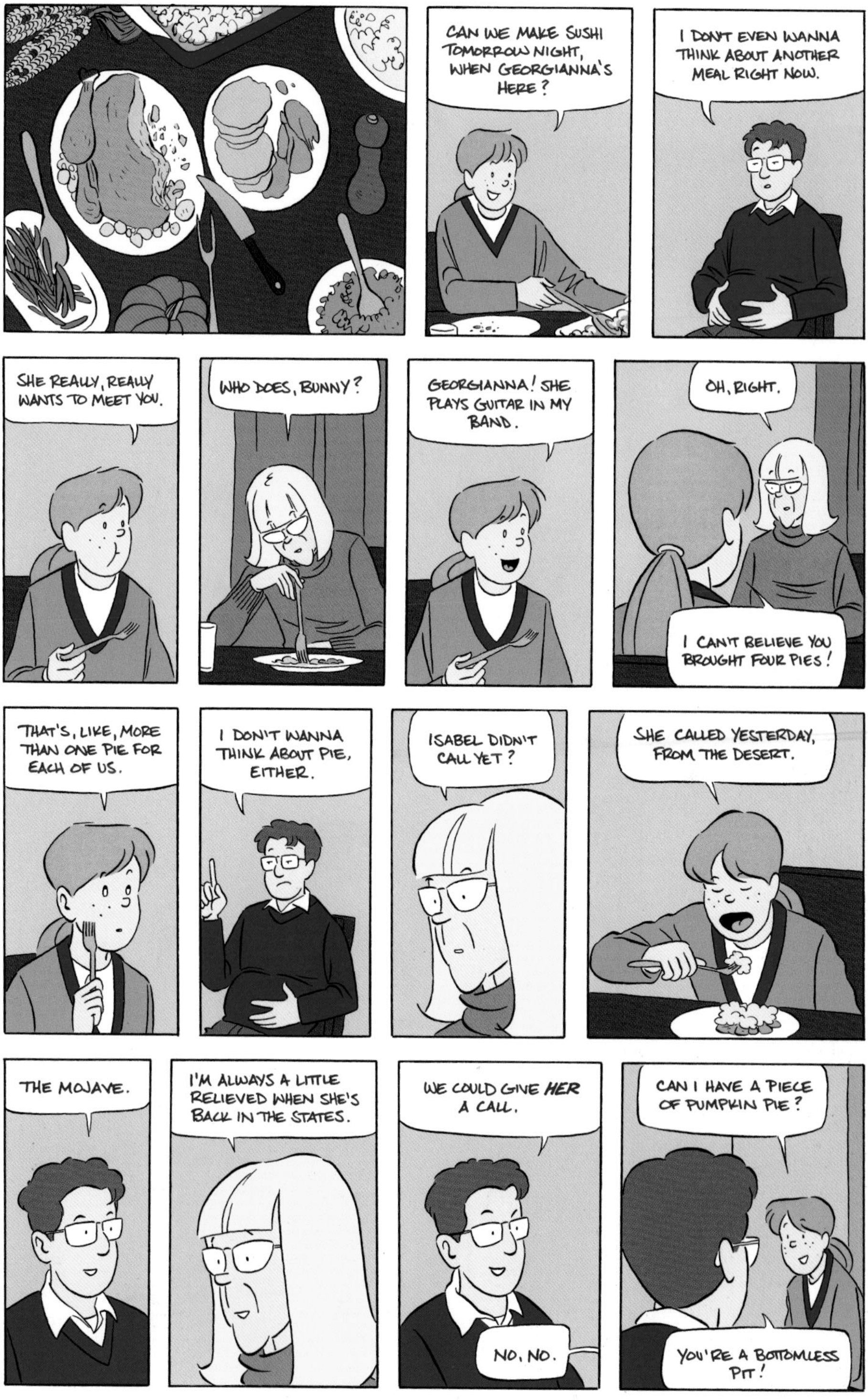
CAN WE MAKE SUSHI TOMORROW NIGHT, WHEN GEORGIANNA'S HERE?
I DON'T EVEN WANNA THINK ABOUT ANOTHER MEAL RIGHT NOW.
SHE REALLY, REALLY WANTS TO MEET YOU.
WHO DOES, BUNNY?
GEORGIANNA! SHE PLAYS GUITAR IN MY BAND.
OH, RIGHT.
I CAN'T BELIEVE YOU BROUGHT FOUR PIES!
THAT'S, LIKE, MORE THAN ONE PIE FOR EACH OF US.
I DON'T WANNA THINK ABOUT PIE, EITHER.
ISABEL DIDN'T CALL YET?
SHE CALLED YESTERDAY, FROM THE DESERT.
THE MOJAVE.
I'M ALWAYS A LITTLE RELIEVED WHEN SHE'S BACK IN THE STATES.
WE COULD GIVE *HER* A CALL.
NO, NO.
CAN I HAVE A PIECE OF PUMPKIN PIE?
YOU'RE A BOTTOMLESS PIT!

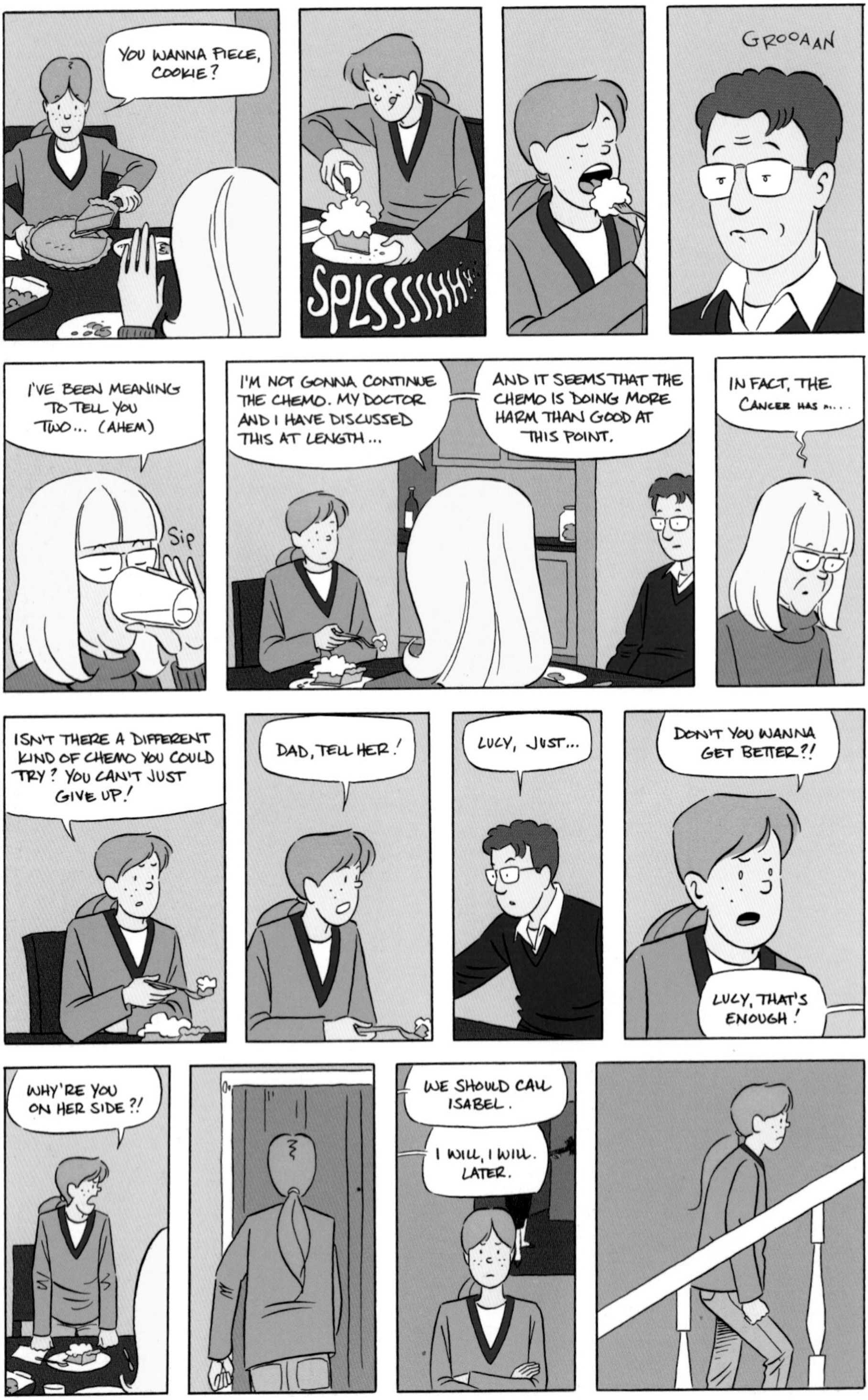
YOU WANNA PIECE, COOKIE?
SPLSSSSHH
GROOAAN
I'VE BEEN MEANING TO TELL YOU TWO... (AHEM)
SIP
I'M NOT GONNA CONTINUE THE CHEMO. MY DOCTOR AND I HAVE DISCUSSED THIS AT LENGTH...
AND IT SEEMS THAT THE CHEMO IS DOING MORE HARM THAN GOOD AT THIS POINT.
IN FACT, THE CANCER HAS...
ISN'T THERE A DIFFERENT KIND OF CHEMO YOU COULD TRY? YOU CAN'T JUST GIVE UP!
DAD, TELL HER!
LUCY, JUST...
DON'T YOU WANNA GET BETTER?!
LUCY, THAT'S ENOUGH!
WHY'RE YOU ON HER SIDE?!
WE SHOULD CALL ISABEL.
I WILL, I WILL. LATER.

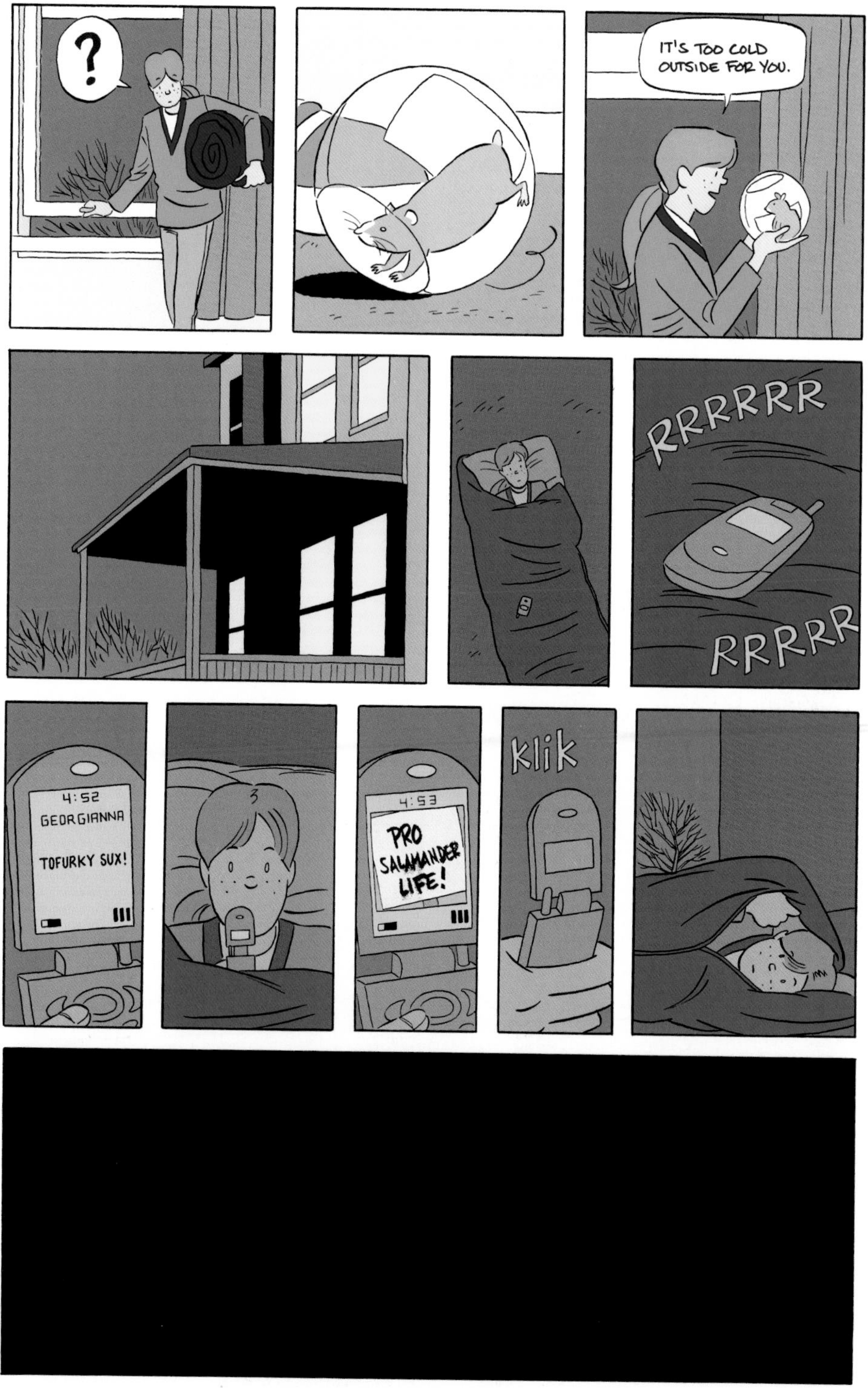
?
IT'S TOO COLD OUTSIDE FOR YOU.
RRRRRR
RRRRR
4:52
GEORGIANNA
TOFURKY SUX!
4:53
PRO SALAMANDER LIFE!
klik

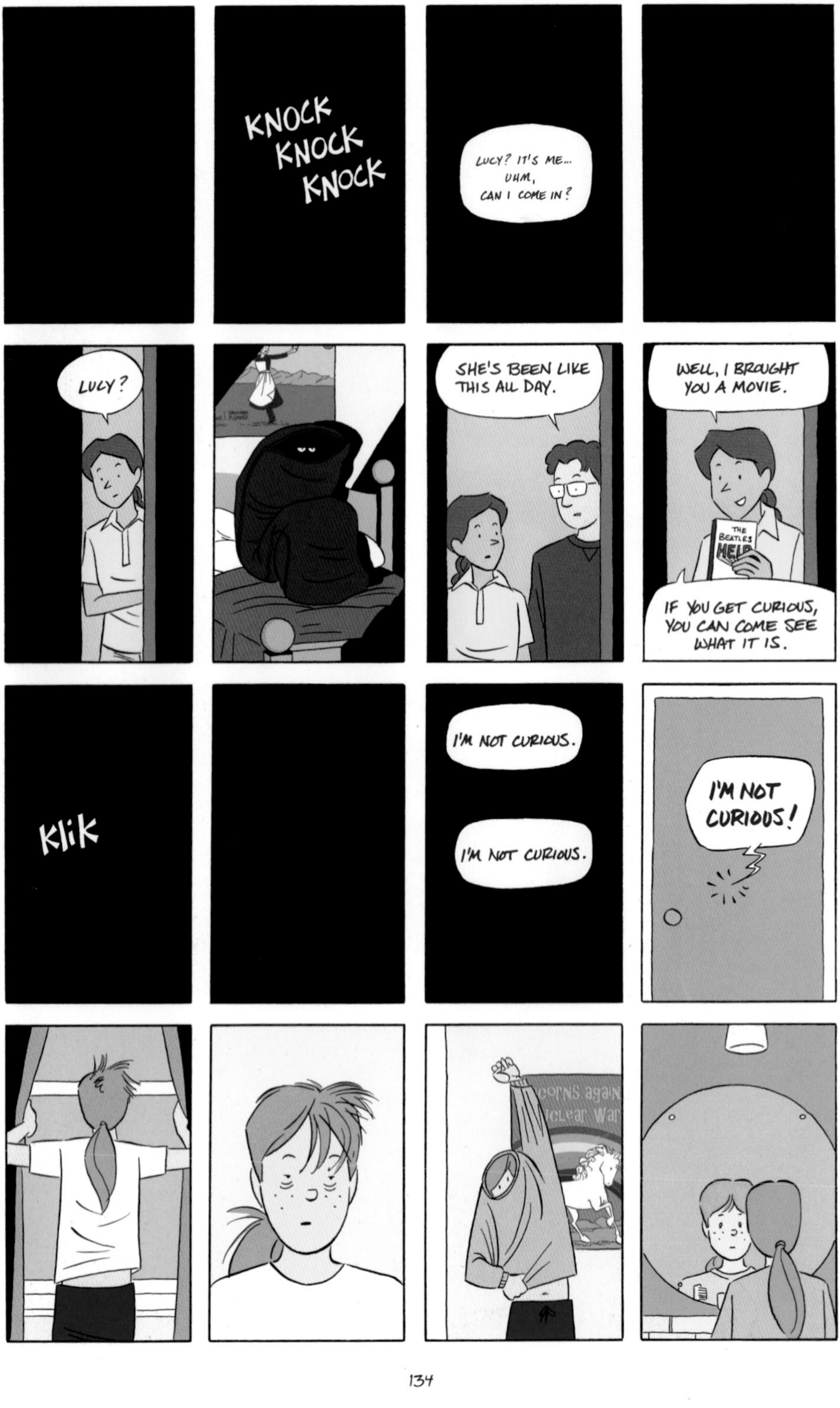
KNOCK
KNOCK
KNOCK
LUCY? IT'S ME... UHM, CAN I COME IN?
LUCY?
SHE'S BEEN LIKE THIS ALL DAY.
WELL, I BROUGHT YOU A MOVIE.
THE BEATLES HELP
IF YOU GET CURIOUS, YOU CAN COME SEE WHAT IT IS.
KLIK
I'M NOT CURIOUS.
I'M NOT CURIOUS.
I'M NOT CURIOUS!

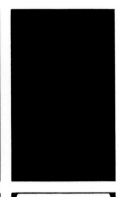

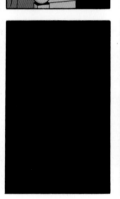

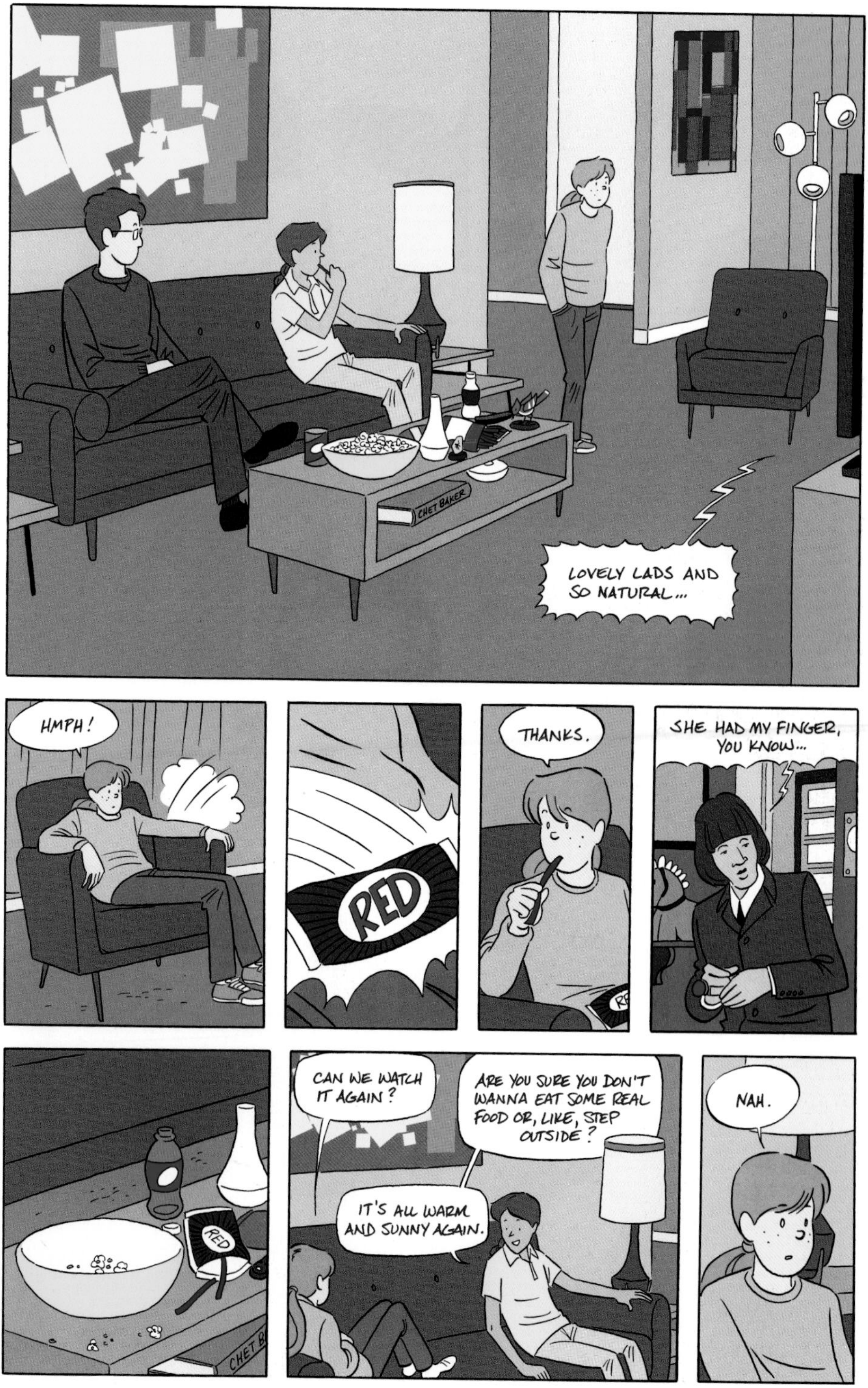
CHET BAKER
LOVELY LADS AND SO NATURAL...
HMPH!
RED
THANKS.
SHE HAD MY FINGER, YOU KNOW...
RED
CHET B
CAN WE WATCH IT AGAIN?
ARE YOU SURE YOU DON'T WANNA EAT SOME REAL FOOD OR, LIKE, STEP OUTSIDE?
IT'S ALL WARM AND SUNNY AGAIN.
NAH.

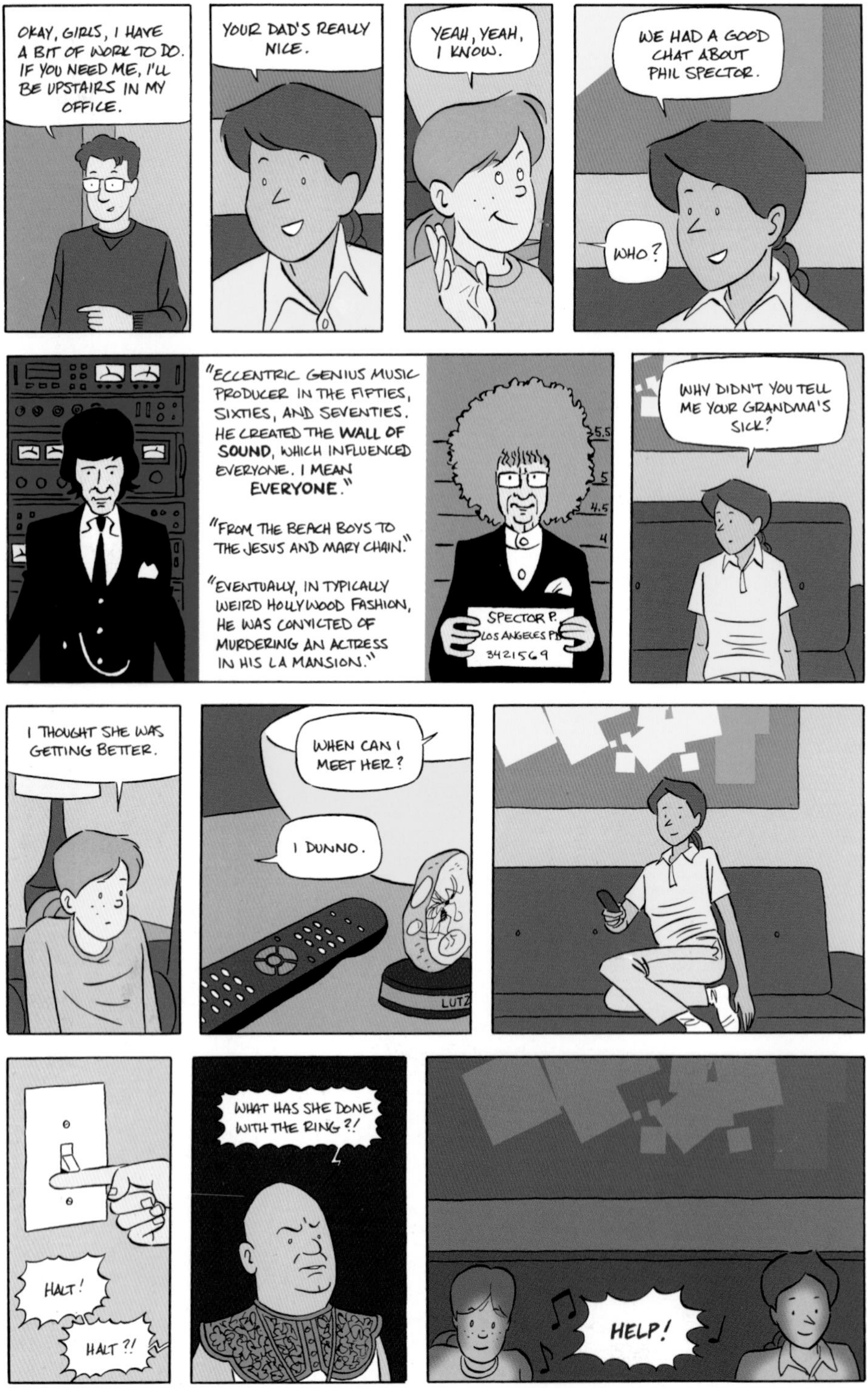
OKAY, GIRLS, I HAVE A BIT OF WORK TO DO. IF YOU NEED ME, I'LL BE UPSTAIRS IN MY OFFICE.
YOUR DAD'S REALLY NICE.
YEAH, YEAH, I KNOW.
WE HAD A GOOD CHAT ABOUT PHIL SPECTOR.
WHO?
"ECCENTRIC GENIUS MUSIC PRODUCER IN THE FIFTIES, SIXTIES, AND SEVENTIES. HE CREATED THE WALL OF SOUND, WHICH INFLUENCED EVERYONE. I MEAN EVERYONE."
"FROM THE BEACH BOYS TO THE JESUS AND MARY CHAIN."
"EVENTUALLY, IN TYPICALLY WEIRD HOLLYWOOD FASHION, HE WAS CONVICTED OF MURDERING AN ACTRESS IN HIS LA MANSION."
5.5
5
4.5
4
SPECTOR P.
LOS ANGELES PD
3421569
WHY DIDN'T YOU TELL ME YOUR GRANDMA'S SICK?
I THOUGHT SHE WAS GETTING BETTER.
WHEN CAN I MEET HER?
I DUNNO.
LUTZ
HALT!
HALT?!
WHAT HAS SHE DONE WITH THE RING?!
HELP!

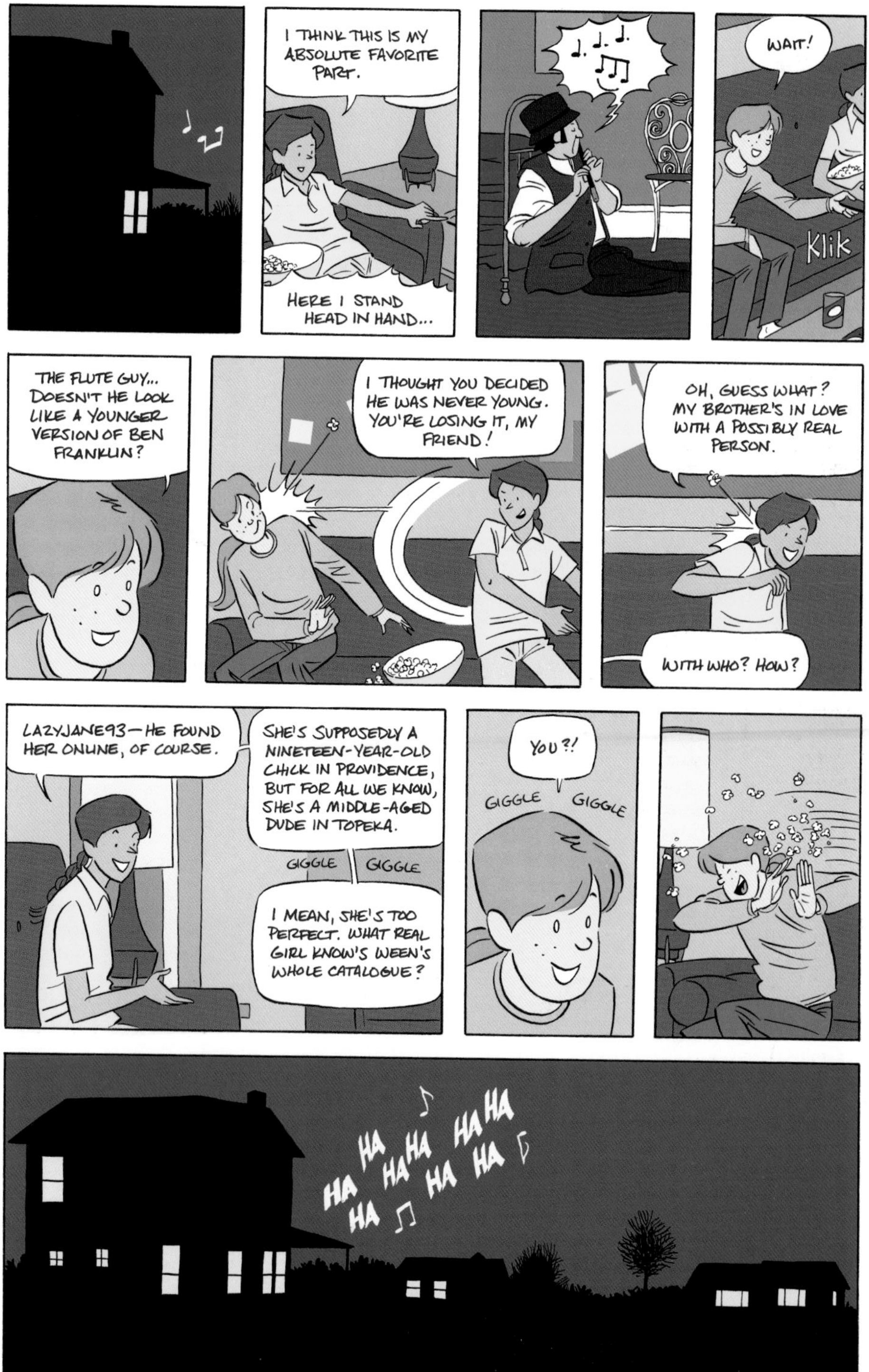
I THINK THIS IS MY ABSOLUTE FAVORITE PART.
HERE I STAND HEAD IN HAND...
WAIT!
KLIK
THE FLUTE GUY... DOESN'T HE LOOK LIKE A YOUNGER VERSION OF BEN FRANKLIN?
I THOUGHT YOU DECIDED HE WAS NEVER YOUNG. YOU'RE LOSING IT, MY FRIEND!
OH, GUESS WHAT? MY BROTHER'S IN LOVE WITH A POSSIBLY REAL PERSON.
WITH WHO? HOW?
LAZYJANE93—HE FOUND HER ONLINE, OF COURSE.
SHE'S SUPPOSEDLY A NINETEEN-YEAR-OLD CHICK IN PROVIDENCE, BUT FOR ALL WE KNOW, SHE'S A MIDDLE-AGED DUDE IN TOPEKA.
GIGGLE GIGGLE
I MEAN, SHE'S TOO PERFECT. WHAT REAL GIRL KNOW'S WEEN'S WHOLE CATALOGUE?
YOU?!
GIGGLE GIGGLE
HA HA HA HA HA HA HA HA HA HA

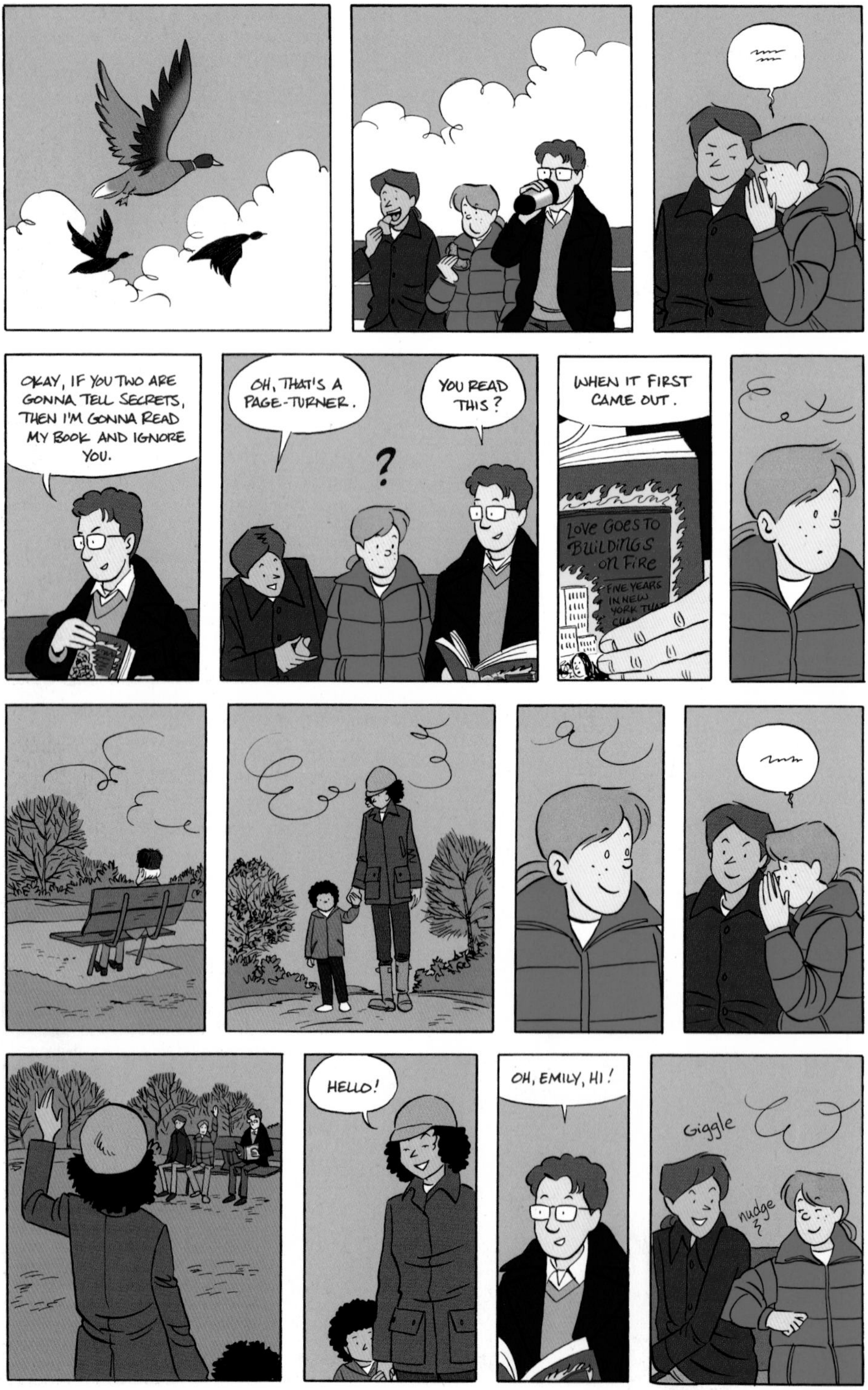
OKAY, IF YOU TWO ARE GONNA TELL SECRETS, THEN I'M GONNA READ MY BOOK AND IGNORE YOU.
OH, THAT'S A PAGE-TURNER.
?
YOU READ THIS?
WHEN IT FIRST CAME OUT.
Love Goes to Buildings on Fire
FIVE YEARS IN NEW YORK THAT
HELLO!
OH, EMILY, HI!
Giggle
nudge

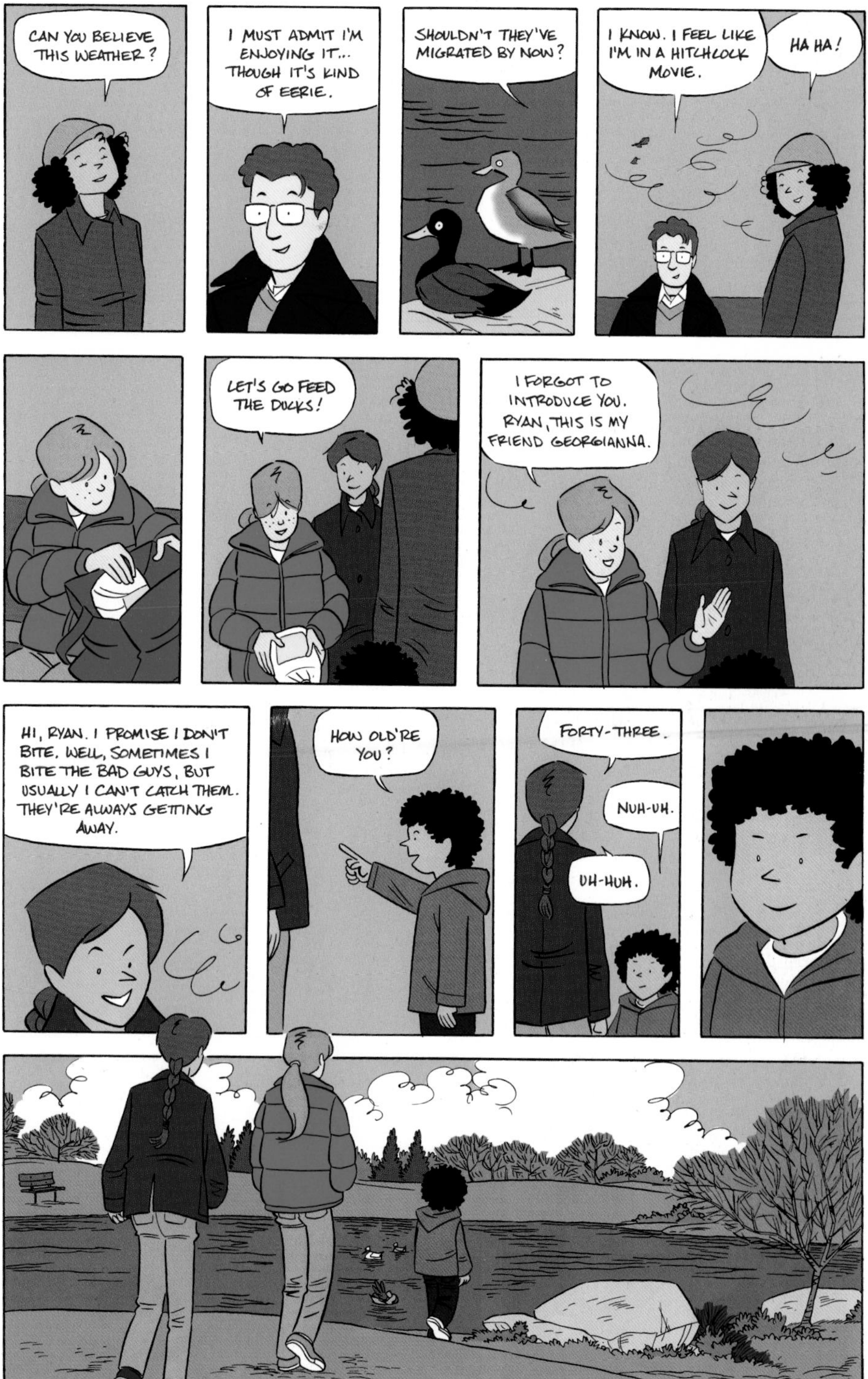
CAN YOU BELIEVE THIS WEATHER?
I MUST ADMIT I'M ENJOYING IT... THOUGH IT'S KIND OF EERIE.
SHOULDN'T THEY'VE MIGRATED BY NOW?
I KNOW. I FEEL LIKE I'M IN A HITCHCOCK MOVIE.
HA HA!
LET'S GO FEED THE DUCKS!
I FORGOT TO INTRODUCE YOU. RYAN, THIS IS MY FRIEND GEORGIANNA.
HI, RYAN. I PROMISE I DON'T BITE. WELL, SOMETIMES I BITE THE BAD GUYS, BUT USUALLY I CAN'T CATCH THEM. THEY'RE ALWAYS GETTING AWAY.
HOW OLD'RE YOU?
FORTY-THREE.
NUH-UH.
UH-HUH.

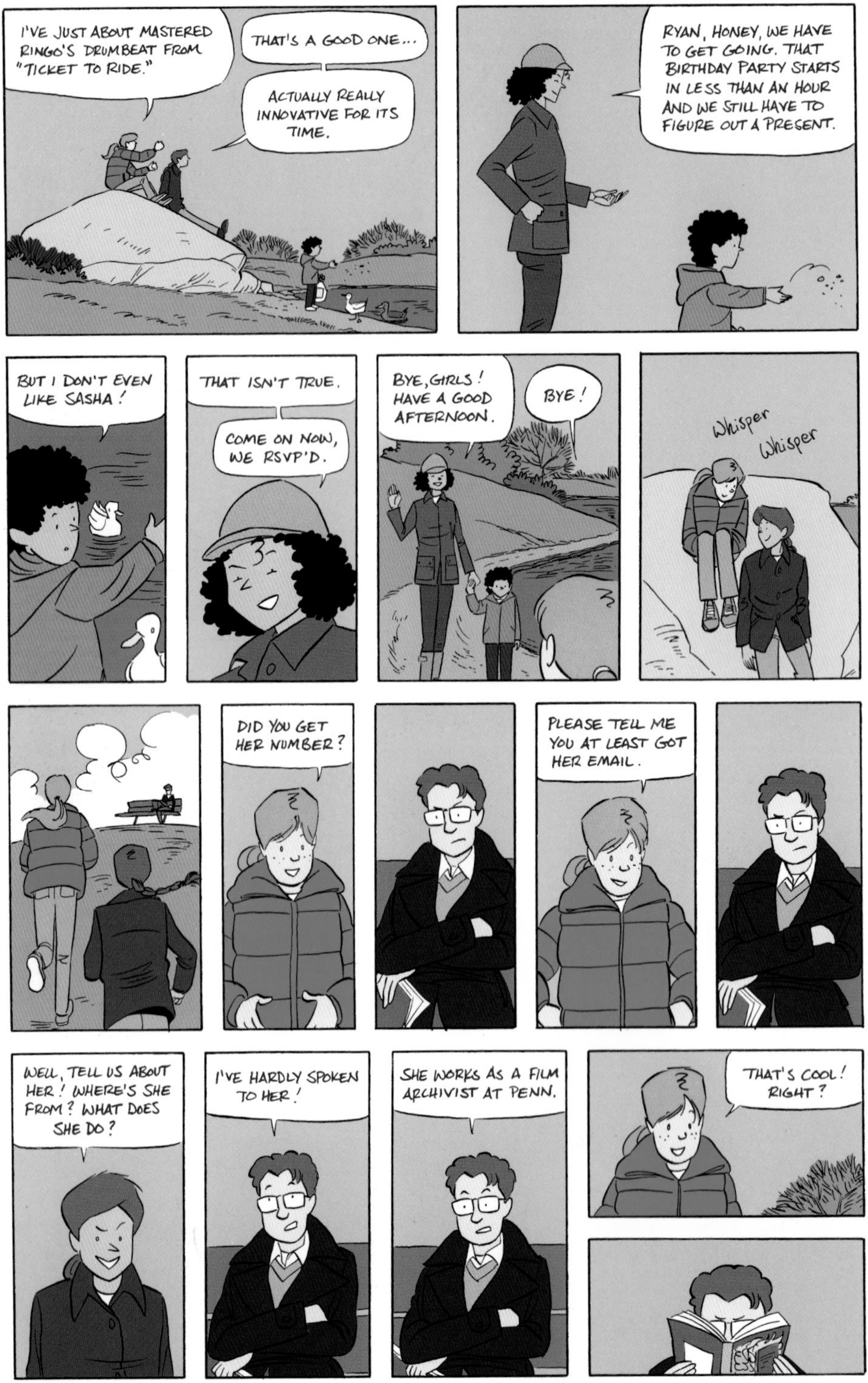
I'VE JUST ABOUT MASTERED RINGO'S DRUMBEAT FROM "TICKET TO RIDE."
THAT'S A GOOD ONE...
ACTUALLY REALLY INNOVATIVE FOR ITS TIME.
RYAN, HONEY, WE HAVE TO GET GOING. THAT BIRTHDAY PARTY STARTS IN LESS THAN AN HOUR AND WE STILL HAVE TO FIGURE OUT A PRESENT.
BUT I DON'T EVEN LIKE SASHA!
THAT ISN'T TRUE.
COME ON NOW, WE RSVP'D.
BYE, GIRLS! HAVE A GOOD AFTERNOON.
BYE!
Whisper
Whisper
DID YOU GET HER NUMBER?
PLEASE TELL ME YOU AT LEAST GOT HER EMAIL.
WELL, TELL US ABOUT HER! WHERE'S SHE FROM? WHAT DOES SHE DO?
I'VE HARDLY SPOKEN TO HER!
SHE WORKS AS A FILM ARCHIVIST AT PENN.
THAT'S COOL! RIGHT?

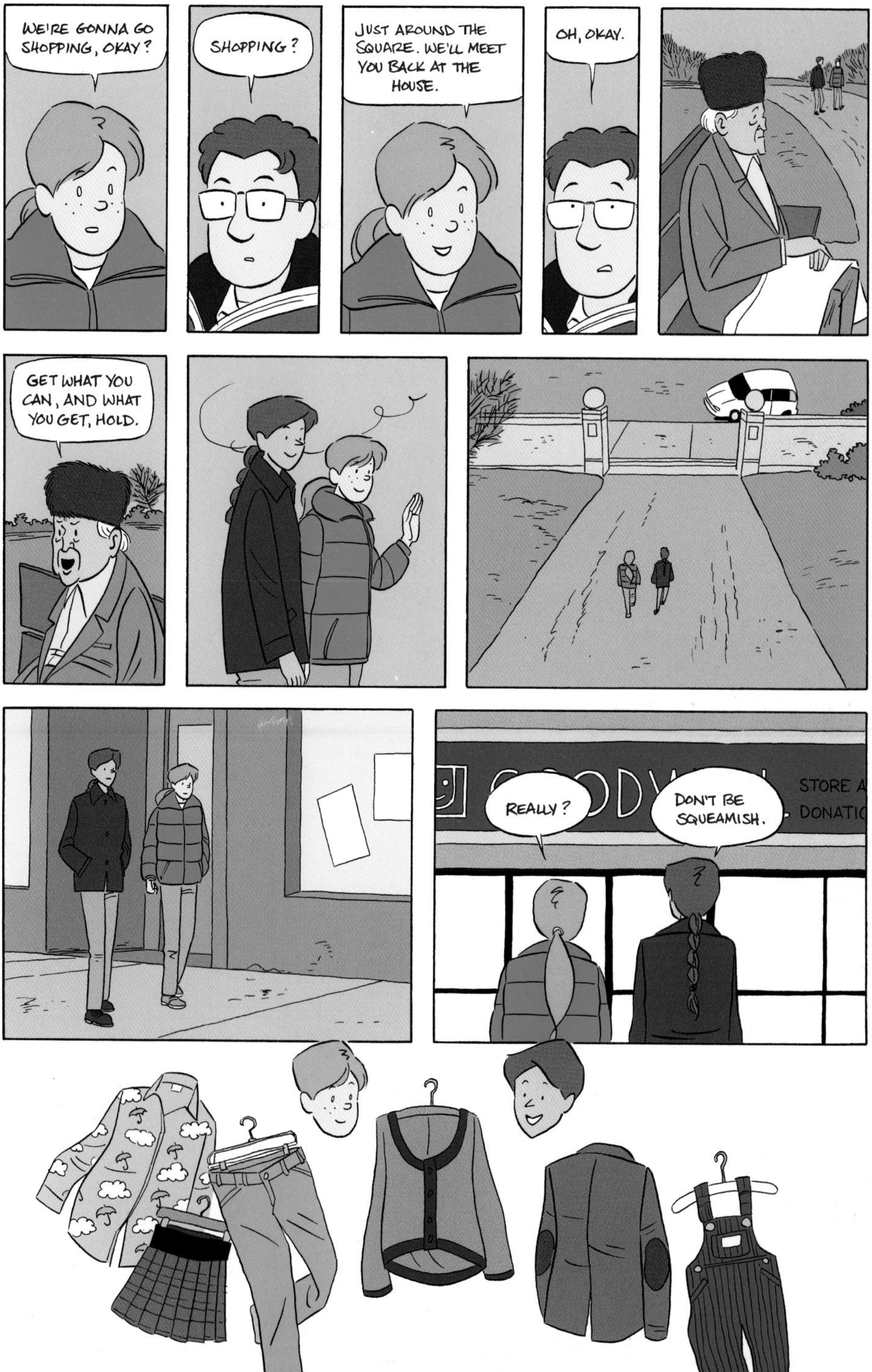
WE'RE GONNA GO SHOPPING, OKAY?
SHOPPING?
JUST AROUND THE SQUARE. WE'LL MEET YOU BACK AT THE HOUSE.
OH, OKAY.
GET WHAT YOU CAN, AND WHAT YOU GET, HOLD.
REALLY?
DON'T BE SQUEAMISH.

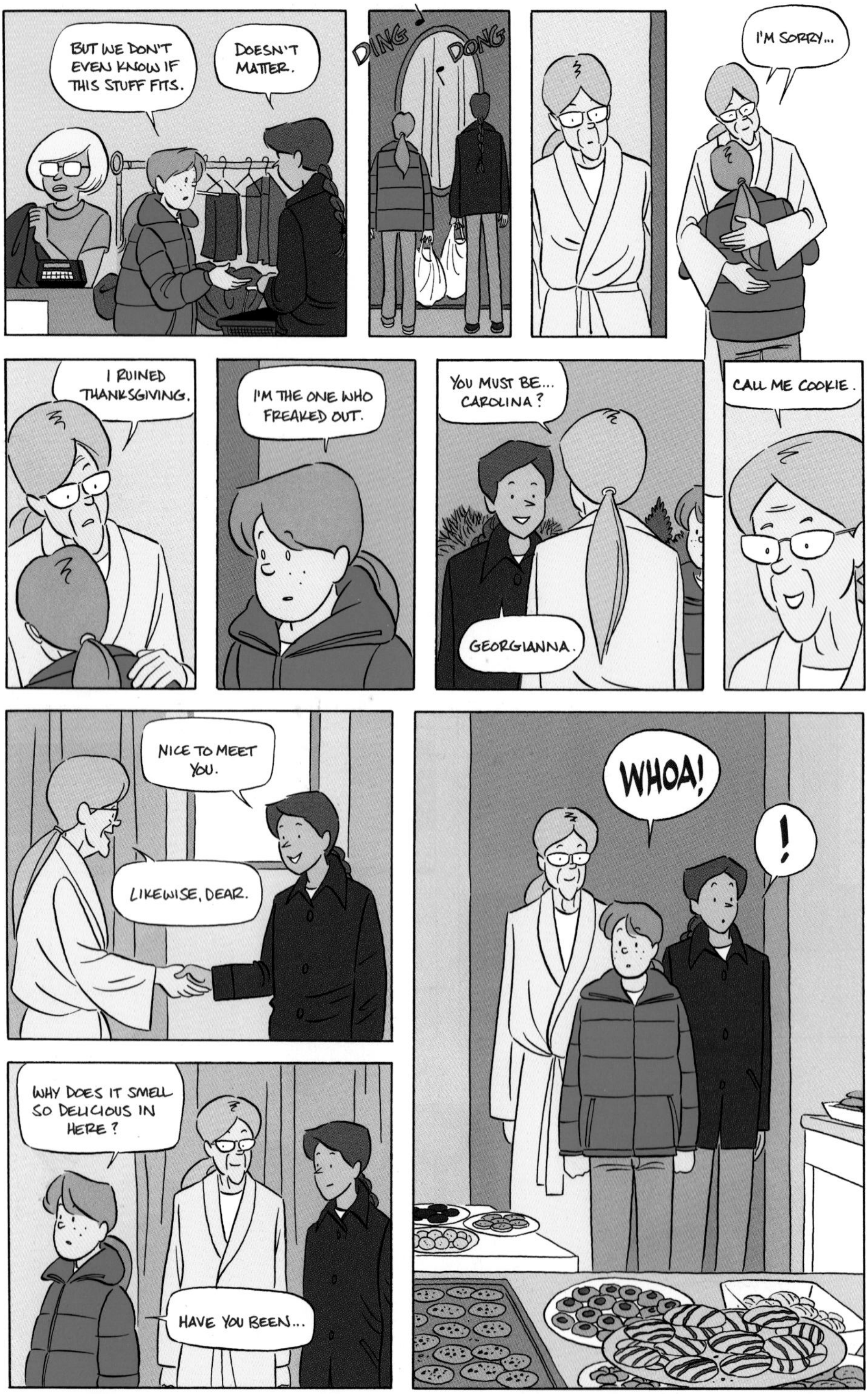
BUT WE DON'T EVEN KNOW IF THIS STUFF FITS.
DOESN'T MATTER.
DING DONG
I'M SORRY...
I RUINED THANKSGIVING.
I'M THE ONE WHO FREAKED OUT.
YOU MUST BE... CAROLINA?
GEORGIANNA.
CALL ME COOKIE.
NICE TO MEET YOU.
LIKEWISE, DEAR.
WHY DOES IT SMELL SO DELICIOUS IN HERE?
HAVE YOU BEEN...
WHOA!
!

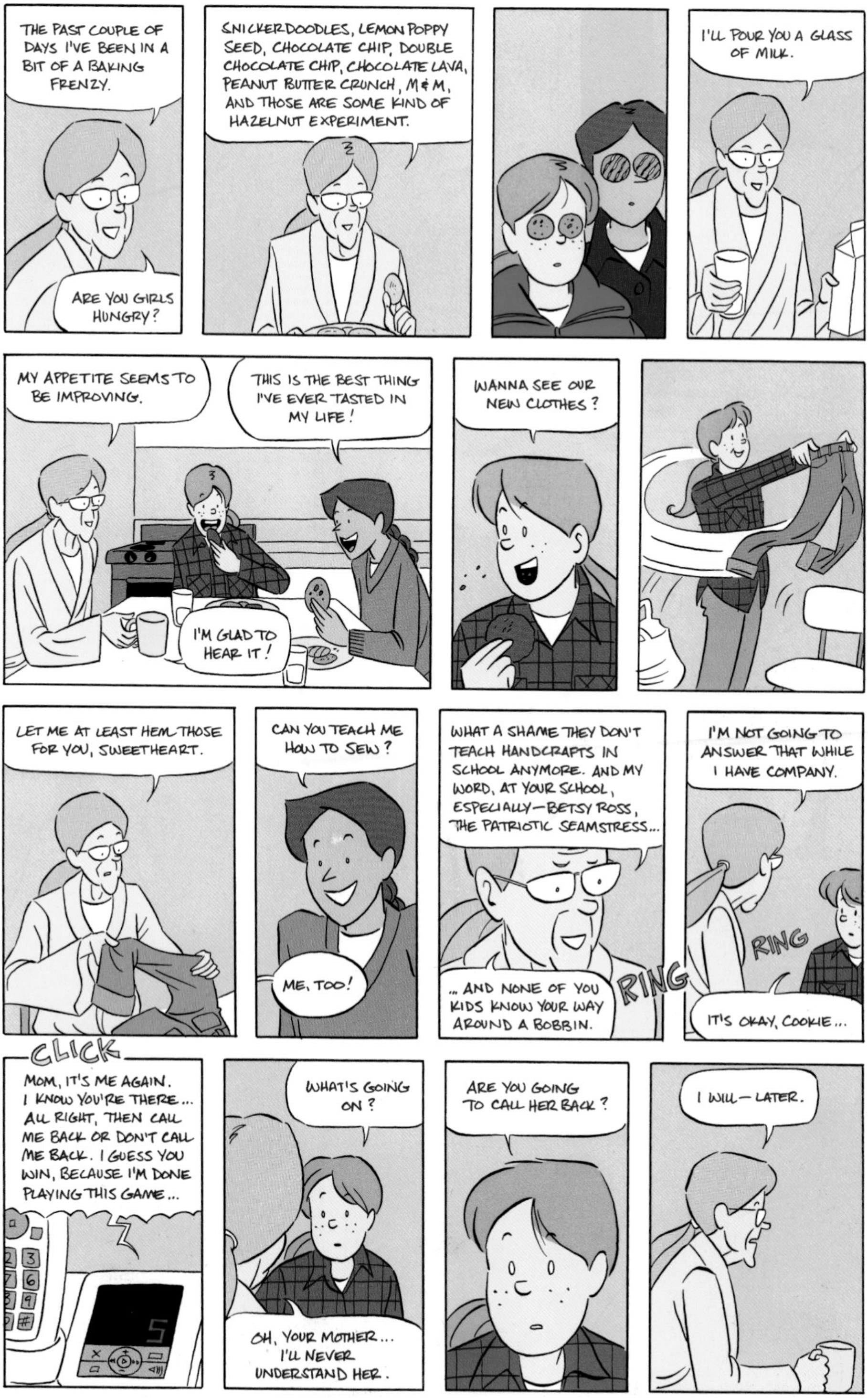
THE PAST COUPLE OF DAYS I'VE BEEN IN A BIT OF A BAKING FRENZY.
ARE YOU GIRLS HUNGRY?
SNICKERDOODLES, LEMON POPPY SEED, CHOCOLATE CHIP, DOUBLE CHOCOLATE CHIP, CHOCOLATE LAVA, PEANUT BUTTER CRUNCH, M&M, AND THOSE ARE SOME KIND OF HAZELNUT EXPERIMENT.
I'LL POUR YOU A GLASS OF MILK.
MY APPETITE SEEMS TO BE IMPROVING.
THIS IS THE BEST THING I'VE EVER TASTED IN MY LIFE!
I'M GLAD TO HEAR IT!
WANNA SEE OUR NEW CLOTHES?
LET ME AT LEAST HEM THOSE FOR YOU, SWEETHEART.
CAN YOU TEACH ME HOW TO SEW?
ME, TOO!
WHAT A SHAME THEY DON'T TEACH HANDCRAFTS IN SCHOOL ANYMORE. AND MY WORD, AT YOUR SCHOOL, ESPECIALLY—BETSY ROSS, THE PATRIOTIC SEAMSTRESS...
... AND NONE OF YOU KIDS KNOW YOUR WAY AROUND A BOBBIN.
RING
I'M NOT GOING TO ANSWER THAT WHILE I HAVE COMPANY.
RING
IT'S OKAY, COOKIE...
CLICK
MOM, IT'S ME AGAIN. I KNOW YOU'RE THERE... ALL RIGHT, THEN CALL ME BACK OR DON'T CALL ME BACK. I GUESS YOU WIN, BECAUSE I'M DONE PLAYING THIS GAME...
5
WHAT'S GOING ON?
OH, YOUR MOTHER... I'LL NEVER UNDERSTAND HER.
ARE YOU GOING TO CALL HER BACK?
I WILL—LATER.

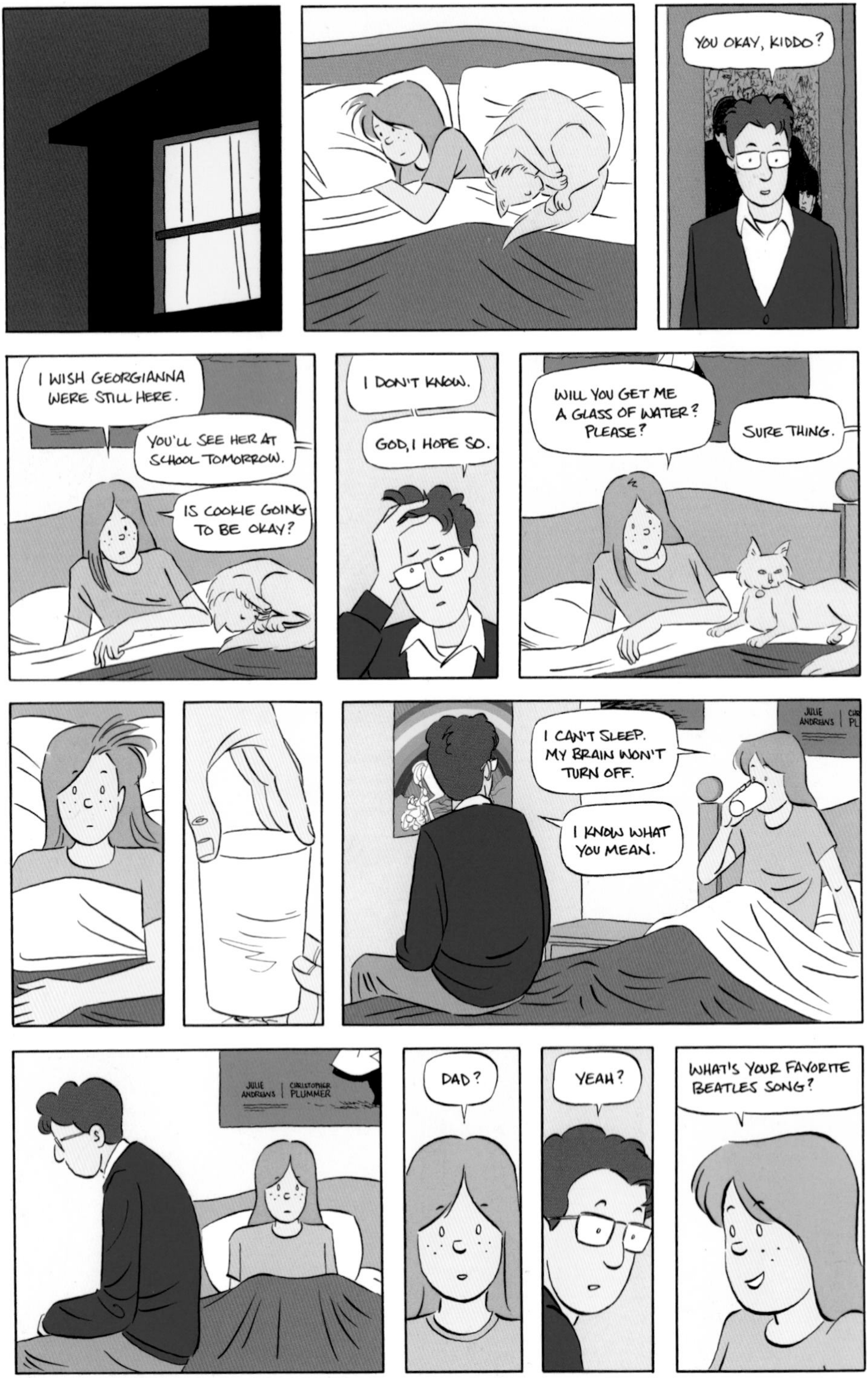
YOU OKAY, KIDDO?
I WISH GEORGIANNA WERE STILL HERE.
YOU'LL SEE HER AT SCHOOL TOMORROW.
IS COOKIE GOING TO BE OKAY?
I DON'T KNOW.
GOD, I HOPE SO.
WILL YOU GET ME A GLASS OF WATER? PLEASE?
SURE THING.
I CAN'T SLEEP. MY BRAIN WON'T TURN OFF.
I KNOW WHAT YOU MEAN.
JULIE ANDREWS
CHRISTOPHER PLUMMER
DAD?
YEAH?
WHAT'S YOUR FAVORITE BEATLES SONG?

OH, GOOD, ANOTHER QUESTION I CAN'T ANSWER.

WHY NOT?

BECAUSE MY FAVORITE SONG PROBABLY CHANGES EVERY DAY, EVERY MINUTE, ALL DEPENDING ON MY MOOD.

WELL, WHAT'S YOUR FAVORITE SONG RIGHT NOW, THIS VERY SECOND?

HANG ON...

YAWN

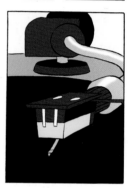

I ONCE HAD A GIRL...

THIS SONG MAKES ME FEEL LIKE WALKING AROUND BAREFOOT AND GROWING A BEARD.

YOU ALREADY HAVE A BEARD, MR. FUZZHEAD.

MRROW

THAT'S A SITAR, RIGHT?

DOES THIS RING MEAN ANYTHING TO YOU?

UH HUH.

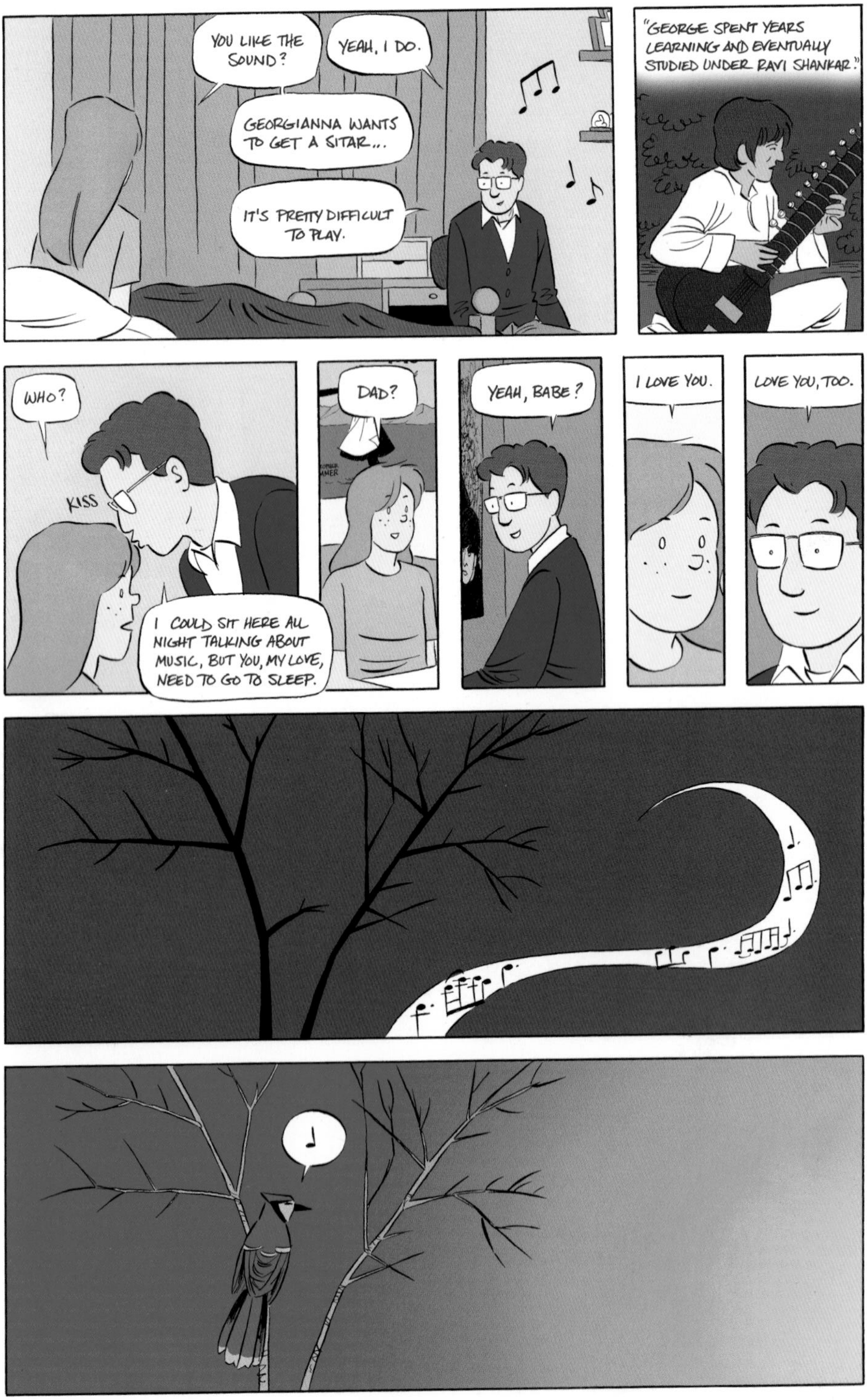
YOU LIKE THE SOUND?
YEAH, I DO.
GEORGIANNA WANTS TO GET A SITAR...
IT'S PRETTY DIFFICULT TO PLAY.
"GEORGE SPENT YEARS LEARNING AND EVENTUALLY STUDIED UNDER RAVI SHANKAR."
WHO?
KISS
I COULD SIT HERE ALL NIGHT TALKING ABOUT MUSIC, BUT YOU, MY LOVE, NEED TO GO TO SLEEP.
DAD?
YEAH, BABE?
I LOVE YOU.
LOVE YOU, TOO.

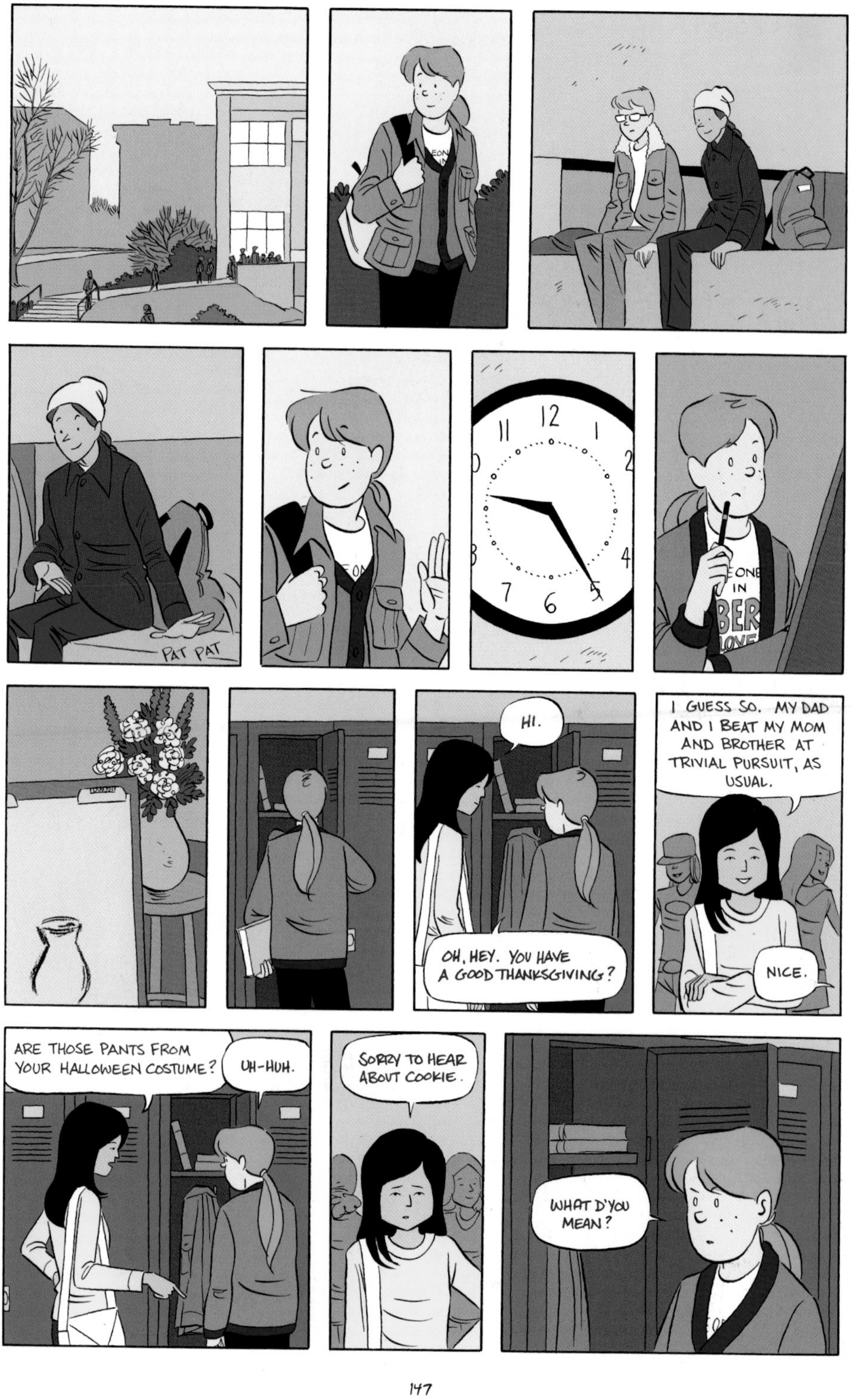
PAT PAT
HI.
OH, HEY. YOU HAVE A GOOD THANKSGIVING?
I GUESS SO. MY DAD AND I BEAT MY MOM AND BROTHER AT TRIVIAL PURSUIT, AS USUAL.
NICE.
ARE THOSE PANTS FROM YOUR HALLOWEEN COSTUME?
UH-HUH.
SORRY TO HEAR ABOUT COOKIE.
WHAT D'YOU MEAN?

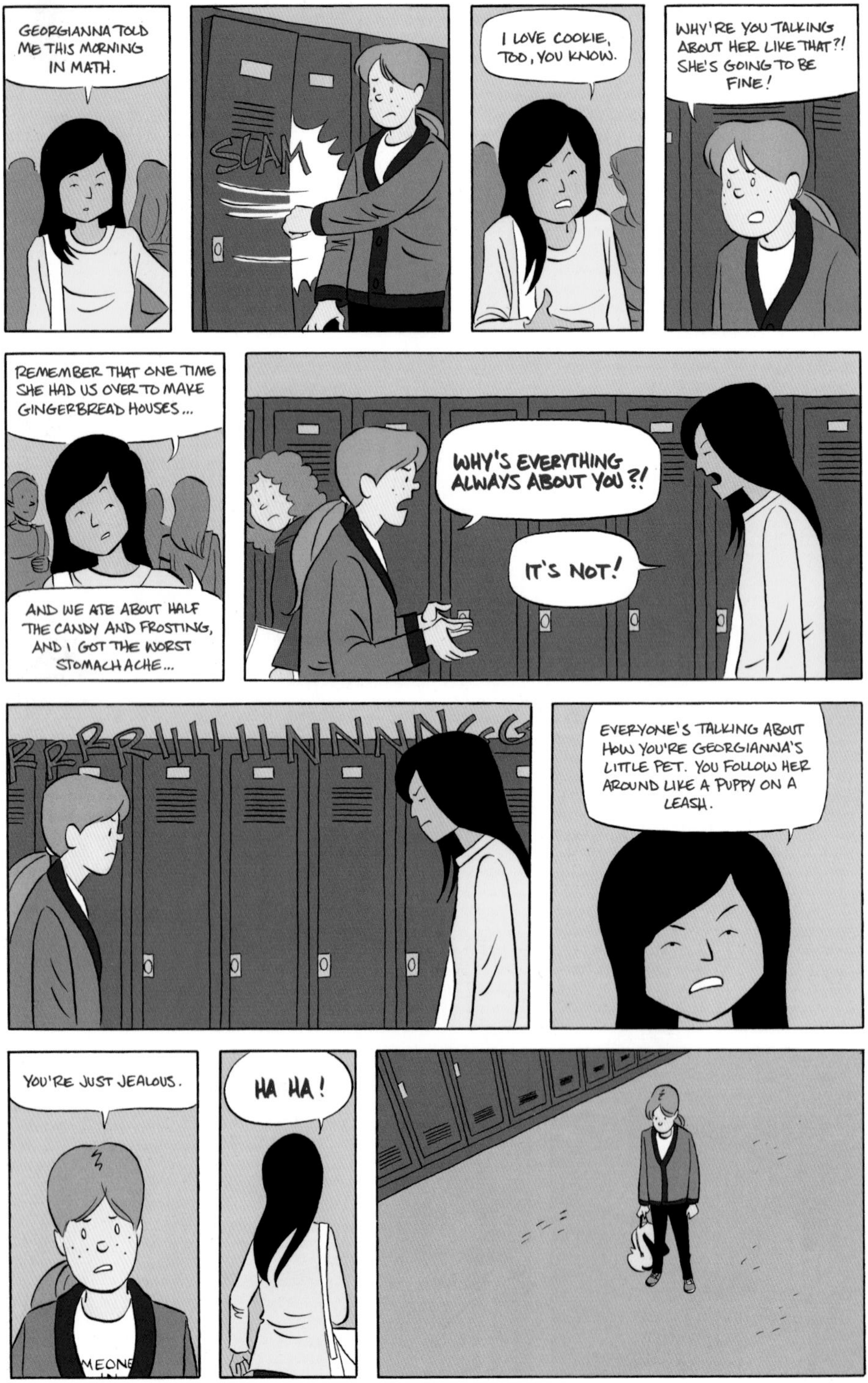
GEORGIANNA TOLD ME THIS MORNING IN MATH.
SLAM
I LOVE COOKIE, TOO, YOU KNOW.
WHY'RE YOU TALKING ABOUT HER LIKE THAT?! SHE'S GOING TO BE FINE!
REMEMBER THAT ONE TIME SHE HAD US OVER TO MAKE GINGERBREAD HOUSES...
AND WE ATE ABOUT HALF THE CANDY AND FROSTING, AND I GOT THE WORST STOMACHACHE...
WHY'S EVERYTHING ALWAYS ABOUT YOU?!
IT'S NOT!
RRRRIIIIIINNNNNGG
EVERYONE'S TALKING ABOUT HOW YOU'RE GEORGIANNA'S LITTLE PET. YOU FOLLOW HER AROUND LIKE A PUPPY ON A LEASH.
YOU'RE JUST JEALOUS.
HA HA!

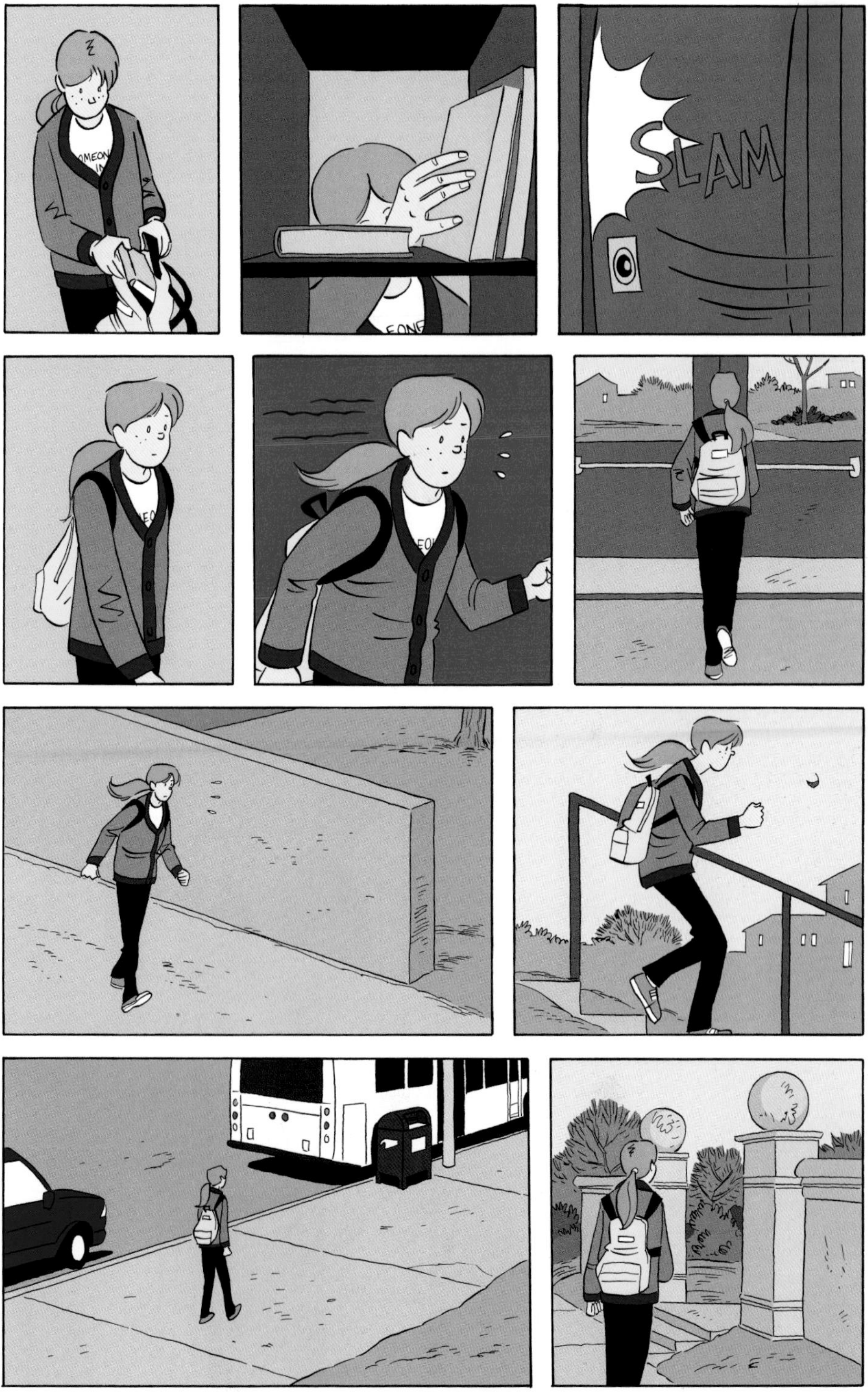
SLAM

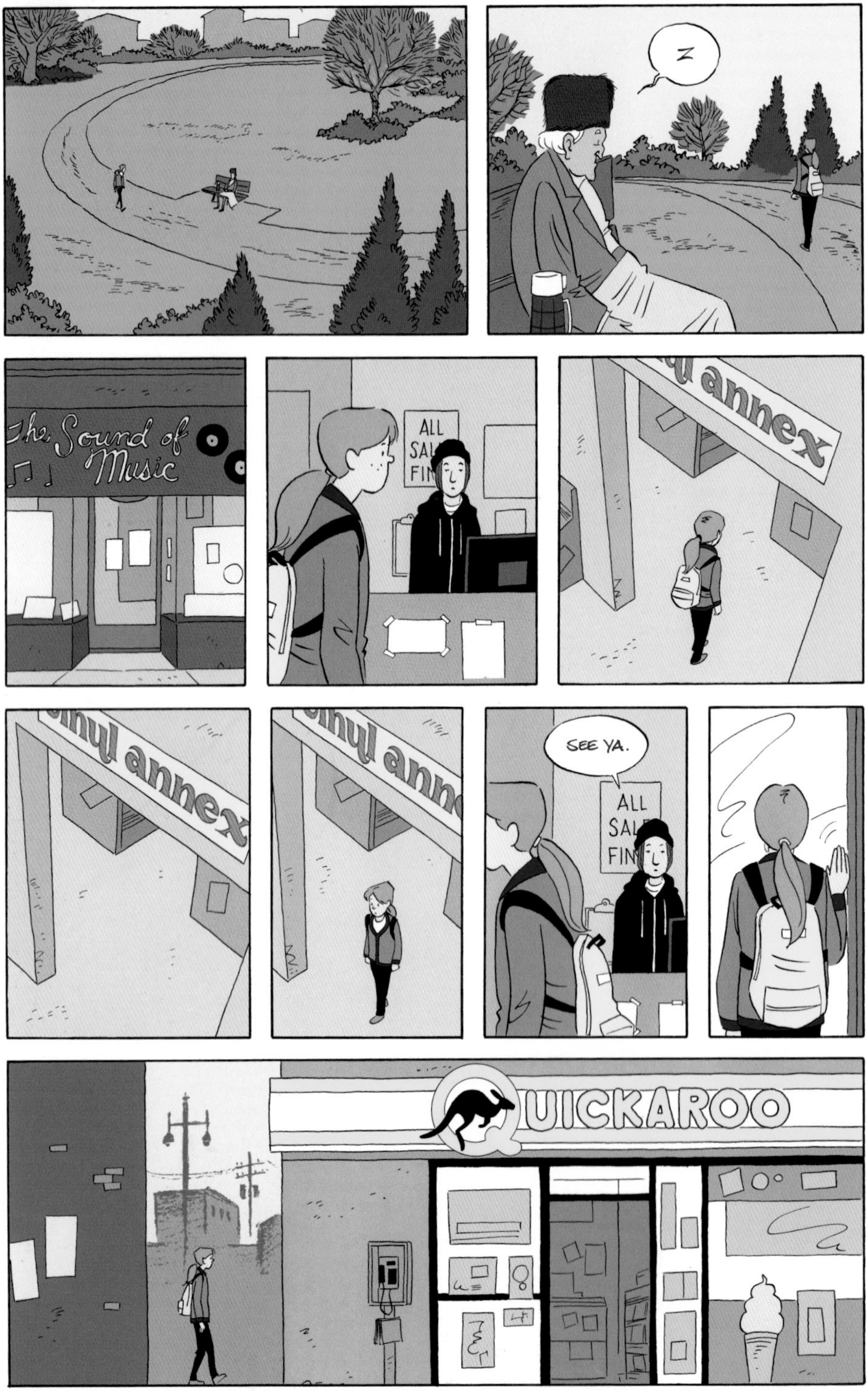
Z
The Sound of Music
ALL SALE FIN
...nyl annex
...nyl annex
...nyl annex
SEE YA.
ALL SALE FIN
QUICKAROO

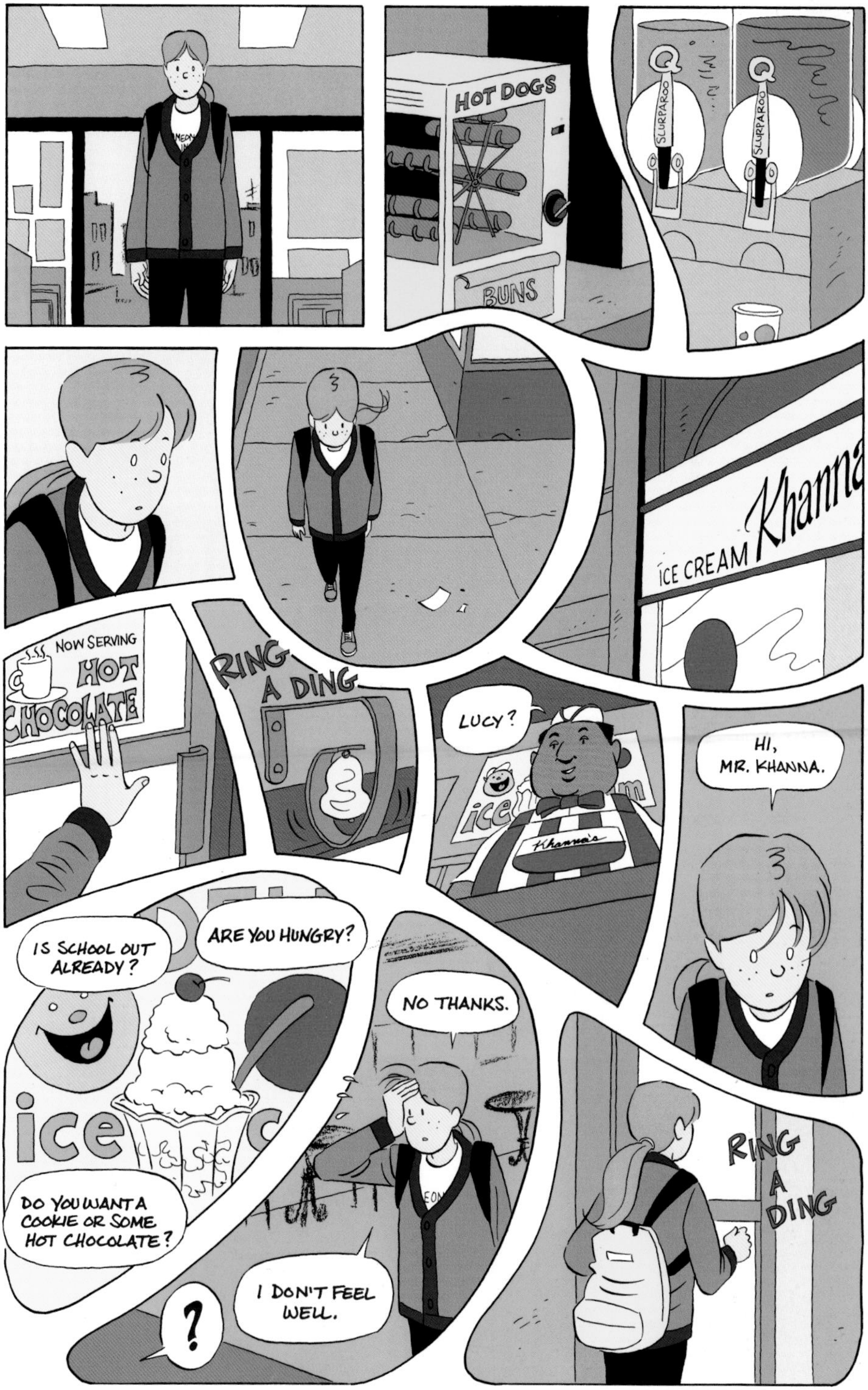
HOT DOGS
BUNS
SLURPAROO
SLURPAROO
ICE CREAM Khanna
NOW SERVING HOT CHOCOLATE
RING A DING
LUCY?
Khanna's
HI, MR. KHANNA.
IS SCHOOL OUT ALREADY?
ARE YOU HUNGRY?
DO YOU WANT A COOKIE OR SOME HOT CHOCOLATE?
NO THANKS.
?
I DON'T FEEL WELL.
RING A DING

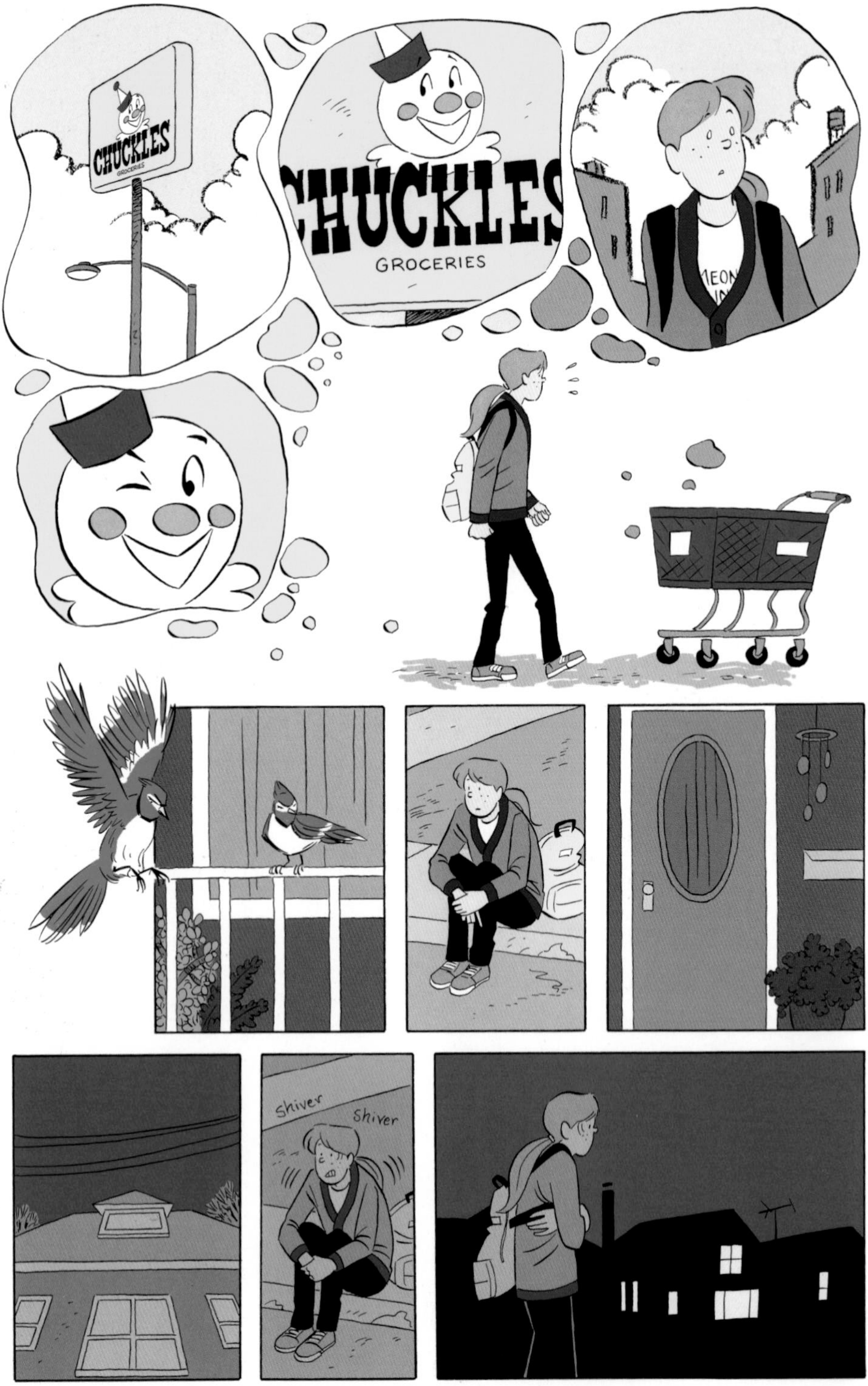
CHUCKLES
GROCERIES
CHUCKLES
GROCERIES
Shiver
Shiver

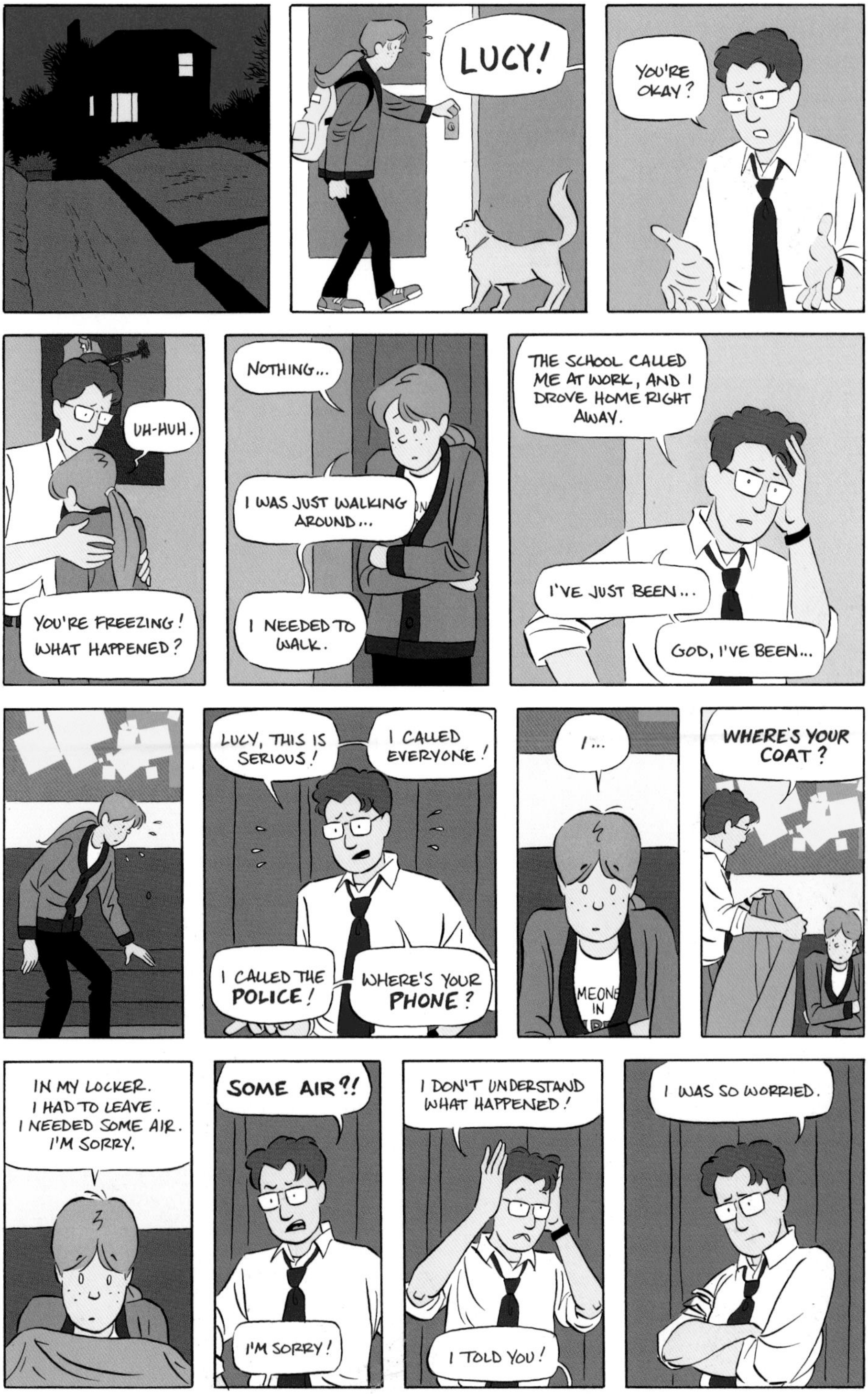
LUCY!
YOU'RE OKAY?
UH-HUH.
YOU'RE FREEZING! WHAT HAPPENED?
NOTHING...
I WAS JUST WALKING AROUND...
I NEEDED TO WALK.
THE SCHOOL CALLED ME AT WORK, AND I DROVE HOME RIGHT AWAY.
I'VE JUST BEEN...
GOD, I'VE BEEN...
LUCY, THIS IS SERIOUS!
I CALLED EVERYONE!
I CALLED THE POLICE!
WHERE'S YOUR PHONE?
I...
WHERE'S YOUR COAT?
IN MY LOCKER. I HAD TO LEAVE. I NEEDED SOME AIR. I'M SORRY.
SOME AIR?!
I'M SORRY!
I DON'T UNDERSTAND WHAT HAPPENED!
I TOLD YOU!
I WAS SO WORRIED.

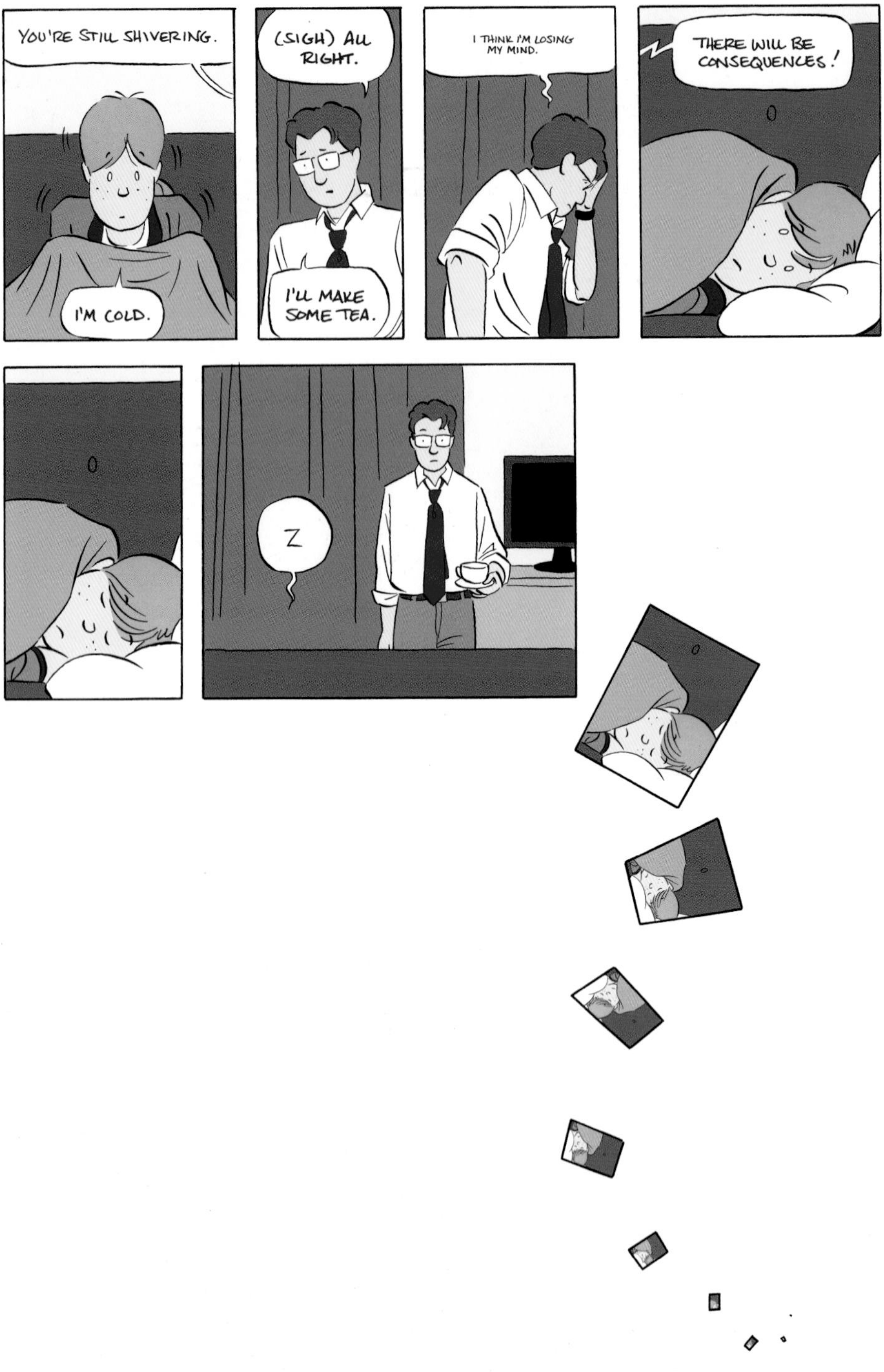
YOU'RE STILL SHIVERING.
I'M COLD.
(SIGH) ALL RIGHT.
I'LL MAKE SOME TEA.
I THINK I'M LOSING MY MIND.
THERE WILL BE CONSEQUENCES!
Z

ALL SALES FINAL

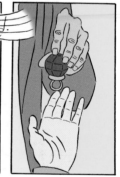

YOU MUST LET ME SLEEP NOW FOR THE WINTER.

WHERE YOU GOING?

TO MY NEST.

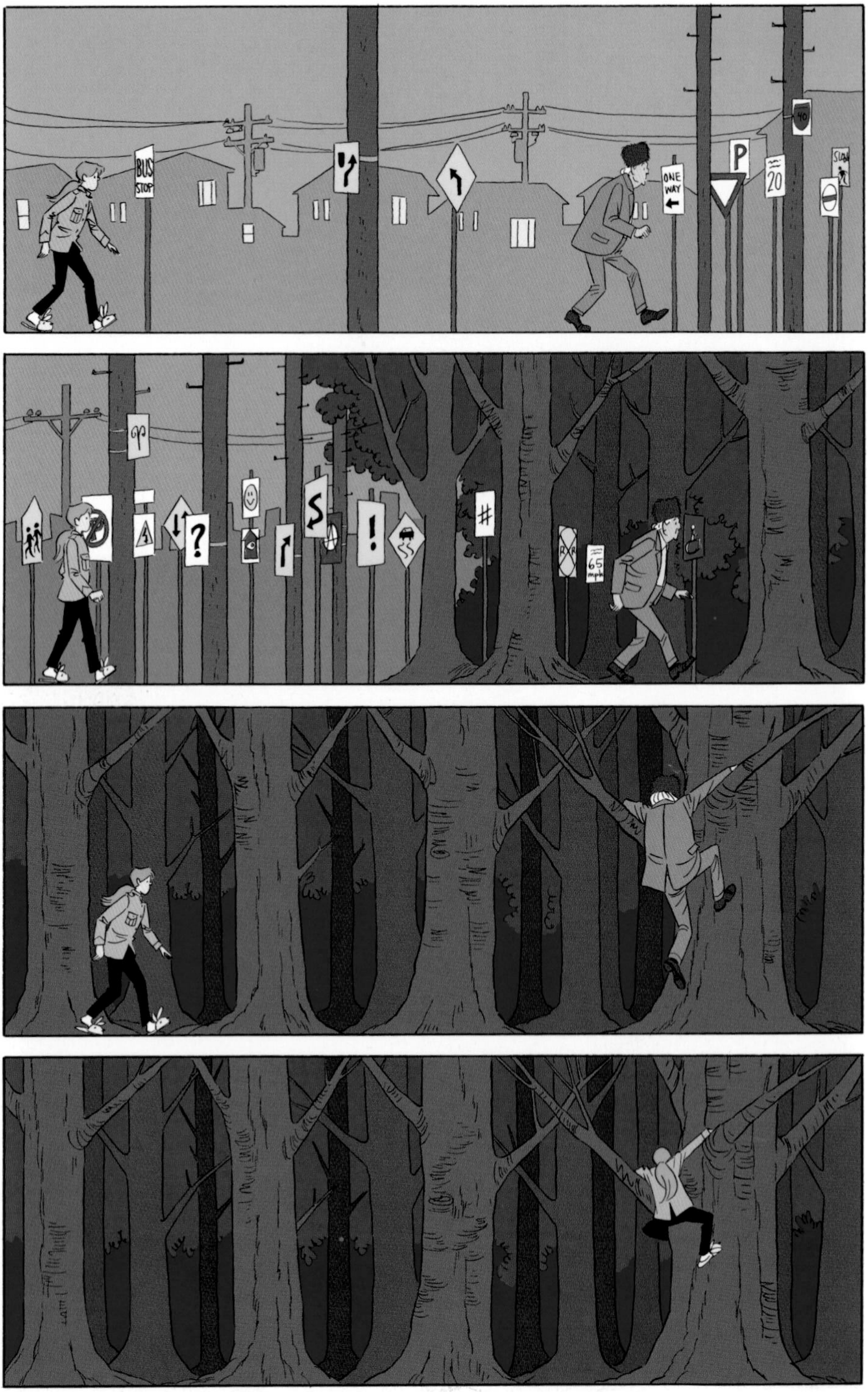
BUS STOP
ONE WAY
P
20
40
SLOW
?
S
!
#
65 mph

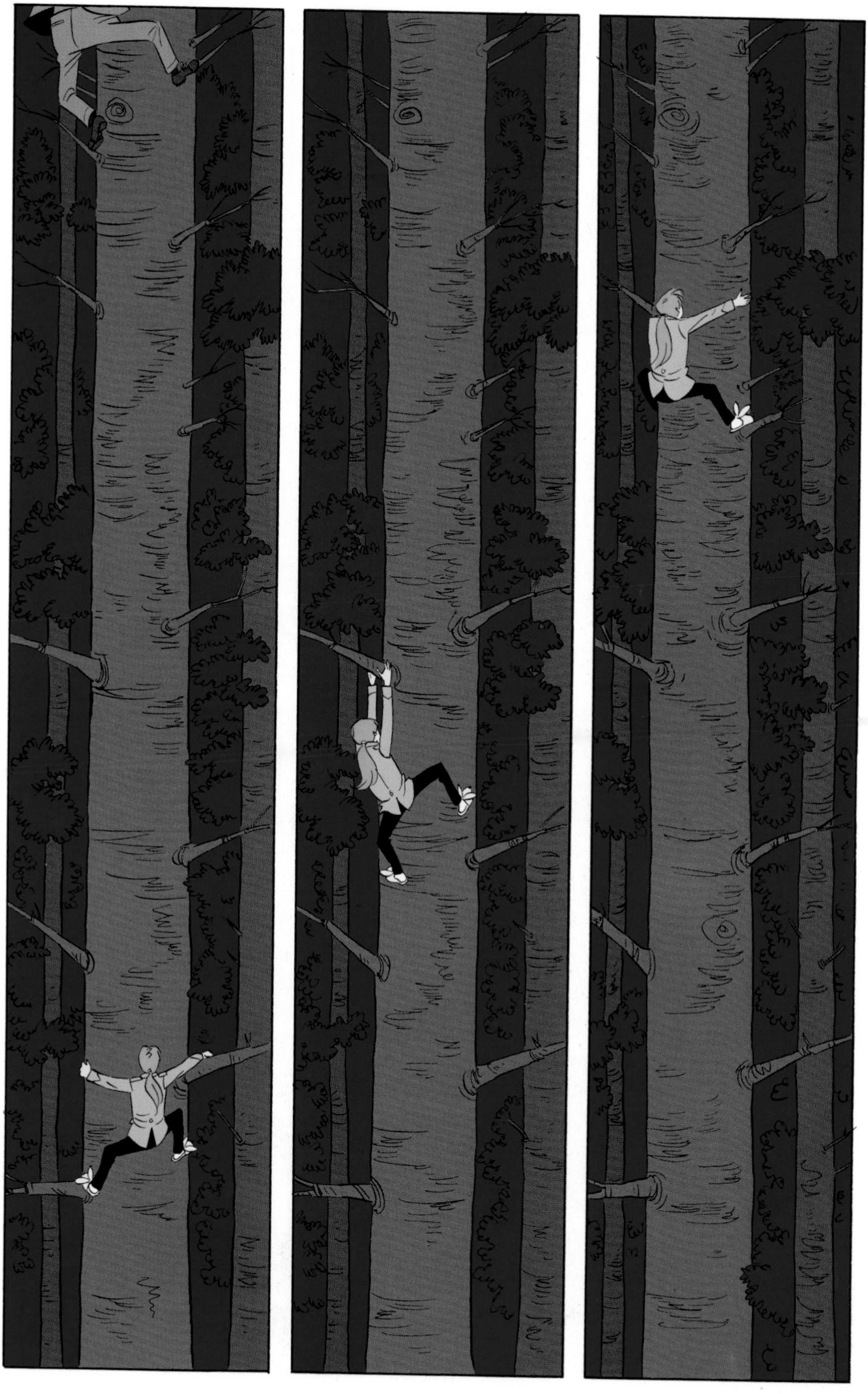

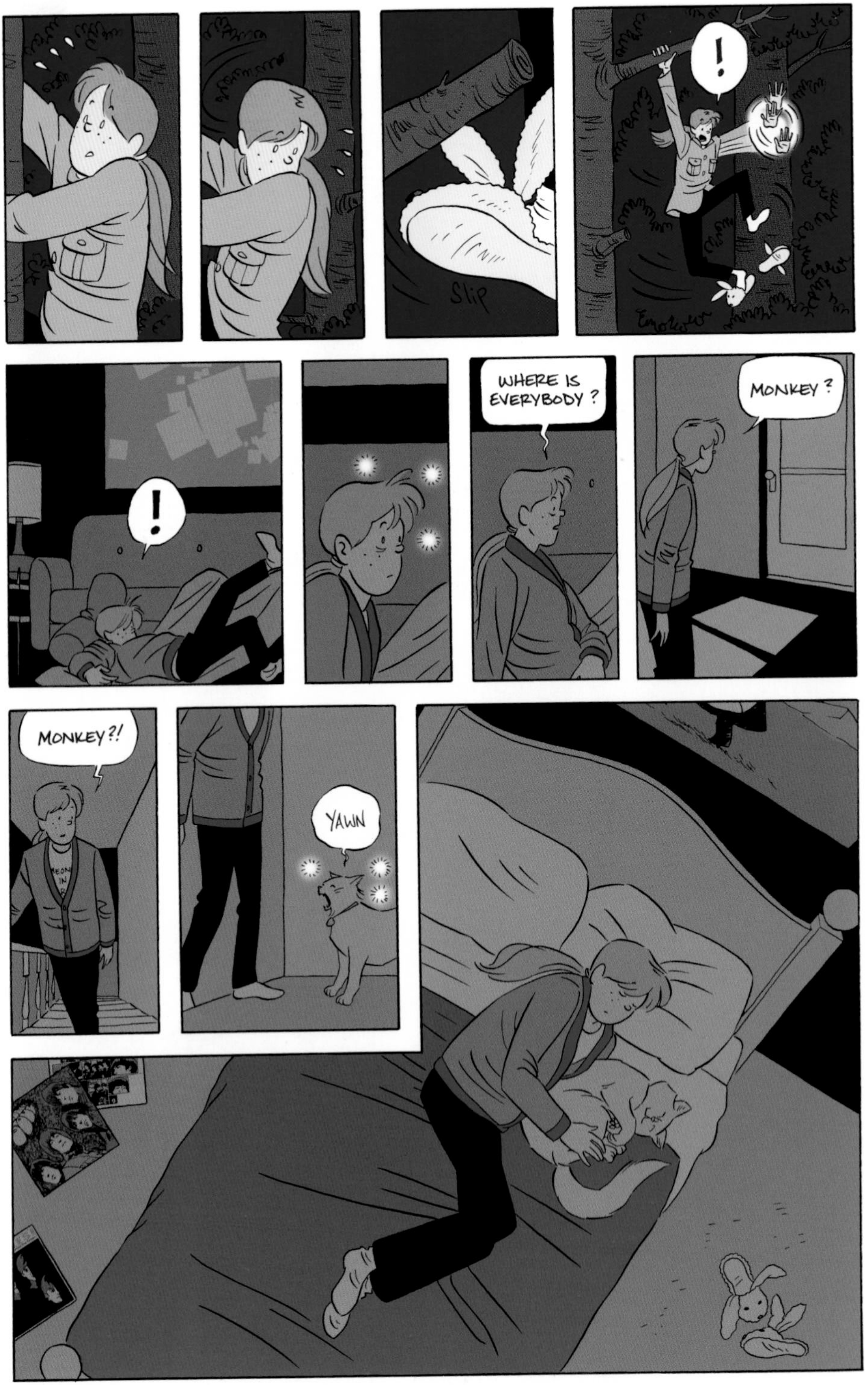

Slip
!
!
WHERE IS EVERYBODY ?
MONKEY ?
MONKEY?!
YAWN

winter

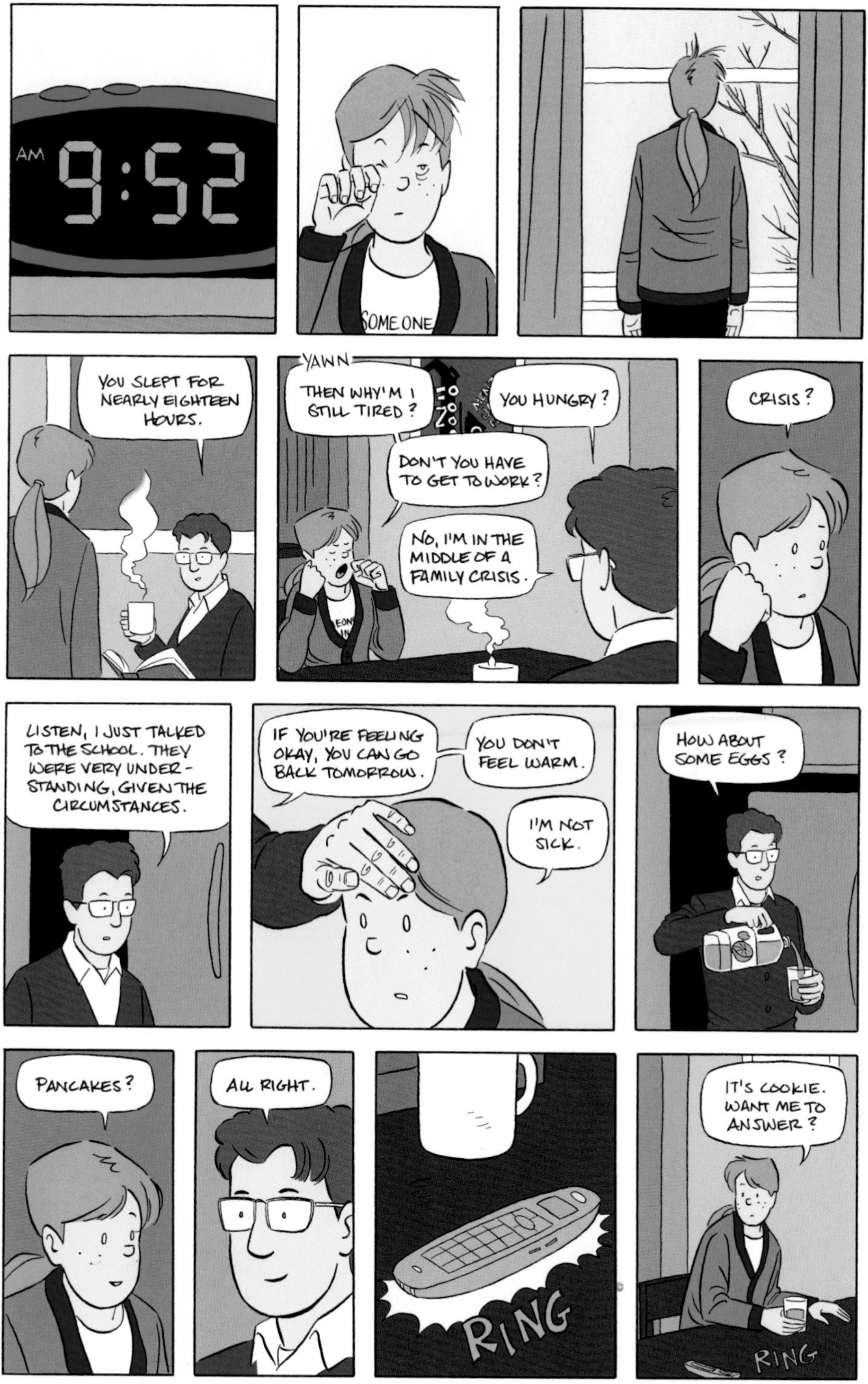
AM 9:52
SOMEONE
YOU SLEPT FOR NEARLY EIGHTEEN HOURS.
YAWN
THEN WHY'M I STILL TIRED?
YOU HUNGRY?
DON'T YOU HAVE TO GET TO WORK?
NO, I'M IN THE MIDDLE OF A FAMILY CRISIS.
CRISIS?
LISTEN, I JUST TALKED TO THE SCHOOL. THEY WERE VERY UNDER-STANDING, GIVEN THE CIRCUMSTANCES.
IF YOU'RE FEELING OKAY, YOU CAN GO BACK TOMORROW.
YOU DON'T FEEL WARM.
I'M NOT SICK.
HOW ABOUT SOME EGGS?
PANCAKES?
ALL RIGHT.
RING
IT'S COOKIE. WANT ME TO ANSWER?
RING

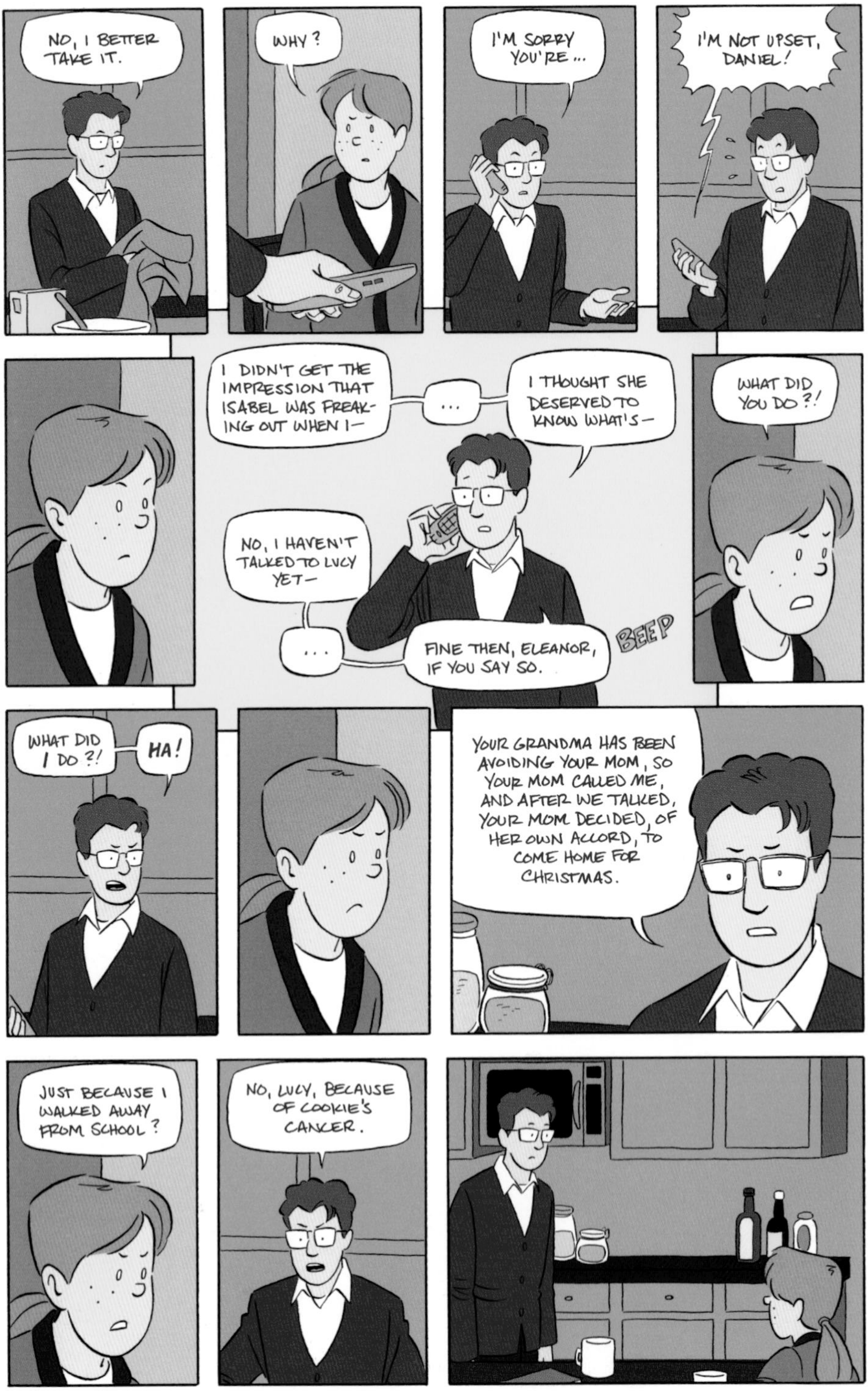
NO, I BETTER TAKE IT.
WHY?
I'M SORRY YOU'RE...
I'M NOT UPSET, DANIEL!
I DIDN'T GET THE IMPRESSION THAT ISABEL WAS FREAKING OUT WHEN I—
...
I THOUGHT SHE DESERVED TO KNOW WHAT'S—
NO, I HAVEN'T TALKED TO LUCY YET—
...
FINE THEN, ELEANOR, IF YOU SAY SO.
BEEP
WHAT DID YOU DO?!
WHAT DID I DO?!
HA!
YOUR GRANDMA HAS BEEN AVOIDING YOUR MOM, SO YOUR MOM CALLED ME, AND AFTER WE TALKED, YOUR MOM DECIDED, OF HER OWN ACCORD, TO COME HOME FOR CHRISTMAS.
JUST BECAUSE I WALKED AWAY FROM SCHOOL?
NO, LUCY, BECAUSE OF COOKIE'S CANCER.

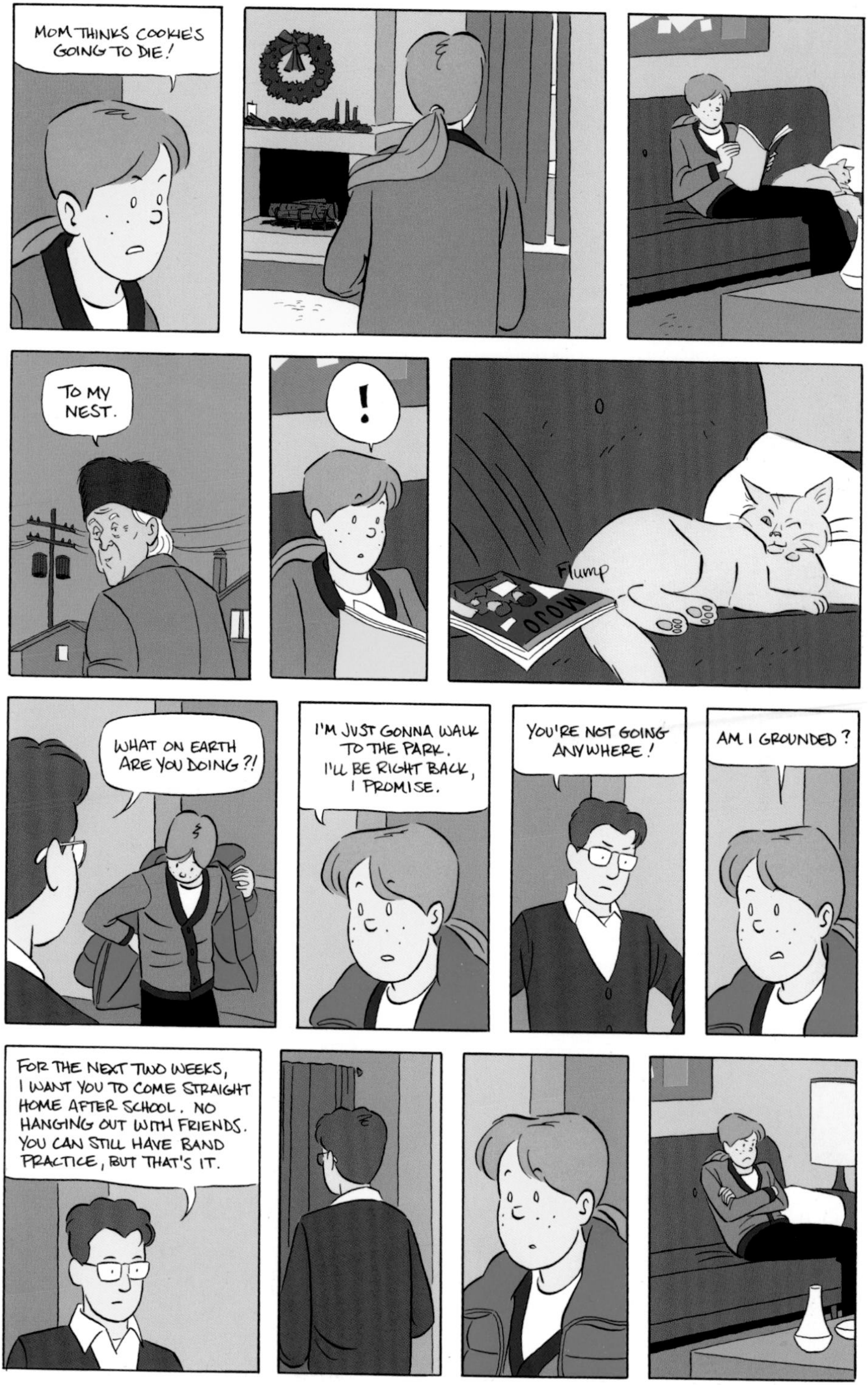
MOM THINKS COOKIE'S GOING TO DIE!
TO MY NEST.
!
Flump
MOJO
WHAT ON EARTH ARE YOU DOING?!
I'M JUST GONNA WALK TO THE PARK. I'LL BE RIGHT BACK, I PROMISE.
YOU'RE NOT GOING ANYWHERE!
AM I GROUNDED?
FOR THE NEXT TWO WEEKS, I WANT YOU TO COME STRAIGHT HOME AFTER SCHOOL. NO HANGING OUT WITH FRIENDS. YOU CAN STILL HAVE BAND PRACTICE, BUT THAT'S IT.

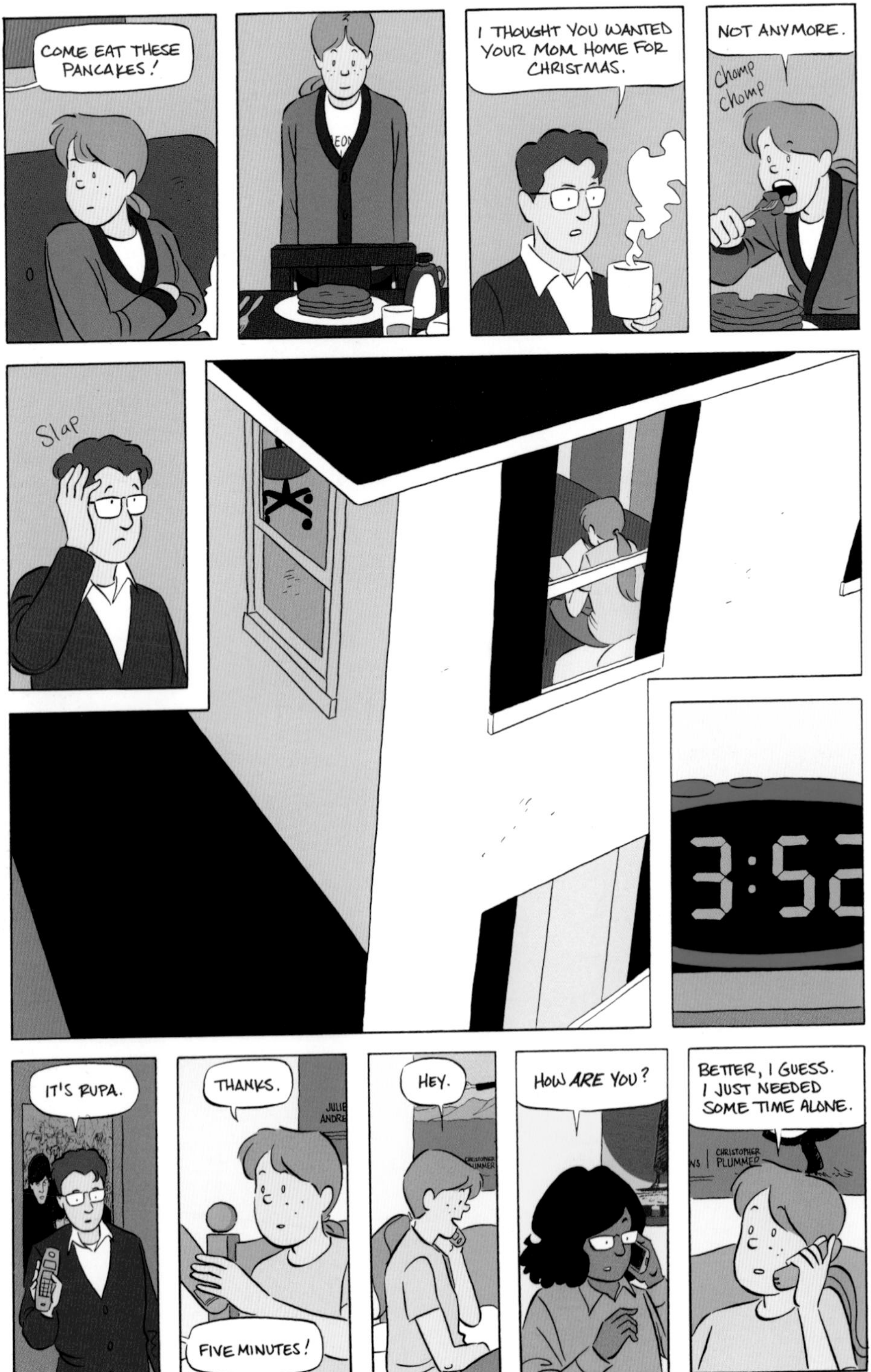
COME EAT THESE PANCAKES!
I THOUGHT YOU WANTED YOUR MOM HOME FOR CHRISTMAS.
NOT ANYMORE.
Chomp Chomp
Slap
3:52
IT'S RUPA.
THANKS.
FIVE MINUTES!
HEY.
CHRISTOPHER PLUMMER
HOW ARE YOU?
BETTER, I GUESS. I JUST NEEDED SOME TIME ALONE.
CHRISTOPHER PLUMMER

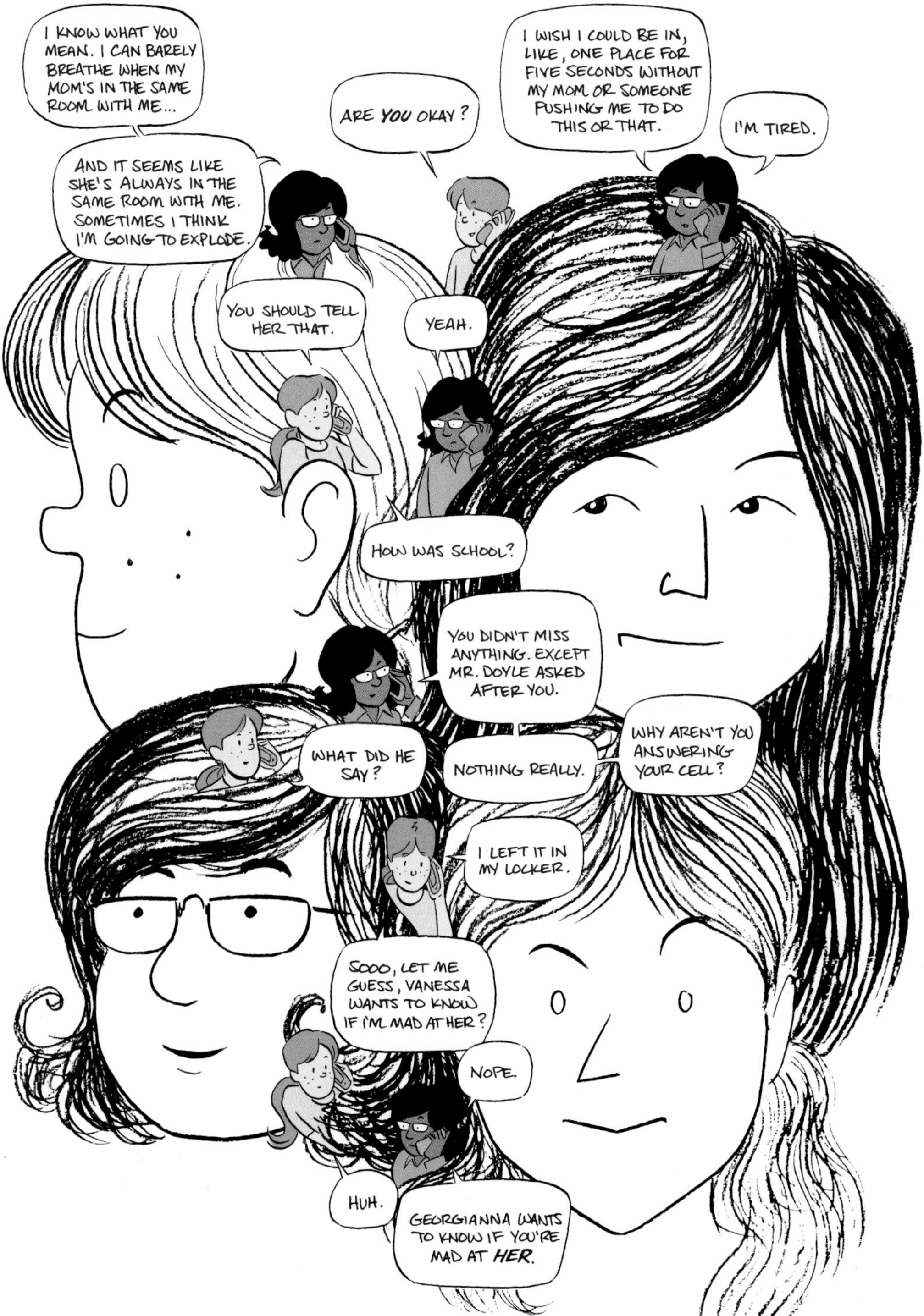
I KNOW WHAT YOU MEAN. I CAN BARELY BREATHE WHEN MY MOM'S IN THE SAME ROOM WITH ME...
AND IT SEEMS LIKE SHE'S ALWAYS IN THE SAME ROOM WITH ME. SOMETIMES I THINK I'M GOING TO EXPLODE.
ARE *YOU* OKAY?
I WISH I COULD BE IN, LIKE, ONE PLACE FOR FIVE SECONDS WITHOUT MY MOM OR SOMEONE PUSHING ME TO DO THIS OR THAT.
I'M TIRED.
YOU SHOULD TELL HER THAT.
YEAH.
HOW WAS SCHOOL?
YOU DIDN'T MISS ANYTHING. EXCEPT MR. DOYLE ASKED AFTER YOU.
WHAT DID HE SAY?
NOTHING REALLY.
WHY AREN'T YOU ANSWERING YOUR CELL?
I LEFT IT IN MY LOCKER.
SOOO, LET ME GUESS, VANESSA WANTS TO KNOW IF I'M MAD AT HER?
NOPE.
HUH.
GEORGIANNA WANTS TO KNOW IF YOU'RE MAD AT *HER*.

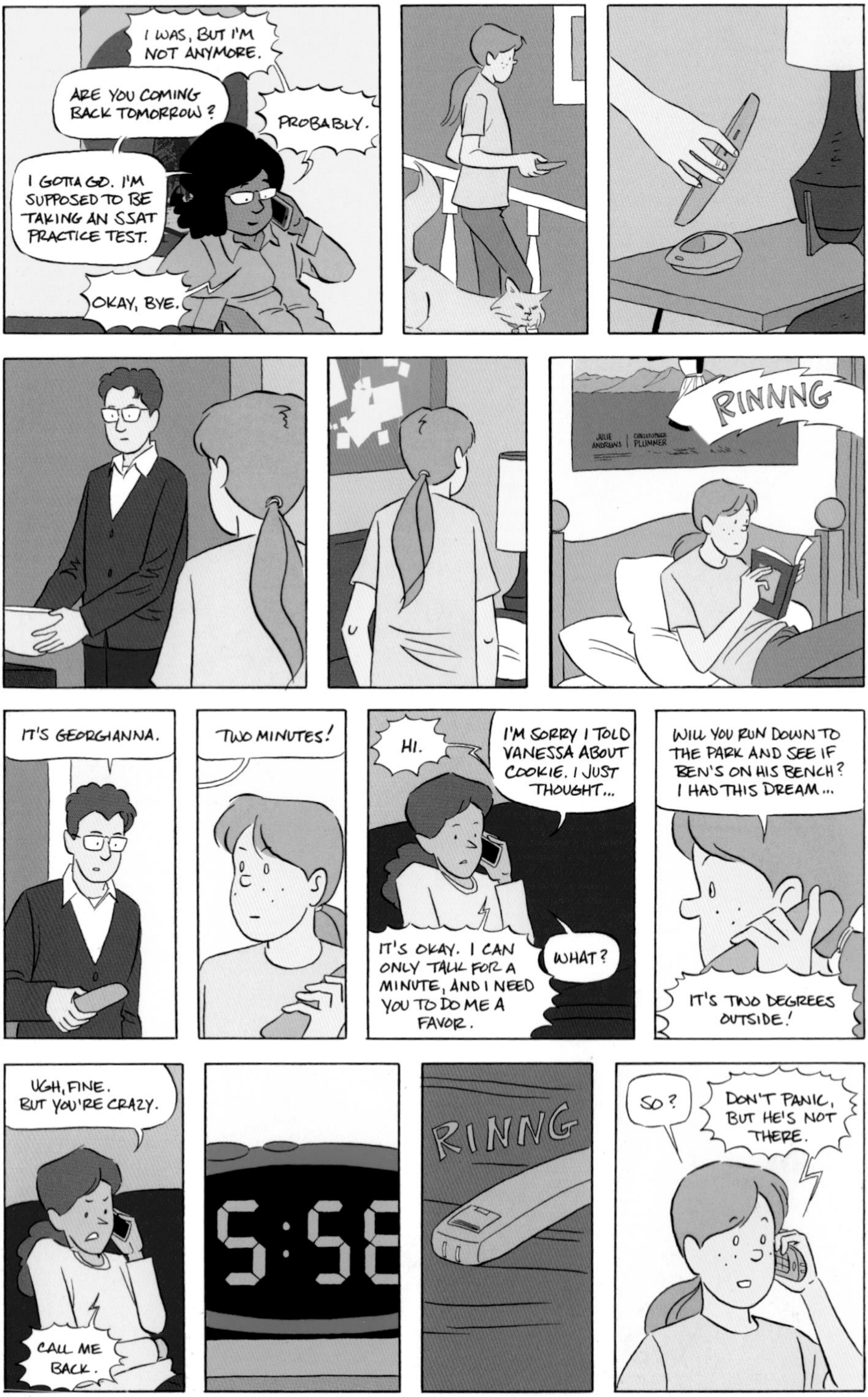
I WAS, BUT I'M NOT ANYMORE.
ARE YOU COMING BACK TOMORROW?
PROBABLY.
I GOTTA GO. I'M SUPPOSED TO BE TAKING AN SSAT PRACTICE TEST.
OKAY, BYE.
JULIE ANDREWS
CHRISTOPHER PLUMMER
RINNNG
IT'S GEORGIANNA.
TWO MINUTES!
HI.
I'M SORRY I TOLD VANESSA ABOUT COOKIE. I JUST THOUGHT...
IT'S OKAY. I CAN ONLY TALK FOR A MINUTE, AND I NEED YOU TO DO ME A FAVOR.
WHAT?
WILL YOU RUN DOWN TO THE PARK AND SEE IF BEN'S ON HIS BENCH? I HAD THIS DREAM...
IT'S TWO DEGREES OUTSIDE!
UGH, FINE. BUT YOU'RE CRAZY.
CALL ME BACK.
5:56
RINNG
SO?
DON'T PANIC, BUT HE'S NOT THERE.

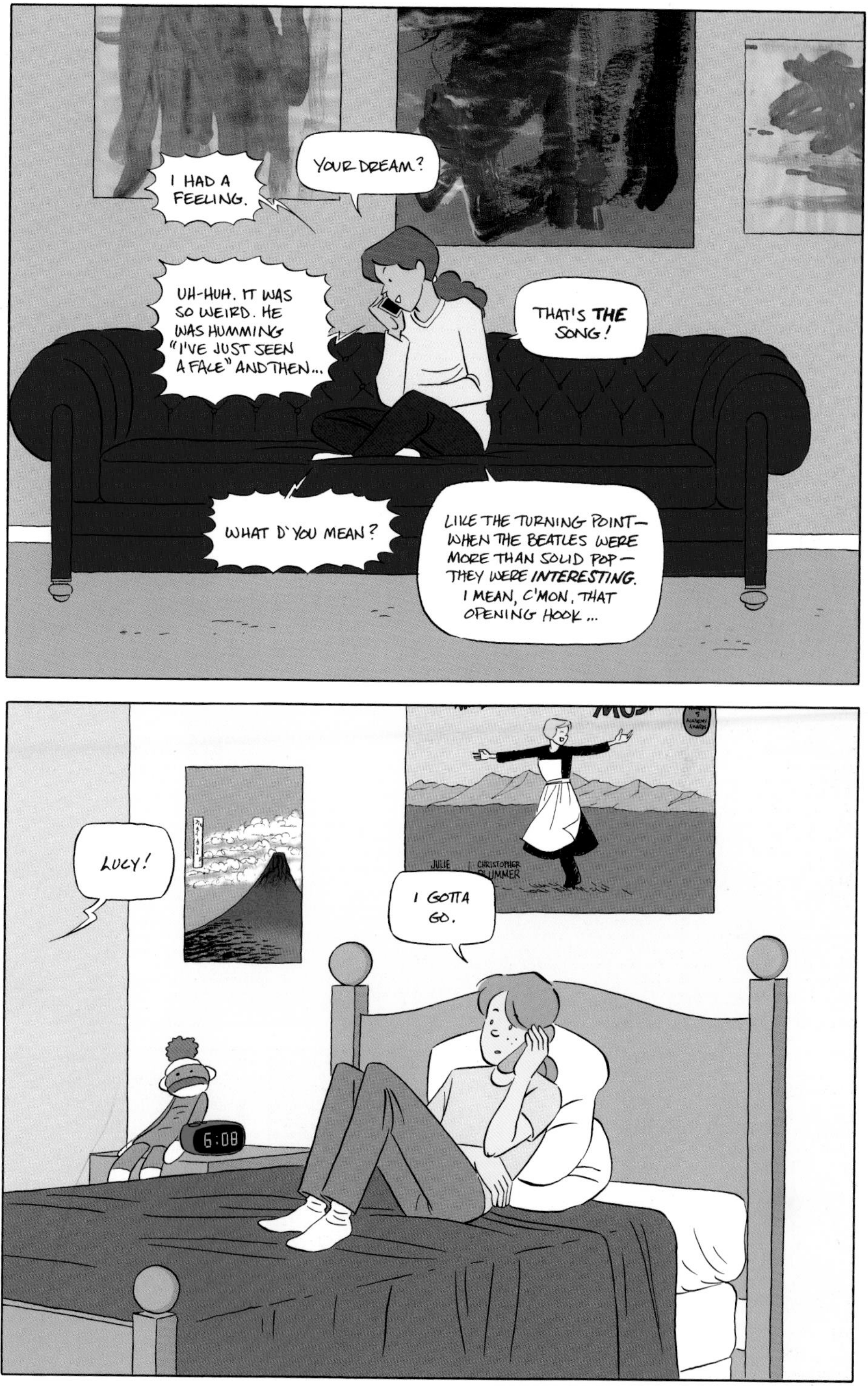
I HAD A FEELING.
YOUR DREAM?
UH-HUH. IT WAS SO WEIRD. HE WAS HUMMING "I'VE JUST SEEN A FACE" AND THEN...
THAT'S **THE** SONG!
WHAT D'YOU MEAN?
LIKE THE TURNING POINT— WHEN THE BEATLES WERE MORE THAN SOLID POP— THEY WERE ***INTERESTING***. I MEAN, C'MON, THAT OPENING HOOK...
JULIE
CHRISTOPHER
LUCY!
I GOTTA GO.
6:08

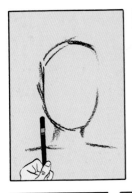

YOU'RE REALLY STRUGGLING WITH THIS.

CAN I DRAW SOMEONE ELSE? LIKE MY MOM, OR MY GRANDMA...

OR ANYONE? PLEASE?

HOW ABOUT IF YOU BEGIN BY DRAWING YOUR MOM OR YOUR GRANDMA AND SEE IF THAT HELPS YOU TO DRAW YOURSELF?

DRAWING IS A PROCESS. YOU HAVE TO LET YOUR-SELF TRUST THE PROCESS.

I CAN'T.

NO, YOU DON'T WANT TO, WHICH IS VERY DIFFERENT.

I NEED A BOOK ABOUT SURREAL ART.

SURE.

FOLLOW ME THIS WAY.

?

BOOK RETURN

DALI

FRIDA KHALO

I'M PROBABLY GONNA FAIL ART.

I DON'T THINK THAT'S POSSIBLE.

ANYTHING'S POSSIBLE IF YOU PUT YOUR MIND TO IT.

I *NEED* A PIECE OF GUM.

!

IS THAT SO?

I HAVE A.D.D., AND CHEWING HELPS ME CONCENTRATE.

OH, I'VE BEEN MEANING TO TELL YOU—I ALWAYS THOUGHT THE TIME SERIES WAS A TRILOGY, BUT IT TURNS OUT THERE ARE TWO MORE BOOKS AFTER *A SWIFTLY TILTING PLANET*, WHICH MAKES IT, WHAT, A QUINTET, I GUESS.

RIGHT. *MANY WATERS* AND *AN ACCEPTABLE TIME*.

YOU'VE READ THEM?

NOT YET.

WHY NOT?

BECAUSE I'M SAVING THEM... FOR LATER.

YOU'RE A REAL ENIGMA, LUCY SUTCLIFFE.

BEEP

I KNOW. CAN I PLEASE HAVE A PIECE OF GUM.?

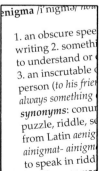

enigma /iˈnigmə/ nou

1. an obscure spee
writing 2. somethi
to understand or (
3. an inscrutable (
person (*to his frie*
always something (
synonyms: conur
puzzle, riddle, se
from Latin *aenigm*
ainigmat- ainigm
to speak in ridd
first known use

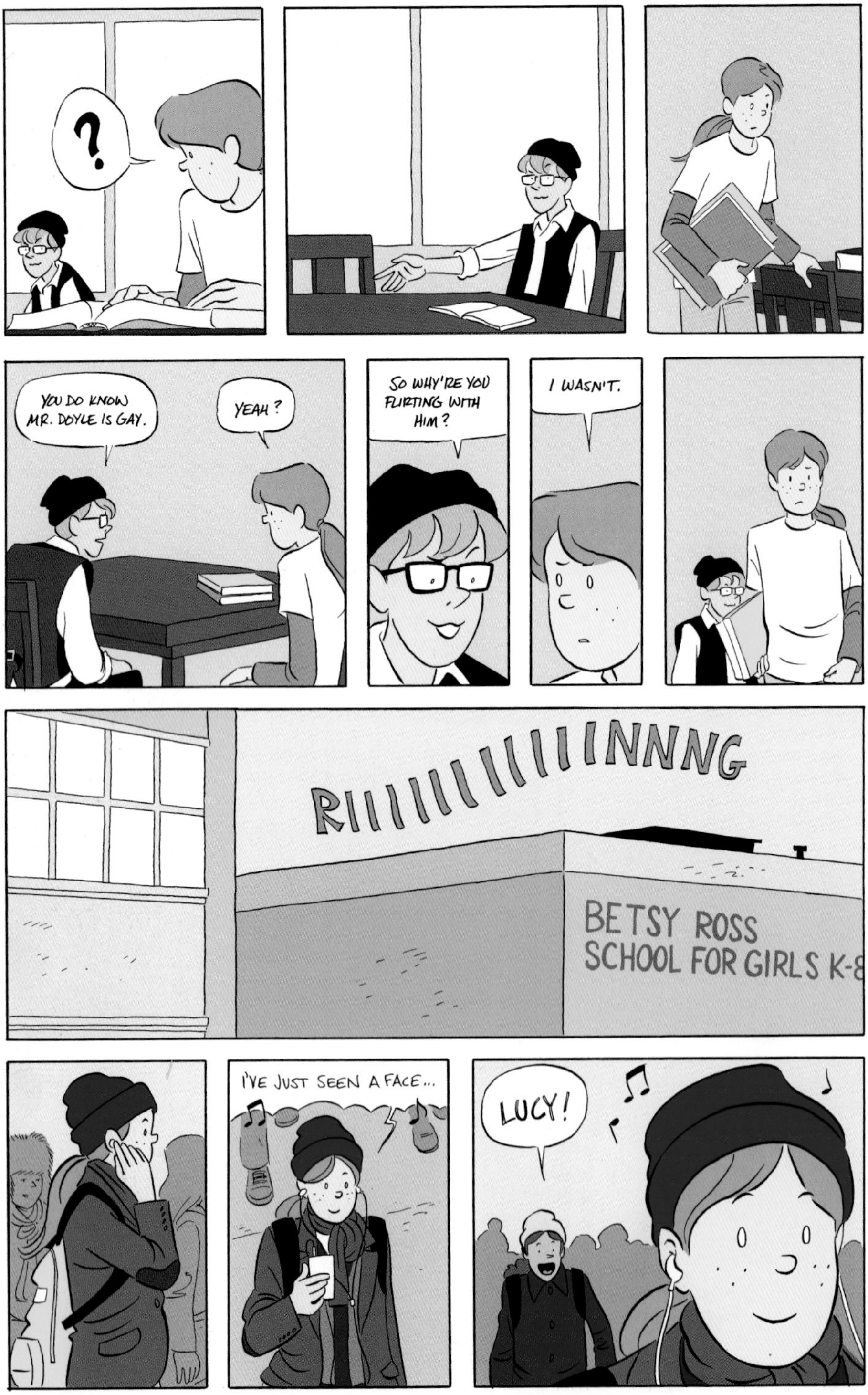
?
YOU DO KNOW MR. DOYLE IS GAY.
YEAH?
SO WHY'RE YOU FLIRTING WITH HIM?
I WASN'T.
RIIIIIIIIIIIINNNG
BETSY ROSS SCHOOL FOR GIRLS K-8
I'VE JUST SEEN A FACE...
LUCY!

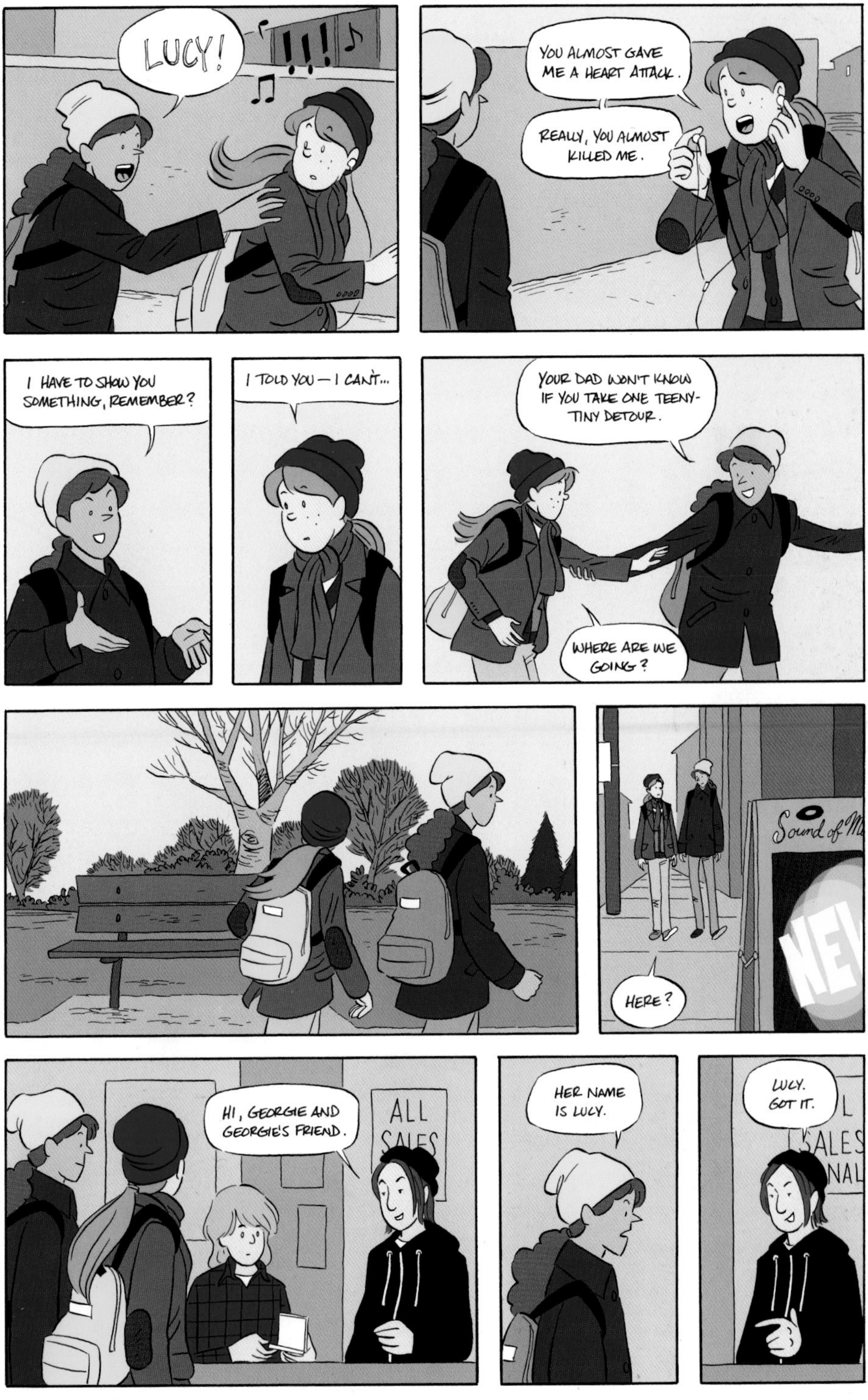
LUCY!
!!!
YOU ALMOST GAVE ME A HEART ATTACK.
REALLY, YOU ALMOST KILLED ME.
I HAVE TO SHOW YOU SOMETHING, REMEMBER?
I TOLD YOU — I CAN'T...
YOUR DAD WON'T KNOW IF YOU TAKE ONE TEENY-TINY DETOUR.
WHERE ARE WE GOING?
Sound of M
NEW
HERE?
HI, GEORGIE AND GEORGIE'S FRIEND.
ALL SALES
HER NAME IS LUCY.
LUCY. GOT IT.

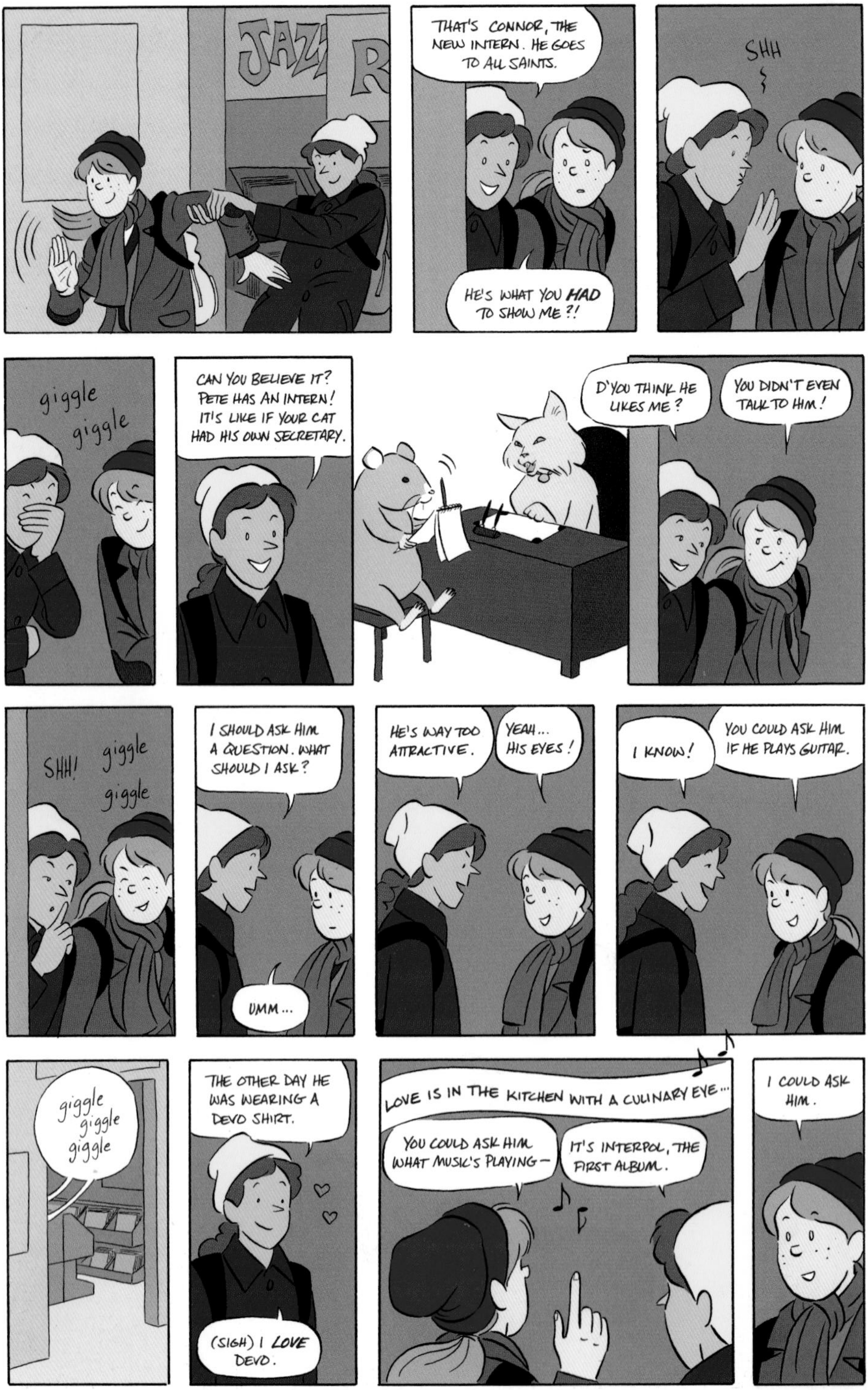
THAT'S CONNOR, THE NEW INTERN. HE GOES TO ALL SAINTS.
HE'S WHAT YOU HAD TO SHOW ME?!
SHH
giggle giggle
CAN YOU BELIEVE IT? PETE HAS AN INTERN! IT'S LIKE IF YOUR CAT HAD HIS OWN SECRETARY.
D'YOU THINK HE LIKES ME?
YOU DIDN'T EVEN TALK TO HIM!
SHH! giggle giggle
I SHOULD ASK HIM A QUESTION. WHAT SHOULD I ASK?
UMM...
HE'S WAY TOO ATTRACTIVE.
YEAH... HIS EYES!
I KNOW!
YOU COULD ASK HIM IF HE PLAYS GUITAR.
giggle giggle giggle
THE OTHER DAY HE WAS WEARING A DEVO SHIRT.
(SIGH) I LOVE DEVO.
LOVE IS IN THE KITCHEN WITH A CULINARY EYE...
YOU COULD ASK HIM WHAT MUSIC'S PLAYING—
IT'S INTERPOL, THE FIRST ALBUM.
I COULD ASK HIM.

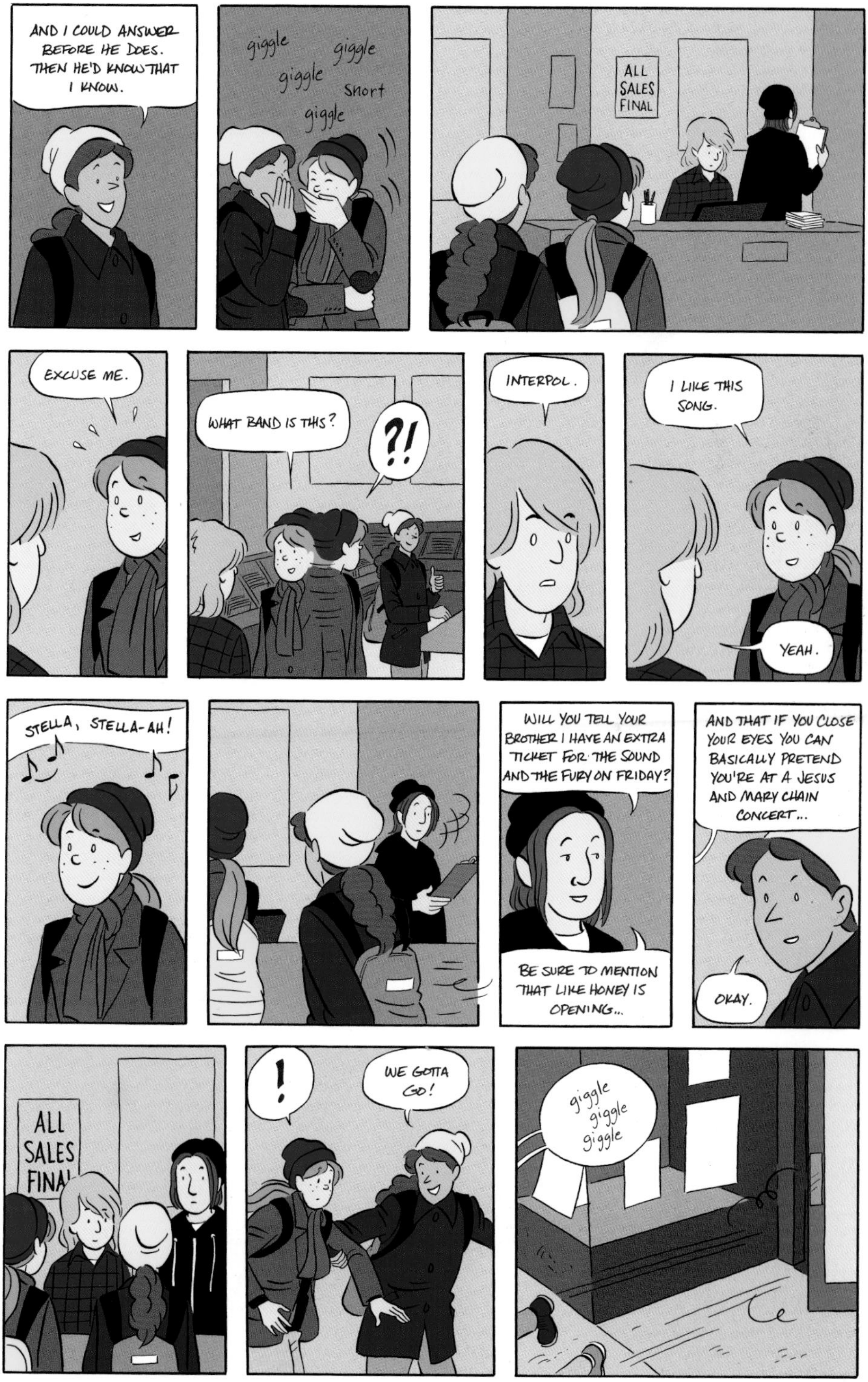
AND I COULD ANSWER BEFORE HE DOES. THEN HE'D KNOW THAT I KNOW.
giggle giggle giggle snort giggle
ALL SALES FINAL
EXCUSE ME.
WHAT BAND IS THIS?
?!
INTERPOL.
I LIKE THIS SONG.
YEAH.
STELLA, STELLA-AH!
WILL YOU TELL YOUR BROTHER I HAVE AN EXTRA TICKET FOR THE SOUND AND THE FURY ON FRIDAY?
BE SURE TO MENTION THAT LIKE HONEY IS OPENING...
AND THAT IF YOU CLOSE YOUR EYES YOU CAN BASICALLY PRETEND YOU'RE AT A JESUS AND MARY CHAIN CONCERT...
OKAY.
ALL SALES FINA
!
WE GOTTA GO!
giggle giggle giggle

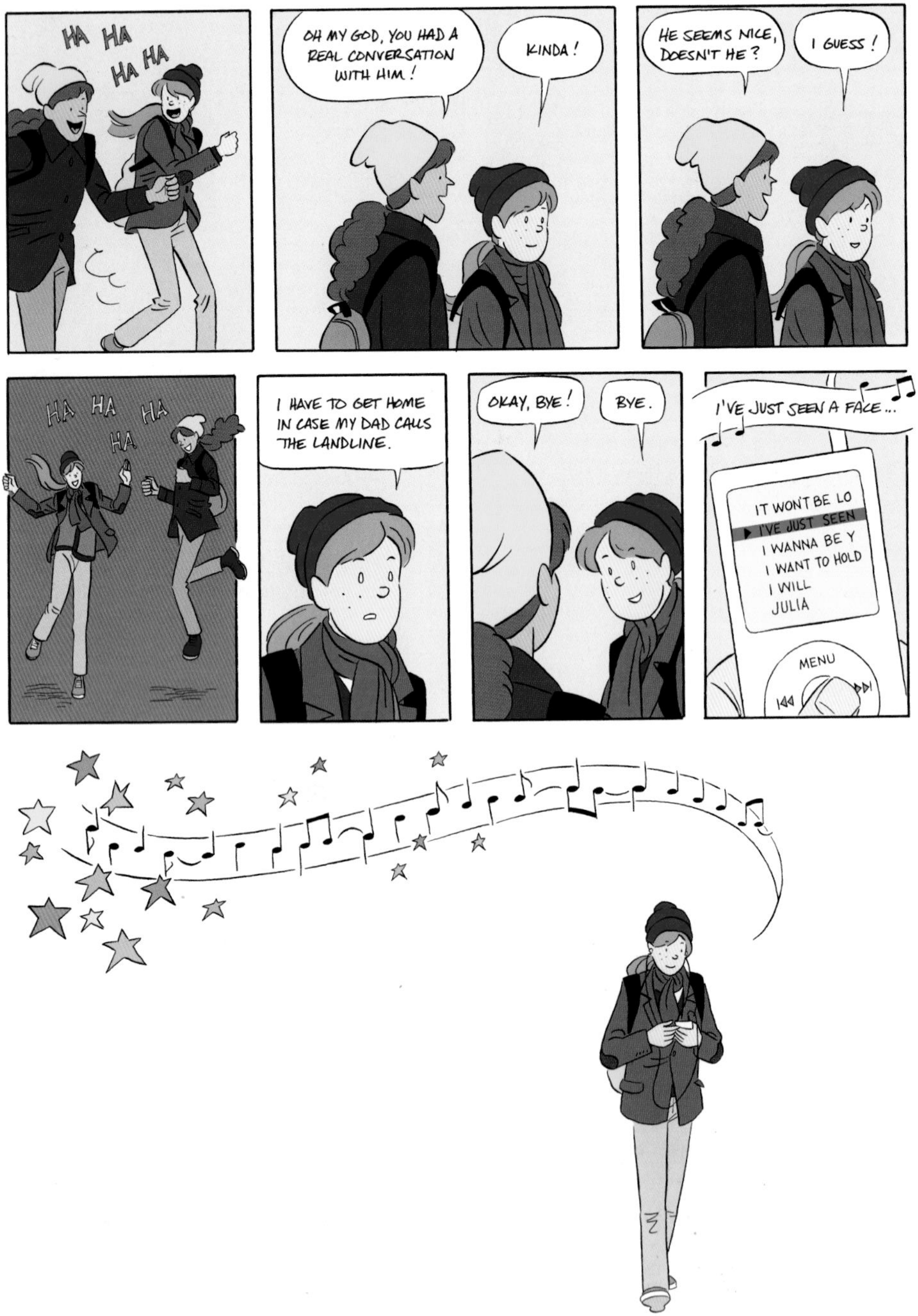
HA HA
HA HA
OH MY GOD, YOU HAD A REAL CONVERSATION WITH HIM!
KINDA!
HE SEEMS NICE, DOESN'T HE?
I GUESS!
HA HA HA
HA
I HAVE TO GET HOME IN CASE MY DAD CALLS THE LANDLINE.
OKAY, BYE!
BYE.
I'VE JUST SEEN A FACE...
IT WON'T BE LO
I'VE JUST SEEN
I WANNA BE Y
I WANT TO HOLD
I WILL
JULIA
MENU

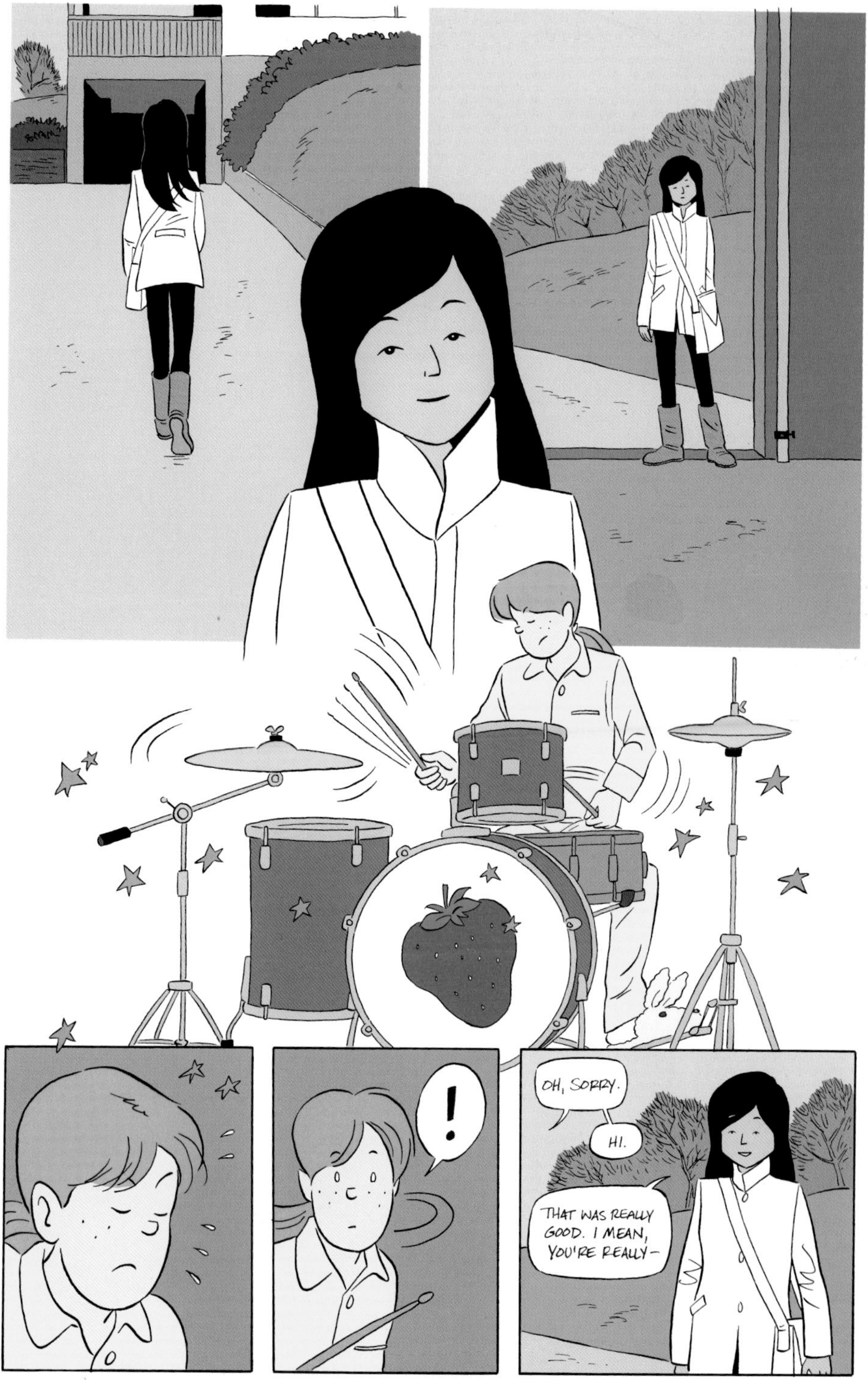
!
OH, SORRY.
HI.
THAT WAS REALLY GOOD. I MEAN, YOU'RE REALLY—

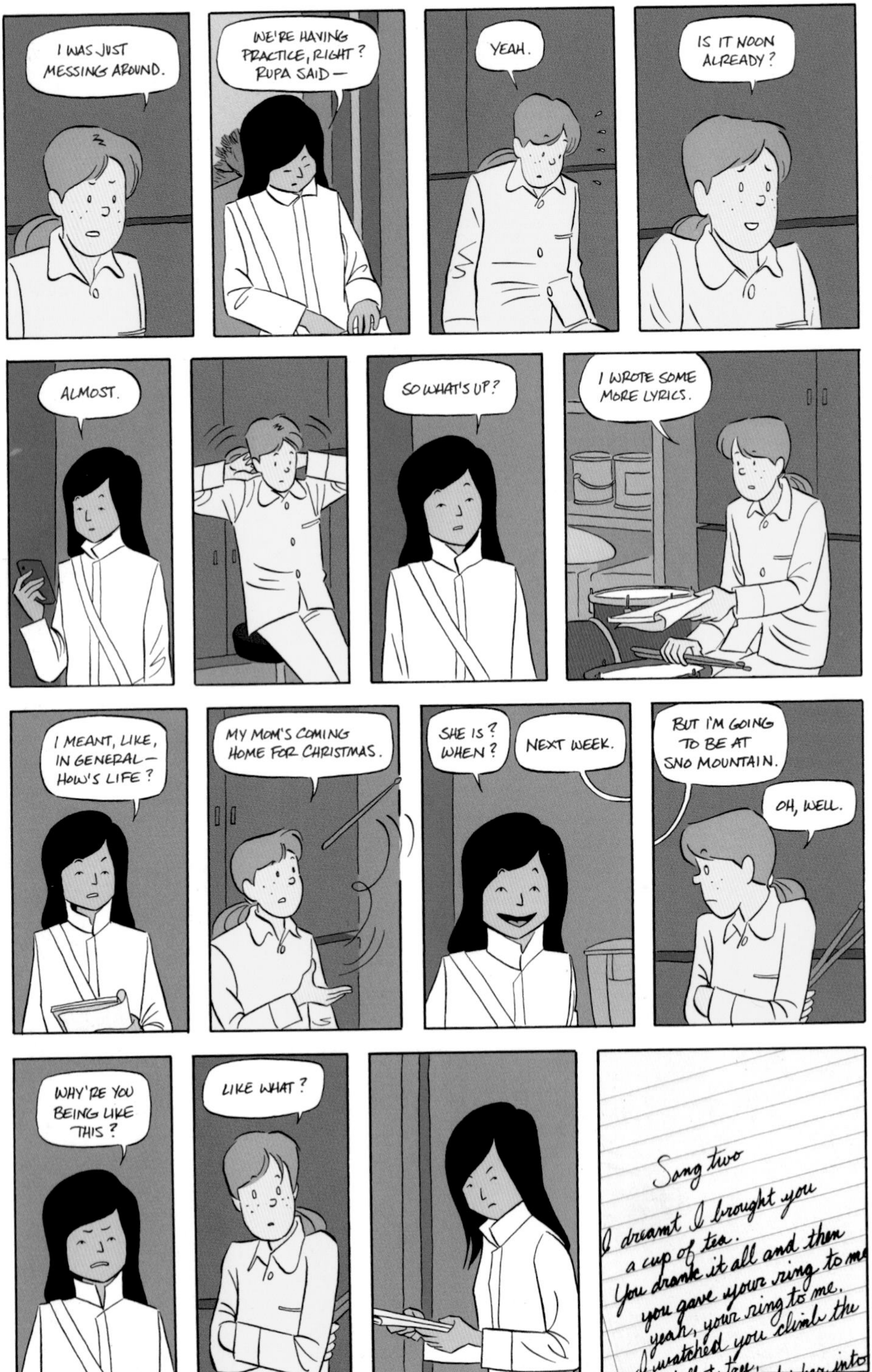
I WAS JUST MESSING AROUND.
WE'RE HAVING PRACTICE, RIGHT? RUPA SAID—
YEAH.
IS IT NOON ALREADY?
ALMOST.
SO WHAT'S UP?
I WROTE SOME MORE LYRICS.
I MEANT, LIKE, IN GENERAL— HOW'S LIFE?
MY MOM'S COMING HOME FOR CHRISTMAS.
SHE IS? WHEN?
NEXT WEEK.
BUT I'M GOING TO BE AT SNO MOUNTAIN.
OH, WELL.
WHY'RE YOU BEING LIKE THIS?
LIKE WHAT?
Song two
I dreamt I brought you
a cup of tea.
You drank it all and then
you gave your ring to me
yeah, your ring to me.
I watched you climb the

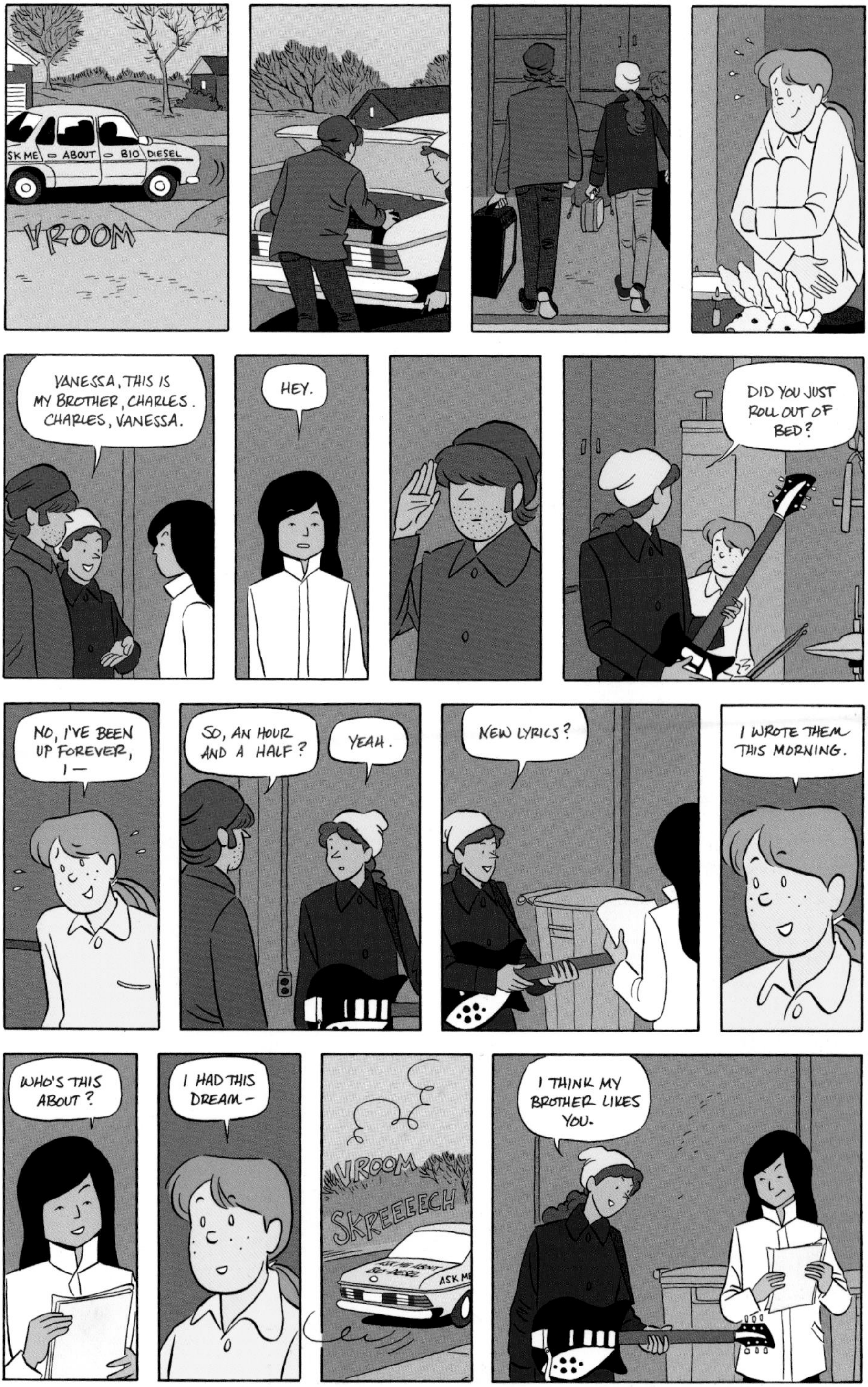
SK ME ABOUT BIO DIESEL
VROOM
VANESSA, THIS IS MY BROTHER, CHARLES. CHARLES, VANESSA.
HEY.
DID YOU JUST ROLL OUT OF BED?
NO, I'VE BEEN UP FOREVER, I —
SO, AN HOUR AND A HALF?
YEAH.
NEW LYRICS?
I WROTE THEM THIS MORNING.
WHO'S THIS ABOUT?
I HAD THIS DREAM-
VROOM
SKREEEECH
ASK ME
I THINK MY BROTHER LIKES YOU.

I KNOW WHO...

WE FOUND A REAL-LIFE MUSE. HE WORKS AT...

IT'S NOT ABOUT CONNOR.

CONNOR?

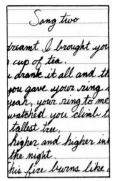

Song two

dreamt I brought you
a cup of tea.
drank it all and th
you gave your ring
yeah, your ring to me
watched you climb t
tallest tree,
higher and higher in
the night.
his fire burns like

LUCY AND CONNOR SITTING IN A TREE!

K-I-S-S-I-N-G.

"THIS FIRE BURNS LIKE A TIGER."

WILLIAM BLAKE, REMEMBER?

"TYGER TYGER, BURNING BRIGHT."

MRS. CLARKE WOULD BE SO PROUD.

SHUT UP!

NO, I LIKE IT!

ME, TOO.

YOU DO?

YEAH.

VRRM

I THINK THE BUNNY SLIPPERS SHOULD BE A THING.

!

LIKE, YOU SHOULD WEAR THEM IF WE EVER PLAY OUTSIDE THIS GARAGE.

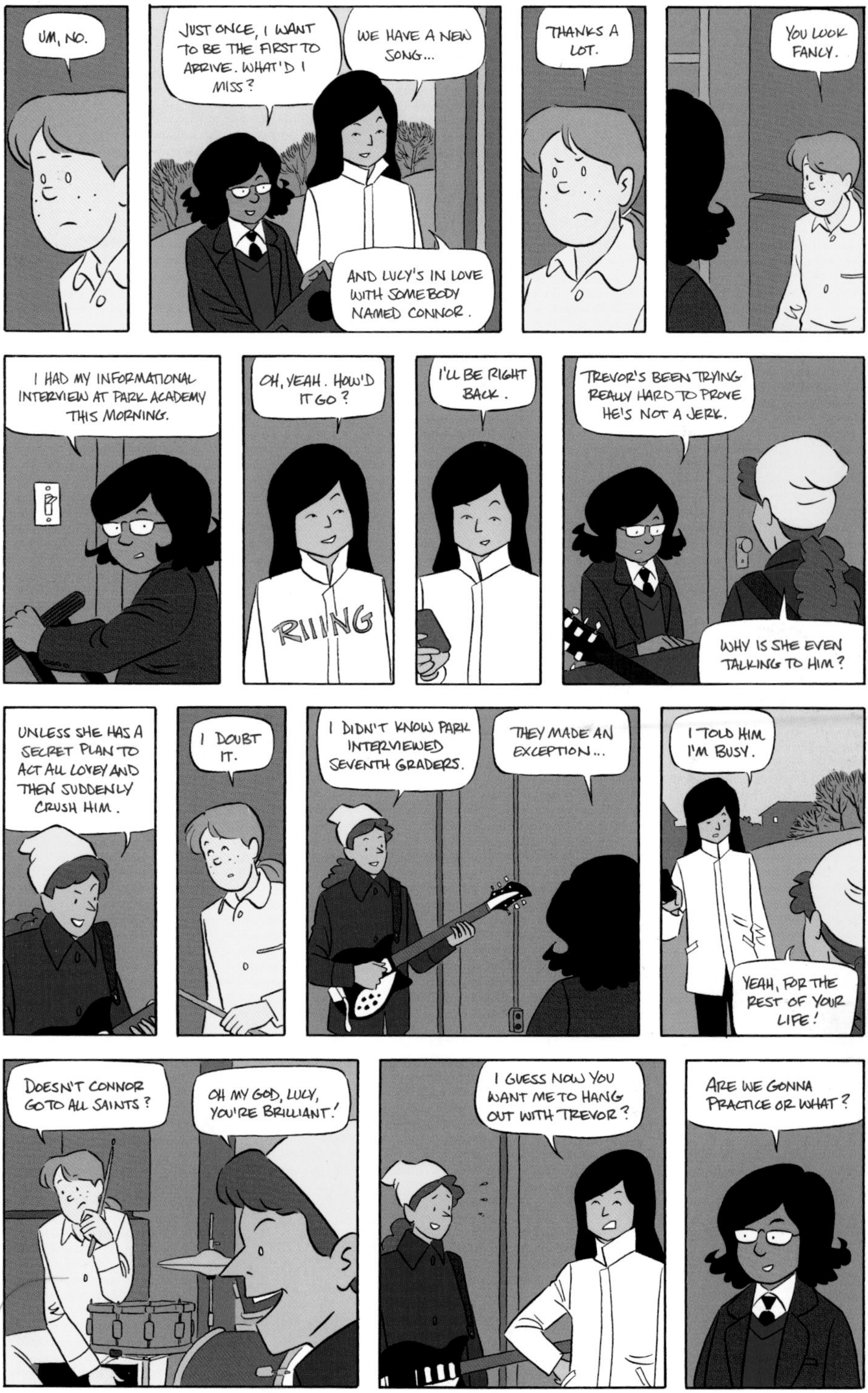
UM, NO.
JUST ONCE, I WANT TO BE THE FIRST TO ARRIVE. WHAT'D I MISS?
WE HAVE A NEW SONG...
AND LUCY'S IN LOVE WITH SOMEBODY NAMED CONNOR.
THANKS A LOT.
YOU LOOK FANCY.
I HAD MY INFORMATIONAL INTERVIEW AT PARK ACADEMY THIS MORNING.
OH, YEAH. HOW'D IT GO?
RIIING
I'LL BE RIGHT BACK.
TREVOR'S BEEN TRYING REALLY HARD TO PROVE HE'S NOT A JERK.
WHY IS SHE EVEN TALKING TO HIM?
UNLESS SHE HAS A SECRET PLAN TO ACT ALL LOVEY AND THEN SUDDENLY CRUSH HIM.
I DOUBT IT.
I DIDN'T KNOW PARK INTERVIEWED SEVENTH GRADERS.
THEY MADE AN EXCEPTION...
I TOLD HIM I'M BUSY.
YEAH, FOR THE REST OF YOUR LIFE!
DOESN'T CONNOR GO TO ALL SAINTS?
OH MY GOD, LUCY, YOU'RE BRILLIANT!
I GUESS NOW YOU WANT ME TO HANG OUT WITH TREVOR?
ARE WE GONNA PRACTICE OR WHAT?

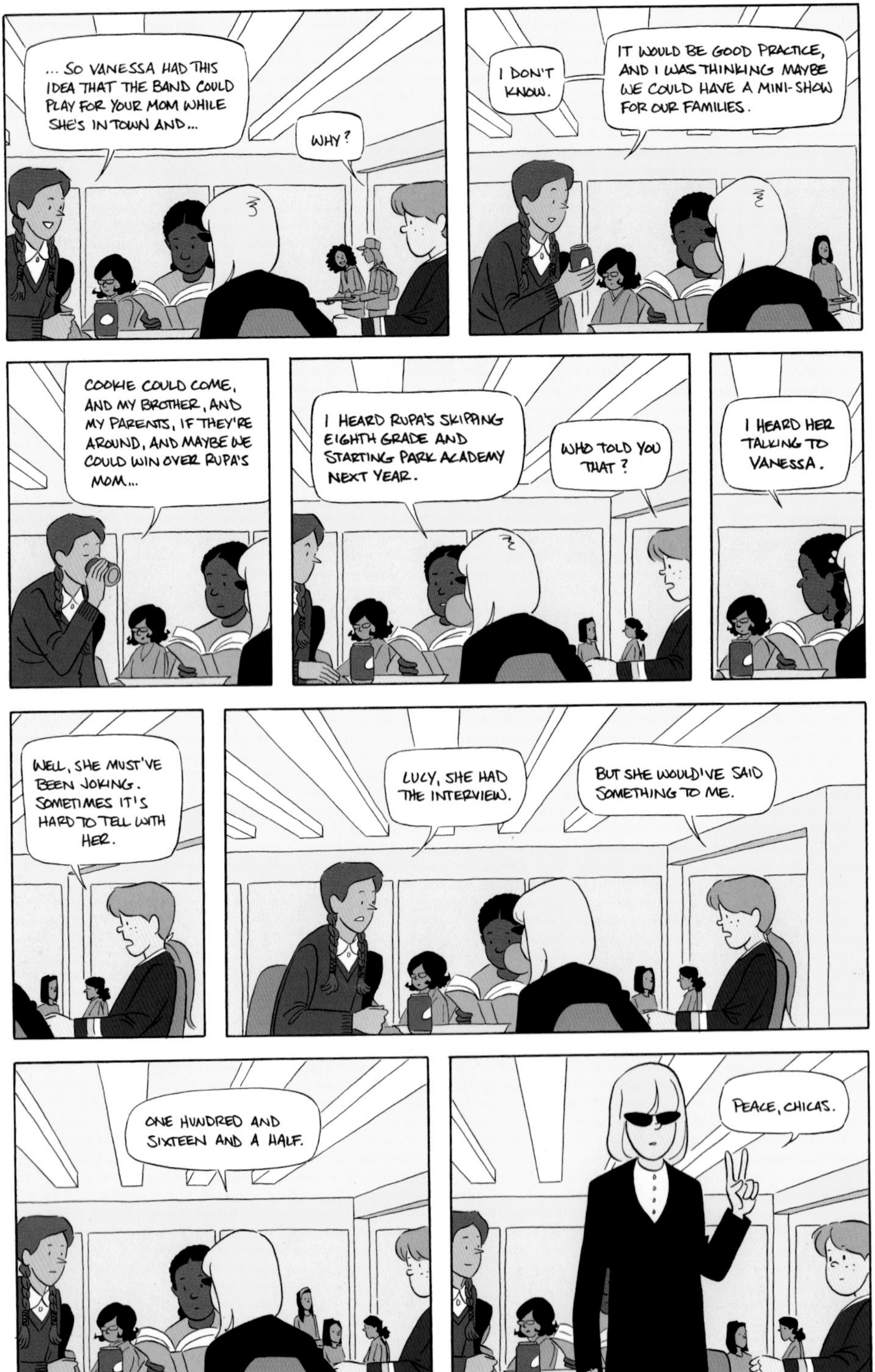
... SO VANESSA HAD THIS IDEA THAT THE BAND COULD PLAY FOR YOUR MOM WHILE SHE'S IN TOWN AND...
WHY?
I DON'T KNOW.
IT WOULD BE GOOD PRACTICE, AND I WAS THINKING MAYBE WE COULD HAVE A MINI-SHOW FOR OUR FAMILIES.
COOKIE COULD COME, AND MY BROTHER, AND MY PARENTS, IF THEY'RE AROUND, AND MAYBE WE COULD WIN OVER RUPA'S MOM...
I HEARD RUPA'S SKIPPING EIGHTH GRADE AND STARTING PARK ACADEMY NEXT YEAR.
WHO TOLD YOU THAT?
I HEARD HER TALKING TO VANESSA.
WELL, SHE MUST'VE BEEN JOKING. SOMETIMES IT'S HARD TO TELL WITH HER.
LUCY, SHE HAD THE INTERVIEW.
BUT SHE WOULD'VE SAID SOMETHING TO ME.
ONE HUNDRED AND SIXTEEN AND A HALF.
PEACE, CHICAS.

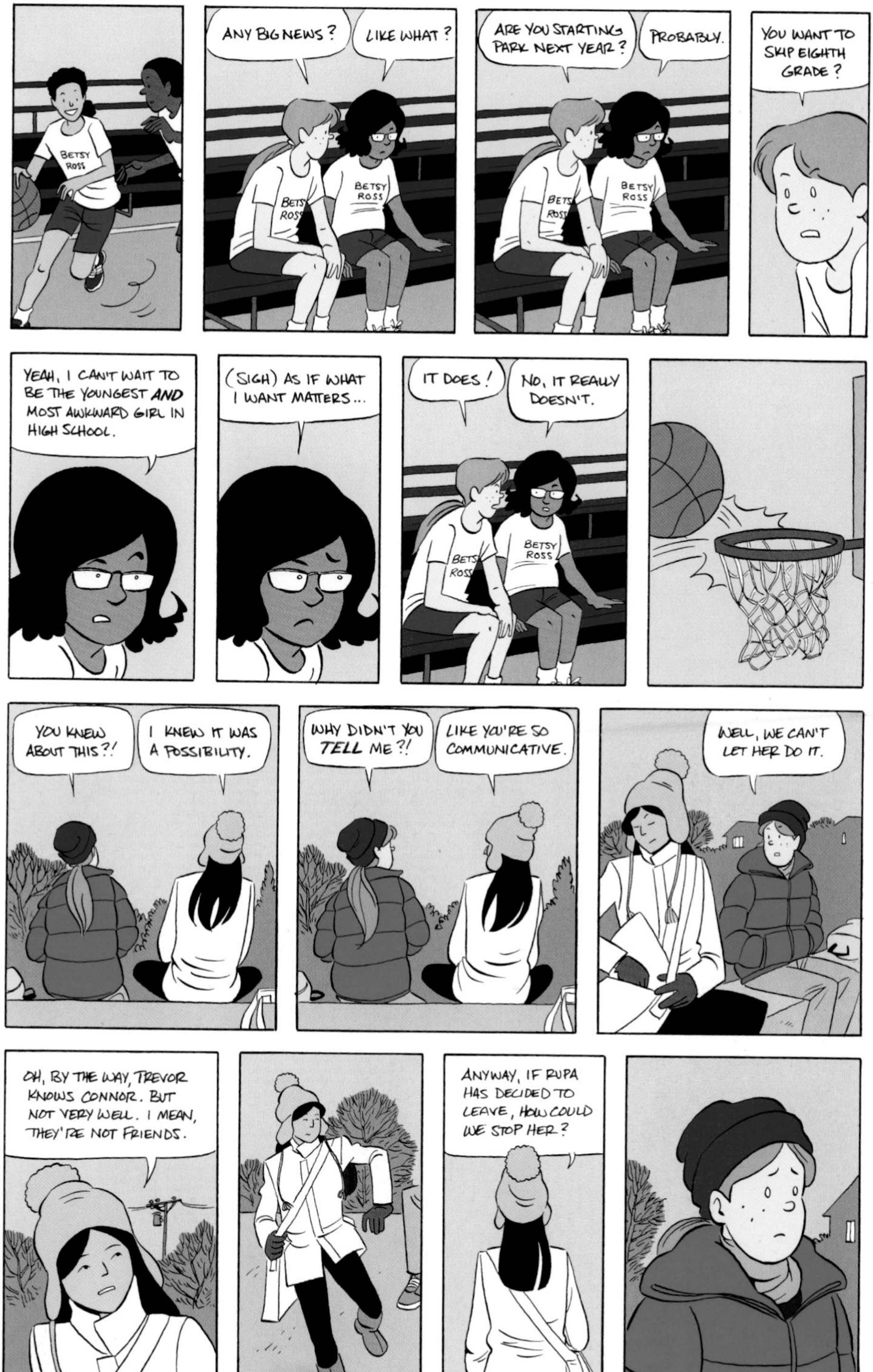
BETSY ROSS
ANY BIG NEWS?
LIKE WHAT?
ARE YOU STARTING PARK NEXT YEAR?
PROBABLY.
YOU WANT TO SKIP EIGHTH GRADE?
YEAH, I CAN'T WAIT TO BE THE YOUNGEST **AND** MOST AWKWARD GIRL IN HIGH SCHOOL.
(SIGH) AS IF WHAT I WANT MATTERS...
IT DOES!
NO, IT REALLY DOESN'T.
YOU KNEW ABOUT THIS?!
I KNEW IT WAS A POSSIBILITY.
WHY DIDN'T YOU **TELL** ME?!
LIKE YOU'RE SO COMMUNICATIVE.
WELL, WE CAN'T LET HER DO IT.
OH, BY THE WAY, TREVOR KNOWS CONNOR. BUT NOT VERY WELL. I MEAN, THEY'RE NOT FRIENDS.
ANYWAY, IF RUPA HAS DECIDED TO LEAVE, HOW COULD WE STOP HER?

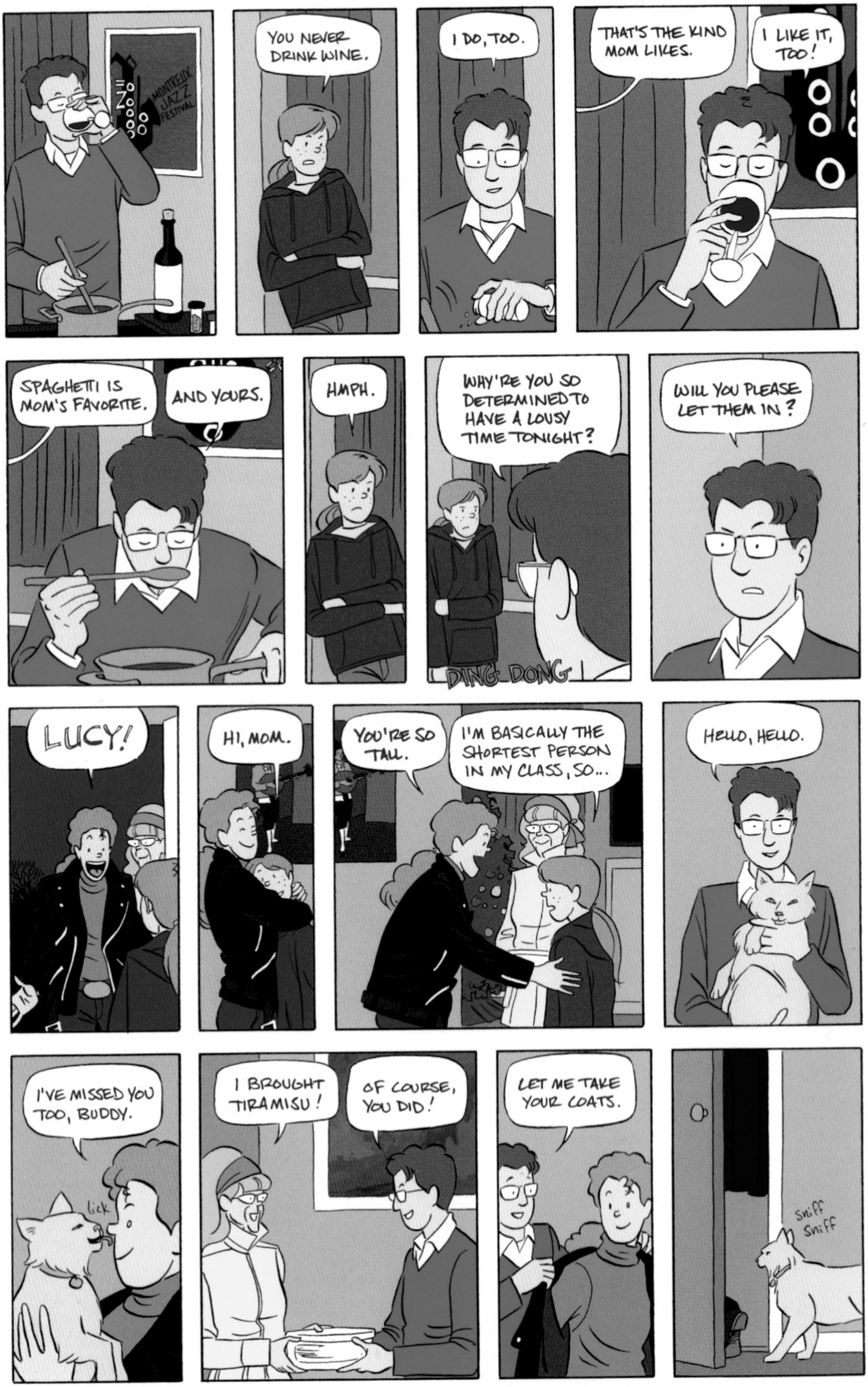
YOU NEVER DRINK WINE.
I DO, TOO.
THAT'S THE KIND MOM LIKES.
I LIKE IT, TOO!
SPAGHETTI IS MOM'S FAVORITE.
AND YOURS.
HMPH.
WHY'RE YOU SO DETERMINED TO HAVE A LOUSY TIME TONIGHT?
DING DONG
WILL YOU PLEASE LET THEM IN?
LUCY!
HI, MOM.
YOU'RE SO TALL.
I'M BASICALLY THE SHORTEST PERSON IN MY CLASS, SO...
HELLO, HELLO.
I'VE MISSED YOU TOO, BUDDY.
lick
I BROUGHT TIRAMISU!
OF COURSE, YOU DID!
LET ME TAKE YOUR COATS.
sniff sniff

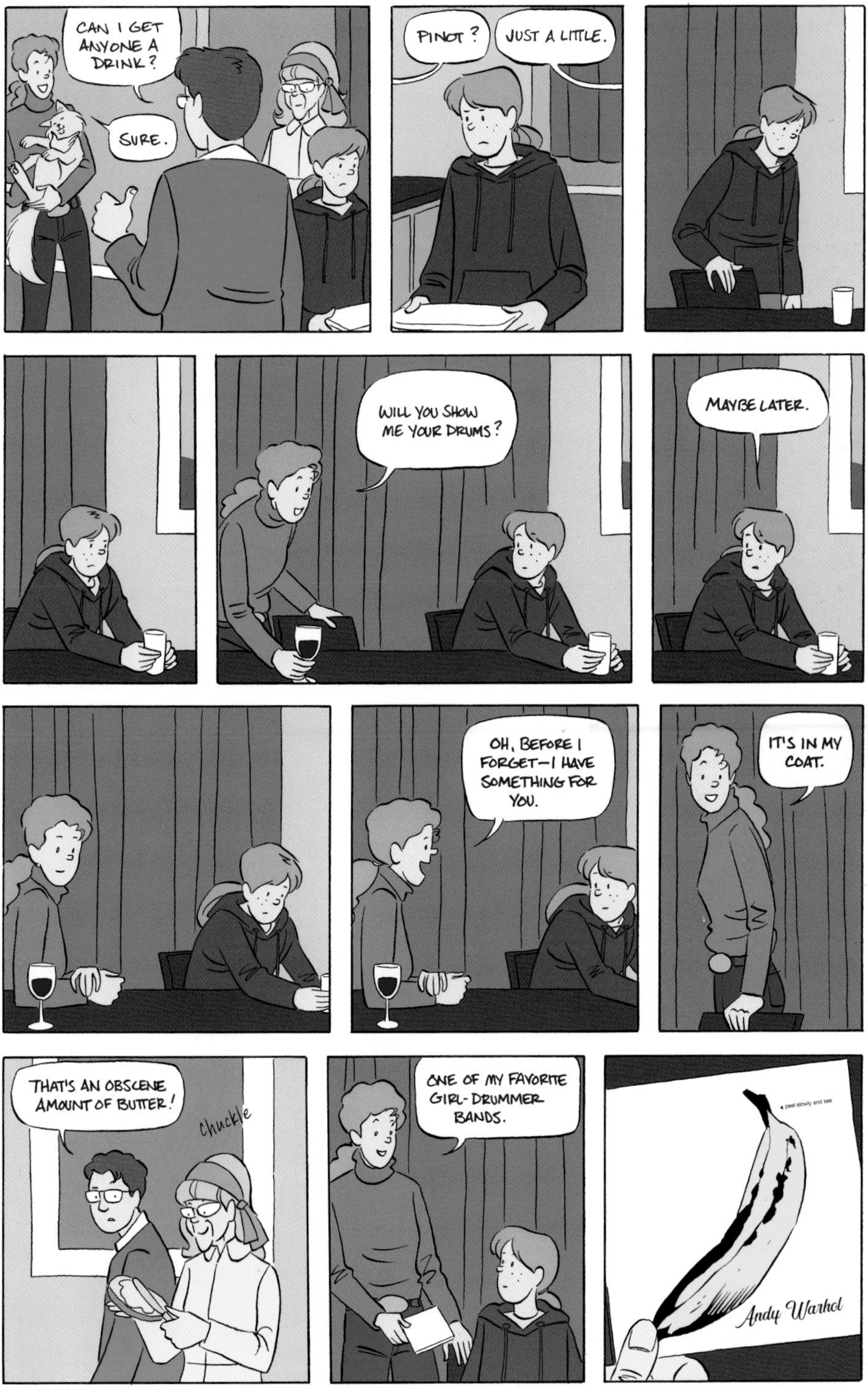
CAN I GET ANYONE A DRINK?
SURE.
PINOT?
JUST A LITTLE.
WILL YOU SHOW ME YOUR DRUMS?
MAYBE LATER.
OH, BEFORE I FORGET—I HAVE SOMETHING FOR YOU.
IT'S IN MY COAT.
THAT'S AN OBSCENE AMOUNT OF BUTTER!
chuckle
ONE OF MY FAVORITE GIRL-DRUMMER BANDS.
Andy Warhol

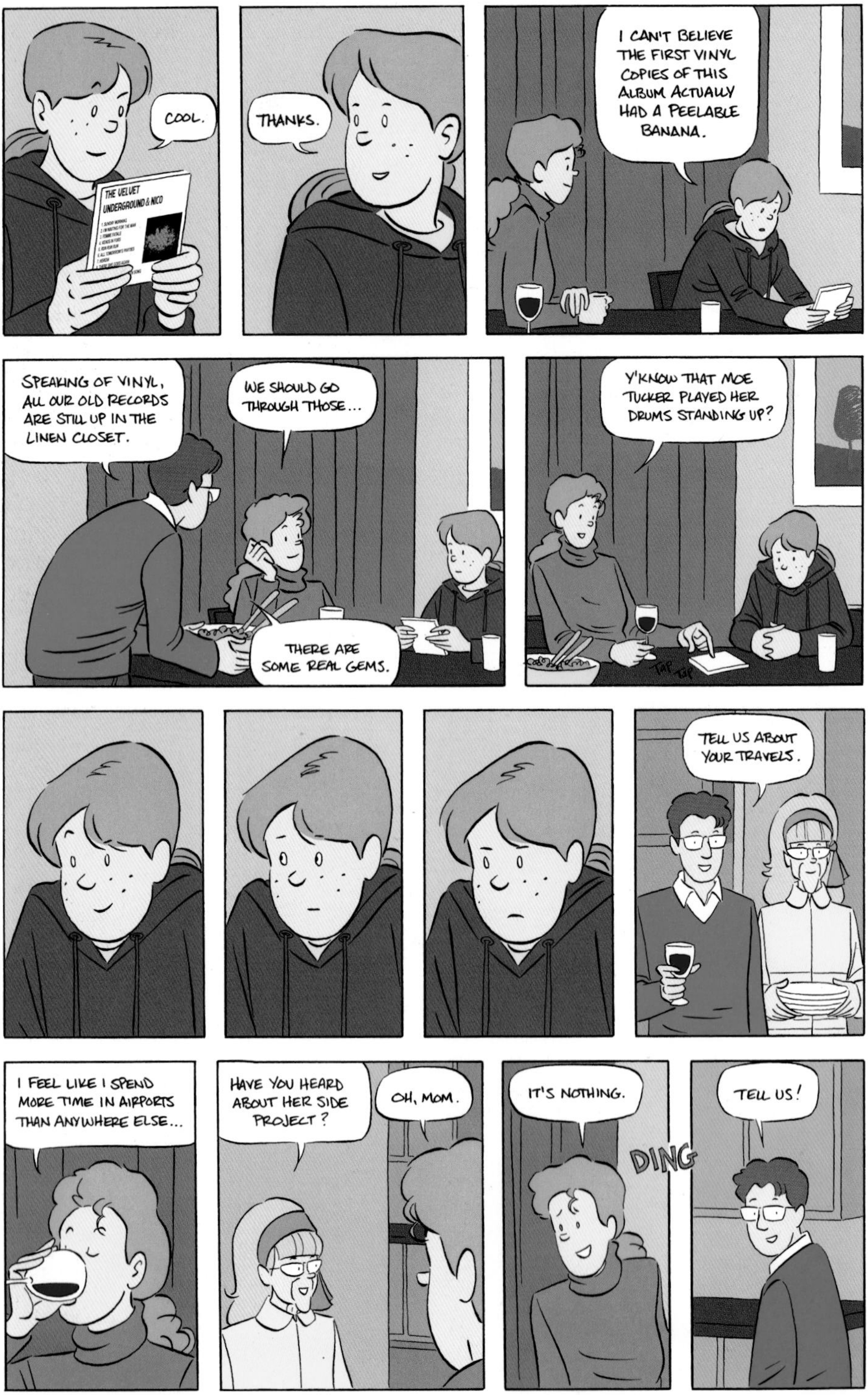
COOL.
THE VELVET UNDERGROUND & NICO
THANKS.
I CAN'T BELIEVE THE FIRST VINYL COPIES OF THIS ALBUM ACTUALLY HAD A PEELABLE BANANA.
SPEAKING OF VINYL, ALL OUR OLD RECORDS ARE STILL UP IN THE LINEN CLOSET.
WE SHOULD GO THROUGH THOSE...
THERE ARE SOME REAL GEMS.
Y'KNOW THAT MOE TUCKER PLAYED HER DRUMS STANDING UP?
TAP TAP
TELL US ABOUT YOUR TRAVELS.
I FEEL LIKE I SPEND MORE TIME IN AIRPORTS THAN ANYWHERE ELSE...
HAVE YOU HEARD ABOUT HER SIDE PROJECT?
OH, MOM.
IT'S NOTHING.
DING
TELL US!

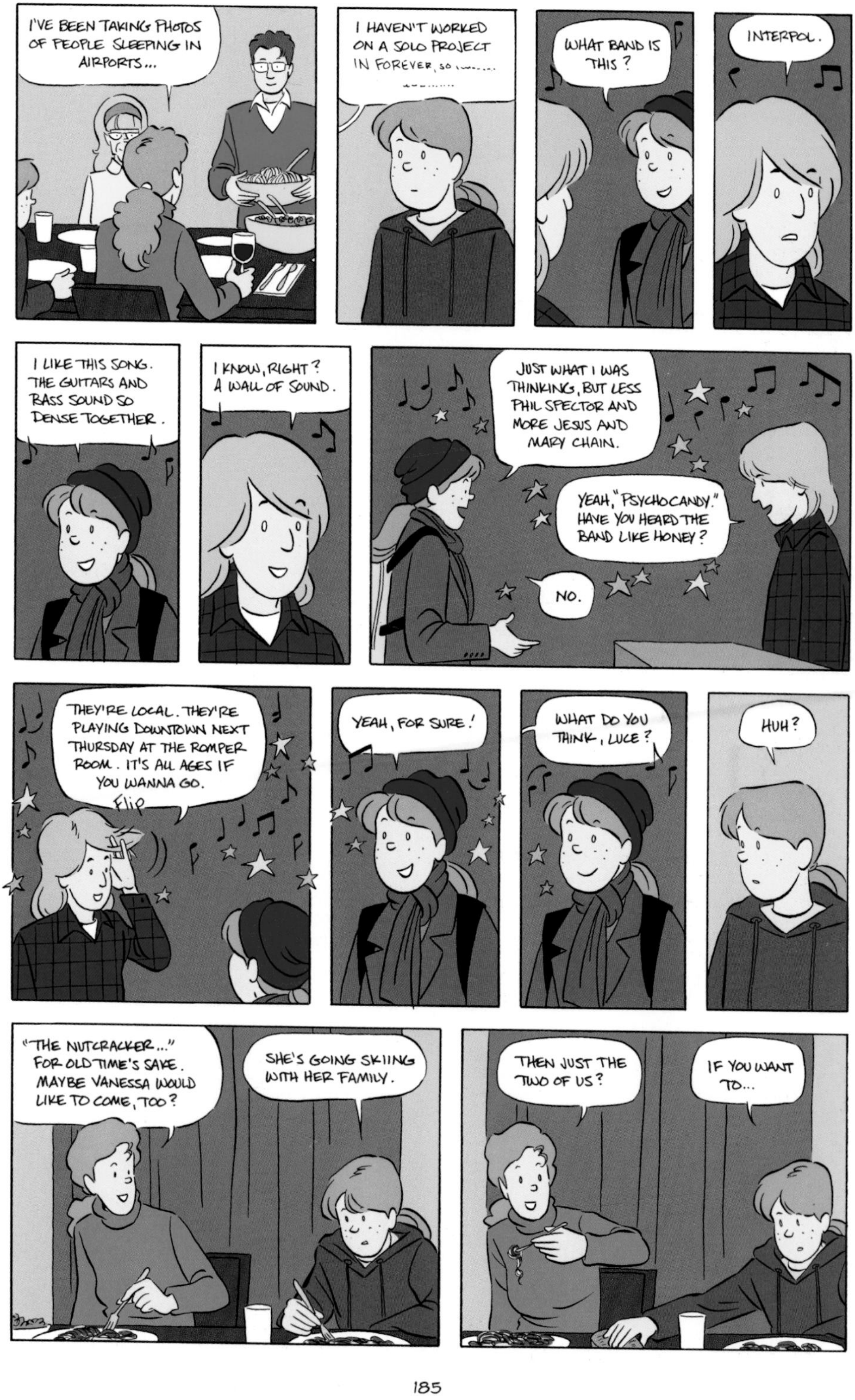
I'VE BEEN TAKING PHOTOS OF PEOPLE SLEEPING IN AIRPORTS...
I HAVEN'T WORKED ON A SOLO PROJECT IN FOREVER, SO I......
WHAT BAND IS THIS?
INTERPOL.
I LIKE THIS SONG. THE GUITARS AND BASS SOUND SO DENSE TOGETHER.
I KNOW, RIGHT? A WALL OF SOUND.
JUST WHAT I WAS THINKING, BUT LESS PHIL SPECTOR AND MORE JESUS AND MARY CHAIN.
YEAH, "PSYCHOCANDY." HAVE YOU HEARD THE BAND LIKE HONEY?
NO.
THEY'RE LOCAL. THEY'RE PLAYING DOWNTOWN NEXT THURSDAY AT THE ROMPER ROOM. IT'S ALL AGES IF YOU WANNA GO.
Flip
YEAH, FOR SURE!
WHAT DO YOU THINK, LUCE?
HUH?
"THE NUTCRACKER..." FOR OLD TIME'S SAKE. MAYBE VANESSA WOULD LIKE TO COME, TOO?
SHE'S GOING SKIING WITH HER FAMILY.
THEN JUST THE TWO OF US?
IF YOU WANT TO...

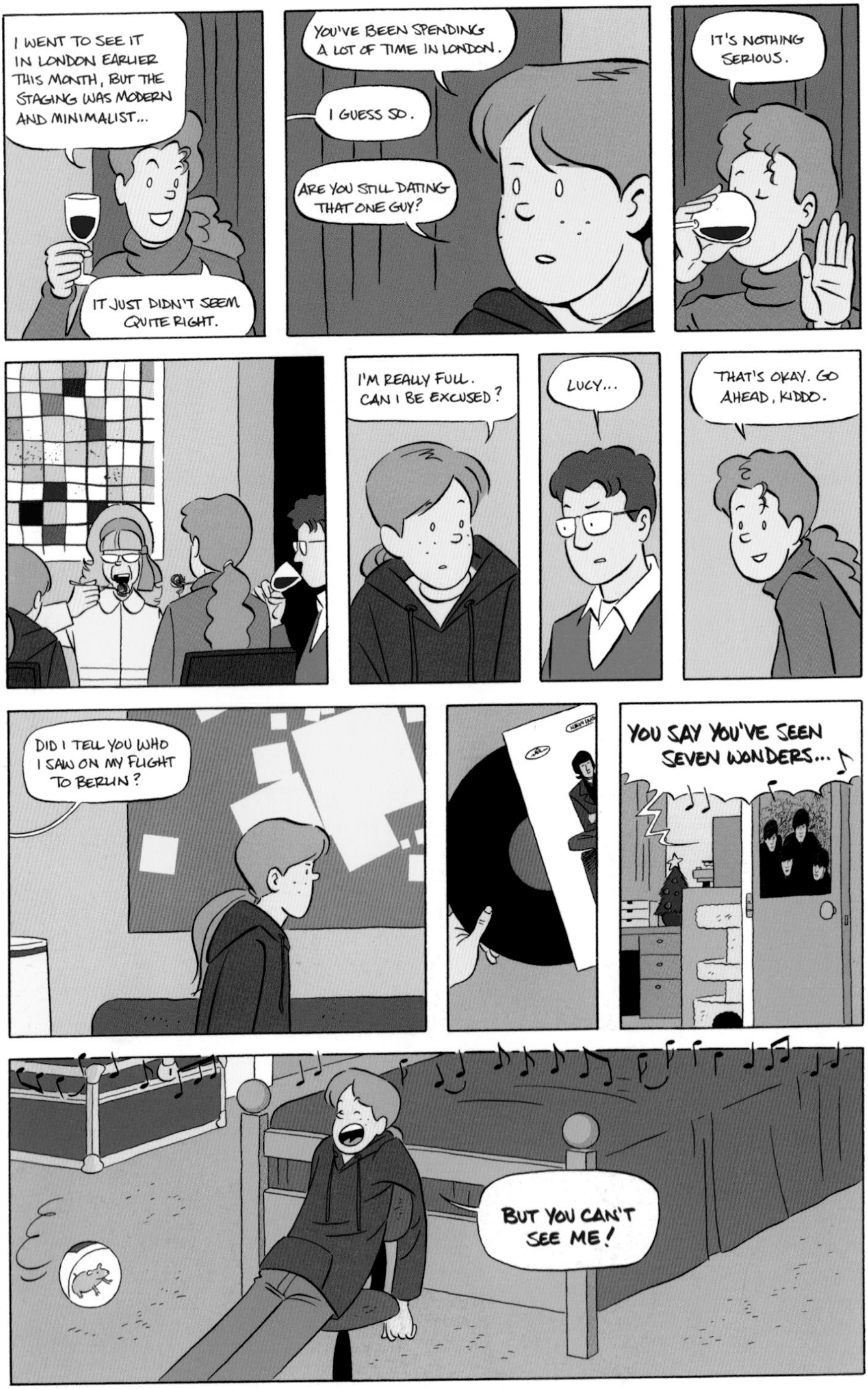
I WENT TO SEE IT IN LONDON EARLIER THIS MONTH, BUT THE STAGING WAS MODERN AND MINIMALIST...
IT JUST DIDN'T SEEM QUITE RIGHT.
YOU'VE BEEN SPENDING A LOT OF TIME IN LONDON.
I GUESS SO.
ARE YOU STILL DATING THAT ONE GUY?
IT'S NOTHING SERIOUS.
I'M REALLY FULL. CAN I BE EXCUSED?
LUCY...
THAT'S OKAY. GO AHEAD, KIDDO.
DID I TELL YOU WHO I SAW ON MY FLIGHT TO BERLIN?
YOU SAY YOU'VE SEEN SEVEN WONDERS...
BUT YOU CAN'T SEE ME!

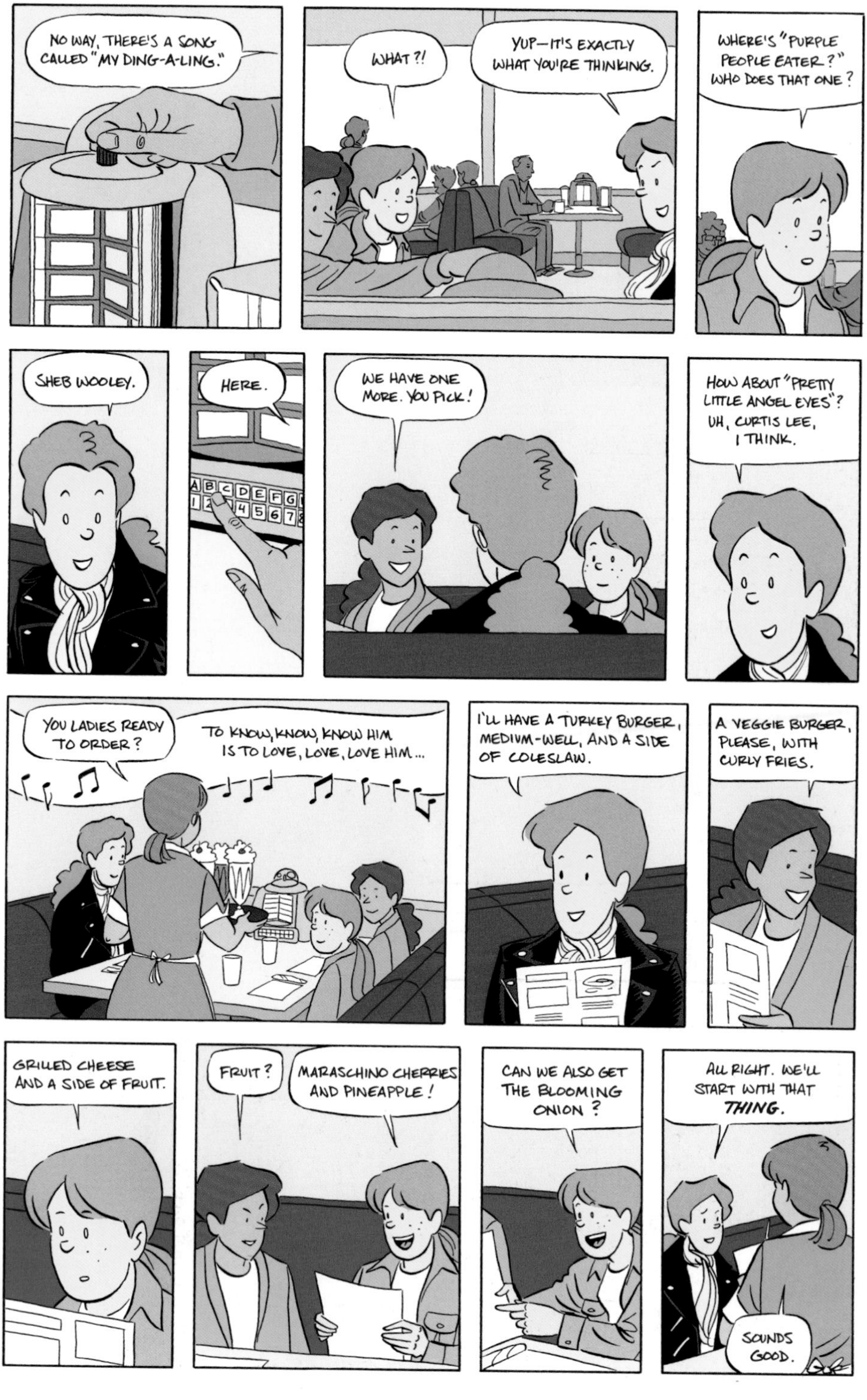
NO WAY, THERE'S A SONG CALLED "MY DING-A-LING."
WHAT?!
YUP—IT'S EXACTLY WHAT YOU'RE THINKING.
WHERE'S "PURPLE PEOPLE EATER?" WHO DOES THAT ONE?
SHEB WOOLEY.
HERE.
WE HAVE ONE MORE. YOU PICK!
HOW ABOUT "PRETTY LITTLE ANGEL EYES"? UH, CURTIS LEE, I THINK.
YOU LADIES READY TO ORDER?
TO KNOW, KNOW, KNOW HIM IS TO LOVE, LOVE, LOVE HIM...
I'LL HAVE A TURKEY BURGER, MEDIUM-WELL, AND A SIDE OF COLESLAW.
A VEGGIE BURGER, PLEASE, WITH CURLY FRIES.
GRILLED CHEESE AND A SIDE OF FRUIT.
FRUIT?
MARASCHINO CHERRIES AND PINEAPPLE!
CAN WE ALSO GET THE BLOOMING ONION?
ALL RIGHT. WE'LL START WITH THAT *THING*.
SOUNDS GOOD.

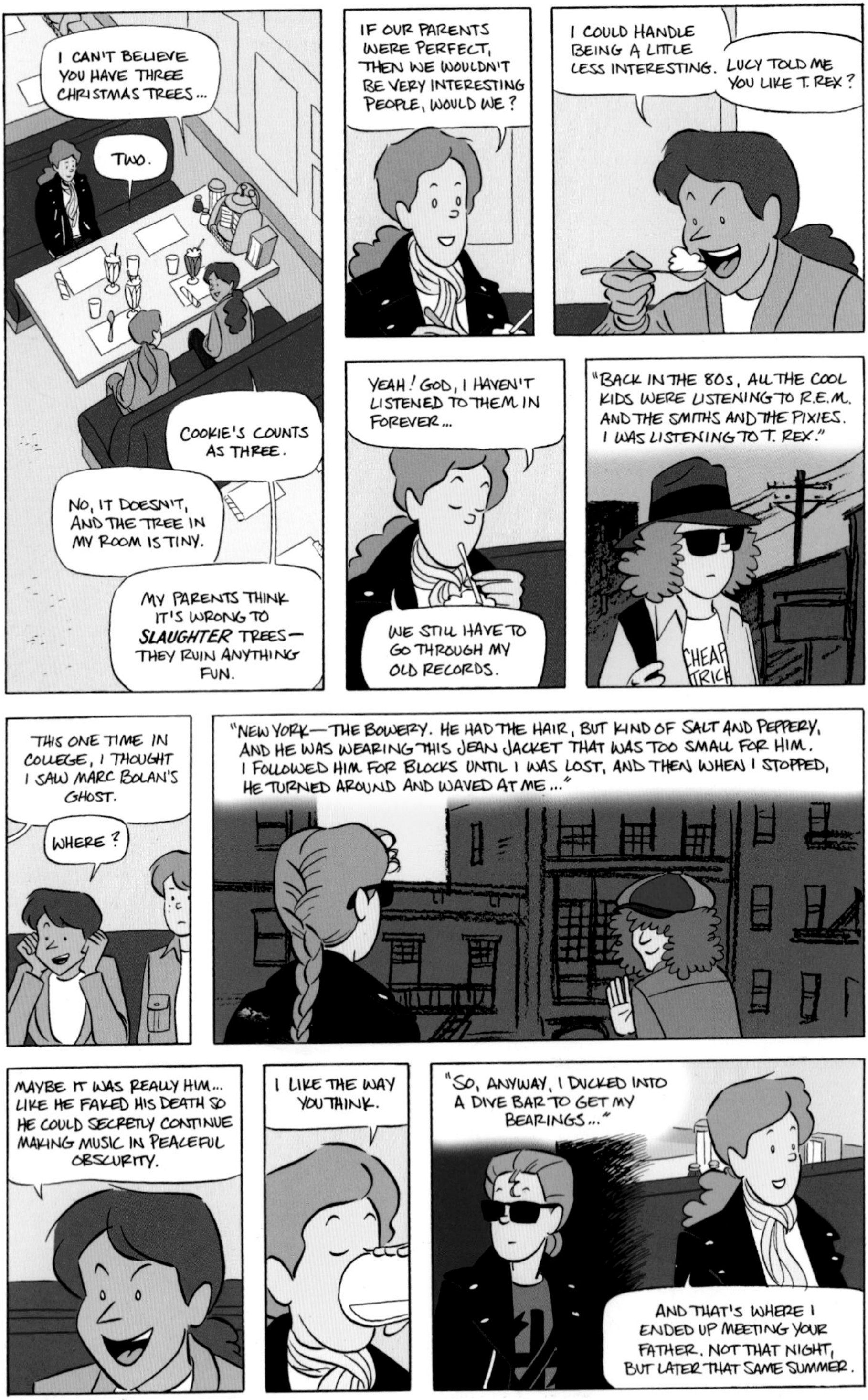
I CAN'T BELIEVE YOU HAVE THREE CHRISTMAS TREES...
TWO.
COOKIE'S COUNTS AS THREE.
NO, IT DOESN'T, AND THE TREE IN MY ROOM IS TINY.
MY PARENTS THINK IT'S WRONG TO SLAUGHTER TREES— THEY RUIN ANYTHING FUN.
IF OUR PARENTS WERE PERFECT, THEN WE WOULDN'T BE VERY INTERESTING PEOPLE, WOULD WE?
I COULD HANDLE BEING A LITTLE LESS INTERESTING.
LUCY TOLD ME YOU LIKE T. REX?
YEAH! GOD, I HAVEN'T LISTENED TO THEM IN FOREVER...
WE STILL HAVE TO GO THROUGH MY OLD RECORDS.
"BACK IN THE 80s, ALL THE COOL KIDS WERE LISTENING TO R.E.M. AND THE SMITHS AND THE PIXIES. I WAS LISTENING TO T. REX."
CHEAP TRICK
THIS ONE TIME IN COLLEGE, I THOUGHT I SAW MARC BOLAN'S GHOST.
WHERE?
"NEW YORK— THE BOWERY. HE HAD THE HAIR, BUT KIND OF SALT AND PEPPERY, AND HE WAS WEARING THIS JEAN JACKET THAT WAS TOO SMALL FOR HIM. I FOLLOWED HIM FOR BLOCKS UNTIL I WAS LOST, AND THEN WHEN I STOPPED, HE TURNED AROUND AND WAVED AT ME..."
MAYBE IT WAS REALLY HIM... LIKE HE FAKED HIS DEATH SO HE COULD SECRETLY CONTINUE MAKING MUSIC IN PEACEFUL OBSCURITY.
I LIKE THE WAY YOU THINK.
"SO, ANYWAY, I DUCKED INTO A DIVE BAR TO GET MY BEARINGS..."
AND THAT'S WHERE I ENDED UP MEETING YOUR FATHER. NOT THAT NIGHT, BUT LATER THAT SAME SUMMER.

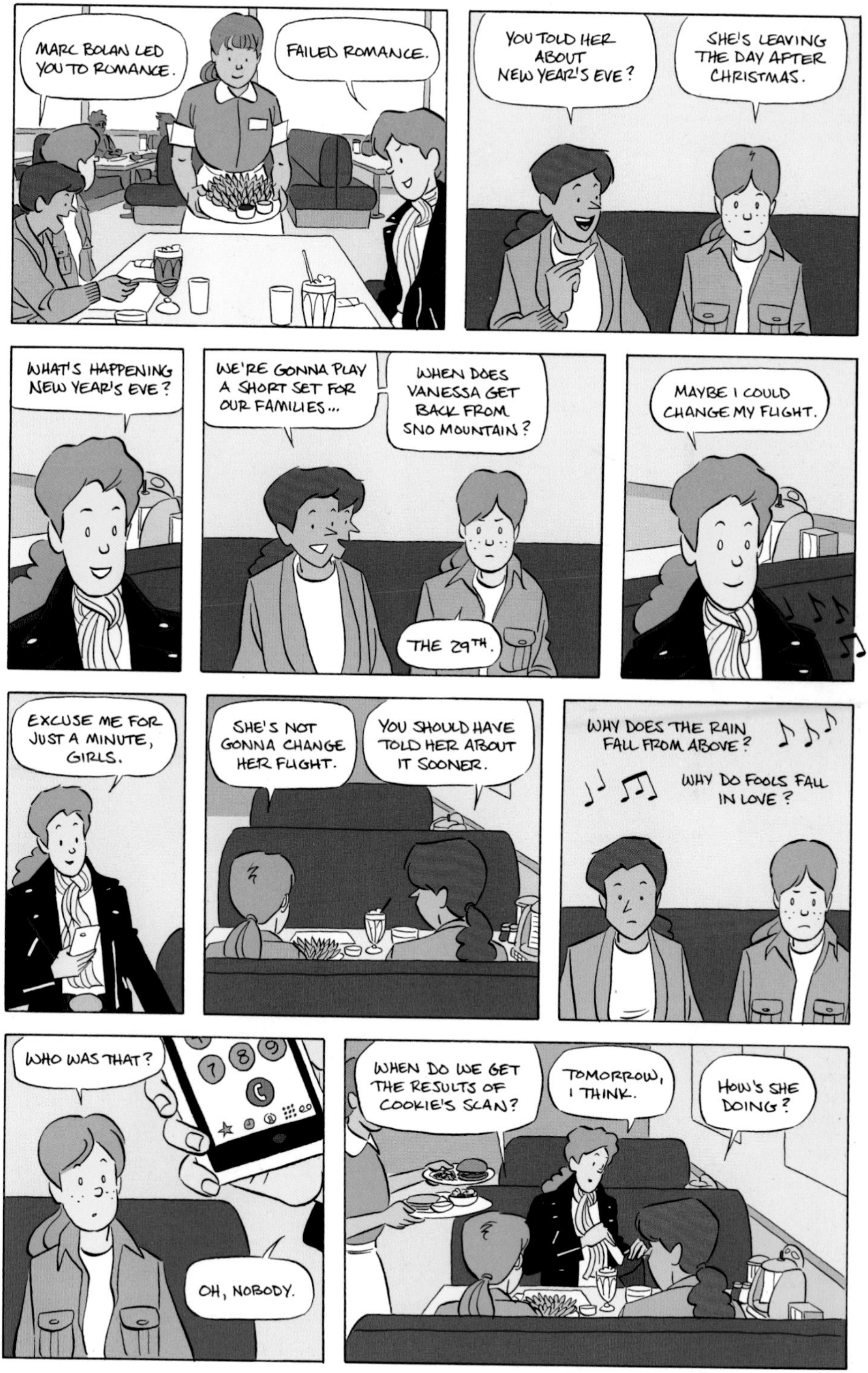
MARC BOLAN LED YOU TO ROMANCE.
FAILED ROMANCE.
YOU TOLD HER ABOUT NEW YEAR'S EVE?
SHE'S LEAVING THE DAY AFTER CHRISTMAS.
WHAT'S HAPPENING NEW YEAR'S EVE?
WE'RE GONNA PLAY A SHORT SET FOR OUR FAMILIES...
WHEN DOES VANESSA GET BACK FROM SNO MOUNTAIN?
THE 29TH.
MAYBE I COULD CHANGE MY FLIGHT.
EXCUSE ME FOR JUST A MINUTE, GIRLS.
SHE'S NOT GONNA CHANGE HER FLIGHT.
YOU SHOULD HAVE TOLD HER ABOUT IT SOONER.
WHY DOES THE RAIN FALL FROM ABOVE?
WHY DO FOOLS FALL IN LOVE?
WHO WAS THAT?
OH, NOBODY.
WHEN DO WE GET THE RESULTS OF COOKIE'S SCAN?
TOMORROW, I THINK.
HOW'S SHE DOING?

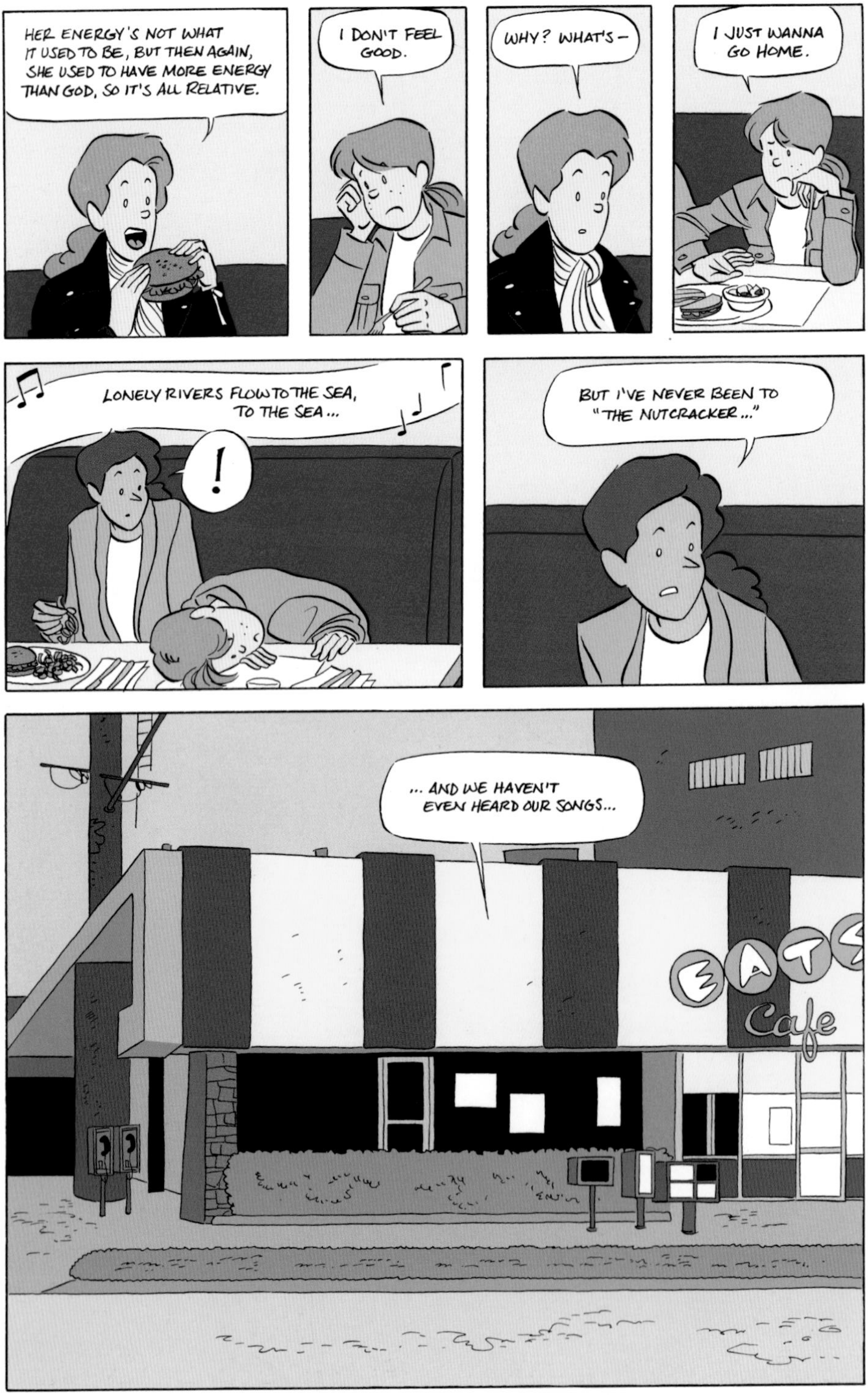
HER ENERGY'S NOT WHAT IT USED TO BE, BUT THEN AGAIN, SHE USED TO HAVE MORE ENERGY THAN GOD, SO IT'S ALL RELATIVE.
I DON'T FEEL GOOD.
WHY? WHAT'S –
I JUST WANNA GO HOME.
LONELY RIVERS FLOW TO THE SEA, TO THE SEA...
!
BUT I'VE NEVER BEEN TO "THE NUTCRACKER..."
... AND WE HAVEN'T EVEN HEARD OUR SONGS...
EATS
Cafe

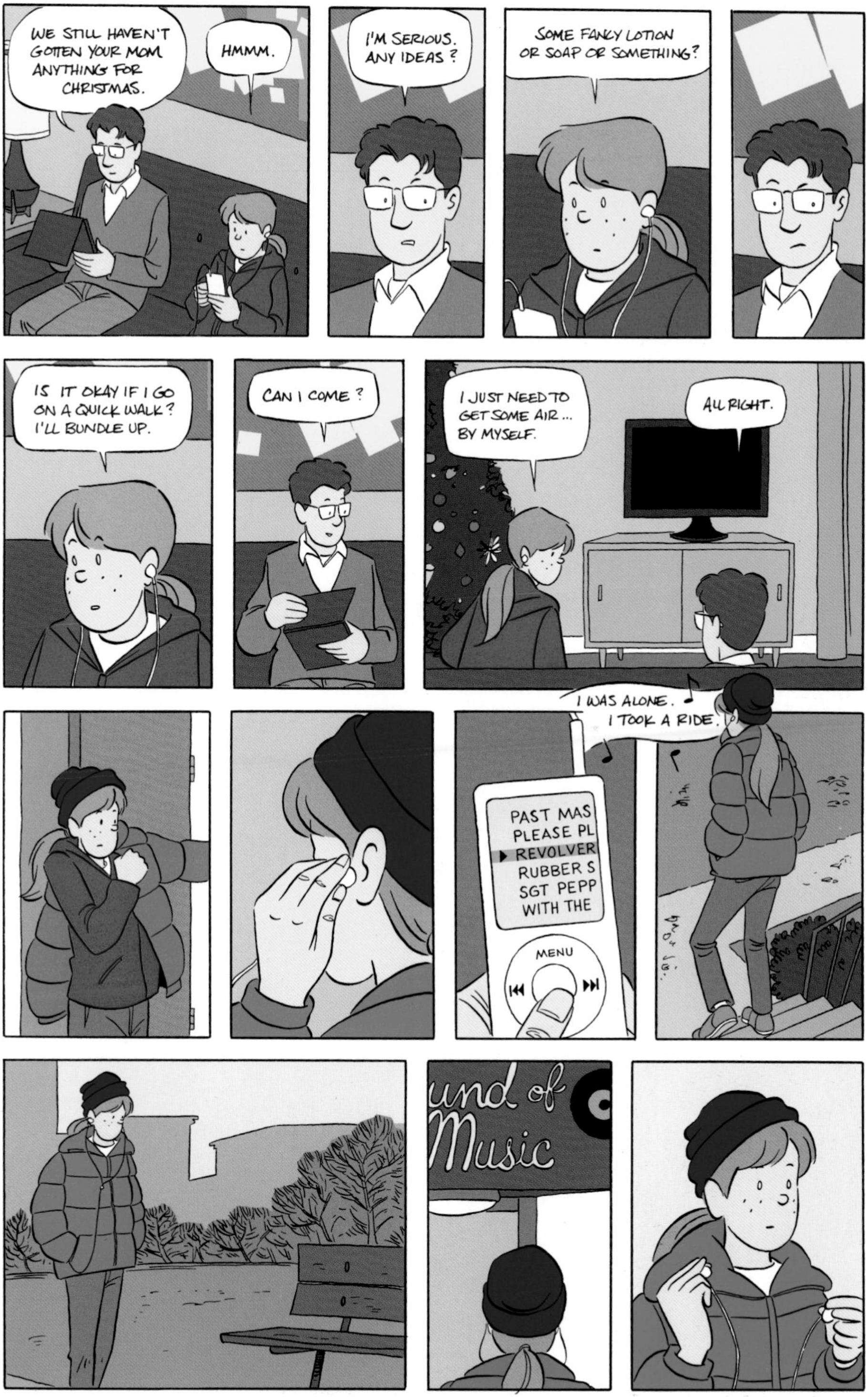
WE STILL HAVEN'T GOTTEN YOUR MOM ANYTHING FOR CHRISTMAS.
HMMM.
I'M SERIOUS. ANY IDEAS ?
SOME FANCY LOTION OR SOAP OR SOMETHING?
IS IT OKAY IF I GO ON A QUICK WALK? I'LL BUNDLE UP.
CAN I COME ?
I JUST NEED TO GET SOME AIR... BY MYSELF.
ALL RIGHT.
I WAS ALONE. I TOOK A RIDE.
PAST MAS
PLEASE PL
REVOLVER
RUBBER S
SGT PEPP
WITH THE
MENU
und of
Music

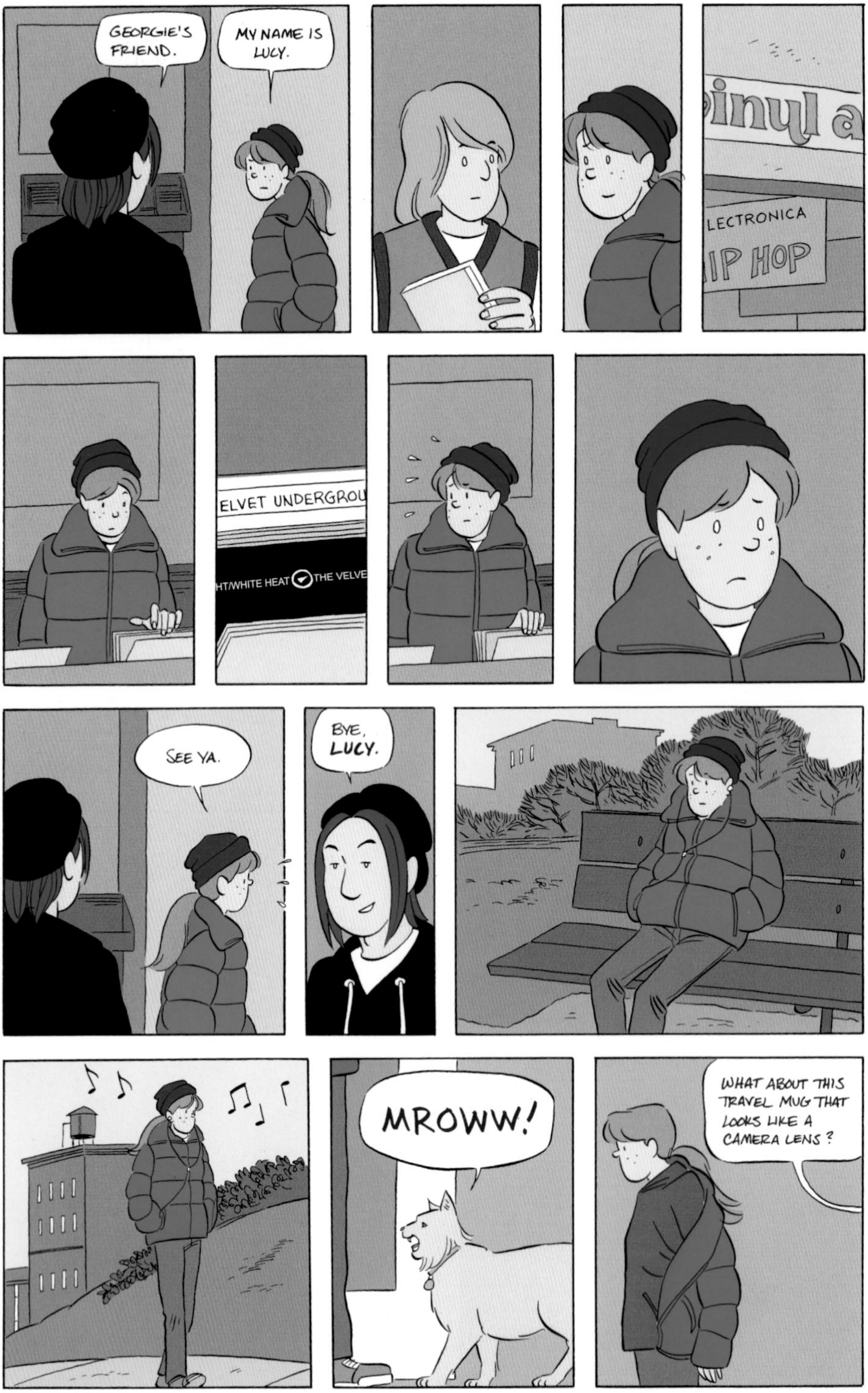
GEORGIE'S FRIEND.
MY NAME IS LUCY.
ELECTRONICA
IP HOP
ELVET UNDERGROU
HT/WHITE HEAT
THE VELVE
SEE YA.
BYE, LUCY.
MROWW!
WHAT ABOUT THIS TRAVEL MUG THAT LOOKS LIKE A CAMERA LENS?

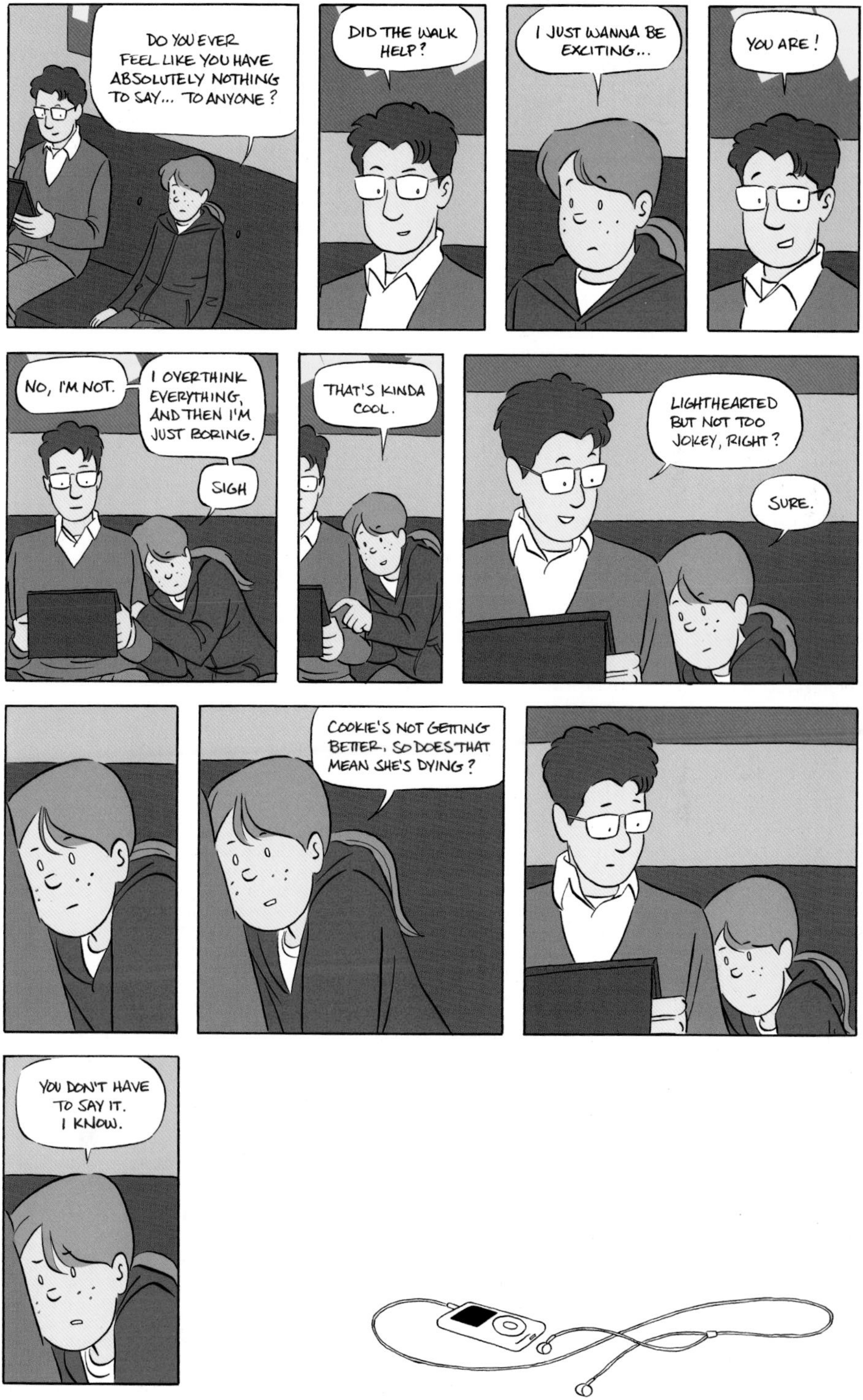
DO YOU EVER FEEL LIKE YOU HAVE ABSOLUTELY NOTHING TO SAY... TO ANYONE?
DID THE WALK HELP?
I JUST WANNA BE EXCITING...
YOU ARE!
NO, I'M NOT.
I OVERTHINK EVERYTHING, AND THEN I'M JUST BORING.
SIGH
THAT'S KINDA COOL.
LIGHTHEARTED BUT NOT TOO JOKEY, RIGHT?
SURE.
COOKIE'S NOT GETTING BETTER, SO DOES THAT MEAN SHE'S DYING?
YOU DON'T HAVE TO SAY IT. I KNOW.

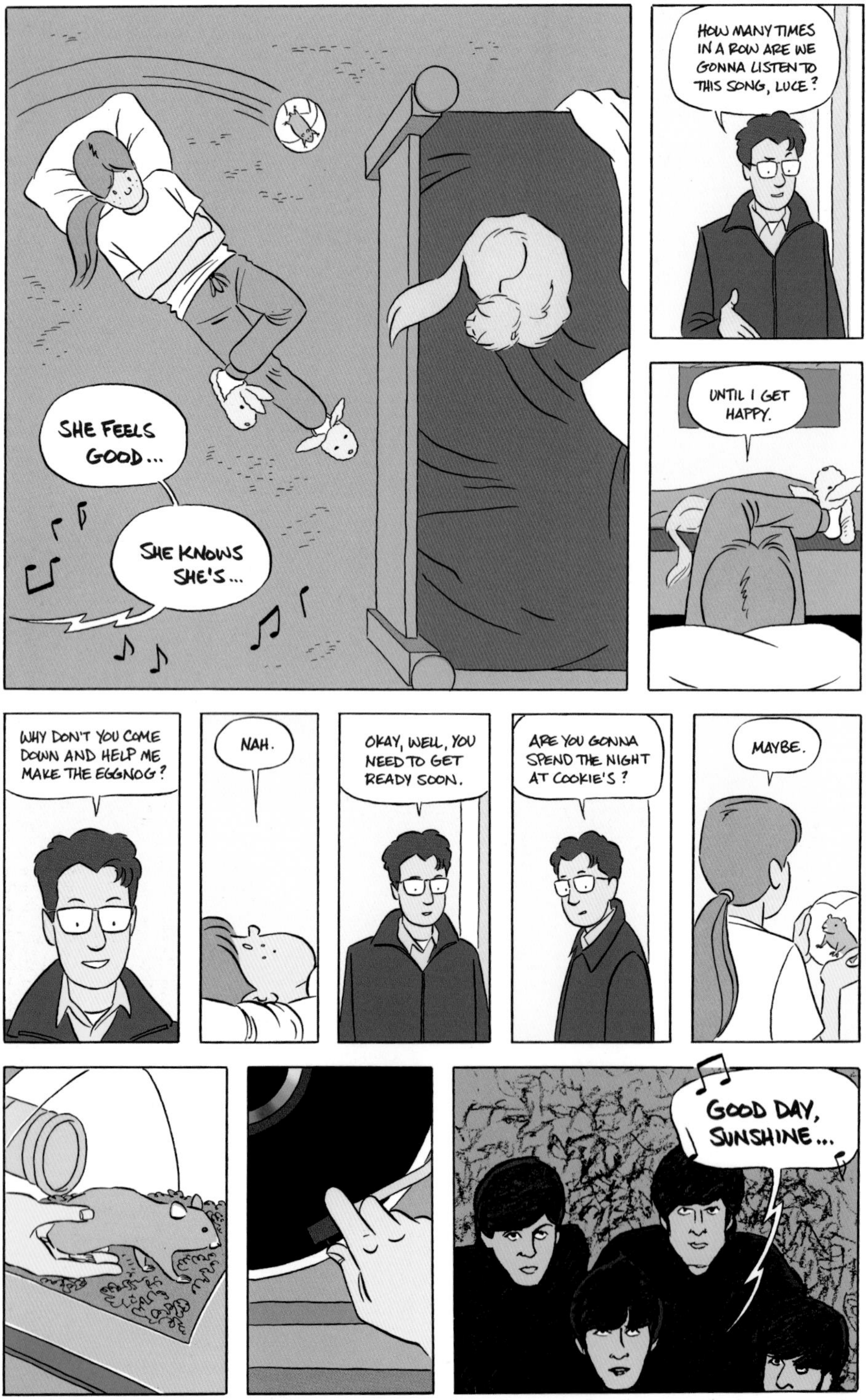
SHE FEELS GOOD...
SHE KNOWS SHE'S...
HOW MANY TIMES IN A ROW ARE WE GONNA LISTEN TO THIS SONG, LUCE?
UNTIL I GET HAPPY.
WHY DON'T YOU COME DOWN AND HELP ME MAKE THE EGGNOG?
NAH.
OKAY, WELL, YOU NEED TO GET READY SOON.
ARE YOU GONNA SPEND THE NIGHT AT COOKIE'S?
MAYBE.
GOOD DAY, SUNSHINE...

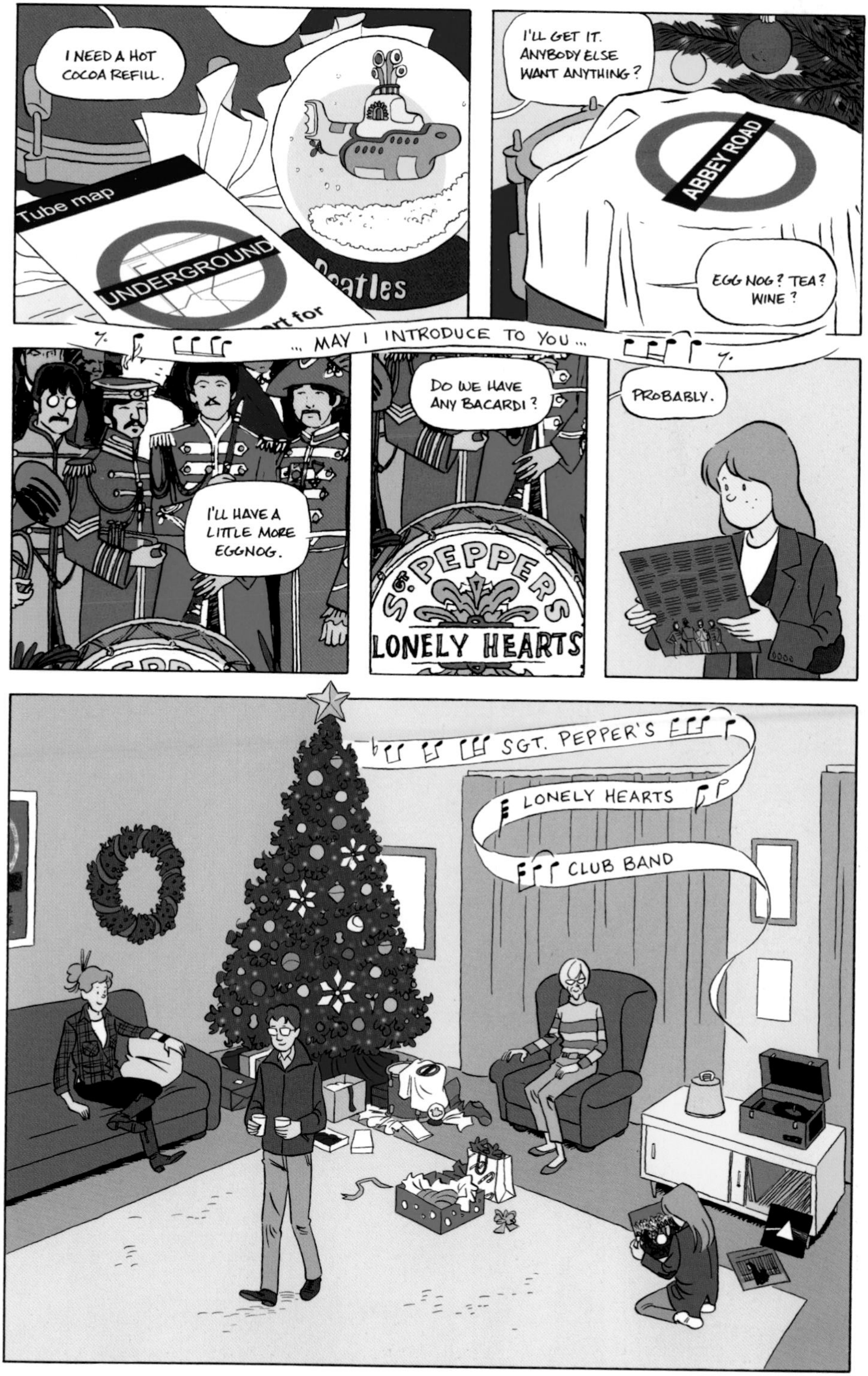
I NEED A HOT COCOA REFILL.
Tube map
UNDERGROUND
Beatles
I'LL GET IT. ANYBODY ELSE WANT ANYTHING?
ABBEY ROAD
EGG NOG? TEA? WINE?
... MAY I INTRODUCE TO YOU...
I'LL HAVE A LITTLE MORE EGGNOG.
DO WE HAVE ANY BACARDI?
SGT. PEPPERS
LONELY HEARTS
PROBABLY.
SGT. PEPPER'S
LONELY HEARTS
CLUB BAND

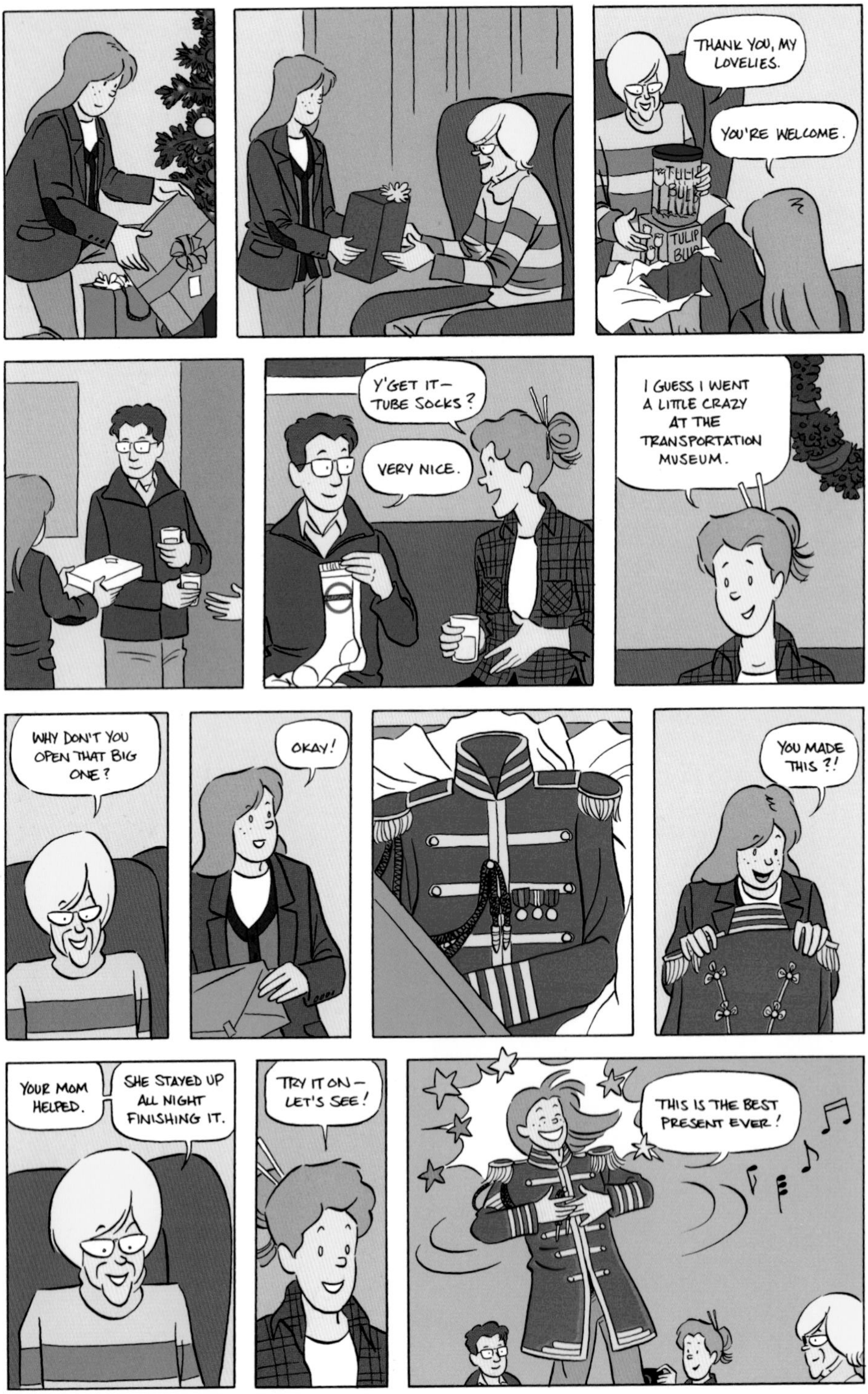
THANK YOU, MY LOVELIES.
YOU'RE WELCOME.
TULIP BULB
TULIP BULB
Y'GET IT— TUBE SOCKS?
VERY NICE.
I GUESS I WENT A LITTLE CRAZY AT THE TRANSPORTATION MUSEUM.
WHY DON'T YOU OPEN THAT BIG ONE?
OKAY!
YOU MADE THIS?!
YOUR MOM HELPED.
SHE STAYED UP ALL NIGHT FINISHING IT.
TRY IT ON— LET'S SEE!
THIS IS THE BEST PRESENT EVER!

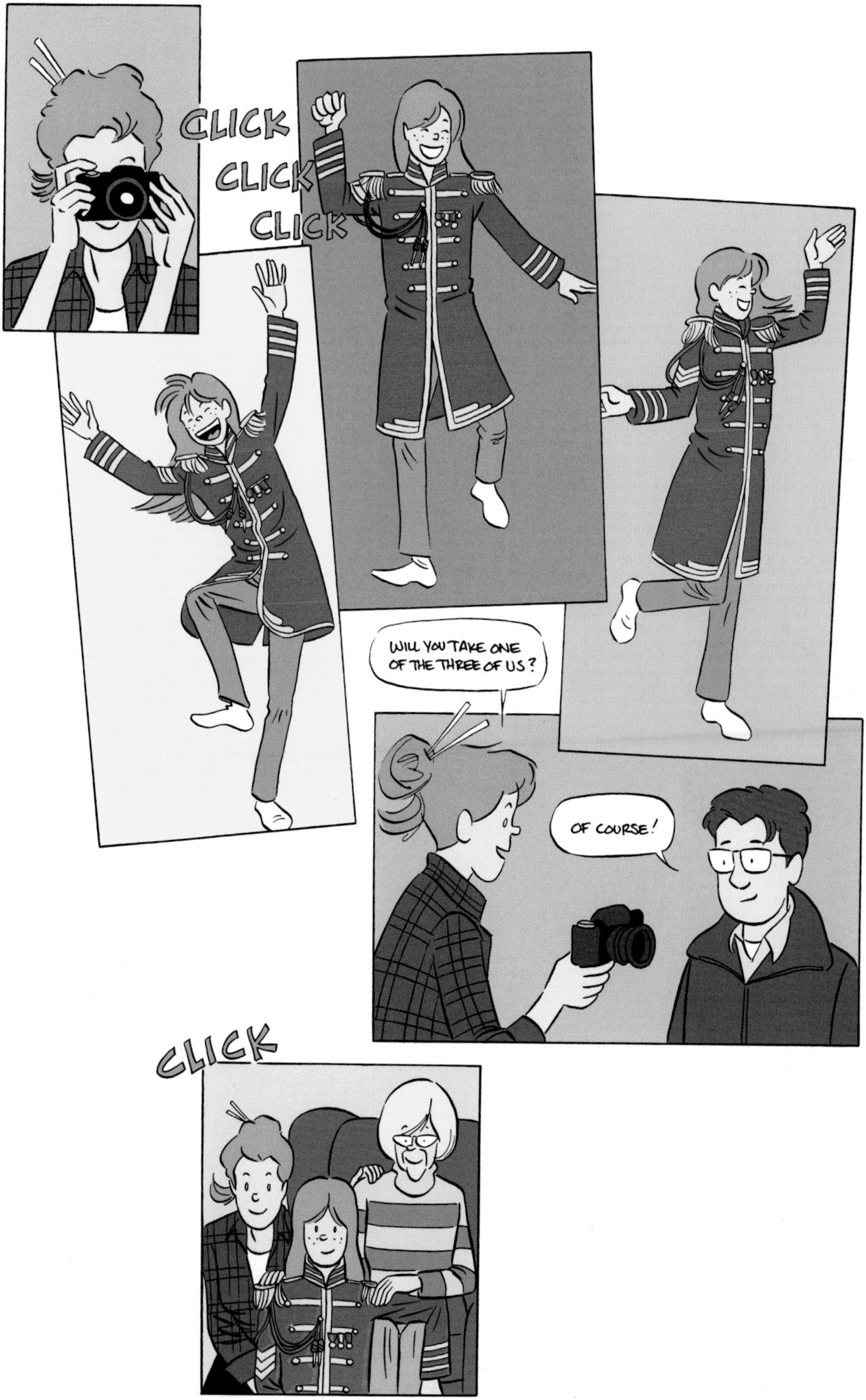
CLICK
CLICK
CLICK
WILL YOU TAKE ONE OF THE THREE OF US?
OF COURSE!
CLICK

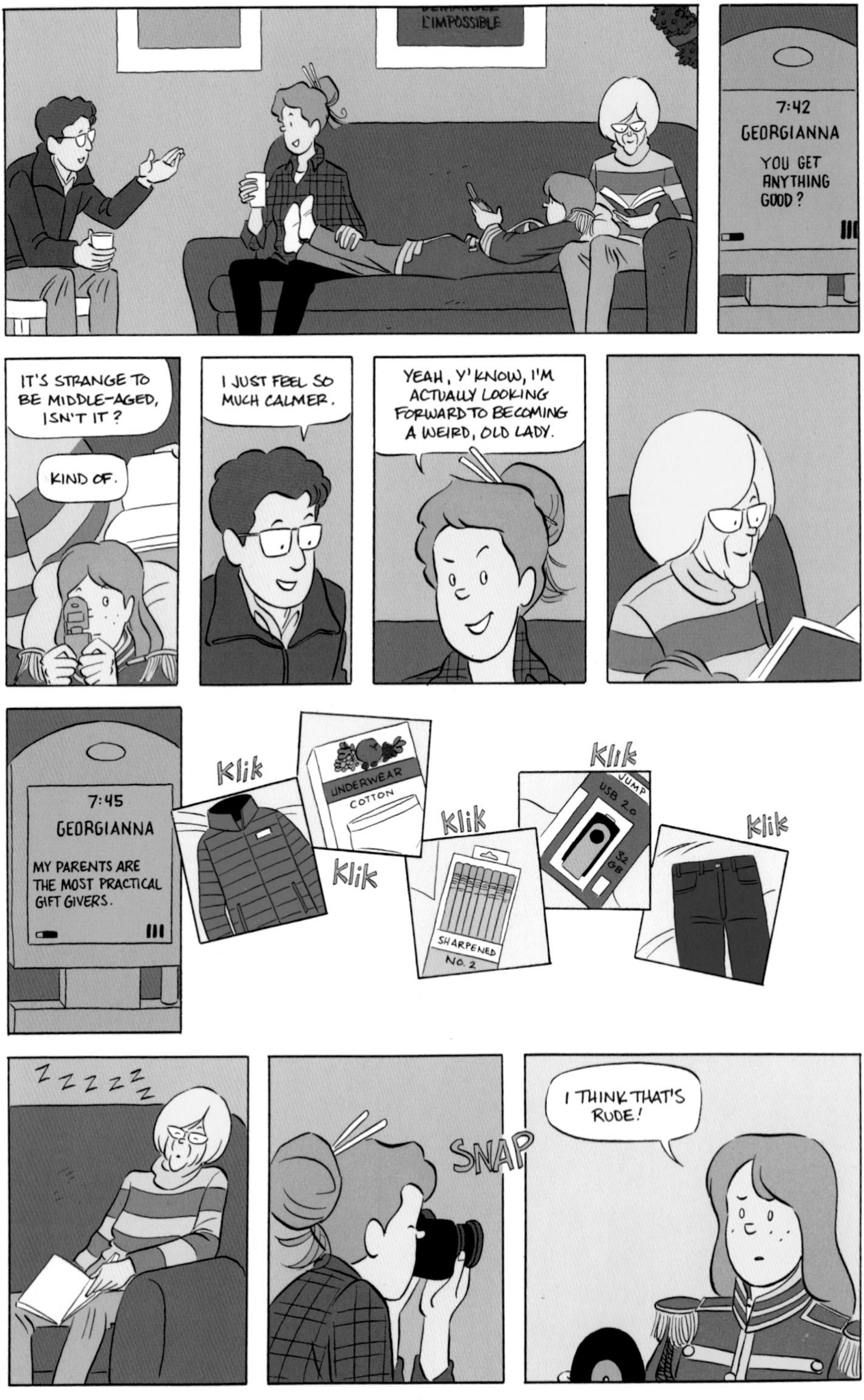
L'IMPOSSIBLE
7:42
GEORGIANNA
YOU GET ANYTHING GOOD?
IT'S STRANGE TO BE MIDDLE-AGED, ISN'T IT?
KIND OF.
I JUST FEEL SO MUCH CALMER.
YEAH, Y'KNOW, I'M ACTUALLY LOOKING FORWARD TO BECOMING A WEIRD, OLD LADY.
7:45
GEORGIANNA
MY PARENTS ARE THE MOST PRACTICAL GIFT GIVERS.
KLIK
UNDERWEAR
COTTON
KLIK
KLIK
SHARPENED
NO. 2
KLIK
JUMP
USB 2.0
32 GB
KLIK
ZZZZZZ
SNAP
I THINK THAT'S RUDE!

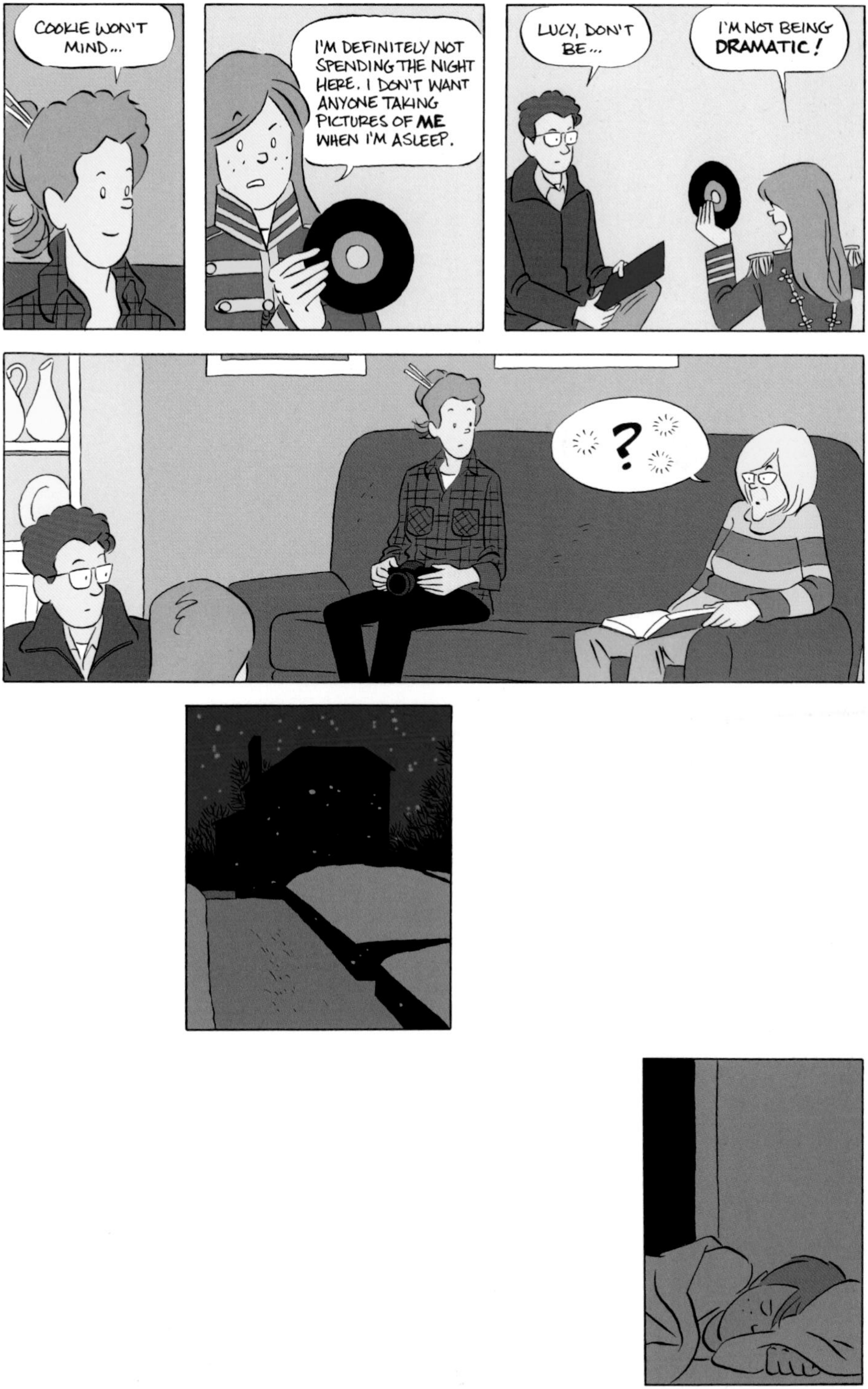
COOKIE WON'T MIND...
I'M DEFINITELY NOT SPENDING THE NIGHT HERE. I DON'T WANT ANYONE TAKING PICTURES OF **ME** WHEN I'M ASLEEP.
LUCY, DON'T BE...
I'M NOT BEING **DRAMATIC!**
?

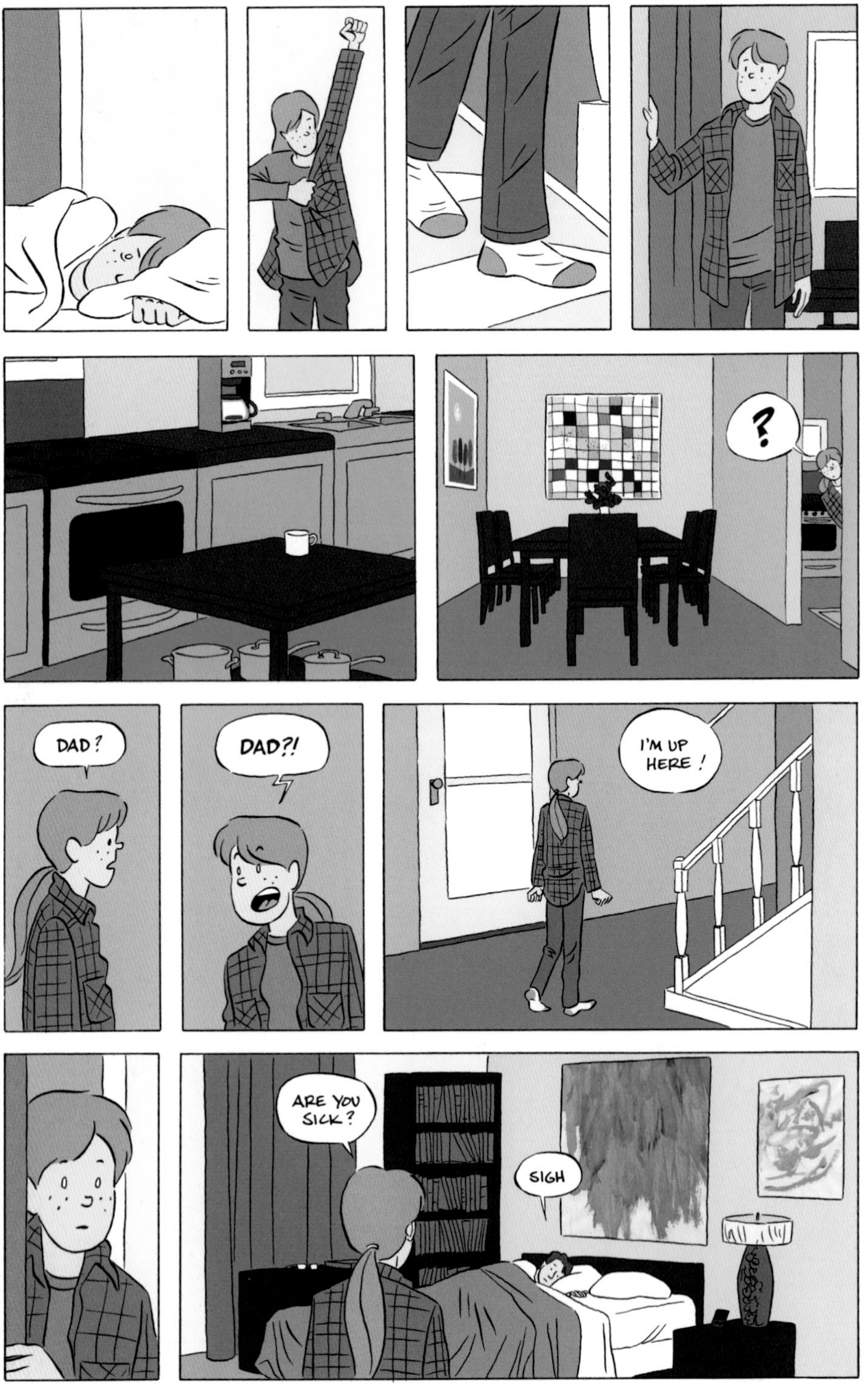
?
DAD?
DAD?!
I'M UP HERE!
ARE YOU SICK?
SIGH

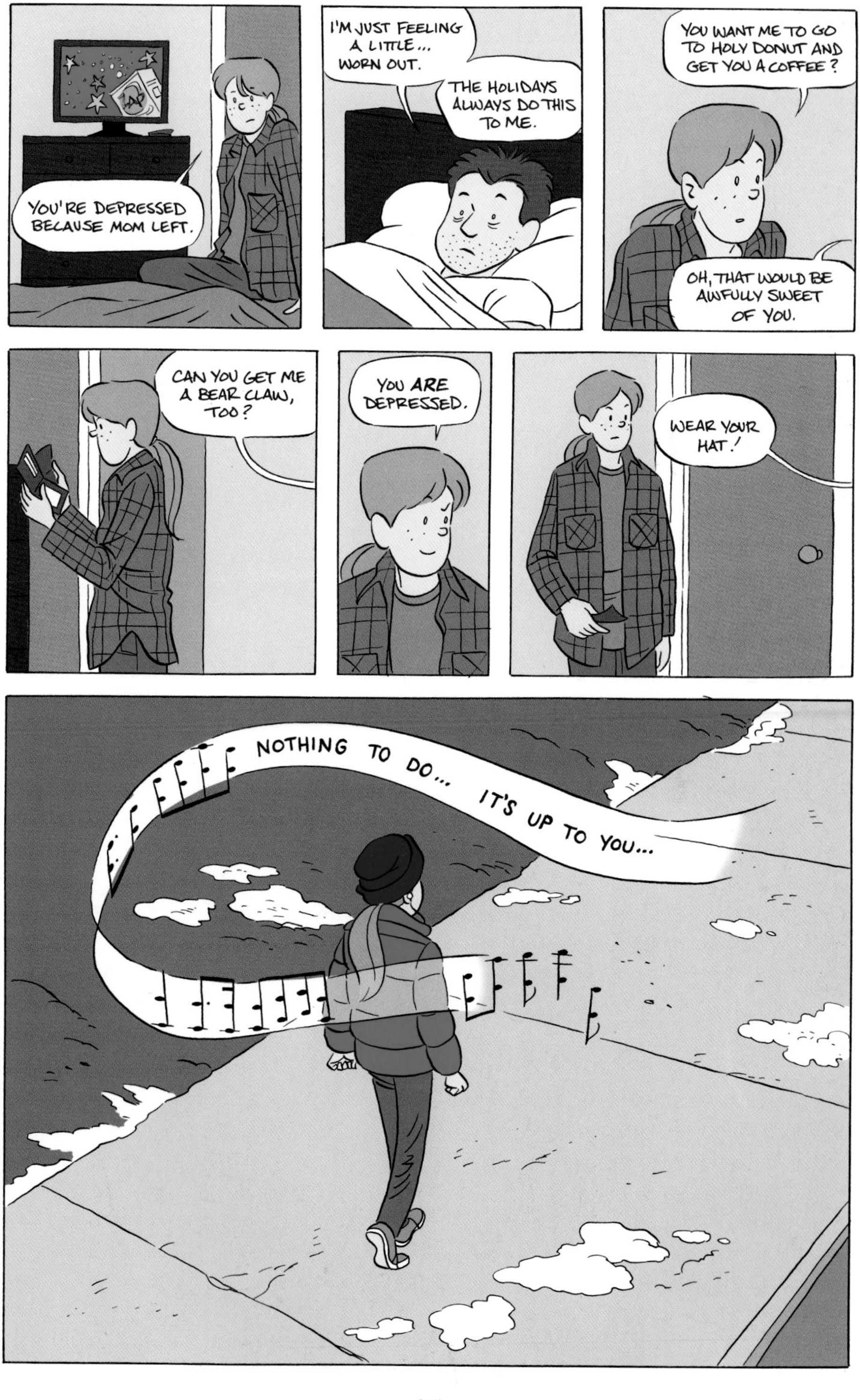
YOU'RE DEPRESSED BECAUSE MOM LEFT.
I'M JUST FEELING A LITTLE... WORN OUT.
THE HOLIDAYS ALWAYS DO THIS TO ME.
YOU WANT ME TO GO TO HOLY DONUT AND GET YOU A COFFEE?
OH, THAT WOULD BE AWFULLY SWEET OF YOU.
CAN YOU GET ME A BEAR CLAW, TOO?
YOU ARE DEPRESSED.
WEAR YOUR HAT!
NOTHING TO DO... IT'S UP TO YOU...

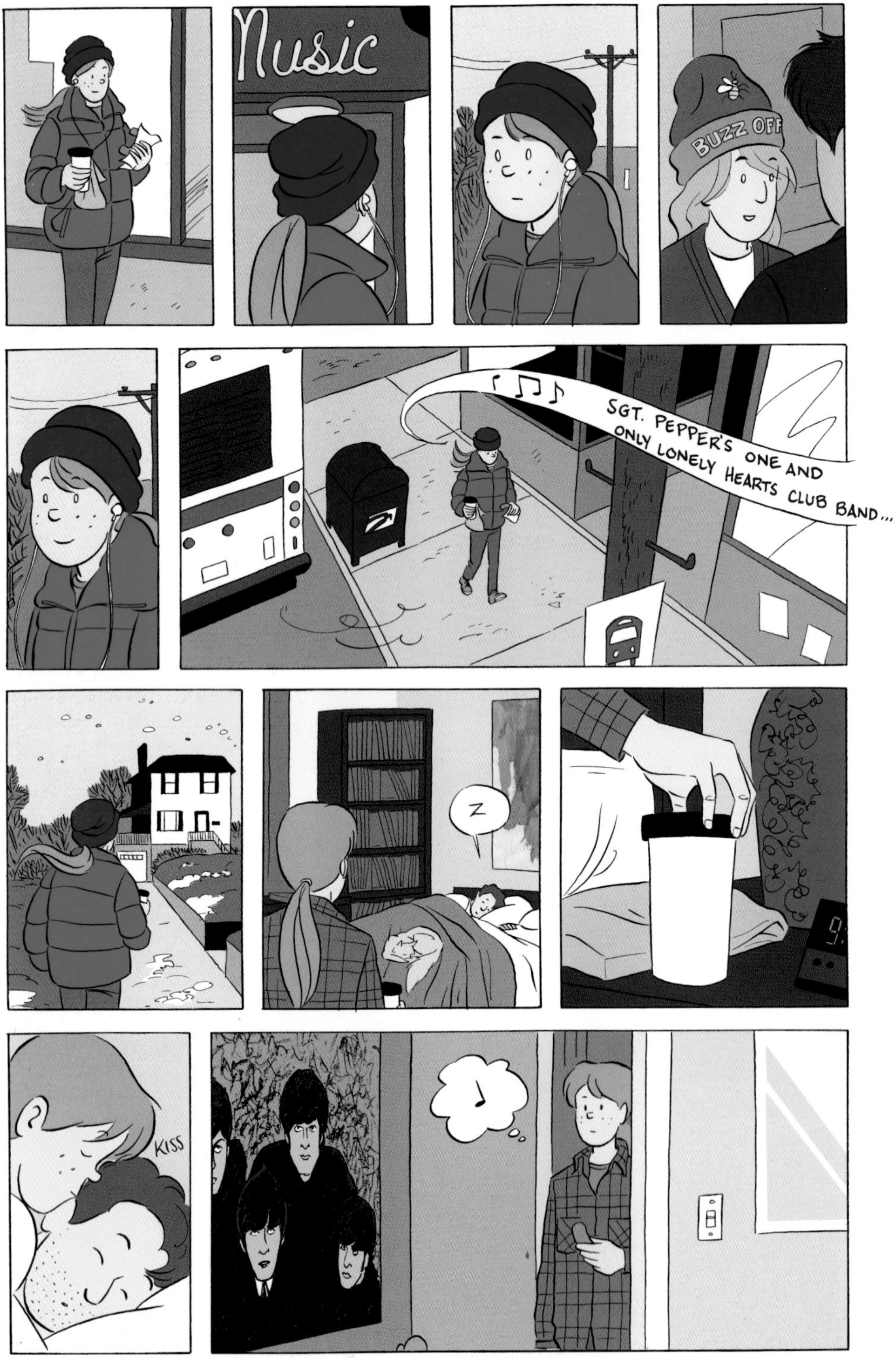
Music
BUZZ OFF
SGT. PEPPER'S ONE AND ONLY LONELY HEARTS CLUB BAND...
Z
KISS

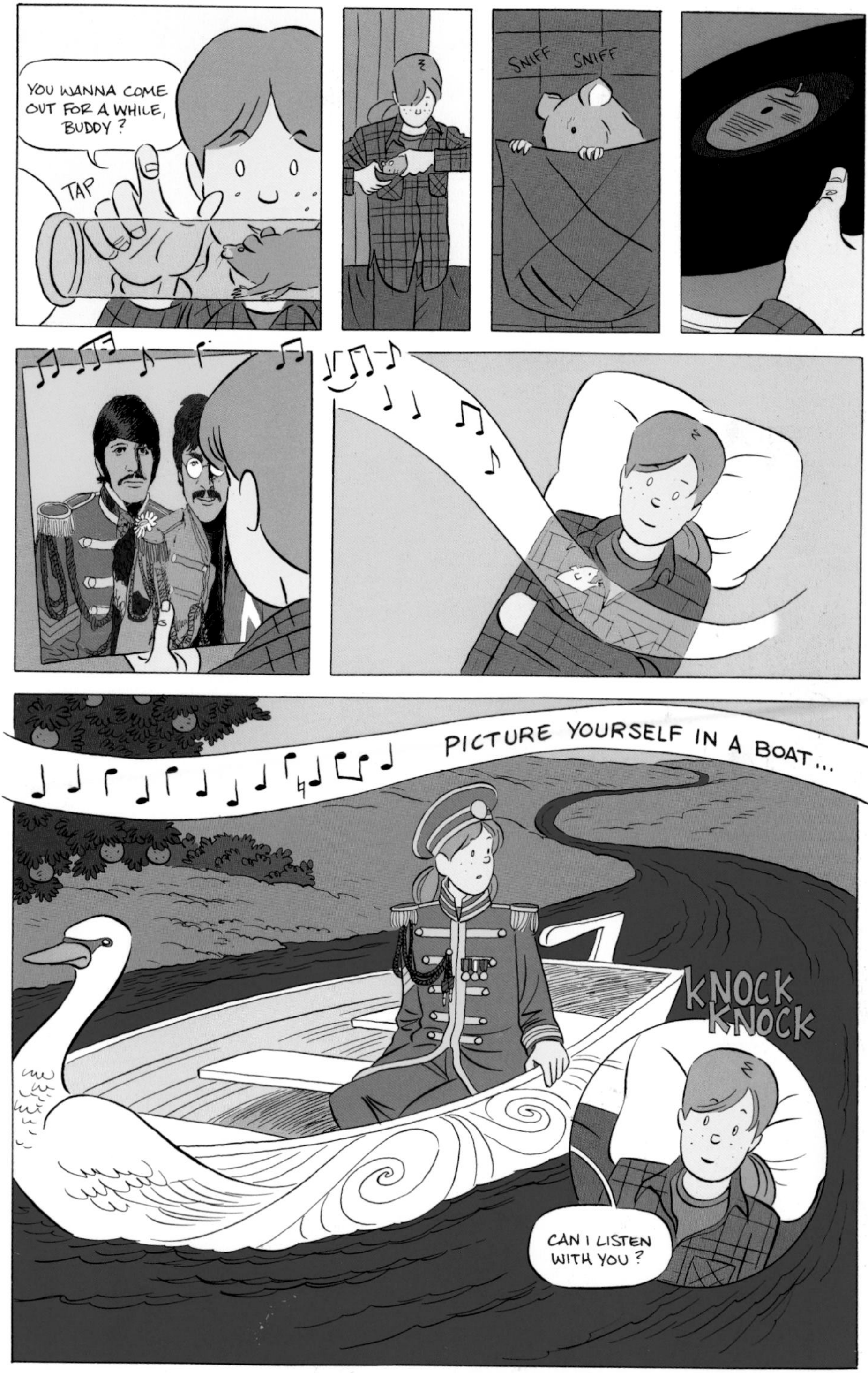
YOU WANNA COME OUT FOR A WHILE, BUDDY?
TAP
SNIFF SNIFF
PICTURE YOURSELF IN A BOAT...
KNOCK KNOCK
CAN I LISTEN WITH YOU?

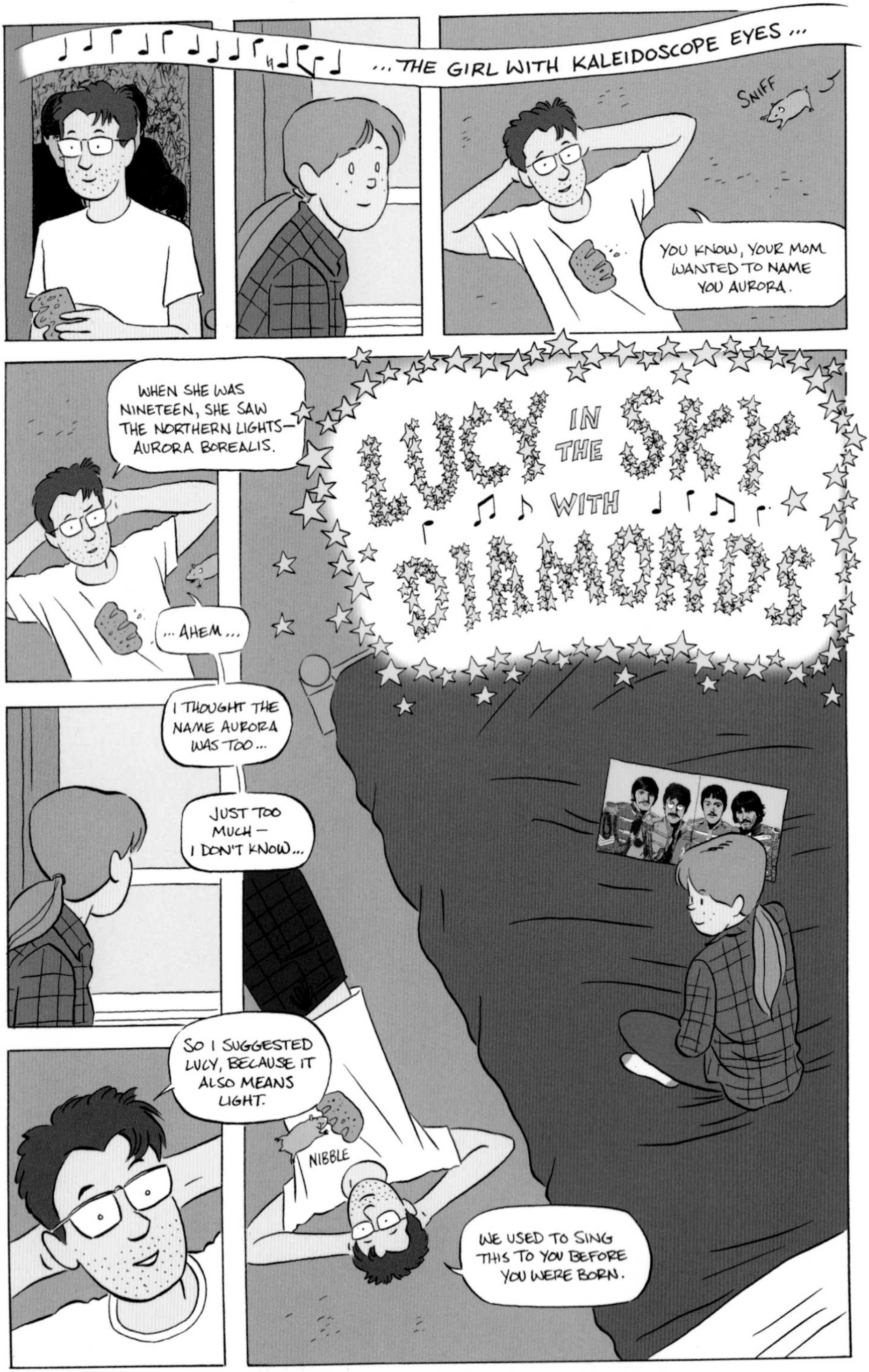
...THE GIRL WITH KALEIDOSCOPE EYES...
SNIFF
YOU KNOW, YOUR MOM WANTED TO NAME YOU AURORA.
WHEN SHE WAS NINETEEN, SHE SAW THE NORTHERN LIGHTS— AURORA BOREALIS.
LUCY IN THE SKY WITH DIAMONDS
...AHEM...
I THOUGHT THE NAME AURORA WAS TOO...
JUST TOO MUCH— I DON'T KNOW...
SO I SUGGESTED LUCY, BECAUSE IT ALSO MEANS LIGHT.
NIBBLE
WE USED TO SING THIS TO YOU BEFORE YOU WERE BORN.

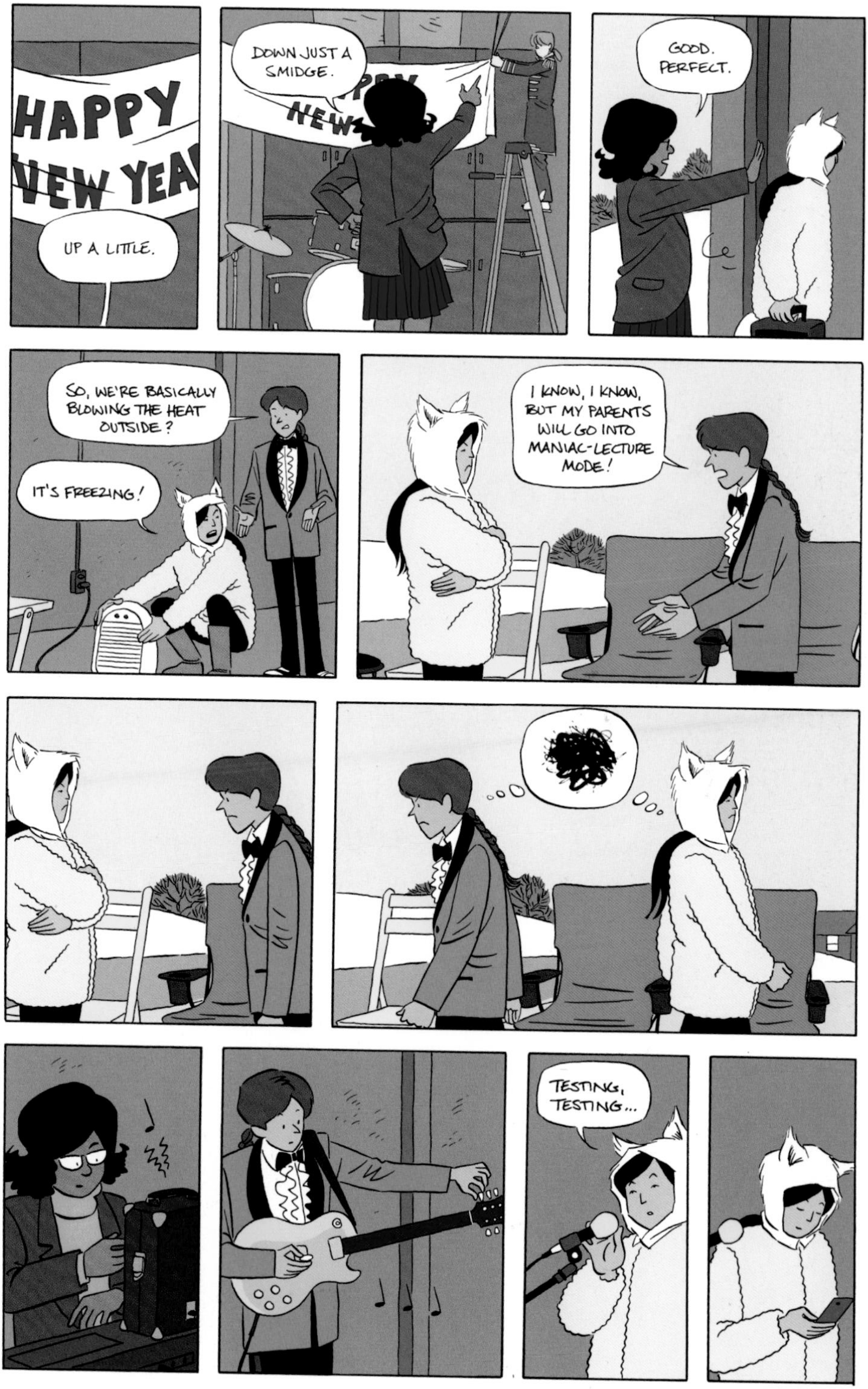
HAPPY NEW YEA
UP A LITTLE.
DOWN JUST A SMIDGE.
GOOD. PERFECT.
SO, WE'RE BASICALLY BLOWING THE HEAT OUTSIDE?
IT'S FREEZING!
I KNOW, I KNOW, BUT MY PARENTS WILL GO INTO MANIAC-LECTURE MODE!
TESTING, TESTING...

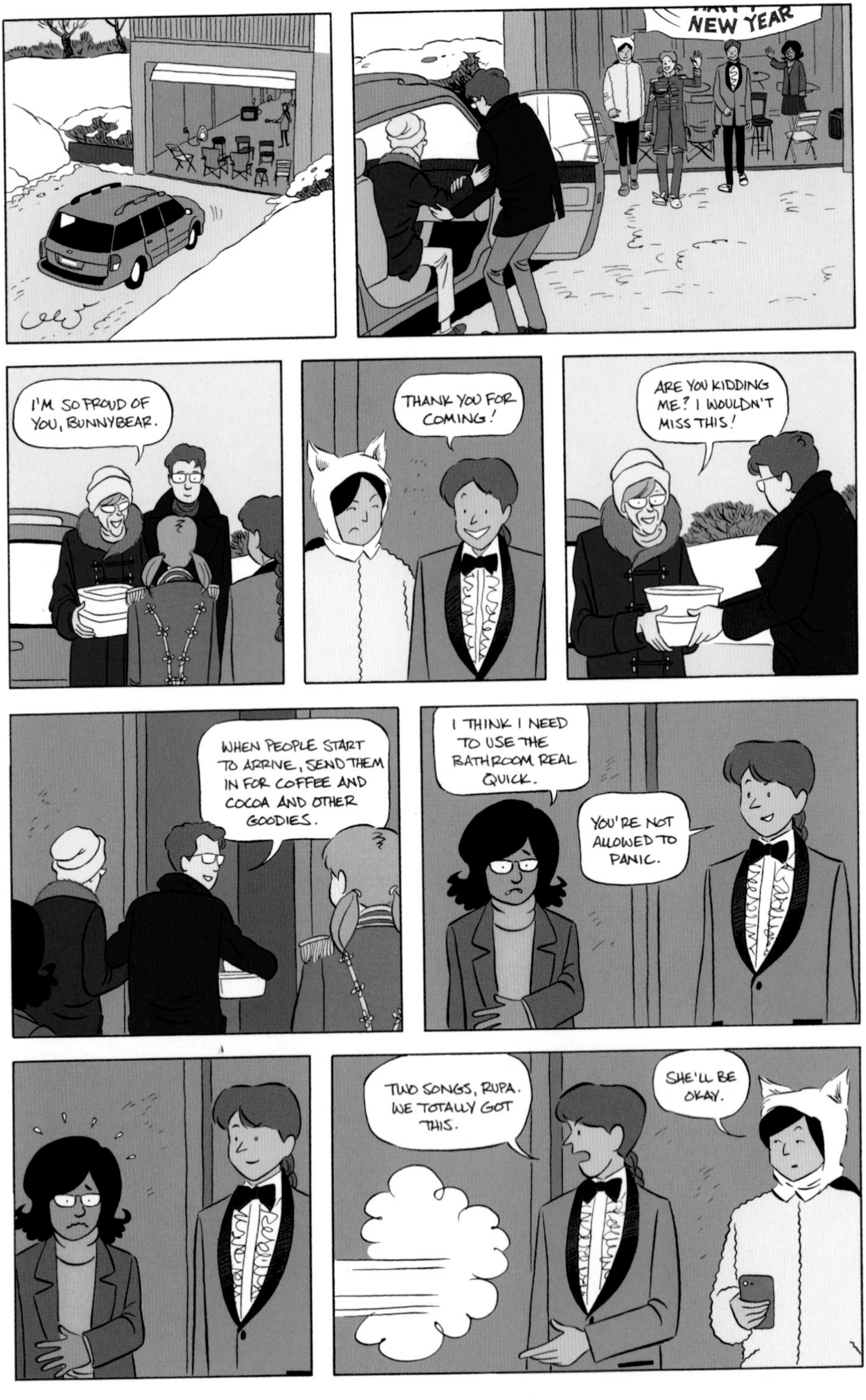
NEW YEAR
I'M SO PROUD OF YOU, BUNNYBEAR.
THANK YOU FOR COMING!
ARE YOU KIDDING ME? I WOULDN'T MISS THIS!
WHEN PEOPLE START TO ARRIVE, SEND THEM IN FOR COFFEE AND COCOA AND OTHER GOODIES.
I THINK I NEED TO USE THE BATHROOM REAL QUICK.
YOU'RE NOT ALLOWED TO PANIC.
TWO SONGS, RUPA. WE TOTALLY GOT THIS.
SHE'LL BE OKAY.

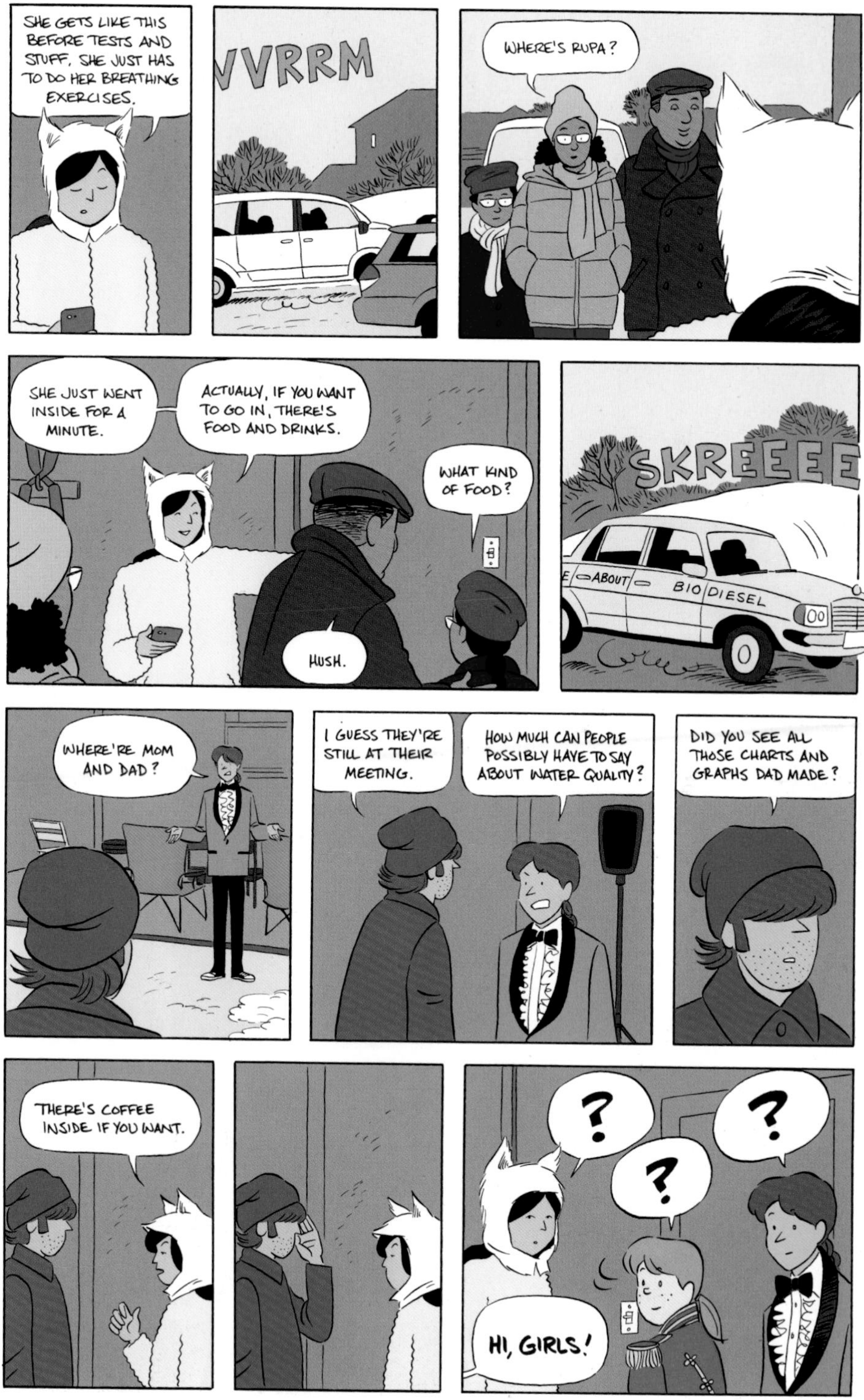
SHE GETS LIKE THIS BEFORE TESTS AND STUFF. SHE JUST HAS TO DO HER BREATHING EXERCISES.
VVRRM
WHERE'S RUPA?
SHE JUST WENT INSIDE FOR A MINUTE.
ACTUALLY, IF YOU WANT TO GO IN, THERE'S FOOD AND DRINKS.
WHAT KIND OF FOOD?
HUSH.
SKREEEE
ABOUT BIO DIESEL
WHERE'RE MOM AND DAD?
I GUESS THEY'RE STILL AT THEIR MEETING.
HOW MUCH CAN PEOPLE POSSIBLY HAVE TO SAY ABOUT WATER QUALITY?
DID YOU SEE ALL THOSE CHARTS AND GRAPHS DAD MADE?
THERE'S COFFEE INSIDE IF YOU WANT.
?
?
?
HI, GIRLS!

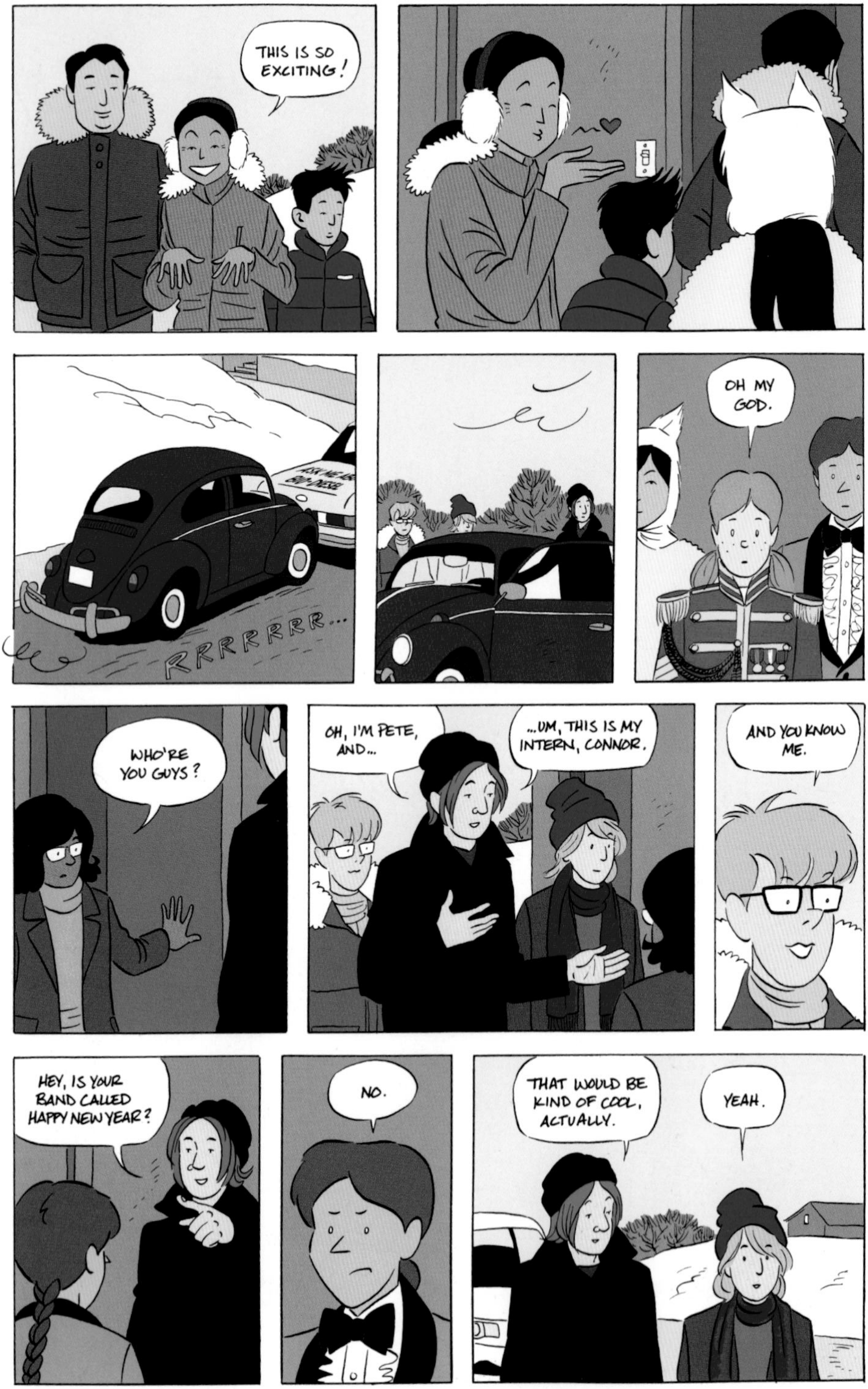
THIS IS SO EXCITING!
RRRRRRRR...
OH MY GOD.
WHO'RE YOU GUYS?
OH, I'M PETE, AND...
...UM, THIS IS MY INTERN, CONNOR.
AND YOU KNOW ME.
HEY, IS YOUR BAND CALLED HAPPY NEW YEAR?
NO.
THAT WOULD BE KIND OF COOL, ACTUALLY.
YEAH.

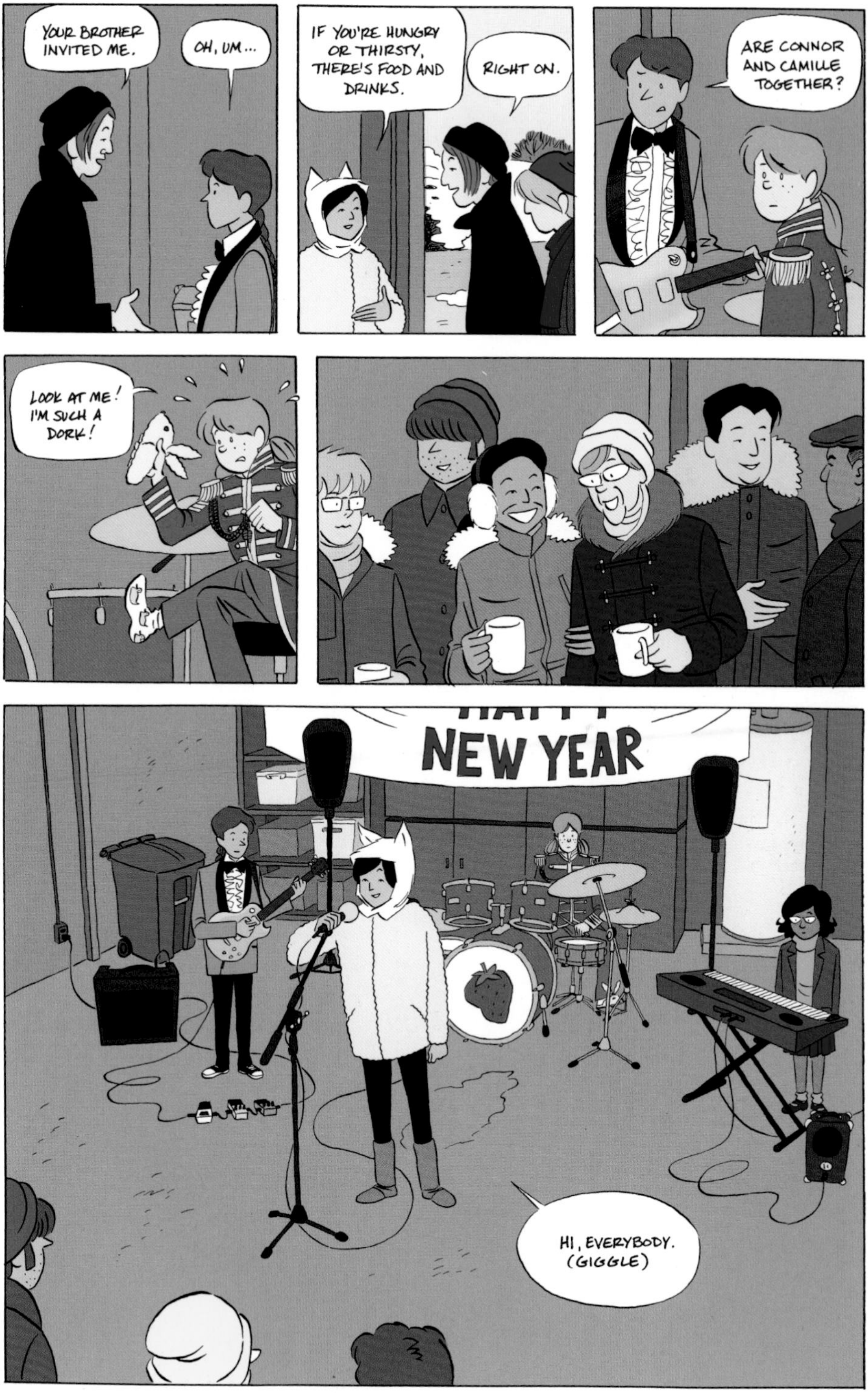
YOUR BROTHER INVITED ME.
OH, UM...
IF YOU'RE HUNGRY OR THIRSTY, THERE'S FOOD AND DRINKS.
RIGHT ON.
ARE CONNOR AND CAMILLE TOGETHER?
LOOK AT ME! I'M SUCH A DORK!
NEW YEAR
HI, EVERYBODY. (GIGGLE)

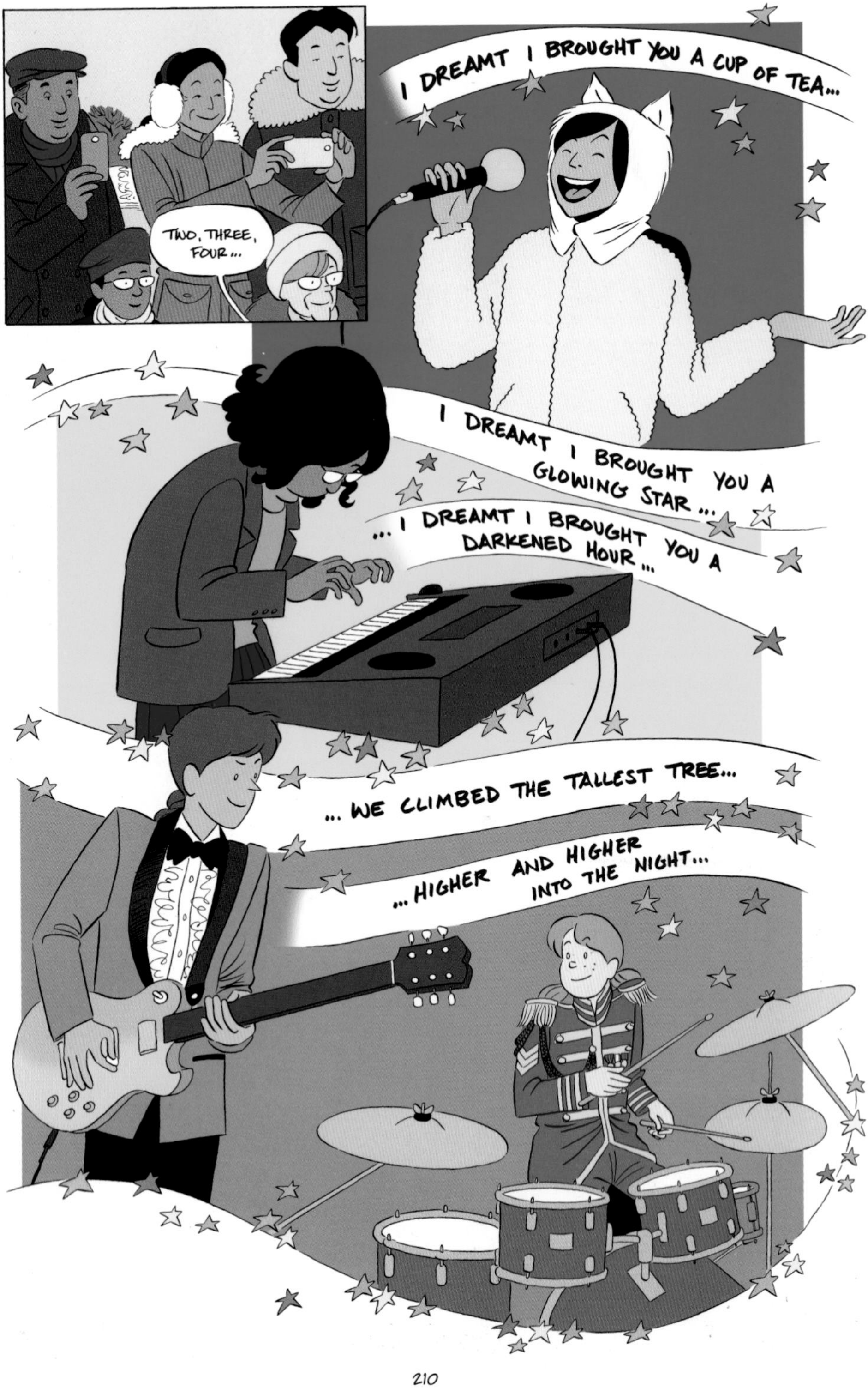
TWO, THREE, FOUR...
I DREAMT I BROUGHT YOU A CUP OF TEA...
I DREAMT I BROUGHT YOU A GLOWING STAR...
...I DREAMT I BROUGHT YOU A DARKENED HOUR...
...WE CLIMBED THE TALLEST TREE...
...HIGHER AND HIGHER INTO THE NIGHT...

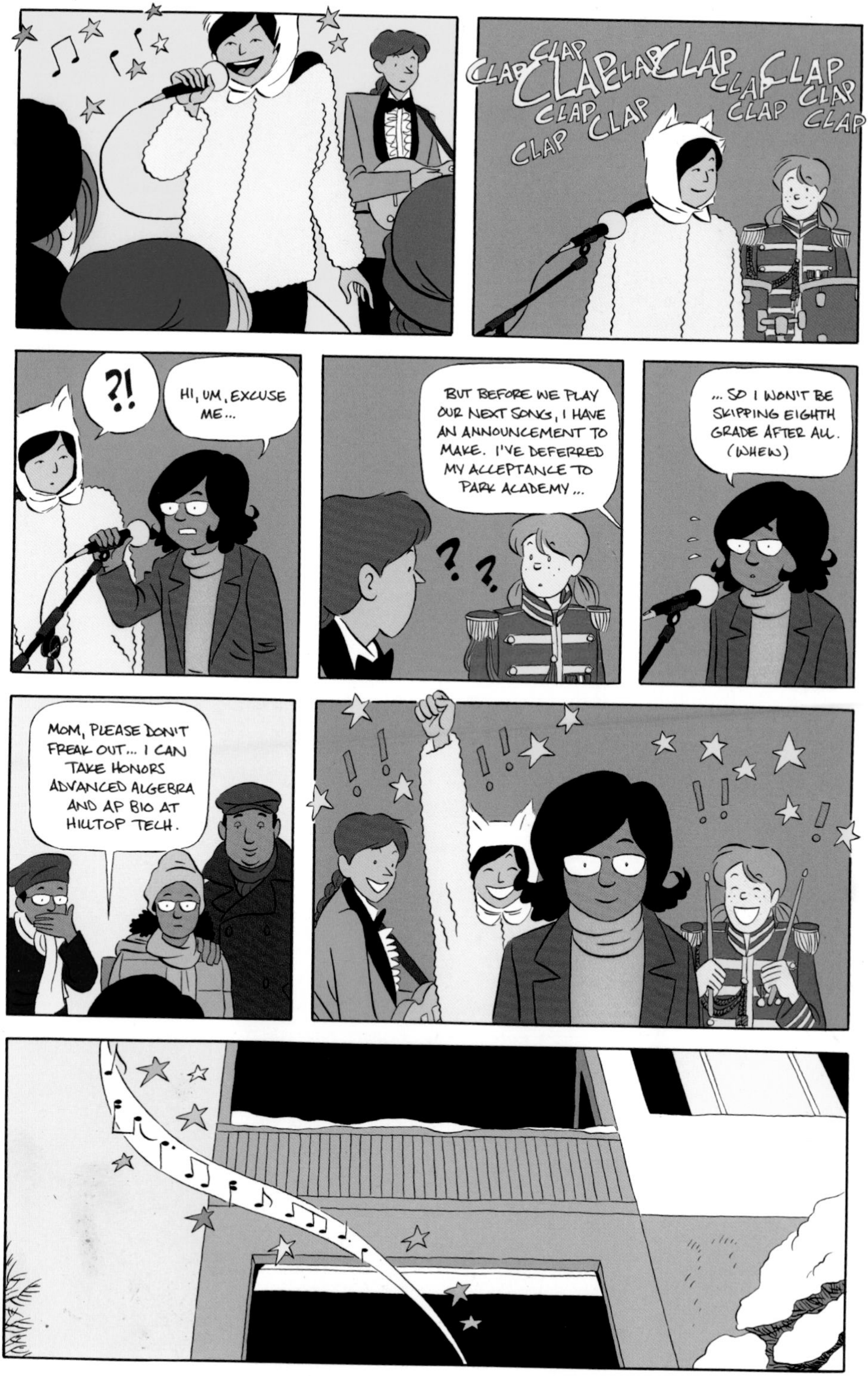
CLAP CLAP CLAP CLAP CLAP CLAP CLAP CLAP CLAP CLAP CLAP CLAP CLAP
?!
HI, UM, EXCUSE ME...
BUT BEFORE WE PLAY OUR NEXT SONGS, I HAVE AN ANNOUNCEMENT TO MAKE. I'VE DEFERRED MY ACCEPTANCE TO PARK ACADEMY...
??
...SO I WON'T BE SKIPPING EIGHTH GRADE AFTER ALL. (WHEW)
MOM, PLEASE DON'T FREAK OUT... I CAN TAKE HONORS ADVANCED ALGEBRA AND AP BIO AT HILLTOP TECH.
!! !! !! !

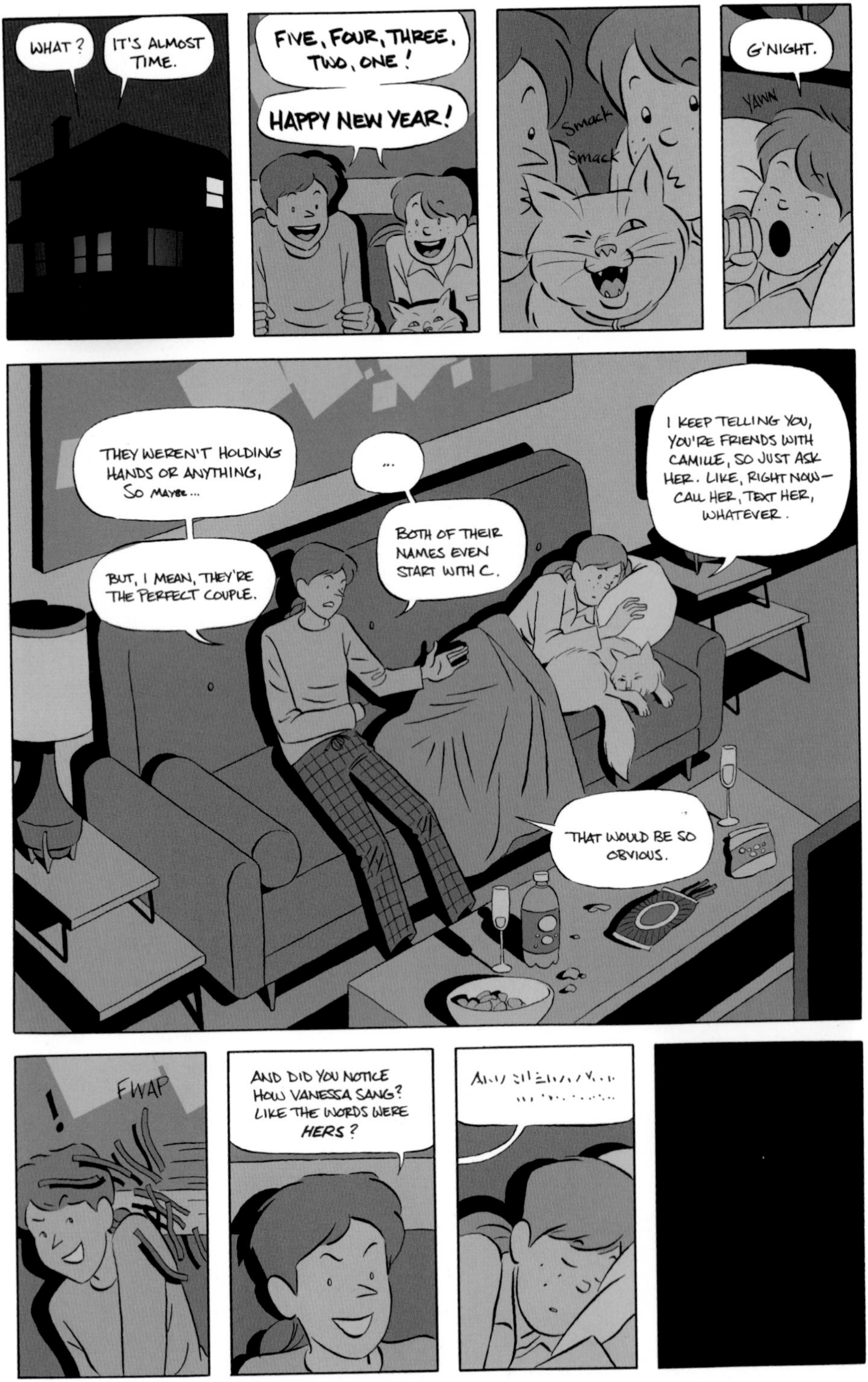
WHAT?
IT'S ALMOST TIME.
FIVE, FOUR, THREE, TWO, ONE!
HAPPY NEW YEAR!
Smack
Smack
G'NIGHT.
YAWN
THEY WEREN'T HOLDING HANDS OR ANYTHING, SO MAYBE...
BUT, I MEAN, THEY'RE THE PERFECT COUPLE.
...
BOTH OF THEIR NAMES EVEN START WITH C.
I KEEP TELLING YOU, YOU'RE FRIENDS WITH CAMILLE, SO JUST ASK HER. LIKE, RIGHT NOW— CALL HER, TEXT HER, WHATEVER.
THAT WOULD BE SO OBVIOUS.
!
FWAP
AND DID YOU NOTICE HOW VANESSA SANG? LIKE THE WORDS WERE HERS?

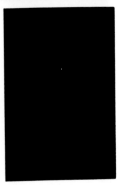

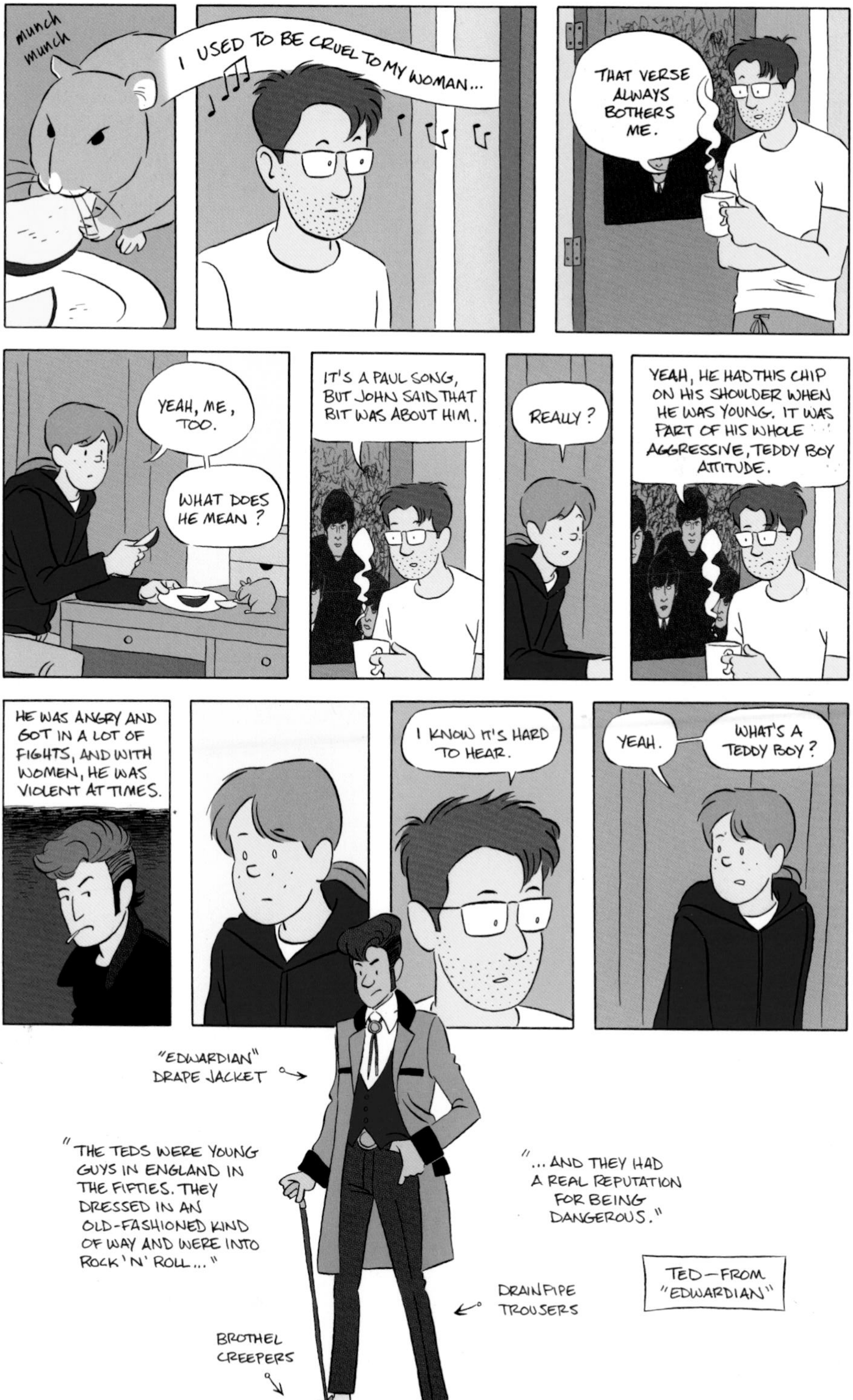
munch munch
I USED TO BE CRUEL TO MY WOMAN...
THAT VERSE ALWAYS BOTHERS ME.
YEAH, ME, TOO.
WHAT DOES HE MEAN ?
IT'S A PAUL SONG, BUT JOHN SAID THAT BIT WAS ABOUT HIM.
REALLY ?
YEAH, HE HAD THIS CHIP ON HIS SHOULDER WHEN HE WAS YOUNG. IT WAS PART OF HIS WHOLE AGGRESSIVE, TEDDY BOY ATTITUDE.
HE WAS ANGRY AND GOT IN A LOT OF FIGHTS, AND WITH WOMEN, HE WAS VIOLENT AT TIMES.
I KNOW IT'S HARD TO HEAR.
YEAH.
WHAT'S A TEDDY BOY ?
"EDWARDIAN" DRAPE JACKET
"THE TEDS WERE YOUNG GUYS IN ENGLAND IN THE FIFTIES. THEY DRESSED IN AN OLD-FASHIONED KIND OF WAY AND WERE INTO ROCK 'N' ROLL..."
"...AND THEY HAD A REAL REPUTATION FOR BEING DANGEROUS."
TED—FROM "EDWARDIAN"
DRAINPIPE TROUSERS
BROTHEL CREEPERS

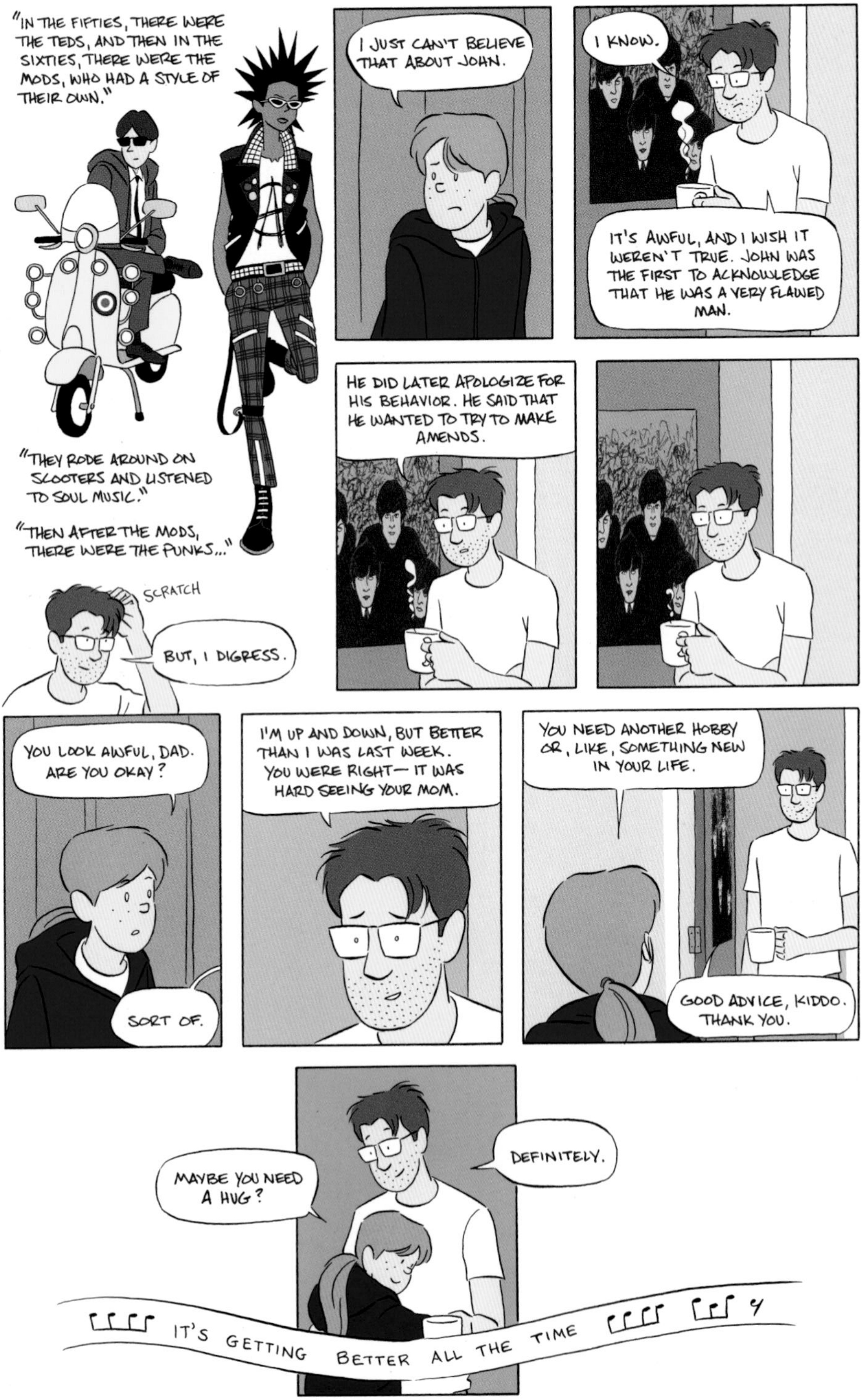
"IN THE FIFTIES, THERE WERE THE TEDS, AND THEN IN THE SIXTIES, THERE WERE THE MODS, WHO HAD A STYLE OF THEIR OWN."
"THEY RODE AROUND ON SCOOTERS AND LISTENED TO SOUL MUSIC."
"THEN AFTER THE MODS, THERE WERE THE PUNKS..."
SCRATCH
BUT, I DIGRESS.
I JUST CAN'T BELIEVE THAT ABOUT JOHN.
I KNOW.
IT'S AWFUL, AND I WISH IT WEREN'T TRUE. JOHN WAS THE FIRST TO ACKNOWLEDGE THAT HE WAS A VERY FLAWED MAN.
HE DID LATER APOLOGIZE FOR HIS BEHAVIOR. HE SAID THAT HE WANTED TO TRY TO MAKE AMENDS.
YOU LOOK AWFUL, DAD. ARE YOU OKAY?
SORT OF.
I'M UP AND DOWN, BUT BETTER THAN I WAS LAST WEEK. YOU WERE RIGHT— IT WAS HARD SEEING YOUR MOM.
YOU NEED ANOTHER HOBBY OR, LIKE, SOMETHING NEW IN YOUR LIFE.
GOOD ADVICE, KIDDO. THANK YOU.
MAYBE YOU NEED A HUG?
DEFINITELY.
IT'S GETTING BETTER ALL THE TIME

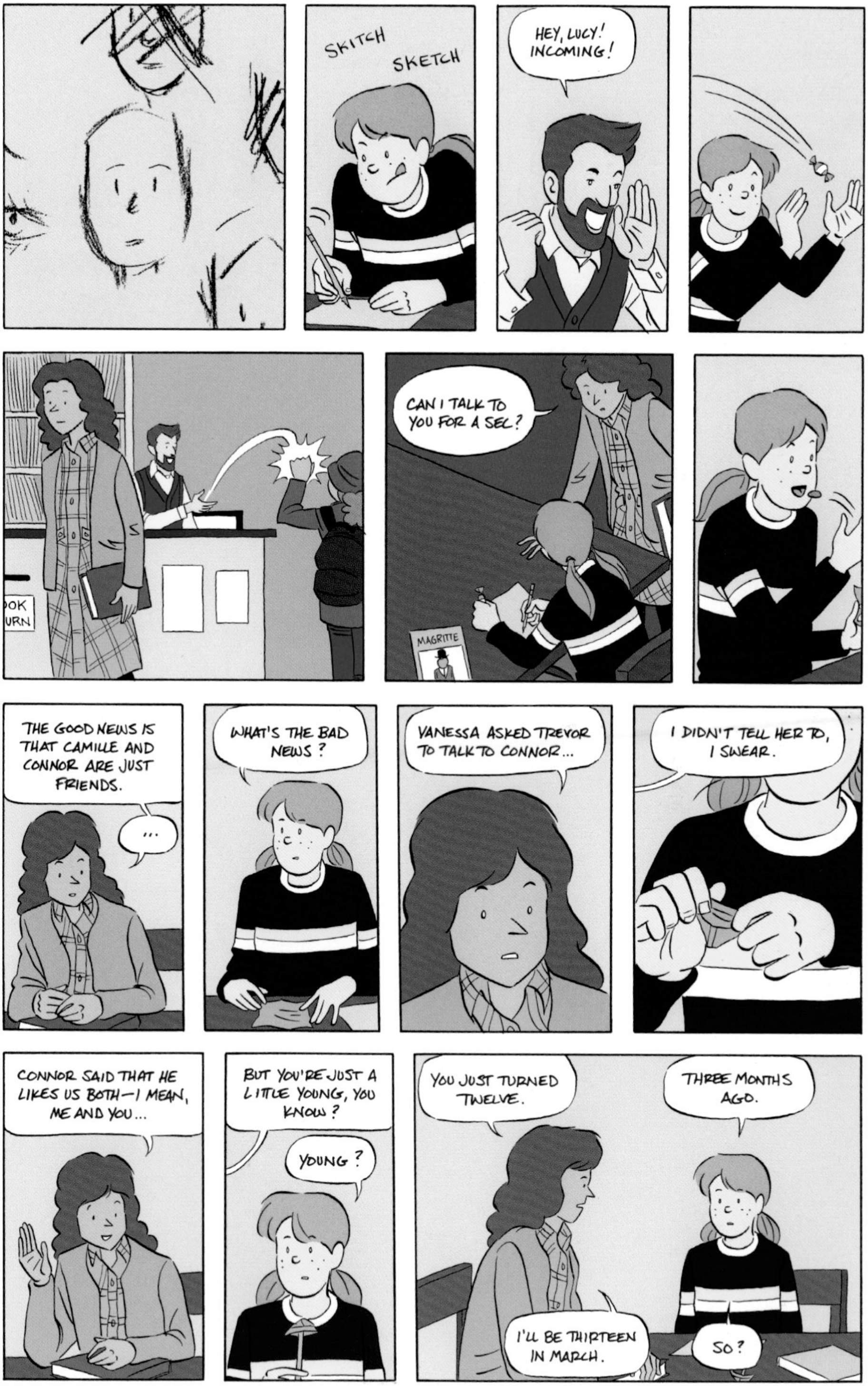

SKITCH
SKETCH
HEY, LUCY! INCOMING!
CAN I TALK TO YOU FOR A SEC?
MAGRITTE
THE GOOD NEWS IS THAT CAMILLE AND CONNOR ARE JUST FRIENDS.
...
WHAT'S THE BAD NEWS?
VANESSA ASKED TREVOR TO TALK TO CONNOR...
I DIDN'T TELL HER TO, I SWEAR.
CONNOR SAID THAT HE LIKES US BOTH—I MEAN, ME AND YOU...
BUT YOU'RE JUST A LITTLE YOUNG, YOU KNOW?
YOUNG?
YOU JUST TURNED TWELVE.
THREE MONTHS AGO.
I'LL BE THIRTEEN IN MARCH.
SO?

THE FOUR OF US ARE GONNA HANG OUT THIS WEEKEND.

WAIT — WHAT?

ME AND CONNOR AND VANESSA AND TREVOR.

YOU HATE VANESSA.

I DON'T *HATE* HER.

WHATEVER.

I GUESS I'LL SEE YOU AT LUNCH?

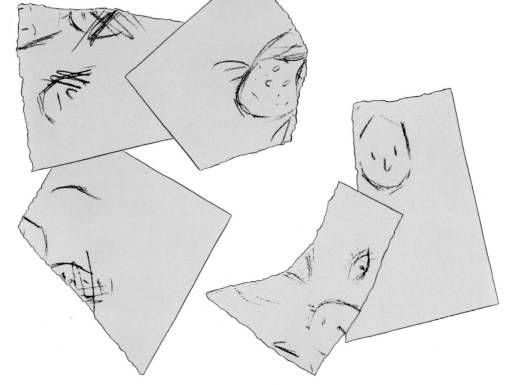

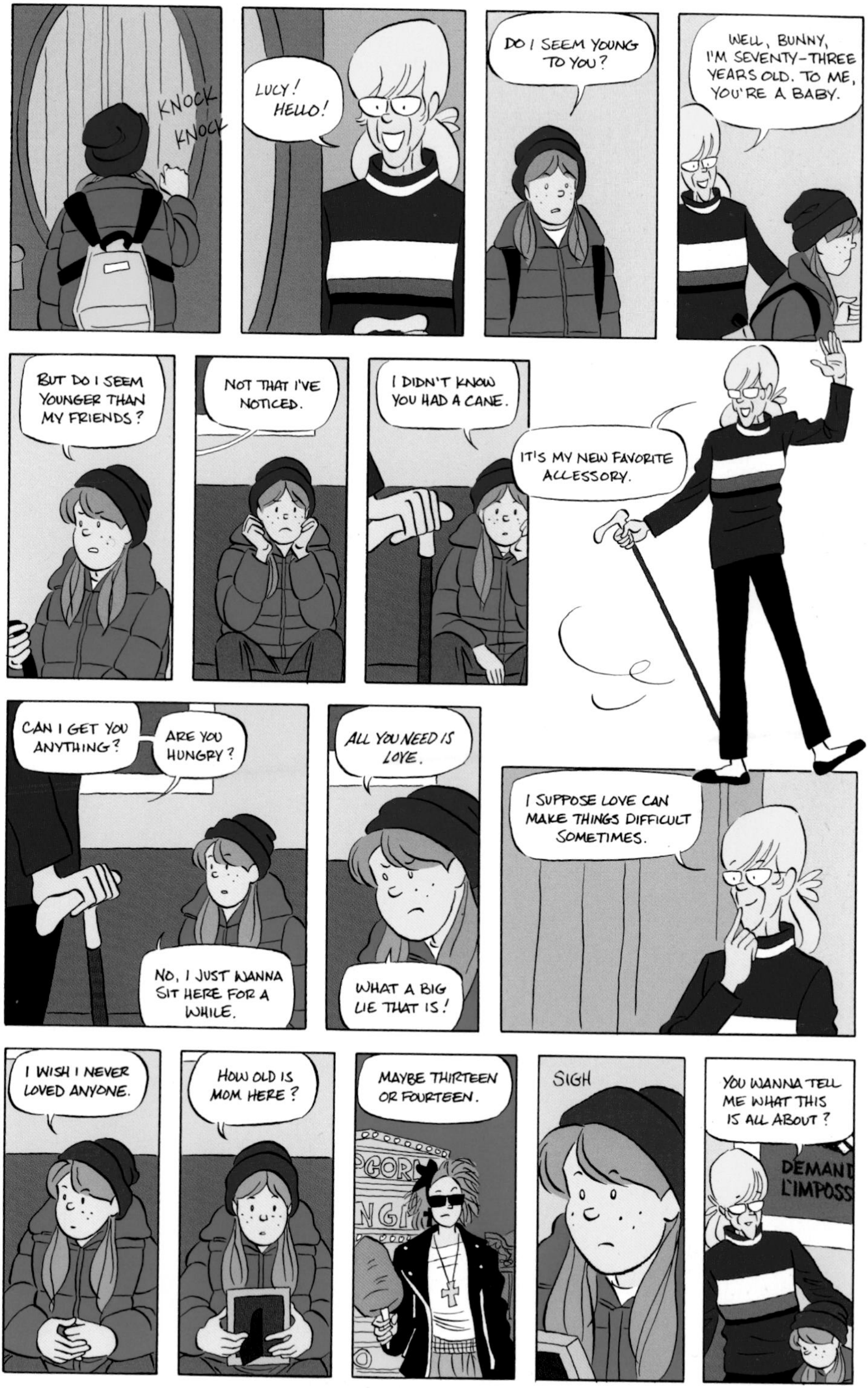
KNOCK KNOCK
LUCY! HELLO!
DO I SEEM YOUNG TO YOU?
WELL, BUNNY, I'M SEVENTY-THREE YEARS OLD. TO ME, YOU'RE A BABY.
BUT DO I SEEM YOUNGER THAN MY FRIENDS?
NOT THAT I'VE NOTICED.
I DIDN'T KNOW YOU HAD A CANE.
IT'S MY NEW FAVORITE ACCESSORY.
CAN I GET YOU ANYTHING?
ARE YOU HUNGRY?
NO, I JUST WANNA SIT HERE FOR A WHILE.
ALL YOU NEED IS LOVE.
WHAT A BIG LIE THAT IS!
I SUPPOSE LOVE CAN MAKE THINGS DIFFICULT SOMETIMES.
I WISH I NEVER LOVED ANYONE.
HOW OLD IS MOM HERE?
MAYBE THIRTEEN OR FOURTEEN.
SIGH
YOU WANNA TELL ME WHAT THIS IS ALL ABOUT?
DEMAND L'IMPOSS

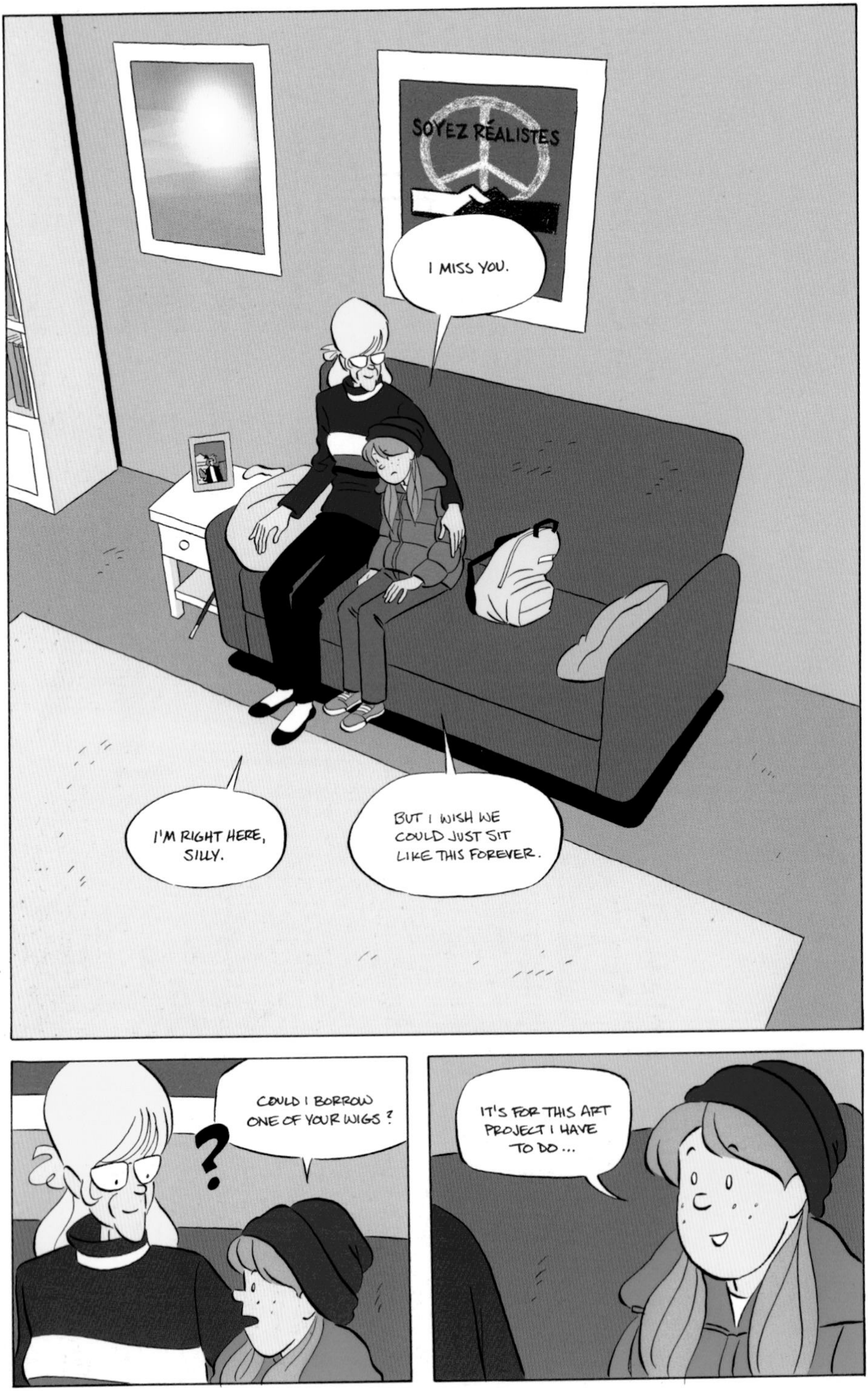
SOYEZ RÉALISTES
I MISS YOU.
I'M RIGHT HERE, SILLY.
BUT I WISH WE COULD JUST SIT LIKE THIS FOREVER.
?
COULD I BORROW ONE OF YOUR WIGS?
IT'S FOR THIS ART PROJECT I HAVE TO DO...

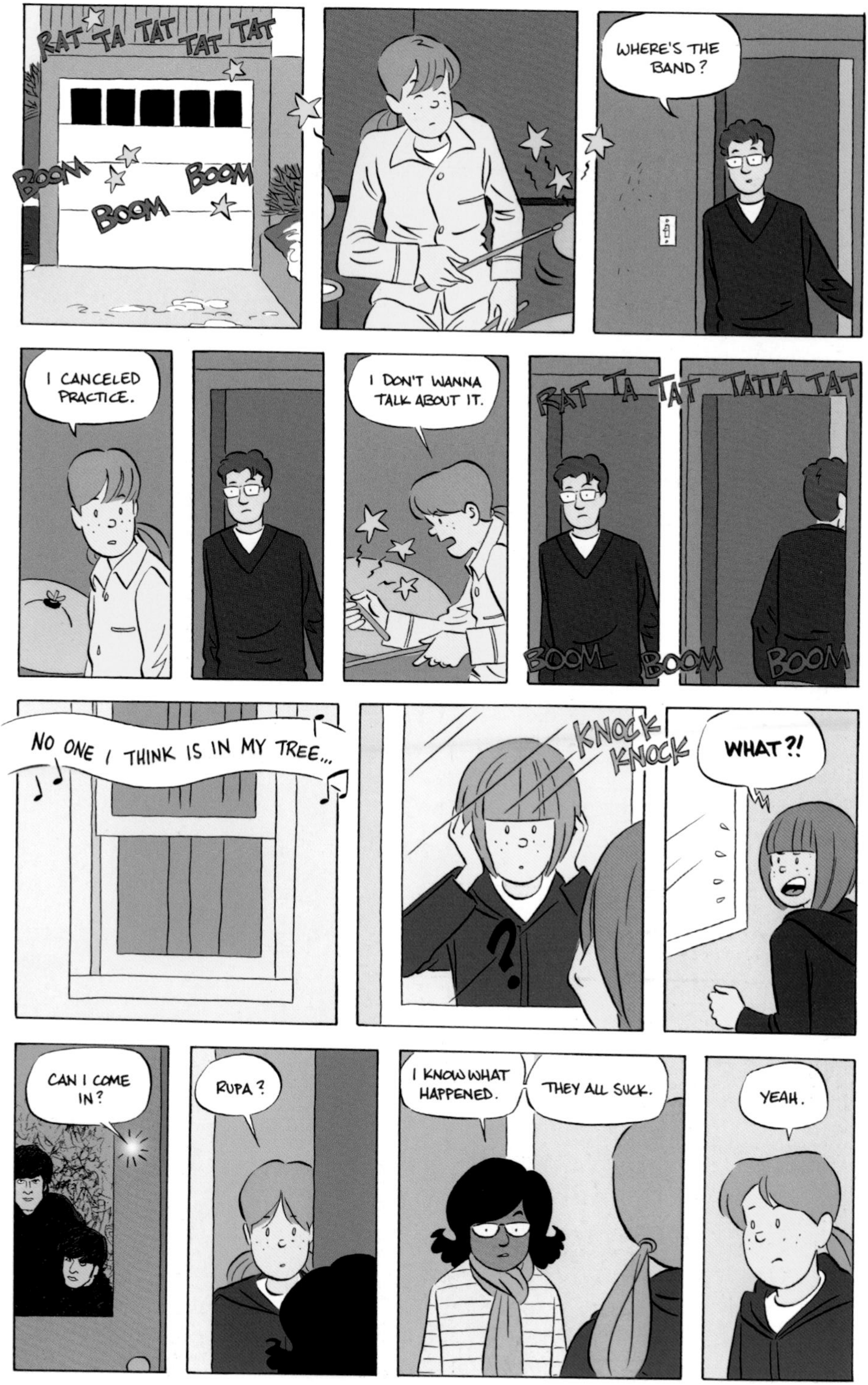
RAT TA TAT TAT TAT
BOOM
BOOM
BOOM
WHERE'S THE BAND?
I CANCELED PRACTICE.
I DON'T WANNA TALK ABOUT IT.
RAT TA TAT TATTA TAT
BOOM
BOOM
BOOM
NO ONE I THINK IS IN MY TREE...
KNOCK KNOCK
WHAT?!
CAN I COME IN?
RUPA?
I KNOW WHAT HAPPENED.
THEY ALL SUCK.
YEAH.

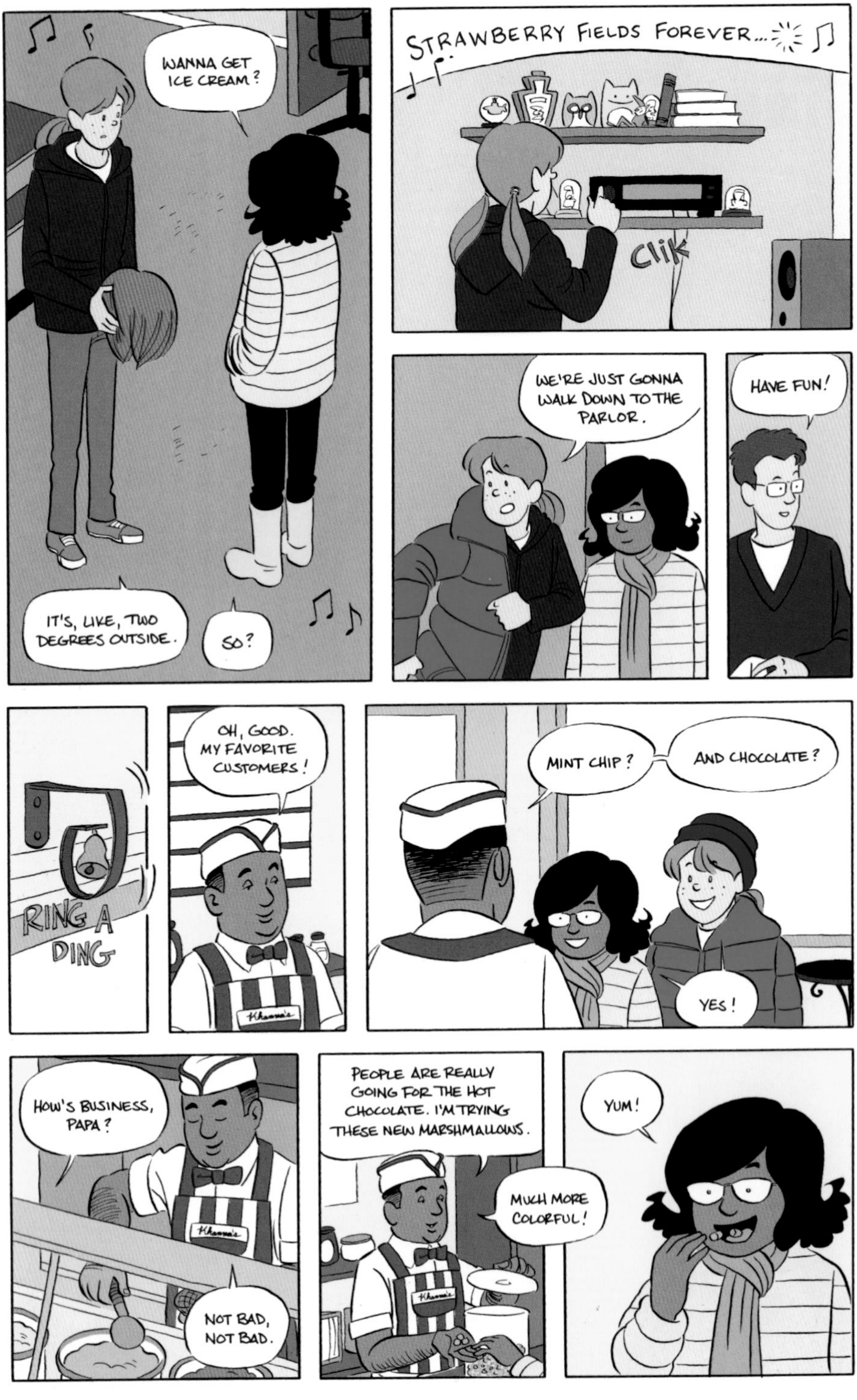
WANNA GET ICE CREAM?
IT'S, LIKE, TWO DEGREES OUTSIDE.
SO?
STRAWBERRY FIELDS FOREVER...
CLIK
WE'RE JUST GONNA WALK DOWN TO THE PARLOR.
HAVE FUN!
RING A DING
OH, GOOD. MY FAVORITE CUSTOMERS!
MINT CHIP?
AND CHOCOLATE?
YES!
HOW'S BUSINESS, PAPA?
NOT BAD, NOT BAD.
PEOPLE ARE REALLY GOING FOR THE HOT CHOCOLATE. I'M TRYING THESE NEW MARSHMALLOWS.
MUCH MORE COLORFUL!
YUM!

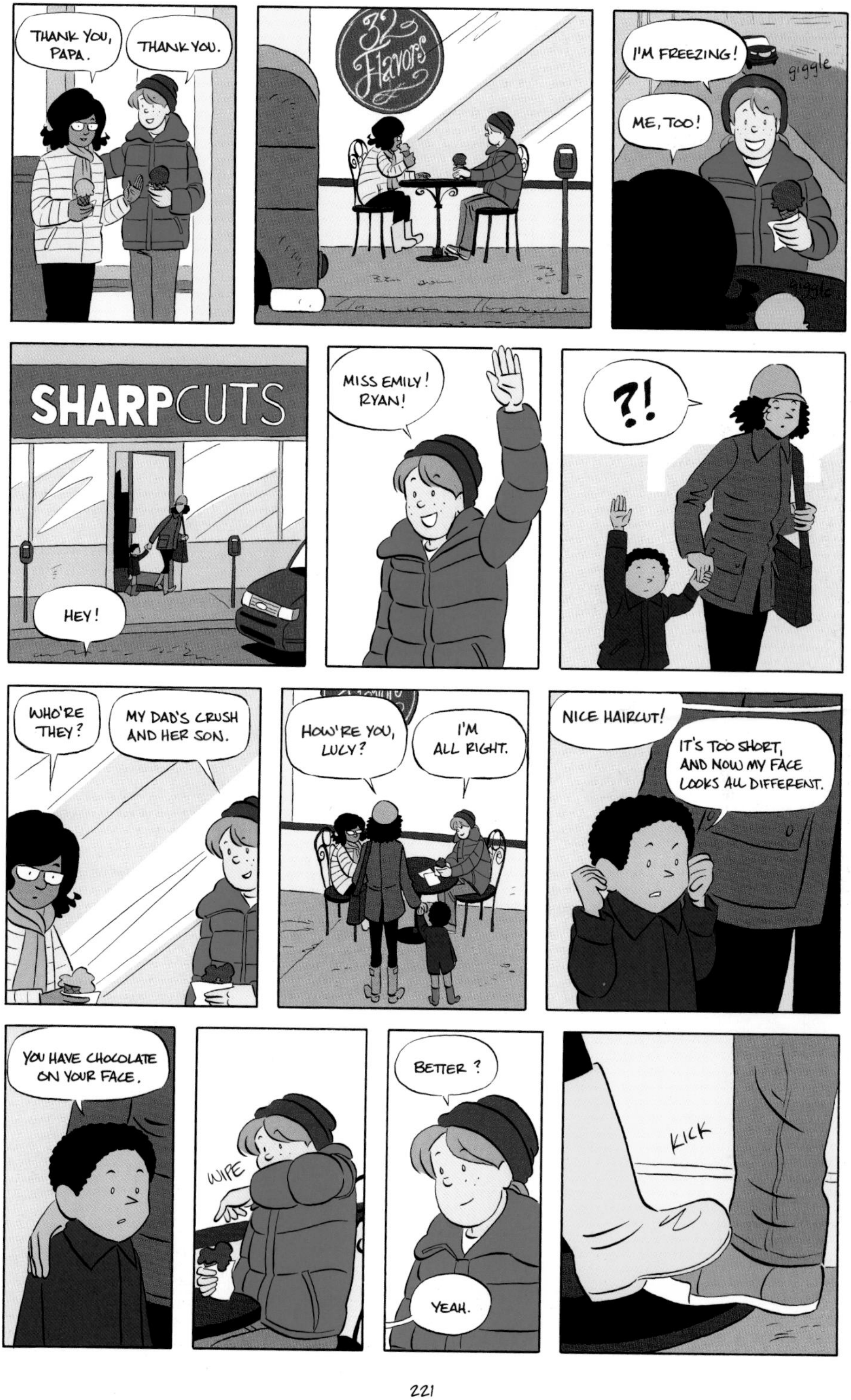
THANK YOU, PAPA.
THANK YOU.
32 Flavors
I'M FREEZING!
giggle
ME, TOO!
giggle
SHARPCUTS
HEY!
MISS EMILY! RYAN!
?!
WHO'RE THEY?
MY DAD'S CRUSH AND HER SON.
HOW'RE YOU, LUCY?
I'M ALL RIGHT.
NICE HAIRCUT!
IT'S TOO SHORT, AND NOW MY FACE LOOKS ALL DIFFERENT.
YOU HAVE CHOCOLATE ON YOUR FACE.
WIPE
BETTER?
YEAH.
KICK

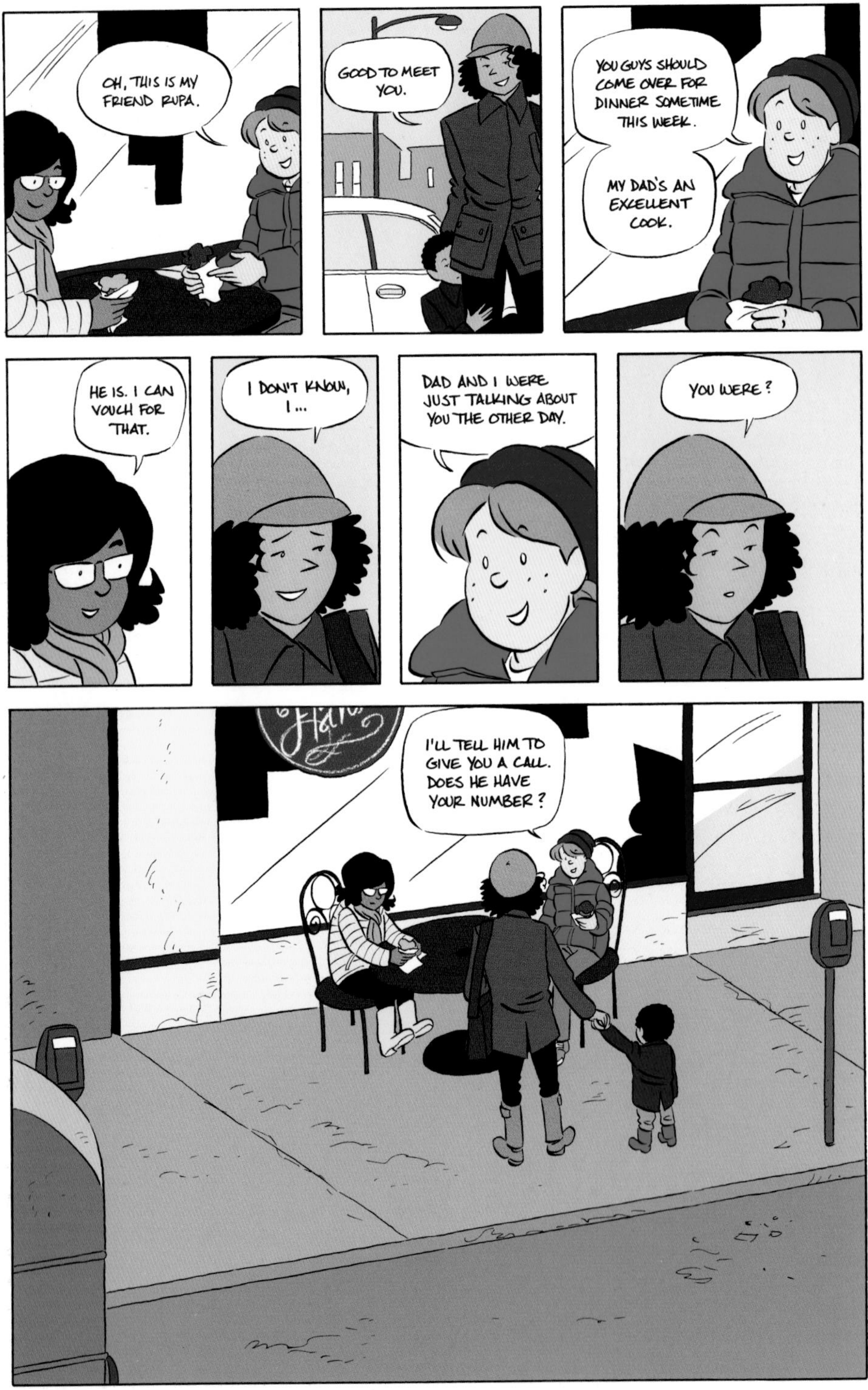
OH, THIS IS MY FRIEND RUPA.
GOOD TO MEET YOU.
YOU GUYS SHOULD COME OVER FOR DINNER SOMETIME THIS WEEK.
MY DAD'S AN EXCELLENT COOK.
HE IS. I CAN VOUCH FOR THAT.
I DON'T KNOW, I...
DAD AND I WERE JUST TALKING ABOUT YOU THE OTHER DAY.
YOU WERE?
I'LL TELL HIM TO GIVE YOU A CALL. DOES HE HAVE YOUR NUMBER?

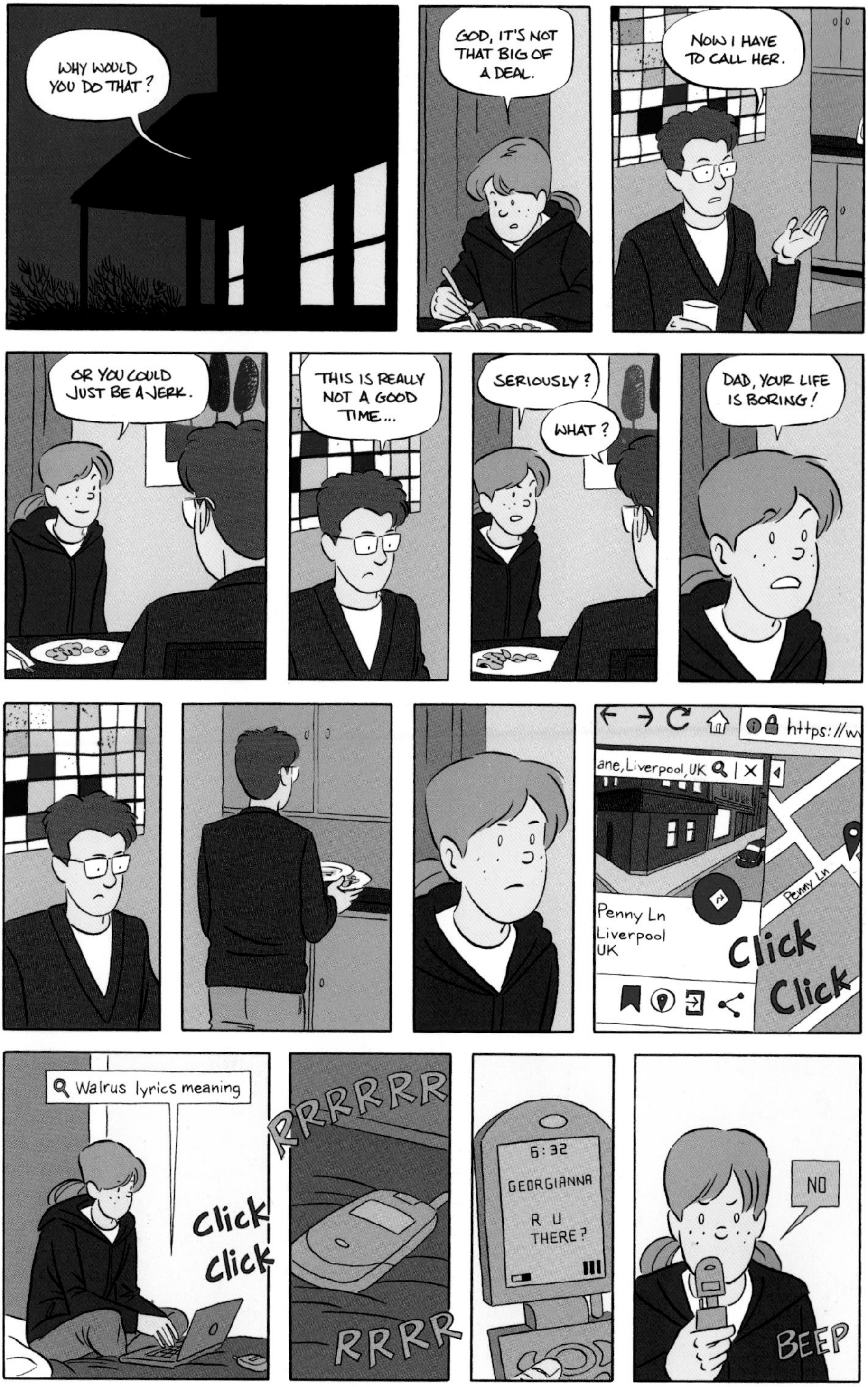
WHY WOULD YOU DO THAT?
GOD, IT'S NOT THAT BIG OF A DEAL.
NOW I HAVE TO CALL HER.
OR YOU COULD JUST BE A JERK.
THIS IS REALLY NOT A GOOD TIME...
SERIOUSLY?
WHAT?
DAD, YOUR LIFE IS BORING!
https://w
ane, Liverpool, UK
Penny Ln
Penny Ln
Liverpool
UK
Click
Click
Walrus lyrics meaning
Click
Click
RRRRRR
RRRR
6:32
GEORGIANNA
R U THERE?
NO
BEEP

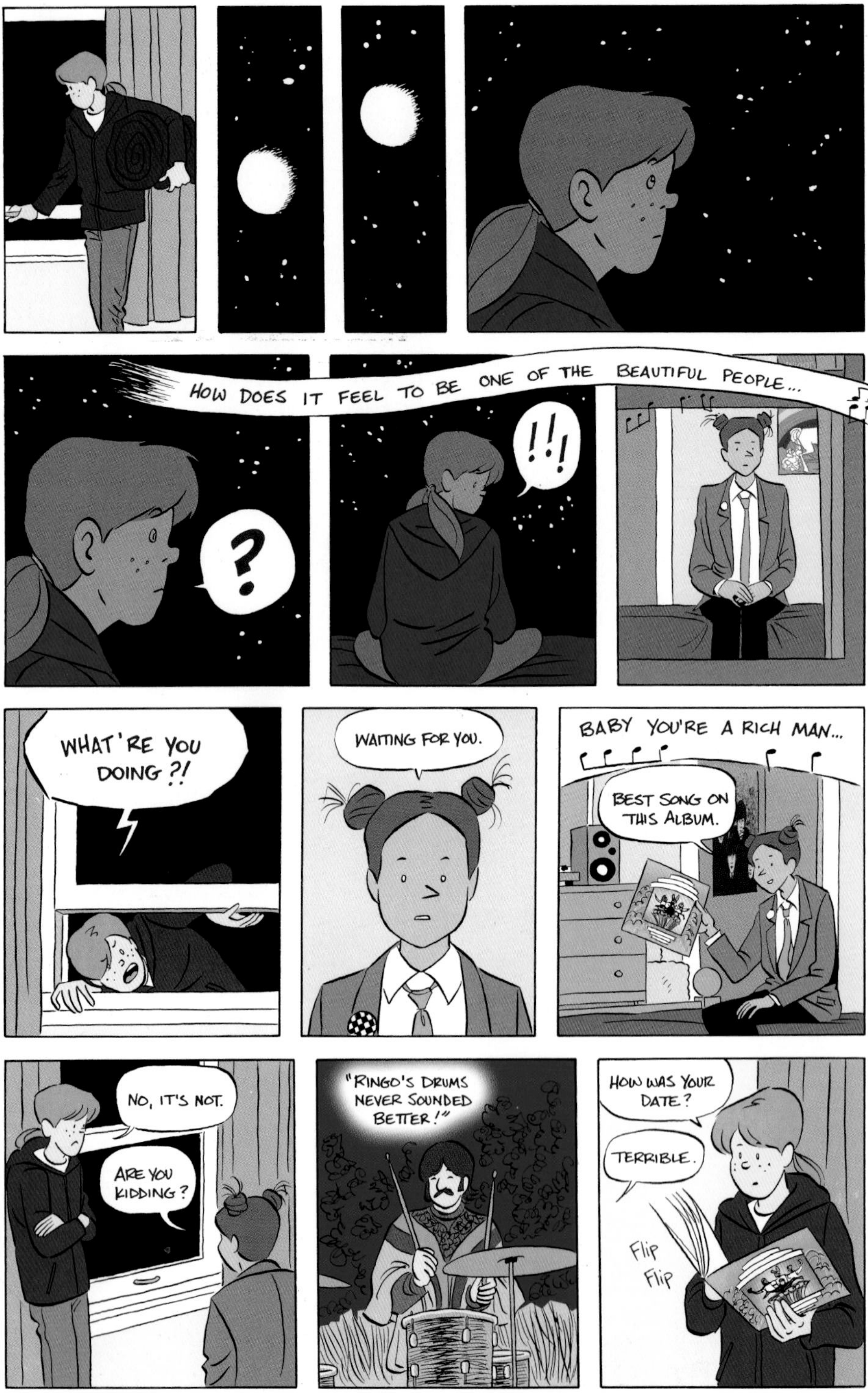
HOW DOES IT FEEL TO BE ONE OF THE BEAUTIFUL PEOPLE...
?
!!!
WHAT'RE YOU DOING ?!
WAITING FOR YOU.
BABY YOU'RE A RICH MAN...
BEST SONG ON THIS ALBUM.
NO, IT'S NOT.
ARE YOU KIDDING?
"RINGO'S DRUMS NEVER SOUNDED BETTER!"
HOW WAS YOUR DATE?
TERRIBLE.
Flip
Flip

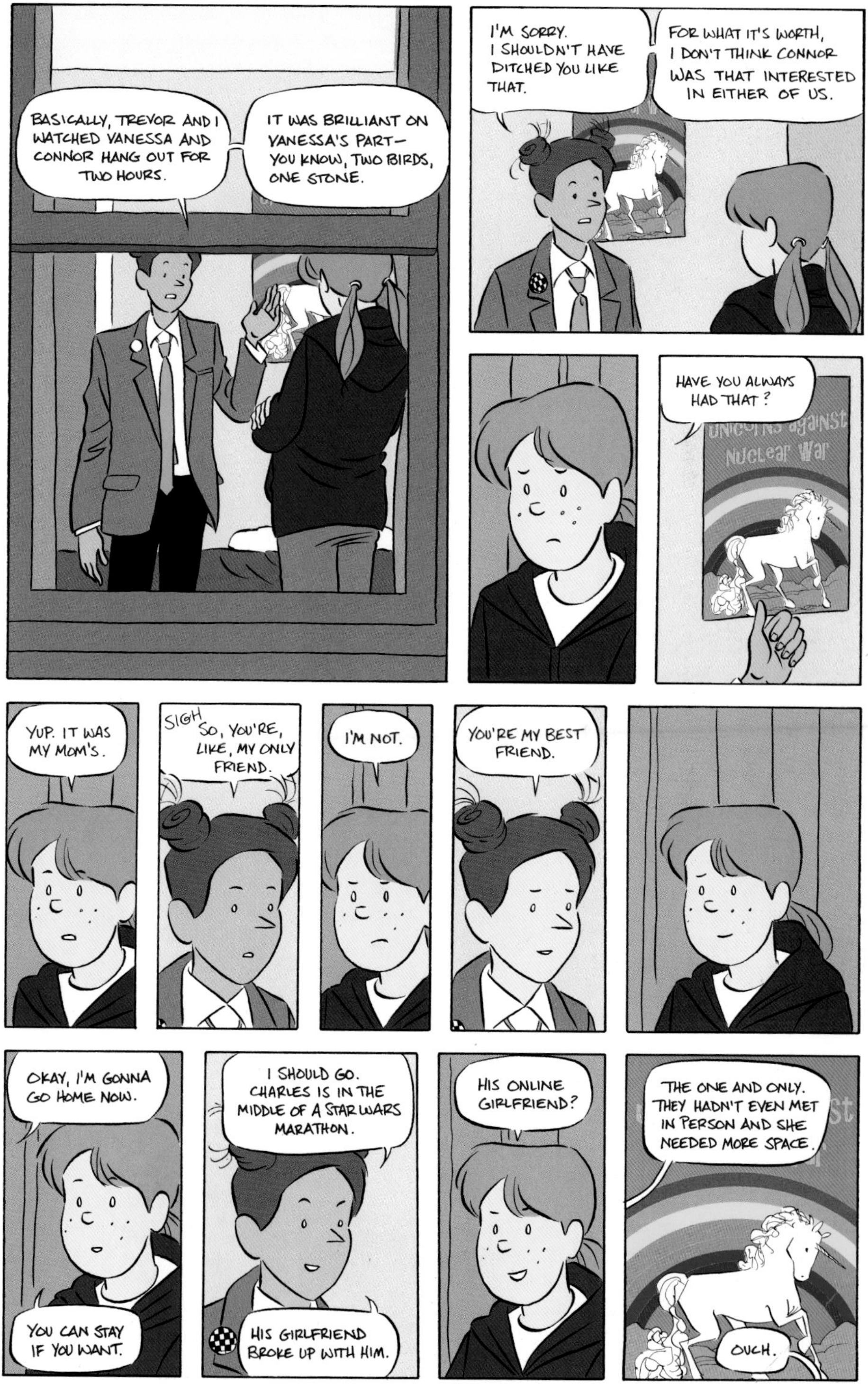
BASICALLY, TREVOR AND I WATCHED VANESSA AND CONNOR HANG OUT FOR TWO HOURS.
IT WAS BRILLIANT ON VANESSA'S PART— YOU KNOW, TWO BIRDS, ONE STONE.
I'M SORRY. I SHOULDN'T HAVE DITCHED YOU LIKE THAT.
FOR WHAT IT'S WORTH, I DON'T THINK CONNOR WAS THAT INTERESTED IN EITHER OF US.
HAVE YOU ALWAYS HAD THAT?
Unicorns against Nuclear War
YUP. IT WAS MY MOM'S.
SIGH
SO, YOU'RE, LIKE, MY ONLY FRIEND.
I'M NOT.
YOU'RE MY BEST FRIEND.
OKAY, I'M GONNA GO HOME NOW.
YOU CAN STAY IF YOU WANT.
I SHOULD GO. CHARLES IS IN THE MIDDLE OF A STAR WARS MARATHON.
HIS GIRLFRIEND BROKE UP WITH HIM.
HIS ONLINE GIRLFRIEND?
THE ONE AND ONLY. THEY HADN'T EVEN MET IN PERSON AND SHE NEEDED MORE SPACE.
OUCH.

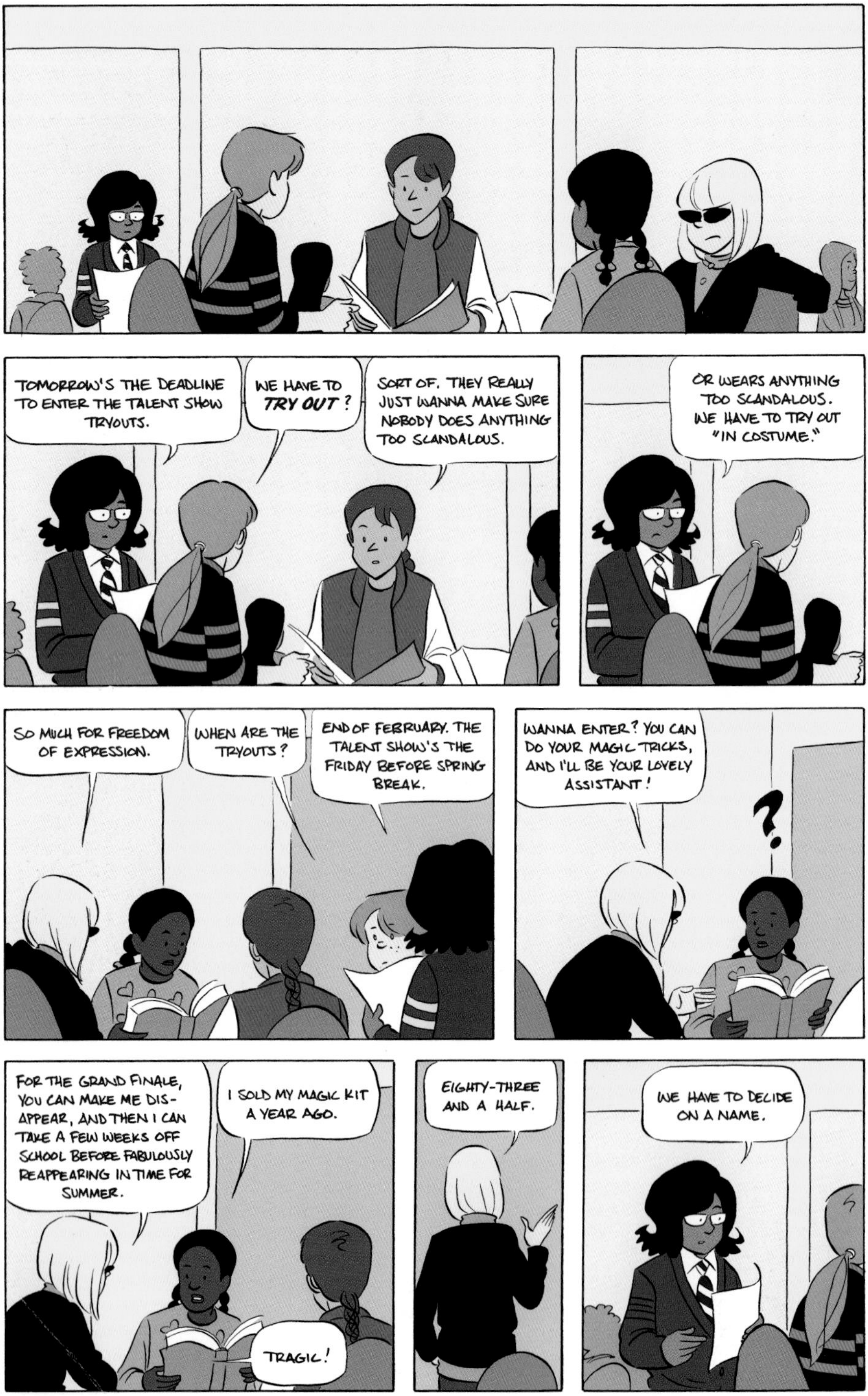
TOMORROW'S THE DEADLINE TO ENTER THE TALENT SHOW TRYOUTS.
WE HAVE TO *TRY OUT*?
SORT OF. THEY REALLY JUST WANNA MAKE SURE NOBODY DOES ANYTHING TOO SCANDALOUS.
OR WEARS ANYTHING TOO SCANDALOUS. WE HAVE TO TRY OUT "IN COSTUME."
SO MUCH FOR FREEDOM OF EXPRESSION.
WHEN ARE THE TRYOUTS?
END OF FEBRUARY. THE TALENT SHOW'S THE FRIDAY BEFORE SPRING BREAK.
WANNA ENTER? YOU CAN DO YOUR MAGIC TRICKS, AND I'LL BE YOUR LOVELY ASSISTANT!
?
FOR THE GRAND FINALE, YOU CAN MAKE ME DIS-APPEAR, AND THEN I CAN TAKE A FEW WEEKS OFF SCHOOL BEFORE FABULOUSLY REAPPEARING IN TIME FOR SUMMER.
I SOLD MY MAGIC KIT A YEAR AGO.
TRAGIC!
EIGHTY-THREE AND A HALF.
WE HAVE TO DECIDE ON A NAME.

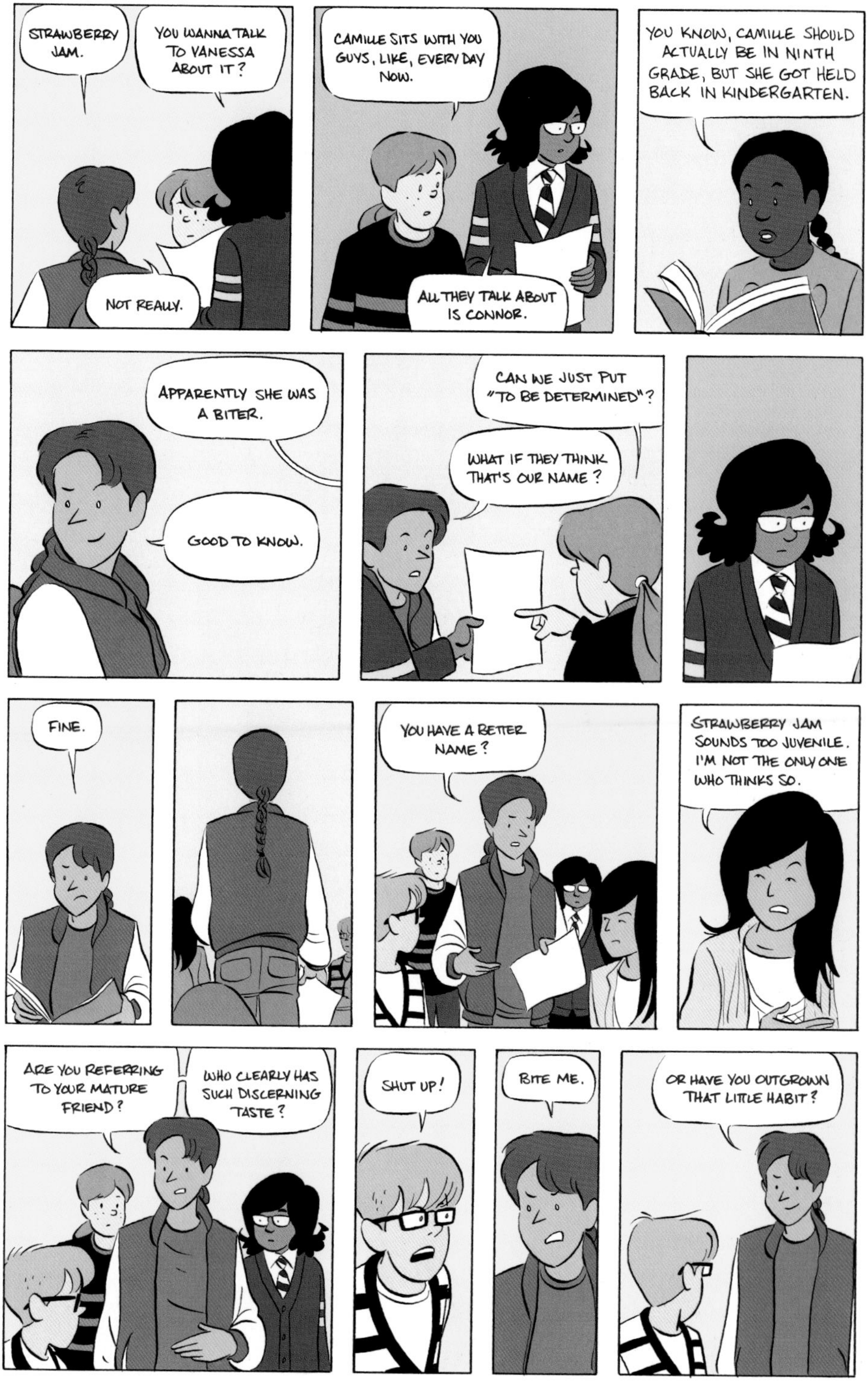
STRAWBERRY JAM.
YOU WANNA TALK TO VANESSA ABOUT IT?
NOT REALLY.
CAMILLE SITS WITH YOU GUYS, LIKE, EVERY DAY NOW.
ALL THEY TALK ABOUT IS CONNOR.
YOU KNOW, CAMILLE SHOULD ACTUALLY BE IN NINTH GRADE, BUT SHE GOT HELD BACK IN KINDERGARTEN.
APPARENTLY SHE WAS A BITER.
GOOD TO KNOW.
CAN WE JUST PUT "TO BE DETERMINED"?
WHAT IF THEY THINK THAT'S OUR NAME?
FINE.
YOU HAVE A BETTER NAME?
STRAWBERRY JAM SOUNDS TOO JUVENILE. I'M NOT THE ONLY ONE WHO THINKS SO.
ARE YOU REFERRING TO YOUR MATURE FRIEND?
WHO CLEARLY HAS SUCH DISCERNING TASTE?
SHUT UP!
BITE ME.
OR HAVE YOU OUTGROWN THAT LITTLE HABIT?

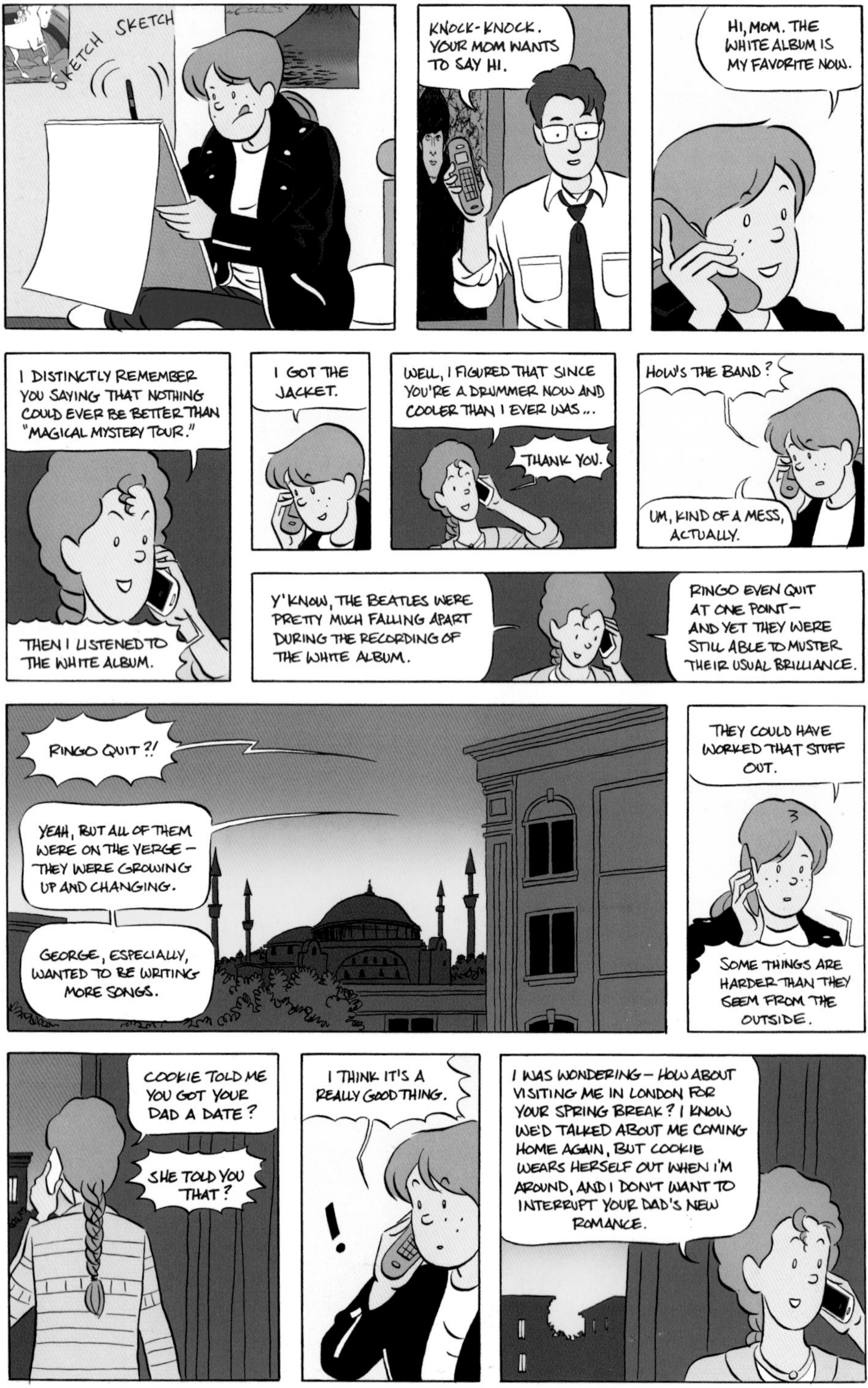
SKETCH SKETCH
KNOCK-KNOCK. YOUR MOM WANTS TO SAY HI.
HI, MOM. THE WHITE ALBUM IS MY FAVORITE NOW.
I DISTINCTLY REMEMBER YOU SAYING THAT NOTHING COULD EVER BE BETTER THAN "MAGICAL MYSTERY TOUR."
THEN I LISTENED TO THE WHITE ALBUM.
I GOT THE JACKET.
WELL, I FIGURED THAT SINCE YOU'RE A DRUMMER NOW AND COOLER THAN I EVER WAS...
THANK YOU.
HOW'S THE BAND?
UM, KIND OF A MESS, ACTUALLY.
Y'KNOW, THE BEATLES WERE PRETTY MUCH FALLING APART DURING THE RECORDING OF THE WHITE ALBUM.
RINGO EVEN QUIT AT ONE POINT— AND YET THEY WERE STILL ABLE TO MUSTER THEIR USUAL BRILLIANCE.
RINGO QUIT?!
YEAH, BUT ALL OF THEM WERE ON THE VERGE— THEY WERE GROWING UP AND CHANGING.
GEORGE, ESPECIALLY, WANTED TO BE WRITING MORE SONGS.
THEY COULD HAVE WORKED THAT STUFF OUT.
SOME THINGS ARE HARDER THAN THEY SEEM FROM THE OUTSIDE.
COOKIE TOLD ME YOU GOT YOUR DAD A DATE?
SHE TOLD YOU THAT?
I THINK IT'S A REALLY GOOD THING.
!
I WAS WONDERING— HOW ABOUT VISITING ME IN LONDON FOR YOUR SPRING BREAK? I KNOW WE'D TALKED ABOUT ME COMING HOME AGAIN, BUT COOKIE WEARS HERSELF OUT WHEN I'M AROUND, AND I DON'T WANT TO INTERRUPT YOUR DAD'S NEW ROMANCE.

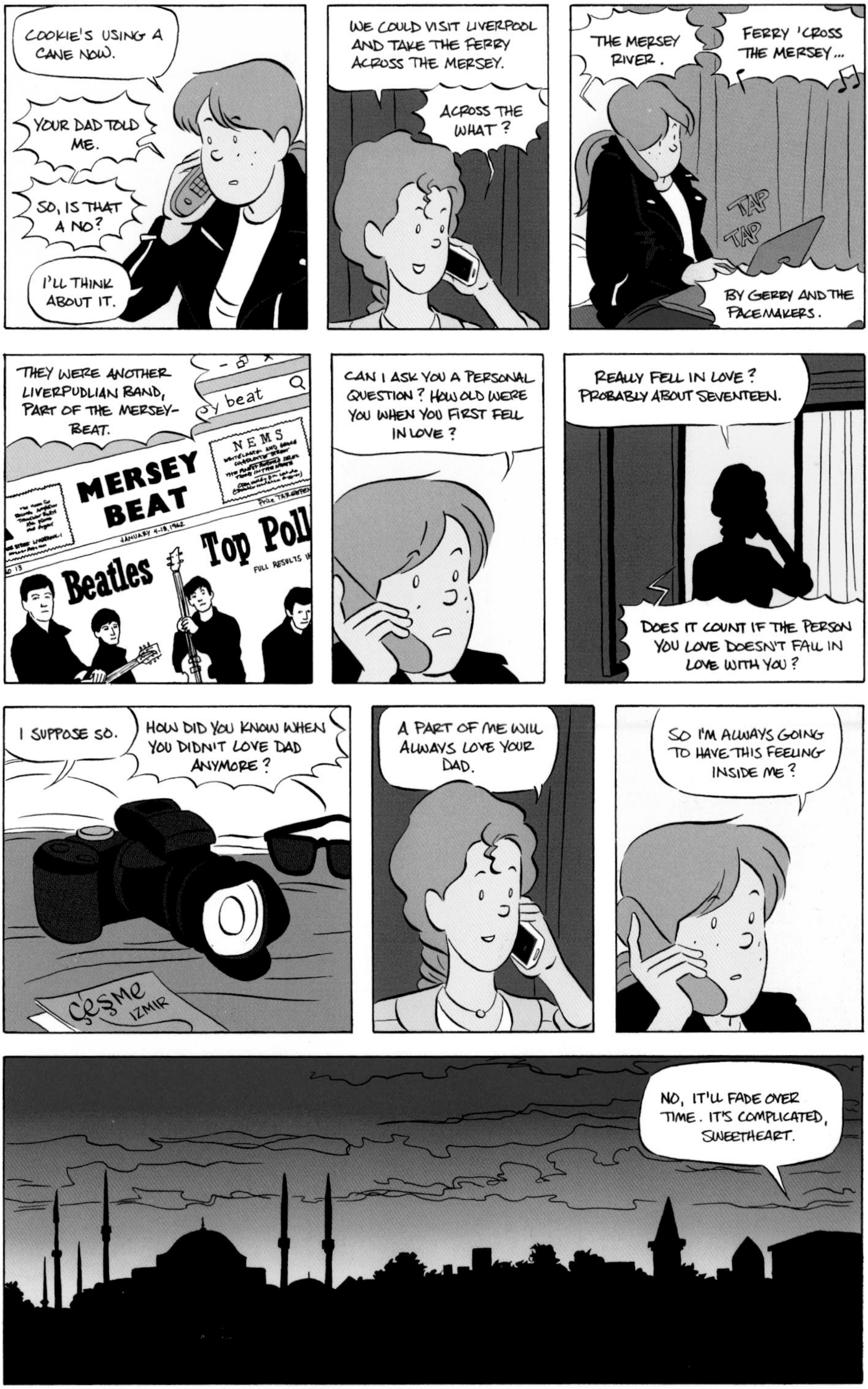
COOKIE'S USING A CANE NOW.
YOUR DAD TOLD ME.
SO, IS THAT A NO?
I'LL THINK ABOUT IT.
WE COULD VISIT LIVERPOOL AND TAKE THE FERRY ACROSS THE MERSEY.
ACROSS THE WHAT?
THE MERSEY RIVER.
FERRY 'CROSS THE MERSEY...
TAP TAP
BY GERRY AND THE PACEMAKERS.
THEY WERE ANOTHER LIVERPUDLIAN BAND, PART OF THE MERSEY-BEAT.
y beat
NEMS
MERSEY BEAT
JANUARY 4-18, 1962
Top Poll
Beatles
CAN I ASK YOU A PERSONAL QUESTION? HOW OLD WERE YOU WHEN YOU FIRST FELL IN LOVE?
REALLY FELL IN LOVE? PROBABLY ABOUT SEVENTEEN.
DOES IT COUNT IF THE PERSON YOU LOVE DOESN'T FALL IN LOVE WITH YOU?
I SUPPOSE SO.
HOW DID YOU KNOW WHEN YOU DIDN'T LOVE DAD ANYMORE?
ÇeşMe
IZMIR
A PART OF ME WILL ALWAYS LOVE YOUR DAD.
SO I'M ALWAYS GOING TO HAVE THIS FEELING INSIDE ME?
NO, IT'LL FADE OVER TIME. IT'S COMPLICATED, SWEETHEART.

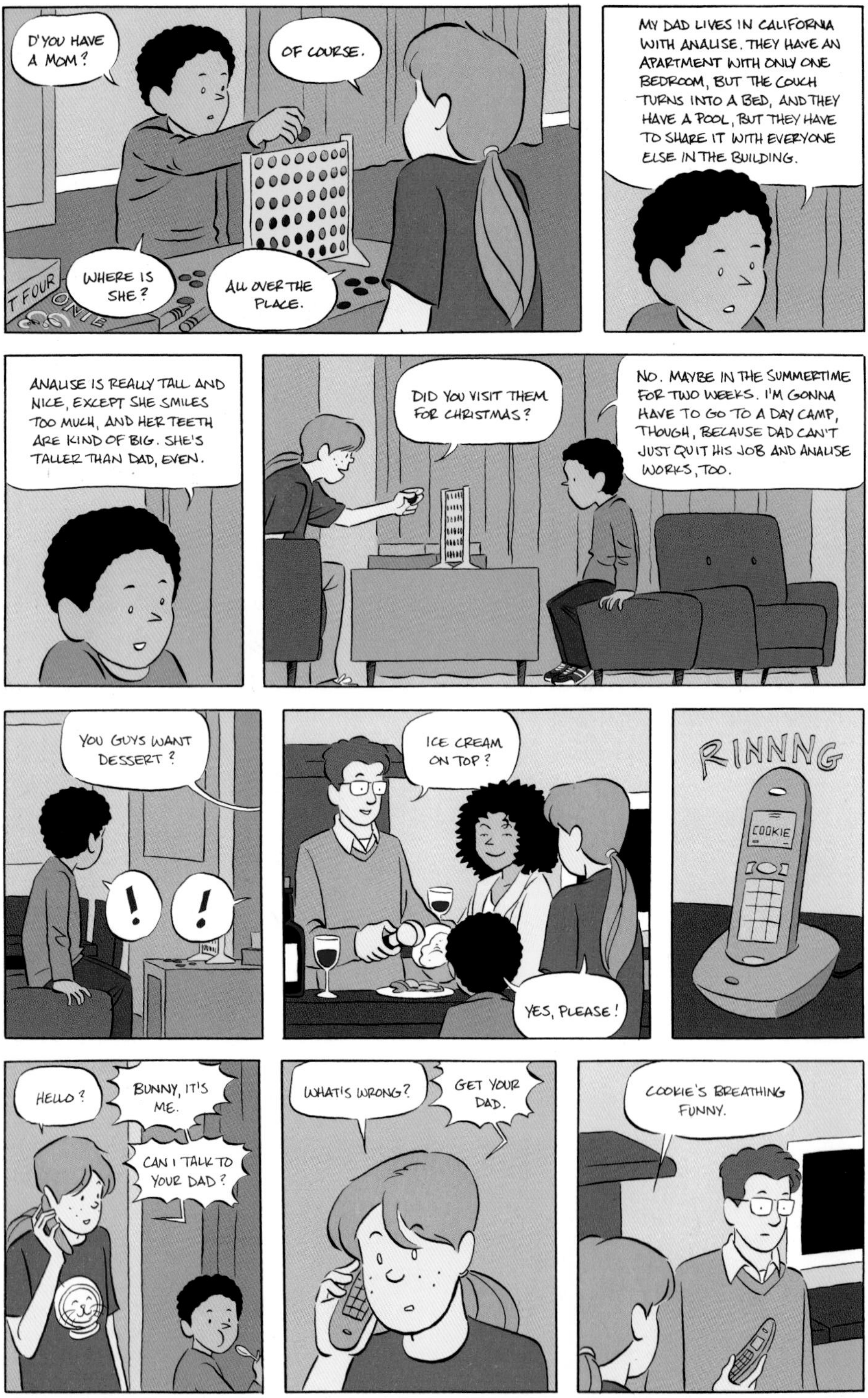
D'YOU HAVE A MOM?
OF COURSE.
WHERE IS SHE?
ALL OVER THE PLACE.
MY DAD LIVES IN CALIFORNIA WITH ANALISE. THEY HAVE AN APARTMENT WITH ONLY ONE BEDROOM, BUT THE COUCH TURNS INTO A BED, AND THEY HAVE A POOL, BUT THEY HAVE TO SHARE IT WITH EVERYONE ELSE IN THE BUILDING.
ANALISE IS REALLY TALL AND NICE, EXCEPT SHE SMILES TOO MUCH, AND HER TEETH ARE KIND OF BIG. SHE'S TALLER THAN DAD, EVEN.
DID YOU VISIT THEM FOR CHRISTMAS?
NO. MAYBE IN THE SUMMERTIME FOR TWO WEEKS. I'M GONNA HAVE TO GO TO A DAY CAMP, THOUGH, BECAUSE DAD CAN'T JUST QUIT HIS JOB AND ANALISE WORKS, TOO.
YOU GUYS WANT DESSERT?
!
!
ICE CREAM ON TOP?
YES, PLEASE!
RINNNG
COOKIE
HELLO?
BUNNY, IT'S ME.
CAN I TALK TO YOUR DAD?
WHAT'S WRONG?
GET YOUR DAD.
COOKIE'S BREATHING FUNNY.

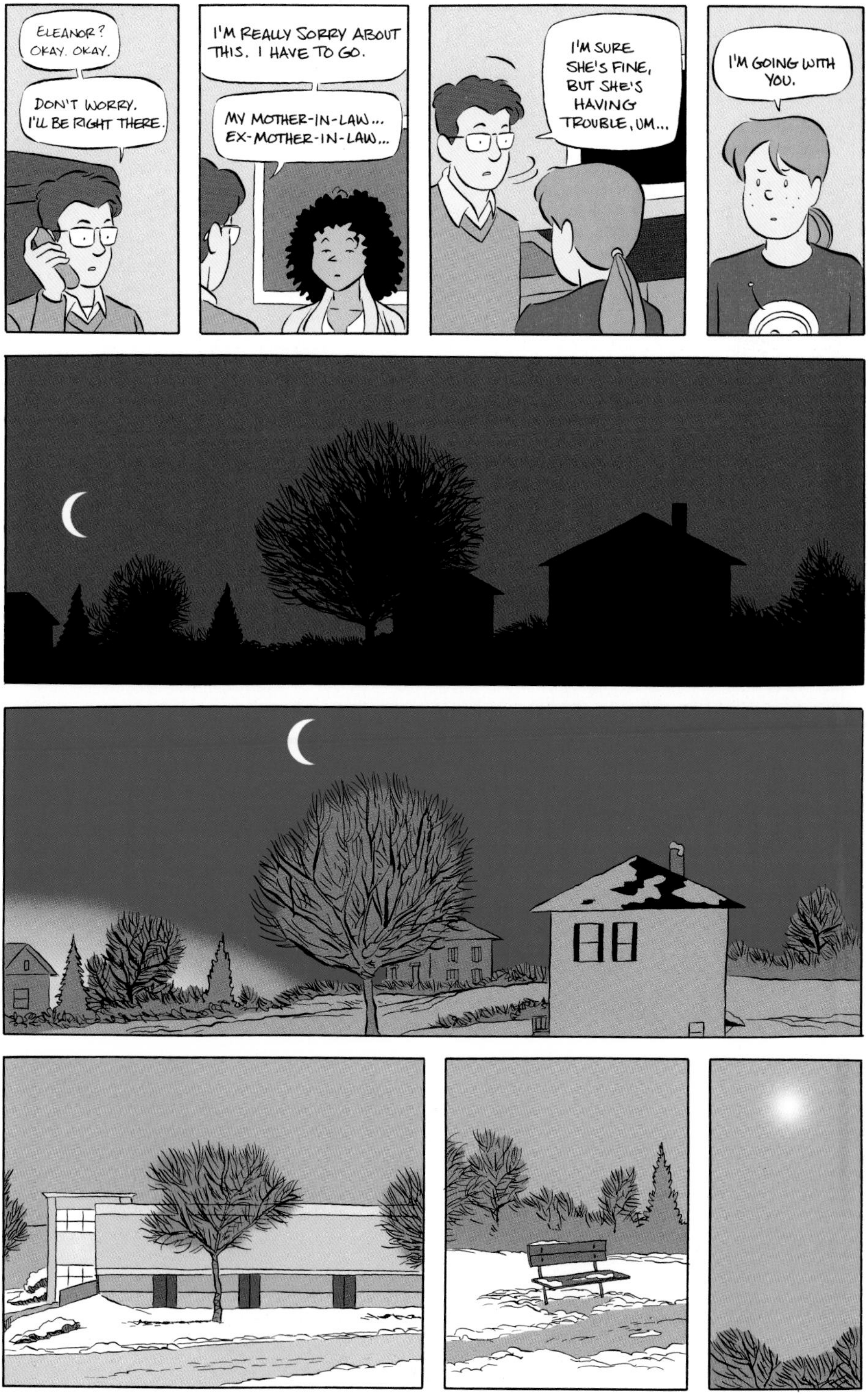
ELEANOR? OKAY. OKAY.
DON'T WORRY. I'LL BE RIGHT THERE.
I'M REALLY SORRY ABOUT THIS. I HAVE TO GO.
MY MOTHER-IN-LAW... EX-MOTHER-IN-LAW...
I'M SURE SHE'S FINE, BUT SHE'S HAVING TROUBLE, UM...
I'M GOING WITH YOU.

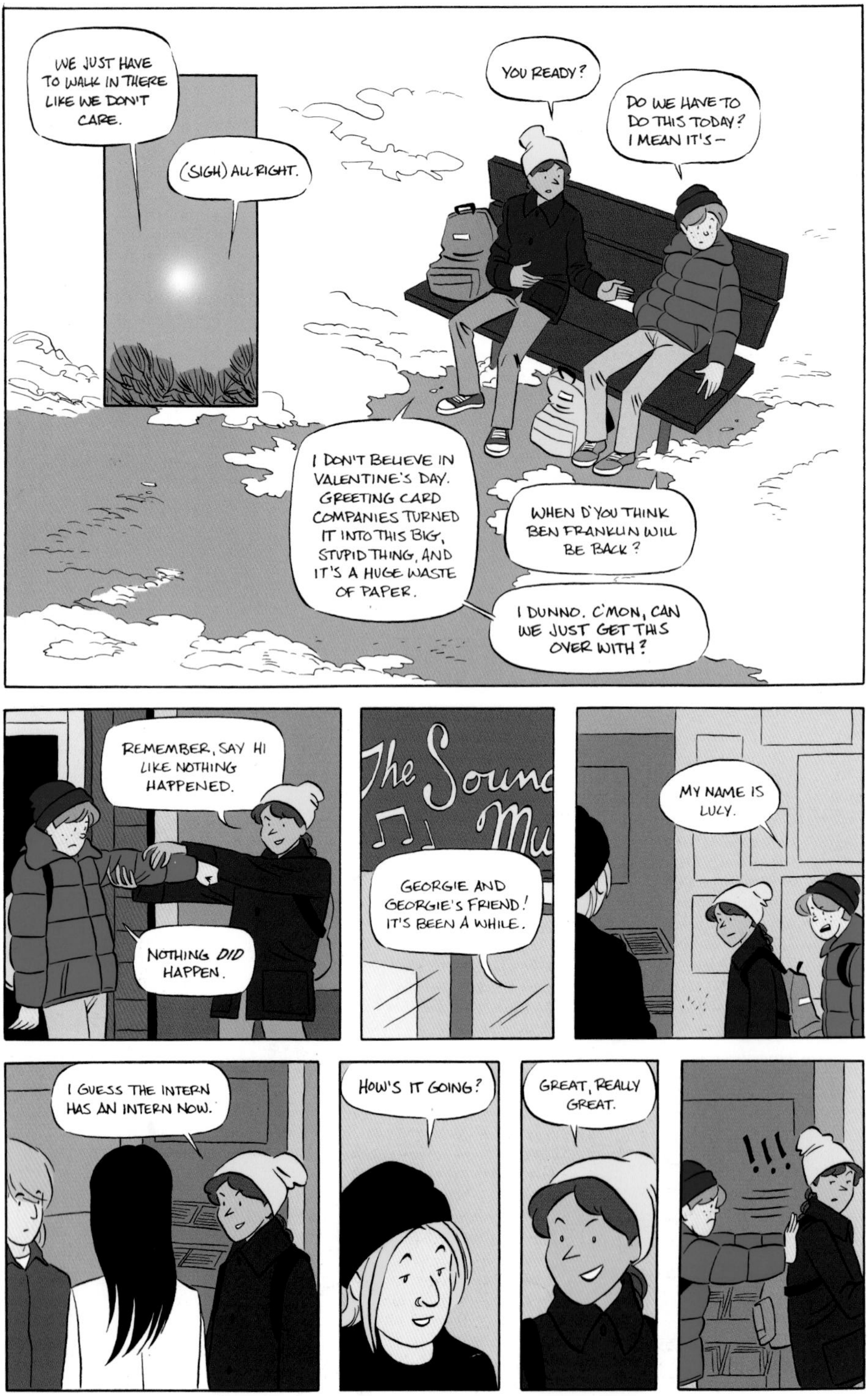
WE JUST HAVE TO WALK IN THERE LIKE WE DON'T CARE.
(SIGH) ALL RIGHT.
YOU READY?
DO WE HAVE TO DO THIS TODAY? I MEAN IT'S –
I DON'T BELIEVE IN VALENTINE'S DAY. GREETING CARD COMPANIES TURNED IT INTO THIS BIG, STUPID THING, AND IT'S A HUGE WASTE OF PAPER.
WHEN D'YOU THINK BEN FRANKLIN WILL BE BACK?
I DUNNO. C'MON, CAN WE JUST GET THIS OVER WITH?
REMEMBER, SAY HI LIKE NOTHING HAPPENED.
NOTHING *DID* HAPPEN.
The Sound Mu
GEORGIE AND GEORGIE'S FRIEND! IT'S BEEN A WHILE.
MY NAME IS LUCY.
I GUESS THE INTERN HAS AN INTERN NOW.
HOW'S IT GOING?
GREAT, REALLY GREAT.
!!!

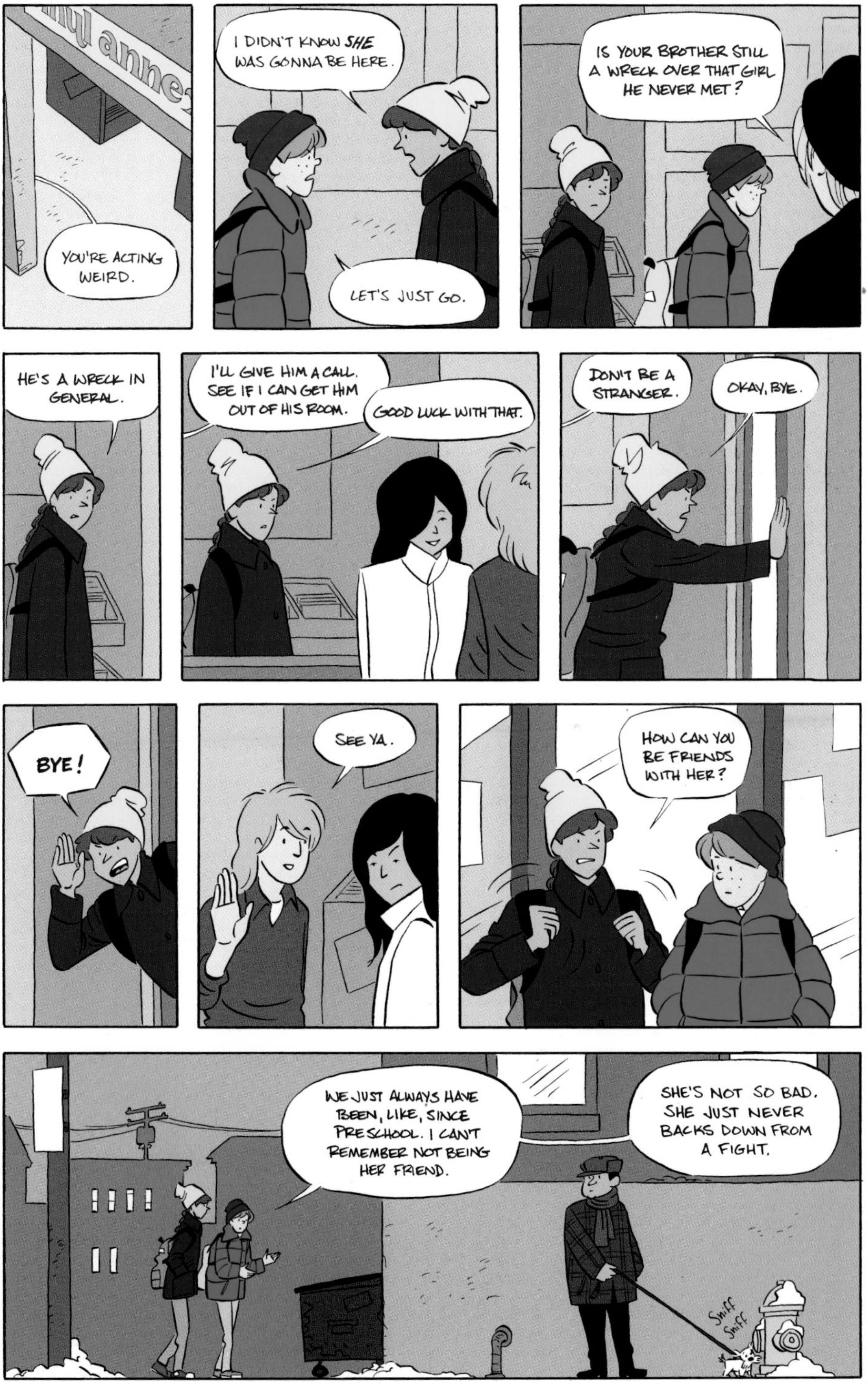

YOU'RE ACTING WEIRD.
I DIDN'T KNOW SHE WAS GONNA BE HERE.
LET'S JUST GO.
IS YOUR BROTHER STILL A WRECK OVER THAT GIRL HE NEVER MET?
HE'S A WRECK IN GENERAL.
I'LL GIVE HIM A CALL. SEE IF I CAN GET HIM OUT OF HIS ROOM.
GOOD LUCK WITH THAT.
DON'T BE A STRANGER.
OKAY, BYE.
BYE!
SEE YA.
HOW CAN YOU BE FRIENDS WITH HER?
WE JUST ALWAYS HAVE BEEN, LIKE, SINCE PRESCHOOL. I CAN'T REMEMBER NOT BEING HER FRIEND.
SHE'S NOT SO BAD. SHE JUST NEVER BACKS DOWN FROM A FIGHT.
Sniff Sniff

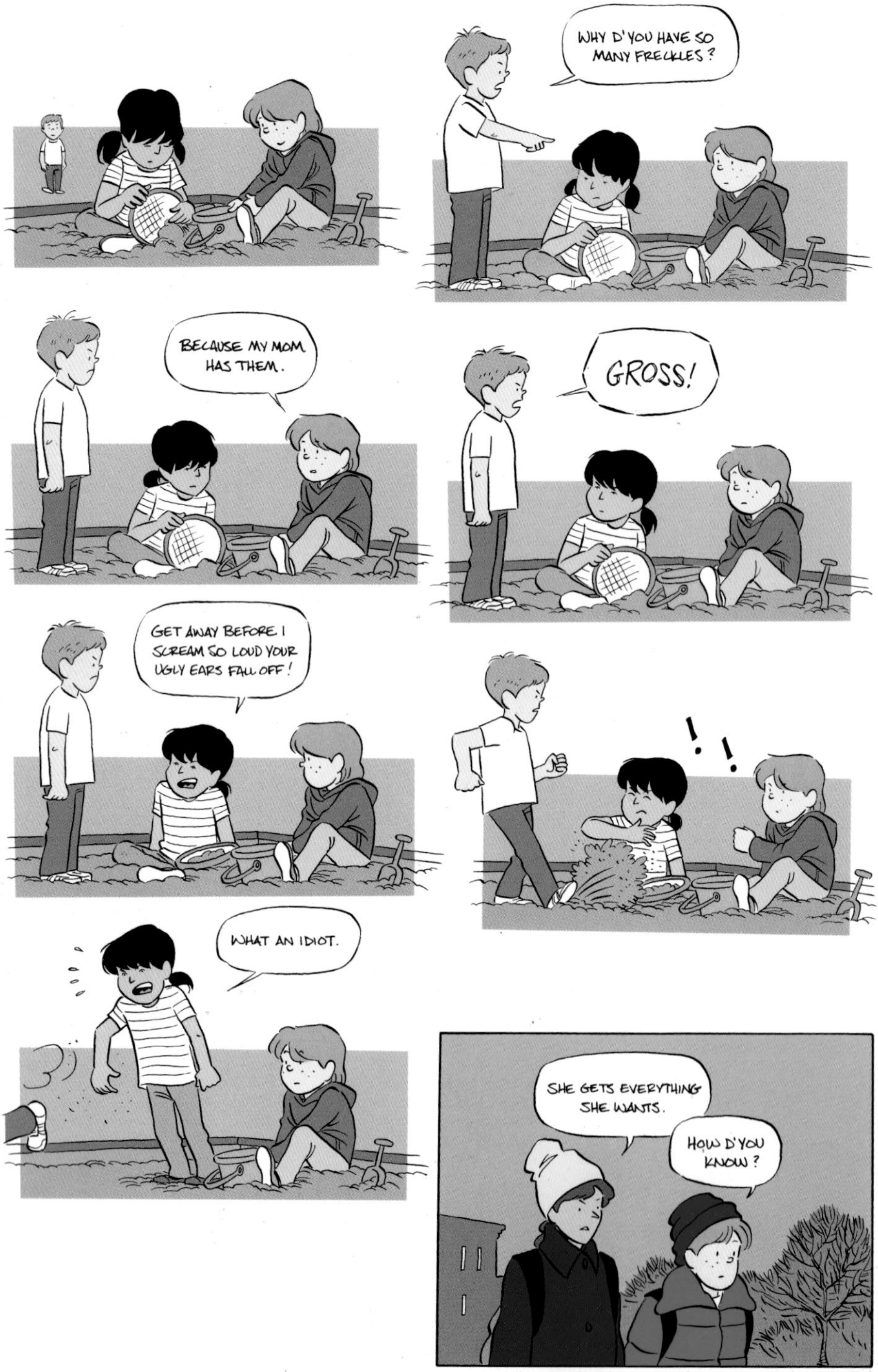
WHY D'YOU HAVE SO MANY FRECKLES?
BECAUSE MY MOM HAS THEM.
GROSS!
GET AWAY BEFORE I SCREAM SO LOUD YOUR UGLY EARS FALL OFF!
!
!
WHAT AN IDIOT.
SHE GETS EVERYTHING SHE WANTS.
HOW D'YOU KNOW?

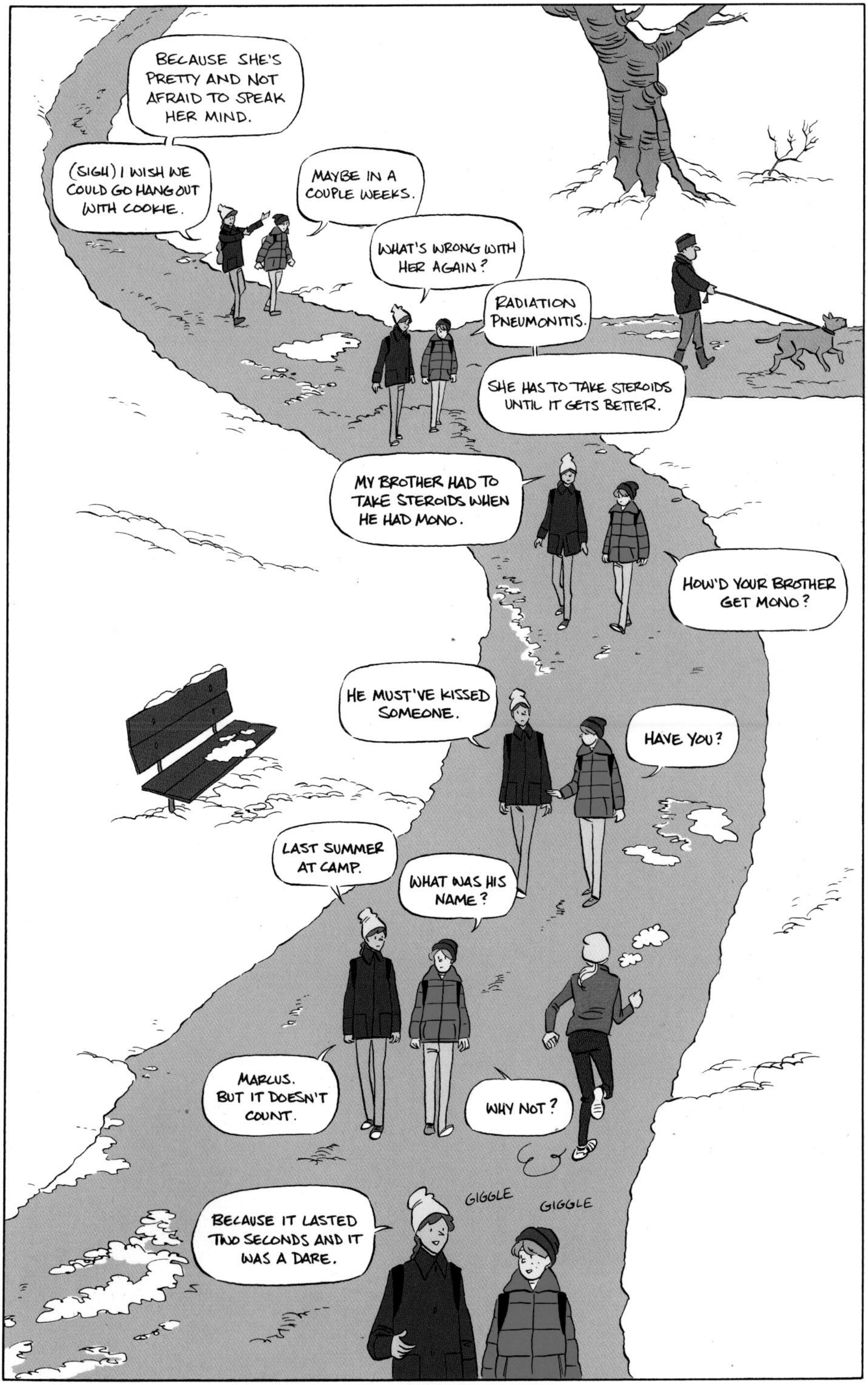
BECAUSE SHE'S PRETTY AND NOT AFRAID TO SPEAK HER MIND.
(SIGH) I WISH WE COULD GO HANG OUT WITH COOKIE.
MAYBE IN A COUPLE WEEKS.
WHAT'S WRONG WITH HER AGAIN?
RADIATION PNEUMONITIS.
SHE HAS TO TAKE STEROIDS UNTIL IT GETS BETTER.
MY BROTHER HAD TO TAKE STEROIDS WHEN HE HAD MONO.
HOW'D YOUR BROTHER GET MONO?
HE MUST'VE KISSED SOMEONE.
HAVE YOU?
LAST SUMMER AT CAMP.
WHAT WAS HIS NAME?
MARCUS. BUT IT DOESN'T COUNT.
WHY NOT?
BECAUSE IT LASTED TWO SECONDS AND IT WAS A DARE.
GIGGLE
GIGGLE

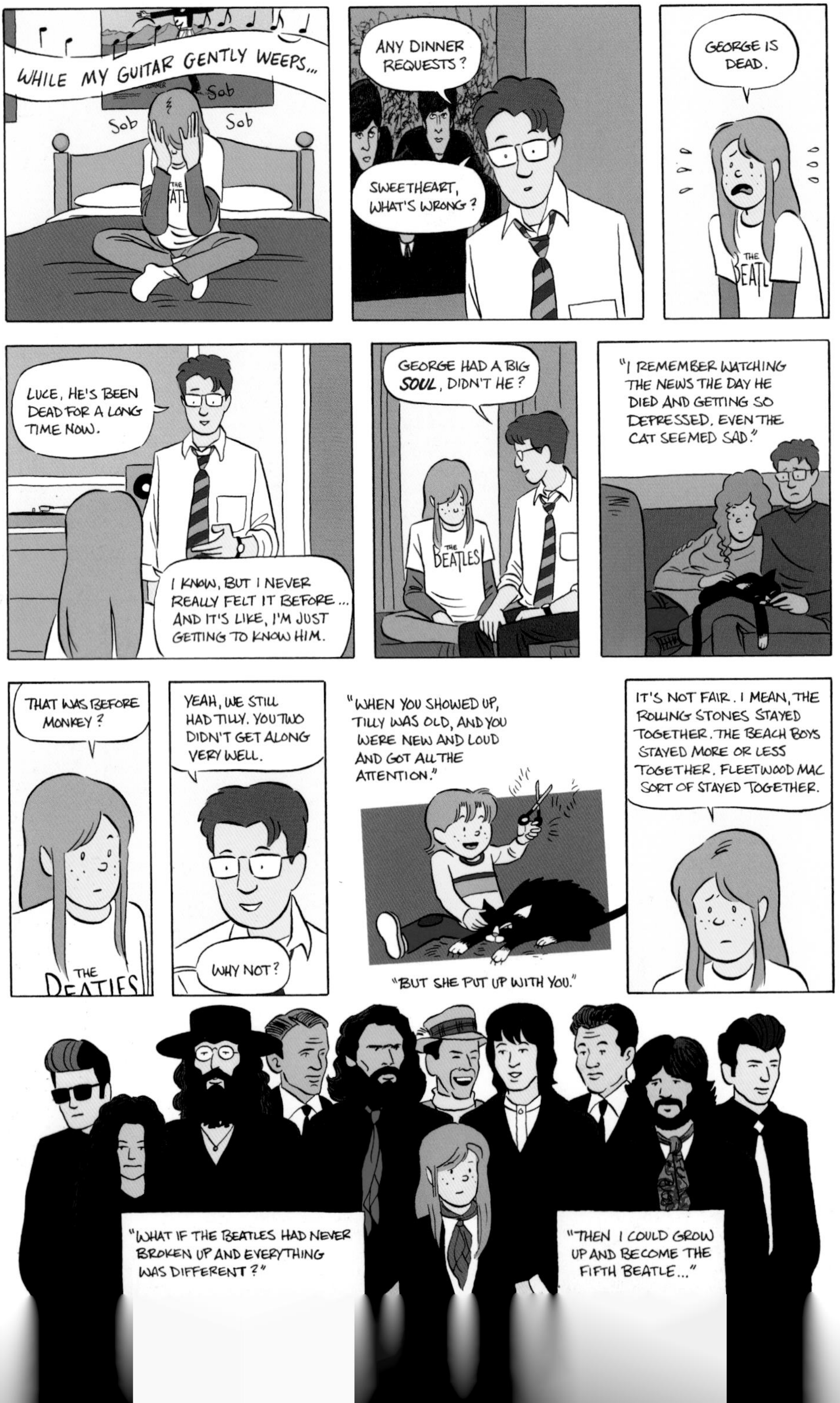
WHILE MY GUITAR GENTLY WEEPS...
Sob
Sob
Sob
ANY DINNER REQUESTS?
SWEETHEART, WHAT'S WRONG?
GEORGE IS DEAD.
LUCE, HE'S BEEN DEAD FOR A LONG TIME NOW.
I KNOW, BUT I NEVER REALLY FELT IT BEFORE... AND IT'S LIKE, I'M JUST GETTING TO KNOW HIM.
GEORGE HAD A BIG SOUL, DIDN'T HE?
"I REMEMBER WATCHING THE NEWS THE DAY HE DIED AND GETTING SO DEPRESSED. EVEN THE CAT SEEMED SAD."
THAT WAS BEFORE MONKEY?
YEAH, WE STILL HAD TILLY. YOU TWO DIDN'T GET ALONG VERY WELL.
WHY NOT?
"WHEN YOU SHOWED UP, TILLY WAS OLD, AND YOU WERE NEW AND LOUD AND GOT ALL THE ATTENTION."
"BUT SHE PUT UP WITH YOU."
IT'S NOT FAIR. I MEAN, THE ROLLING STONES STAYED TOGETHER. THE BEACH BOYS STAYED MORE OR LESS TOGETHER. FLEETWOOD MAC SORT OF STAYED TOGETHER.
"WHAT IF THE BEATLES HAD NEVER BROKEN UP AND EVERYTHING WAS DIFFERENT?"
"THEN I COULD GROW UP AND BECOME THE FIFTH BEATLE..."

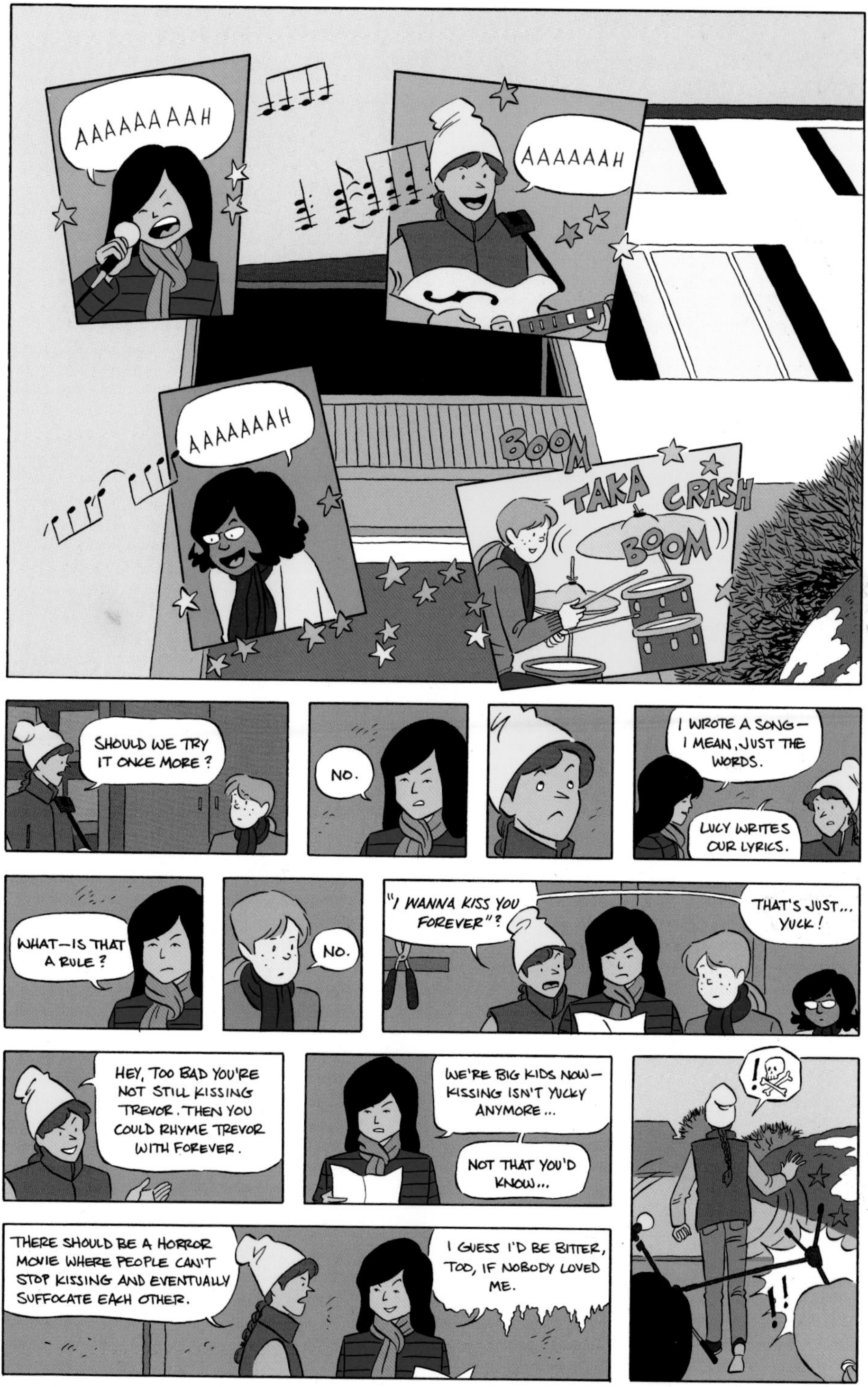
AAAAAAAAH
AAAAAAH
AAAAAAAH
BOOM
TAKA
CRASH
BOOM
SHOULD WE TRY IT ONCE MORE?
NO.
I WROTE A SONG— I MEAN, JUST THE WORDS.
LUCY WRITES OUR LYRICS.
WHAT—IS THAT A RULE?
NO.
"I WANNA KISS YOU FOREVER"?
THAT'S JUST... YUCK!
HEY, TOO BAD YOU'RE NOT STILL KISSING TREVOR. THEN YOU COULD RHYME TREVOR WITH FOREVER.
WE'RE BIG KIDS NOW— KISSING ISN'T YUCKY ANYMORE...
NOT THAT YOU'D KNOW...
THERE SHOULD BE A HORROR MOVIE WHERE PEOPLE CAN'T STOP KISSING AND EVENTUALLY SUFFOCATE EACH OTHER.
I GUESS I'D BE BITTER, TOO, IF NOBODY LOVED ME.
!
!!

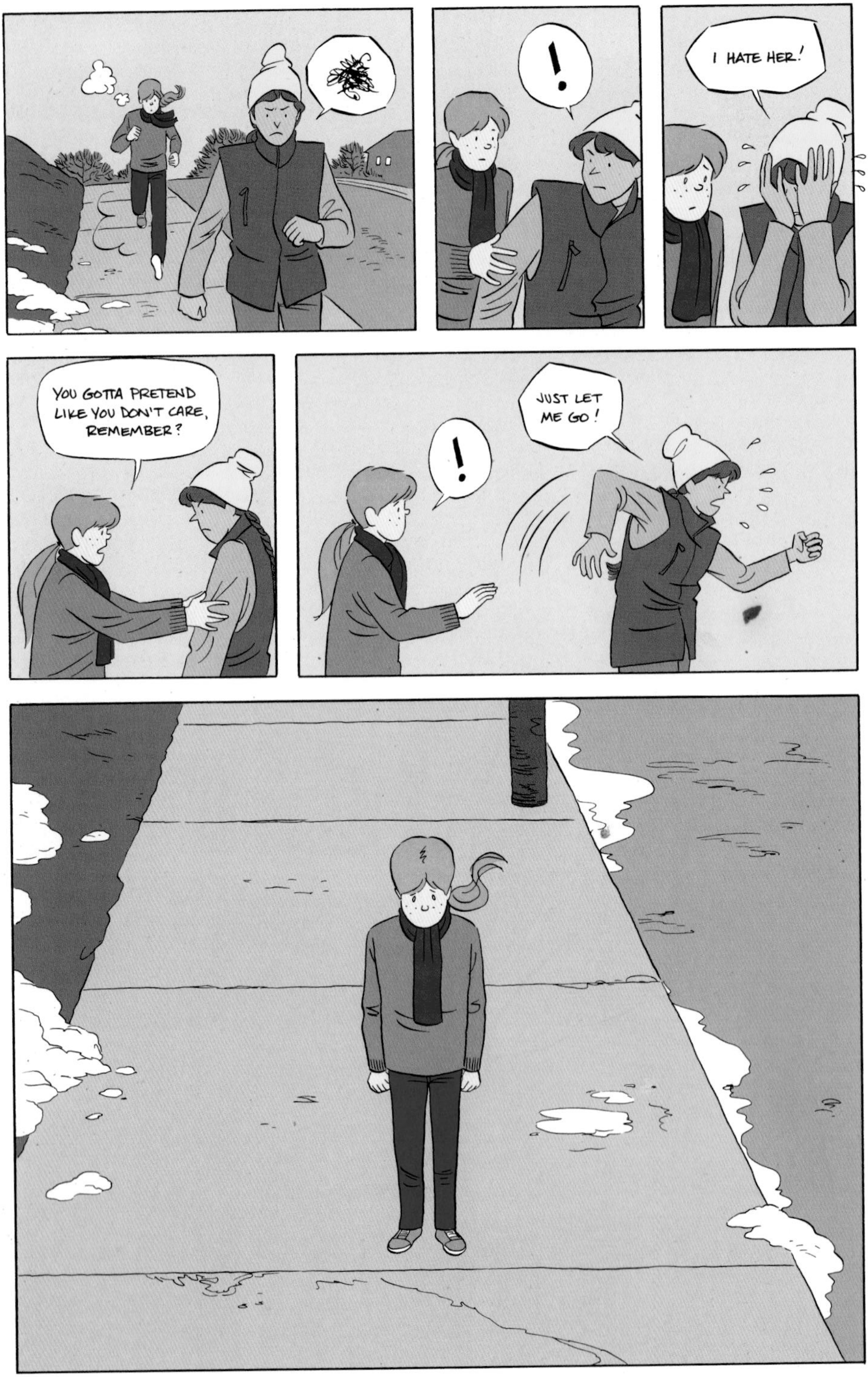
!
I HATE HER!
YOU GOTTA PRETEND LIKE YOU DON'T CARE, REMEMBER?
!
JUST LET ME GO!

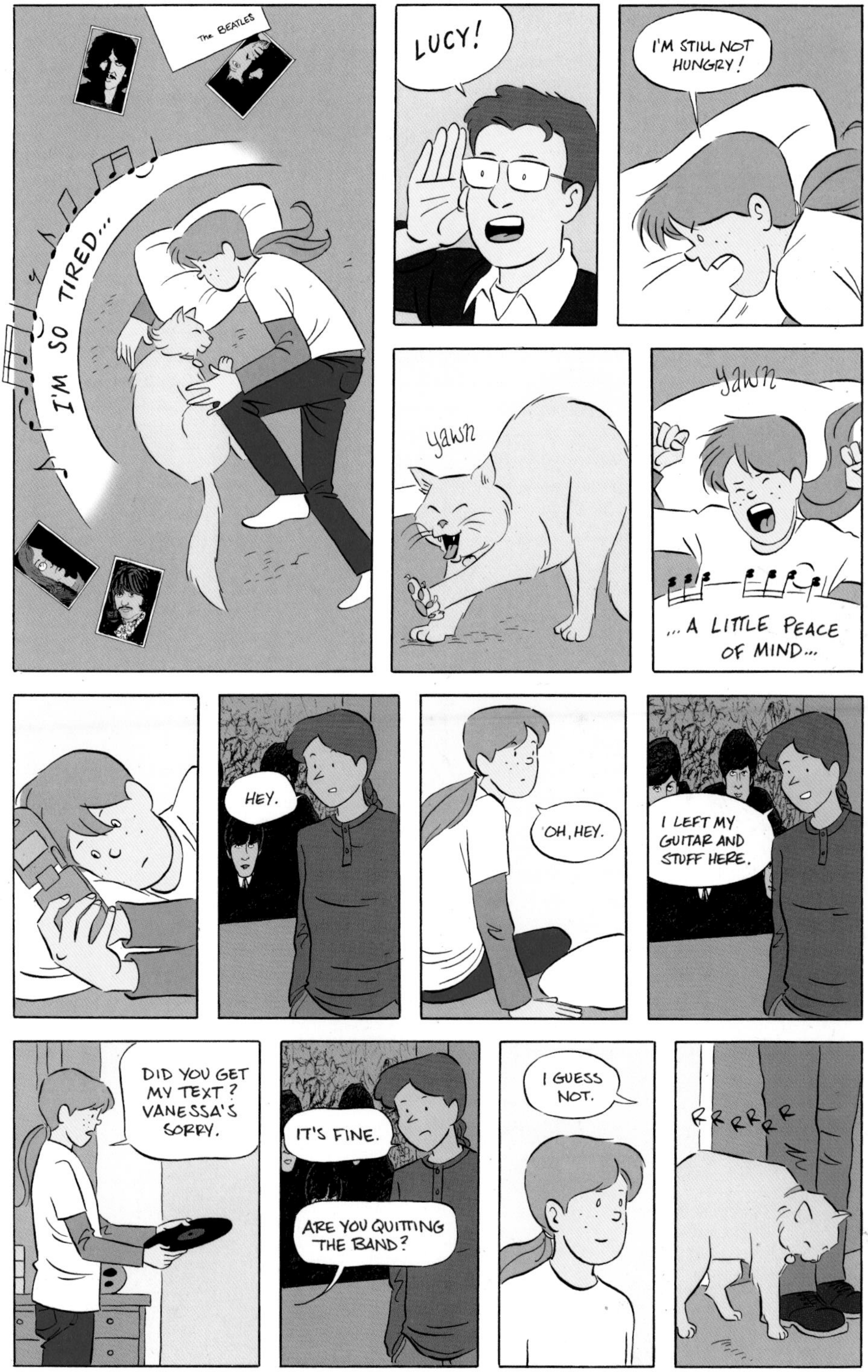
The BEATLES
I'M SO TIRED...
LUCY!
I'M STILL NOT HUNGRY!
yawn
yawn
... A LITTLE PEACE OF MIND...
HEY.
OH, HEY.
I LEFT MY GUITAR AND STUFF HERE.
DID YOU GET MY TEXT? VANESSA'S SORRY.
IT'S FINE.
ARE YOU QUITTING THE BAND?
I GUESS NOT.
RRRRRR

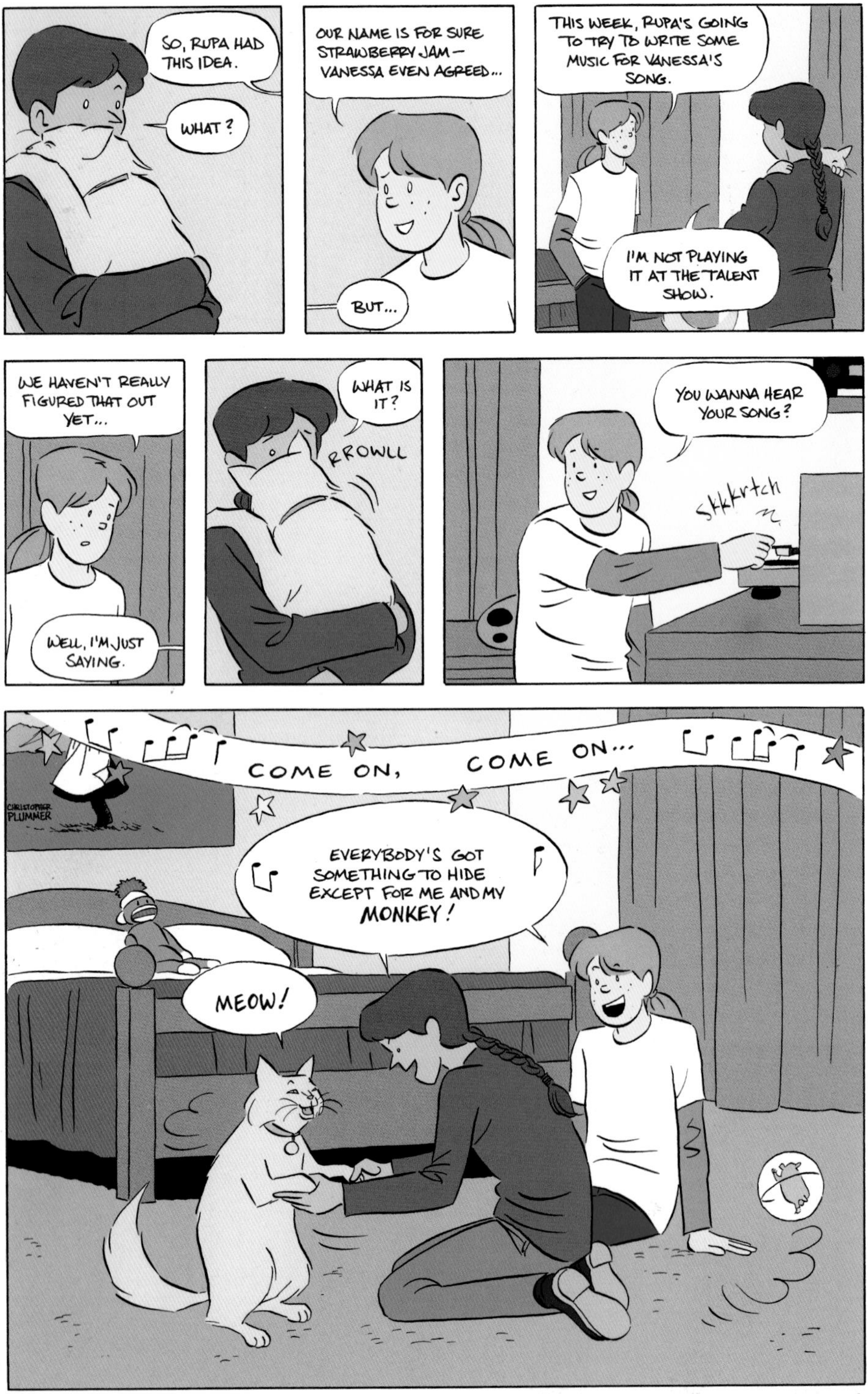
SO, RUPA HAD THIS IDEA.
WHAT?
OUR NAME IS FOR SURE STRAWBERRY JAM— VANESSA EVEN AGREED...
BUT...
THIS WEEK, RUPA'S GOING TO TRY TO WRITE SOME MUSIC FOR VANESSA'S SONG.
I'M NOT PLAYING IT AT THE TALENT SHOW.
WE HAVEN'T REALLY FIGURED THAT OUT YET...
WELL, I'M JUST SAYING.
WHAT IS IT?
RROWLL
YOU WANNA HEAR YOUR SONG?
SKKKRTCH
COME ON, COME ON...
CHRISTOPHER PLUMMER
EVERYBODY'S GOT SOMETHING TO HIDE EXCEPT FOR ME AND MY MONKEY!
MEOW!

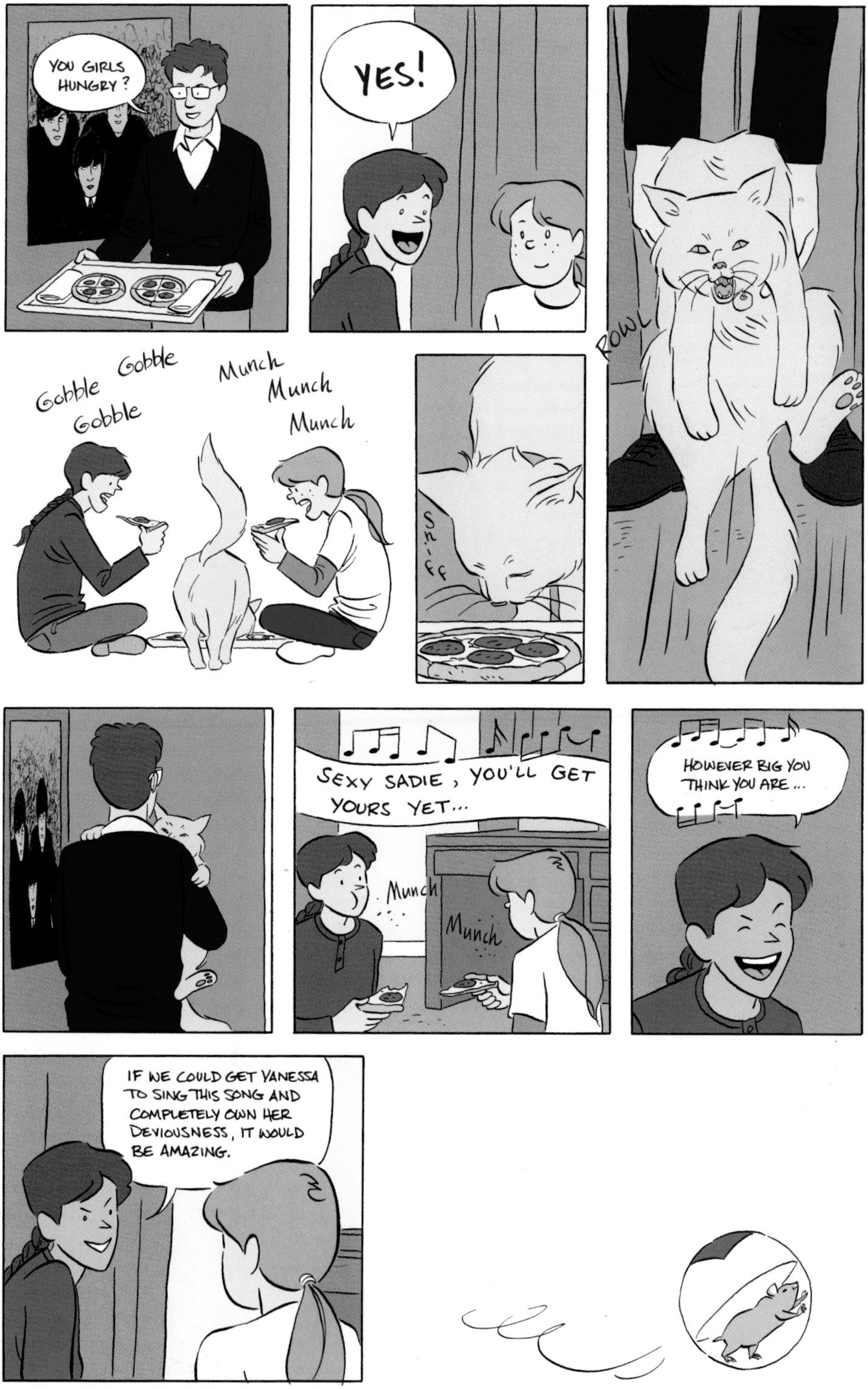

YOU GIRLS HUNGRY?
YES!
ROWL
Gobble Gobble Gobble
Munch Munch Munch
Sniff
SEXY SADIE, YOU'LL GET YOURS YET...
Munch
Munch
HOWEVER BIG YOU THINK YOU ARE...
IF WE COULD GET VANESSA TO SING THIS SONG AND COMPLETELY OWN HER DEVIOUSNESS, IT WOULD BE AMAZING.

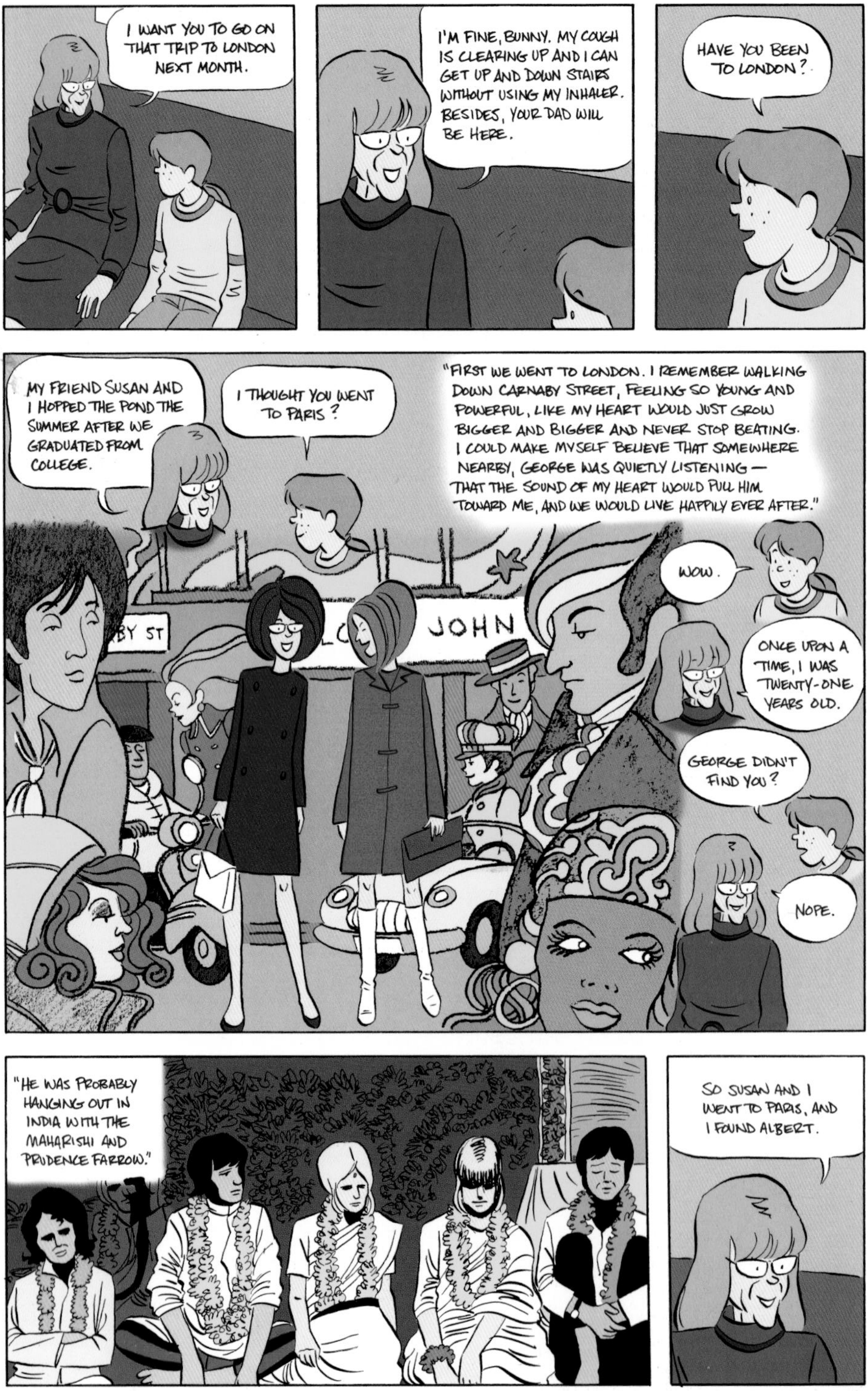
I WANT YOU TO GO ON THAT TRIP TO LONDON NEXT MONTH.
I'M FINE, BUNNY. MY COUGH IS CLEARING UP AND I CAN GET UP AND DOWN STAIRS WITHOUT USING MY INHALER. BESIDES, YOUR DAD WILL BE HERE.
HAVE YOU BEEN TO LONDON?
MY FRIEND SUSAN AND I HOPPED THE POND THE SUMMER AFTER WE GRADUATED FROM COLLEGE.
I THOUGHT YOU WENT TO PARIS?
"FIRST WE WENT TO LONDON. I REMEMBER WALKING DOWN CARNABY STREET, FEELING SO YOUNG AND POWERFUL, LIKE MY HEART WOULD JUST GROW BIGGER AND BIGGER AND NEVER STOP BEATING. I COULD MAKE MYSELF BELIEVE THAT SOMEWHERE NEARBY, GEORGE WAS QUIETLY LISTENING — THAT THE SOUND OF MY HEART WOULD PULL HIM TOWARD ME, AND WE WOULD LIVE HAPPILY EVER AFTER."
WOW.
BY ST
JOHN
ONCE UPON A TIME, I WAS TWENTY-ONE YEARS OLD.
GEORGE DIDN'T FIND YOU?
NOPE.
"HE WAS PROBABLY HANGING OUT IN INDIA WITH THE MAHARISHI AND PRUDENCE FARROW."
SO SUSAN AND I WENT TO PARIS, AND I FOUND ALBERT.

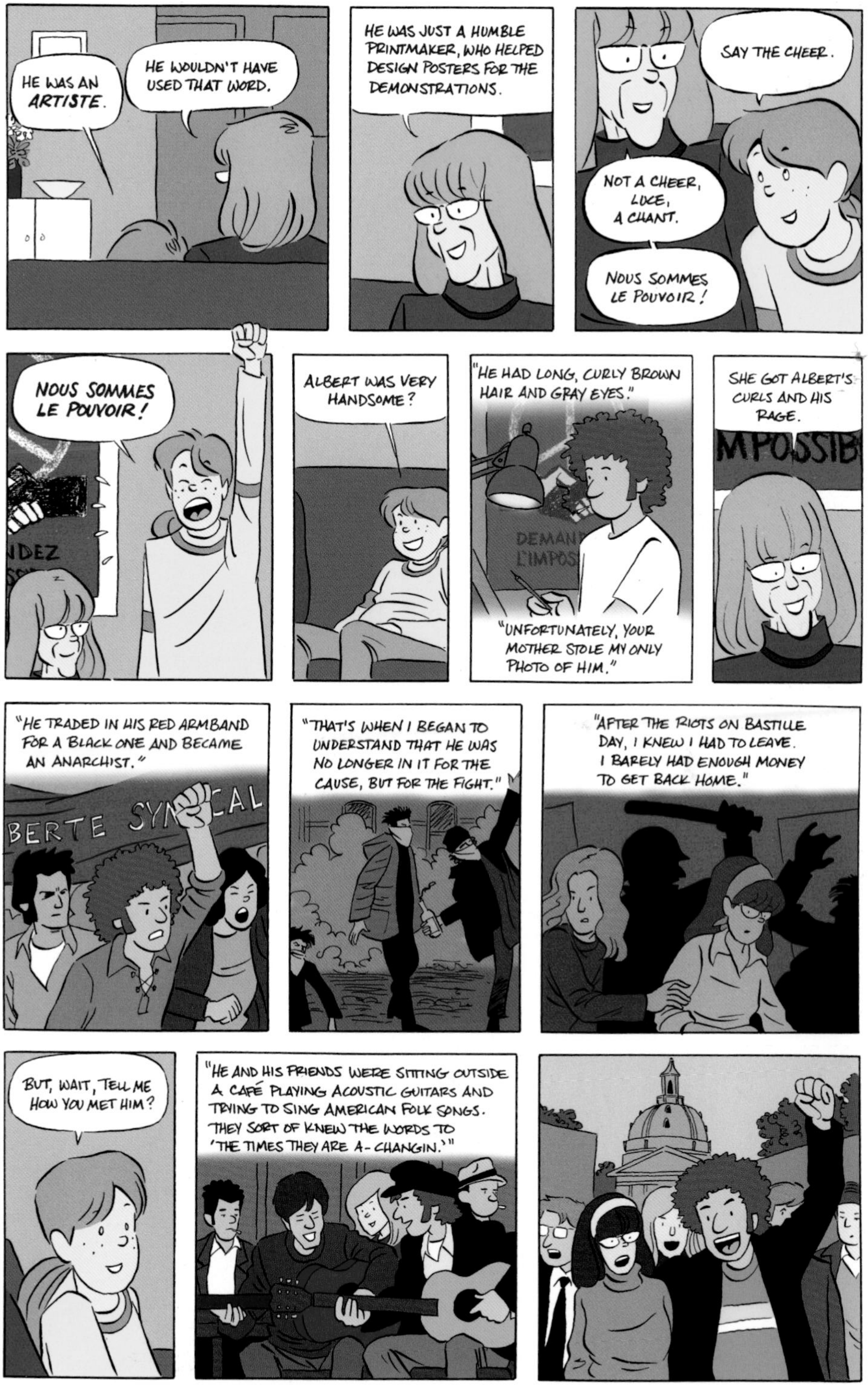
HE WAS AN ARTISTE.
HE WOULDN'T HAVE USED THAT WORD.
HE WAS JUST A HUMBLE PRINTMAKER, WHO HELPED DESIGN POSTERS FOR THE DEMONSTRATIONS.
SAY THE CHEER.
NOT A CHEER, LUCE, A CHANT.
NOUS SOMMES LE POUVOIR!
NOUS SOMMES LE POUVOIR!
ALBERT WAS VERY HANDSOME?
"HE HAD LONG, CURLY BROWN HAIR AND GRAY EYES."
DEMANDEZ L'IMPOSSIBLE
"UNFORTUNATELY, YOUR MOTHER STOLE MY ONLY PHOTO OF HIM."
SHE GOT ALBERT'S CURLS AND HIS RAGE.
"HE TRADED IN HIS RED ARMBAND FOR A BLACK ONE AND BECAME AN ANARCHIST."
"THAT'S WHEN I BEGAN TO UNDERSTAND THAT HE WAS NO LONGER IN IT FOR THE CAUSE, BUT FOR THE FIGHT."
"AFTER THE RIOTS ON BASTILLE DAY, I KNEW I HAD TO LEAVE. I BARELY HAD ENOUGH MONEY TO GET BACK HOME."
BUT, WAIT, TELL ME HOW YOU MET HIM?
"HE AND HIS FRIENDS WERE SITTING OUTSIDE A CAFÉ PLAYING ACOUSTIC GUITARS AND TRYING TO SING AMERICAN FOLK SONGS. THEY SORT OF KNEW THE WORDS TO 'THE TIMES THEY ARE A-CHANGIN.'"

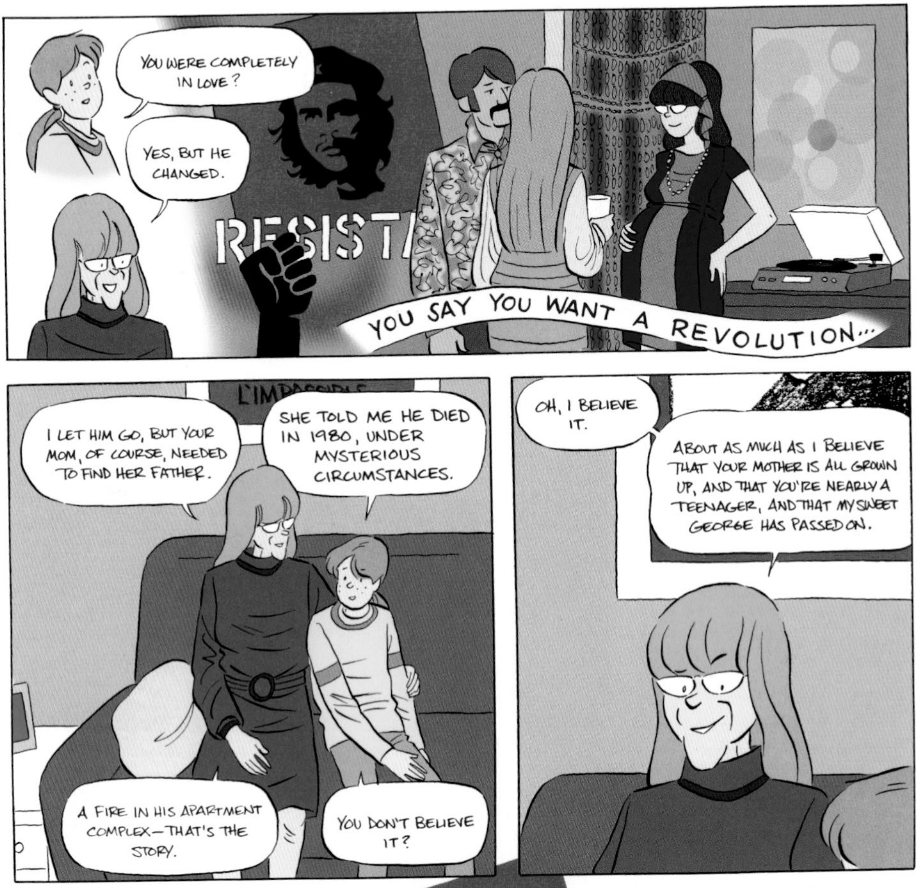
YOU WERE COMPLETELY IN LOVE?
YES, BUT HE CHANGED.
RESIST
YOU SAY YOU WANT A REVOLUTION...
I LET HIM GO, BUT YOUR MOM, OF COURSE, NEEDED TO FIND HER FATHER.
SHE TOLD ME HE DIED IN 1980, UNDER MYSTERIOUS CIRCUMSTANCES.
A FIRE IN HIS APARTMENT COMPLEX—THAT'S THE STORY.
YOU DON'T BELIEVE IT?
OH, I BELIEVE IT.
ABOUT AS MUCH AS I BELIEVE THAT YOUR MOTHER IS ALL GROWN UP, AND THAT YOU'RE NEARLY A TEENAGER, AND THAT MY SWEET GEORGE HAS PASSED ON.

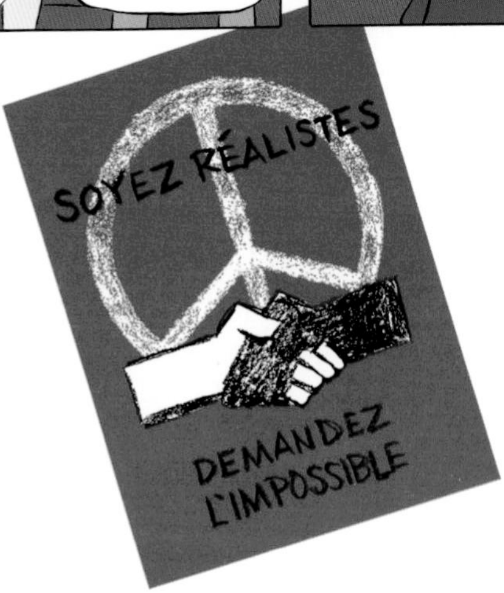
SOYEZ RÉALISTES
DEMANDEZ L'IMPOSSIBLE

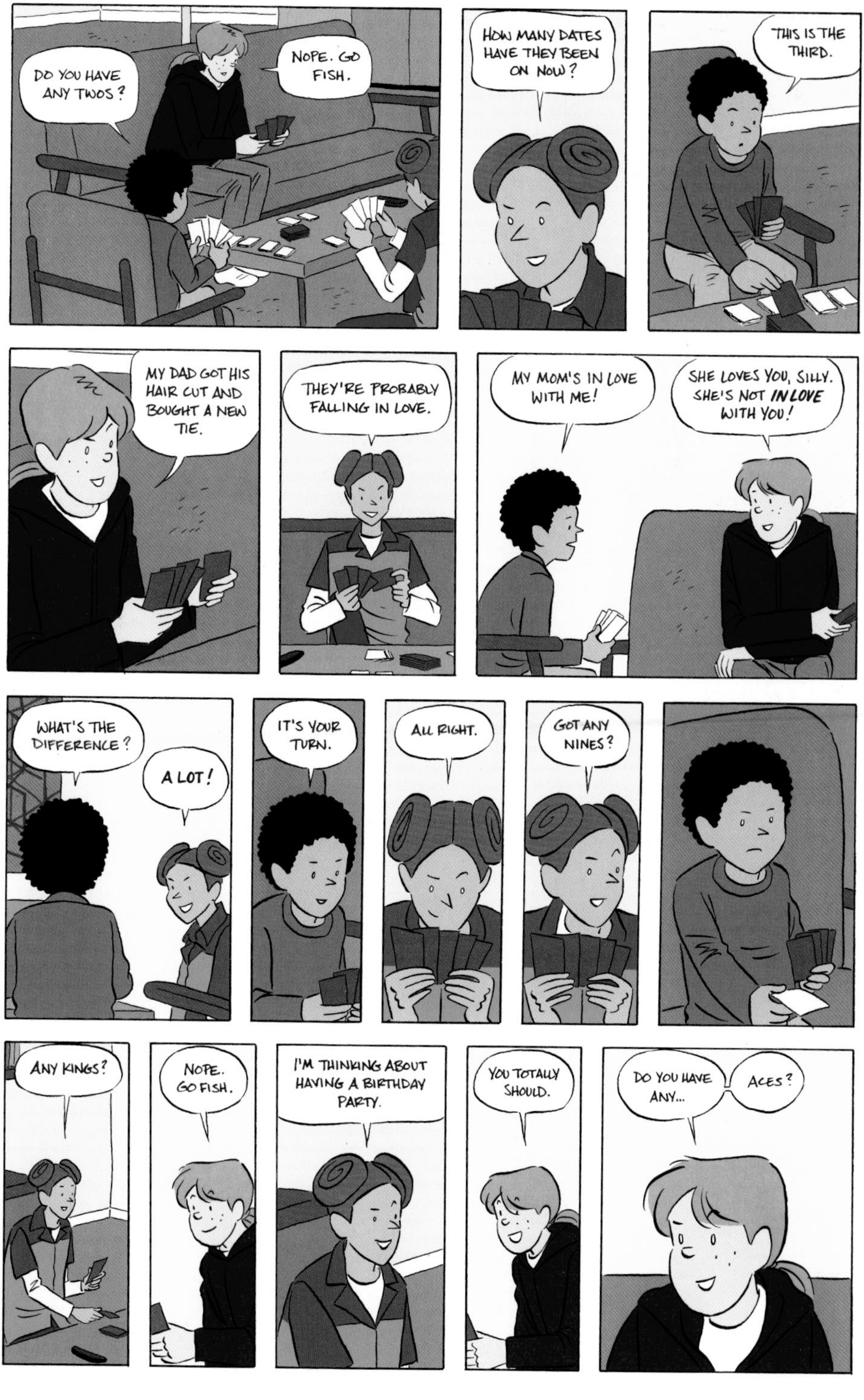
DO YOU HAVE ANY TWOS?
NOPE. GO FISH.
HOW MANY DATES HAVE THEY BEEN ON NOW?
THIS IS THE THIRD.
MY DAD GOT HIS HAIR CUT AND BOUGHT A NEW TIE.
THEY'RE PROBABLY FALLING IN LOVE.
MY MOM'S IN LOVE WITH ME!
SHE LOVES YOU, SILLY. SHE'S NOT IN LOVE WITH YOU!
WHAT'S THE DIFFERENCE?
A LOT!
IT'S YOUR TURN.
ALL RIGHT.
GOT ANY NINES?
ANY KINGS?
NOPE. GO FISH.
I'M THINKING ABOUT HAVING A BIRTHDAY PARTY.
YOU TOTALLY SHOULD.
DO YOU HAVE ANY...
ACES?

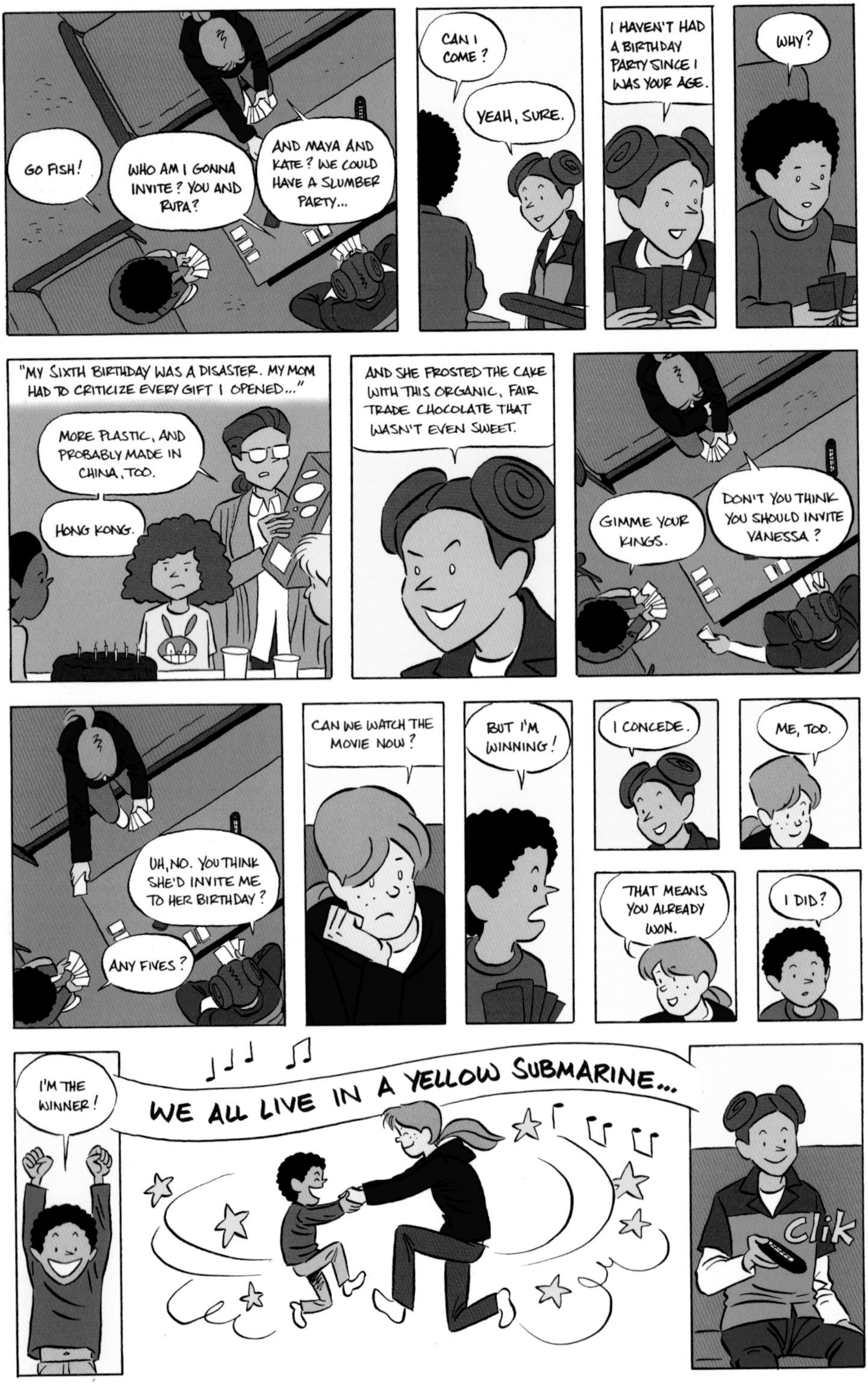
GO FISH!
WHO AM I GONNA INVITE? YOU AND RUPA?
AND MAYA AND KATE? WE COULD HAVE A SLUMBER PARTY...
CAN I COME?
YEAH, SURE.
I HAVEN'T HAD A BIRTHDAY PARTY SINCE I WAS YOUR AGE.
WHY?
"MY SIXTH BIRTHDAY WAS A DISASTER. MY MOM HAD TO CRITICIZE EVERY GIFT I OPENED..."
MORE PLASTIC, AND PROBABLY MADE IN CHINA, TOO.
HONG KONG.
AND SHE FROSTED THE CAKE WITH THIS ORGANIC, FAIR TRADE CHOCOLATE THAT WASN'T EVEN SWEET.
GIMME YOUR KINGS.
DON'T YOU THINK YOU SHOULD INVITE VANESSA?
UH, NO. YOU THINK SHE'D INVITE ME TO HER BIRTHDAY?
ANY FIVES?
CAN WE WATCH THE MOVIE NOW?
BUT I'M WINNING!
I CONCEDE.
ME, TOO.
THAT MEANS YOU ALREADY WON.
I DID?
I'M THE WINNER!
WE ALL LIVE IN A YELLOW SUBMARINE...
CLIK

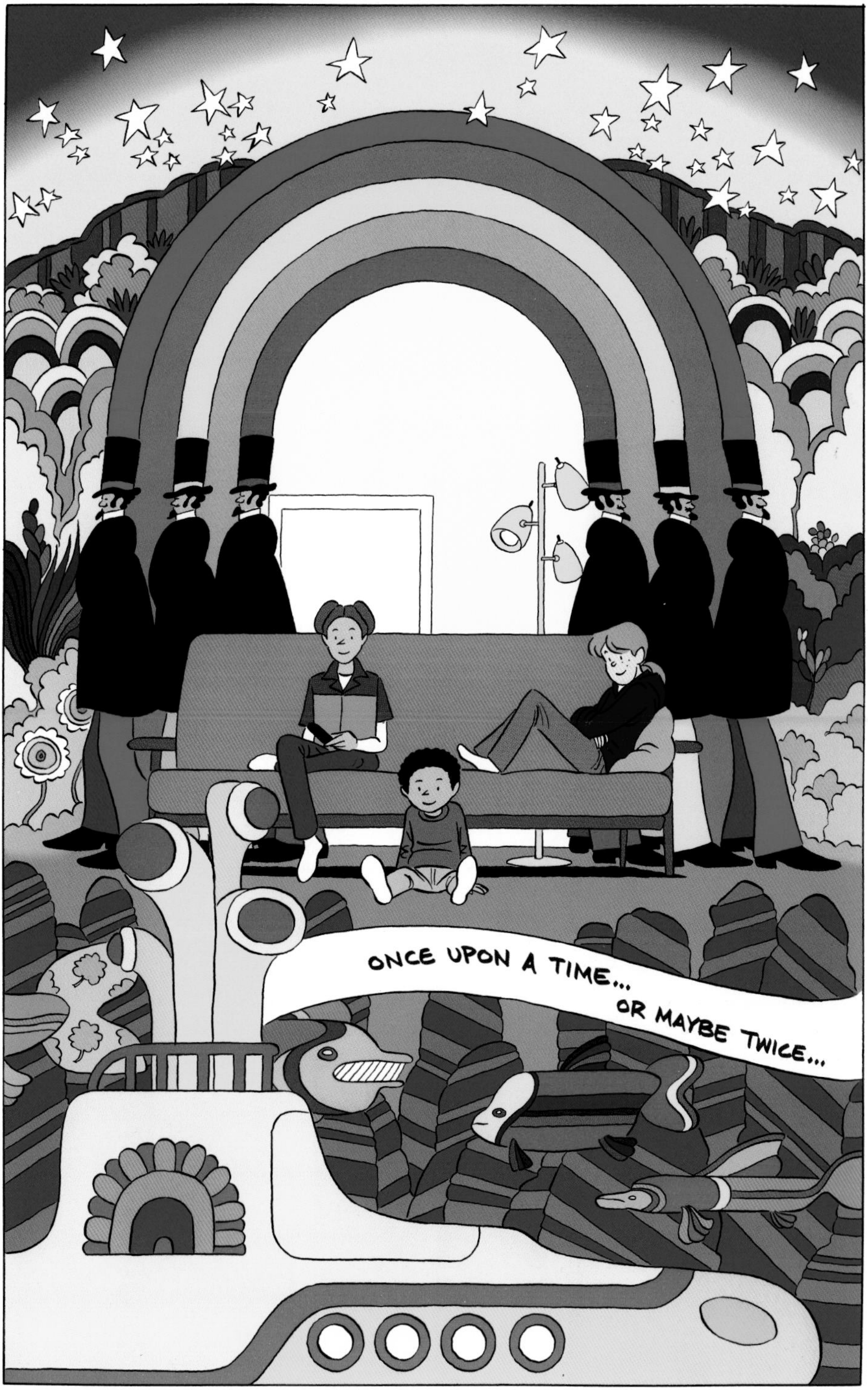
ONCE UPON A TIME...
OR MAYBE TWICE...

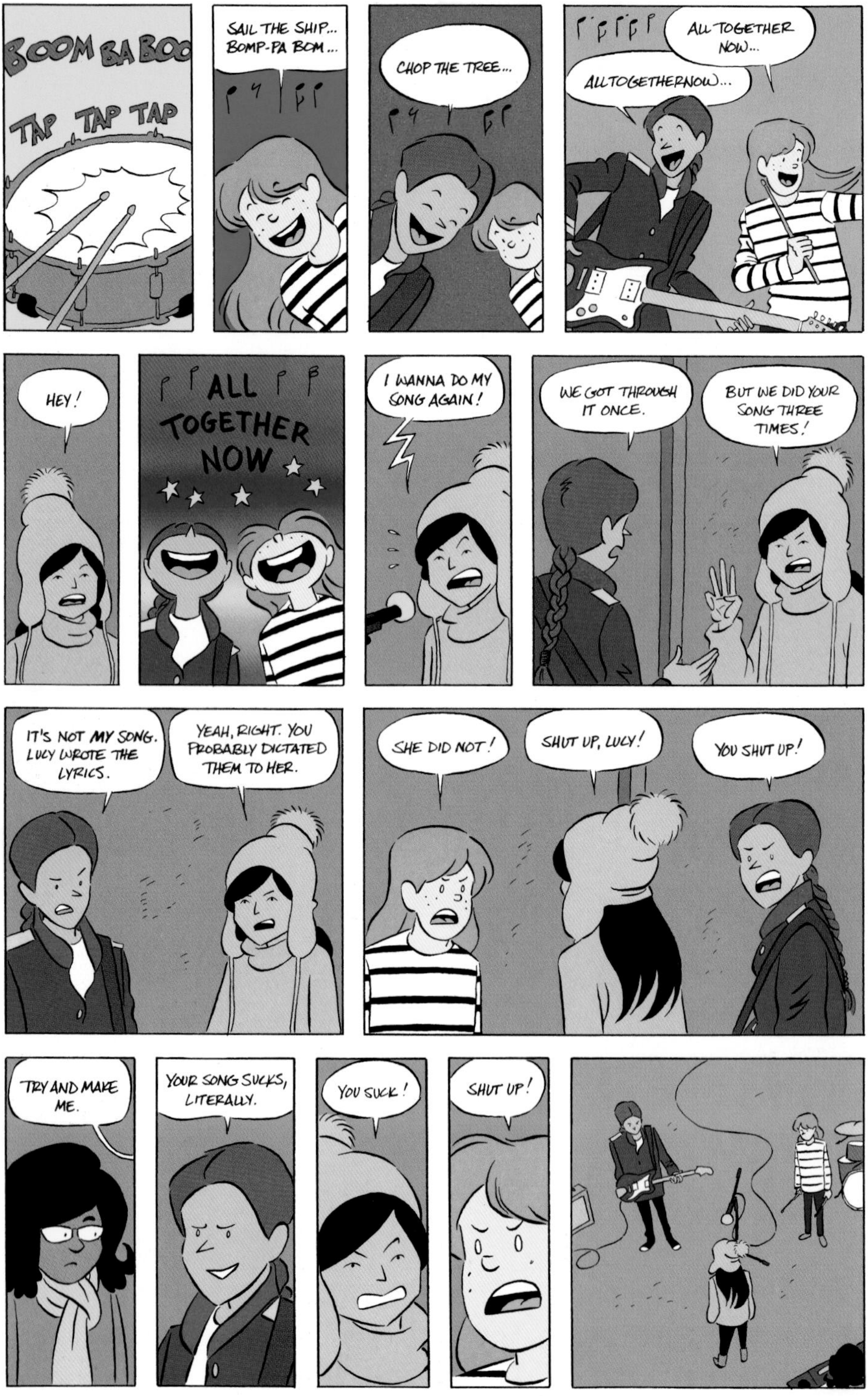
BOOM BA BOO
TAP TAP TAP
SAIL THE SHIP... BOMP-PA BOM...
CHOP THE TREE...
ALL TOGETHER NOW...
ALLTOGETHERNOW...
HEY!
ALL TOGETHER NOW
I WANNA DO MY SONG AGAIN!
WE GOT THROUGH IT ONCE.
BUT WE DID YOUR SONG THREE TIMES!
IT'S NOT MY SONG. LUCY WROTE THE LYRICS.
YEAH, RIGHT. YOU PROBABLY DICTATED THEM TO HER.
SHE DID NOT!
SHUT UP, LUCY!
YOU SHUT UP!
TRY AND MAKE ME.
YOUR SONG SUCKS, LITERALLY.
YOU SUCK!
SHUT UP!

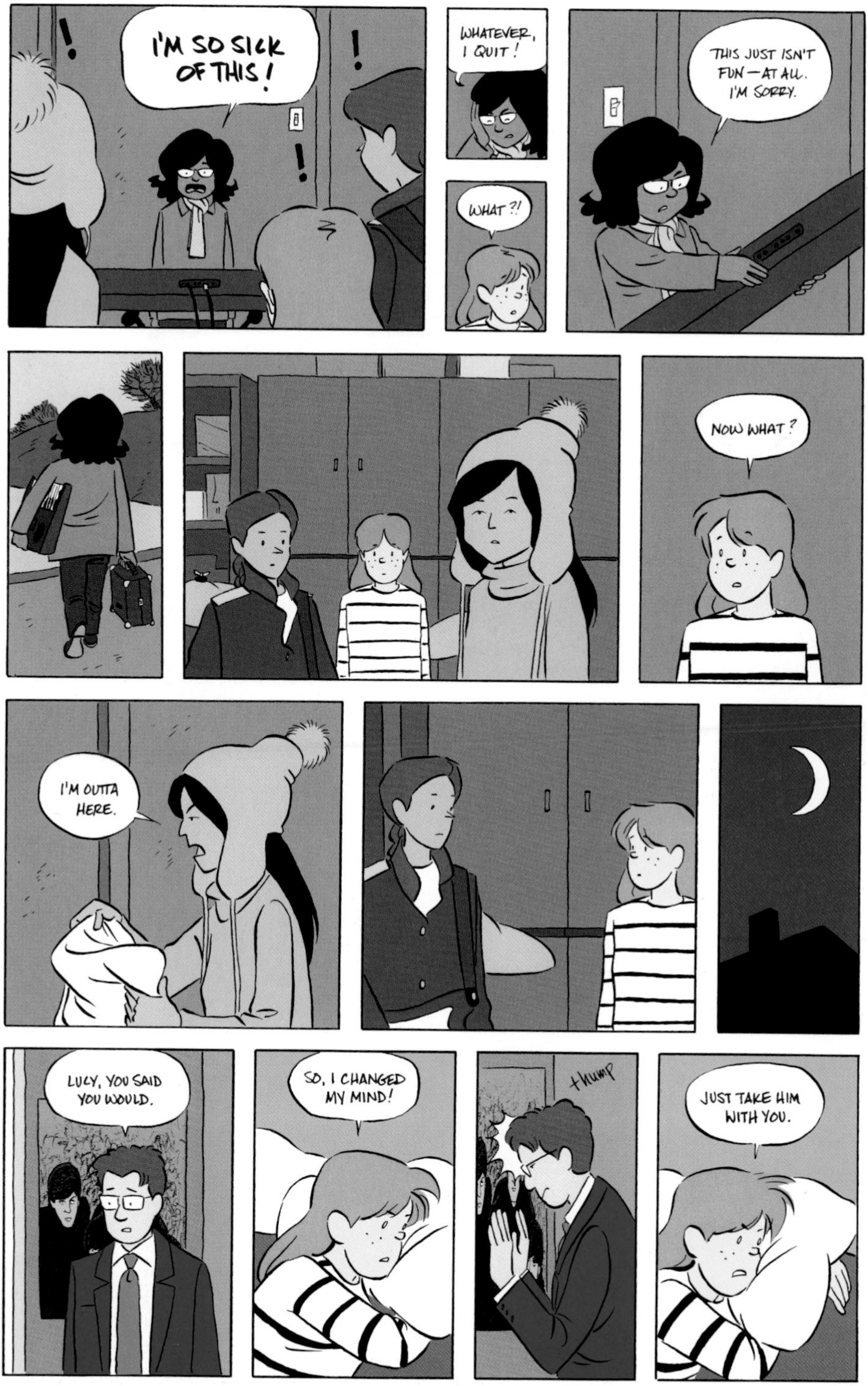
I'M SO SICK OF THIS!
WHATEVER, I QUIT!
WHAT?!
THIS JUST ISN'T FUN—AT ALL. I'M SORRY.
NOW WHAT?
I'M OUTTA HERE.
LUCY, YOU SAID YOU WOULD.
SO, I CHANGED MY MIND!
thump
JUST TAKE HIM WITH YOU.

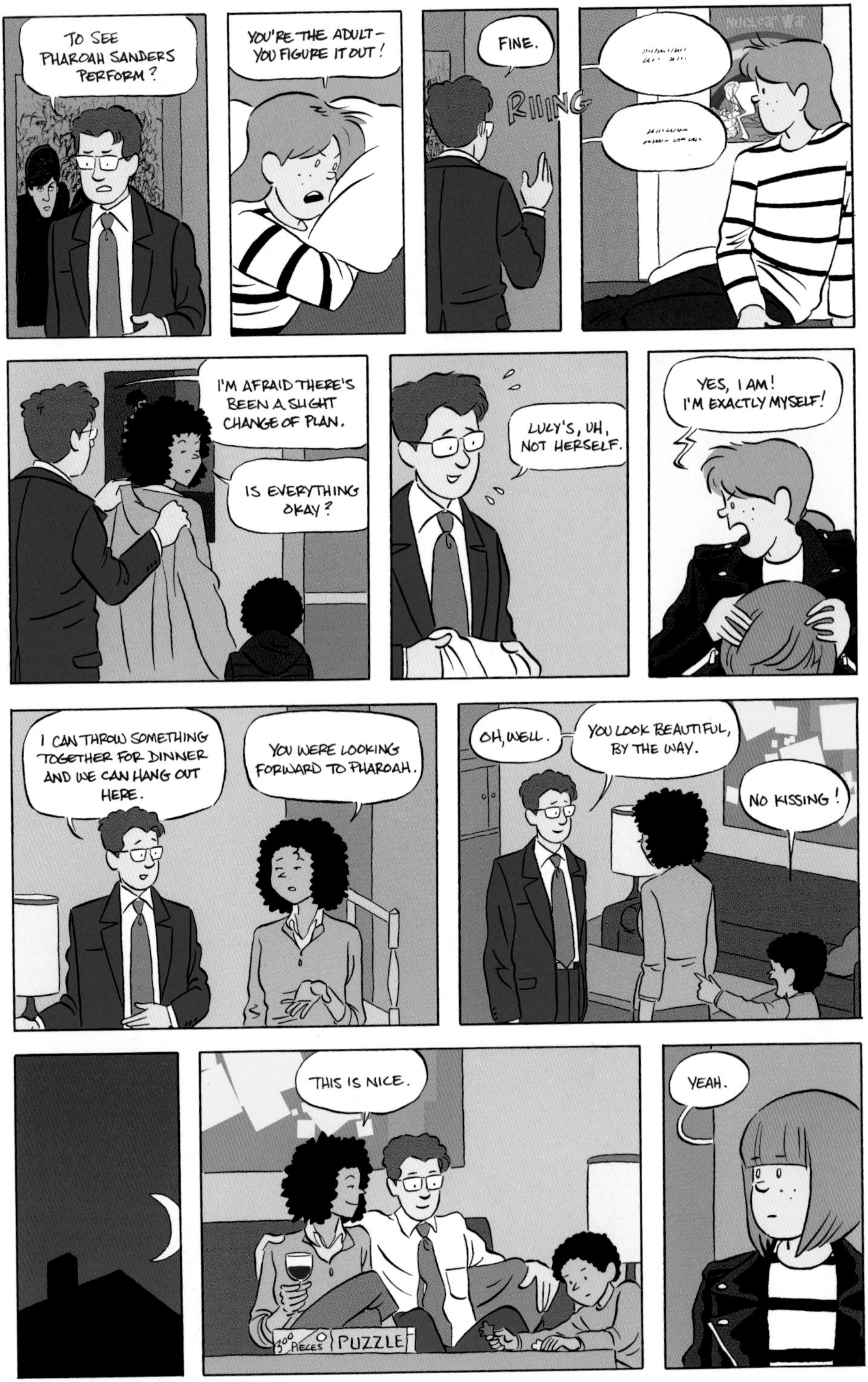
TO SEE PHAROAH SANDERS PERFORM?
YOU'RE THE ADULT– YOU FIGURE IT OUT!
FINE.
RIIING
Nuclear War
I'M AFRAID THERE'S BEEN A SLIGHT CHANGE OF PLAN.
IS EVERYTHING OKAY?
LUCY'S, UH, NOT HERSELF.
YES, I AM! I'M EXACTLY MYSELF!
I CAN THROW SOMETHING TOGETHER FOR DINNER AND WE CAN HANG OUT HERE.
YOU WERE LOOKING FORWARD TO PHAROAH.
OH, WELL.
YOU LOOK BEAUTIFUL, BY THE WAY.
NO KISSING!
THIS IS NICE.
300 PIECES PUZZLE
YEAH.

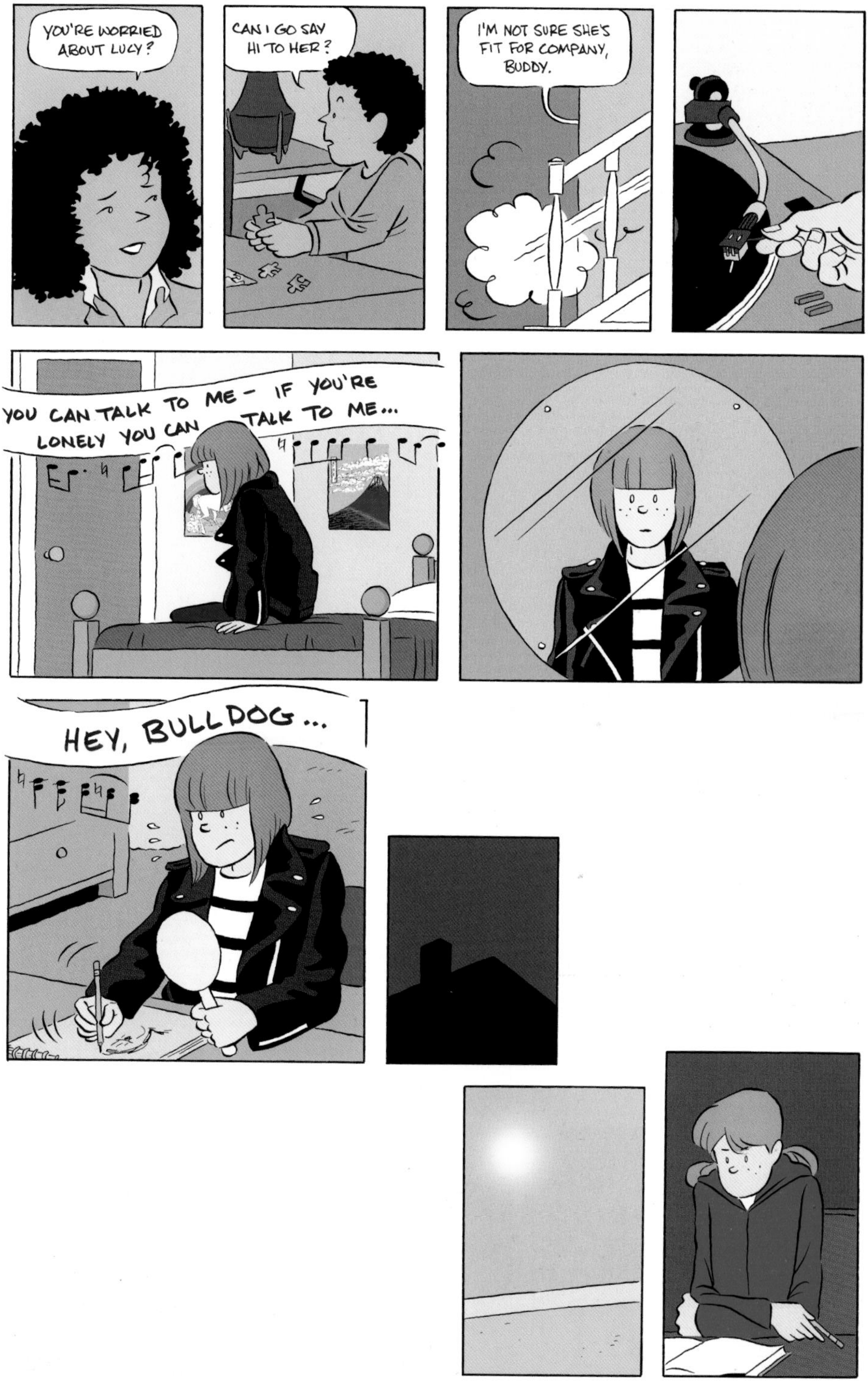
YOU'RE WORRIED ABOUT LUCY?
CAN I GO SAY HI TO HER?
I'M NOT SURE SHE'S FIT FOR COMPANY, BUDDY.
YOU CAN TALK TO ME - IF YOU'RE LONELY YOU CAN TALK TO ME...
HEY, BULLDOG...

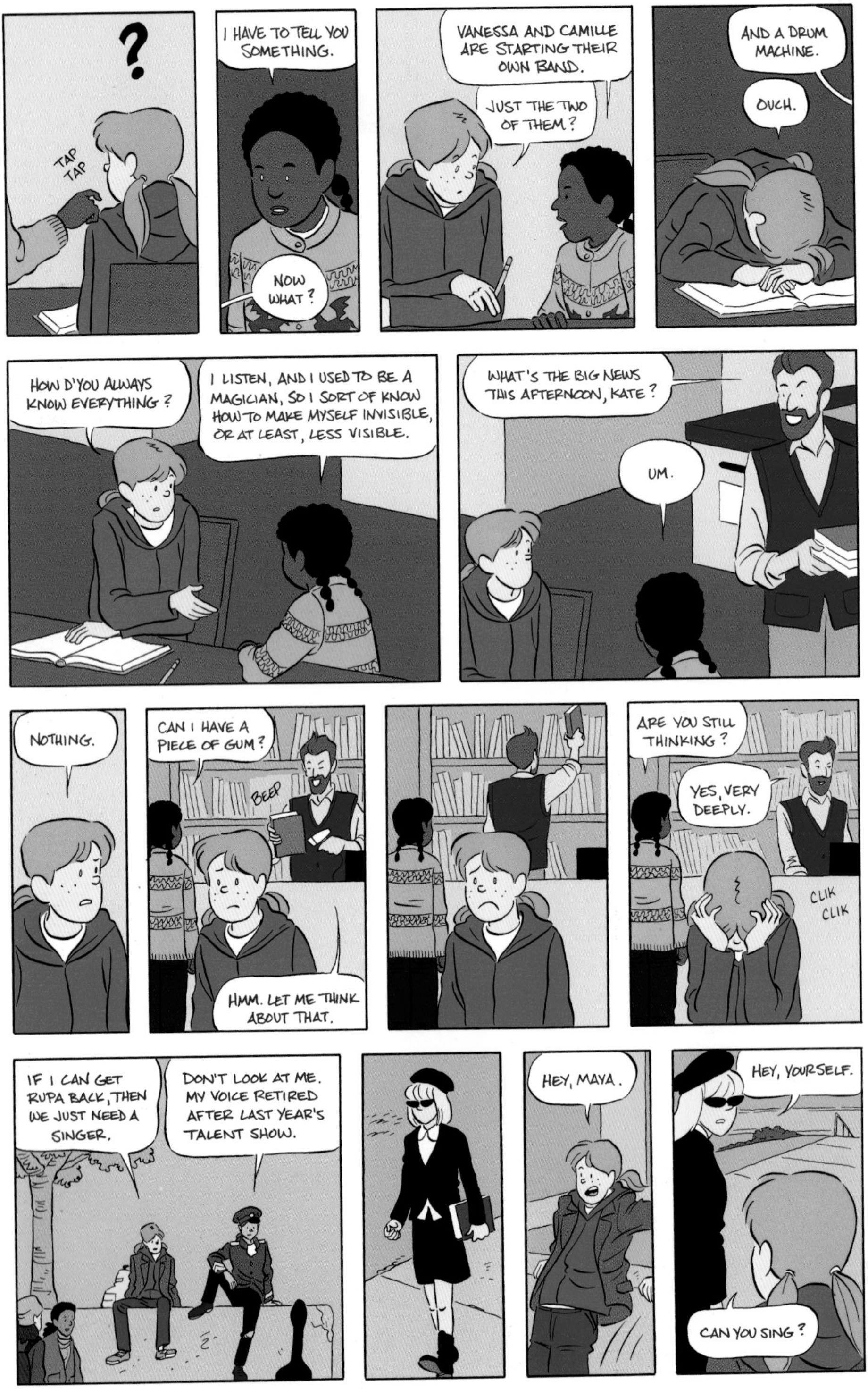
?
TAP TAP
I HAVE TO TELL YOU SOMETHING.
NOW WHAT?
VANESSA AND CAMILLE ARE STARTING THEIR OWN BAND.
JUST THE TWO OF THEM?
AND A DRUM MACHINE.
OUCH.
HOW D'YOU ALWAYS KNOW EVERYTHING?
I LISTEN, AND I USED TO BE A MAGICIAN, SO I SORT OF KNOW HOW TO MAKE MYSELF INVISIBLE, OR AT LEAST, LESS VISIBLE.
WHAT'S THE BIG NEWS THIS AFTERNOON, KATE?
UM.
NOTHING.
CAN I HAVE A PIECE OF GUM?
BEEP
HMM. LET ME THINK ABOUT THAT.
ARE YOU STILL THINKING?
YES, VERY DEEPLY.
CLIK CLIK
IF I CAN GET RUPA BACK, THEN WE JUST NEED A SINGER.
DON'T LOOK AT ME. MY VOICE RETIRED AFTER LAST YEAR'S TALENT SHOW.
HEY, MAYA.
HEY, YOURSELF.
CAN YOU SING?

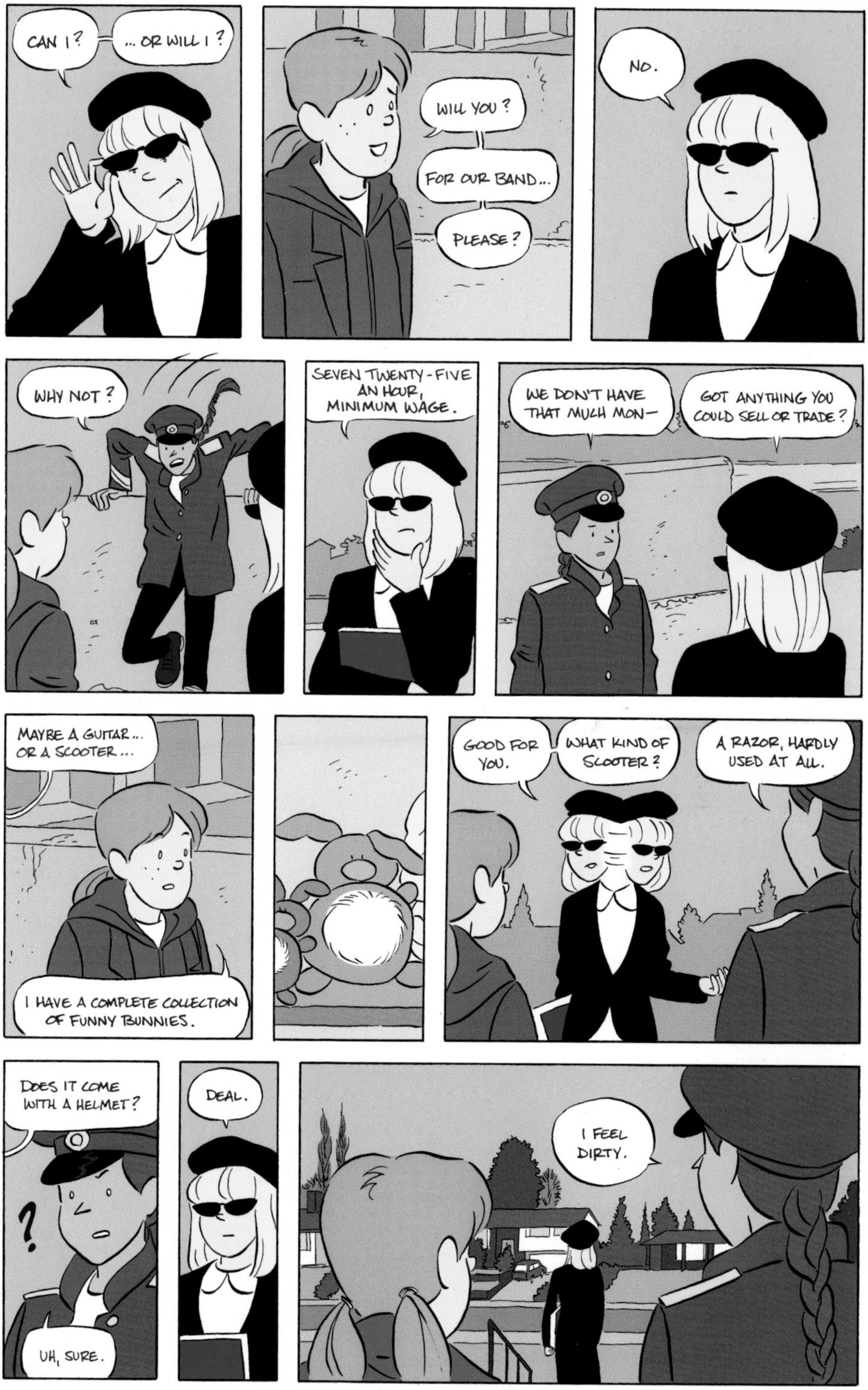
CAN I?
... OR WILL I?
WILL YOU?
FOR OUR BAND...
PLEASE?
NO.
WHY NOT?
SEVEN TWENTY-FIVE AN HOUR, MINIMUM WAGE.
WE DON'T HAVE THAT MUCH MON—
GOT ANYTHING YOU COULD SELL OR TRADE?
MAYBE A GUITAR... OR A SCOOTER...
I HAVE A COMPLETE COLLECTION OF FUNNY BUNNIES.
GOOD FOR YOU.
WHAT KIND OF SCOOTER?
A RAZOR, HARDLY USED AT ALL.
DOES IT COME WITH A HELMET?
UH, SURE.
DEAL.
I FEEL DIRTY.

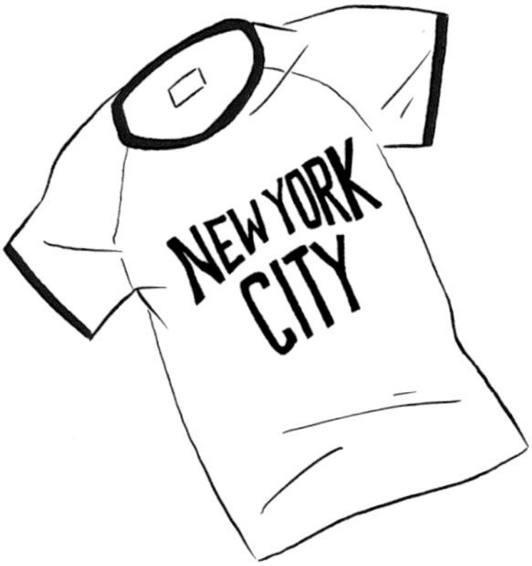
NEW YORK
CITY

spring

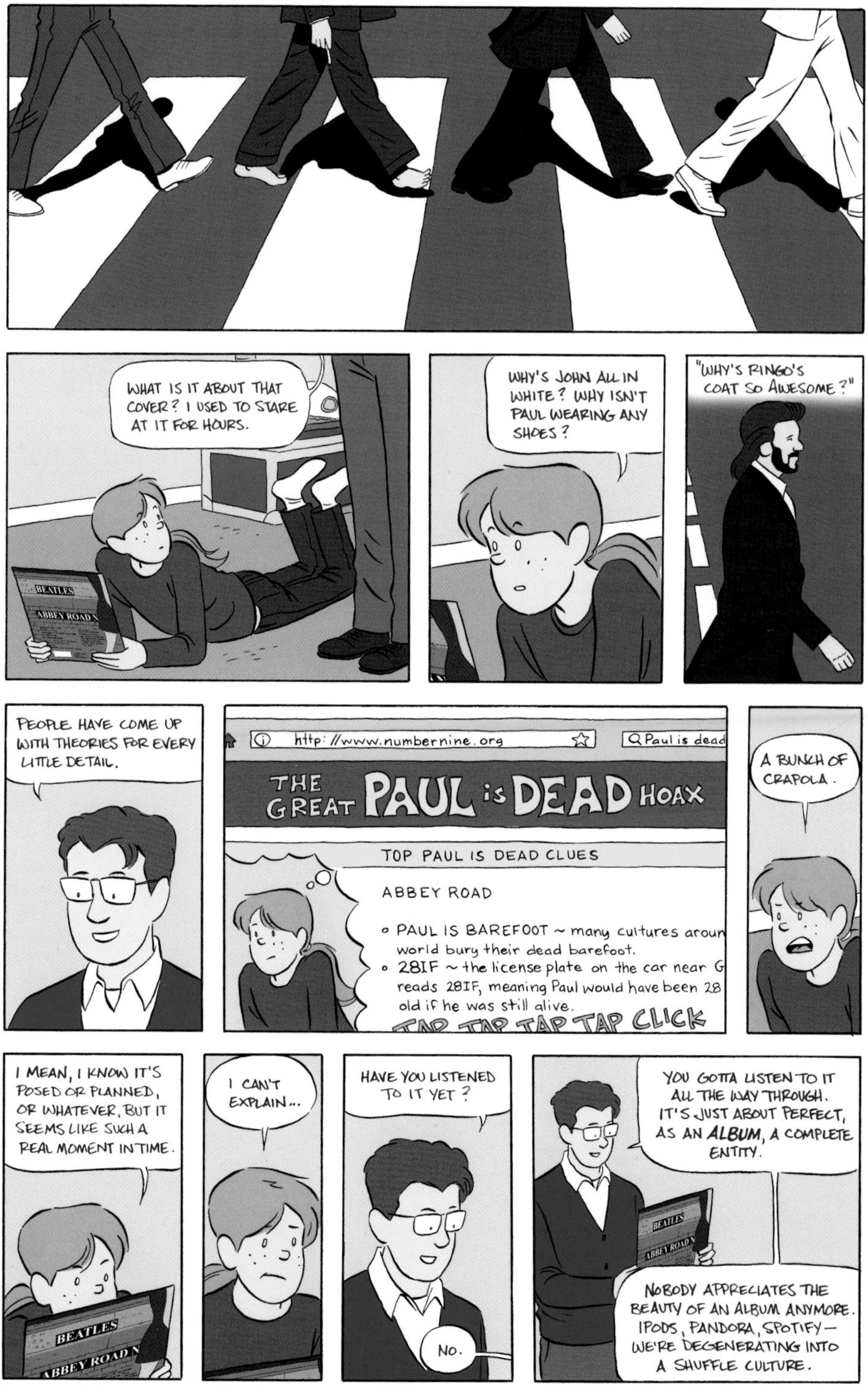
WHAT IS IT ABOUT THAT COVER? I USED TO STARE AT IT FOR HOURS.
WHY'S JOHN ALL IN WHITE? WHY ISN'T PAUL WEARING ANY SHOES?
"WHY'S RINGO'S COAT SO AWESOME?"
PEOPLE HAVE COME UP WITH THEORIES FOR EVERY LITTLE DETAIL.
http://www.numbernine.org
Paul is dead
THE GREAT PAUL is DEAD HOAX
TOP PAUL IS DEAD CLUES
ABBEY ROAD
PAUL IS BAREFOOT ~ many cultures aroun world bury their dead barefoot.
28IF ~ the license plate on the car near G reads 28IF, meaning Paul would have been 28 old if he was still alive.
TAP TAP TAP TAP CLICK
A BUNCH OF CRAPOLA.
I MEAN, I KNOW IT'S POSED OR PLANNED, OR WHATEVER, BUT IT SEEMS LIKE SUCH A REAL MOMENT IN TIME.
I CAN'T EXPLAIN...
HAVE YOU LISTENED TO IT YET?
NO.
YOU GOTTA LISTEN TO IT ALL THE WAY THROUGH. IT'S JUST ABOUT PERFECT, AS AN ALBUM, A COMPLETE ENTITY.
NOBODY APPRECIATES THE BEAUTY OF AN ALBUM ANYMORE. IPODS, PANDORA, SPOTIFY— WE'RE DEGENERATING INTO A SHUFFLE CULTURE.

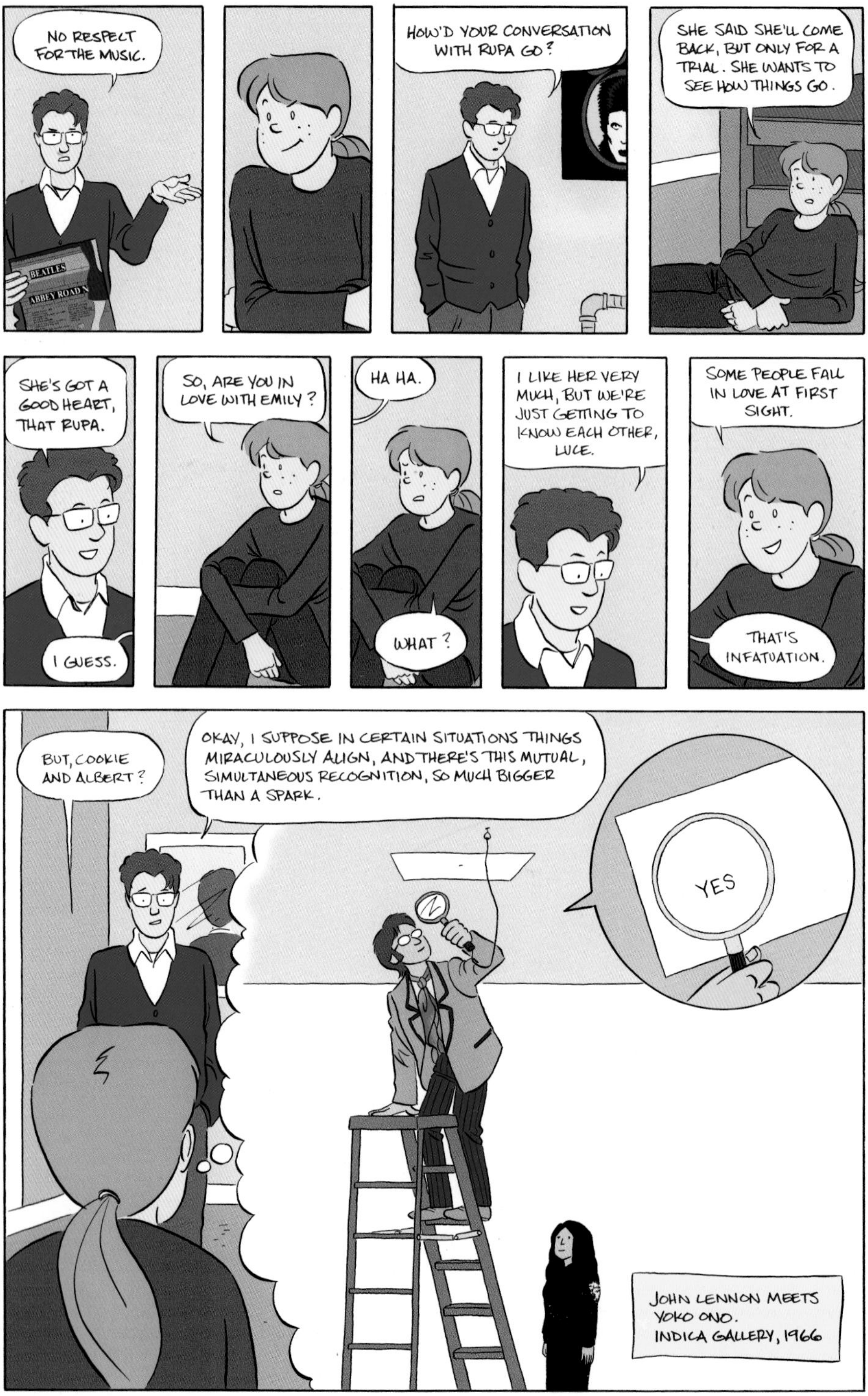
NO RESPECT FOR THE MUSIC.
BEATLES
ABBEY ROAD
HOW'D YOUR CONVERSATION WITH RUPA GO?
SHE SAID SHE'LL COME BACK, BUT ONLY FOR A TRIAL. SHE WANTS TO SEE HOW THINGS GO.
SHE'S GOT A GOOD HEART, THAT RUPA.
I GUESS.
SO, ARE YOU IN LOVE WITH EMILY?
HA HA.
WHAT?
I LIKE HER VERY MUCH, BUT WE'RE JUST GETTING TO KNOW EACH OTHER, LUCE.
SOME PEOPLE FALL IN LOVE AT FIRST SIGHT.
THAT'S INFATUATION.
BUT, COOKIE AND ALBERT?
OKAY, I SUPPOSE IN CERTAIN SITUATIONS THINGS MIRACULOUSLY ALIGN, AND THERE'S THIS MUTUAL, SIMULTANEOUS RECOGNITION, SO MUCH BIGGER THAN A SPARK.
YES
JOHN LENNON MEETS YOKO ONO.
INDICA GALLERY, 1966

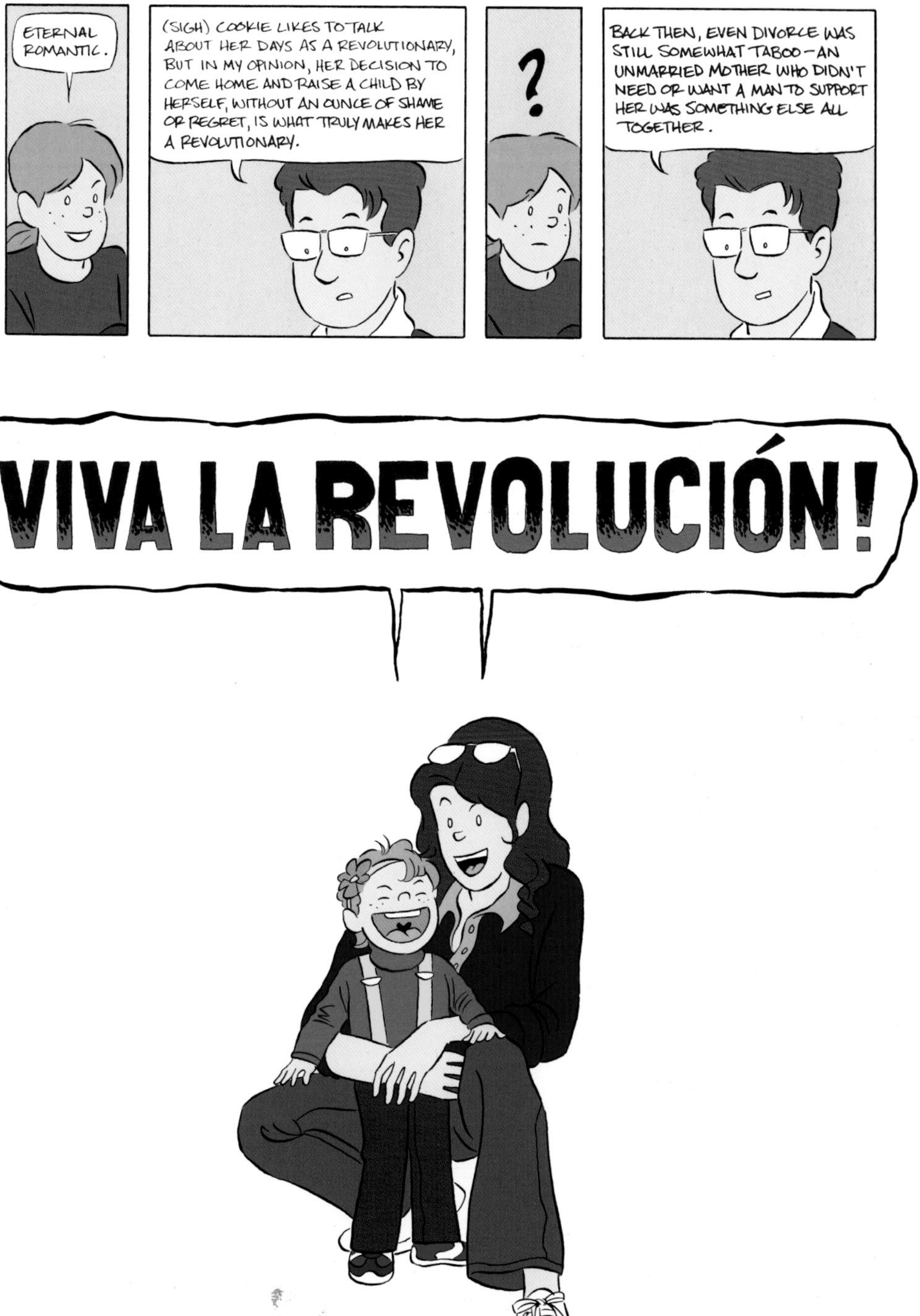

ETERNAL ROMANTIC.
(SIGH) COOKIE LIKES TO TALK ABOUT HER DAYS AS A REVOLUTIONARY, BUT IN MY OPINION, HER DECISION TO COME HOME AND RAISE A CHILD BY HERSELF, WITHOUT AN OUNCE OF SHAME OR REGRET, IS WHAT TRULY MAKES HER A REVOLUTIONARY.
?
BACK THEN, EVEN DIVORCE WAS STILL SOMEWHAT TABOO—AN UNMARRIED MOTHER WHO DIDN'T NEED OR WANT A MAN TO SUPPORT HER WAS SOMETHING ELSE ALL TOGETHER.
VIVA LA REVOLUCIÓN!

chomp

munch munch munch

... SO NOW MAYA'S IN OUR BAND, AND EVEN THOUGH THE DEADLINE WAS LAST MONTH ...

... PRINCIPAL BLAIR'S LETTING VANESSA AND CAMILLE ENTER THE TALENT SHOW...

... AND LAST NIGHT, WE HAD TO TAKE COOKIE TO THE HOSPITAL, BECAUSE HER PNEUMONITIS GOT WORSE AGAIN...

... SHE HAS TO SLEEP WITH AN OXYGEN MASK...

wipe

I'M GLAD YOU'RE BACK.

yawn

IT'S JUST... IT'S BEEN A LONG, COLD, LONELY WINTER.

DO-DO-DO-DO

SOMETIMES I DON'T KNOW HOW ...

LET EACH FOLLOWING DAY CORRECT THE LAST.

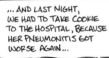

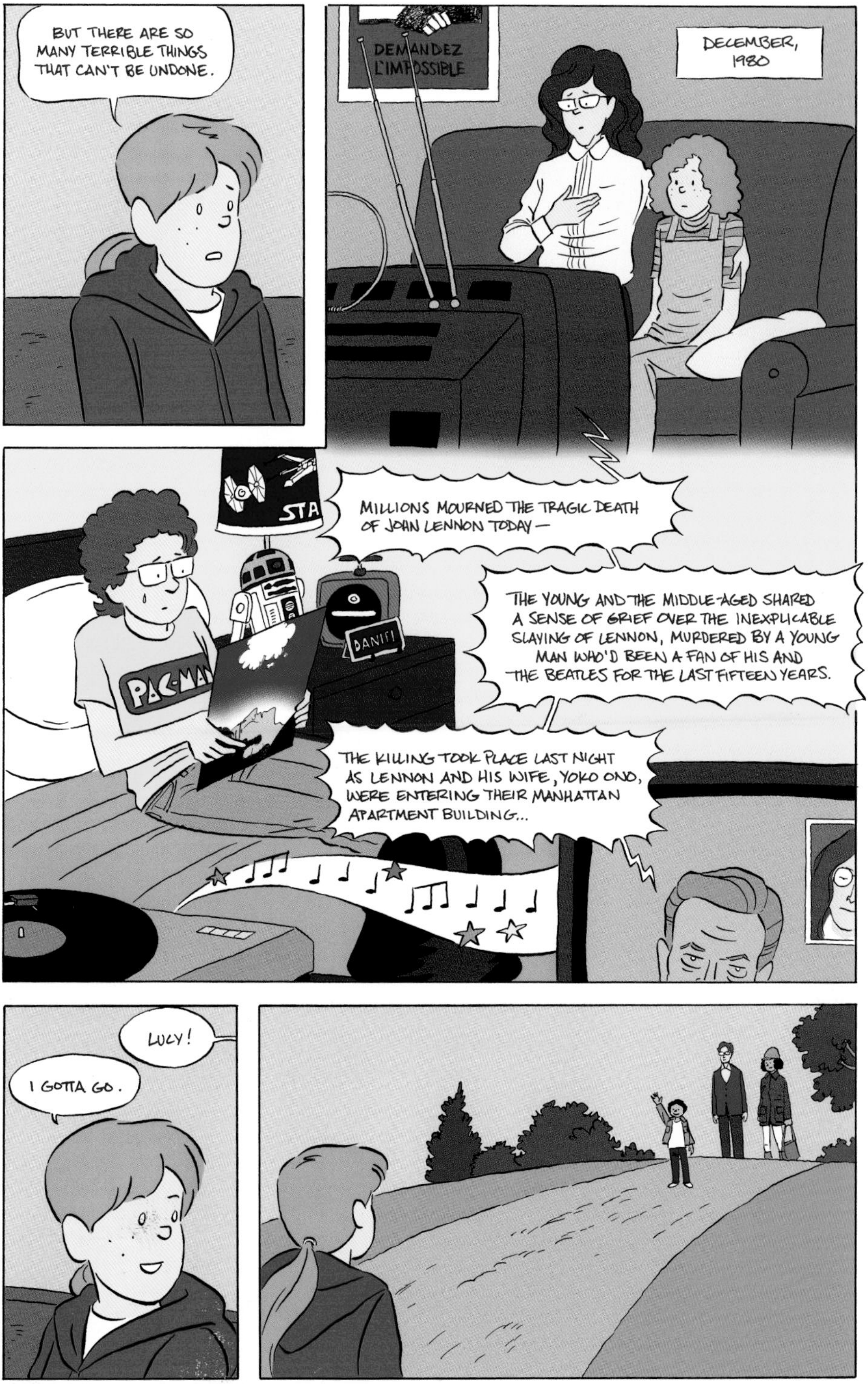
BUT THERE ARE SO MANY TERRIBLE THINGS THAT CAN'T BE UNDONE.
DEMANDEZ L'IMPOSSIBLE
DECEMBER, 1980
STA
MILLIONS MOURNED THE TRAGIC DEATH OF JOHN LENNON TODAY—
THE YOUNG AND THE MIDDLE-AGED SHARED A SENSE OF GRIEF OVER THE INEXPLICABLE SLAYING OF LENNON, MURDERED BY A YOUNG MAN WHO'D BEEN A FAN OF HIS AND THE BEATLES FOR THE LAST FIFTEEN YEARS.
PAC-MAN
DANIEL
THE KILLING TOOK PLACE LAST NIGHT AS LENNON AND HIS WIFE, YOKO ONO, WERE ENTERING THEIR MANHATTAN APARTMENT BUILDING...
LUCY!
I GOTTA GO.

21
MROW!
St. Kilda,
HELLO my name is
Strawberry jam
Lucy,
So far I've resisted buying you a kilt. Can't wait to show you all the tartan I've collected. See you in London!
xoxo, Mom
Lucy Sutcli
21 Junipe
Burgonville
1919
U.S.
GREETINGS FROM
St. Kilda, Scotland
STAC AN ARMIN
ONCE THERE WAS A WAY
TO GET BACK HOMEWARD...

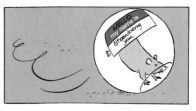

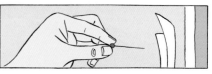

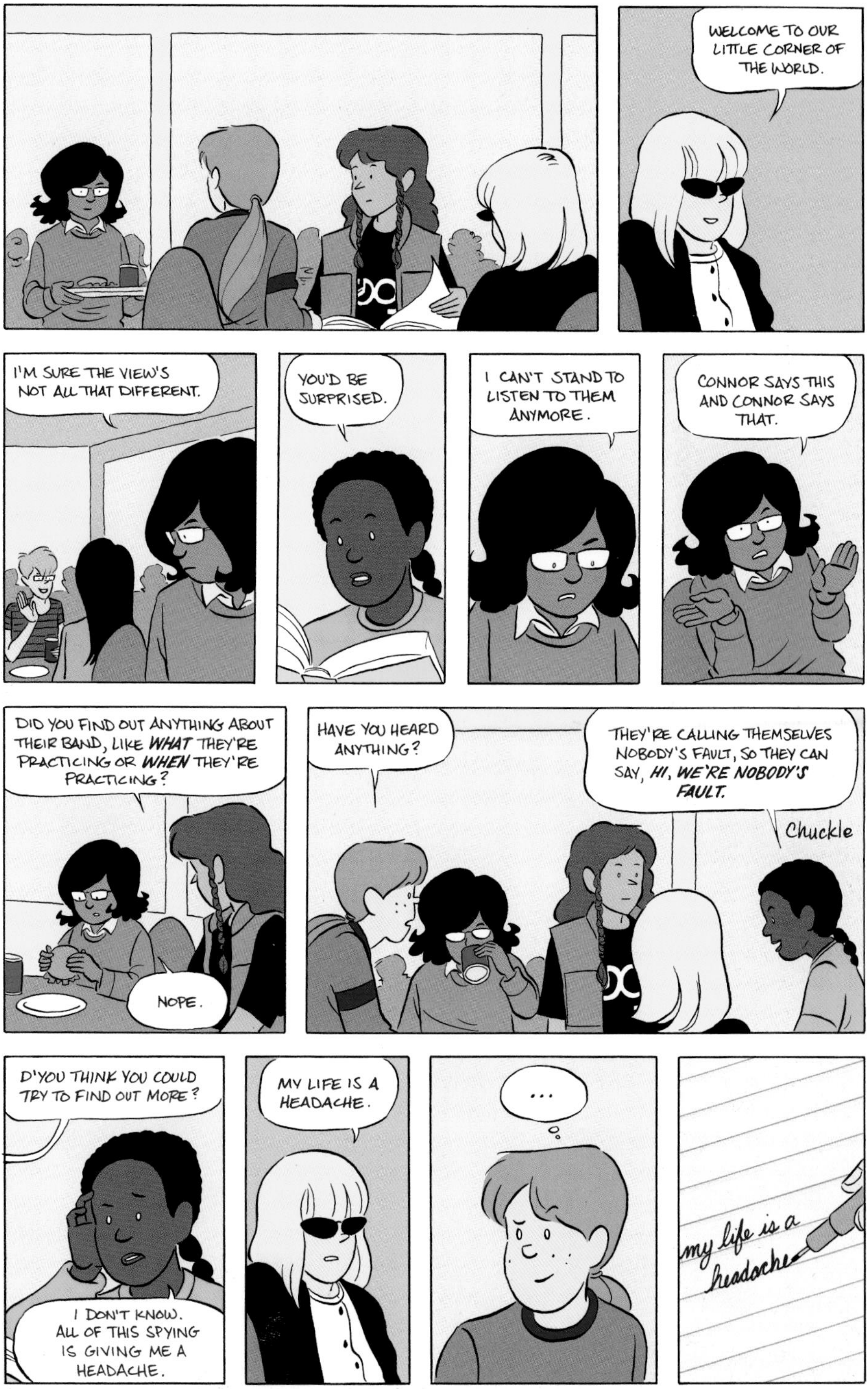
WELCOME TO OUR LITTLE CORNER OF THE WORLD.
I'M SURE THE VIEW'S NOT ALL THAT DIFFERENT.
YOU'D BE SURPRISED.
I CAN'T STAND TO LISTEN TO THEM ANYMORE.
CONNOR SAYS THIS AND CONNOR SAYS THAT.
DID YOU FIND OUT ANYTHING ABOUT THEIR BAND, LIKE *WHAT* THEY'RE PRACTICING OR *WHEN* THEY'RE PRACTICING?
NOPE.
HAVE YOU HEARD ANYTHING?
THEY'RE CALLING THEMSELVES NOBODY'S FAULT, SO THEY CAN SAY, *HI, WE'RE NOBODY'S FAULT.*
Chuckle
D'YOU THINK YOU COULD TRY TO FIND OUT MORE?
I DON'T KNOW. ALL OF THIS SPYING IS GIVING ME A HEADACHE.
MY LIFE IS A HEADACHE.
...
my life is a headache

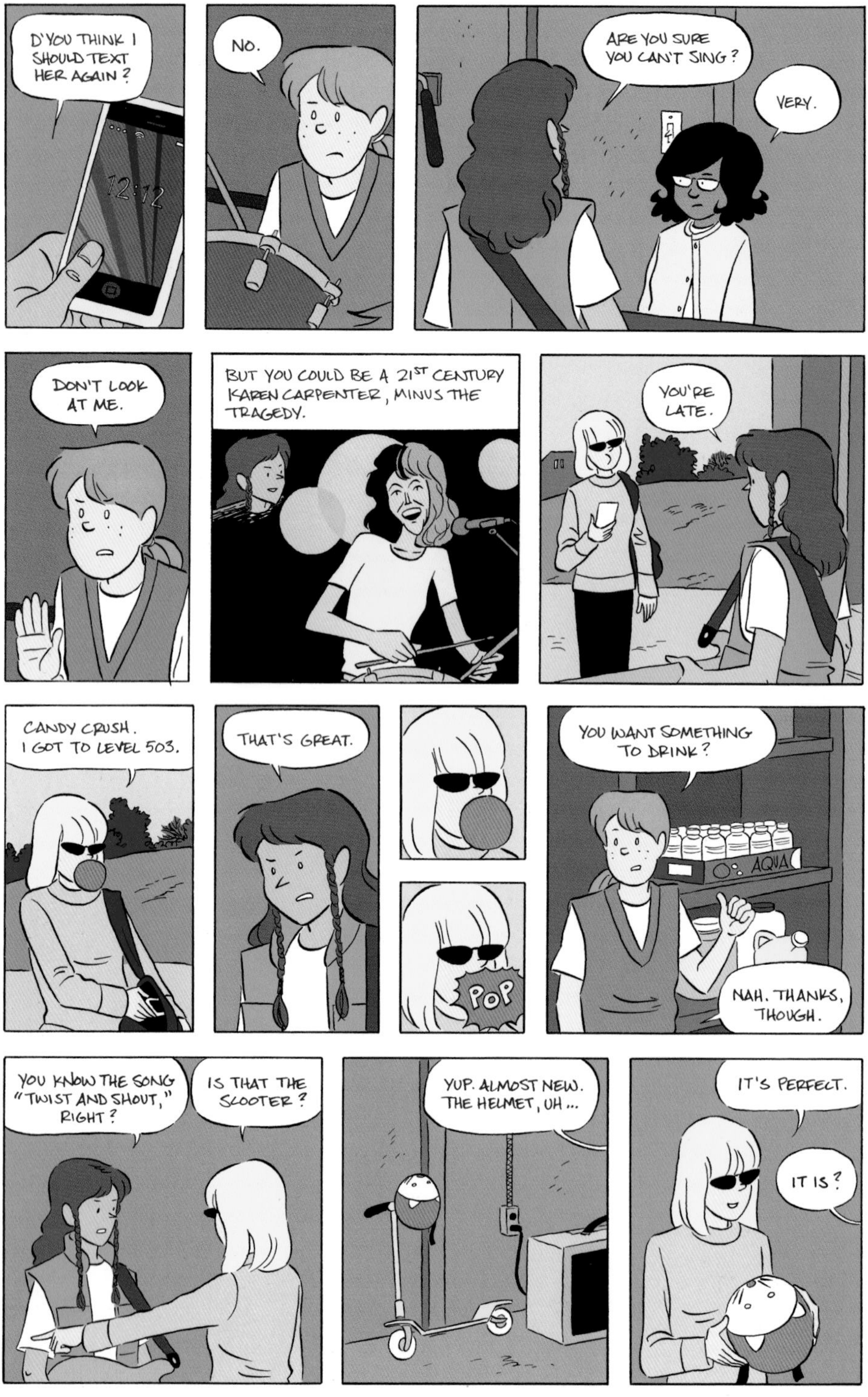
D'YOU THINK I SHOULD TEXT HER AGAIN?
12:12
NO.
ARE YOU SURE YOU CAN'T SING?
VERY.
DON'T LOOK AT ME.
BUT YOU COULD BE A 21ST CENTURY KAREN CARPENTER, MINUS THE TRAGEDY.
YOU'RE LATE.
CANDY CRUSH. I GOT TO LEVEL 503.
THAT'S GREAT.
POP
YOU WANT SOMETHING TO DRINK?
AQUA
NAH. THANKS, THOUGH.
YOU KNOW THE SONG "TWIST AND SHOUT," RIGHT?
IS THAT THE SCOOTER?
YUP. ALMOST NEW. THE HELMET, UH...
IT'S PERFECT.
IT IS?

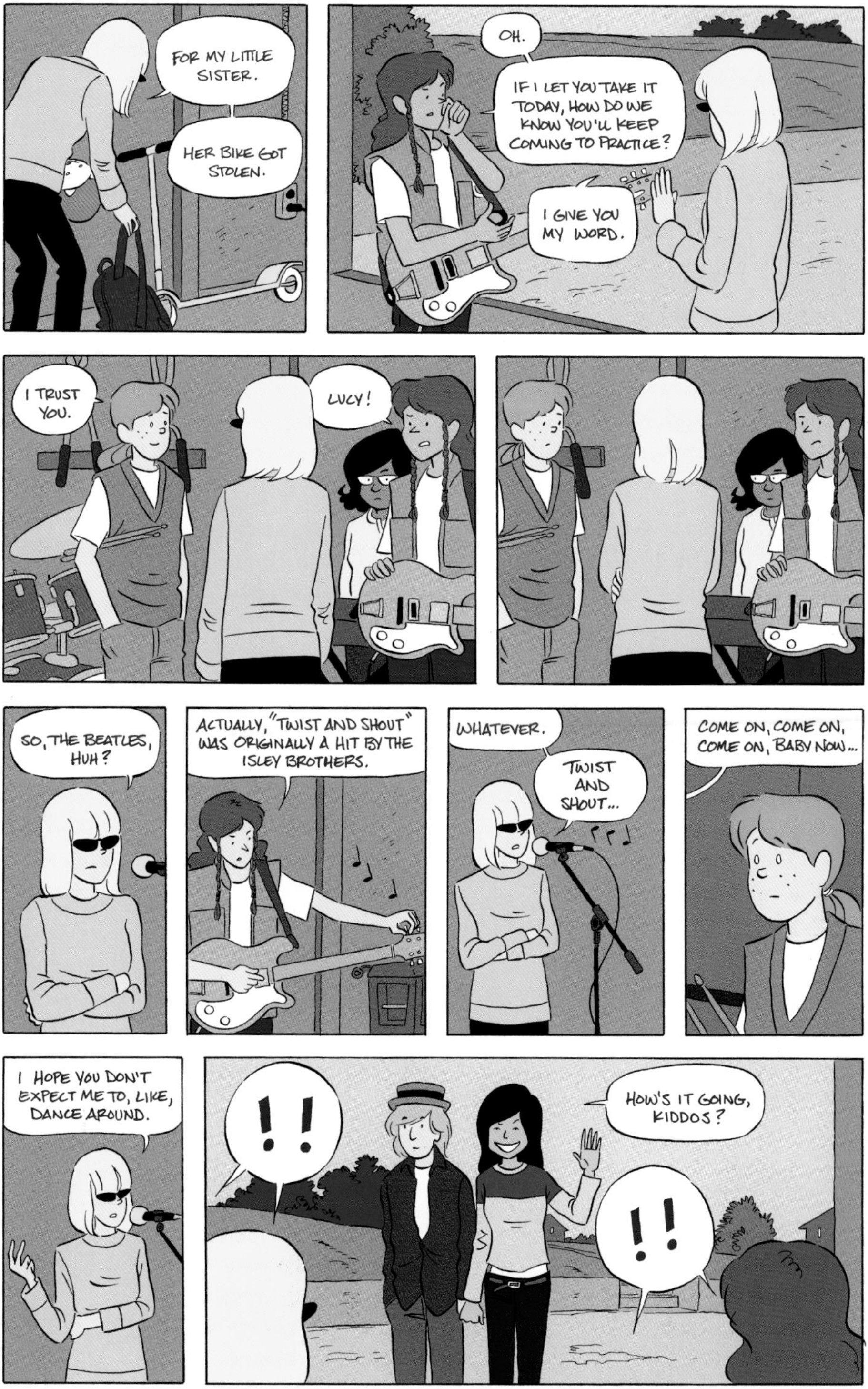
FOR MY LITTLE SISTER.
HER BIKE GOT STOLEN.
OH.
IF I LET YOU TAKE IT TODAY, HOW DO WE KNOW YOU'LL KEEP COMING TO PRACTICE?
I GIVE YOU MY WORD.
I TRUST YOU.
LUCY!
SO, THE BEATLES, HUH?
ACTUALLY, "TWIST AND SHOUT" WAS ORIGINALLY A HIT BY THE ISLEY BROTHERS.
WHATEVER.
TWIST AND SHOUT...
COME ON, COME ON, COME ON, BABY NOW...
I HOPE YOU DON'T EXPECT ME TO, LIKE, DANCE AROUND.
!!
HOW'S IT GOING, KIDDOS?
!!

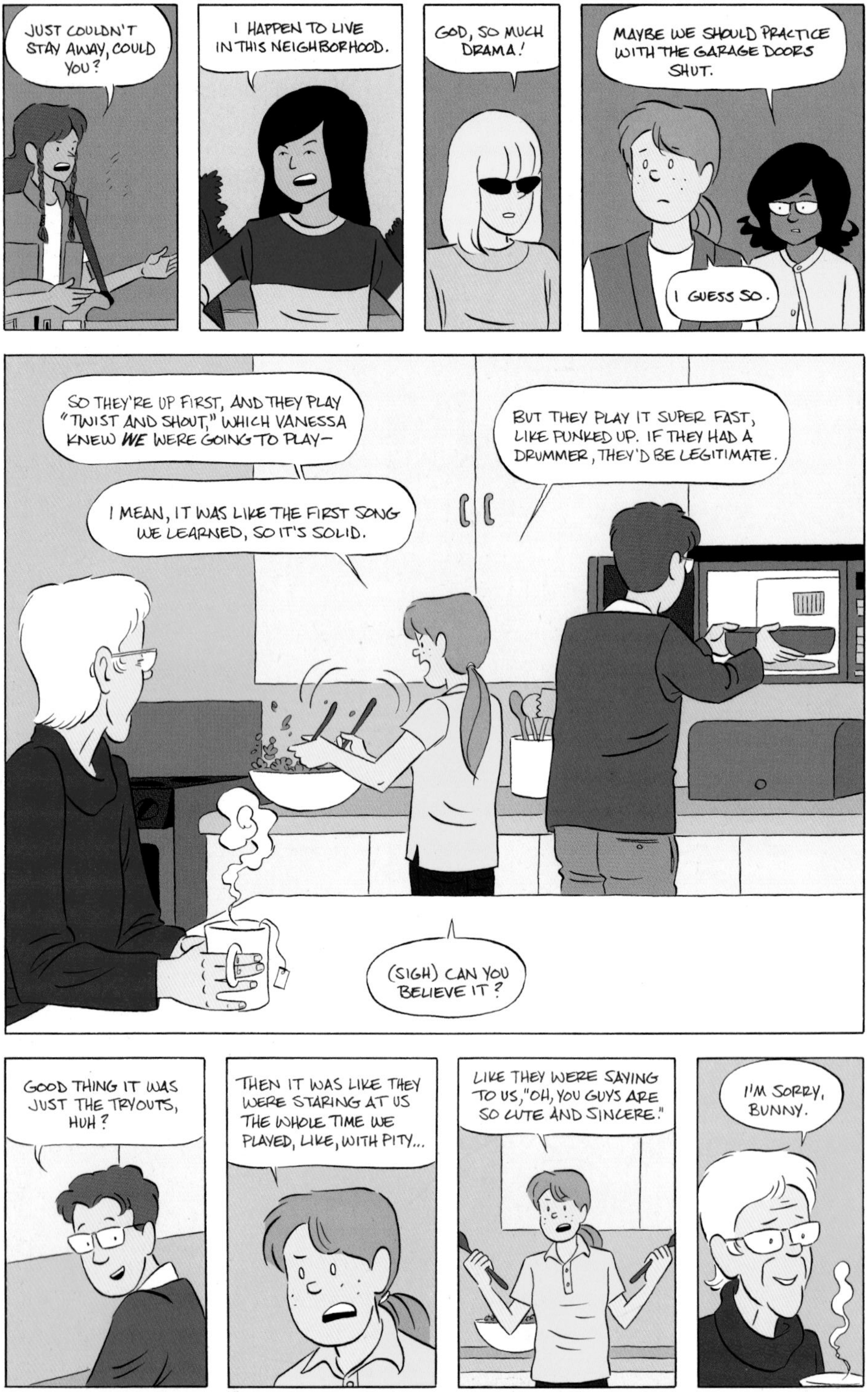
JUST COULDN'T STAY AWAY, COULD YOU?
I HAPPEN TO LIVE IN THIS NEIGHBORHOOD.
GOD, SO MUCH DRAMA!
MAYBE WE SHOULD PRACTICE WITH THE GARAGE DOORS SHUT.
I GUESS SO.
SO THEY'RE UP FIRST, AND THEY PLAY "TWIST AND SHOUT," WHICH VANESSA KNEW WE WERE GOING TO PLAY—
I MEAN, IT WAS LIKE THE FIRST SONG WE LEARNED, SO IT'S SOLID.
BUT THEY PLAY IT SUPER FAST, LIKE PUNKED UP. IF THEY HAD A DRUMMER, THEY'D BE LEGITIMATE.
(SIGH) CAN YOU BELIEVE IT?
GOOD THING IT WAS JUST THE TRYOUTS, HUH?
THEN IT WAS LIKE THEY WERE STARING AT US THE WHOLE TIME WE PLAYED, LIKE, WITH PITY...
LIKE THEY WERE SAYING TO US, "OH, YOU GUYS ARE SO CUTE AND SINCERE."
I'M SORRY, BUNNY.

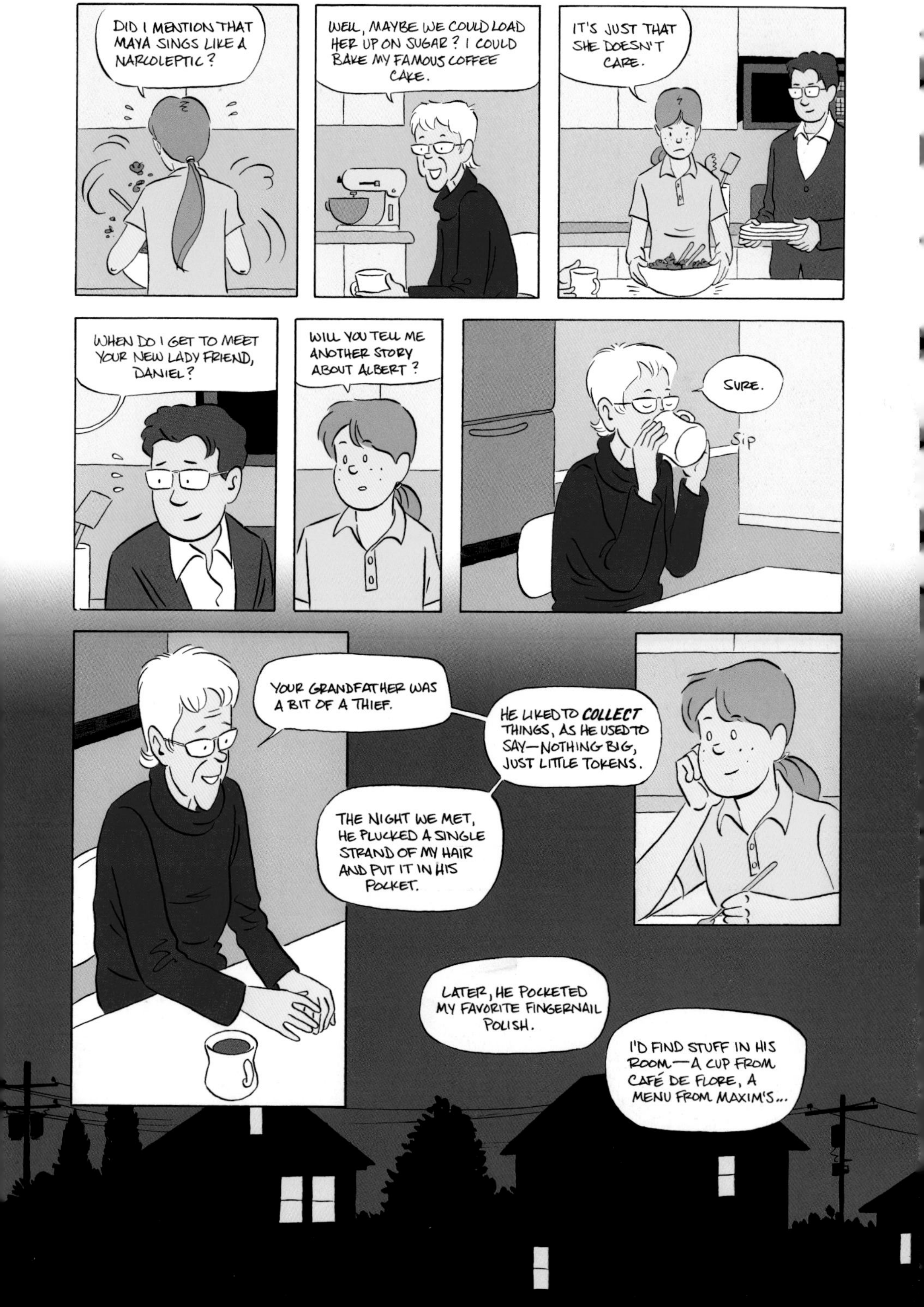
DID I MENTION THAT MAYA SINGS LIKE A NARCOLEPTIC?
WELL, MAYBE WE COULD LOAD HER UP ON SUGAR? I COULD BAKE MY FAMOUS COFFEE CAKE.
IT'S JUST THAT SHE DOESN'T CARE.
WHEN DO I GET TO MEET YOUR NEW LADY FRIEND, DANIEL?
WILL YOU TELL ME ANOTHER STORY ABOUT ALBERT?
SURE.
SIP
YOUR GRANDFATHER WAS A BIT OF A THIEF.
HE LIKED TO COLLECT THINGS, AS HE USED TO SAY—NOTHING BIG, JUST LITTLE TOKENS.
THE NIGHT WE MET, HE PLUCKED A SINGLE STRAND OF MY HAIR AND PUT IT IN HIS POCKET.
LATER, HE POCKETED MY FAVORITE FINGERNAIL POLISH.
I'D FIND STUFF IN HIS ROOM—A CUP FROM CAFÉ DE FLORE, A MENU FROM MAXIM'S...

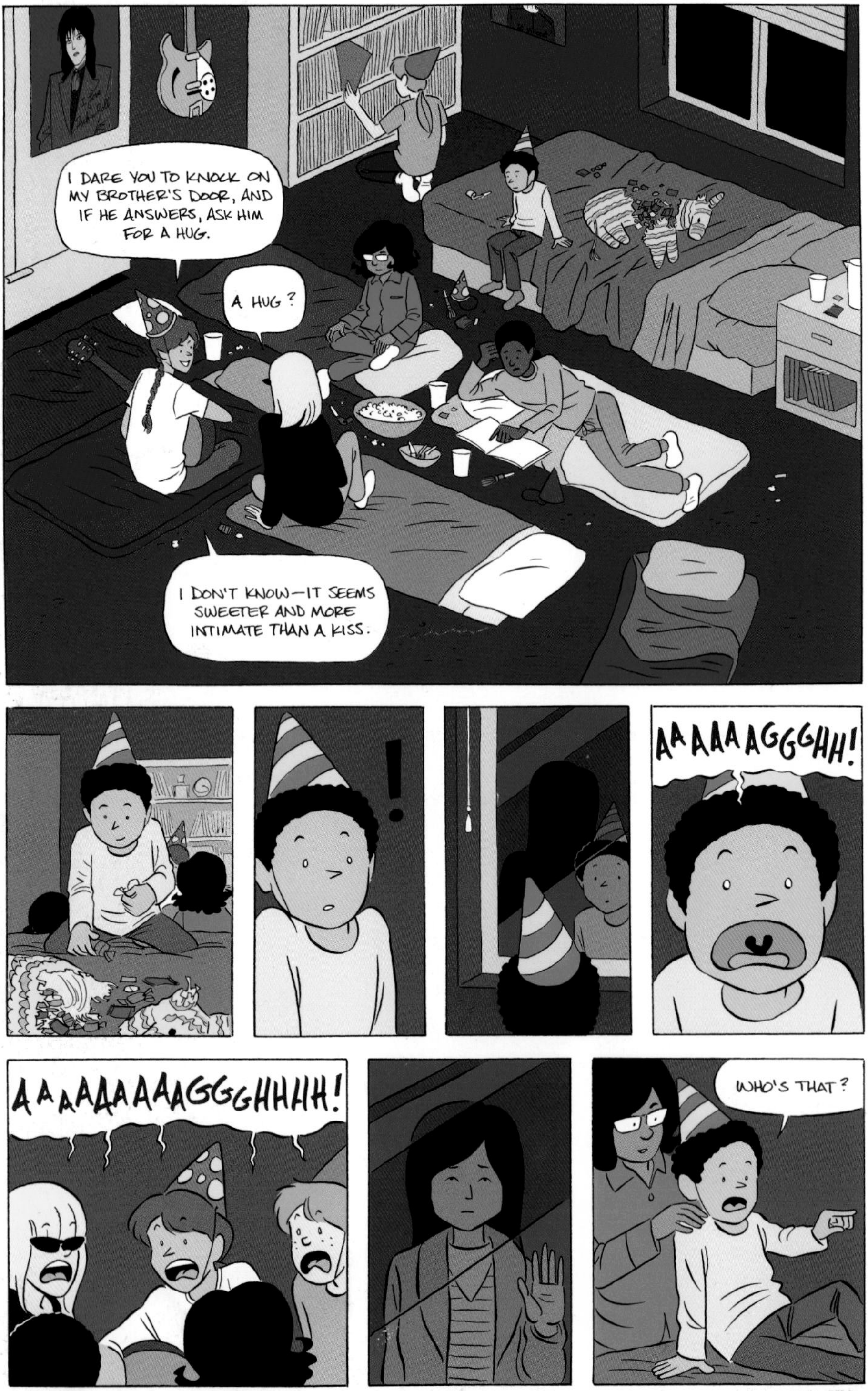
I DARE YOU TO KNOCK ON MY BROTHER'S DOOR, AND IF HE ANSWERS, ASK HIM FOR A HUG.
A HUG?
I DON'T KNOW—IT SEEMS SWEETER AND MORE INTIMATE THAN A KISS.
!
AAAAAAGGGHH!
AAAAAAAAGGGHHHH!
WHO'S THAT?

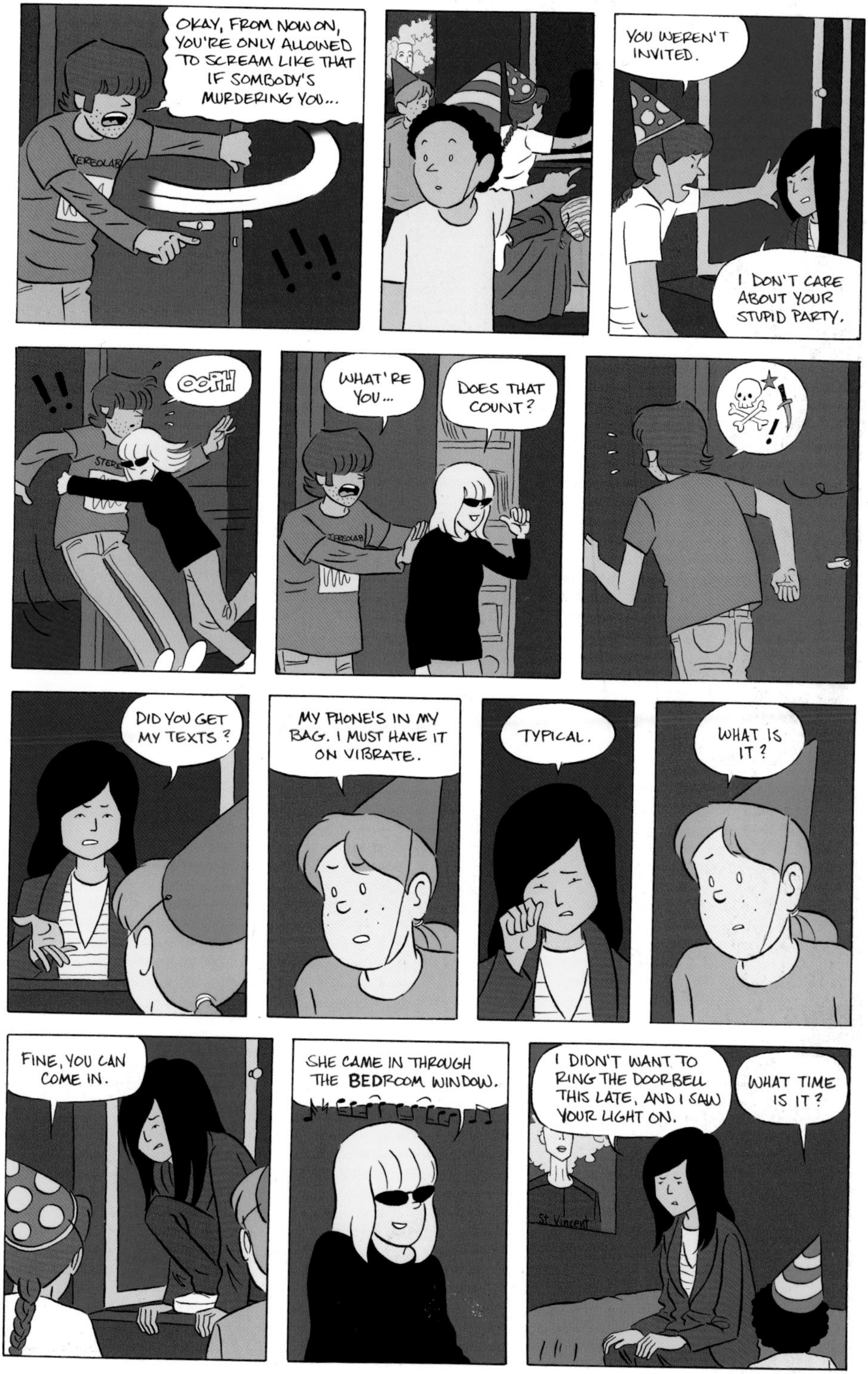
OKAY, FROM NOW ON, YOU'RE ONLY ALLOWED TO SCREAM LIKE THAT IF SOMBODY'S MURDERING YOU...
STEREOLAB
!!!
YOU WEREN'T INVITED.
I DON'T CARE ABOUT YOUR STUPID PARTY.
!!
OOPH
STEREO
WHAT'RE YOU...
DOES THAT COUNT?
STEREOLAB
!
DID YOU GET MY TEXTS?
MY PHONE'S IN MY BAG. I MUST HAVE IT ON VIBRATE.
TYPICAL.
WHAT IS IT?
FINE, YOU CAN COME IN.
SHE CAME IN THROUGH THE BEDROOM WINDOW.
I DIDN'T WANT TO RING THE DOORBELL THIS LATE, AND I SAW YOUR LIGHT ON.
WHAT TIME IS IT?
St Vincent

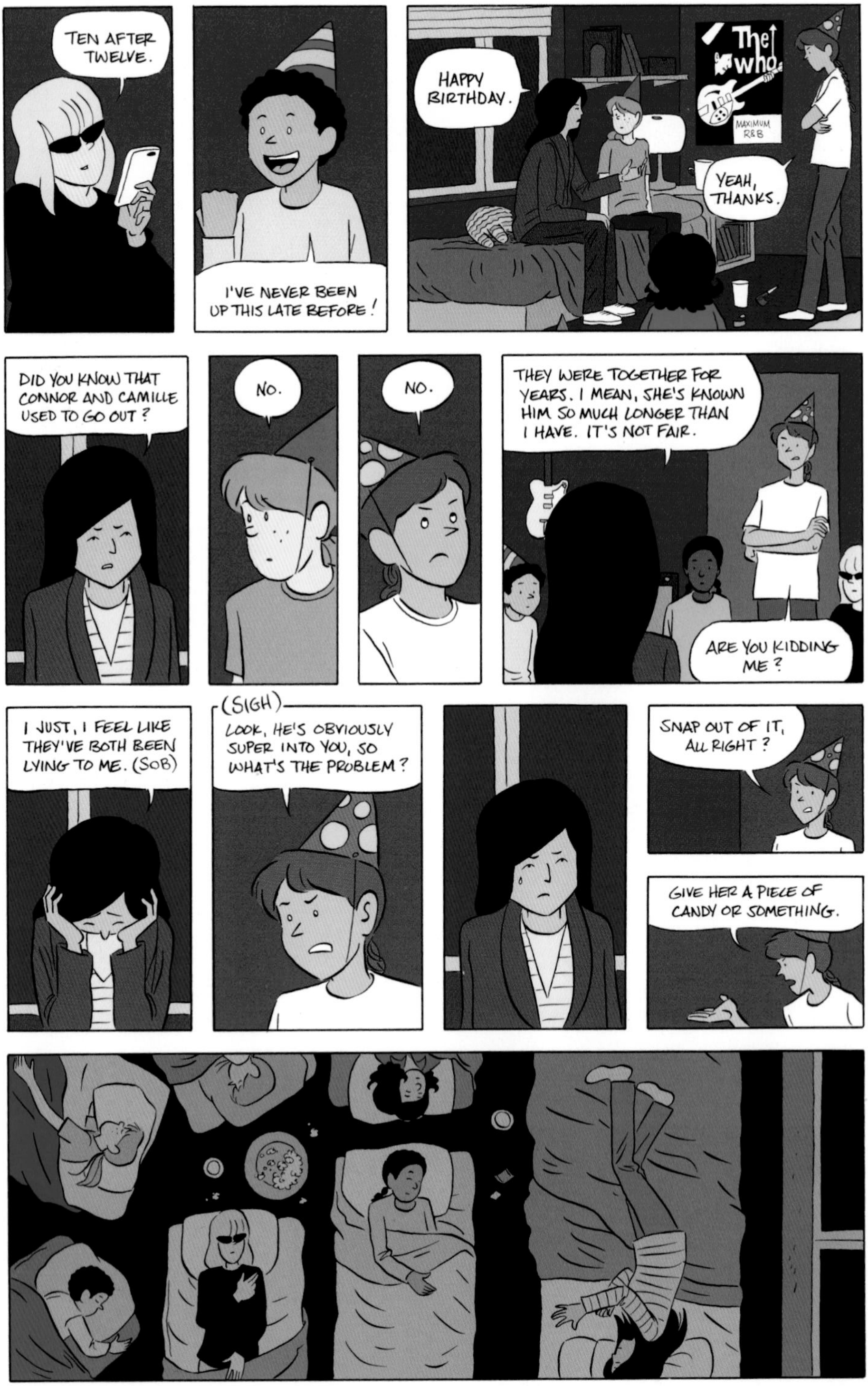
TEN AFTER TWELVE.
I'VE NEVER BEEN UP THIS LATE BEFORE!
HAPPY BIRTHDAY.
The Who
MAXIMUM R&B
YEAH, THANKS.
DID YOU KNOW THAT CONNOR AND CAMILLE USED TO GO OUT?
NO.
NO.
THEY WERE TOGETHER FOR YEARS. I MEAN, SHE'S KNOWN HIM SO MUCH LONGER THAN I HAVE. IT'S NOT FAIR.
ARE YOU KIDDING ME?
I JUST, I FEEL LIKE THEY'VE BOTH BEEN LYING TO ME. (SOB)
(SIGH)
LOOK, HE'S OBVIOUSLY SUPER INTO YOU, SO WHAT'S THE PROBLEM?
SNAP OUT OF IT, ALL RIGHT?
GIVE HER A PIECE OF CANDY OR SOMETHING.

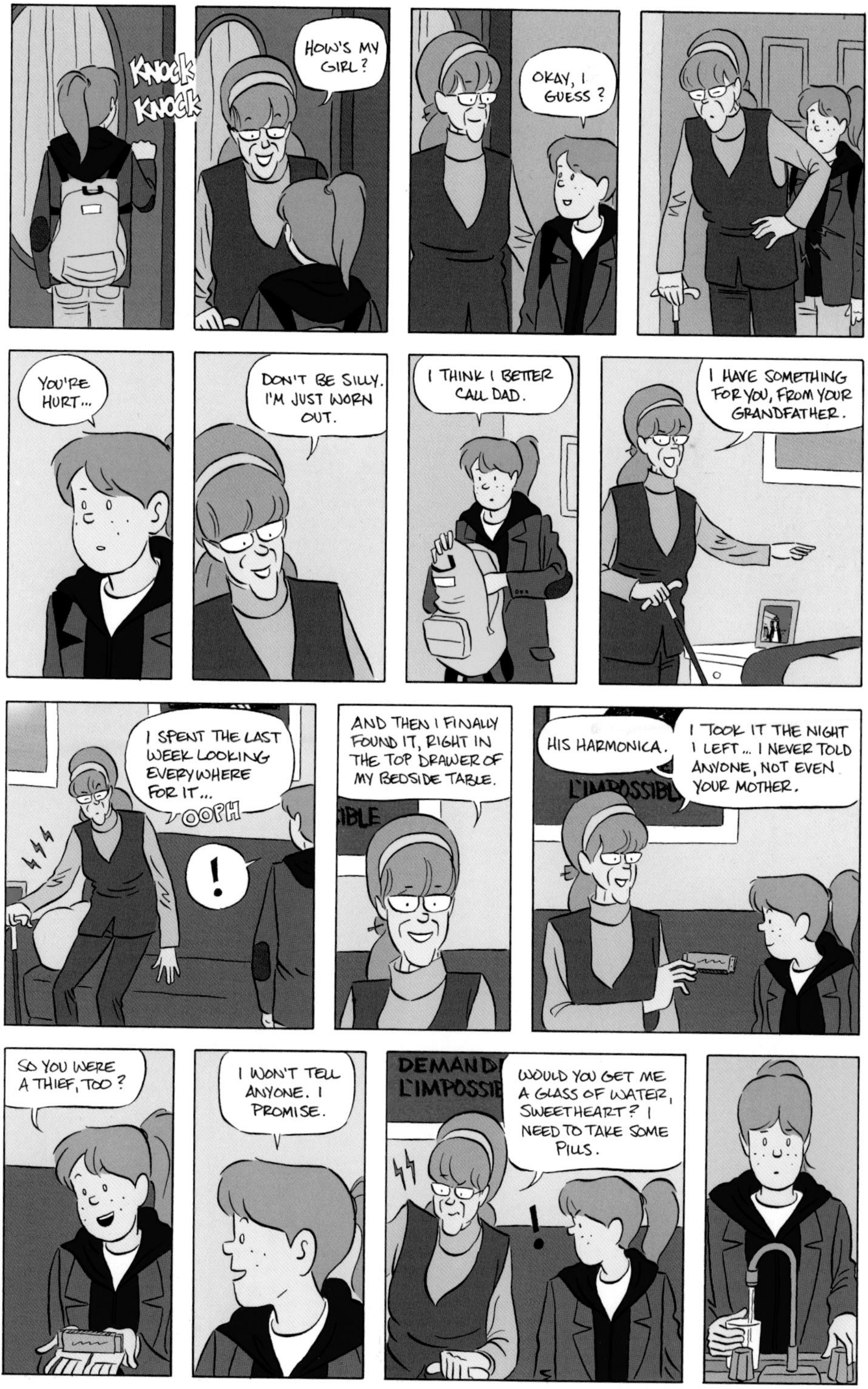
KNOCK KNOCK
HOW'S MY GIRL?
OKAY, I GUESS?
YOU'RE HURT...
DON'T BE SILLY. I'M JUST WORN OUT.
I THINK I BETTER CALL DAD.
I HAVE SOMETHING FOR YOU, FROM YOUR GRANDFATHER.
I SPENT THE LAST WEEK LOOKING EVERYWHERE FOR IT...
OOPH
!
AND THEN I FINALLY FOUND IT, RIGHT IN THE TOP DRAWER OF MY BEDSIDE TABLE.
HIS HARMONICA.
I TOOK IT THE NIGHT I LEFT... I NEVER TOLD ANYONE, NOT EVEN YOUR MOTHER.
SO YOU WERE A THIEF, TOO?
I WON'T TELL ANYONE. I PROMISE.
DEMAND
L'IMPOSSIB
WOULD YOU GET ME A GLASS OF WATER, SWEETHEART? I NEED TO TAKE SOME PILLS.
!

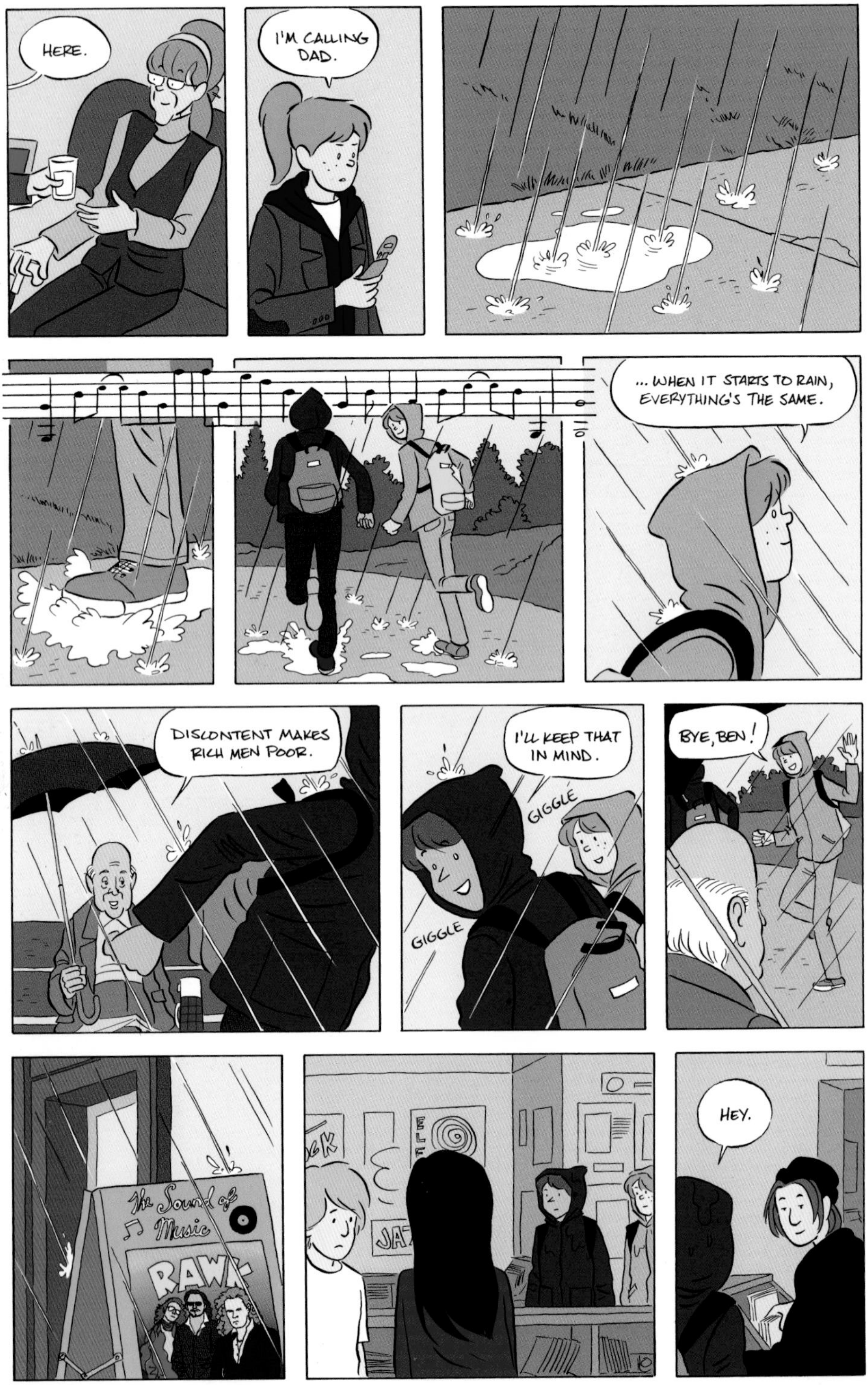
HERE.
I'M CALLING DAD.
... WHEN IT STARTS TO RAIN, EVERYTHING'S THE SAME.
DISCONTENT MAKES RICH MEN POOR.
I'LL KEEP THAT IN MIND.
GIGGLE
GIGGLE
BYE, BEN!
The Sound of Music
HEY.

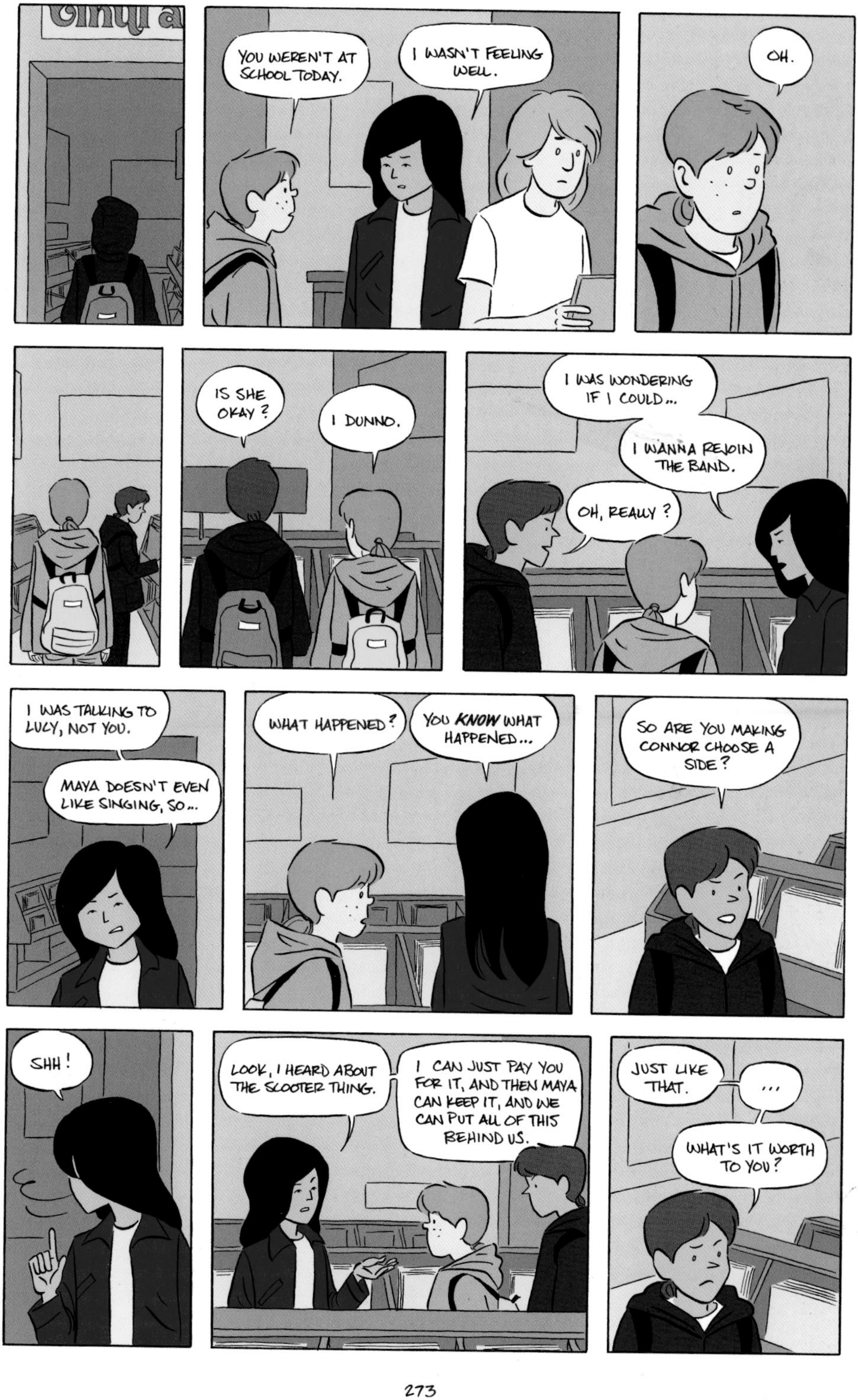
YOU WEREN'T AT SCHOOL TODAY.
I WASN'T FEELING WELL.
OH.
IS SHE OKAY?
I DUNNO.
I WAS WONDERING IF I COULD...
I WANNA REJOIN THE BAND.
OH, REALLY?
I WAS TALKING TO LUCY, NOT YOU.
MAYA DOESN'T EVEN LIKE SINGING, SO...
WHAT HAPPENED?
YOU *KNOW* WHAT HAPPENED...
SO ARE YOU MAKING CONNOR CHOOSE A SIDE?
SHH!
LOOK, I HEARD ABOUT THE SCOOTER THING.
I CAN JUST PAY YOU FOR IT, AND THEN MAYA CAN KEEP IT, AND WE CAN PUT ALL OF THIS BEHIND US.
JUST LIKE THAT.
...
WHAT'S IT WORTH TO YOU?

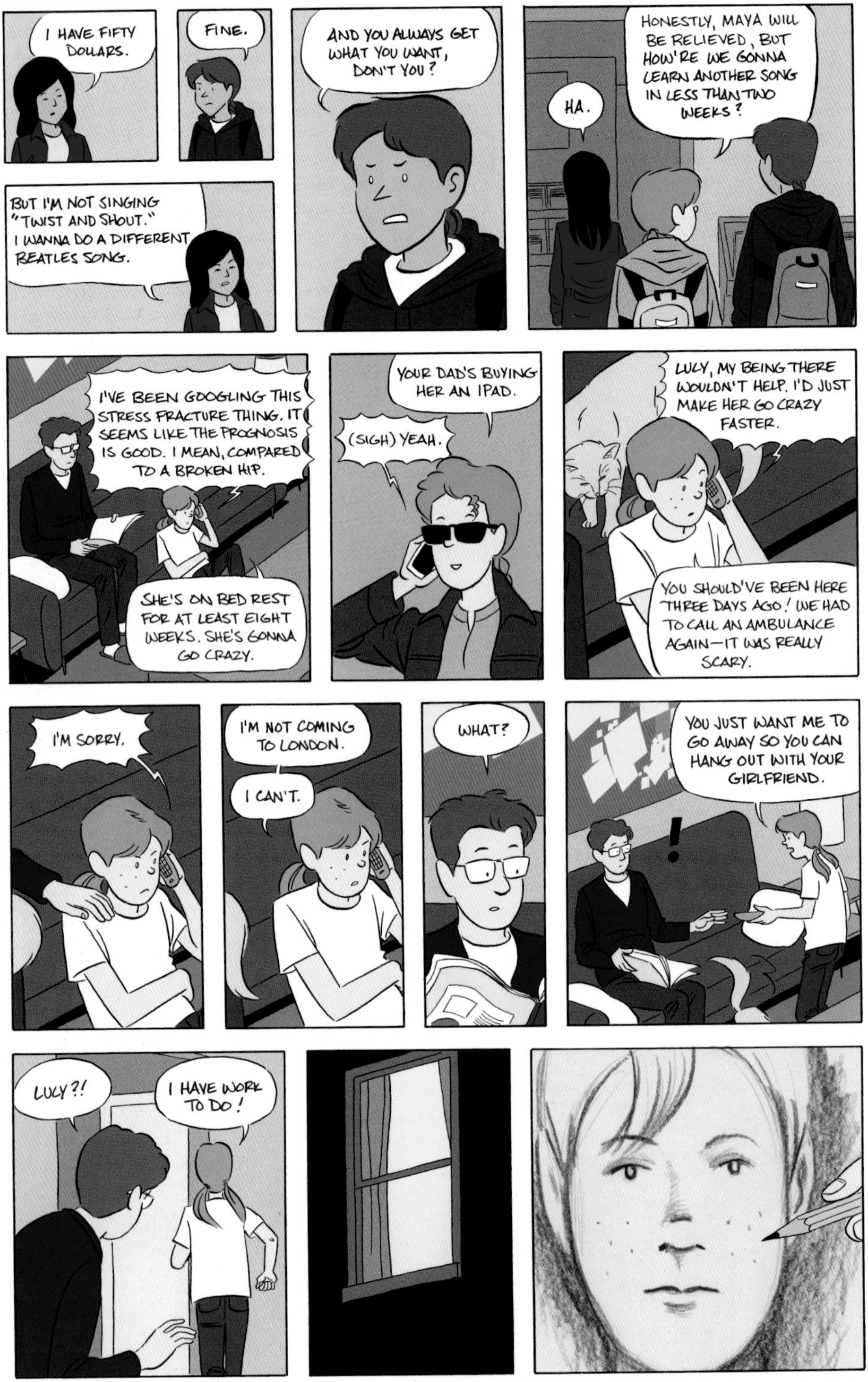
I HAVE FIFTY DOLLARS.
FINE.
BUT I'M NOT SINGING "TWIST AND SHOUT." I WANNA DO A DIFFERENT BEATLES SONG.
AND YOU ALWAYS GET WHAT YOU WANT, DON'T YOU?
HA.
HONESTLY, MAYA WILL BE RELIEVED, BUT HOW'RE WE GONNA LEARN ANOTHER SONG IN LESS THAN TWO WEEKS?
I'VE BEEN GOOGLING THIS STRESS FRACTURE THING. IT SEEMS LIKE THE PROGNOSIS IS GOOD. I MEAN, COMPARED TO A BROKEN HIP.
SHE'S ON BED REST FOR AT LEAST EIGHT WEEKS. SHE'S GONNA GO CRAZY.
YOUR DAD'S BUYING HER AN IPAD.
(SIGH) YEAH.
LUCY, MY BEING THERE WOULDN'T HELP. I'D JUST MAKE HER GO CRAZY FASTER.
YOU SHOULD'VE BEEN HERE THREE DAYS AGO! WE HAD TO CALL AN AMBULANCE AGAIN—IT WAS REALLY SCARY.
I'M SORRY.
I'M NOT COMING TO LONDON.
I CAN'T.
WHAT?
YOU JUST WANT ME TO GO AWAY SO YOU CAN HANG OUT WITH YOUR GIRLFRIEND.
!
LUCY?!
I HAVE WORK TO DO!

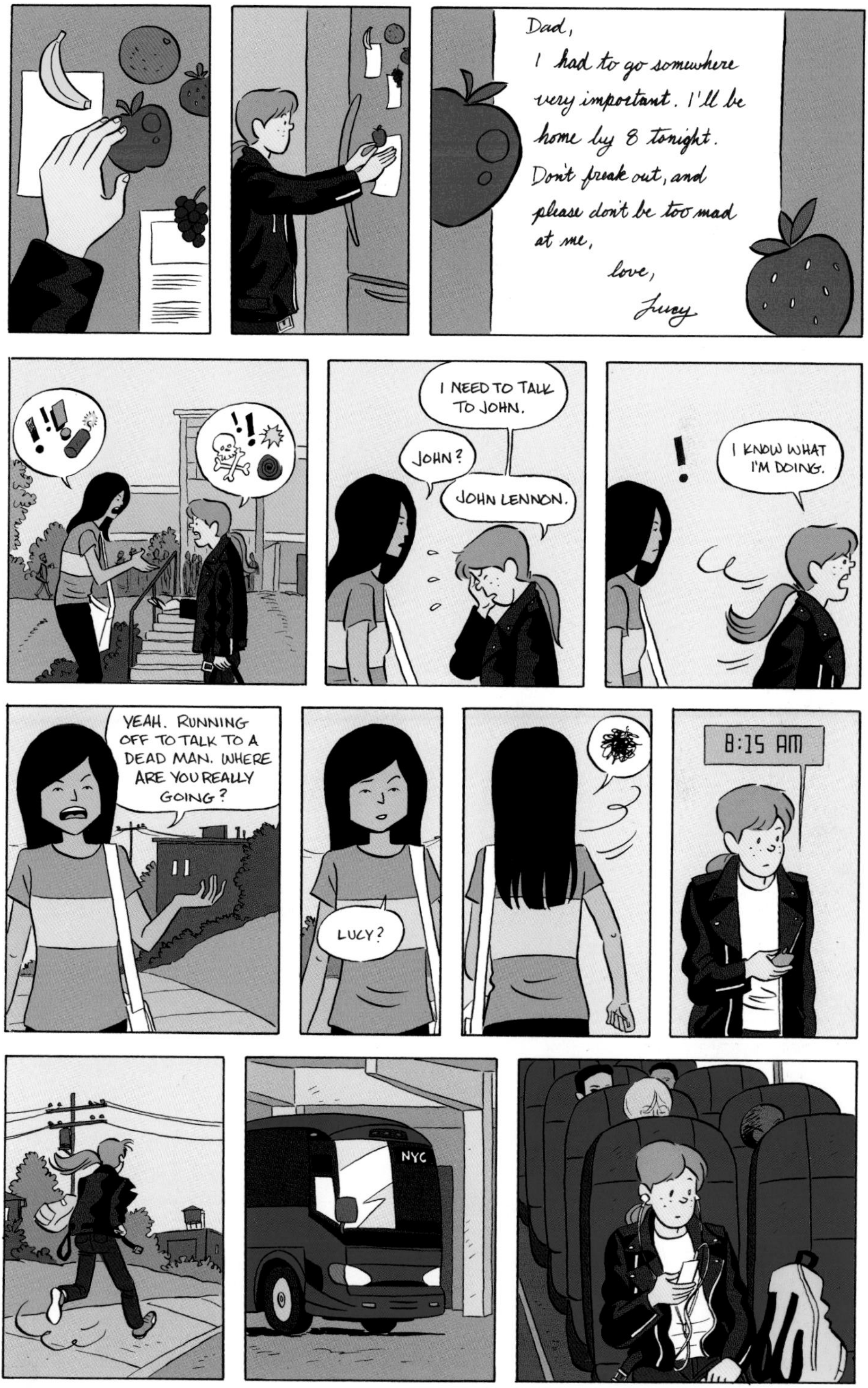
Dad,
I had to go somewhere very important. I'll be home by 8 tonight. Don't freak out, and please don't be too mad at me,
love,
Lucy
I NEED TO TALK TO JOHN.
JOHN?
JOHN LENNON.
!
I KNOW WHAT I'M DOING.
YEAH. RUNNING OFF TO TALK TO A DEAD MAN. WHERE ARE YOU REALLY GOING?
LUCY?
8:15 AM
NYC

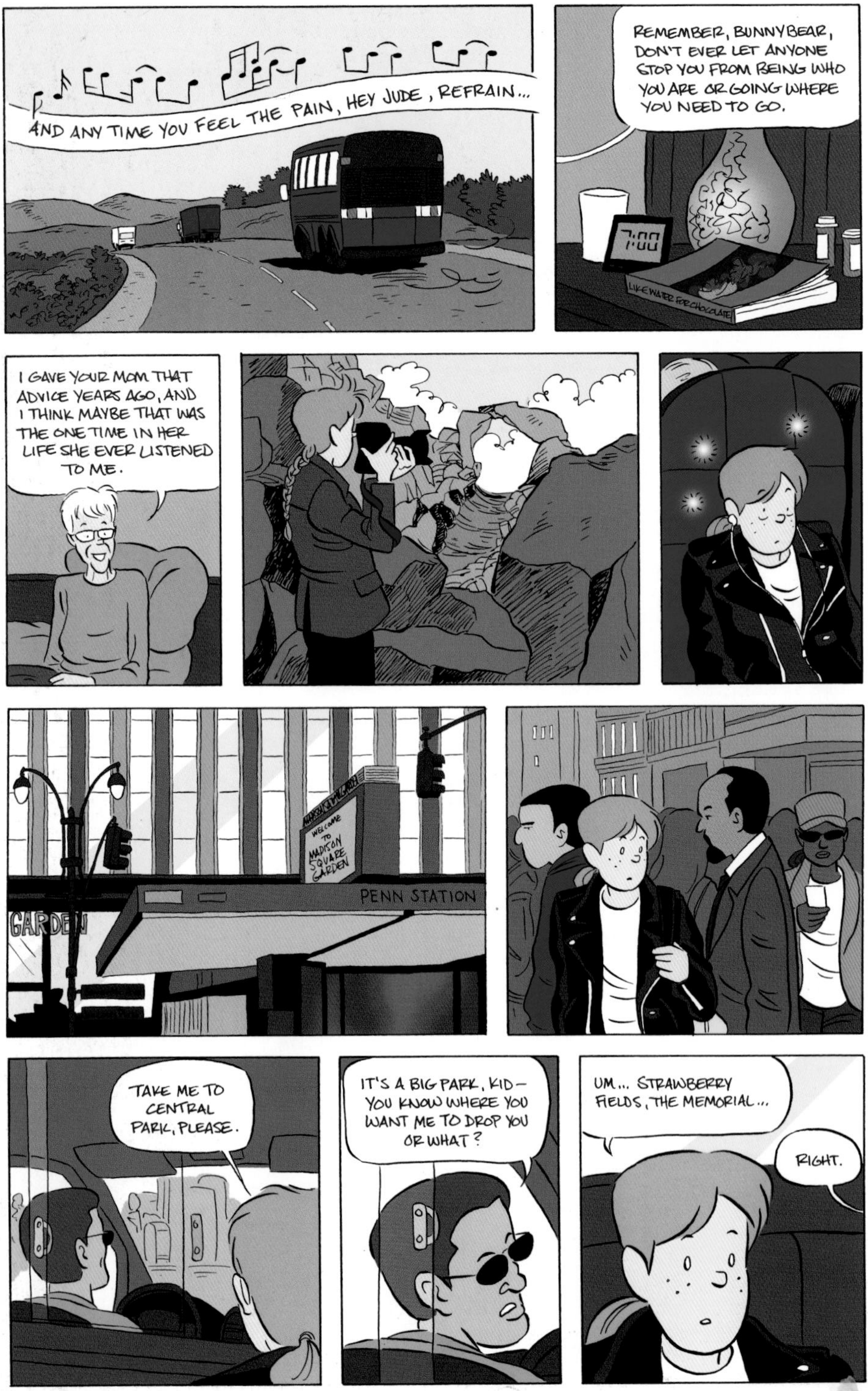
AND ANY TIME YOU FEEL THE PAIN, HEY JUDE, REFRAIN...
REMEMBER, BUNNYBEAR, DON'T EVER LET ANYONE STOP YOU FROM BEING WHO YOU ARE OR GOING WHERE YOU NEED TO GO.
7:00
LIKE WATER FOR CHOCOLATE
I GAVE YOUR MOM THAT ADVICE YEARS AGO, AND I THINK MAYBE THAT WAS THE ONE TIME IN HER LIFE SHE EVER LISTENED TO ME.
WELCOME TO MADISON SQUARE GARDEN
PENN STATION
GARDEN
TAKE ME TO CENTRAL PARK, PLEASE.
IT'S A BIG PARK, KID— YOU KNOW WHERE YOU WANT ME TO DROP YOU OR WHAT?
UM... STRAWBERRY FIELDS, THE MEMORIAL...
RIGHT.

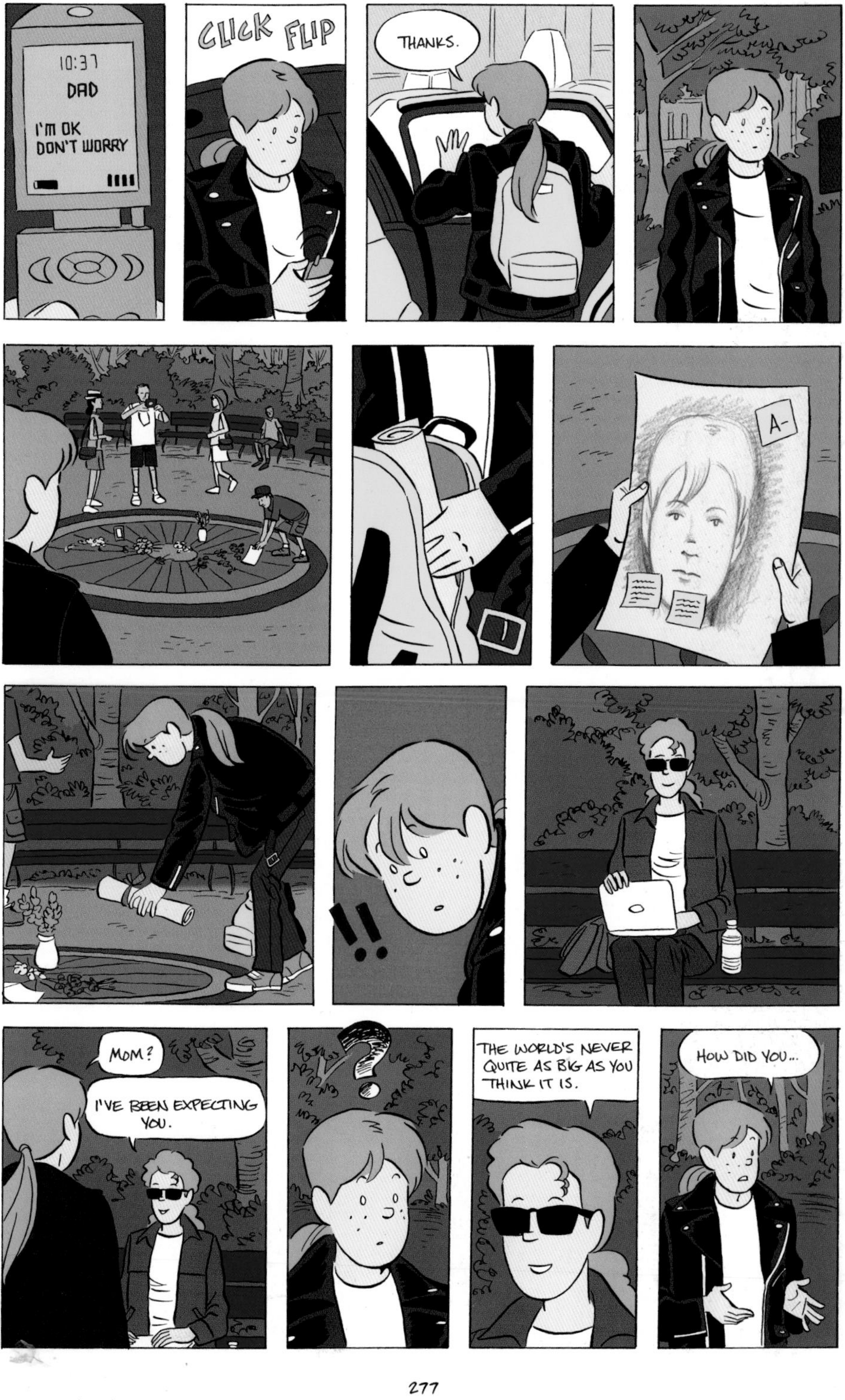
10:37
DAD
I'M OK
DON'T WORRY
CLICK
FLIP
THANKS.
A-
!!
MOM?
I'VE BEEN EXPECTING YOU.
?
THE WORLD'S NEVER QUITE AS BIG AS YOU THINK IT IS.
HOW DID YOU...

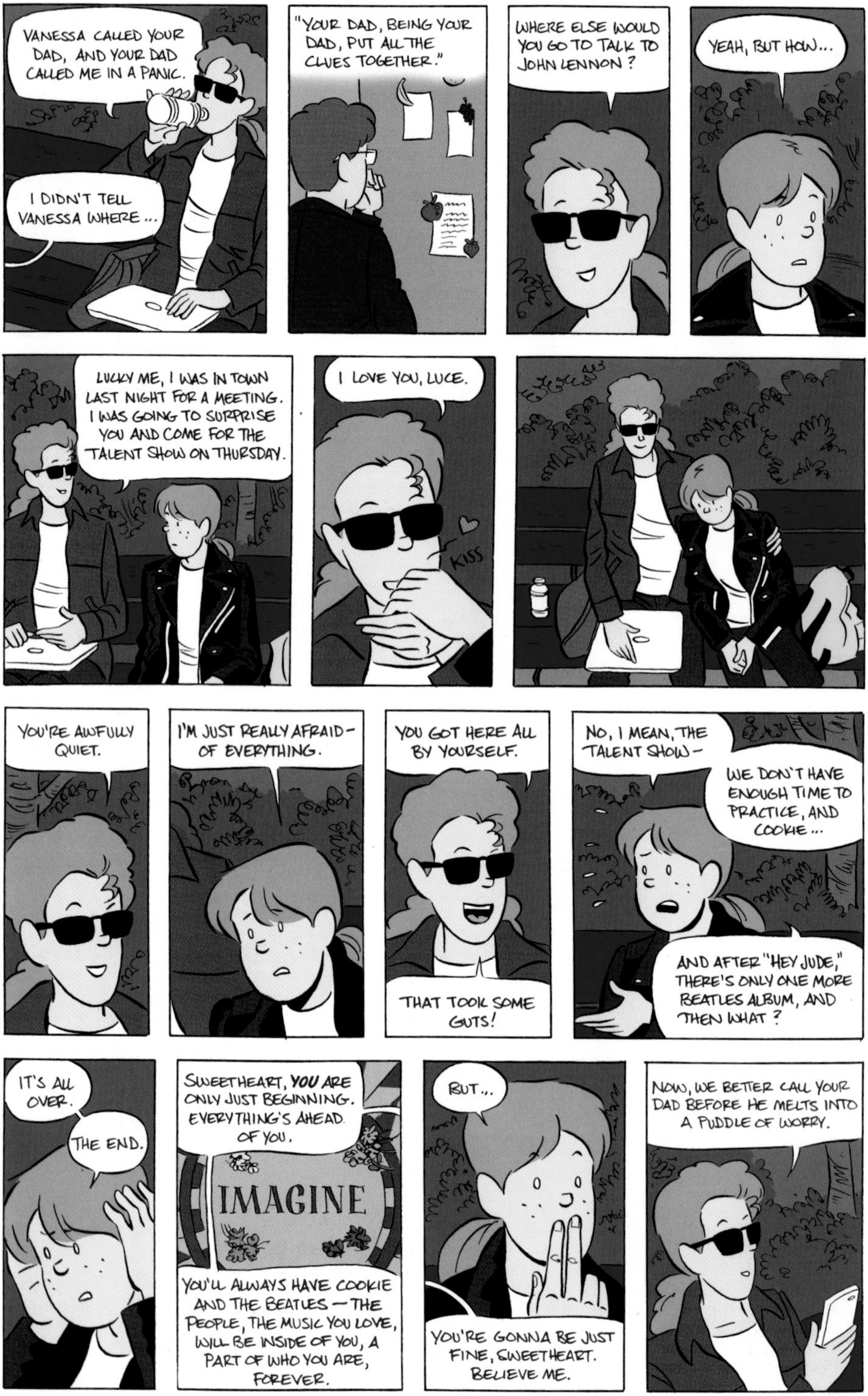
VANESSA CALLED YOUR DAD, AND YOUR DAD CALLED ME IN A PANIC.
I DIDN'T TELL VANESSA WHERE...
"YOUR DAD, BEING YOUR DAD, PUT ALL THE CLUES TOGETHER."
WHERE ELSE WOULD YOU GO TO TALK TO JOHN LENNON?
YEAH, BUT HOW...
LUCKY ME, I WAS IN TOWN LAST NIGHT FOR A MEETING. I WAS GOING TO SURPRISE YOU AND COME FOR THE TALENT SHOW ON THURSDAY.
I LOVE YOU, LUCE.
KISS
YOU'RE AWFULLY QUIET.
I'M JUST REALLY AFRAID- OF EVERYTHING.
YOU GOT HERE ALL BY YOURSELF.
THAT TOOK SOME GUTS!
NO, I MEAN, THE TALENT SHOW-
WE DON'T HAVE ENOUGH TIME TO PRACTICE, AND COOKIE...
AND AFTER "HEY JUDE," THERE'S ONLY ONE MORE BEATLES ALBUM, AND THEN WHAT?
IT'S ALL OVER.
THE END.
SWEETHEART, YOU ARE ONLY JUST BEGINNING. EVERYTHING'S AHEAD OF YOU.
IMAGINE
YOU'LL ALWAYS HAVE COOKIE AND THE BEATLES — THE PEOPLE, THE MUSIC YOU LOVE, WILL BE INSIDE OF YOU, A PART OF WHO YOU ARE, FOREVER.
BUT...
YOU'RE GONNA BE JUST FINE, SWEETHEART. BELIEVE ME.
NOW, WE BETTER CALL YOUR DAD BEFORE HE MELTS INTO A PUDDLE OF WORRY.

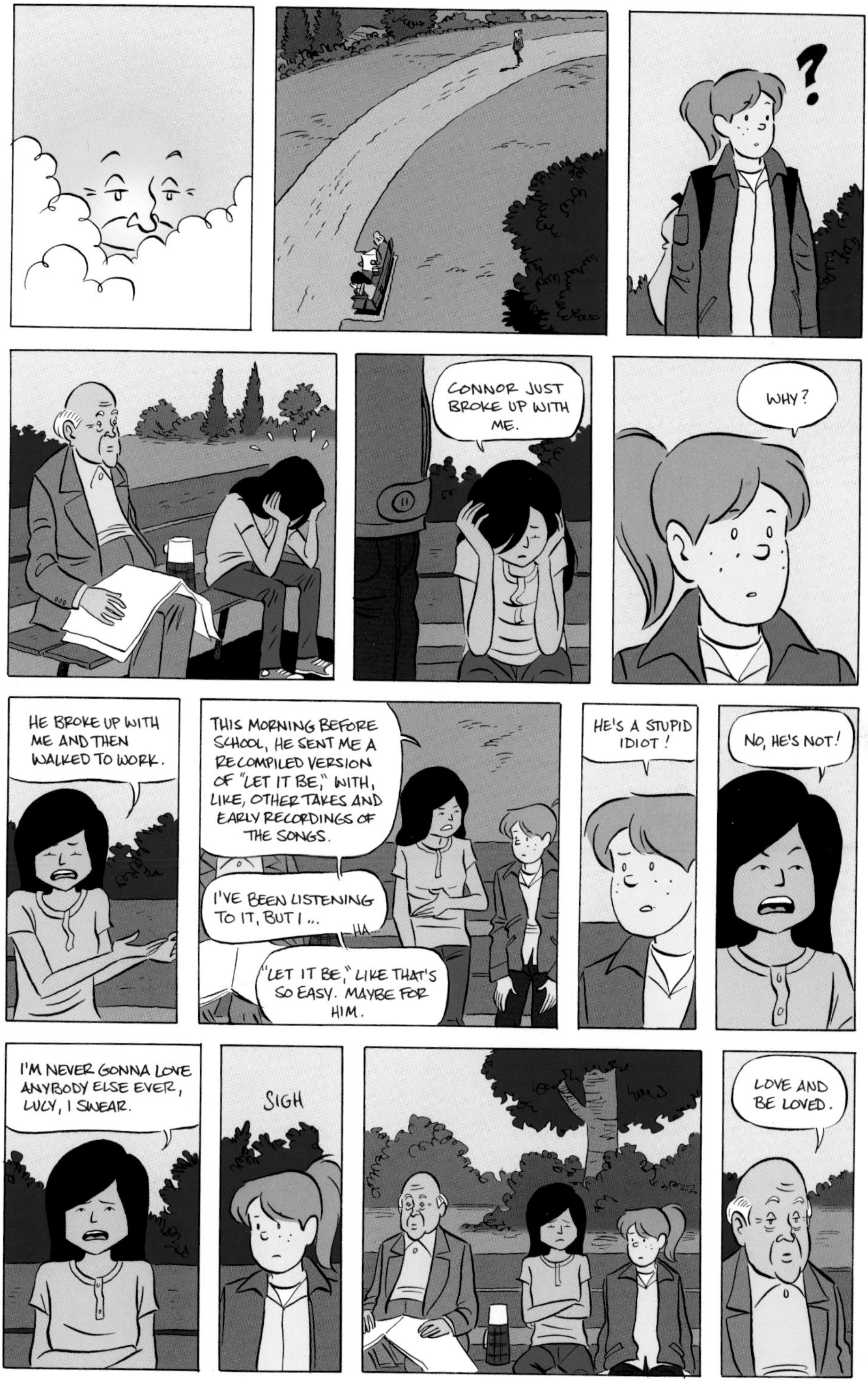
CONNOR JUST BROKE UP WITH ME.
WHY?
HE BROKE UP WITH ME AND THEN WALKED TO WORK.
THIS MORNING BEFORE SCHOOL, HE SENT ME A RECOMPILED VERSION OF "LET IT BE," WITH, LIKE, OTHER TAKES AND EARLY RECORDINGS OF THE SONGS.
I'VE BEEN LISTENING TO IT, BUT I ...
HA...
"LET IT BE," LIKE THAT'S SO EASY. MAYBE FOR HIM.
HE'S A STUPID IDIOT!
NO, HE'S NOT!
I'M NEVER GONNA LOVE ANYBODY ELSE EVER, LUCY, I SWEAR.
SIGH
LOVE AND BE LOVED.

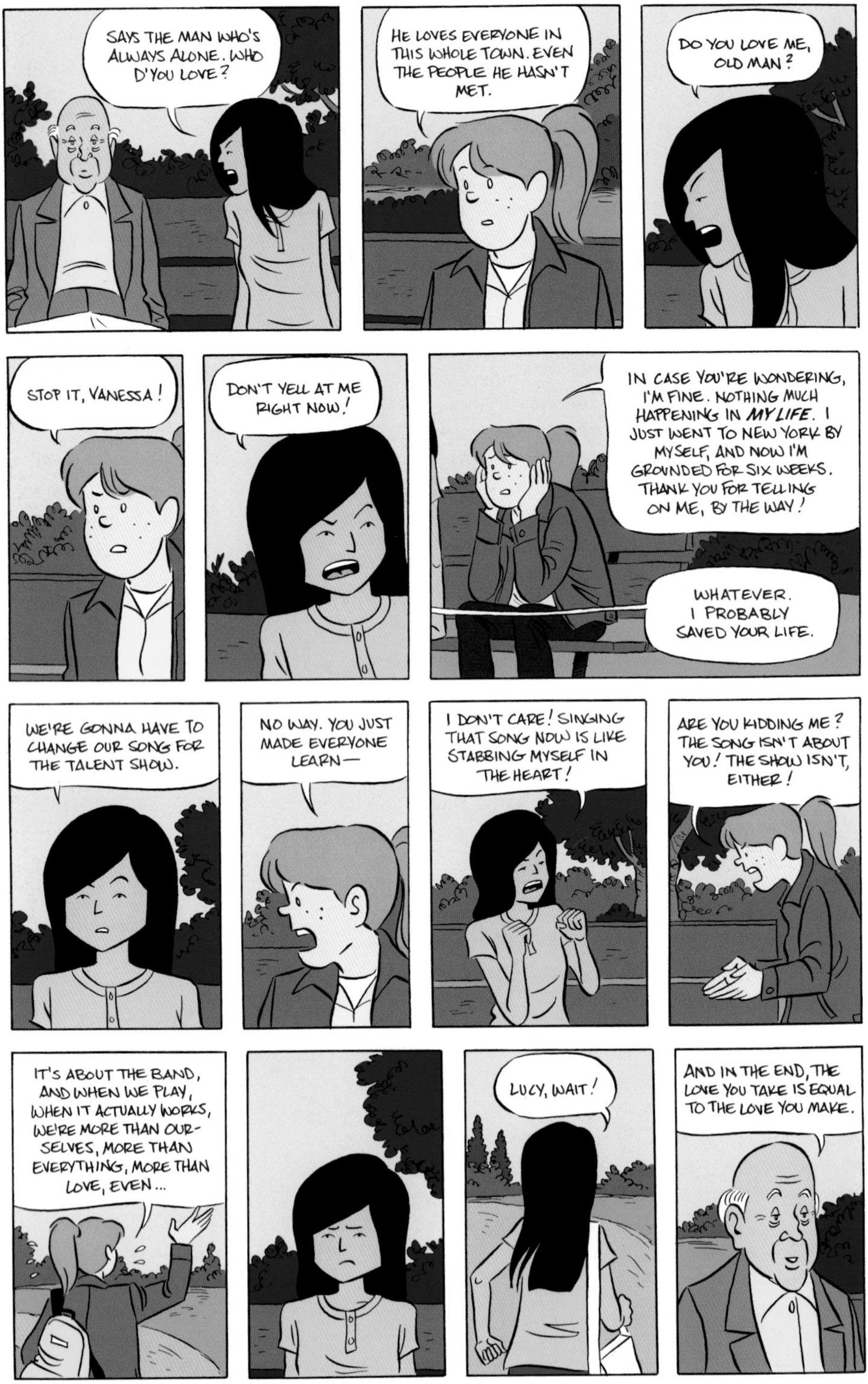
SAYS THE MAN WHO'S ALWAYS ALONE. WHO D'YOU LOVE?
HE LOVES EVERYONE IN THIS WHOLE TOWN. EVEN THE PEOPLE HE HASN'T MET.
DO YOU LOVE ME, OLD MAN?
STOP IT, VANESSA!
DON'T YELL AT ME RIGHT NOW!
IN CASE YOU'RE WONDERING, I'M FINE. NOTHING MUCH HAPPENING IN *MY LIFE*. I JUST WENT TO NEW YORK BY MYSELF, AND NOW I'M GROUNDED FOR SIX WEEKS. THANK YOU FOR TELLING ON ME, BY THE WAY!
WHATEVER. I PROBABLY SAVED YOUR LIFE.
WE'RE GONNA HAVE TO CHANGE OUR SONG FOR THE TALENT SHOW.
NO WAY. YOU JUST MADE EVERYONE LEARN—
I DON'T CARE! SINGING THAT SONG NOW IS LIKE STABBING MYSELF IN THE HEART!
ARE YOU KIDDING ME? THE SONG ISN'T ABOUT YOU! THE SHOW ISN'T, EITHER!
IT'S ABOUT THE BAND, AND WHEN WE PLAY, WHEN IT ACTUALLY WORKS, WE'RE MORE THAN OURSELVES, MORE THAN EVERYTHING, MORE THAN LOVE, EVEN...
LUCY, WAIT!
AND IN THE END, THE LOVE YOU TAKE IS EQUAL TO THE LOVE YOU MAKE.

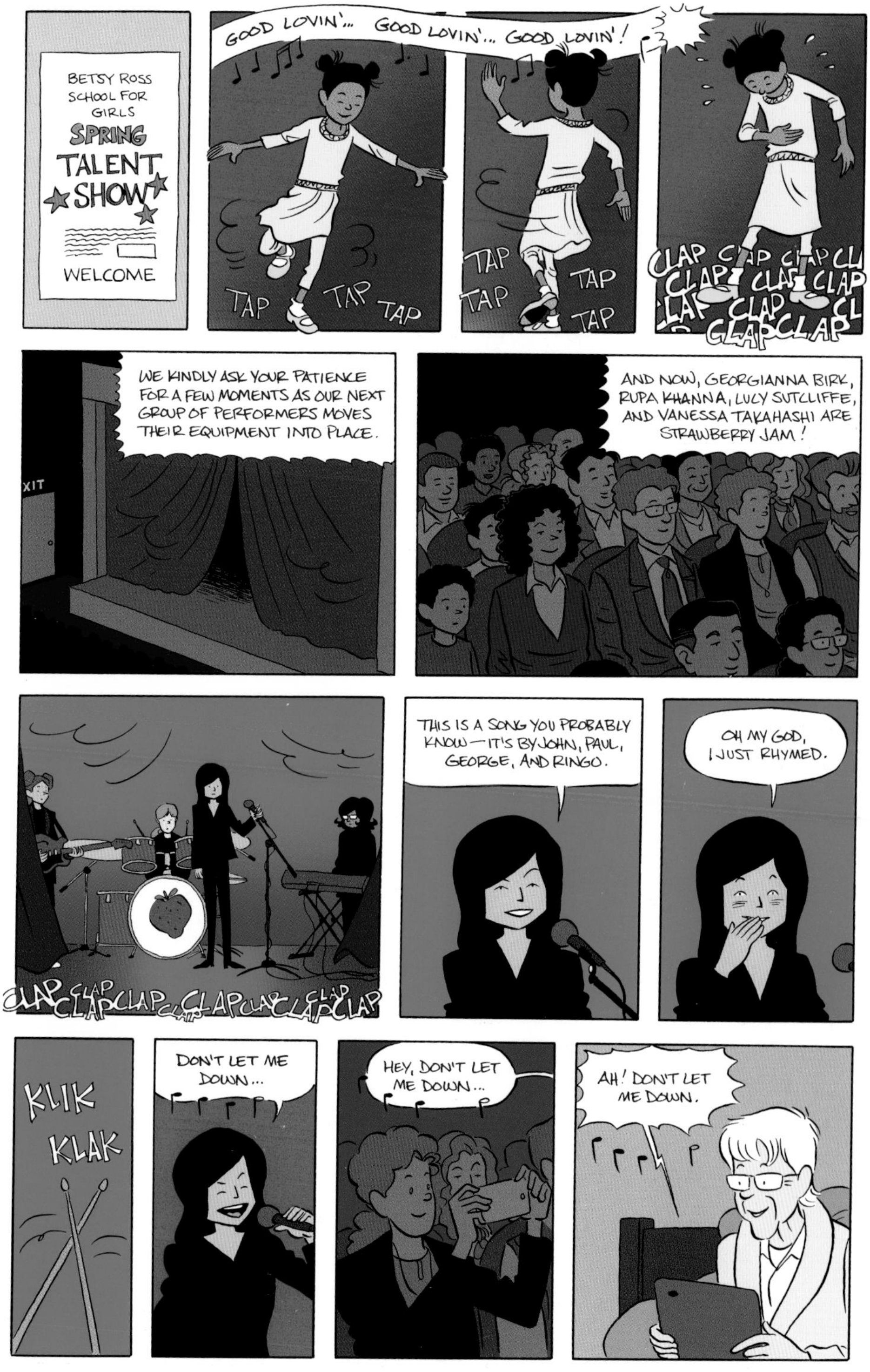
BETSY ROSS SCHOOL FOR GIRLS
SPRING TALENT SHOW
WELCOME
GOOD LOVIN'... GOOD LOVIN'... GOOD LOVIN'!
TAP TAP TAP
TAP TAP TAP TAP
CLAP CLAP CLAP CLAP CLAP CLAP CLAP CLAP CLAP CLAP
WE KINDLY ASK YOUR PATIENCE FOR A FEW MOMENTS AS OUR NEXT GROUP OF PERFORMERS MOVES THEIR EQUIPMENT INTO PLACE.
EXIT
AND NOW, GEORGIANNA BIRK, RUPA KHANNA, LUCY SUTCLIFFE, AND VANESSA TAKAHASHI ARE STRAWBERRY JAM!
CLAP CLAP CLAP CLAP CLAP CLAP CLAP CLAP CLAP
THIS IS A SONG YOU PROBABLY KNOW — IT'S BY JOHN, PAUL, GEORGE, AND RINGO.
OH MY GOD, I JUST RHYMED.
KLIK KLAK
DON'T LET ME DOWN...
HEY, DON'T LET ME DOWN...
AH! DON'T LET ME DOWN.

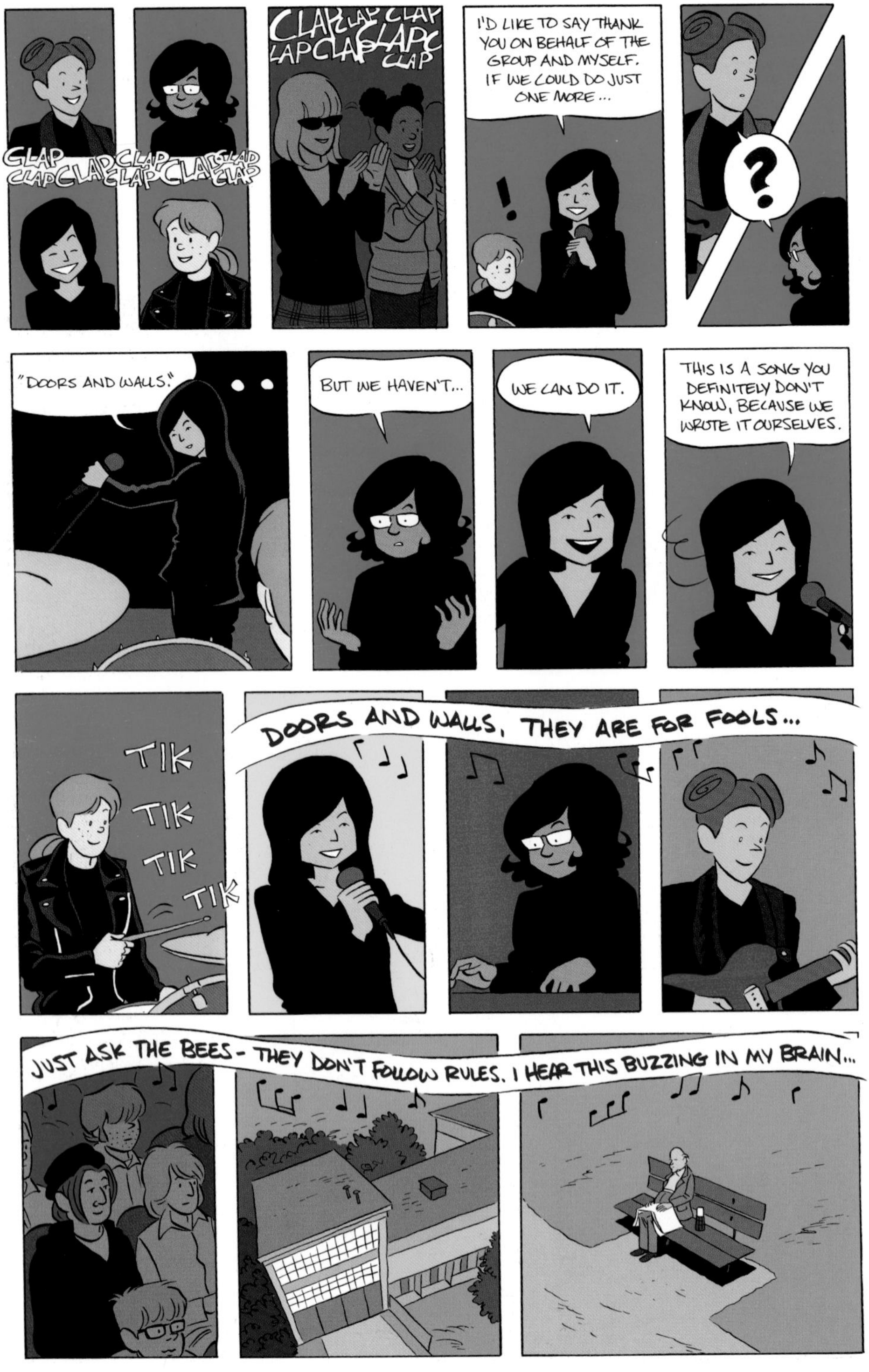
CLAP CLAP CLAP CLAP CLAP CLAP CLAP CLAP
CLAP CLAP CLAP CLAP CLAP CLAP CLAP
I'D LIKE TO SAY THANK YOU ON BEHALF OF THE GROUP AND MYSELF. IF WE COULD DO JUST ONE MORE...
!
?
"DOORS AND WALLS."
BUT WE HAVEN'T...
WE CAN DO IT.
THIS IS A SONG YOU DEFINITELY DON'T KNOW, BECAUSE WE WROTE IT OURSELVES.
TIK TIK TIK TIK
DOORS AND WALLS, THEY ARE FOR FOOLS...
JUST ASK THE BEES - THEY DON'T FOLLOW RULES. I HEAR THIS BUZZING IN MY BRAIN...

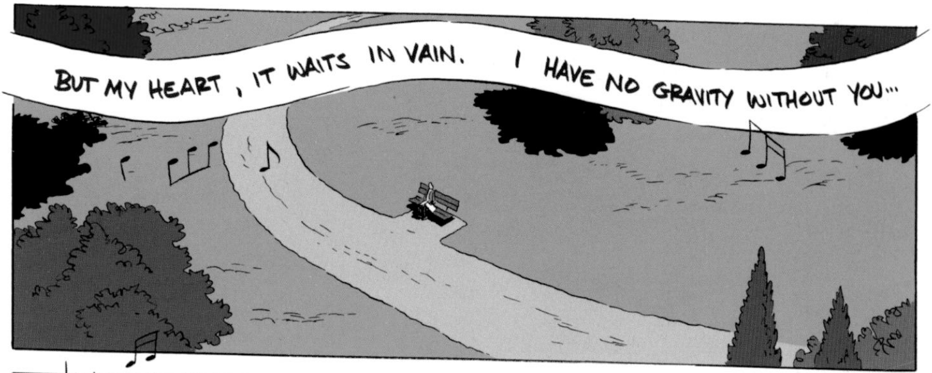
BUT MY HEART, IT WAITS IN VAIN. I HAVE NO GRAVITY WITHOUT YOU...

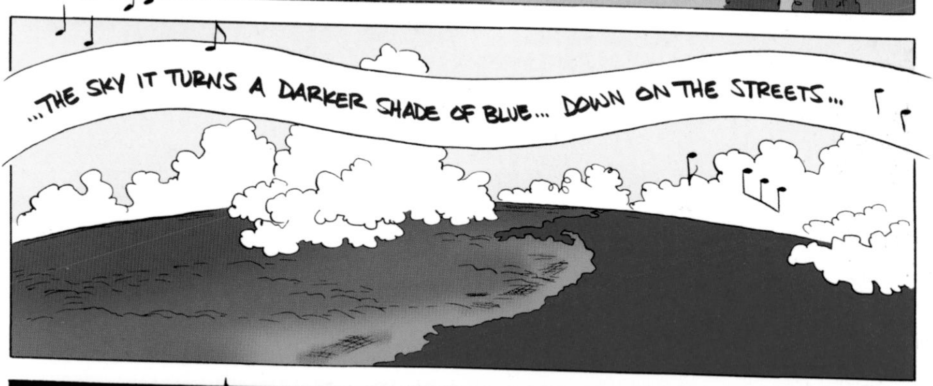
...THE SKY IT TURNS A DARKER SHADE OF BLUE... DOWN ON THE STREETS...

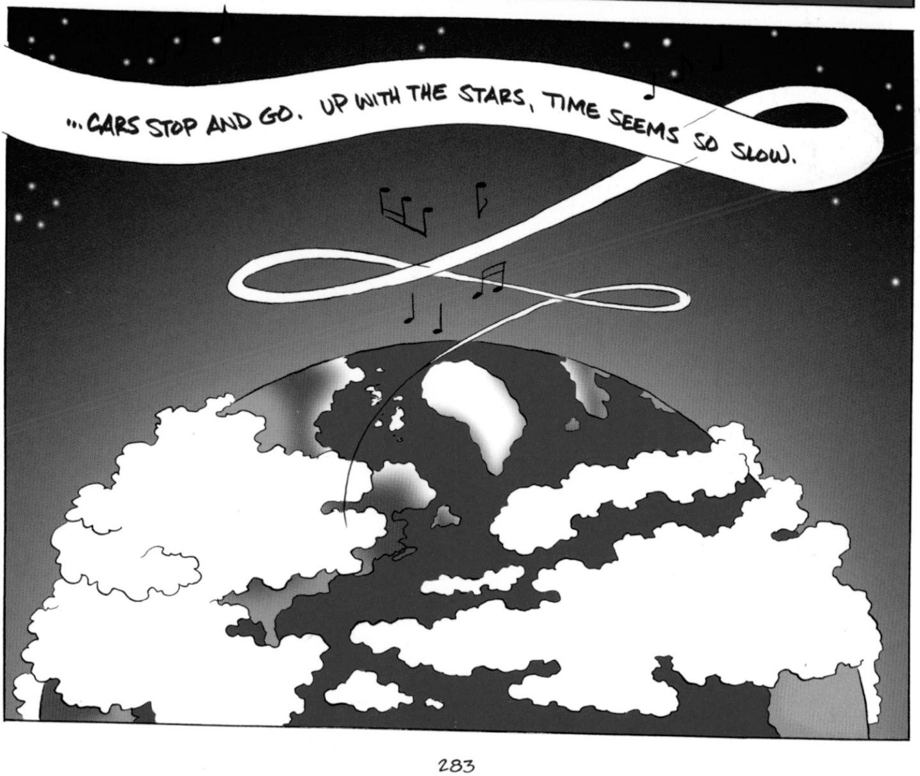
...CARS STOP AND GO. UP WITH THE STARS, TIME SEEMS SO SLOW.

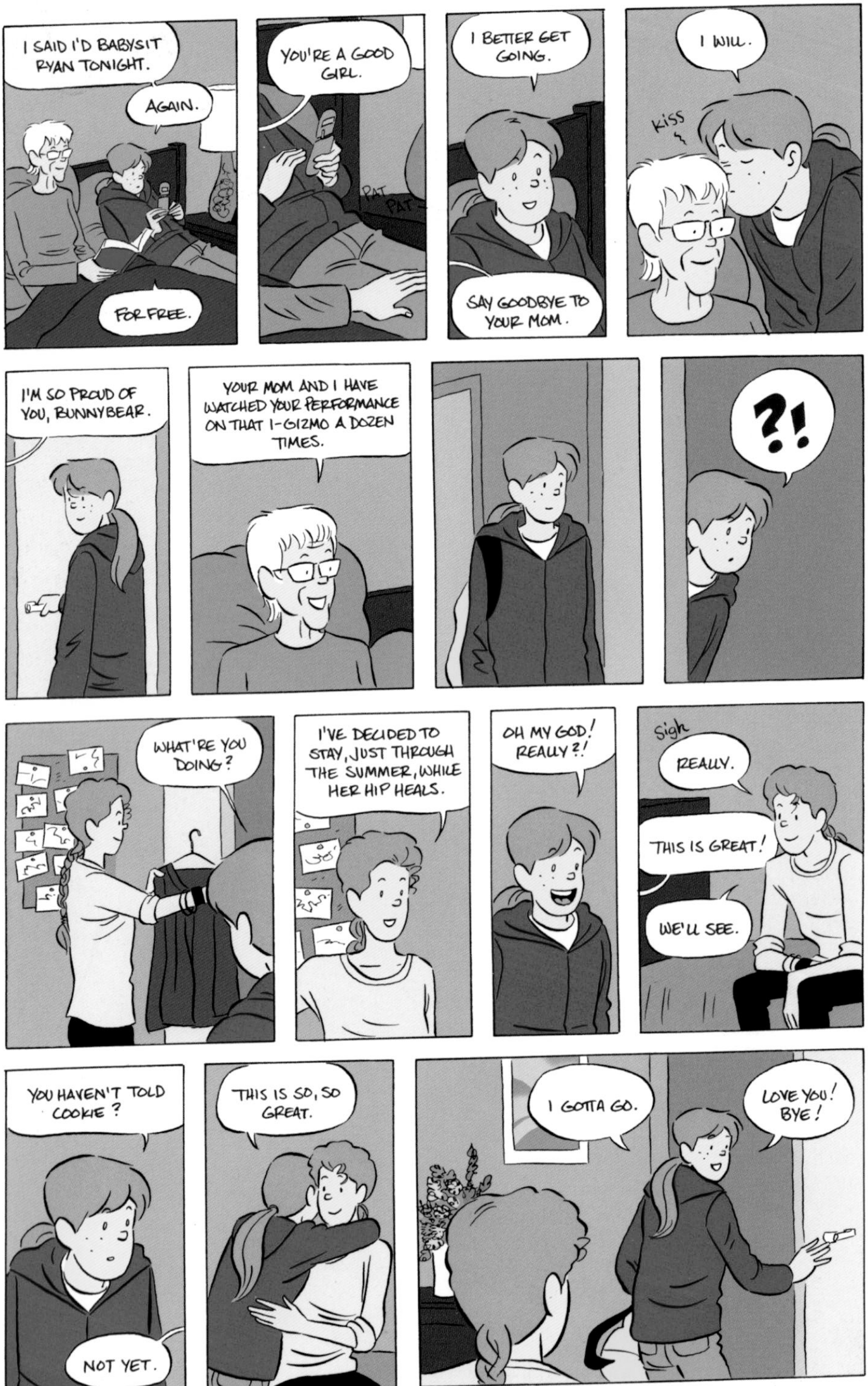
I SAID I'D BABYSIT RYAN TONIGHT.
AGAIN.
FOR FREE.
YOU'RE A GOOD GIRL.
PAT PAT
I BETTER GET GOING.
SAY GOODBYE TO YOUR MOM.
I WILL.
KISS
I'M SO PROUD OF YOU, BUNNYBEAR.
YOUR MOM AND I HAVE WATCHED YOUR PERFORMANCE ON THAT I-GIZMO A DOZEN TIMES.
?!
WHAT'RE YOU DOING?
I'VE DECIDED TO STAY, JUST THROUGH THE SUMMER, WHILE HER HIP HEALS.
OH MY GOD! REALLY?!
Sigh
REALLY.
THIS IS GREAT!
WE'LL SEE.
YOU HAVEN'T TOLD COOKIE?
NOT YET.
THIS IS SO, SO GREAT.
I GOTTA GO.
LOVE YOU! BYE!

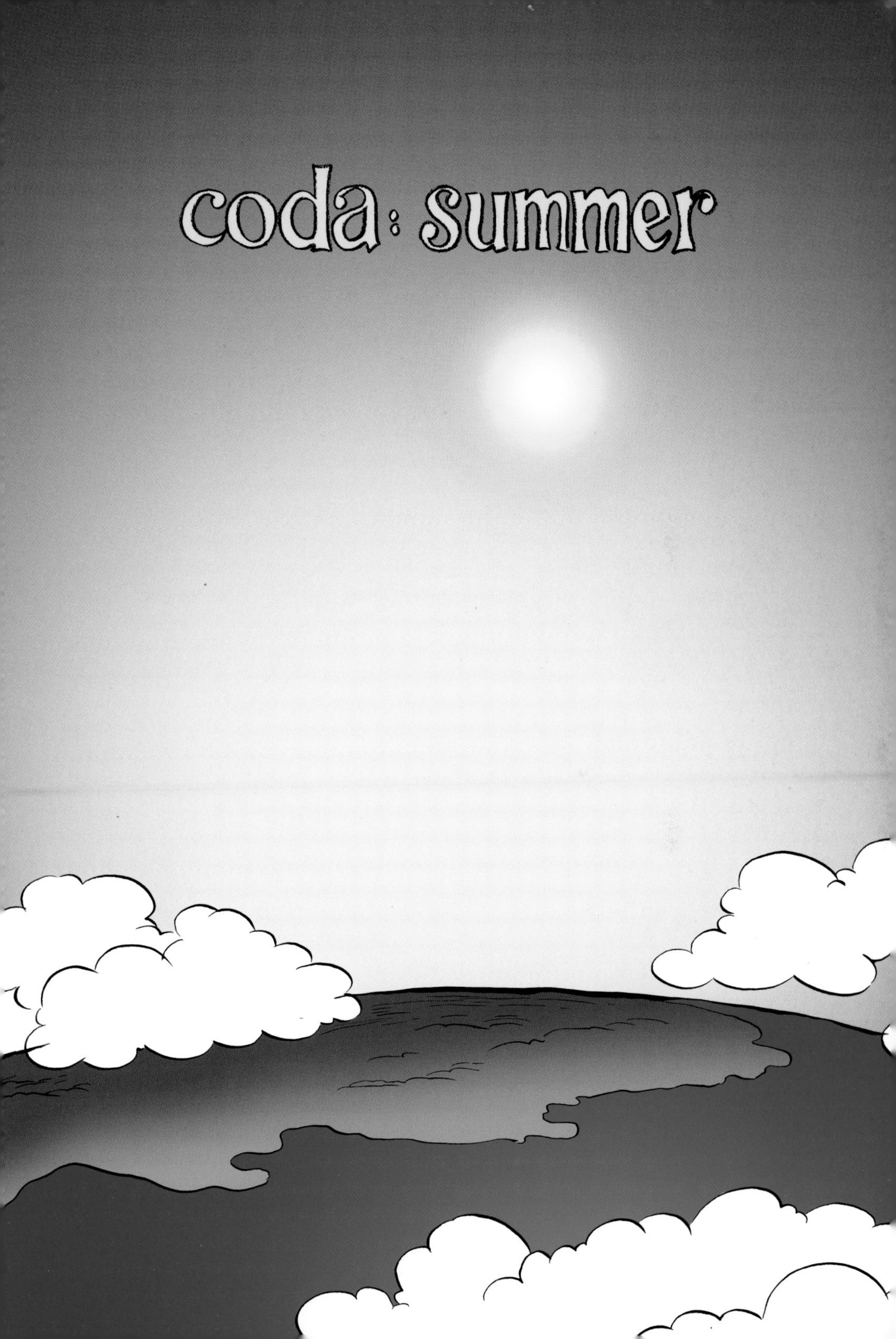
coda: summer

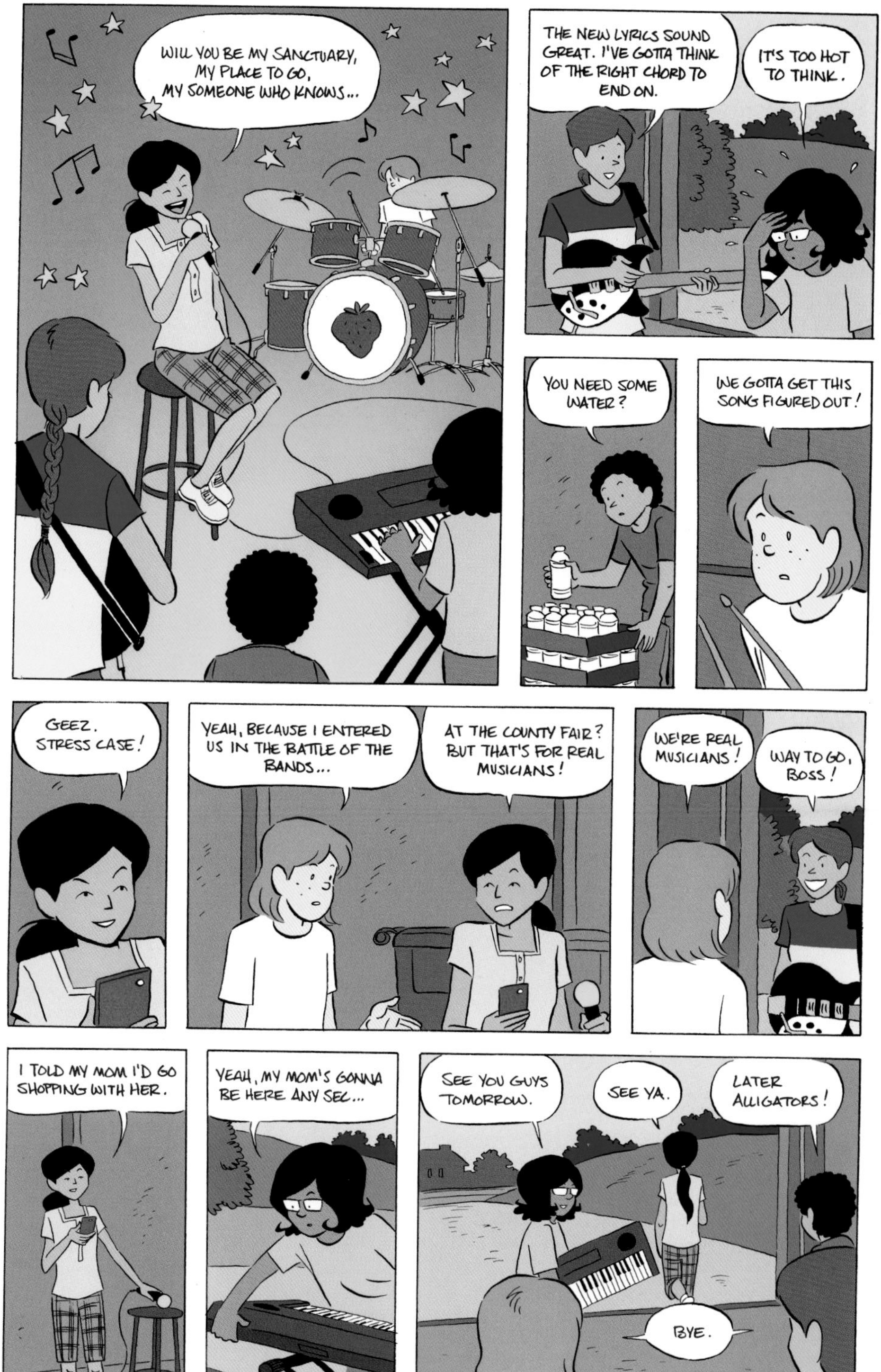
WILL YOU BE MY SANCTUARY, MY PLACE TO GO, MY SOMEONE WHO KNOWS...
THE NEW LYRICS SOUND GREAT. I'VE GOTTA THINK OF THE RIGHT CHORD TO END ON.
IT'S TOO HOT TO THINK.
YOU NEED SOME WATER?
WE GOTTA GET THIS SONG FIGURED OUT!
GEEZ. STRESS CASE!
YEAH, BECAUSE I ENTERED US IN THE BATTLE OF THE BANDS...
AT THE COUNTY FAIR? BUT THAT'S FOR REAL MUSICIANS!
WE'RE REAL MUSICIANS!
WAY TO GO, BOSS!
I TOLD MY MOM I'D GO SHOPPING WITH HER.
YEAH, MY MOM'S GONNA BE HERE ANY SEC...
SEE YOU GUYS TOMORROW.
SEE YA.
LATER ALLIGATORS!
BYE.

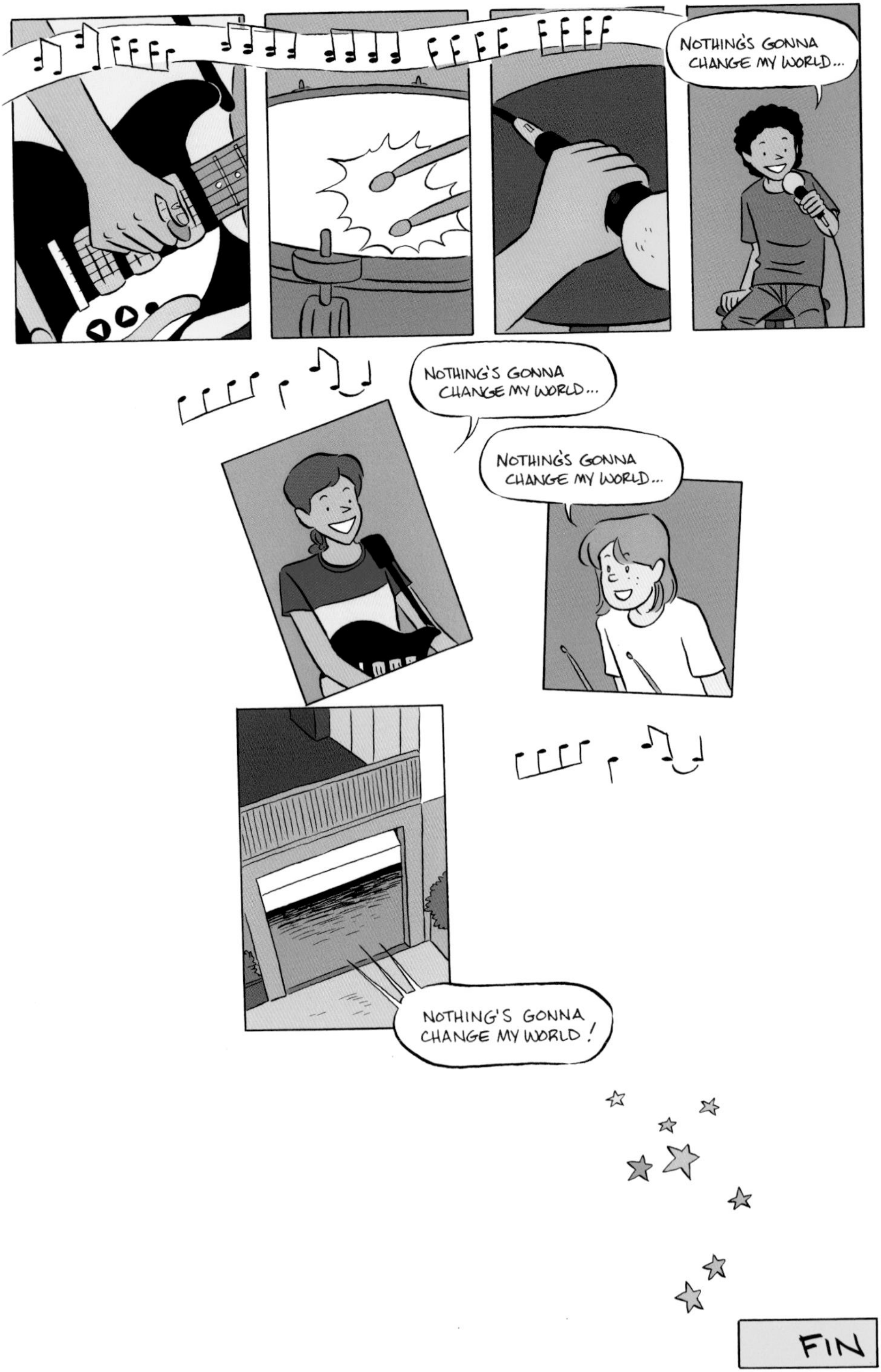
NOTHING'S GONNA CHANGE MY WORLD...
NOTHING'S GONNA CHANGE MY WORLD...
NOTHING'S GONNA CHANGE MY WORLD...
NOTHING'S GONNA CHANGE MY WORLD!
FIN

AFTERWORD

I was fourteen when John Lennon was murdered. I heard the news at school from a friend, who, knowing I was a huge Beatles fan, offered his sincere condolences. Of course, Lennon's death hit me hard, but looking back, it seems as if it didn't hit me quite as hard as it should have. Already, my musical interests were moving in other directions.

When I was very young, my dad had given me his Beatles albums and an old guitar from his college years, along with a book of guitar chords. It didn't take me long to learn a few chords and start to figure out some Beatles songs. Those albums were, more or less, the soundtrack to my childhood. By the time I reached high school, I knew all the songs by heart, both the big hits and the filler (if any Beatles songs can really be called filler). But by then, I had discovered punk rock, and new wave, and all those bands that were a part of the second British invasion of the 1980s. So, I put away my Beatles albums, for a while, as I joined my own band and tried to discover myself.

In my twenties, I began to rebuild my music collection on CD and rediscovered the Beatles, this time on the albums as they were originally released in the UK. I found I still knew the words to every song. It was like they were in my blood, an essential part of my being. Listening to them with mature ears, I appreciated the Beatles' genius and their ability to compose near-perfect pop songs.

My story is not so different from the millions of other people who feel that same connection to the Fab Four's music. It was not a surprise that I should meet and marry someone who shared my love for them. And, as my dad planted the seeds of my Beatlemania in me, Kiara's passion for the Beatles came through her dad, Bill.

In July of 2019, we took our then three-year-old daughter, Esmé, to see Paul McCartney. Grandpa Bill came with us. It was the first time both Esmé and I saw a Beatle. Over that past year, she and I had learned to sing and play the song "Blackbird," and when we realized it was part of Paul's set that night, we all turned to one another with looks of simultaneous recognition. This was heightened by the fact that this one perfect moment was happening in the midst of what had otherwise been a difficult year for us due to a health scare. There we were, three generations, equally enthralled and touched by this music, which was now fifty years old. I could not have imagined the same scene with my own grandfather.

Pop music today is no longer synonymous with rock 'n' roll, like it was when I was a kid. Guitar music has become a genre once more, no longer the mainstream. But there's still something special about getting together with a few friends in a garage, turning your instruments up loud, and working it out. Who knows if Esmé or her siblings will take up an instrument or join a band, but music is such a given in their lives. It is all around them. It is a natural presence for them. I can see it in the unselfconscious way they sing. And that is how it should be.

Music was clearly the lifeblood of the four lads from Liverpool as well. None of them knew any other professional life, and it's a bit crazy to consider that by the time they had reached the age of thirty, their careers as Beatles were over. When I was in my thirties myself, I sat down to watch the movie *Imagine*, about the life of John Lennon, and I finally broke down and cried like I felt I should have back in high school—both for John's death, and the fact that the Beatles were no more. But I also remember something John said about people mourning the Beatles—that if you still wanted to hear them, all you had to do was play their records. He said it in a way that was flip and slightly callous, and it was during a time when he was trying to demystify the Beatles, both for himself and others. But those records *are* a gift, greater than he was probably willing to admit, for millions of folks who have been touched by their deceptively simple genius, and for millions more still waiting to hear them and be inspired by them.

Sean Chiki

Albany, California

SOUNDTRACK

What follows is a list of songs, albums, and artists listened to, sung, or referred to in the story. The page number is indicated first, followed by artist, song, album, and label. Regarding Beatles songs—since Lucy is listening to her dad's old LPs, the American vinyl release of the song is listed first, followed by the UK release, and in a few cases, the current CD release.

Note: Fictional songs are marked with an asterisk.

1 *One 4 All, "I Love You More," *Strength in Numbers* (Brinki)
5 *One 4 All, "Together Forever," *One For All* (Brinki)
11 *One 4 All, "Say Goodbye, Baby," *The More the Merrier* (Brinki)
18 Pharoah Sanders, "Yemenja," *Journey to the One* (Theresa Records)
30 The Beatles, "I Saw Her Standing There," *Introducing the Beatles* (Veejay), *Meet the Beatles* (Capitol), *Please Please Me* (Parlophone)
33 The Beatles, "Misery," *Introducing the Beatles* (Veejay), *Please Please Me* (Parlophone)
36 "Castle on a Cloud," *Les Miserables*
36 *Miss Deed, "Do The Deed," *Do the Deed* (Brinki)
37 Carly Rae Jepsen, "Call Me Maybe," *Curiosity* (School Boy, Interscope)
38 The Beatles, "Till There Was You," *Meet the Beatles!* (Capitol), *With the Beatles* (Parlophone)
46 The Beatles, "It Won't Be Long," *Meet the Beatles!* (Capitol), *With the Beatles* (Parlophone)
51 John's Children, "Desdemona," UK single (Track)
52 Cat Power, *Sun* (Matador)
55 The Archies, "Sugar, Sugar," *Everything's Archie* (Calendar)
56 The Beach Boys, *Pet Sounds* (Capitol)
56 Gram Parsons, *Grievous Angel* (Reprise)
63 The Beatles, "Roll Over Beethoven," *The Beatles Second Album* (Capitol), *With the Beatles* (Parlophone)
74 Jimmie Davis and Charles Mitchell (authorship disputed) "You Are My Sunshine"
78 The Beatles, "A Hard Day's Night," *A Hard Day's Night* (Capital, Parlophone)
84 The Beatles, "Komm Gib Mir Deine Hand," *Something New* (Capitol), German single (Odeon Records), *Past Masters* (Apple, CD release)

93 *Strawberry Jam, "Doors and Walls"

96 The Beatles, "Honey Don't," *Beatles '65* (Capitol), *Beatles for Sale* (Parlophone)

97 The Beatles, "She's a Woman," *Beatles '65* (Capitol), UK single (Parlophone), *Past Masters* (Apple, CD release)

97 The Beatles, "I Feel Fine," *Beatles '65* (Capitol), UK single (Parlophone), *Past Masters* (Apple, CD release)

101 The Velvet Underground, "Sweet Jane," *Loaded* (Atlantic)

106 Ray Parker, Jr., "Ghostbusters," *Ghostbusters: Original Soundtrack Album* (Arista)

106 *Phresh Phace, "Hello," *Heartbeatz* (Brinki)

107 *Miss Deed, "Unicorn," *Do The Deed* (Brinki)

109 *One 4 All, "Say Goodbye, Baby," *The More the Merrier* (Brinki)

110 *Tom Fool, "Easy," *The Riddler* (Brinki)

110 *Miss Deed, "Do the Deed," *Do the Deed* (Brinki)

111 The Beatles, "Twist and Shout," *The Early Beatles* (Capitol), *Please Please Me* (Parlophone)

115 The Beatles, "Eight Days a Week," *Beatles VI* (Capitol), *Beatles for Sale* (Parlophone)

136 The Beatles, "Help," *Help* (Capitol, Parlophone)

137 The Beatles, "You've Got to Hide Your Love Away," *Help* (Capitol, Parlophone)

145 The Beatles, "Norwegian Wood," *Rubber Soul* (Capitol, Parlophone)

167 The Beatles, "I've Just Seen a Face," *Rubber Soul* (Capitol, Parlophone)

172 Interpol, "Stella Was a Diver and She Was Always Down," *Turn On the Bright Lights* (Matador)

183 The Velvet Underground and Nico, *The Velvet Underground and Nico* (Verve)

185 The Jesus and Mary Chain, *Psychocandy* (Blanco y Negro)

186 The Beatles, "And Your Bird Can Sing," *Yesterday and Today* (Capitol), *Revolver* (Parlophone)

187 Chuck Berry, "My Ding-a-Ling," *The London Chuck Berry Sessions* (Chess)

187 Sheb Wooley, "Purple People Eater," single (MGM)

187 Teddy Bears, "To Know Him Is to Love Him," single (Doré)

189 Frankie Lymon and the Teenagers, "Why Do Fools Fall in Love," *The Teenagers Featuring Frankie Lymon* (Gee)

190 The Righteous Brothers, "Unchained Melody," *Just Once In My Life* (Philles)

191 The Beatles, "Got to Get You into My Life," *Revolver* (Capitol, Parlophone)

194 The Beatles, "Good Day Sunshine," *Revolver* (Capitol, Parlophone)

195 The Beatles, "Sgt. Pepper's Lonely Hearts Club Band," *Sgt. Pepper's Lonely Hearts Club Band* (Capitol, Parlophone)

201 The Beatles, "Good Morning," *Sgt. Pepper's Lonely Hearts Club Band* (Capitol, Parlophone)

202 The Beatles, "Sgt. Pepper's Lonely Hearts Club Band (Reprise)," *Sgt. Pepper's Lonely Heart's Club Band* (Capitol, Parlophone)

203 The Beatles, "Lucy in the Sky with Diamonds," *Sgt. Pepper's Lonely Hearts Club Band* (Capitol, Parlophone)

210 *Strawberry Jam, "Song Two"
214 The Beatles, "Getting Better," *Sgt. Pepper's Lonely Hearts Club Band* (Capitol, Parlophone)
220 The Beatles, "Strawberry Fields Forever," *Magical Mystery Tour* (Capitol, Parlophone)
223 The Beatles, "Penny Lane," *Magical Mystery Tour* (Capitol, Parlophone)
223 The Beatles, "I Am the Walrus," *Magical Mystery Tour* (Capitol, Parlophone)
224 The Beatles, "Baby You're a Rich Man," *Magical Mystery Tour* (Capitol, Parlophone)
229 Gerry and the Pacemakers, "Ferry Cross the Mersey," single (Columbia)
236 The Beatles, "While My Guitar Gently Weeps," *The Beatles* (Apple)
237 The Beatles, "Twist and Shout," *The Early Beatles* (Capitol), *Please Please Me* (Parlophone)
239 The Beatles, "I'm So Tired," *The Beatles* (Apple)
240 The Beatles, "Everybody's Got Something to Hide Except Me and My Monkey," *The Beatles* (Apple)
241 The Beatles, "Sexy Sadie," *The Beatles* (Apple)
243 Bob Dylan, "The Times They Are a-Changin'," *The Times They Are a-Changin'* (Columbia)
244 The Beatles, "Revolution 1," *The Beatles* (Apple)
246 The Beatles, "Yellow Submarine," *Revolver* (Capitol, Parlophone), *Yellow Submarine* (Apple)
247 The Beatles, "All Together Now," *Yellow Submarine* (Apple)
251 The Beatles, "Hey Bulldog," *Yellow Submarine* (Apple)
260 The Beatles, "Here Comes the Sun," *Abbey Road* (Apple)
262 The Beatles, "Golden Slumbers," *Abbey Road* (Apple)
269 The Beatles, "She Came in Through the Bathroom Window," *Abbey Road* (Apple)
272 The Beatles, "Rain," *Hey Jude* (Apple), UK single (Apple), *Past Masters* (Apple, CD release)
276 The Beatles, "Hey Jude," *Hey Jude* (Apple), UK single (Apple), *Past Masters* (Apple, CD release)
280 The Beatles, "The End," *Abbey Road* (Apple)
281 The Young Rascals, "Good Lovin'," *The Young Rascals* (Atlantic)
281 The Beatles, "Don't Let Me Down," *Hey Jude* (Apple), UK single (Apple), *Past Masters* (Apple, CD release)
282 *Strawberry Jam, "Doors and Walls,"
287 *Strawberry Jam, "Sanctuary"
288 The Beatles, "Across the Universe," *Let It Be* (Apple)

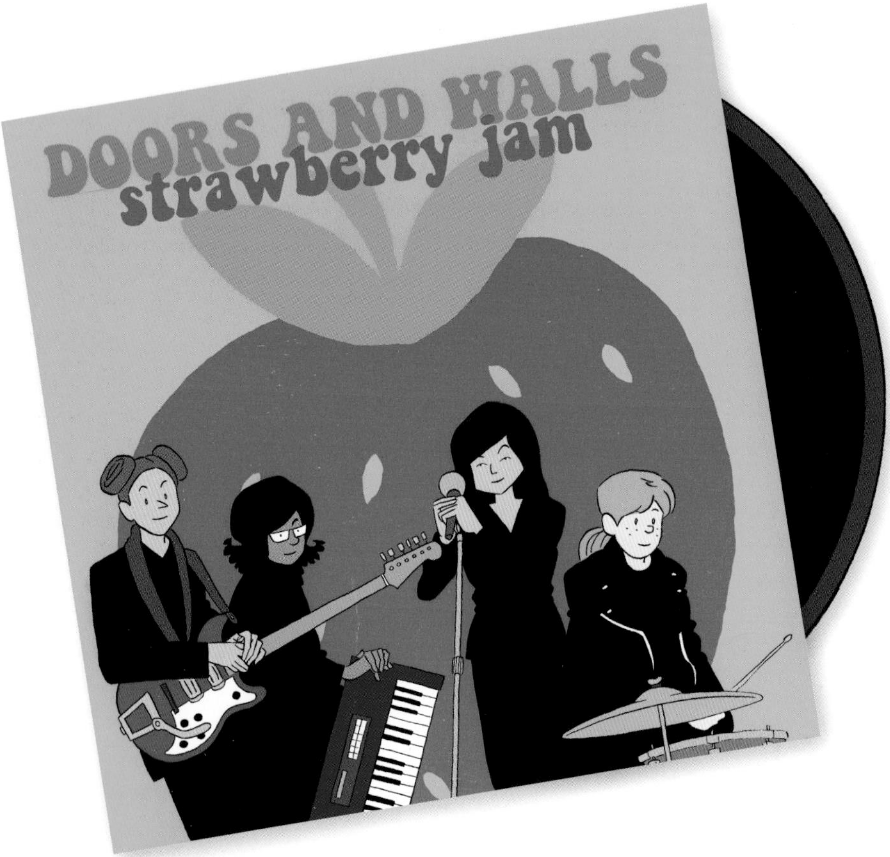
DOORS AND WALLS
strawberry jam

ACKNOWLEDGMENTS

Over the past five years, as *Lucy in the Sky* has come together, our little family has grown into a big family. Pregnancy, childbirth, and life with babies and toddlers have sometimes slowed our writing and illustrating progress, so we would like to thank everyone involved with this book for their patience. More importantly, though, we would like to thank our children for allowing Mama and Dada the necessary time to work. Esmé, Arthur, and Julian, we love you more than words can say, more than there are stars in the sky, and even more than the Beatles.

It is hard to imagine where we would be without our steadfast agent, Alice Tasman, who first suggested we try our hand at a middle grade book. Also, many, many thanks to everyone at First Second, especially Calista Brill, Robyn Chapman, Kirk Benshoff, and Molly Johanson for their enthusiasm and dedication to *Lucy*.

We are forever grateful to our own parents for their love and support, and, of course, for raising us with the Beatles. Bill Brinkman (aka Popsie), you are the most loving "manny" in the world—we couldn't have finished this book without you!

Our Waldorf community has supported us with encouragement, kindness, childcare, and delicious meals. Sharon Lacay, you are an inspiration!

Finally, thank you to our dear friends Augusta Meill, Alyson Brown, Jeremy Greco, Andy Peters, and the good people (past and present) at the Booksmith in San Francisco, including you, Aileen Long.

FRIENDS! MUSIC! MYSTERIES!

These great graphic novels have it all!

BE PREPARED
VERA BROSGOL

BE PREPARED
by Vera Brosgol

Come along with Vera as she goes to summer camp for the first time ever!

Jen Wang
STARGAZING

STARGAZING
by Jen Wang

Meet Christine and Moon, two friends who have a lot in common, but who couldn't be more different!

From the author of Pashmina
JUKEBOX
Nidhi Chanani

JUKEBOX
by Nidhi Chanani

Fly through music history with Shaheen and Tannaz in this time-traveling adventure!

Cici's journal
JORIS CHAMBLAIN
AURÉLIE NEYRET

CICI'S JOURNAL
by Joris Chamblain and Aurélie Nyret

Join Cici as she explores the secrets and mysteries hidden in her hometown!

Great graphic novels for every reader